*For Mr. Barfuss*

STRIND

Leigh

DRONODAN

INTERISLAND WATERS

Marow

# THE
# SHATTERED
# REALM
## OF
# ARDOR BENN

KINGDOM OF GRIT: BOOK TWO

# TYLER
# WHITESIDES

www.orbitbooks.net

ORBIT

First published in Great Britain in 2020 by Orbit

1 3 5 7 9 10 8 6 4 2

Copyright © 2020 by Tyler Whitesides

Map by Serena Malyon

Excerpt of *Age of Assassins* by RJ Barker
Copyright © 2017 by RJ Barker

A CIP catalogue record for this book
is available from the British Library.

ISBN 978-0-356-51101-6

Printed and bound in Great Britain by Clays Ltd, Elcograf S.p.A.

Papers used by Orbit are from well-managed forests
and other responsible sources.

Orbit
An imprint of
Little, Brown Book Group
Carmelite House
50 Victoria Embankment
London EC4Y 0DZ

An Hachette UK Company
www.hachette.co.uk

www.orbitbooks.net

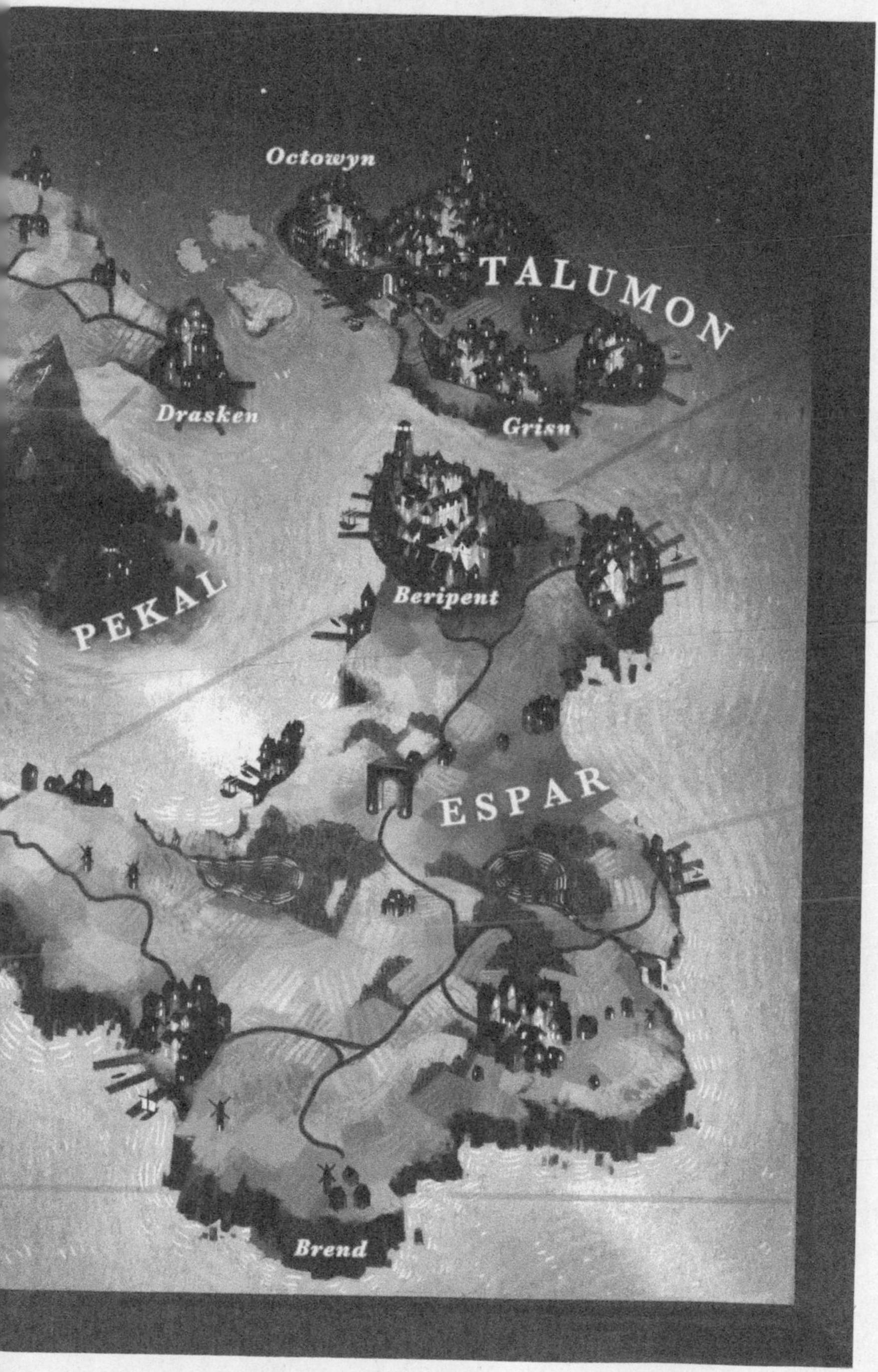
Octowyn
TALUMON
Drasken
Grisn
PEKAL
Beripent
ESPAR
Brend

# PART I

---

The journey to the Homeland is long, and many shall perish ere they reach that holy shore. From port, send thine aid. But glory, starboard, for it shall mark thy way to everlasting perfection.

—*Wayfarist Voyage, vol. 1*

Do not judge us by the high mountain peaks of our ancestors. They pushed up soil against the Moon in fear, but we come in obeisant supplication.

—*Ancient Agrodite poem*

# CHAPTER

# 1

Ardor Benn tried very hard to lie still, but this coffin was blazing uncomfortable. It was about three inches too short, giving him a real crick in the neck. General Nelbet must have been a rather small man. Or perhaps the carpenter who made the coffin took into account the fact that the top four inches of the general's head had been blown off by a cannonball.

Whichever the case, *Ard's* head was wholly intact and now pressed awkwardly against the top of the hard oak casket. Oh, the things he was willing to do for a thousand Ashings. At least there was a pillow. Apparently, even the dead needed a luxurious place to lay half their skull.

"Citizens of Beripent, of the Archkingdom!"

About time this ceremony got started.

"On this, the sixth day of the Ninth Cycle..." The speaker had a powerful voice to reach the crowd standing on the palace grounds. He was likely wearing black, reading from a scroll. And he probably had a big nose.

"We gather to mourn the death of General Yul Nelbet."

Yeah. Big nose. That kind of voice would belong to someone with hair sprouting from his ears, too.

"He fell to cannon fire aboard the warship *Restrain*, while engaging enemy vessels from the rebellious Sovereign States. General

Nelbet died honorably, and his service to the crown will not be dimmed or forgotten in this savage war for reunification."

Ard had practically forgotten him already. The particular naval battle that was the general's demise hadn't accomplished anything spectacular. In fact, Ard was pretty sure the Archkingdom had lost miserably. Regardless of how the war turned out, the history books weren't likely to put a lot of emphasis on that little skirmish.

"General Nelbet is remembered alongside the twenty-one soldiers who lost their lives in the same confrontation."

The speaker continued by reading down the list of names.

Sparks, war was ugly. And to think that just over a year and a half ago, the islands of the Greater Chain had been enjoying one of the longest spans of peace in recorded history. Of course, Ardor Benn had to go and blow it all.

For a moment, things had looked promising. The councils had selected a king who might have actually turned out to be a decent fellow. But all it took was a slit throat and suddenly Remium Agaul's hotheaded cousin, Termain, was sitting in his place. Within a cycle, the island nations of Dronodan and Talumon had seceded, allying themselves with the banished Trothian nation and declaring themselves the independent Sovereign States.

Ard told himself that those were the kinds of things that started a war. Not stealing the royal regalia, disproving Wayfarist doctrine, becoming a Paladin Visitant, and feeding the beloved crusader monarch to a dragon.

The speaker finished reading the names of the fallen, and Ard figured it was time to get ready. Reaching his gloved hand alongside his face, he grabbed the hem of the carefully positioned cloth bag and pulled it down over his head.

Raek would say that the bag had greatly improved his looks, since Ard hadn't had a decent shave or haircut in well over a year. The unkempt appearance certainly wasn't an attempt to be fashionable. He was doing it solely for the benefit of anonymity. See, standing on the palace steps and calling out the king for his secret crimes tended to garner attention. And while Ardor Benn loved attention, he didn't so much care for recognition. Especially by the Regulators.

He'd had to lie low in the weeks following Pethredote's death, and he'd only felt good about emerging once his beard had grown in. Even then, he didn't dare give his own name, what with all the rumors flying around the palace.

In essence, he had been forced to retire Ardor Benn for a spell. In his dealings with everyone but Raek, he was now Androt Penn, or one of a half dozen other aliases he had paperwork for.

"It is with great solemnity," continued the speaker, "that King Termain Agaul bestows upon this body the highest of military honors—the Stalwart Heart."

Ard quickly tied the head-bag securely around his neck, the strings slipping twice before he managed to get it snug around the collar of his general's uniform. The gloves were ridiculously silky. No wonder the general had died. Poor guy was probably trying to pull the trigger on his Roller, but his finger just kept slipping off.

Outside the coffin, Ard heard a latch releasing. Quickly, he crossed his hands across his chest in the deadest of fashion, leveling his breathing and lying as still as the grave.

The casket's lid swung open on silent hinges. Ard kept his eyes open, though he couldn't see much through the bag on his head. It was a cold winter night, but the light that poured in had the steady glow of Light Grit detonations.

A shadow loomed over him. That would be King Termain, royal imbecile of the highest order.

"Homeland keep you, General." He spoke softly enough that Ard was likely the only one in earshot. "You served well."

And there it was.

King Termain slipped the Stalwart Heart medallion into Ard's gloved hand, tucking it tightly against his uniformed breast. Ard's client would be ecstatic about that little piece of metal. And that meant he and Raek would finally get paid.

Trumpets. Drums. A salute of six gunshots.

Then the casket's lid swung shut and Ard relaxed, hearing the latch lock him securely into the darkness once more. It wasn't far from the palace grounds to the cemetery, but the procession would need to cut through the upper end of the Central Quarter.

Under the head-bag, Ardor Benn grinned. His portion of the ruse had gone incredibly smoothly. Ard felt like he could list his portrayal of a dead general among his most flawless performances. Of course, the most complicated bit was yet to come, but that was up to Raekon Dorrel.

This way of traveling was actually much smoother than a typical carriage ride. Ard knew his coffin was set atop a palanquin, carried on the shoulders of eight strong Regulators. Almost made a fellow feel like dozing off with this fine pillow under his head.

The procession made another turn. Left this time. Ard was supposed to keep track of where they were in the route, but sparks, he had a hard enough time doing that when he wasn't in a coffin with a bag over his head.

A typical Beripent funeral procession for a man of the general's standing would be led by mounted Regulators, sent ahead to make sure the streets were properly cleared and prepared. Several blocks behind them was the carried casket. Another set of mounted Regulators would take up the rear, keeping the wake of citizens a respectful distance behind the coffin.

Tonight, Ard expected quite a significant following. General Nelbet was a war hero, after all. Every citizen of Espar and Strind knew someone fighting in the war. Honoring the fallen was a way for each person to thank the Homeland that it wasn't their acquaintance in the coffin.

The procession came to a halt. Careful not to let his movement shake the coffin, Ard reached up and untied the drawstring at his neck. Pushing the head-bag up past his eyebrows, he drew in a breath of cool air, unfiltered by the lavender-scented fabric. He could hear better with the bag off his head, although everything was still muffled through the wooden casket.

"Blazing oxcart overturned in the street ahead," said a woman's voice.

Okay. Ard knew exactly where they were now.

"That's *your* job to clear it out!" The man's response was a touch on the whiny side for Ard's liking. But then, a wrinkle in the routine often made people panic. Some people got whiny when they panicked.

"It was carrying Grit pots," she hissed. "Road's blocked from both ways with half a dozen Prolonged Barrier clouds spanning the intersection. By my estimate, they won't burn out for another twelve minutes."

*Sixteen*, Ard mentally corrected. Unless Gard and Sigg had overturned the cart early. A likely possibility, with those two. Ard didn't like contracting those boorish thugs, but Raek couldn't be in two places at once.

"We can't backtrack the processional," said the whiner. "Of all the unprofessional…"

"We're dealing with it," the woman cut in. "There's an alleyway up ahead. Pello's clearing it out as we speak."

"This is General Yul Nelbet," he replied. "We're not parading his body down some Homeland-forsaken alley."

"It cuts directly over to Key Street," the woman explained. "The procession is turning there in half a block anyway."

The whiner clucked his tongue disapprovingly. "If anything should go wrong…"

Ard heard the woman's horse turn away, and the whole procession started forward again.

Nothing was going to go wrong in the narrow alleyway between Harson and Key. It was going to go exactly as Ard and Raek intended.

He felt the palanquin make the turn and counted twenty-two seconds before he heard the loud caw of a crow. At least, that's what the sound was supposed to be. From here, Raek sounded more like a soprano getting punched in the throat. Still, it was better than that time Raek had insisted on the signal being a goat's bleat. They had been in a pasture of sheep, for Homeland's sake! How was he supposed to sort all that out?

Ardor Benn reached up and knocked on the coffin.

The palanquin came to a jolting halt. Good. He had their attention. Ard knocked again, five crisp raps on the sturdy wooden lid.

It took only a moment for the palanquin to come off the bearers' shoulders. Ard felt himself lowered all the way down to the alley's dirt floor. Murmured conversations sounded on all sides, but Ard was only listening to the release of the latch.

It was all up to his partner now. Their success would rest in that brief moment between the next two seconds.

Ard heard the shattering of clay Grit pots, followed by exclamations from the Regulators surrounding his casket. He threw open the lid of the coffin and sat up, the lavender-scented head-bag slipping down over his face again. He heard the clicking of Slagstone gun hammers, but gratefully, the whiny voice of their commander shrieked, "Don't shoot!" The last thing they wanted to do was gun down General Nelbet if he had somehow made a miraculous recovery on his way to the cemetery.

Witnessing the rising dead had the potential to be quite traumatizing. But in a matter of minutes, these Regulators wouldn't remember a thing about this experience. The shattering pot Ard had heard, launched from a window high above, had been full of Memory Grit. The detonation was expensive, but the narrow alleyway gave them a little extra coverage, as the buildings' walls would push the Memory cloud to fill the space. To prevent outsiders from looking in, Raek had also detonated small pots of Shadow Grit at either end of the alley. And if anyone stepped through the dark clouds to investigate, they'd find themselves in the blast radius of the Memory Grit, soon to forget the whole ordeal.

Ard took advantage of the hesitation to smash his own clay pot against the side of the coffin. A small cloud of highly Compounded Light Grit sprang up next to him, but Ard was the only one prepared for the blinding brightness in the dark alleyway, his eyes squinted behind the cloth bag.

With all other eyes shut or diverted from the glaring orb, Ard leapt from the coffin, quickly scanning the narrow alleyway to see where to go. There was plenty of clutter along the walls, and clotheslines crisscrossed overhead like the beginnings of spiderwebs. But the spot he was looking for was a deep pocket of utter darkness just below that window.

It was another cloud of Shadow Grit, carefully placed by Raek to keep its contents concealed. The moment Ard entered it, he could see what was inside, finally pulling the head-bag completely off.

General Nelbet's stiff corpse was propped awkwardly in a large wheelbarrow. His hands were crossed upon his uniformed chest, and an identical head-bag was tied securely around his neck.

Ard wasted no time, taking hold of the wheelbarrow's handles. He gave it a good shove toward the coffin, letting go and watching it careen out of the Shadow cloud and topple, spilling the corpse onto the hardened dirt beside the palanquin.

By now, there was sufficient chaos in the alleyway, as some of the Reggies exclaimed that the casket was empty. Ard pushed open the window and hoisted himself out of the Shadow cloud and into the tenement building.

He paused in the empty room, suddenly wondering how he'd arrived here as his memories from the alleyway vanished. But he knew what the plan had been, and the fact that he wasn't shot was a good sign. Glancing back into the disturbed alley, Ard saw that the general's body was in place. Perfect.

Ard sprinted across the empty room and up two flights of stairs.

The door at the top was unlocked and he quietly slipped inside, shutting it behind him.

Raekon Dorrel was seated in a chair at the third-story window, a crossbow in one hand and a bag of fried potatoes in the other. He turned as Ard entered the room.

"Oh, hey, General," he said through a mouthful. "How was your afternoon?"

Ard pulled off the silky gloves and tossed them into the hearth, where Raek had a nice fire going to ward off the winter chill.

"Not bad. Luxurious ride. Lots of women and children weeping for me. And the king awarded me the Stalwart Heart for getting my skull knocked open."

Ard took his first look at the medallion. It was about the size of an Ashing, but made entirely of gold. One side was smooth, but the other was stamped with the outline of Espar ringed about by the words BRAVE. INTREPID. STALWART.

That definitely wasn't what they'd stamped on the fake medallion tucked into the general's cold hand. Ard was still surprised that they'd been able to fit a word as long as *nincompoop*.

Raek pointed out the window. "You're missing the show."

Ard crossed quietly and squinted down into the alley. His bright cloud of Light Grit still beamed from the coffin, providing plenty of illumination to the scene below. Most of the Regulators were surrounding the general's body, scratching their heads, their chins, and anything else that might release answers to their questions when scratched.

Everyone below was talking at once, and Ard could only hear bits of sentences floating up to the third-story window. It was a lane of confusion and upset. To Ard and Raek it seemed pure comedy.

After several moments of hysteria, the whiner regained control. "Obviously, we need to pick up the general and put him back in the casket."

"How do we know he's dead?" one of the bearers dared. "I saw him sit up."

"Of course he's dead, you idiot!" cried the whiner. "He's missing half his head!"

"How do we know that's really him?" asked another.

"He's wearing the uniform," reasoned the whiner. "He's got the Stalwart Heart right there in his hand." He pointed to the glint of metal.

"Something feels off," said another bearer. "How did he ignite that Light Grit? And how did he get out of the coffin?"

"He didn't!" the whiner cried. "You dropped the casket. He tumbled out...I don't know!"

"And now to prove the obvious," Raek narrated in a whispered voice, "the little man removes the head-bag."

Sure enough, the Regulator stepped forward and untied the drawstring at the general's neck. With one swift movement, he whisked off the bag.

Even from the third-story window, Ard had to look away from the gruesome sight. When he regained the stomach to look again, the whiner had tossed the empty head-bag to one of the bearers and was storming off, calling over his shoulder.

"No more questions! Just load the body back into the coffin and let's forget this ever happened."

"Literally," Raek whispered, passing his partner the bag of fried potatoes. "In about two minutes."

The bearer stuffed the bag over the mangled head of the general and tied it closed. The others positioned the palanquin nearer, moving the coffin away from the brightly glowing Light cloud.

Ard reached for a potato, only to find that Raek had eaten them all and had passed him an empty bag. He crumpled it up and tossed it into the fire, the greasy paper going up in a gush of flames.

Below, the general was finally in the casket and the lid was latched once more. Dazed and frightened faces returned to their positions and the palanquin was raised. Falling in to their familiar pace, the procession continued down the alley, the Memory cloud extinguishing as they exited onto the busy thoroughfare of Key Street.

"And now we can add 'grave robbers' to our list of dirty deeds." Raek reached out and swiped the medallion from Ard's grasp, turning it under his careful eye.

"That wasn't grave robbing," Ard said. "It was an intricate, complex ruse. We've been over this, Raek."

"We stole from a dead guy."

"Not true," Ard rebutted. "General Nelbet was never awarded the Stalwart Heart. I was."

Raek rolled his eyes. "You're sure there wasn't a misunderstanding?"

"Nope." Ard unbuttoned his general's coat. "I distinctly heard him say that—quote—'King Termain Agaul bestows upon *this body* the highest of military honors—the Stalwart Heart.'"

"Congratulations." Raek's voice was deadpan. "You're a war hero."

"And soon we'll have spending money again." Ard removed his boots and pants, tossing the latter into the crackling hearth to destroy the evidence of his disguise. Now that he stood in nothing but his undershorts, he wondered aloud. "Did you bring that bag I packed?"

Raek absently gestured to a duffel in the corner, his attention still on the medallion. The alley suddenly went dark below, Ard's little Compounded cloud of Light Grit extinguishing without so much as a flicker.

"Anyone who knows Lord Stend will think he's a crazy old coot when he starts showing this off." Raek twirled the medallion between his fingers. "Pretending like he earned it more than forty years ago."

"Anyone who knows Lord Stend *already* thinks he's a crazy old coot," Ard corrected, rummaging in the duffel bag. "But he's a crazy old coot that's going to pay us."

"Those are my favorite kinds." Raek stuffed the medallion into his pocket and began packing his array of crossbow Grit bolts.

"I can't find my pants," Ard muttered. "Did you take them out?"

"I'm ashamed to say that I didn't think of that," Raek answered. "I don't know what load of slag you threw in there, but that bag was a lot heavier than a change of clothes."

"Extra stuff," Ard said. "You know, in case things went sideways."

"What are you talking about? It never goes sideways."

The door flew open, Gard and Sigg appearing with Rollers drawn. The hired thugs had sneers on their ugly faces as they strode into the room, full of self-importance and misplaced confidence.

"Hey, there, fellas." Raek's tone wavered. "Everything all right?"

"You told them where to find us?" Ard shrieked at his partner.

"An Ashing goes a long way with the street urchins," said the bigger man. That was Gard. Not quite Raek's height, but equally bald. "Little brat told us right where you was hiding out."

"Sounds like the oxcart worked out," Raek tried. "Diverted the whole funeral procession."

"We's here to collect." Sigg spat on the wooden floor. He was stocky—nearly square, with pale skin and a royal mess of a tattoo on his forearm. Was that supposed to be a woman's face or a pile of unfired dragon slag?

"And we's decided we want double," added Gard. "And we want it now, Fuse."

Androt Penn and the Lit Fuse.

Raek had been the first to point out the obvious likeness to their original names. But that was the point! Confusion through similarity. If anyone suspected their true identities, Ard could quickly explain that they were often mistaken for those legendary ruse artists, Ardor Benn and the Short Fuse. And this way, when the real

Ardor Benn was ready to return, he could retroactively claim any notable deeds done by his pseudonym.

"Hey, now," Raek began. "You know that's not how this works. We had an agreement."

"Agreements change," said Gard. "And you gots to—"

Raek lunged for the crossbow and string of Grit bolts beside the chair. Sigg's Roller cracked, a lead ball smashing into the floorboards beside the weaponry.

Raek jerked back sharply and Gard closed the distance, seizing him and leveling his Roller barrel against Raek's temple.

"I knew we shouldn't have hired these guys," Ard said. During the brief skirmish, he had drawn both of his own Rollers from his duffel bag. Now he stood in the corner of the room, sorely underdressed for a gunfight, but appropriately armed.

"It was short notice," Raek said. "We didn't have a lot of options."

"One more reason to move to the Sovereign States." Ard took an aggressive step forward. "They say all the honest criminals have gone to Dronodan. Nothing but lowlifes left in Beripent."

"Not another step!" Gard pressed the barrel tighter against Raek's head. He had backed the two of them against the wall next to the window.

"If you shoot my partner, then I shoot yours," Ard reasoned.

"Then I shoot you," Gard said.

"Then you definitely won't get paid," Raek pointed out.

That seemed to puzzle them nicely. Ard took advantage of the stupor to take three swift steps across the room, stopping just arm's length from Raek. Gard instantly shrank behind the bigger man, making himself completely unseen by gripping the back of Raek's shirt and repositioning the Roller at the base of his skull.

Ard looked at his partner. They were pushing their luck. Sigg had a clear line of fire on Ard, and the goon was obviously itching to pull the trigger.

"Smoke in the chimney?" Ard asked.

Raek groaned. "Last time I ended up with two broken ribs."

"Well, maybe this time I'll only break one." He cocked the Roller in his right hand.

"Hey!" Sigg shook his gun in Ard's direction. "You put that down!"

But Ard was aiming his gun directly at Raekon Dorrel, the tip of the barrel hovering just inches from Raek's chest. "Fourth button down?"

"Just a hair lower," Raek replied.

Ard pulled the trigger.

The ball tore through Raek's shirt just below the fourth button. There was a splatter of blood and Gard slumped against the wall, gasping his final breaths in silent pain.

Raek fell to his knees, gripping his chest, but Ard spun without hesitation, sending the shot from his other Roller through Sigg's thigh. The injured man let out an earsplitting cry, dropping his gun to grip the wound.

"Consider that your payment," Ard said as Sigg scooted across the floor and all but tumbled out of sight down the stairs.

"How'd it go?" Ard turned to check on Raek. The big man was on his feet once more, the grimace on his face actually less than what Ard had expected. Raek ripped open his shirt to expose the piece of pipe that ran through his torso and exited out the back.

"Oh, good." Ard sighed. "You still only have one hole in your chest."

The pipe was compliments of the palace healers, under the orders of King Pethredote himself. It had been embedded into Raek's chest as an experimental means of reviving him from the brink of death. The front of the pipe had a slightly wider mouth, like a funnel, enabling carefully measured amounts of Health Grit to be poured directly into his torso.

When Ard had rescued Raek from the palace dungeon, the back of the pipe had been plugged, allowing the healer to adjust the exact location of the detonation's center inside the patient.

The sides of the pipe were perforated with dozens of small holes, once allowing the Health cloud to make direct contact with Raek's insides. Of course, the whole thing was now a mess of rigid scars, making the pipe impossible to safely extract.

Raek was perfectly healthy now, but the "chimney," as Ard liked to call it, still had its uses. Like shooting someone hiding behind your friend. Or carrying snacks.

"Mostly a clean pass this time." Wincing, Raek dropped into the chair by the window and rummaged through his sash of Grit bolts. "Just grazed the right side a bit." He opened a pocket and withdrew a pair of corks and a small paper cartridge with the ends twisted closed.

"I was even a few inches away," Ard said. On his first attempt at "smoke in the chimney" he had all but pressed the gun barrel into Raek's chest.

"And this time you warned me." Raek handed one of the corks to Ard and leaned forward, pulling up his shirt. "Flames, you're a considerate guy."

The hole was bleeding, and Raek grunted as Ard shoved the cork into the back of the pipe. Leaning in his chair, Raek untwisted the paper roll and poured a little Grit into the funneled front of the pipe before using the other cork to seal it off. He gave it a sharp rap, which must have detonated the Grit, and sighed in relief as the cloud formed, fully contained within his body.

"Where'd you get that Health Grit?" Ard asked.

Raek's eyes were closed and he rolled his head back. "I brought it just in case things went sideways." A little grin pulled at the corners of his mouth.

Movement in the dark alley below suddenly caught Ard's attention. He maneuvered himself in front of Raek and peered straight down over the windowsill.

Sparks! There were three Reggies down there, weapons drawn as they positioned themselves against the wall of the building.

"Raek!" Ard hissed, ducking his head back inside. "We've got company."

Raek's eyes snapped open. He, too, leaned out the window only to draw back the moment he saw the Reggies. "Folks in this part of town must not be used to gunshots."

"I've also heard that an Ashing goes a long way with the street urchins," Ard said. It was likely that the same unfortunate orphans who'd spied for Gard and Sigg shared their knowledge with the local Regulators.

See, that was why no one could be trusted.

"It won't take them long to find Sigg," Raek surmised.

"Which leads them to us. Literally a trail of blood straight here," said Ard. "So, what do we do?"

"Well, I think you should start by putting on some pants." Raek was strapping on his sash of Grit bolts and winding his crossbow.

Ard staggered back to his duffel bag and upended the contents onto the wooden floor. Seriously, no trousers? Of all the things to forget...

Ard had just pulled his shirt over his head when a commotion sounded from the stairwell. Raek reached back and hurled a Grit pot through the doorway. Ard heard it bounce once before effectively shattering with enough force to spark the Slagstone fragment and ignite the Grit inside.

That was probably Barrier Grit to block the stairwell. But if the blast didn't completely fill the space, the Reggies would still be able to shoot into the room.

Ard tugged on his vest and stomped into his comfortable pair of boots. Much better than those shiny things he'd had to wear as the decorated general. He grabbed his wide leather Grit belt and scampered over to the window to consult with Raek.

The big man was loading a bolt into his crossbow, the clay tip dyed green. He cast a reluctant sidelong glance at Ard's attire.

"It's a little brisk for winter," Ard admitted. "But I'm trying to make a statement."

"What about the general's pants?" He took aim out the window.

"I threw those in the fire," Ard said. "In retrospect, not my most brilliant decision."

"We'll have to Drift Jump across the alley to that window and escape through the other building."

"Whoa! Have you seen me Drift Jump unaided?" Ard asked.

The window Raek was aiming at was even smaller than the one they'd be jumping from. And the face of the opposing building was flat and notably ledge-less. If Ard didn't line up his jump perfectly, he'd splat into the bricks and fall three stories to the Reggies waiting below.

"Would you complain about jumping if Quarrah were here?" Raek took the shot, Grit bolt speeding across the alleyway and smashing open just above the far window.

"No!" Ard quickly retorted. At least Quarrah would have held his hand so he didn't spiral out of control like a wounded pigeon.

The Drift cloud filled the space between the two buildings, but the shattering bolt surely would have attracted the attention of the Reggies positioned below. They needed to jump *now*!

Raek poked his head out the window, withdrawing it when a gunshot sounded from below.

"There's a clothesline just overhead," Raek reported. "It won't have to bear our weight in the Drift cloud, and we can use it as a guide to get over to the other window."

Okay. Not as good as Quarrah Khai holding his hand, but better than nothing.

Raek quickly reached out and snatched something off the line. "The Homeland is merciful today." He threw the item in Ard's face. Raek backed up, sprinted a few steps, and leapt from the window, catching hold of a towel draped over the clothesline.

His large figure sped across the alleyway, instantly drawing gunfire from below. The towel in his hands skimmed unnaturally across the clothesline, guiding Raek in a straight shot while scattering the few linens remaining on the line.

Ard saw him tuck his feet up and sail through the small open window on the other side, letting go of the towel at the last minute and tumbling out of sight into the far room.

A gunshot sounded from the stairwell behind, biting into the wooden ceiling above Ard's head. He flinched, finally looking down at the item that Raek had tossed him.

It was a pair of trousers.

Never mind that they looked quite small and definitely tailored for a woman. There was no time to put them on now, anyway.

Strapping his Grit belt around his middle, Ard sprinted forward as another gun fired from the stairs. He leapt out the window, flinging one of the pant legs over the clothesline and tethering himself to the guide.

Raek must have drawn all the fire from the Reggies below. Or maybe they were already moving to surround the building across the way. Either way, only one ball whizzed past Ardor Benn as he glided across the alleyway, damp linens spiraling lazily through the air around him.

The clothesline guided him true, and his momentum practically threw him through the window, pulling the pants along with him. He tumbled into the dim room, Raek hoisting him to his feet before his head had stopped spinning.

Ard instantly kicked off his boots and began tugging on the trousers, awkwardly hopping across the room.

"Don't mind us, ma'am," Raek said. "We're just performing a routine laundry inspection."

Ard looked up, noticing for the first time the gray-haired woman sitting at the table in the corner. Her eyes were wide, unblinking, and she held a slice of bread like a defensive shield.

"It would seem everything is just fine here," Ard said, sliding back into his boots. It was less than fine, really. He couldn't come close to fastening the top three buttons of these pants.

Raek pushed open the woman's door and the two of them moved out, quickly finding a stairwell at the end of the hallway.

"Next time, could you find me a *dry* pair of pants?"

"Next time?" Raek replied, his long legs taking the stairs three at a time. "You intend for this to happen again?"

They sprinted down another flight of stairs, and by the time they reached the bottom, Ard was thoroughly turned around. The landing placed them at the end of a long, narrow hallway pocked with doors on either side and lit only by a dimly Prolonged Light cloud up ahead.

Ard pushed open the nearest door on the right and charged into the apartment. There were two kids playing with a set of wooden horses, a small orb of Light Grit hanging in one corner.

The mother screamed, and the kids seemed frozen. Ard and Raek barreled past them, making for the dark window over a padded bench seat.

"This is going to put us back in the alley we just came from," said Raek.

"They won't be expecting that." Ard unlatched the window and pushed it open. "We can cut back over to Harson and disappear."

Raek grunted in approval as Ard stepped up onto the bench, struggling to throw his leg over the windowsill.

"So blazing tight..." he muttered.

"Folks," Raek said to the family, "just be grateful that he's wearing pants at all."

They ripped right up the crotch, and Ard suddenly had the mobility he needed to get out the window and drop into the quiet alleyway. Overhead, their cloud of Drift Grit still shimmered, but the Regulators had moved out to swarm the buildings on both sides of the alley.

They were almost to Harson Street when they heard a shout of pursuit. Ard and Raek turned their jog into a sprint, suddenly less interested in subtlety and more interested in getting the blazes out of there.

They crossed Harson, ducking down another side alley and merging onto Lanler Avenue. The duo was far enough ahead to outdistance any Reggies on foot, but someone on horseback was giving chase. Ard could hear the whistle, the shouts, and the hooves on the cobblestones.

Darkness was their ally, and Ard and Raek were familiar enough with the wealthy upper end of the Central Quarter to get off the major roadways, where Light Grit streetlamps would give them away.

They'd be safe once they reached the Char. From there, they could hire a carriage to take them back to their slum of an apartment in the lower Western Quarter.

Ard led them around another corner, losing all sense of direction, but pushing forward nonetheless. He didn't question his route. In fact, he was filled with a strange sense of confidence that he was going the right way.

The two escapees had just turned onto a little street, quiet and unlit, when Raek grabbed his arm to demand a breather.

The big Mixer didn't appear to be doing well, doubling over the moment they stopped running, gasping so hard it turned into a cough. Raek's endurance definitely wasn't what it used to be, reminding Ard of the toll Pethredote's blade had taken on his partner.

Ard drew his Roller at the sound of approaching horse hooves. Wheezing, Raek pointed down the street. "Got to keep moving…"

Ard glanced back the way they'd come, noticing a carriage they'd passed in their haste. The single horse's head was downcast as though the animal were catching a quick nap between routes.

At once, Ard was seized with a powerful feeling. It twisted up his insides as though the thought of doing anything other than hiding in that carriage would make him sick.

"This way," he hissed to Raek, moving back in the direction they'd come. Moving *toward* the sounds of those still searching for them.

"Are you out of your mind?" Raek cried. Still, he moved to follow, his breathing finally under control.

"Trust me," Ard responded. "It's just an—"

"Don't you say 'Urging,'" Raek cut him off.

But it was. Ard wondered if the Homeland had been Urging him to this hiding spot from the very moment they'd begun their escape.

The Urgings weren't what the Islehood taught—at least not for Ardor Benn. But he'd experienced driving feelings more and more since the night he'd traveled through time. And when he *did* feel them, wasn't it his responsibility to follow through? To keep this timeline intact and moving forward?

There was no driver on the bench, so it wasn't likely that the carriage was for hire. He cracked open the door and poked his head inside.

Sparks! It was occupied!

There was a single woman seated inside, her cowled figure almost swallowed up by the darkness of the carriage's interior.

*We're caught if she screams,* Ard thought, quickly withdrawing. He could hear the Reggie's horse just around the corner. But the woman didn't make a sound, and as Ard swung the carriage door shut, she reached out to stop him.

"Inspector Stringer?" Her voice was soft, anxious.

Ard glanced at Raek. Around the corner, a Regulator whistle chirped that the search was still on.

"Yes?" Ard said.

"Oh, flames," muttered Raek.

"I was beginning to think you weren't coming," said the woman.

"I apologize. My assistant and I were … strung out to dry, so to speak." Ard climbed into the carriage, his impossibly tight pants protesting the movement. He waved quickly for Raek to follow.

"Come along, good chap. We shouldn't keep the lady waiting any longer."

Raek rolled his eyes and squeezed through the doorway, making it suddenly look small before he pulled it shut, plunging the three of them into complete darkness.

"I have a few granules of Light Grit here," spoke the woman.

"Please," insisted Ard, "we prefer to operate in the shadows."

"This is more than a shadow," Raek's voice sounded.

"I appreciate you meeting me under these circumstances," she said.

"We appreciate you having the carriage ready," answered Ard in all truthfulness. The Reggie whistle tweeted again, and the horse sounded like it was just outside their carriage. In a moment the sweep would be complete and he and Raek could be safely on their way.

"As I stated in my letter," she said, "I am willing to pay handsomely for any information you can uncover."

Well, this just got interesting!

"How handsomely?" Ard asked.

"Price really isn't an issue," she said. "If you can find out what happened to my son, you can all but name your price."

Raek coughed in the darkness beside him.

*Name your price?* Ard was glad he'd followed the Homeland's Urging tonight!

"So, how about that Light Grit you mentioned?" Ard suggested, suddenly desperate to see the face of the woman who could make such outlandish promises. The sounds of the searching Reggie had moved past, so a little illumination wouldn't hurt.

A Slagstone ignitor sparked and a fist-sized orb of Light Grit flared to life on the seat beside the woman. Ard blinked a few times as she reached up and removed her hood.

For some reason, the woman looked vaguely familiar, but not enough for Ard to put a name to her face. Her brown hair was woven into intricate braids, its length unknown as it vanished down her back. She looked to be a few years older than Ard, with skin as pale and smooth as cream.

At the sight of Raekon Dorrel in full light, the woman stiffened. "Do you always keep such...formidable company?"

Ard glanced at his big friend, crossbow laid across his lap and a long knife on his thigh. His shirt was torn open, but luckily the bolt sash covered the ghastly-looking "chimney."

"Oh, this is my assistant," Ard said. "He...assists me with things."

"Your Majesty," Raek said, light glinting off his inclined bald head.

Ard burst into laughter at the statement, falling promptly silent when Raek shot him a sideways glance that said he was not joking.

Oh, sparks! *That* was why she looked familiar!

Queen Abeth Ostel Agaul, widow of the late Remium, cousin-in-law to King Termain Agaul.

"So, you..." Ard floundered. "What brings you back to Beripent?"

Ard tried not to follow politics too closely, but the last he had heard, Lady Abeth had fled to her native island of Dronodan after the assassination of her husband and son.

Wait...Now she was seeking information regarding her son's death? Regardless of who had been arrested for the murders, everyone knew King Termain was responsible.

"I'm sure you are aware that tonight was the funeral of General Yul Nelbet," Abeth said.

Ard nodded slowly. "So I heard."

"Termain respected him greatly," she continued, "even before the war. As plans for his burial were finalized, my contacts reached out. We had lived at the palace for nearly eight years while my husband served as advisor to King Pethredote. There are many who remain loyal to the line of Remium Agaul."

"We list ourselves among them," Ard said.

It was true. Had he been allowed to rule for more than the space of a few hours, Remium could have been like a noncorrupt version of Pethredote: stable, progressive, and benevolent.

Queen Abeth smiled, but it was a flicker; short-lived and back to business. "I do not think the citizens of the Archkingdom are aware of the significance of the general's burial site."

Ard cocked his head. "The cemetery on the shoreline of the upper Central Quarter. I haven't heard specifics."

"The Tertiary Mausoleum," she replied. "Second deck, ninth niche."

She said it with such passion, but it didn't mean anything to Ard. He glanced at Raek, hoping for some insight. Confronted with flat stares, the lady finally whispered.

"My son's niche."

Ard felt his fist balling up. He knew Termain had recklessly abandoned longstanding policies, disregarded counsel, and generally did whatever the blazes he wanted. But removing the prince's remains to bury his general pal... this was another level of boneheadedness.

"Want us to stop the interment?" Raek hefted his crossbow. "Might not be too late. We could just lob the general's casket over the shoreline cliff."

Lady Abeth's eyes grew round, bulging like quickly rising pastry dough. "Homeland, no!" She swallowed hard. "They've already moved my son's casket to a lower mausoleum. That is what brought me back to Beripent."

"I'm sorry your visit was inspired by such insulting circumstances," Ard said.

"It was not easy for me to return to Espar," she explained. Ard imagined not. Her association with Dronodan had forced her to become an expatriate to the Archkingdom. "I am not likely to return again unless the war should end favorably, so I wanted to leave the Agaul family ring with my son's body."

"Don't tell me you cracked open that casket," Raek muttered.

Lady Abeth nodded. "You may call it a morbid desire, but I considered it an Urging from the Homeland. However you deem it, my glimpse into that casket is what brought us together tonight."

"How so?" Ard asked.

The lady leaned forward. "Inspector," Abeth whispered, "that body is not my son's."

"You're certain of this?" asked Ard.

"Your Highness," Raek cut in, "with all due respect, the body has been there for over a year. You aren't bound to recognize much."

"It was his teeth," Abeth said. "Decay had peeled back his lips and I saw into the corpse's mouth. My Shad had been suffering a cracked molar just days prior to his death. He was terrified of the Healers and begged me not to tell them. I was waiting to see if his pain would subside naturally, when he was killed by the blast in his bedroom. But the body I saw in my son's casket yesterday had no cracked tooth."

The magnitude of this conversation, which had been revealing itself little by little like gentle waves washing sand away from a buried seashell, was suddenly wholly visible. If Shad Agaul, rightful heir to the throne, was not in his casket, then where was he?

"And what, exactly, do you need me to…inspect?" Ard asked.

"Find my son," Lady Abeth said. "Or whatever information you can about his true whereabouts. I will provide you with any needed resources and compensate you generously for your time. I suspect Termain to be behind this, and uncovering the truth could tip the scales enough to remove him from the throne and unify the islands once again."

The carriage fell into contemplative silence. Raek gave Ard an unmistakable look. It seemed to say, *Don't you dare, Ardor Benn. This is bigger than our usual petty ruses. Remember what happened last time you bit off more than you could chew?*

"Very well," Ard said, recapturing some of the stuffy-inspector voice he had dialed in when they'd first climbed into the carriage. Beside him, Raek let out a not-so-subtle sigh. "I believe we are exactly the men for your job."

~

*This is our final testament... Should we die up there, our glory shall not be forgotten, for this shall remain forever incorruptible.*

# CHAPTER

# 2

Portsend Wal let his mixing scales balance, glancing over the rim of his spectacles to check the progress of his students. He could see only the tops of their heads, bent over those long tables, scribing charcoals clacking against the pages of their notebooks.

They were all good students. *Wartime* students. While their friends were off fighting, they had chosen to stay and learn. Each day, Portsend saw optimism in their faces. The hope that the war wouldn't last their whole lifetime, and that their studies would actually be worth something in a postwar society.

Portsend turned his attention back to his balanced scales. Ah, well. Turned out his scribing charcoal weighed nine granules. He had guessed eleven.

It had nothing to do with the arithmetic his students were working out, it was just something he did to pass the time. He couldn't simply stand around waiting. That would be too Settled for him. Portsend believed he should constantly be refining and improving his skills. It wasn't just good Wayfarist doctrine, it was his progressive mentality that had landed him this teaching position at the Southern Quarter College of Beripent.

It wasn't the University in Helizon, of course. Portsend had been on track for a position there. He'd met the right people and even toured the expansive campus. Sparks, he'd heard that the university's headmaster herself had read his paper on theoretical containment of uncontainable Grit types. And of course it helped to have a glowing letter of recommendation from the Holy Isless who was now serving as Prime of all Wayfarism.

But none of that mattered now. The University in Helizon was on Talumon. As a citizen of the Archkingdom, he couldn't so much as step foot on Talumon, let alone teach at a university there.

His classroom here was more than sufficient. The demonstration table at the front of the room was supplied with the finest mixing equipment, and the framed blackboard slate covered nearly the entire wall behind him. Seating for the students was laid out in rising tiers, and Light Grit lanterns supplemented the natural skylight, providing plenty of illumination for reading and writing.

One could say his classroom was lacking only the prestige of Helizon's university. But Portsend believed it was the quality of the instruction that made excellent students, not the name of the institution. His students would be no less equipped just because they were schooled in Beripent—a city known for commerce and trade, but not particularly for education.

Portsend glanced up again. Most of the students had finished now. Just waiting on a handful. This particular course had been filled to capacity with sixty-five students. Today, nearly a third of them were absent. Students had a way of disappearing as the term wore on. Like driftwood, caught for a while in a river's eddy, bobbing in and out before being swept downstream in pursuit of something else.

To Portsend Wal, there was nothing else. This was Introduction to Practical Grit Mixing. This was where it all began! What other topic could possibly be interesting enough to lure them away?

Portsend cleared his throat. "Let us conclude." That lifted the remaining heads. Perhaps they had already worked it out and were merely checking their work. Or doodling.

The older he got, the harder it was for Portsend to gauge the difficulty of the equations he set out for his students. It seemed he couldn't remember a time when he didn't know how to calculate the waning effect of Prolonging Grit.

"The answer you should have arrived at is nineteen granules of Prolonging Grit," Portsend said. "That will sustain the given cloud of Light Grit for forty-three minutes."

As he spoke, he noticed several of the students begin to gather their belongings. He glanced at the large hourglass on the shelf beside the door. Still a few minutes of sand left. He'd heard that, as of this year, the University in Helizon had a genuine clock in every classroom. No, Portsend wasn't jealous. That incessant ticking would probably have driven him mad.

The unauthorized, premature adjournment spread through the tiers, but Portsend wasn't finished. Those final minutes were his, and these youngsters needed to learn patience.

"Let us theorize that a panweight of Drift Grit becomes contaminated." Portsend raised his voice, causing the buzz to subside as the students realized that class was not dismissed. "Assuming the original panweight was pure, how do you calculate the loss in quality?"

"We would need to know how many granules of the contaminant were introduced into the Grit," said Tobal on the front tier. "Which could be done by weighing the whole thing again, and calculating the difference."

Portsend held up a finger. "That's well and good in some situations. But let us suppose that the panweight of Drift Grit falls from the back of a wagon and breaks open on a dirt road. It would be impossible to recover every pinch. In this scenario, you are dealing with introduced contaminants, as well as loss of product."

"You could use a sifter to separate the impurities," suggested Kella.

"No." This was from Lomaya Vans on the second tier. Her confident tone made Portsend smile. She was among the brightest he'd seen in his career.

"Drift Grit is pulverized bone," Lomaya expounded. "If it has mingled with soil, even the finest Sifter wouldn't be able to separate the contaminants."

"There is no way to calculate the loss of quality without a practical test," said San Green.

Yes. Very good. There was a reason his class was called Introduction to *Practical* Grit Mixing.

"I mean, the duration of the cloud will tell you exactly how contaminated the Grit was," San continued. "Sometimes you've just got to detonate it."

"So you perform a test," Portsend said, nodding, "and the resulting cloud, derived from a single granule, burns out at eight minutes and twenty seconds. How much contamination would there be in the entire panweight?"

Portsend found the question perfectly stimulating, but all eyes had gone to the hourglass beside the door. Well, those few minutes had sure whisked by.

He sniffed again. "Class dismissed."

The students rose, shuffling down the stairwell aisle and making for the exit. Portsend quickly busied himself, wiping down the blackboard with a dusty rag.

"Professor Wal?"

He turned sharply, glasses slipping to the tip of his nose. San

Green was standing across the demonstration table, satchel slung over one shoulder. Behind him, the tiered seating was empty and most of the students were clustered at the doorway, pressing to slip through like the sands of his hourglass.

"I wonder if I could speak with you for a moment," the young man said.

Portsend always found it difficult to speak with students one-on-one. He thoroughly enjoyed them as a whole, but in single conversation, he had a hard time striking the proper tone. Too friendly and he could lose their respect. Too stern and he could embitter them against this wonderful field of study.

"Now is a good time," Portsend said. "Do you have a concern?"

"I've decided to leave the college," answered San.

Portsend studied the lad. This was indeed unexpected. San was a solid student, with a clever approach to problem-solving that Portsend didn't see in many. But come to think of it, the lad had started the term with much more enthusiasm than he'd shown lately.

"May I ask why?"

"My friends are..." San hesitated, his eyes flicking to the doorway where the last of the students were disappearing. Then he lowered his voice. "I'm going to the war. It's where I should have been all along, but my parents had set aside Ashings for my schooling since I was young."

Sparks, he was *still* young. San couldn't have been much older than seventeen—fresh out of local school. Portsend had been teaching for longer than this kid had been alive!

"What do you expect to do in the war, San?"

The lad shrugged. "A fellow from my hometown is part of the navy. He might be able to get me onto a fighting ship. If not, most of my friends are in the infantry. Infantry is always taking recruits."

Infantrymen were dying out a lot faster than the recruits were coming in, from what Portsend had heard. "Why do you want to fight?"

"It's what I'm supposed to be doing," San repeated.

Portsend scratched his chin. "You believe in this war?"

"I believe Dronodan and Talumon need to rejoin the Archkingdom," he said.

"They were never part of the *Archkingdom*," replied Portsend calmly. "That is a construct named by King Termain Agaul. Under the crusader monarch, there were no divisive names among the kingdom. We were simply the Greater Chain."

Technically, each of the four islands was its own kingdom, governed by its own rulers subject to Espar. But King Pethredote had tried to do away with labels like that, referring instead to the whole of the kingdom as the Greater Chain, which excluded only the smattering of sandy, Trothian islets.

"Call it what you want," San said, "their leaving is costing a lot of lives and resources."

"Do you believe it was wrong for the Sovereign States to secede?"

"It was wrong for them to defy the king."

San was smart, but he was showing the inexperience of his age. The hotheaded naivety of youth.

King Termain shouldn't have been on the throne at all. Had the noble councils been considering him, they would have found him sorely incompetent and voted him down.

His presence on the throne had been something of a loophole, and his refusal to allow his competence to be judged by the noble councils was really what had started this whole war. Now good students like San Green were trading their scribing charcoals for spears.

"Have you stopped to consider that you may be more valuable to your infantry friends by completing your schooling and getting a certification?" Portsend tried. "You reasoned through that final question very well."

San shook his head. "That was just theoretical. I want to be out there doing something useful."

"All worthwhile things start theoretically," said Portsend. "But a spilled keg of Drift Grit on the battlefield is a daily reality that someone has to deal with. Just think, in five more terms you could enlist as a Field Mixer. *That* would be doing something useful."

Portsend could see the young man considering it. He would be sorry to see San go, but sorrier still if he went without fully considering his options. Education was a long game, but it made for more powerful players.

"Come to class until the end of the week," Portsend invited. "Give me three more lectures. If I can't convince you to stay, then you can leave with my blessing."

San nodded. "Thank you. You're the first professor to challenge my decision. The others simply waved me off."

*Probably because many of the others think this is a war worth fighting,* Portsend thought. He nodded to the youth and turned his attention back to wiping the chalkboard. San took the nonverbal dismissal and exited the classroom, pulling the door shut behind him.

There was a knock at the door. Students always left in such a hurry that he wasn't surprised when one had to double back to the classroom for a forgotten belonging. Or perhaps it was San, already come to his senses.

"Enter!" he called, finishing a dusty swipe as the door swung inward.

"Portsend Wal."

That got his attention. It was a voice he hadn't heard in many cycles, and one he certainly never expected to hear within the walls of his classroom. His heart hammered in his chest as he tried to peer coolly over the rims of his glasses at the woman in the doorway.

"Prime Isless Gloristar," he finally croaked.

Portsend hadn't seen her since her ascension to Prime Isless after Frid Chauster's assassination a year and a half ago. Now she was here, draped in the velvety purple robes of her high station. The hems were trimmed in white lace, a large anchor embroidered on the chest.

"Won't you invite me in?" Even as she asked it, she strode toward him, seeming to float with her feet concealed beneath that dark robe. She was his exact age, although her black hair had not yet been touched by gray. Her skin was not as dark as his, just a smooth rich brown.

She looked thinner than when he'd last seen her. Understandable, with the weight of all Wayfarism on her shoulders. And he was probably fatter, despite lugging books to his top floor classroom day after day.

So caught up in seeing Gloristar, Portsend hadn't noticed the Regulators in the doorway until they pulled the door shut, leaving the professor and the Prime Isless alone.

Portsend stood rooted. What was proper protocol when greeting the head of Wayfarism? Would she expect such formalities after all the years they'd known each other? He decided on a low nod, reciting the common phrase that began a guidance session in the Mooring.

"Homeland guide and watch us until that blessed day when we return."

Gloristar smiled, her teeth straight and white. "We're not in the Mooring, Portsend." Her tone was gentle. "And I am no longer your compass."

He felt suddenly foolish for the formal greeting. But then, that was how he had greeted her for three years on the cove dock as he'd sought spiritual guidance. Gloristar had always been there for Portsend. Guiding him through the grief he'd felt at the death of his son and subsequent abandonment by his wife.

Portsend's visits to the Mooring had become frequent and regular, and much more had been discussed in Cove 14 than his spiritual well-being. He and Gloristar had grown as close as the Islehood's restrictions would allow. It had always been platonic between them. Always decorous and restrained.

Well, except for that one night.

"You seem to have a shortage of students." Gloristar waved her hand at the large vacant room.

"I've never paused my lectures long enough to notice," he replied.

Homeland, what was she doing here?

"Are you well?" he asked, feet shuffling nervously.

"As well as can be expected," Gloristar answered. "I am convinced there is no worse time to be Prime Isless."

She made a fair point. Wayfarism was under more scrutiny now than ever before. No sooner had Prime Isle Chauster been accused of being a crooked conspirator than shadow was cast on the doctrine of the Holy Torch. Widespread rumors had stretched out like thirsty roots, claiming that the dragons were the true shield against Moonsickness.

This was further aggravated by rumors of Moonsickness reaching the shores of the Greater Chain. It had started almost two years ago with a small township on the southernmost tip of Espar. Supposedly, the villagers had torn each other to shreds.

This story had prompted evacuations from several other distant coastal villages that feared they were located too far from the Holy Torch. Sparks, Portsend had even heard rumors of Moonsick people ravaging bigger cities lately. Just last cycle, the students were abuzz about two deranged Moonsick individuals terrorizing Beripent's Central Quarter.

Portsend didn't believe any of these ever-increasing accounts. Such heresy couldn't shake him from a lifetime of faith, but these ripples of disbelief upset many people to the core.

And if the rumors weren't enough, Gloristar was attempting to lead Wayfarism across war-torn island borders, under the direction of a king no one thought should be ruling.

"We are going to lose this war, Portsend," Gloristar suddenly said as if getting plainly to business. "It is only a matter of time.

King Termain knows it, I think, but he's too stubborn to relent. Things will worsen in the coming years, and eventually Dronodan and Talumon will overpower us."

Years more? A cycle of war was too long.

"I'm here because King Termain is exploiting every resource in the Archkingdom to gain the upper hand."

Portsend stiffened. And here he had fooled himself into thinking she'd paid him a social visit. He didn't want to discuss this with her. The king had the support of the Prime Isless, and with it came the unquestioning loyalty of so many Wayfarists. Gloristar's continued endorsements of King Termain had kept Portsend awake many a night, wondering if she'd really changed that much. Or maybe he'd misread her all along...

"You're here to help him exploit the college's resources?" he asked flatly.

"I'm not here for him," she whispered. "I need your help, Portsend."

He turned to her then, his disdain for her political affiliations melting away as he saw the frightened look on her face.

"There is no one else I can turn to with this. No one I trust." There were suddenly tears in her eyes. "I am sure beyond any doubt that the Homeland has Urged me to you. I believe you will feel it as well. Or have you forgotten our verse?"

Their verse. Was it inappropriate to feel so bonded with another person over an ancient passage of scripture?

He felt the unmistakeable Urging from the Homeland that Gloristar had mentioned. "It has always been you who have helped me," he whispered.

"Well, now it is time to set our verse straight."

Portsend nodded. Their relationship was as complex and delicate as cross-mixed Grit on the balance scales. He had little doubt that they'd be together if she weren't a Holy Isless. Or if he *were* one. Those within the Islehood could marry each other, and he'd honestly considered joining for that sole purpose. But he feared it would have been a Settled decision, driven by such a disingenuous motive.

"I don't think you heard me, Portsend…King Termain is exploiting *every* resource." Gloristar didn't truly cry, the tears disappearing as quickly as they had appeared.

"You?" Portsend felt an anger burning within his chest. King or commoner, if Termain Agaul had touched her in any way…

"I'm sure you have wondered about my endorsements of his rule." She shook her head. "I hope you know me well enough to realize that they have not been given willingly."

Portsend said nothing, but a harbored fear died at her words, like a ray of sunshine piercing into a shadowy corner of his mind.

"In some ways, I feel like little more than Termain's puppet in the Mooring," she continued. "Without the backing of Wayfarism, he knows he could not hold the throne."

That was probably the truth. A denouncement from Gloristar might even bring about a swift end to the war. Likely, the citizens of the Archkingdom would rise up against him internally, and the Sovereign States would quickly take control. Wouldn't that outcome be preferable to years of war? After all, there was more than one way to unify the Greater Chain. Maybe it was radical thinking, but Espar didn't have to come out on top, so long as a good person took the throne.

"Termain has…assured a way to get the endorsement of Wayfarism," she said.

"What has he done?" Portsend's question was forceful, and filled with a growing acrimony.

"I will admit that Wayfarism has its flaws," said Gloristar. "If it were perfect, what would we have to strive for? But of all its weaknesses, perhaps the greatest is the manner of passing the mantel of Prime. I now understand this better than anyone."

"You're referring to the Anchored Tome?" Portsend assumed. He didn't know the details about it. The ancient book was kept in a holy room in Cove 1 at the end of the Mooring. Only the Prime Isle was allowed to enter the Sanctum and read from the Anchored Tome. The book contained information that imbued the Primes with power and knowledge to lead Wayfarism and protect all of civilization.

Gloristar nodded. "Although a system may function sufficiently for centuries, it doesn't mean it cannot be destroyed in the blink of an eye. Perhaps the position of Prime Isle is not so different from that of the Bull Dragon Patriarchy."

"Termain destroyed the Anchored Tome?" Portsend cried.

Gloristar shook her head. "That would have only driven me to spurn him without providing any leverage over me."

"What, then?"

"King Termain forced entry into the Sanctum and stole the Anchored Tome. And he has sworn to destroy it if it looks like he is about to lose the war, or his throne."

"This is ludicrous! He cannot expect *you* to win the war for him," said Portsend.

"And yet he does," she said. "He believes that whoever controls Wayfarism will always have the upper hand. Historically, there is some truth to that."

"Can't you copy down what was written in the Tome?" Portsend asked. "If you could reproduce the book, he would have nothing over you."

"The Anchored Tome is massive and complex," she said. "I was only able to study it for a few days before Termain took it. The Prime Isles are forbidden from taking notes in the Sanctum for fear that sacred information could leave the room. I have tried my best to write everything I can remember, but it will not be close to comprehensive."

"He's threatening all of Wayfarism," Portsend said. "If Termain destroys the Tome, you would become the final Prime Isless."

"He may not destroy it. He says he will return the book once the

Archkingdom of Espar and Strind wins this war. We need to make Termain Agaul victorious." She took a steadying breath. "That is why I have come to you."

What? Gloristar spoke as if he had some great power. He was a professor at a minor college. A simple Grit Mixer, if he boiled himself down. What could he possibly do to turn the tides in a war that he didn't think the Archkingdom deserved to win?

Prime Isless Gloristar reached into her violet robe and withdrew a small item. It was a hardened leather tube—the kind meant for carrying scrolls. The leather was the same deep purple as her attire, with a matching white anchor tooled on the cap.

Gloristar handed it to him. "The scroll contains some of the information I was able to remember from the Anchored Tome."

*Sparks!* Portsend nearly dropped the leather tube. "These are sacred secrets, Gloristar. You can't share this with me." He tried to pass it back, but she held out her hand.

"It is a list of materials that are known to have some connection with developing Grit."

Portsend reluctantly looked at the scroll tube again. "You're talking about source materials?"

"Not the ones you'll be familiar with," she replied. "The Anchored Tome contained a list of new materials, to be kept forever private."

"Then why are you giving this to me?" This seemed a huge breach of her station. What in Homeland's name was Gloristar thinking, sharing information from the Tome?

"I don't know if this is every item from the list, but the ones I have included in the scroll I am sure of. I need you to experiment with the listed materials. Portsend." She reached out and gripped his arm. "I need you to develop *new* Grit."

New Grit.

The scroll felt almost warm in his hand, like its secrets were burning his palm. Portsend Wal knew the Grit Classification

Tables by heart. There were fifteen Grit types—five common and ten specialty. It had been over two hundred years since anyone had discovered a new one. And now this scroll held the key to more?

"Why would something like this be kept in the Anchored Tome?" Portsend asked quietly.

"The Prime Isles have always been responsible for the well-being of the general population." Gloristar dropped her hand from his arm. "According to the text recorded in the Tome, these particular materials could lead to Grit types more powerful than anything the Greater Chain has ever seen."

Portsend was shaking his head. This was madness! Why was he holding this scroll?

"Don't you see?" Gloristar said. "This will give us the advantage over Dronodan and Talumon."

He took a small step back as if to study her. "Are you the Prime Isless of Wayfarism?" he whispered. "Or are you a war general?"

Gloristar stared at him, unblinking. "Sometimes, a woman in my position must be both."

Portsend saw the hidden struggle in her wide eyes and he was suddenly seized with a desperate desire to reach out and hold her. But that kind of behavior would have been inappropriate when she was a simple Isless, let alone the Prime. It was a desire he had learned to quash, and suppressing it now was like slipping into a pair of old shoes.

"You know I will do anything for you," he settled on saying.

This brought a smile to Gloristar's lips, albeit a sad one. "That's why I'm here, Portsend."

He gripped the scroll tube tightly, overwhelmed and admittedly excited by its possibilities. Now that he had agreed to keep it, Portsend felt anxious to delve into its mysteries. New types of Grit...By the Homeland, this was a curious time to be alive.

He glanced over his empty classroom once more. What of his position here? What of the students?

"I will submit my resignation papers to the college at once," he said. "But the administration will expect me to see out the term."

"Oh, Portsend." Gloristar was smiling again, but this time he could tell it was at his expense. "I wouldn't ask you to give this up. Teaching has been your constant through all your challenges. I know what it means to you, and you are far too good at what you do."

"Then I am to work on the materials here?" he said. "At the college?"

She nodded. "It will be safer than bringing you to the palace. The farther you are from King Termain, the more effective I think you will be. I understand that your experiments could take time, but he will not. Better for both our sakes if he isn't breathing down the back of your neck. Besides, I've already taken the liberty of dropping off the first round of materials at your campus laboratory."

"Materials?"

"From the scroll," she answered. "And if you need more, just let me know with at least a cycle's notice. We'll get the materials out to Pekal, and through a dragon as quickly as possible. King Termain is fully invested in this project."

"Then he's read the Tome?" That seemed utterly blasphemous. "He knows about the list?"

"He would never dare," she said.

"Well, at least the king has *some* degree of veneration."

"Nothing so noble, I'm afraid," she answered. "The Anchored Tome is believed to be protected by all the Paladin Visitants. If the book is opened outside the Sanctum, they will appear in fiery justice to destroy whoever attempts to read it. That's a risk not even Termain Agaul is willing to take."

"Then how does he know about this project?" Portsend held up the leather scroll tube.

"After his latest round of threats against me, I admitted to having knowledge that could help us produce new Grit. He doesn't know about the list, and he doesn't know about you yet. But he's willing to fund anything I say, so long as it gets results."

"I will do my best." Portsend didn't know what else to say.

"Keep me informed of every development."

"How am I supposed to reach you?"

"You know your way to the Mooring," Gloristar said. "Although, records show that you have been there less and less since my ascension to Prime Isless. I hope your faith has not been waning like that of countless others."

"I assure you, my belief and trust in the Homeland burns as brightly as ever," he answered. "I've just had a hard time adjusting to a new compass."

"Well, perhaps this will give us a chance to connect once again," she said. "I will have the Isles at the dock move your name to a different ledger. That will allow you to visit me in Cove One."

"You can do that?" He thought only other Isles were allowed to enter Cove 1.

"I can do whatever I want," she said. "I'm the Prime Isless of Wayfarism." Gloristar straightened her robes as though to indicate that she was ready to go. "I'm leaving two Regulators to watch over you."

"Gloristar," he protested. "That won't be necessary."

"Didn't you hear what I just said? I can do whatever I want." She raised an eyebrow as if challenging him to rebut.

"I thought we were going for secrecy," Portsend said. "Students have a penchant for gossip, and the sudden appearance of two Regulators stationed at my classroom door is hardly subtle."

"You'll barely notice them," Gloristar said. "They won't be in uniform. I don't expect you to do this alone. The king supports you financially, I support you spiritually, the Regulators will keep an eye on you, and I'm sure you'll need an assistant in the lab."

"You have someone in mind?"

"Homeland, no," she said. "That's your area of expertise. I imagine a fellow professor would have the skills you need."

Portsend ran through the college faculty in his mind, ruling out the majority right away. Tensa Fentall was a possibility. She was a professor of mathematics. Or the physicist, Grend Opal. As brilliant as both of them were, Portsend had a hard time imagining a successful collaboration in which he didn't lose control of the project. Professors of advanced schooling could be headstrong and opinionated. At least, that was what had landed Portsend his job. He needed bright minds that were eager and fresh, not so set in their ways that the things they thought they knew would become roadblocks to the theoretical.

"I trust you to exercise discretion in your choice of assistants," Gloristar said.

Portsend was nodding. He knew a couple of eager minds.

~

*We were no strangers to conflicts, but we resolved them in our own way, without the meddling of gods.*

# CHAPTER

# 3

Would you look at that?" Ard was staring at the sign on the shopfront, a cart full of fruit passing behind him. "Inspector Ardour Stringer. It's almost as if the man is *asking* me to impersonate him."

"It's almost as if Ardor isn't the most common male name in the Greater Chain," Raek pointed out.

"Spelled the old Dronodanian way." Ard stepped forward and tapped the *ou* in the name. "Seems unnecessarily fancy."

Two days had passed since their accidental meeting with Lady Abeth. Raek was quick to point out that they'd never really nailed down exactly how much she was going to pay them. Ard wasn't worried, with such a highbrow employer.

After all, if he had learned anything from Halavend's million-Ashing job, it was that promised payment could easily turn into no payment. All Ard could really control was getting the job done well. And that meant eliminating liabilities like the real Inspector Stringer—a risky unknown thread that could unravel the whole tapestry as fast as they could weave it.

Raek had done some asking around and they'd located the inspector's office, deciding to swing by and tie up that loose end before heading to their next meeting with Lady Abeth at the Agauls' Guesthouse Adagio in the Eastern Quarter.

Ard flipped back the tails of his leather coat and pushed open the door. The pair of Rollers holstered on his hips were no longer illegal for a common civilian to carry. That had been one of the first laws King Termain had scratched. Maybe it was his way of making the civilians feel safe during a time of war. But Ard doubted that much consideration had gone into the change. Termain acted. He didn't necessarily *think*.

Inspector Stringer's office wasn't much to look at. The whole room was smaller than a cove in the Mooring. One window, two chairs, a hard bench, and a desk covered in ripped and crumpled papers.

Behind the desk sat a portly man with a bristly mustache and a wicked-looking black eye. He looked up, stiffening as Ard and Raek entered. One hand vanished under the desk, and Ard knew he was going for a gun.

Ard held his hands up to show that he had no intention of using his Rollers. "Inspector Ardour Stringer?"

"That's what the sign says." His voice was raspy and somewhat irritable.

"Hey, now," Ard soothed. Something had obviously rattled this guy. "That's no way to greet new clients."

Stringer relaxed a little, but Ard couldn't tell if he'd let go of the unseen gun. "Have a seat."

Ard took him up on the empty chair, while Raek plopped himself down on the bench, the wooden wall protesting as he leaned against it.

"My rates have gone up from what you might have seen posted," Stringer said, smoothing out a wrinkly paper that had clearly been recently wadded up. "I already have a full roster of clients, and I'm up to my chin in paperwork."

Ard noticed two torn pieces of paper pieced back together. The inspector seemed to be copying the text onto a new sheet, scribing charcoal worn to little more than a stub.

"That paperwork looks like it packs a mean right hook," Ard said, touching his own eye as if it were swollen.

"Nobody said being a private inspector was free of risks," Stringer said.

"Angry client?" Ard pressed.

Stringer shook his head. "I'd never seen the chap before."

"What did he look like?"

"Blazing big," answered Stringer. "Bigger than your pal there." He pointed at Raek, who raised an eyebrow skeptically. Surely that was an exaggeration.

"He just came in here and started tearing the place up?" Ard assumed the attacker was also responsible for the shredded documents.

"I'd closed the office early. It was the night of the general's funeral and I thought I'd head over to see the interment," Stringer said. "Didn't get to the end of the block when I saw somebody breaking through my front door. I hurried back to find that thug in here, ripping my documents to tatters."

All right, so the funeral was his excuse for closing early the night he was supposed to have had his secret rendezvous with Lady Abeth. And his encounter with the vandal would explain why he had been so late, if he'd ever shown up at all. This didn't seem like a coincidence.

"Do you have any idea who might have sent the thug to trash your office?" Ard asked.

"It could have been any number of..." Stringer trailed off, making an exasperated sigh. "What? Is this an interrogation now? Who's the inspector here?"

That *did* seem to be the question they had come to establish.

"We are merely concerned clients," said Raek. "Concerned about what an intrusion into your office could mean for the privacy of our information."

"I don't have any of your personal information," Stringer said. "You're not even my clients!"

"And I regret to inform you that we never will be." Ard stood, waving for Raek. "Come along. We'll take our case elsewhere."

Inspector Ardour Stringer didn't even try to stop them. His hand finally came above the desk and he started writing again with a heavy sigh on his lips.

"Bigger than me?" Raek scoffed as they merged onto the busy street and headed north. There were thunderclouds to the east. One of those cold winter rainstorms rolling in.

"You know attackers always seem bigger in the memory of the victims," Ard said. "He was probably a pip-squeak. I don't imagine Stringer putting up much of a fight."

"Well, the goon obviously wasn't there looking for information," Raek said. "Tearing up papers makes them awfully hard to read."

"Right." Ard hailed a carriage, but it rattled past them. "And a good criminal would have at least waited until Stringer was out of sight. Sacking the office was just a tactic to keep him detained."

"So, whoever hired the man knew that he was supposed to meet Lady Abeth that night."

"My money is on King Termain," Ard said. "He could have easily caught wind that his cousin-in-law was illegally back in town."

"Maybe he had someone follow her to the inspector's office."

"Except she obviously never met Stringer in person," Ard said, "since she assumed that I was the inspector."

"You do bear a striking resemblance," said Raek. "I think it's the double chin."

"So all of Abeth's communication with Stringer must have been written," Ard said, ignoring the jab. "Termain could have intercepted a message and realized that Abeth was snooping around her son's grave."

"And Termain could put a quick stop to her snooping by roughing up the inspector and making him miss his appointment." Raek hailed another carriage, and this time it stopped. "Upper Eastern Quarter," he said to the driver. "It's a ways out of town. Near the Creekstone Watermill."

Raek knew right where they were going, having scouted around the guesthouse yesterday while Ard once again counted their earnings from having turned the Stalwart Heart medallion over to Lord Stend.

A thousand Ashings would keep them comfortable for a good while. But despite their string of successful ruses, it seemed like the money vanished quicker these days. Shortages from the war made the cost of living rise steadily. Wealthy one day, paupers the next. Isle Halavend's job was supposed to have set them up for life.

Oh, well. Maybe this one would.

They climbed into the carriage and it lurched forward. Ard considered how much more comfortable the seat was when wearing appropriately sized pants.

Although Isle Halavend's job had left him without an Ashlit, in debt to pirates and poachers, Ardor Benn had gained something valuable.

Knowledge about the Homeland.

After coercing King Pethredote with a false Paladin Visitant, Ard and Raek had learned things that the common man was never meant to know—the true nature of the Paladin Visitants as time-traveling impetuses of change. The Homeland existing not as a place but as a perfected version of the future. The Urgings, as the future's way of coaxing people down certain paths so the timeline would unfold in a better way.

The fact that Raek knew the same information didn't seem to affect his big friend. Raekon Dorrel had never been a believer in Wayfarism, and he was probably secretly pleased that much of what they'd learned scientifically disproved major points of the religion.

Ard wondered if his brief experience as a Paladin Visitant had enhanced his ability to detect these Urgings. Or perhaps it had just caused him to be more conscientious—interpreting any gut feeling as a warning from the future.

"Why him?" Raek asked, bringing Ard back to the topic at hand. "In a city full of inspectors, why did Lady Abeth choose Stringer?"

"Maybe they were secret lovers once," Ard joked.

"Yeah. A lover whose face she's never seen," Raek added. "And she wanted to tell him that the missing prince was actually his."

Ard smiled. "The spelling of his name would imply that he was from Dronodan. That gets some instant trust from Dronodanian royalty like Abeth, who is an Ostel by blood. And since she suspects Termain of having assassinated her family, she probably didn't feel like she could trust any of the palace inspectors."

"I suppose it doesn't matter how she chose him," said Raek. "All that matters is stopping her from communicating with him again."

"And him with her," Ard added, though that way was probably more unlikely. Letters didn't go from the Archkingdom to the

Sovereign States without being read by authorities. Especially if it was addressed to Lady Abeth at the palace in Leigh.

Stringer was probably waiting on the courier with hopes that he'd have another chance to meet Abeth. But the queen had already moved on, directing Ard and Raek to her guesthouse, where they would receive all future communications. The issue was probably resolved, but it wouldn't hurt to cover their bases.

"We should forge a letter to Stringer from Lady Abeth," Ard suggested. "We can tell him that he missed his chance and she has taken her case elsewhere. 'Do not write back, as any further communication could put me at risk.'"

"Postscript—'I miss the scratch of your pine-bristle mustache across my tender lips.'"

"You're a poet, Raekon. Don't let anyone tell you otherwise."

This was quite the scenic route, Ard realized, looking out the window to the northeast. Rolling greenery swept from the roadside all the way to the shoreline cliff, unobstructed by buildings of any kind. Beyond, it was nothing but endless ocean. Eastern Espar was windward, and Ard hoped they'd be inside the guesthouse before that storm broke.

"After meeting Stringer, I'm worried I don't look *inspectory* enough." Ard popped the collar of his jacket.

"I'm not sure there's a standard look," Raek said. "Besides, you fooled the former queen in torn, skintight trousers."

"Still, I feel like I need a neat hat, or something."

The carriage came to a halt and the two men climbed out. As Raek settled with the driver, Ard turned his attention to the Guesthouse Adagio, private property of the late Remium Agaul.

Guesthouses were common among the nobility, ranging widely in size and niceties. They were intended as comfortable accommodations for visitors coming from other cities or islands. More often, Ard figured they were used for illicit rendezvous. Homeland knew there would be plenty of beds to choose from.

The carriage rattled away as a low peal of thunder sounded to the east.

"He could have at least dropped us at the front door," Ard remarked. They stood outside the stone wall at the perimeter of the property. The gate was open, so the two of them started up the inclined gravel roadway.

The Guesthouse Adagio was a genuine estate with landscaped grounds, a lavish main structure, carriage house, stables, and a smattering of quaint cottages for visitors. It was a coveted piece of shoreline property, with a perfectly unobstructed view of the sea— a true rarity in Beripent, the largest city in the Greater Chain.

"This place is downright silly," Raek muttered.

Ard followed his gaze to the pink-and-white stone structure of the main guesthouse. Protruding off the edge of the roof, high above the front door, was a full-scale stone statue of a bull dragon head. Moss and mildew had colored it green, giving it an almost furry texture.

Ard shrugged. Grotenisk was much scarier. Of course, one had to travel two hundred and fifty years back in time to see his fiery face.

The two men moved up the pink stone stairs. As though by magic, the door swung open when they reached the top step. Standing in the threshold was a slender man, his wispy gray hair combed over his balding scalp. His nose was small, sitting atop a manicured mustache, but his face was long, with heavy brows that seemed to press down on his blue eyes.

"Good day, gentlemen," he said. "You must be Inspector Stringer and associate."

"Ha," Raek said. "I'm an associate."

"Ardor." Ard stuck out his hand to shake. "This is Raekon Peed-enyersoup." If Ard would be going by his real first name, then at least he could afford Raek the same luxury. It wasn't like this butler was expecting any trickery.

"Pleasure." He nodded. "Codley Hattingson at your service. I've been in the Agauls' employ for some thirty years, serving as principal butler for the last twenty. Istil's line, of course."

Ugh. There were too many Agauls to keep track of. That had become woefully apparent after Pethredote's untimely demise. Ard was pretty sure Istil had been one of the good guys.

"Please, come in," Codley said, peering eastward over their shoulders. "It would appear a spot of rain is forthcoming."

"Fancy chap for a fancy place, I see," said Raek, who instinctively ducked his head in all doorways even though this one was plenty high. Codley shut the door and barred it securely.

"We're here to meet with Lady Abeth," Ard said.

"Her Majesty is not here," replied the butler.

Ard scratched his head. "That seems kind of funny, because I definitely remember her asking us to meet here today. What is it, Wednesday?"

"Thursday," Codley corrected.

"Yeah," Ard said. "That's what I meant."

"The queen's visit to Beripent was, of necessity, very brief," Codley said. "She has returned to the relative safety of Dronodan for now, leaving me express instructions to aid you in your investigation."

"Now, wait a minute," Raek cut in. "This sounds fishy to me."

"*Cod* fishy," Ard chimed, smirking at the awful pun.

"How do we know you didn't toss the good lady over the shoreline and lure us here to dispatch us?" In one swift motion, Raek drew his long knife.

Ard was ninety percent sure that Codley wet himself a little, but he regained his composure with startling speed, reaching one white-gloved hand into his vest and withdrawing a letter.

"You'll note the official seal of Her Majesty." Codley proffered it to Ard. "As well as her own hand, which you'll recognize from your prior correspondences."

Ard took the letter and broke the wax seal. As much as they were testing Codley, perhaps the manservant was testing them. Identifying Abeth's handwriting was something the real Ardour Stringer would be able to do without hesitation.

But Codley Hattingson didn't seem like much of a bluffer.

"Yeah," Ard said. "This seems legitimate."

"Well, what does it say?" Raek pressed, sheathing his blade.

Ard cleared his throat and read aloud. "'Dear Inspector Stringer, I extend my most heartfelt gratitude to you and your companion for accepting the difficult task I set before you. My faithful servant, Codley Hattingson, will be available to assist you in any and all ways. He is very familiar with the events that surrounded Shad's murder, and will be happy to answer any questions you may have about it. Also, we can continue corresponding through Codley, as he has established ways of moving letters between Beripent and Leigh without unwanted eyes.'"

"That's our man!" Raek cried, slapping Codley on the back so hard he nearly fell on his face.

Ard continued reading. "'Please keep me apprised of any information you may uncover regarding the true whereabouts of my son. As you undertake this highly dangerous task, I invite you to reside here, at the Guesthouse Adagio.'"

Ard had taken the liberty of inventing that last sentence on the spot, but he was quite pleased with how queenly it sounded as it rolled off his tongue.

"What?" Raek snatched the letter out of Ard's hands as the butler's eyes grew to the size of dinner plates.

"'...here, at the Guesthouse Adagio,'" Raek mumbled as though rereading Ard's made-up sentence, sealing the lie and tying poor Codley Hattingson's undershorts into an even tighter knot. Raek looked up, nodding solemnly. "Her Majesty's generosity is truly astounding."

"Yes." Codley tugged at his high collar. "Well, that is what the guesthouse is for. To make comfortable the true friends of the Agaul family." With a deep breath, he gestured to another doorway down a wide hallway beyond the foyer. "Come. Let me show you around. Make yourselves...at home."

Raek folded the letter and handed it back to Ard, who slipped it into his vest pocket. They needed to make sure Codley never got his hands on that. The handwriting would also prove helpful to craft a convincing response in order to cut off the real Inspector Stringer. They'd need a good forger to fool a trained eye like the inspector's.

As lavish as the foyer had appeared, with draperies on the walls and a high chandelier, it seemed little more than a coat closet when compared to the vast social room down the hallway. The space was designed to host a gathering, with clusters of padded furniture dotting the large room.

*Quarrah would love to rob this place*, Ard thought. And it probably wouldn't be difficult. The east wall was composed entirely of glass panes that reached from floor to ceiling. Not very practical, but it provided an indisputably breathtaking view of the open sea. The dark storm clouds were rolling closer, blotting the afternoon light and making it feel as though dusk were setting on too soon. There were about ten feet of easement from the glass wall to the edge of the clifftop, and a warning wind ruffled the tall ornamental grasses that clung to the ledge.

Ard crossed the room to a door marked with a tall A-shaped star. He cracked it open, peering into a large boudoir with a poster bed and a loft. "I think I found my room."

Codley coughed. "You are welcome to stay in any of the visitor cottages on the grounds, but I must draw the line at the royal suite." He stepped past Ard and pulled the door shut.

"I'm thinking I ought to get a hat like this one." Raek's voice caused Ard to turn to a wall lined with large portrait paintings. Raek was studying a man with a ruddy complexion and a hat the size of a small sailboat.

"Not sure your neck is wide enough to hold that up," Ard

replied. "That fellow there's got three or four extra chins propping his gourd upright."

"Master Ardor!" Codley scolded. "I expect a certain level of decorum when speaking of the Agaul family."

"My apologies." Ard tugged the bottom of his vest. They shouldn't rile the butler too much.

"The man whom you disgrace," continued Codley, "is none other than Prince Fidor Agaul, younger brother to King Barrid Agaul."

"Barrid." Ard scanned the wall of portraits. "I don't see that old gent up here anywhere."

"We do not display the"—Codley cleared his throat indignantly— "family tyrant."

"Yeah," Raek said. "We took ours off the wall, too."

King Barrid had ruled terribly, some forty years ago, denouncing Wayfarism and really sparking off the Prime Isless at the time. Dronodan and Talumon had seceded from the kingdom until Pethredote had put an end to Barrid and his rule with a Paladin Visitant, reuniting the Greater Chain as a crusader monarch.

"So, one of these blokes would have been king if Pethredote hadn't taken the throne?" Ard asked.

"The crusader monarch merely served as a placeholder," Codley said, "working hand in hand with the Prime Isle, but knowing that rule of the kingdom would eventually return to the Agaul line if the voting council deemed the heir competent."

"The heir being Remium?" he clarified.

"Correct," said Codley. "Which was why he and his family had lived in the palace all those years, with Remium serving as an advisor to King Pethredote. When the noble councils from each of the islands convened after Pethredote's death, they didn't need to select a new ruler. The monarchy was always intended to pass to Remium if he won the vote of competence to resume the Agaul bloodline as primary ruler over all the Greater Chain."

Ard had heard about the two weeks of council meetings, involving every significant nobleman and -woman from all four islands. The councils had happened in Beripent, held in a wing of the palace that the dragon hadn't destroyed. Sounded like enough hot air in one room to lift the whole group skyward like the balloon of a Trans-Island Carriage.

"So Termain wasn't even a real candidate during the royal councils?" Raek asked.

"Indeed. As the elder cousin, the rule was set to go to Remium so long as he was voted competent," said Codley. "If he hadn't been, Termain's competence would have been evaluated next."

"Which he would have failed," assumed Ard.

"Without a doubt," the butler said. "Which was likely why things unfolded as they did. King Remium and his son were both killed within eighteen hours of the crowning. By then, the rule had officially returned to the bloodline, putting Termain on the throne by default."

"And that wasn't disputed?" Ard cried.

"It certainly was," Codley replied. "Dronodan and Talumon had insisted that the councils reconvene for a vote of Termain's competence. In essence, the Greater Chain was divided into those who upheld classic tradition and those who simply wanted a better king. That, gentlemen, is the foundation of the very war we're currently fighting."

Ard had heard lots of reasons for the war. Some said it was over the Trothian banishment. Some said it was over Remium's death. Others said it had to do with the splintering of Wayfarism and Prime Isless Gloristar's endorsement of Termain.

"What about Strind?" Raek asked.

"Termain's mother." Codley pointed to a portrait of a woman with a broad face and an ample chin. A mole dotted her upper lip like a beauty mark, and her obviously dyed hair was mostly hidden under a stylish hat. "The queen dowager, Fabra Ment. She is a lady of the most noble bloodline of Strind, and the primary reason that island sided with Espar in the war."

"Sounds like she's part of the problem," said Raek.

"Fabra Ment is quite harmless." Codley waved him off. "You cannot blame a person for their lineage. She was married to the late Gond Agaul in a political union, which is obviously serving its purpose. Her only real crime was producing that impulsive, asinine jackanapes we now know as King Termain."

He said that last part in one breath, followed immediately by lifting a gloved hand to his lips. "Please forgive my language, gentlemen. I am a citizen of the Archkingdom. I should not speak of the king in such a way."

"We won't report you to the Regulation this time." Raek shook a finger at him.

Ard found Codley's description of Termain to be quite fitting. In fact, that had been one of Pethredote's big motivators in eliminating all dragon shell to prevent another Paladin Visitant. Pethredote had been swept away by the success of his reign and was terrified of what would happen when rule passed back to one of Barrid's great nephews. He'd been so worried that the Agauls would destroy what he'd built that Pethredote had ended up destroying much of it himself.

Now the islands were in a war much like the one King Barrid had started some forty years earlier. Only this time, the new Prime Isless couldn't authorize a crusader to carry Visitant Grit against the tyrant. Ard had used every last granule to travel back in time. And while reports stated that the bull egg had hatched on Pekal, the little dragon wouldn't be developed enough to fertilize eggs for at least another year. Thus, no more Paladin Visitants.

Probably for the best. The last thing Ard wanted was for someone to go tinkering with the timeline and erase their very existence.

"Is that the kid we're looking for?" Raek pointed to the portrait of a young, fair-haired boy, who couldn't have been more than eight years old.

Codley nodded. "Shad Agaul, son of Remium and Abeth, rightful heir to the throne. He was a sweet young lad, and I believe he would have ruled as graciously as his father, had either of them been given the chance."

"I'm guessing his first mandate would have been free toys for all his peers," Raek jested.

Codley shot him a stern glance. "He would not have been a child monarch. That portrait is several years outdated. He was twelve at the time of his death. And still, Prince Shad would not have been eligible to rule until his fourteenth birthday."

"Okay, phew," said Raek. "It seems much better to have a fourteen-year-old in charge of the world."

"I sense your sarcasm, Master Raekon," Codley said. "It is not appreciated."

"I quite appreciated it," Ard admitted.

"What is this bell for?" Raek asked. It was mounted just outside a closed doorway. He gave it a little ring before Codley could protest.

"In your opinion," Ard said, "if Shad had survived to rule after his father's assassination, would Dronodan and Talumon have seceded?"

"I believe that Shad's rule could have kept the Greater Chain unified," Codley said. "Although I will admit, that is a loaded question. The lad was on track to being an upstanding ruler. He was a well-grounded Wayfarist, an attentive student with a thirst for knowledge. But even if he had not been an outstanding monarch, his lineage alone could have held the islands together."

"Right," Ard mused. Because Shad's mother was royalty from Dronodan.

The door beside Raek suddenly opened, and a young man

appeared. His hair was almost to his shoulders, stick straight and black. His skin was fair and his small frame looked tiny next to Raek.

"You called?" he asked, looking from Raek to Ard as though awaiting instructions.

"Well..." Raek said, reaching out to touch the bell in reverent admiration.

"Gentlemen," Codley said, "may I introduce Bannit Lagaday. I suppose he will be cooking for you during your stay at the guesthouse."

"Ring it again," Ard said. "See if someone else comes to do our laundry!" Raek gave it a go.

Codley held up his hand. "I'm afraid Bannit does the work of a dozen servants these days."

"Rather, there's a twelfth of the work to be done," Bannit replied with a nervous laugh. "Staff's been scaled back since Termain took the throne."

"Not much use for a guesthouse belonging to the assassinated cousin of the king," said Codley. "But it is the last property of Remium Agaul's estate that Termain has not claimed. We are few, here at the Guesthouse Adagio, but we are stalwart."

"Tea," Raek said, placing an abrupt order with Bannit. "No milk. Nine granules of sugar."

The slight servant looked delighted to be given an order. "So, is that, say, a spoonful?"

"Now, that would depend on the spoon, wouldn't it?"

Bannit burst into excited laughter, turning to Codley. "Wonderful! This is simply wonderful, isn't it?"

"I don't suppose you have any fresh pastries back there?" Ard asked. "Maybe a doughnut or a scone?"

"I have..." Bannit began, as though he were about to make some grand announcement. "A slice of bread! I could sprinkle it with a touch of sugar. Oh! Perhaps add a dash of cinnamon..."

The little man trailed away, scurrying off into the kitchen. Ard glanced at Raek and gave a bemused shrug. If he and Raek were truly going to make this place their base of operations, then Bannit Lagaday could be a critical asset.

"When eliminating the staff, I decided to keep Bannit because he didn't have an area of expertise, but was moderately skilled in every station," Codley explained, in what Ard considered to be a rather backhanded compliment. "He handles the cooking, cleaning, laundry, heating, and lighting. It's usually not much for the three of us, but his workload will definitely increase with your stay."

"Three of you?" Ard asked. "Who's the other?"

"The groundskeeper, Hedma Sallis," answered Codley. "She is also serving as our equerry, should you need to use the stables or carriages."

This arrangement just kept getting better! He and Raek wouldn't have to "borrow" horses anymore.

Ard turned away from the portrait wall to see that a smattering of raindrops had found the big windows. He strode across the room and seated himself on a long velvet chaise that faced eastward. Ard watched one little raindrop stream along the glass, merging with others, using their established paths to take the easiest way down. Not unlike the methods of a ruse artist.

"I'd like to hear more about the alleged death of the prince," Ard said as Raek took up a padded chair beside him.

Codley remained standing, ever stiff and proper. But he did reposition himself so they could see his face while looking out the window at the storm. "The boy was murdered in his bed on the twenty-first night of the Second Cycle."

More trouble in the palace. Remium Agaul had had his throat slit in one of the council chambers—that much had been made known to the citizens. But none of the details regarding Shad's assassination had ever been released.

"Cause of death?" Ard asked.

"An explosion of Blast Grit," answered Codley. "It was detonated somewhere in his room at close proximity to the sleeping boy."

"That makes Lady Abeth's suspicions feasible," Raek said. "Blast Grit could have blown the boy's face clean off, so no one could truly identify him."

"So, who lit the Grit?" Ard mused.

"If we knew that," said Codley, "things would likely be very different. And if a dozen of Beripent's best inspectors couldn't crack the case when it was fresh, it gives me great pause regarding Her Majesty's decision to hire you."

"You're saying I'm not among the best in Beripent?" Ard asked, fishing for any other motive Abeth might have had in reaching out to Stringer specifically.

Codley sniffed. "Her Majesty thought it wise to select an inspector with fresh eyes. One who had not been involved in the original investigation a year and a half ago."

"Don't be so quick to write us off," Ard said. "The case may be stale, but we have information that changes the game."

*Plus, we think like criminals and have connections that legitimate inspectors would shudder at.*

"Did anything unusual happen in the days leading up to the assassination?" Raek asked.

"The prince received a new mattress," answered Codley. "It was delivered to his room around noon, just twelve hours before the explosion."

Ard and Raek shared a glance. Maybe their stay in the Guesthouse Adagio would be over before it started.

"Well, there you go," said Ard. "Was it straw? No," he quickly corrected himself. "Goose down." A prince wouldn't sleep on anything else. "They smuggled the corpse and keg of Blast Grit into the room inside the new mattress."

"Bravo," Codley said. "You've managed to come to the same conclusion as every other inspector in Beripent."

"I sense your sarcasm," Raek said. "And it's not appreciated."

"It was generally accepted that the Blast Grit was brought into the room via the new mattress," said Codley. "The mattress maker, Von Storret, and his entire delivery crew were arrested and found guilty."

"What do *you* think about that?" Ard could see that something was bothering the butler.

"I think it was awfully convenient," replied Codley. "I think that the eight inspectors who found Von Storret guilty were anxious to collect their significant rewards from Termain. And the two inspectors that considered the mattress maker's innocence were met with unfortunate accidents in the cycles that followed."

Ard leaned back and tapped his chin. "So we've got another dirty-conspirator king."

"Another?" Codley asked.

"Yeah," Raek answered. "Pethredote picked off a lot of folks—anyone who came close to knowing about how he poisoned the Bull Dragon Patriarchy."

"Surely, you don't buy into all that gossip about the crusader monarch," Codley remarked. "Those claims were made by a madman on the step of the palace, during a tumultuous night."

"I hope the madman you're referring to was King Pethredote," answered Ard, "and not that handsome devil they say commanded the sow dragon to eat him."

Ard had made sure that the general public found out about Pethredote's crimes. The poisoning of the dragons, the murder of Isle Halavend, the conspiracies with Prime Isle Chauster to eliminate all stores of dragon shell. And he had made known the truth about the Holy Torch—that the dragons were the ones shielding mankind from Moonsickness.

But there were some truths that Ard had not wanted Cinza and Elbrig to spread that night. The truth about the Paladin Visitants and the Homeland. All that had seemed too much for a kingdom still reeling from having their beloved ruler exposed and eaten by the first dragon ever to willingly leave Pekal.

"I suppose you are entitled to your own radical opinions," Codley said. "Returning to the matter at hand, it is my conclusion that King Termain had his cousin and the prince murdered so he could assume the throne now that the bloodline rule had been reestablished by the council vote."

"Yes," Ard replied. "It would seem that way. And Lady Abeth said the same. But that doesn't tell us what really happened to Shad Agaul."

"Let's suppose the mattress folks were innocent," said Raek. "They still could have been the means by which the keg of Blast Grit and decoy body were moved into the prince's room."

"Someone planted the items without telling the moving crew." Ard nodded. "They surely would have noticed the weight increase, but it wasn't like they were going to slice open the mattress on the way to the palace."

"An opportunist?" Codley wondered.

"Not likely," said Raek. "Too much of a coincidence that Shad happened to get his new mattress on the same day his father was assassinated. This was premeditated."

"So Termain sent someone into Von Storret's under cover of darkness to plant the Grit," Codley surmised. "That is an untraceable shadow."

"Then we'll have to trace a different shadow," said Ard, pondering. "If the mattress was delivered before noon, what time did the explosion occur?"

"Exactly at midnight," answered Codley.

"A fuse?" Ard asked Raek.

The Mixer shook his head. "No fuse I know of could burn for twelve hours unnoticed. Someone would have had to slip into the prince's room and light it after he was asleep."

"No doubt somehow smuggling out the real Shad at the same

time," Ard said. "Who might have gone into the boy's room after he retired?"

"No one," answered Codley. "The boy's door was barred from within. The palace Regulators had to remove the hinges to get inside. By then, the body in the ruined bed had been burned beyond recognition."

"Was there a window?" Raek asked.

"Yes."

"Was it broken?"

"No," answered Codley. "The glass was intact. It, too, was latched and locked from the inside. No signs of forced entry."

"What about a chimney?" Ard asked. "I hear people can squeeze through chimneys to escape." He and Quarrah had used that very method, moving through Grotenisk's skull and fleeing the throne room.

"He had only a Heat Grit hearth in his room," Codley said. "No chimney."

The three of them turned as Bannit reentered, a steaming cup on a saucer in one hand and a porcelain plate with a slice of bread in the other.

"I hope the tea is sweetened to your liking." Bannit handed the cup and saucer to Raek, which suddenly looked miniature in the big man's hands. "And I decided to warm the bread a bit for you." Ard accepted the plate. The offering didn't look like much. Certainly not as delectable as the pastries from their old bakery hideout on Humont Street.

Bannit Lagaday looked out at the storm, sighing contentedly. "Ah. This is just the perfect weather for a warm slice of tea and a cup of bread." Then he scurried away, as if it suddenly dawned on him that he was slacking off.

"What do Bannit and the groundskeeper know about all this?" Ard asked.

"They are extremely loyal to Queen Abeth," Codley said, "and suspect, as we do, that Termain was behind the assassinations."

"But they don't know that the prince's body was replaced?" Raek took a sip of the tea, expressing only moderate disapproval.

"That is correct," said Codley. "Although they have both been notified that you were coming to the guesthouse to reopen the investigation into young Shad's death."

Ard took a bite off the corner of the sweet bread. It actually wasn't as stale as he'd expected it to be.

"What time did the boy usually turn in for the night?" Ard asked.

"He had a well-established routine," said Codley. "But that evening, it being the day of the coronation of his father, his schedule was fairly altered."

"Understandable," Ard said. "I remember staying up a little later the night my dad was crowned king."

"He didn't stay up later," Codley said, ignoring the ridiculous statement. "He retired to his room just after the banquet so he could practice his harp."

"That's dedication," Raek said.

"The prince was scheduled to perform at a public celebration the next morning," explained Codley. "He was rightfully nervous."

"So he kissed his mother and father and went to his room around sunset," summarized Ard, "locked the window and door from within, practiced his harp, and then died in an explosion several hours later. But he didn't really die because the burned corpse in his bed was not him."

Codley held up a finger. "Except he didn't kiss his mother good night that particular evening. In fact, no one recalls the prince bidding them a good evening at all. Troubled, Queen Abeth went to his room, but paused outside his door. She didn't want to interrupt his practicing, so she simply stood and listened. It has become one of Her Majesty's most tender memories."

"Was he any good at the instrument?" Ard asked.

"The sounds Shad Agaul made on his harp were *almost* akin to real music."

Raek almost spit his tea. Codley Hattingson was more brutal than Ard realized, delivering insults that somehow nearly sounded like compliments.

"How long did he practice that night?" asked Ard.

"It is impossible to be sure."

Ard sighed. He didn't know what to make of any of this. What was he doing, playing inspector? His skills lay in getting people to give him what he wanted. In this case, he wanted information about the prince, but from whom? It was like running a ruse where he knew *what* he was trying to steal but didn't know who had it!

"I don't think the boy ever went into his room." Raek swirled his steaming tea gently in the cup.

"But his mother heard him playing the harp," said Codley.

"More than one person knows how to play a harp," Raek replied.

"You're suggesting that someone else was *posing* as the prince?"

"Makes sense," seconded Ard. "If the door and window were barred from within, and only one body was discovered in the room, then it must have been a suicide job."

"With a twelve-year-old boy?" Raek asked. "I find it unlikely that whoever planned this meticulous assassination would allow the whole thing to ride on a young kid sparking the Grit."

"Maybe the double didn't know," continued Ard. "They could have found a boy who knew how to play the harp, told him to close himself in the prince's room, play his harp for an hour, dress himself in the prince's clothes, and have a nice night's sleep on his new bed."

"While, unbeknownst to the double," Raek said, "there was Blast Grit hidden in the mattress."

"That still doesn't tell us who lit it," Ard said.

Codley sniffed. "And the poor unsuspecting double is simply another shadow we cannot trace."

"Hmm." Raek stared out the window at the falling rain. "Where was Shad's father during all of this?"

"King Remium was dead already, his throat slit in the council chamber," answered Codley. "Although, in the confusion of the explosion, his body would not be discovered for another two hours."

"So our assassins used the chaos of the Blast Grit to silently dispatch the king," Ard said. "This strike was well timed and coordinated, leaving no traceable record beyond the mattress maker, Von Storret, and the delivery crew."

"There has to be something we've overlooked," Raek said. "Something we can trace that happened before the assassination."

Ard nodded slowly. "What prompted the prince to get a new mattress?"

"Why, his old one became infested with bedbugs," answered Codley.

Ard lowered the bread before taking another bite. "That's it!"

"That's what, exactly?"

"Any good criminal knows that sometimes you must *create* a problem in order to resolve it the way you want it to be resolved," Ard said. Just look at the overturned oxcart requiring General Nelbet's funeral procession to divert through that alleyway.

"What are you suggesting?" Codley asked.

"How does a prince's mattress get bedbugs?" Ard asked. "Was he out among the public much?"

Codley shook his head. "The boy rarely went beyond the palace grounds."

"Did he have any, you know...nighttime companionship?" Raek asked.

"Homeland! Please!" Codley cried, blushing. "He was twelve years old!"

"How long were the parasites in his bed before the mattress was replaced?" Ard asked.

"Three or four days. Perhaps longer," said the steward. "It is difficult to identify the exact moment, since the boy didn't think to mention the bites until they became quite severe. It was rather unfortunate."

"More than unfortunate," Ard said. "What if those parasites were planted on the prince's bed intentionally?"

Codley clucked his tongue disapprovingly. "By whom?"

"Someone with access to the prince's room, several days *before* the explosion."

"That is a small list," Codley said. "The king and queen, myself, and three very trusted servants responsible for the linens, chamber pot, and general tidying."

"And the harp teacher," Raek said.

"No," answered Codley. "The prince's daily lessons took place on a lower level of the palace."

"You moved his harp downstairs and back every day?" Ard asked.

"Homeland, no," answered Codley. "There was a second harp in place for his lessons. But that does remind me. Every few days, a tuner would be let into Shad's room so she could retune his practice harp."

"Now, this harp tuner didn't happen to be a twelve-year-old boy, did she?" Raek asked.

Codley raised one bushy eyebrow. "I'm afraid not."

"Then she's not our double," said Raek.

"But she might be the one who planted the bedbugs on Shad Agaul's old mattress," said Ard. "And if she wasn't the double, then that means she might be alive to give us answers." Ard stood up, smoothing his vest as he turned to Codley. "I don't believe Shad Agaul ever made it to his room after supper. Someone abducted him elsewhere in the palace, which is why no one remembers him telling them good night."

"But his mother heard the harp..."

"Sparks, Codley!" Ard snapped. "We don't have all the answers yet! But I'd say we're actually pretty good at this, Raek."

"I should hope," Codley said. "It is your job, after all."

"We need a name," Raek said. "If we can track down the tuner, we might be able to get more information."

Codley nodded. "I agree, this could be worth further investigation. At the very least, it's something new. You should be able to acquire the name of the tuner from the palace registrars without attracting too much suspicion."

"Me?" cried Ard.

"You *are* the inspector," Codley pointed out. "If your paperwork and licensure is current, you should have no trouble obtaining that information."

"Yeah, no. That's great," Ard said. "I just thought maybe *you* would remember her name."

"I never associated directly with the harp tuner," said Codley.

"You seem to remember a lot of other random details," Raek pointed out.

"I was in charge of overseeing all the investigations," Codley replied. "I kept careful ledgers and I committed much of the relevant information to memory in order to speed coordination with the various inspectors looking into the murders. But, as I mentioned, this is a new avenue. I hope it yields results."

"I believe that is why Lady Abeth hired us." Ard glanced at Raek, who was finishing off his tea. "We always get results."

~

*We were wronged, but from that mistreatment came our strength.*

# CHAPTER

# 4

Finding the harp tuner was proving more difficult than expected. They'd started by obtaining the proper inspector paperwork from a forger in the Western Quarter who went by the name of the Scribe. She was an established contractor that Ard and Raek had used on many occasions—brilliant and convincing with legal paperwork. It had taken her four full days to get all the documents in order, but the Scribe had sped along the forged note from Lady Abeth to Inspector Ardour Stringer, informing him that he'd lost his chance to meet her and forbidding him from sending any sort of rebuttal message.

The letter had been delivered as soon as the ink had dried, and Ard felt confident that the real Stringer would not give them any trouble going forward.

Once in possession of the forged inspector papers, Ard had paid a visit to the palace to learn the name of the harp tuner. He'd kept his head low as the registrar had thoroughly examined the papers. Time made people forget faces, and Ard's bearded, unkempt appearance would also help. But he had duped a lot of folks at the palace, and it had been quite surreal to return there.

Much had not been salvageable after the dragon's destruction, and the extensive remodel almost made the palace look like a completely different building. But the steps were unchanged. Those same stone steps where Ard had denounced King Pethredote and seen him eaten. The same steps where Ard had stared into the deep green eyes of that mother dragon and watched her take flight, bearing her egg to the wilds of Pekal...

The name he'd learned from the registrar was Beska Falay.

From there, he and Raek had gone to Beska's last-known address. That was where they'd heard the first comment about the tuner's hands.

"Gnarled twigs for fingers," said the man who'd purchased the house from her more than eight cycles ago. At first, Ard had been sure they weren't talking about the same person. The man explained that it was indeed the harp tuner. She was crippled, out of work, out of Ashings, deeply in debt, and desperate to sell her house.

In Ard's experience, people with that kind of preamble ended up roving the rougher parts of Beripent in little more than rags. For the past three days, he and Raek had taken to the streets, asking any vagrant or beggar they came across. Or at least the ones that looked the most coherent.

"A cross-eyed fellow under that awning said he might have seen someone matching Beska's description passing through this morning," Ard said to Raek, the two of them joining up on Dwil Street. It had been another long morning of chasing leads. "You learn anything?"

Side by side on horses taken from the Guesthouse Adagio, they sat high above the majority of the foot traffic, affording them a good look at the people around.

"I talked to an old toothless lady," Raek replied. "Said she last saw Beska over on Winding Street. Made another comment about her hands."

Ard navigated his horse in the direction Raek had pointed. Hadn't they just come from Winding Street?

It was surprising what the homeless saw. And their memories had a way of improving with every Ashlit Ard dropped in their hat. Over the last three days, word had sent them all around Beripent, ultimately landing them in the lower Northern Quarter. They were close to finding her now, Ard could feel it.

They emerged onto Winding Street and Ard wrinkled his nose at a sudden pungent smell. This really wasn't the nicest part of town. The two men rode northward slowly, scanning the crowd in search of another beggar who might steer them in the right direction.

They passed a tavern, and Ard stopped his horse, peering down one of those dank little cuts between buildings where the sun probably never touched. Halfway through, there were several figures, their specific shapes and sizes masked by the loose rags that draped their bodies to ward off the winter chill.

"I'm going to have a word with the locals." Ard swung down from the saddle and handed the reins to Raek.

"I'll keep my eye on the street." Raek uncorked his water skin.

Ard only needed to take a few steps before realizing what was going on. There were three—no, four—beggars huddled under a ventilation slot in the wall on the side of the tavern. The stone wall was smeared with grease from unwanted scraps, and the vagrants were crouched beside it, picking over scraps like street dogs.

"Good afternoon!" Ard called, stepping over a dark puddle. His words fell on them like a spark on Grit. The four figures whirled. One ran, two huddled farther into their own rags, and the last, a bearded man, faced Ard defiantly.

"Ain't causing no trouble, we," he said, something soggy in his cupped hand. "Throws this stuff out here for us. Honest. Owner said so hisself. Said he throw out the scraps if'n we don't go begging at the tavern front. Bad for business, that."

"Look," Ard said. "I'm not here to chase you off. In fact, I'll give you an Ashlit if you can help me find someone. Name's Beska Falay."

One of the two huddled figures suddenly looked up sharply. Her eyes met Ard's for a moment, crooked hands clutching a scrap of bread just below her chin. Then she took off at a sprint.

"I'm not here to hurt you!" Ard tried, but the woman wasn't slowing. "Ah, flames." He set off after her, pushing past the two remaining street folk.

Beska took a right out of the alley, Ard gaining fast. She cut across the street, rags trailing behind her like a shredded cape. Ard dodged to the side, barely missing a mule laden with bags. Beska may have had the advantage of knowing these streets, but Ard could see that she wasn't wearing shoes. His footwear on this cold, uneven terrain had to count for something.

She darted across once more, making for another alley that led back to Winding Street. She would have made it, too, if a hefty fellow with a tall hat hadn't seen the fleeing woman and seized her by the arm.

"Here's your pickpocket, sir," the man said, assuming, as Ard arrived on the scene, huffing. He shoved Beska toward Ard and nodded, as though he'd done some great deed.

"Many thanks," Ard said in dismissal, leading Beska down the alleyway she had been aiming for.

The woman was no older than Ard, rail thin, with pale skin that was covered in a layer of soot and grime. Beneath it all, Ard saw a face that might have once been attractive if it were not distorted by that sneer. And her hands...the comments had all been true. Beska's fingers were so gnarled and crooked that Ard wondered if she could even move them.

Beska tried to pull away from Ard, but he held her fast. "I know you are Beska Falay," Ard said quietly, "former harp tuner to Prince Shad Agaul."

She stopped struggling, but her breathing was heavy. "I haven't said anything," she whispered. "I swear to the Homeland, by all the holy Paladin Visitants, I haven't said a word."

What a way to start a conversation! Now Ard was sure that she'd played some part in Shad's assassination. He just needed her to talk. And this cold alleyway definitely wasn't setting the right mood.

"Can I buy you some dinner?" he asked.

Beska turned and looked him squarely in the face. "What?"

"Dinner," he repeated. "It's that meal that happens after lunch and before you go to sleep."

The two of them emerged onto Winding Street once more. Ahead, he saw Raek standing beside the horses at the tavern's hitching post, his bald head noticeable above the flow of pedestrians.

"Raek, I'd like you to meet Beska Falay," Ard said. "She thinks we're trying to kill her, so I thought we'd grab a bite to eat so we can prove that we're the friendly type."

Busy hitching the horses, Raek gave a dismissive little wave without looking up. "You two go ahead."

"Maybe you didn't hear me," Ard replied. "I said we're getting *food.*"

"You also said she thinks someone's trying to kill her," Raek said from behind the horse. "So I thought it might be a good idea to keep my eye on the tavern door in case she's right."

"Your sacrifice is noted," Ard said, steering Beska toward the tavern entrance.

"He's your henchman?" It was the first thing Beska had said that came out steady.

"He's my partner," Ard answered. "Only bad guys have henchmen."

He pushed open the tavern door and was greeted by a rush of warmth and the pleasant smell of frying bacon and bread.

"You've got to be hungry," Ard said. "Get whatever you want."

They leaned up against the wooden bar, a big man with a dirty apron standing behind it. He finished refilling a mug of ale from a tankard and turned his attention to Ard and Beska.

"Got any wine?" Beska asked.

"Oh, a fancy gal," replied the bartender with a toothy smile, clearly recognizing her from the back alley. "Half a bottle of Thodare. But it'll cost you." His eyes flicked between Ard and Beska. "Five Ashings."

"Five..." Ard took a deep breath. In a more reputable place, he could get a full bottle of Thodare for three.

"Imports ain't cheap with the war on," the bartender insisted.

Ha. This had nothing to do with imports. Thodare was an Esparian wine. The bartender was quicker than he looked. He clearly realized that Ard was working on getting something from the beggar. A little exploitation on top of exploitation.

"We'll take it," Ard said.

"Soup," Beska said. "And corn bread. And any of that roast if you've still got it."

The bartender chuckled. "She knows the menu."

*Well, she ought to,* Ard thought, *having been dining on scraps outside that ventilation slot in the alley.*

"Seven Ashings," he said.

Ouch. That was still a gouge for food from a tavern like this one. Ard dug in his vest for his money pouch. Opening the top, he plucked out an Ashing. The coin, once a rough dragon scale, was smooth and shiny, seven little indentations stamped into the middle. Wordlessly, Ard placed it on the bar and the man snatched it up.

"Take a seat where you like," he said. "I'll bring it out."

Ard was pleased to find a vacant table in the corner, fit squarely against two walls so only a pair of diners could sit. Great for private conversation, speaking into a dim corner, but not so good if you were the type to worry about leaving your back open. At least Raek was standing watch outside.

They settled into their seats, Beska staring straight ahead at the wall, her dirty face expressionless, crippled hands beneath the table.

"My name is Androt Penn," he said quietly. "I'm sorry about what they did to your hands." The statement was carefully crafted to show that he knew her mangled fingers were no accident. "We could have a healer look at those."

"Healers tried," Beska answered flatly. "Left me with a slagload of debt and an endless hunger for Heg."

*Heg.* Street slang for Health Grit. Prolonged exposure, especially if Compounded, could lead to serious addiction. These days, there were plenty of crooked healers willing to get you hooked, take your money, and then become your supplier.

"Who did this?" Ard asked.

No response.

"Look, you can talk to me. I'm not here to cause you any harm."

"You already have," she said. "They're going to kill me for this."

"Who's going to kill you?"

Beska shook her head. There were tears in her eyes.

"You'll be in trouble for coming in here with me?" Ard assumed. "They don't have to know you said anything."

"Doesn't matter. Soon as they find out, I'm dead."

The bartender startled Ard with his sudden approach. He set a short glass and the bottle of Thodare in the middle of the table, followed by a plate of steaming pork roast with a square of corn bread on the side.

Ard let Beska dive in, saddened to see that she went for the wine first. The woman didn't bother to pour it, but tipped the whole bottle back, gulping it down so quickly that Ard was sure she couldn't really taste it. In a moment, it was empty. She wiped her mouth with a ratty sleeve and picked up a fork, struggling to hold it in her bent fingers.

She ate quickly, desperately, but not wholly barbarously. Ard could see traces of refinement behind the beggar's exterior—the very fact that she used the available fork, as difficult as it clearly was. This was obviously someone who had fallen, not an urchin raised on the streets. To think that just over a year ago, this woman had been tuning the prince's own harp.

Beska was halfway through the roast when the bartender returned with a hot bowl of soup. She slowed then, as if to pace herself now that she could see the full menu arrayed.

"Who did this to you?" Ard asked.

Beska paused, looking over at him. Then she turned back to her meal without an answer.

"We can protect you, my friend and I," Ard offered. "But you've got to tell me who did this." He exhaled in resignation. "Look, my name isn't actually Androt Penn." He decided to go with the truth here, hoping his reputation would give him some clout. "My name is Ardor Benn."

She glanced over at him, but Ard couldn't tell if that was a glimmer of recognition in her eyes.

"That's not a very good alias," Beska said. "Those names sound almost exactly the same."

Ard resisted an exasperated sigh. "That's what I was going for. I use it to confuse people in case they recognize me."

"Seems like it could work the other way," she said. "Tip them off."

"You know what…" He didn't need to explain this to her. "Doesn't matter. The point is that I am actually a highly successful ruse artist. My partner and I have a track record of accomplishing things that normal people consider impossible."

Her eyes flashed with the first flicker of hope. "Can you get me off Espar?"

"Where to?"

"Talumon," she answered through a mouthful of corn bread.

Lots of big cities to panhandle in Talumon. Or maybe Beska just thought that the people who wanted her dead wouldn't trouble her in the Sovereign States.

The war made it much harder to move between islands, but Ard had a few channels in place for emergencies like this. "Of course. It'll take a few days, but…"

"I won't live a few days out here."

Ard took a deep breath and hoped he wouldn't regret his next offer. "We can shelter you while we get your passage arranged."

"Where?" She stopped eating to stare at him.

"Somewhere so upscale that whoever wants you dead won't

think to look for you there." Plenty of extra cottages on the guest-house property. And Codley could keep an eye on her until she was ready to go.

"They weren't always like this." Beska lifted her hands, the fork wedged between crippled fingers. "I did everything they asked."

"You planted the bugs on the prince's bed," Ard whispered.

She looked over at him, a puzzled expression on her filthy face. "They told me to drop a handkerchief on his mattress while I tuned the harp. Took it with me when I left."

Clever. Not even Beska really knew what she had done.

"That's all I did. I thought I was done, but they wouldn't let him go."

"Wouldn't let who go?" Ard pressed.

"Waed. One of my students," she answered.

"You were a teacher?"

"Individual harp lessons," she said, "when I wasn't tuning the prince's instrument."

"And they were holding one of your students to make sure you did what they wanted?"

Beska nodded. In a series of clicks, the pieces started falling together.

"How old was this student?" Ard asked.

"Just a lad of twelve," she answered. "He wasn't from a wealthy family. I was teaching him because he showed real talent."

"Did they ever let him go?"

She shook her head. "They took him into the palace on the day of the coronation. That was the last I ever saw him."

*Looks like we found our double for Shad Agaul,* Ard thought. It was too great a coincidence to think that a boy of the prince's same age and skill set would be last seen in the palace on the very day of the assassination. The only thing that remained was finding out if he had detonated the Blast Grit or not.

"What was your young student like?" Ard asked.

"Waed was a bright ray of sunshine," Beska said. "The lad never seemed down or disappointed. He was extremely polite and always expressed his thanks to me for teaching him."

That didn't sound like someone who would willingly light a fuse on a Grit keg under his own bed. Not to say it couldn't happen, but Ard still felt like he was missing something crucial about the actual explosion.

"I don't understand," said Ard. "If you did everything they asked, then..." He glanced at her hands. "What happened?"

"He said they were doing me a favor," answered Beska. "That I would thank them when suspicion about the assassination fell on me."

"Did it ever?"

She shook her head. Of course not. Codley had said the harp tuner was a new lead, overlooked by all the original inspectors on the case.

"They were giving you an alibi," Ard said. "In case anyone suspected that you had been in the prince's room playing his harp that night."

"I was to tell them that it couldn't have been me," Beska held up her hands. "That these were crushed in a carriage accident on my way home from tuning the harp three days before. He even gave me the name of a carriage driver that would confirm my story if anyone asked."

Ard decided not to tell Beska that her abducted student was likely the one who had done the actual playing. Her hands had been crushed so she would lose her job. So no one would trace the missing student to the harp tuner, and the harp tuner back to Shad Agaul's bedroom.

"Who did this?" Ard asked again.

"I never knew his name. He was a big fellow," she said. "Bigger than your henchman out there."

Ard froze. This was the second person in just over a week to attribute their abuse to a man of that description. And "bigger than Raekon Dorrel" wasn't a large pool.

"Can you tell me anything else about him?" Ard asked.

"Ugly as pitch," she answered. "A tattoo on his forearm. A lizard of some kind."

At least that was something more to go on. "What about the name of the carriage driver who was supposed to corroborate your story?"

"Daldon Voria," she said. "I tried to find him after my hands had healed. I would have slit his throat."

"He wasn't there?"

"It had been five cycles since the assassination," she replied. "The company said he had quit driving for them shortly before. I didn't want to attract attention, so I didn't ask where he had gone."

"I'll look into it." Ard noticed her worry and added, "Once you're safely in Talumon." Although Ard doubted her situation would improve much just by leaving Beripent. Poor woman's life had been stripped away from her. And the struggles she now faced were more than some unnamed thug waiting for her to slip up and talk.

"There was something else," Beska said. "I heard the big man mention it more than once. 'The Realm.' Sounded like a place he'd go to get information about his jobs. Maybe a pub or a tavern."

"'The Realm,'" Ard repeated thoughtfully. The name wasn't familiar to him. "We'll look into it, as well." He stood up and pulled off his long jacket. "Put this on. If someone is watching, we want to make you as unrecognizable as possible."

Beska stood, and Ard draped the jacket over her shoulders. It was a disguise so poor that Cinza and Elbrig would have wet themselves over it, but hopefully it would be enough to get Beska safely back to the Guesthouse Adagio.

She reached down and picked up the wooden bowl of soup with her gnarled hands. It took Ard a moment to realize that she intended to take it.

He plucked it from her grasp and set it back on the table. "Where we're going," he said, "you won't have to worry about finding food."

She tensed. "Not back to the palace."

"Of course not," Ard said, leading her out of the tavern. "We can't risk having anyone recognize you." Not to mention, the palace probably held some rather unpleasant memories for her.

Raek was waiting by the horses with his back to them. He didn't turn around until Beska was situated on the back of Ard's horse.

"What the blazes are you doing?" Raek hissed.

"We're taking her to the guesthouse," answered Ard.

"Like slag we are!" he retorted. "Whoever hired her could be watching. She could lead them right to us."

Raek and Beska stared at each other for a long moment. "What's your name?" she finally asked, squinting at him.

He turned away again, pulling himself into the saddle while muttering, "This is a bad idea."

"We'll take the long way back," Ard said. That would help shake any possible followers. "Keep your eyes peeled for a big brute, Raek. Bigger than you." The look on Raek's face told Ard that he'd caught the reference.

Ard nudged his horse forward, Beska gripping the back of his vest as they started toward the Guesthouse Adagio.

⌒

*We have hidden in the depths, but no longer.*

# CHAPTER

# 5

Today it was Portsend Wal who anxiously watched the hourglass beside the classroom door. He'd set a precedent for not releasing his students early, and he was going to stand by that. But Homeland, it was hard to focus on this lecture!

Portsend absently ran a hand across his chest, bumping the corner of the small scroll tube just to reassure himself that it was still nestled snuggly in his vest pocket. That sort of obsessive checking had already become a nervous habit.

The information on the scroll had been extremely simple. A list of seven materials with potential to become new Grit. Gloristar had written no other instructions, because she likely didn't have any. It was impressive that she'd even been able to remember these items from all she'd read in the Anchored Tome.

Finally, the last grains of sand fell through the hourglass and Portsend dismissed the class. He hadn't seen San at today's lecture. The lad had promised to see out the week before making his decision, but he must have grown impatient. Portsend was sorry to lose such a promising student to the war. Well, he'd have to get by with just one assistant.

In the hubbub of dismissal, Portsend moved around the long demonstration table and caught Lomaya Vans as she was standing up.

"Do you have a moment?" he asked the student.

"Am I in trouble?" Lomaya asked.

"Oh, no!" Had his tone been off? "Not at all."

"It was just that expression on your face," she said, loosening up. "Bearer of bad news."

Ah. Not his tone. His face. What he wanted to share with her wasn't necessarily *bad* news. But it *was* serious.

"You have a sharp mind, Lomaya."

"Thank you, Professor."

"I have need of such a mind," he replied. "Would you be interested in some extracurricular studies?"

"What sort of thing?" she asked, a flattered smile creeping onto her face.

"I'm putting together an experimental laboratory," answered Portsend. He felt more comfortable saying it out loud now that the classroom was mostly empty. "A chance to work with real Grit in a variety of applications." For a first-year student like Lomaya, this would surely be a tempting offer.

"I..." she faltered. "I have to write a paper."

This kind of response was partly why Portsend felt confident in recruiting her. A student like Lomaya clearly had her priorities straight.

"And I'll expect your paper to be turned in on time," said Portsend. "What I'm offering will not replace your studies. But I hope it will augment them."

The room was empty now, and Portsend could almost hear the young woman mulling it over. "What would be the time commitment?"

"I can work around your schedule," said Portsend. "But I hope the lab will be exciting enough to motivate you to put in a couple of hours each evening."

"Not sure my boyfriend will be too excited about that," Lomaya said. "How many of us will be involved?"

There was a knock on the open doorframe and Portsend turned

to see San Green standing in the threshold. There was no book satchel over his shoulder, and his coat was buttoned.

"Just the three of us, I imagine." Portsend answered Lomaya's question. "San. Come in."

The young man stepped forward, nodding to Lomaya as he spoke to Portsend. "I've come to let you know that I'll be heading out in the morning."

"You didn't keep your end of the bargain," answered Portsend.

"I couldn't make it to the lecture today," San said. "Packing."

"But you still took the time to bid me farewell."

"I've enjoyed your class," said San. "Seemed like the right thing, to stop by."

Or perhaps the Homeland had Urged the lad to Portsend's doorway. Given the professor one more chance to change his mind. "You know Lomaya Vans?"

The two students shared a pleasant smile. "I believe we have a biology class together as well," San said to her. "Or, we *did*."

"Lomaya and I were just heading down to the Grit laboratories on the east side of campus," said Portsend, habitually checking for the scroll in his breast pocket. "I'd like you to see my lab before you head out."

San tilted his head to the side. "I've got a few more rounds to make yet. People I'd like to see before I go."

*In case he doesn't come home*, Portsend thought. *I may yet convince him to stay.*

"It won't take long," said Portsend. "You owe it to yourself to see where a career in this field could have taken you." He let the offer dangle until the young man nodded.

Portsend crossed the room and plucked his coat from a hook. The two students followed him into the hallway and he locked the classroom door.

Brase was waiting for him, seated in one of the corridor chairs beside the stairwell. The Regulator was out of uniform, of course, and his Rollers were totally concealed beneath a long jacket. The two guards that Gloristar had assigned to watch him were quiet fellows. Portsend had learned their names and little else. They looked young—probably fresh out of Outpost training.

Luthe was standing at the bottom stair, and casually moved aside to let them pass. Portsend led Lomaya and San down one more flight to the main floor, knowing that Brase and Luthe would be following at a respectful distance.

"What sort of things will we be working on?" Lomaya asked as they moved outside, the brisk winter air a blast of refreshment to Portsend. They cut across the patio and moved onto a walkway that led to the campus's central courtyard.

"Practical Grit Mixing, primarily." He wasn't sure what else to call it. If he told them they'd be mixing and altering source materials with the end goal of finding new Grit, they'd call him a lunatic and he'd be on his own for sure.

"We'll be testing detonations, introducing contaminants, studying source materials, and analyzing effects." All true. Only, the effects, contaminants, and source materials would be things not usually tested.

They reached the courtyard, a spacious grassy area surrounded on all sides by campus buildings. The clock tower chimed as they turned eastward, a breeze stirring the rain-sodden leaves on the ground.

As a professor in the field of Grit studies, Portsend was granted a personal laboratory, situated down a gentle slope a safe distance from the other college structures, the stone front dug into the hillside. Others like it dotted the campus's perimeter, open for supervised use by second- and third-year students. Portsend's was much smaller, and the equipment inside much more expensive.

"I think those guys are following us." San glanced over his shoulder as they moved down the slope toward the lab.

"Yes," answered Portsend without looking back. The lad was

very astute, and already thinking like a soldier. And Brase and Luthe were not always as subtle as Gloristar had promised they'd be. "They're my bodyguards."

"Bodyguards?" Lomaya repeated.

"I didn't know grading papers was such a dangerous job," added San lightheartedly.

"I've been told people might kill for cutting-edge information in my field of study." Portsend intentionally made his tone extraserious. He needed to start dropping clues that he was up to more than simple Grit Mixing. These two were smart. By the time he finished showing them around the lab, they'd know that his request for their company was much more than an offer for extracurricular study.

The lab had a narrow door made of a single thick slab of oak. Portsend inserted his key into a padlock and opened the heavy iron latch. Putting his shoulder to the door, he budged it open with a grunt. The overcast afternoon glow peered into the windowless dugout as Portsend reached inside to a familiar rack beside the door. His hand closed around a small Grit pot and he smashed it against the wall, the clay shards falling into a pail as a dome of light appeared, hanging against the wall.

"Would you two do me the favor of igniting some of those lanterns?" Portsend stepped aside to let his pupils enter. He gestured to the dark lanterns against the wall. "Six ought to do."

In the laboratory, Light Grit lanterns were favorable to traditional detonation clouds. With the detonation fully contained, the bright lanterns could be moved and repositioned around the lab however they were needed.

Lomaya and San stood still, barely three steps through the doorway, studying the dim room in silence. They probably felt as though they had suddenly skipped over two entire terms and landed themselves in the second half of their middle year.

Portsend hoped he hadn't made a mistake. They were inexperienced. They didn't even have their detonation licenses.

"Let's give the lanterns enough Prolonging Grit to extend the glow for thirty minutes," Portsend instructed.

Lomaya turned to him. "Where is the Grit?"

The prepared pots for the lanterns, with varying levels of Compounding and Prolonging, were in a cabinet beside the rack, but Portsend didn't tell her about them.

Instead, he stepped inside the lab, leaving the door open to provide additional light. He approached the nearest table and slid a set of balance scales toward the students. "Light Grit is in the yellow canister. Prolonging in the white one." He pointed. "There's an abacus over there, if you need it."

"You want us to mix?" San asked.

"That *is* the purpose of this laboratory." He hoped his answer came off coy, and not belittling.

"We've never done this before," Lomaya pointed out.

"I covered the basics in my first three lectures of the term," answered Portsend.

"Learning about it and doing it are not the same thing," said Lomaya.

"Of course not. But why would anyone spend the time learning, if they didn't intend to do?"

San got started first. Apparently, even his farewells didn't take priority over the opportunity of mixing bulk Grit. Lomaya slipped her book satchel from her shoulder, resting it against the leg of the table as she joined her peer.

In the dimness of the laboratory, Portsend began readying the other materials. It would be difficult to explain why he had so many isolated items that had no connection to Specialty Grit.

Marble and shale. Birchwood, gold, and steel. The vertebrae of a horse, and the teeth of a dragon.

Seven new materials.

Portsend couldn't wait to dive in.

The first lantern ignited, the glow of the Light Grit contained behind the glass. It was Lomaya's. And San had a second one going only moments later. They both took a moment to admire the brightness, and Portsend knew they were seeing more than a glowing lantern. They were seeing accomplishment. There was a level of satisfaction and pride, having Mixed it from scratch. Like how a meal sometimes tasted better to the person who cooked it.

Now that the lanterns were glowing, Portsend pushed the door closed, catching a glimpse of Brase and Luthe loitering under a nearby tree, sharpening their knives. Closing the door didn't just stop the draft of cold air. It was also a subtle way to test San's interest in staying. As the natural afternoon sunlight was shut out, the lad didn't even look up from his task.

Before long, the laboratory was glowing brightly from San and Lomaya's hard work. Portsend arranged the ignited lanterns, hanging them at designated hooks to distribute the illumination across the underground chamber.

"I have some birchwood here," Portsend said, producing one of the canisters that Gloristar had delivered. "It's been to Pekal and back, passed through the digestive tract of a dragon, and subsequently processed into Grit with particular measures taken to keep it isolated and pure."

"More Light Grit, then?" Technically, San was right, but Portsend had been hoping he'd catch the oddity of his description.

"But, why take extra measures to keep the birch separate?"

There. Lomaya had picked up on it immediately. She was still approaching things like a student, while San was trying to retire his critical-thinking skills.

"Isn't birch considered a common wood?" Lomaya continued. Now she was doubting herself, but the young woman was correct, as usual.

Aspen and oak were the only two types of wood considered Specialty. Aspen created Silence Grit, and oak was processed into Shadow Grit. All other wood types were used to make Light Grit, usually a hodgepodge mix of whatever branches and sticks the dragon might have grazed.

Processed birch *would* produce Light Grit—all the science supported it. And to be totally sure, Portsend had tested it just yesterday. The effect was very regular.

So, why had birchwood been written in the Anchored Tome?

It was time to think outside the box—to begin testing Gloristar's materials in unusual ways.

"This is a canister of oak Shadow Grit," said Portsend, producing an ordinary batch from his laboratory stores. "What will happen if we Mix the two?"

"Jonzan's Eighth Truth," answered Lomaya. "The presence of a common wood type will nullify the specialty effect of the oak."

"It won't exactly nullify," corrected Portsend. "Rather, the Specialty Grit will adopt the effect of the common Grit, if they come from the same basic group."

Ten granules of Light Grit, likely including birch in the blend, combined with ten granules of Shadow Grit—oak—would react like twenty granules of regular Light Grit. It wasn't all that complicated, really.

Portsend lifted another canister to the table. "Now, what would happen if we combine the common birchwood with Void Grit?"

"One or the other will become a contaminant," answered San, "depending on the ratio."

Portsend nodded. Contamination ratios were more complex. A cloud of pure Grit always lasted exactly ten minutes. If contaminants came into play, the duration of the cloud could be reduced to seven minutes.

"So, if I have eight granules of Void Grit," said Portsend, "but I contaminate it with two granules of this birchwood"—he couldn't bring himself to call it regular Light Grit, although that's what it technically was; there had to be something unique about it—"how long will my cloud of Void Grit last?"

"Eight minutes," answered San. "You'll lose about two minutes of time, because the contamination makes up twenty percent of the detonation."

It was the easiest set of numbers for a straightforward problem. "And if the contamination was fifty-fifty?" asked Portsend.

"That's within the waste ratio," San answered promptly. "The Grit will yield a null detonation."

He was right. Jonzan's Ninth Truth. Anything more than thirty percent contaminated by sand or soil wouldn't detonate properly. But in many cases, one type of Grit was contaminated by another.

In the problem he had just posed, for example, the two granules of birchwood were acting as the contaminants in the Void Grit. But, if there were more birchwood in the mix, then the Void Grit would be considered the contaminant instead.

In essence, Grit required a minimum level of seventy percent purity in order to ignite at all, with the exception of Prolonging and Compounding Grit.

"I really should be going now," San remarked. "It must be getting late."

But Portsend felt like he was so close to convincing the young man to stay. Maybe another task would keep the lad engaged.

"Grab those scales." Portsend pointed and crossed the lab to produce a canister of Grit. It was another material from the scroll—specifically, horse vertebrae. "Pulverized bone," he said, keeping it intentionally vague. "Let's measure out three granules."

San quickly placed three brass weights in one of the scale pans, while Lomaya scooped out some of the Grit with a clay measuring spoon.

Portsend had no reason to believe that the horse bone would yield anything other than a regular cloud of Drift Grit, as it had done in his first attempt. But inwardly, he hoped for something miraculous. Something to give him a clue about the scroll's secrets and convince his students to stay. Maybe it would react to the time of day, or the relative humidity.

"Does this look all right?" San asked as Portsend returned to their table. The scales were balanced beautifully, and the professor was encouraged that his pupils appeared to be as good in the lab as they were in the classroom.

"Bring the Grit. Let's try it out." Portsend waved his students toward a door at the back of the laboratory.

"But..." Lomaya stammered, rigid. "That's the detonation chamber."

"We'll need to observe it in a controlled area," Portsend explained.

"We'll just be watching from the observation deck, right?" Lomaya asked. Even that would be new to these first-year students.

"I'll need help setting the Grit and running a fuse into the chamber, too," Portsend replied. This really petrified Lomaya, being offered a task usually reserved for the third year's final term. But there was no time for college rules. If he wanted San and Lomaya to become helpful research partners, he needed to get them quickly familiar with all the steps in the process.

"I'm beginning to wonder if this is some sort of test." San lifted the tray of measured Grit, the scales tipping as they unbalanced. "If you're just tempting us to break enough rules so you can throw us out of the program."

Portsend held back a smile. So, the lad still considered himself part of the program...

Snatching one of the glowing lanterns, Portsend pulled open the door and led his students through.

The observation deck was a narrow room with a wooden bench just long enough for half a dozen people to sit and scribe notes. The wall in front of them had a huge cut-out window providing an open-air view into the chamber beyond, a simple, bare room about thirty feet square. The floor and ceiling were made of the same stone slabs as the walls. The only way into the detonation chamber was through a hatch beside the window, an excessive number of bars securing it shut.

Portsend looped the handle of the lantern over a hook in the wall, gesturing to a rack of Grit pots against the far wall. "Barrier Grit," he explained. "We'll detonate some to seal off the observation window as a safety precaution."

"Against Drift Grit?" Lomaya picked up on it immediately. "It's hardly dangerous. And even if it were, a Barrier shell cannot hold back another Grit cloud."

*But it can hold back projectiles in case the nature of the cloud changes. In case it acts like Void Grit, sending scraps of broken pots hurtling in our direction.*

"Standard protocol with new experiments," Portsend explained.

"New for us," San pressed. "I imagine you've ignited hundreds of Drift Grit detonations in your tenure."

They were catching on. Portsend had hoped to have a solid commitment from them before revealing the truth of his experiments. But maybe a taste of the truth would inspire them to make that commitment.

"Please, have a seat." Portsend motioned to the long bench behind them. As they sat, San and Lomaya shared a puzzled glance, probably wondering if they'd done something wrong.

"The powdered bone you measured is not common Drift Grit," Portsend began. At least, he hoped it wasn't. Otherwise, he was chasing a myth.

San looked down at the tray in his hands. "Specialty Grit?"

"Is that human bone?" Lomaya followed up. "Illusion? Memory?" Her voice was excited. "Health?"

Portsend held up a hand to slow her enthusiasm. "It is processed horse vertebrae."

That earned him blank stares until San spoke. "I hate to think of a horse being eaten by a dragon..." He glanced at the Grit. "Still, this should be considered common bone. Drift Grit."

Lomaya held up a finger. "But you've isolated it. Just like you were talking about with birchwood." Her forehead wrinkled. "Why?"

Portsend took a deep breath. "I have been asked to experiment with a variety of isolated materials with hopes of finding"—did he dare say it?—"new Grit."

They didn't laugh at him. Portsend's fellow professors would have called him crazy and left as quick as a spark. But the solemn intrigue on the faces of his students assured him that telling them was the right choice.

"Who is funding this?" San finally asked.

Portsend wrung his hands. "I'm afraid I cannot share that information. But I swear to you that the source is legitimate and trustworthy."

"How many materials do you have?" asked Lomaya.

"Seven."

"And have you discovered anything new?"

"Not yet," Portsend said, afraid it would disappoint them. "But with your help, I—"

"I'll stay," San interrupted.

Lomaya was nodding at his side. "I can be here again tomorrow."

*And the day after that*, Portsend thought. *And the day after that.*

They'd keep at it until something unusual came from the Prime Isless's scrolls. He pictured her concerned expression as she pleaded with him to take this assignment. Portsend owed it to Gloristar to work quickly and efficiently.

"Who else knows about this?" Lomaya asked.

"Just the two of you," admitted Portsend. "And I must ask you to keep it that way."

"A project that warrants two bodyguards..." San remarked. "I'll keep my lips shut." He looked excited, but beside him, Lomaya now wore a strained expression.

"I hate to demand such secrecy." Portsend tried to be understanding. Hadn't she mentioned a boyfriend?

"I understand," she said softly. "I won't tell anyone."

San stood, holding out the tray of powdered bone. "Well, let's find out what this does!"

*Probably nothing unusual.* Portsend kept the thought to himself. He didn't want his pessimism to influence his newly formed research team.

"We'll place the tray in the center of the detonation chamber and run out a length of fuse," Portsend explained, pointing to the hatch entrance.

"Professor?" Lomaya's voice caused him to turn back to the bench. "Thank you for this opportunity."

"Yeah," San seconded. "This is..." He trailed off like he couldn't find the words.

Portsend Wal simply nodded. Never Settle. Keep progressing. Homeland willing, the scroll from the Anchored Tome would open its secrets to them.

~

*For our minds are keener and our bodies pure, even unto a state of utter perfection.*

# CHAPTER

# 6

Ard stacked his fork and knife on the empty plate and scooted it forward, making some room for his elbows on the table. He would have liked to retire to any one of the padded seats around the guesthouse's grand salon, but Beska Falay was still eating.

The beggar woman should have looked a lot better after five days of food and clean water. She'd had a good scrubbing and fresh clothes, but her eyes still looked sunken and tired. Most of the time she had a peaky pallor and an expression to match.

Codley Hattingson stepped forward to clear Ard's plate, shooting him a disapproving glance for his propped-up elbows.

"Mister…" Beska caught Codley's sleeve in her crippled hand. She still hadn't bothered to learn his name. Ard assumed this was a carryover from her previous life as a palace harp tuner, surrounded by servants who barely seemed important.

"Something to drink?" She actually had a nice smile, though Ard could see how painted-on it was.

"I shall pour you another glass of water," Codley replied.

"Anything stronger?" she tried.

"Water will do you much better." Codley tugged his sleeve free and carried Ard's plate away to the kitchen. Ard wondered if they even had any alcohol left, after Beska had smashed open the liquor cabinet on her second night at the guesthouse.

"Codley's right," Ard said. "You need to stay sharp. Tomorrow is going to be a big day."

"It's not like I've never been off Espar," Beska muttered, returning to her food.

"Not during an interisland war, you haven't," Ard pointed out.

It had taken them this long to arrange Beska's travel to Talumon. She hadn't left the guesthouse grounds but seemed quite comfortable in one of the small cottages, only making the trek across the grounds to the salon when accompanied by Ard or Hedma Sallis, the groundskeeper.

Ard glanced across the room. It was completely dark through the picture windows on the east side. It was a kind of flat, endless blackness that stretched out over the ocean.

"We'll see you as far as the docks," Ard said. "First thing in the morning."

"How do I know your contact will make good on his word?" Beska slurped down another bite of noodles.

"Because he doesn't get paid until he gets back from Talumon."

The smuggler Ard was using had already made a dozen successful runs between islands, posing as a common fisherman. He would run out of one harbor, change his flags and swap his papers, and then sail into the opposing island, claiming he'd left from there. It had been riskier at first, but now that harbor Regulators were familiar with him, Ard had no reason to think the trick would fail.

Codley reentered the salon. "It would seem that Master Raekon has returned. I shall meet him at the door."

Raek had been out much later than expected. Ard hoped that meant he had good news on one of the many leads they'd been chasing.

Pushing away from the dining table, Ard stood up. Beska still had half a bowl of dinner and he had grown impatient waiting on the hard chair.

He crossed the room and picked a pastry off a plate on a side table. He was fairly sure it was supposed to be a sugary palmier, but the shape was all wrong. Well, as long as he didn't break his teeth on it…

He bit down, surprised at the flakiness of the pastry. "Bannit?" he muttered. "Where's Bannit? Bannit!"

With alarming speed, the wiry servant appeared. His coarse black hair had fallen forward from his apparent sprint from the kitchen, and the tips of his ears poked through like pale half moons.

"Yes, Master?"

"This…" Ard wagged the morsel in Bannit's direction. "This is the best one yet."

Bannit relaxed, an eager smile spreading over his face. "I chilled the butter," the servant explained. "Everyone in town says that's the secret."

"I don't care what you did," replied Ard, taking a second bite, "just so long as you can do it again."

Going on two weeks, from the time of their arrival, Bannit's enthusiasm hadn't waned. Ard had gladly taken on the responsibility of being the Guesthouse Adagio's official taste tester, and the little cook had been making huge improvements to the menu.

"I knew you'd like it, Master." Bannit nodded. "I'll whip up another three dozen. That ought to last us the week."

"I appreciate your enthusiasm," Ard said, "but pastries are like bathwater—best enjoyed fresh. Small batches, Mister Lagaday. All victories are won in small batches."

"Wisdom," Bannit whispered, nodding thoughtfully. "Pure wisdom." It took the sudden appearance of Codley and Raek to jolt the servant out of his reverie. "Can I get you anything, Master Raekon?"

Raek pressed a hand to the metal chimney in his chest, trying to hide a wince from an obvious twinge of pain. "The usual tea would be great."

The little cook nodded, ducking through the kitchen door.

"You missed dinner," Ard said, finally seating himself on a soft chair.

"I picked up a bite on the street," Raek replied. He scanned the room, his glance moving quickly past the spot where Beska sat eating. It was no secret that Raek didn't trust her. Ard didn't, either. But he believed what she'd told him in the tavern. She and her harp student had played a significant role in the assassination, or abduction, of the prince. But the woman had been terribly manipulated. She was far more of a victim than a conspirator.

"I could go for dessert." Raek crossed to the tray next to Ard and scooped up a little tart.

"Anything this afternoon?" Ard asked.

Raek shook his bald head. "Honestly, at this point I'm not expecting to turn over any new rocks. I've hit all the usual channels. We just don't have enough to go on."

"I still can't believe you don't know him," Ard answered, inferring the man who had destroyed the harp tuner's hands. "Beska said he was bigger than you."

"Just because a person is roughly my size doesn't mean I should know him," Raek pointed out. "You realize how absurd that is, right?"

"I just thought you might go to Big Man conventions, or something," Ard said. "You know, where you talk about how cold your feet get as they dangle off the end of your bed. And you write letters advocating for higher doorframes?"

"Yeah," Raek said. "And we practice getting things down from the top shelf. It's a real hoot."

Ard sighed, finishing off the palmier. "If our contacts aren't turning anything up, then we need to change our methods."

"I'm open to ideas," Raek said.

"Well, if we can't find him," mused Ard, "then maybe *he* can find *us*."

Raek glanced over at the dining table. "You want to use Beska as bait?"

She stopped eating, the fork beginning to tremble in her gnarled hand. "That's not what we agreed on."

"Relax," Ard called. Then to Raek. "She has to leave in the morning. We can find another way to lure him out."

"Might I suggest an audition," chimed Codley.

Sparks, most of the time, Ard forgot he was in the room. The butler could stand frighteningly still for extended periods of time.

"What kind of audition?" Raek asked.

"Something specific to his size," replied Codley, "since it seems to be the only definitive thing we know about him."

"You know we were joking about Big Man conventions, right?" Ard said.

Codley's eyebrows responded with a twitch. "Perhaps an audition for a stage play," he said, "where size of the actor is requisite for the character."

"Codley," Ard began, "the only other thing we know about this guy is that he breaks people's fingers. That doesn't really sound like the type to go around memorizing Dorian's *Lovesick Fisherman*."

"Well, pardon me for thinking outside the box." Codley sniffed.

"What else?" Raek mused, casting a sidelong glance at Beska. "He was muscular, tanned skin, shaved head."

"Was he missing any teeth?" These were questions Ard had asked before, but he knew Beska was sober now, and a few days of comfort might have helped jog her memory.

"Don't remember," she answered from the table. "Tried not to look at his face much."

"What was his voice like?"

"It was sort of...deep."

"Oh," Raek said in mock realization. "So, like a man's voice? And don't forget the lizard tattoo on his forearm. There are probably only tens of thousands of citizens in Beripent who have tattoos."

"Lizard, you say?" interjected Codley. "What variety of lizard?"

Beska sighed, leaning back in her chair. She looked like she was finally finished eating. There was still food on her plate, but that had become common. Beska ate until she was stuffed, often requesting a final plate that she knew she couldn't finish.

"It was small," she said. "That's all I know."

"Of course it was small," Codley rebutted. "The depiction could be no larger than the width of the man's forearm. Was it scaled, or smooth? Bearded? Spines?"

"I told you, I don't know!" answered Beska, standing up.

"It was just a tattoo, Codley," said Raek, "not an actual lizard."

"Ha!" Ard cried. "But it does make me wonder about the artist's ability. Raek's right about the vast number of tattooed citizens, but a lot of those look like a dragon took a slag on the person's arm. Locating the best artists could help to narrow the field. They know their clients, and they're bound to be familiar with one another's work."

It was a stretch, but everyone looked to Beska. "It was detailed," she remembered. "I thought it looked rather realistic." She paused. "Except for the feet."

"What about them?" Ard pressed.

She squinted, as though trying to dig up an old and certainly unpleasant memory. "They were too big for the lizard's body. As though its claws were absurdly massive hooks."

Ard and Raek looked at each other, both of them coming to the same conclusion. Ard was the first to say it out loud.

"That was a fighting Karvan lizard!"

"Come again?" Codley said. "What is this?"

"Karvan lizards," Raek explained. "They're a variety native to Pekal."

"Well, I know *that*," Codley remarked. "But I was under the impression that the Karvan lizard is a rather docile creature. Why, you may not have known this, but the crusader monarch himself kept one as a pet in the palace."

"Yeah," Raek said flatly. "Millguin."

That blazing lizard had foiled their otherwise perfect Paladin Visitant ruse against King Pethredote. For when the pet hadn't burned up in the fake Paladin's presence, the king had put a sword through Raek's chest.

"Female Karvan lizards can be bred to be brutally violent," Raek continued. "There are organized rings right here in Beripent where people can pit their lizards against one another for money."

It was true, although Ard found the sport incredibly distasteful. He'd stumbled upon a fighting ring once, while trying to meet with a potential employer. It was morbidly intriguing, although Ard quickly learned he didn't have the stomach for it.

Furthermore, if Ardor Benn were going to place a bet, he was far more inclined to place it on himself. As they'd learned with the Visitant ruse, animals were unpredictable.

"And how would you know about this?" Codley asked.

"It was a case we did a few years back," Ard lied smoothly. "Locked up a breeder and a whole ring of fighters. Sent the lizards to roam free on Pekal."

"And the big feet?" Codley asked.

"Fighters trim out their lizards with all kinds of accessories," Raek explained. "Armor plating, tail barbs." He pointed at Beska. "Absurdly massive hooks over their claws."

"So, our brute is a lizard fighter," Ard mulled.

"And a dedicated one, if he's tattooing that on his arm," added Raek.

"Now all we have to do is hit up one of the fight rings and start asking around," Ard said.

Raek held up a hand. "Not everybody likes to talk as much as you. We do that, and it might spook him."

"Especially if you were to announce yourself as an inspector," Codley added.

"Obviously, I won't do that," said Ard. "Perhaps I'll go by a false name. What about *Androt Penn*? Rolls nicely off the tongue."

"Then you will enter this criminal cesspool posing as gamblers?" Codley asked. "Do you have sufficient funds for that?"

"I believe Her Majesty does," Ard said.

Codley stiffened. "Absolutely not! Queen Abeth's dwindling funds will not be squandered on *lizard fighting*."

"Hold on," Raek said. "*Dwindling*?"

"Her Majesty's assets, those that weren't usurped by King Termain, have mostly been moved to a secure location in Dronodan," answered Codley.

"Okay, but she still has loads of Ashings, right?" Raek clarified. "I mean, what chance do you think we have of actually getting paid this time?"

"Queen Abeth will deliver as promised," replied Codley, as though shocked that Raek would suggest otherwise. "Nothing short of death would cause her to default on her payment."

"It's the *death* part I'm worried about," admitted Raek.

"Homeland, Master Raekon!" cried Codley. "Why would you say such a thing?"

"Our best clients have a history of dying on us," Ard chimed.

"We'd probably only need a thousand Ashings for the lizard fight." He tried to slide that in smoothly to see if Codley would agree while he was flustered.

"It will not happen, gentlemen," Codley said. "I cannot allow you to gamble with the queen's Ashings."

"How many people do you think typically go to these fights?" Ard asked. Thinking back to the one he'd seen, there were probably over a hundred folks placing bets.

"From what I've seen, the events would be big enough for us to blend in," Raek said. "But not so big that we'd miss seeing the brute if he was there."

"He'll probably be fighting, though," Ard said. "Could make him hard to reach."

"All right," said Raek, catching on. "So, we pose as a fighter. Bring our own lizard with the hope that we can rub shoulders with the big guy."

"We're onto something." Ard could feel that the plan was just a few steps away from working.

"Frightful business is what you're onto," muttered Codley, absently dusting at the mantel above the Heat Grit hearth.

"We won't last more than one fight with a fake lizard before they blackball us," Raek pointed out. "How do we make sure the brute is at the same fight?"

Ard closed his eyes, seeing it all take shape. "We *host* the fight."

He opened his eyes to see Raek nodding slowly. Codley had fully turned his back, no doubt to make some undignified facial expression that he just couldn't hold back.

"We host the lizard fight and we make it an exclusive event," Ard went on. "Only contestants who have a lizard that has won, say, five fights is allowed to enter."

"How could you possibly know if your brute has a lizard that fits those qualifications?" Codley asked, whirling around to face them again.

"That's the gamble," Ard admitted. "But I'm guessing that someone willing to tattoo an illegally trimmed lizard on their forearm isn't a newcomer to the game."

Bannit entered from the kitchen, a steaming cup of tea balanced carefully on a small saucer. "Master Raekon." He handed it to the big man.

"Where and when will this fight take place?" Codley fidgeted.

"We'll need some time to put the word out," answered Raek. "I've got a venue in mind. It's an abandoned granary on the road out to Panes."

"Beginning of next cycle?" Ard asked.

"I think that's doable," he said. "Do we still want a lizard?"

Ard nodded. "I think it'll work best if one of us hosts and the other poses as a fighter. That way we can come at the brute from both angles to make sure we don't miss him."

"Assuming this all works," said Codley, "what exactly do you intend to say to the man?"

"He's probably just the muscle," replied Ard. "We'll find out who hired him."

"Where's Beska?" Raek suddenly asked.

Ard looked to the dining table, where Bannit was clearing away the dishes beside her empty chair. "I told her it was a big day tomorrow. She probably went off to bed early."

Raek scowled. "She's not supposed to cross the grounds unaccompanied." He moved for the door, but Ard held up a hand.

"We're not done here, Raek."

"I'll do it," said Bannit. "I'll check on her." He set down the used dishes and straightened, tugging at the edge of his apron as though volunteering was something incredibly brave.

"See her safely to her cottage," Codley ordered, giving a dismissive nod. Bannit scurried out the back door into the dark night.

"Codley," Ard said. "I think we should let the queen know of our progress."

"To be honest," the butler said, "I do not think she would approve of your methods." He crossed to retrieve a paper and scribing charcoal from the drawer of a small desk.

"We don't have to mention the lizards," Ard said.

Codley took a seat, donning a small pair of spectacles. He dated the corner of the page, and then silently awaited dictation.

"Your Majesty," Ard began, standing to pace as he spoke. "I am pleased to report that our investigation speeds forward with significant progress." He paused, turning sharply to look at the butler. "Was that a scoff, Codley?"

"Merely a tickle in the throat," the lean man replied. "Do carry on."

Ard continued. "One suspect has already been apprehended and detained."

"By 'apprehended and detained,'" Raek cut in, "he means 'invited to stay at the guesthouse until we can illegally smuggle her to Talumon.'"

"Don't get hung up on semantics, Raek," said Ard.

"I assume you meant for me to pause my dictation," Codley said without looking up from the page.

"Use your discretion," answered Ard. "But you can resume now." He began pacing once more. "We have come to conclude that your son was not in the room at the time of the explosion. The body recovered likely belonged to a young harp player whom you heard practicing through the door. As to the actual whereabouts of the prince, we are still searching. We hope soon to have a positive word for your royal ear."

That was appropriately adoring. After all, the real Ardour Stringer was supposed to be Dronodanian.

"During the course of our interrogation, the suspect mentioned something called the Realm," Ard resumed. "Its meaning is still unknown to us, but fortunately, I have a well-laid plan in motion that should soon yield answers."

Ard stopped pacing and looked to Raek. "Anything more?"

"What about something like, 'I miss you terribly. Please come back to me'?"

"Okay." Ard turned sharply away from Raek. "I think we got everything." He crossed to the desk and signed the letter, careful to slip a *u* into the inspector's first name. He'd been practicing the signature for days now, using some of the forging techniques that Elbrig had taught him when he'd trained to be the composer of the Unclaimed Symphony.

Codley Hattingson folded the page and stood up. "With your permission, gentlemen, I shall adjourn for the evening."

"How long until that letter reaches the queen?" Ard asked.

"My couriers can have it in Her Majesty's hand in just two days." That was remarkably fast. "I expect she will send a reply." He nodded again.

"Good night, Codley," Ard said. The butler crossed the grand salon and exited the guesthouse through the north doors.

"Is it a good idea to play pen pals with the former queen of the Greater Chain?" Raek asked.

"Why not?" Ard flopped himself down on a chaise, propping a pillow behind his head.

"Well, for starters, we told the Cod that she gave us permission to live here."

"I burned that first letter," answered Ard. "There's no evidence that she didn't."

"Unless she says something in a letter to Codley. Or if he says something in a letter to her."

"At some point, I'm sure Lady Abeth is going to figure out that we're living in her guesthouse."

"And that's . . . okay?" Raek asked slowly.

"It will be. We're getting results, Raek. So far, we've uncovered more of the truth behind the prince's assassination than a dozen of Beripent's finest inspectors. As long as we stay relevant, I don't think Abeth is going to kick us out. We'll chalk the whole thing up to a misunderstanding." Ard reached behind his head and blindly grabbed a little tart. "Staying here is part of our payment. Try to enjoy yourself."

"I'm enjoying myself plenty. I've got one cottage to eat in, one cottage to sleep in, one cottage with all my mixing equipment. And the best part is, I can't hear you snoring."

The north doors suddenly burst open in a whoosh of cold air. Ard was on his feet in a flash, heart racing. Hedma Sallis stood in the doorway, her chest heaving as though she'd sprinted some distance. Bannit Lagaday arrived a moment after her, his pale face tight with concern.

"It's Beska!" the small cook replied. "She's gone!"

"Gone?" Ard cried.

"She left the property on Keyling, riding bareback," answered Hedma.

"Why would she leave?" Ard muttered. "We were getting her out of here first thing in the morning."

Bannit turned to Raek. "She may have stolen something of yours."

"What?"

"The door to your guest cottage was open," he continued. "Light Grit was still burning inside. The place was ransacked."

"Blazing sparks!" Raek pushed past Bannit and Hedma, disappearing into the night.

"We've got to go after her," Ard said.

The groundskeeper shrugged helplessly. "Keyling's our fastest mount. She's gone, Master Ardor."

~

*On the morrow, we shall go up at last.*

# CHAPTER

# 7

Beska Falay was dead.

Ard thought of her again as he stood outside the abandoned granary, preparing to host his first Karvan lizard ring fight.

The Regulators in the Northern Quarter had found the harp tuner's body the morning after she'd left the guesthouse. Her stolen horse, Keyling, had been recovered not far from her corpse, spattered in dried blood. The Reggies had delivered the traumatized mare back to the Guesthouse Adagio after identifying the brand on her flank—the star-shaped Agaul "A."

Codley Hattingson had been remarkably smooth under pressure, explaining to the Regulators that the stable had been raided in the night by an unidentified vagrant. The Reggies had then broken the news that the suspected thief had been murdered. They described her as a beggar woman with terribly crippled hands, which was enough for Ard to know that it was her.

Two weeks had passed and Ard still couldn't fathom why Beska had fled. The woman had ransacked Raek's cottage, but he'd said she hadn't taken a thing.

Beska's death had been wholly avoidable and it weighed on Ard's conscience. He had promised to help her and everything had been in place for her safe departure. He tried not to let himself feel responsible. After all, it was her own poor choices that had led to her demise. But would she still be alive if Ard hadn't interfered with her life?

He breathed in the cold night air, pushing thoughts of Beska to the back of his mind as he adjusted the cuffs of his black jacket. Talumonian fashion was questionable. It was a wonder they were winning the war, what with the number of times Ard had already snagged his large cuffs.

His disguise was simple, taking a page out of the disguise managers' book. Cinza and Elbrig always said that a good costume was less about hiding one's face and more about drawing attention to a few memorable points—tonight, a large tricornered hat, a patch over his left eye, and his beard tied into two woolly tufts under his chin.

The crowd on the other side of the door was roaring. Ard had even heard a few organized chants. The turnout had been good, and gratefully, Raek had confirmed that their thug was here.

Staug Raifen. Or at least, that was the name the big man was going by when Ard received the list of lizard handlers.

Ard stepped onto the rickety ladder that extended up the exterior of the old granary. When he had almost reached the top, he climbed through a window onto a little platform that overlooked the interior of the building. Raek had secured the dilapidated landing with extra timbers to make sure it wouldn't collapse under Ard's weight.

Setup for this particular ruse had gone rather smoothly. He and Raek had split up, donning a variety of disguises and taking turns visiting as many established lizard fighting rings as they could. The purpose of this was threefold.

First, they hoped that one of them would spot the big thug and they wouldn't have to go through with hosting their own fight. But they hadn't been that lucky in the five matches they'd attended around Beripent.

Second, gossiping at the rings was the best way to make sure everyone knew about the "big fight" coming up at the abandoned granary south of Beripent. Afraid to seem out of touch, nearly everyone they talked to said they were planning on coming. It was a ring of thick-skulled tough guys. It didn't take much to play on their insecurities.

And third, if they were going to host a fight, they better blazing well watch a few to see how these things worked!

Ard had quickly learned that hype was everything at these events. Even more so at this one, since these were experienced lizards with clout, their handlers were known among this circle of lowlifes.

Well, except for Raek and his lizard, Snapjaw, supposedly fresh off a smuggler's boat from Talumon, where the fighting was hot. Androt Penn had come with them, and after finding the ring scene in Beripent to be rather lackluster, decided to host his own exclusive event for veteran lizards.

In reality, Raek had purchased Snapjaw from a vendor in the Char who specialized in exotic imports from Pekal. Nothing dragon-related, of course. Mostly just plants, insects, birds, and the occasional Karvan lizard.

The one in Raek's cage had definitely never seen a fight. Ard wasn't even sure it was a female. Her real name was Sunbeam, probably to entice a parent to buy it as a pet. But "Sunbeam" wasn't likely to strike fear into the hearts of her opponents, so they were going with Snapjaw.

*Time to get this party started.*

Ard tossed a pot of Light Grit ahead, the clay shattering on the edge of his wooden platform. The sudden illumination caught the attention of the crowd below, turning heads and quieting mouths.

*Quite the turnout, indeed,* Ard thought, looking down on the motley crowd.

The fighting arena was circular, marked by waist-high posts, with a web of chains strung between them. Torches flickered, mounted to the posts to provide warmth and an atmospheric light.

The spectators surrounded all but the far side of the circle, where a low deck had been constructed just a single step up from the grain-littered floor. The back half of the deck was covered by a low-strung canvas tent, partitioned into stalls. The lizards were housed there, out of sight from one another, but close enough to hear and smell their opponents. This was supposed to create a festering rage that would be fully unleashed when the creatures were finally released.

Standing shoulder to shoulder on the deck were the eight lizard handlers. From his perch, Ard could easily identify Raek, even with his ridiculous wig in place. Cinza and Elbrig had termed him *undisguiseable*, due to his towering stature. But tonight, Raek wasn't the only big man standing on the deck.

Staug Raifen was every bit the size of Ard's partner. The man's head had a fuzz of hair, and his face was as ugly as Beska had promised. Exuding a sickening level of self-importance, he stood with his hands clasped behind his back, blocking Ard's view of the tattoo. But Raek had confirmed that it was him.

Ard cleared his throat. This wasn't really a "ladies and gentlemen" kind of crowd, so he started things off with more appropriate verbiage.

"Are you Moonsick rats ready for some blood?"

This got an adequate cheer, but the spectators were obviously anxious for Ard to get the formalities out of the way.

"Eight dragons tonight!" he called.

This crowd commonly referred to their lizards as dragons. Ha! If any of them had seen a real dragon, they'd balk at the hyperbole. Last time Ard was on Pekal, he'd actually seen two sows attack each other. That memory made this sort of event seem like awfully small potatoes.

"The matches will be single elimination," Ard shouted, "winners going on to fight winners for a set of three rounds. These are all seasoned beasts, here, and we might want to see them fight again some day, so it's Master's Call tonight."

That was a useful term he'd picked up at one of the earlier fights.

Master's Call meant that the match would end as soon as one of the lizard handlers admitted defeat. This allowed them to resuscitate the creature in a cloud of Health Grit. With any luck, she would heal enough to fight another day.

Ard unfolded the piece of paper in his hand. It was a simple list of names—handlers and their lizards. He had paired them into matches based on the brief information Raek had shared when he delivered the list.

According to the bets made below, it was clear that Staug's lizard, Clutch, was favored to be tonight's winner. Coming in second was Riser, who belonged to a terrifying woman called Patra Bo.

Poor Snapjaw was at the bottom of the betting chart. And rightfully so. She'd probably been bred for lounging in a windowsill, eating flies. No matter. If everything went as planned, Snapjaw wouldn't see any action tonight.

"First up..." Now the crowd was quiet enough that Ard didn't need to yell. "Stride Fenet's champion, Sidebite, versus Patra Bo's Riser!"

Why not get things started with one of the leading lizards? The moment the match was announced, the Tallies began hawking, waving their notebooks in the air and scribbling bets.

Below, Ard saw Raek follow the other handlers off the deck. Only Stride and Patra Bo remained, turning their attention to the tent behind them. Carefully, they retrieved their cages from the canvas stalls, sliding them across the deck toward the ring. The animals inside were thrashing at the sudden sight of each other. Ard wouldn't have been surprised if they'd ripped right through the bars.

The two handlers positioned the rectangular cages side by side, one end dangling off the raised deck leading into the arena.

Ard watched the crowd, giving enough time for bets to be cast and recorded. The Tallies had to close their books the moment the cages opened, so there was a general freneticism as people tried to throw away their Ashings before Ard gave the call. The actual exchange of money wouldn't happen until the end of the night. The Tallies would balance their ledgers and everyone would pay up or get paid on their way out the door.

One of the workers Ard had hired tossed a fuse pot into the air above the arena. It detonated about twelve feet off the ground, bits of shattered clay falling through a perfect orb of light that now lit the ring with noonday clarity.

That was long enough for the bets.

"Dragons ready!"

On the deck, Stride and Patra Bo knelt down next to their animals' cages, hands on their latches.

"Fight!"

The ends of the rectangular cages dropped open and the two creatures emerged, catching each other in a violent embrace even before they hit the arena floor.

They wrestled furiously for a moment, one indistinguishable from the other as the overhead light glinted on their armor plating. After their initial fury, the two creatures pulled apart and Ard watched them circle, tongues flicking out.

These Karvan lizards looked nothing like Pethredote's old pet, Millguin. These were lean and fast. With all their accessories, they even looked different from the wild ones Ard had seen on Pekal.

Sidebite's plating was unpainted shiny metal. Her helm was horned, three long spikes obviously meant for piercing armor. The claws on her front feet were shod with large hooks like crescent moons, but her back legs were left bare. Ard had learned this was common, allowing the lizard to spring from firmly planted hind legs and slash with the front.

Riser's armor had been decorated with messy streaks of red. Her helm was ridged down the middle, clearly designed for blows to glance off. The lizard's belly was covered in hardened molded leather, and barbed metal studs dotted the length of her spine and tail. Riser's claw hooks were clearly bigger than Sidebite's, a testament to the lizard's strength.

The spectators screamed themselves hoarse, and Ard wondered if it even made a difference to the captive lizards. Did they recognize the voices of their handlers, or would they fight just the same in an empty room? The violence had been bred into them through habit, conditioning, and abuse.

Maybe they weren't so different from the humans watching them.

Sidebite lunged, going on hind legs and slashing with her claws. Riser met the attack head on. They grappled for a second before the audience gave a collective gasp. Ard squinted, but from this distance, he couldn't see what had happened. But even from here he could see blood on the grainy floor as the combatants rolled into a different attack.

*Okay, Raek. Your sabotage better work, or this match will be over and we'll have to let two more lizards tear each other up.* Not only that, but in order for the motive to look convincing, Riser needed to be in the ring.

Sidebite and Riser separated. The former was limping, trailing blood. Patra Bo's lizard saw the weakness and struck again, managing to pin Sidebite to the ground before she could turn.

Just then, a third lizard emerged from the tent, breaking free of its cage, and grazing Patra Bo's leg with one of its armored spines as it sped past. The handler screamed, falling to the deck as the lizard leapt into the arena and lunged at Riser's back.

Ard took a deep breath. The plan was really in motion now.

This was Staug Raifen's lizard, Clutch. Her armor was painted blue and trimmed with scraps of serrated metal. She looked like a living saw blade as she slammed into the two creatures already locked in combat.

Clutch's unexpected arrival brought the volume of the crowd to an almost deafening level. Ard looked for Raek down below. Good. His partner was far enough from the cage that no one would have suspected him of tampering with the latch.

Raek's method had been clever—the tiniest dusting of Void Grit under a fragment of wax-coated Slagstone wedged at the top of the cage door. Clutch's own restlessness in her cage had gradually worn away the wax. Once the Slagstone was exposed, all it took was a significant jolt from the lizard to cause a spark, igniting the Void Grit and pushing open the latch.

"Clutch!" One voice rose above the others, and Ard saw Staug Raifen stepping into the arena. "Clutch! Heel!"

But everyone knew Karvan lizards were slow to follow verbal commands, especially the fighting types. Staug stood in the arena, but he couldn't get too close to the three creatures without seriously injuring himself.

"Call the match!" he yelled.

"You filthy cheat!" screamed Patra Bo, on her feet once again and moving toward Staug.

Oh, as much as Ard hated to miss this part, he needed to get down there and move things along before Patra Bo killed their only lead.

Shoving the list into his pocket, Ard ducked back out the window and moved down the ladder, the night wind whipping against his back.

He skipped the last few rungs, jumping to the ground and pulling open the rickety back door. Ard slipped into the granary on the ground floor, greeted by a wash of angry yelling. He ran forward, waving his hands for order.

As he reached the ring, he realized that Clutch and Riser had been detained in separate clouds of Barrier Grit. They were frantically trying to dig out beneath their impenetrable domes, but cumbersome lassos had been looped around their necks before the Grit had detonated. A handful of T-shaped dowels were attached to the collars, making it nearly impossible for the lizards to squeeze through any hole they might dig under the Barrier dome.

The third lizard, Sidebite, wasn't moving at all. Stride Fenet knelt over the bloody lizard, a cloud of Health Grit enveloping the creature with the hope that she'd regain consciousness.

Staug Raifen and Patra Bo faced each other in the middle of the ring, weapons drawn as though they might continue the fight themselves.

Ard pushed through the crowd and stepped over the cordon chains, hands outstretched to make it clear he had come to talk peace. He positioned himself between Staug and Patra Bo, aware that he could now be stabbed from both sides at once.

"Now, now," he said calmly. Outside the arena, the crowd quieted enough to hear the exchange. "Accidents happen."

"That weren't no accident!" Patra Bo hissed. "He released his blazing dragon to break down Riser. Hit her good so she couldn't stand a later fight!"

"That makes no sense, woman!" roared Staug. "If I pulled something like that, I'd be barred from a later fight!"

"Well, sure, you made it look like an accident," said Patra Bo. "I ain't nobody's fool!"

"Calm down!" Ard demanded. Out of the corner of his eye, he saw Raek heading for the back door he had just come through, Snapjaw in her cage under his arm. Raek would have the horses in position shortly.

Now Ard just needed Staug Raifen to punch him.

"I'll agree that things don't look too good for you, Mister Raifen," Ard said.

"I wasn't by ten feet of Clutch's cage," he said, defending himself.

"From my view up top, I'd say no one was," answered Ard.

He crossed the arena quickly and hopped onto the raised deck. No one had touched Clutch's open cage yet, which was lucky. Ard reached into the canvas stall and pulled it out, feeling some strange push and resistance as it passed through the tiny cloud of Void Grit.

Ard pretended to examine the cage, casually palming Raek's little piece of Slagstone. He strode back to the arena, dropping the open cage at the edge of the deck as he stepped into the ring once more.

"Can I offer you some free advice?" Ard asked, coming face-to-face with Staug. Sparks, this man *was* bigger than Raek. The brute merely grunted at Ard's question. "You should learn how to properly latch your lizard cage."

The crowd cooed, and Ard flinched, fully expecting the blow. But Staug's fists remained at his sides, clenched like sizable stones.

Seriously? Ard hadn't expected nearly so much restraint from this guy. He'd just have to pester a little harder. He turned to Patra Bo.

"Was Riser injured in the attack?"

The woman shook her head. "Takes more than a cheating Bloodeye to bring her down."

As much as Ard would have liked to disqualify Staug, the grounds just weren't strong enough to be accepted by the crowd. Especially not when bets had already been placed in Clutch's favor.

Ard faced Staug again, closing the distance between them with a step. "Soon as that Barrier burns out, I want your ugly lizard locked up good and tight in her cage, understood?"

"Riser hooked her," Staug said. "She needs Health Grit before she fights."

Ard shrugged. "I'd recommend Health Grit for you, too, if I thought it would do anything for your looks."

Staug's eyes widened and he stared down at Ard with a puzzled look, like he couldn't quite believe those words had just come out of the ring host's mouth. Based on the sounds the crowd made, they enjoyed a bit of drama.

"My apologies." Ard held up his hands. "I shouldn't insult the hired help."

"Hired help?" he repeated as the crowd crowed.

"I assume that's why you're here," continued Ard. "To clean out the cages after the fight."

This caused a tightening of Staug Raifen's jaw. All right. The way to his fury was through his reputation.

"I'm Clutch's handler." He stated the obvious.

"*Mis*handler, I'd say."

The punch came hard and fast, Staug's arm nothing more than a blurry tattoo of a Karvan lizard. And the fact that Ard was expecting it might have made it hurt worse.

Ard sprawled to the bloody floor, blackness hedging on his eyesight. He lay there dazed for a moment, certain he would black out. The hollering crowd almost faded, only to return at full volume, ringing in Ard's rattled head.

He pushed himself up and dabbed his bloody upper lip. Stepping over to Sidebite, Ard stooped, pushing his face into the Health Grit cloud that surrounded the injured lizard. He felt the pain ease, and the bleeding stopped almost immediately.

Sparks, was this cloud Compounded? It felt amazing, but he couldn't linger.

"I don't know about Beripent," Ard said, yanking his head out of the cloud and turning to face Staug, "but in Talumon, assaulting the ring host is grounds for immediate expulsion from the fight."

The crowd booed, but Ard clapped his hands and pointed across the granary to the back door. "You're coming with me, big guy." He reached out and grabbed Staug's tattooed arm. With his other hand, Ard drew his Roller to show that he meant business.

"Not without Clutch." Staug seemed quite unintimidated by the gun barrel in his ribs.

"We'll throw your beast outside as soon as that Barrier burns out," Ard said, marching Staug to the edge of the ring. The crowd parted as they stepped over the chain, moving for the back door.

"Gritspit and Whiplash fight next," Ard called over his shoulder.

"Handlers, get them ready. I'll call the fight from the platform once I see this brute out."

Ard opened the door and pushed Staug into the night, closing it behind them. Staug startled at the sight of Raek looming in the darkness, already seated atop one of the three horses.

"Get on." Ard pushed the brute toward another mount.

"What is this?" Staug grunted. "You?" It probably took a moment to recognize Raek as his eyes adjusted to the darkness.

"Ride now. Talk later." Raek brushed at his awkward wig and proffered the reins to Staug.

"I'm not going nowhere without Clutch." He folded his arms.

"Fine." Ard stepped past him and climbed into one of the vacant saddles. "You're welcome to stick around here and let the Reggies lock you up. But I'm guessing your jail cell won't fall open like your lizard's cage."

"Reggies?" He looked from Ard to Raek.

"They wear blue coats," Raek explained, "enforce the laws, arrest lizard fighters..."

"I just got word that a whole regiment of Reggies is on its way here," Ard said. "Somebody leaked the location of the fight."

Staug finally stepped toward the available horse, but paused. "What about Clutch?"

"They won't let you keep her at the Stockade, you know," Ard urged.

Staug made a frustrated sound and finally clambered into the saddle.

"We'll make for Panes," Raek said, leading out. "Reggies aren't likely to go that far searching for the others once that granary erupts like an anthill."

The three of them set off at a gallop, Ard letting the grin of success spread across his face. There was no incoming regiment of Regulators, but Staug Raifen's paranoia had paid off nicely.

The lizard tournament would soon devolve into a leaderless ring of chaos, once the people realized that the host had vanished. Ard was hoping they'd assume Staug Raifen had killed him in an angry fit outside the granary and then fled in fear of what the gamblers would do when they found out.

Ard really didn't care how it played out. He had who he needed, and they'd gotten away safely.

"There's an old barn up ahead," Raek called, once they were a good distance down the road. "Don't stop until you get there."

"What about you?" Ard asked, although he already knew the answer.

"I'm going to hang back and keep an eye out for trouble."

Raek peeled away and Ard and Staug continued at a gallop until they saw the barn. Leading their horses off the road, they slowed to a walk before Ard swung out of the saddle and pulled open the big door.

"How'd you know them Reggies was coming to raid?" Staug asked, dismounting once they were both inside. The big man was out of breath from the rush of the ride.

"Perimeter scouts," Ard lied. "Had half a dozen of them set all around, watching for Reggie patrols. Wasn't expecting a whole blazing regiment to come down on us!"

"You should have called a scram!" Staug shouted as Ard closed the barn door, plunging them into darkness.

"There were nearly a hundred people in that building," Ard pointed out, breaking a pot of Light Grit and shedding some light on their surroundings. "With such limited notice, a scram would have turned us against each other. Don't you think Patra Bo would've shot you dead to get out first?"

Staug said nothing for a moment. He knew the cutthroat nature of that group. They were all a bunch of lizards in the ring.

"You tipped off that other fellow with time to get his dragon out," Staug huffed about Raek.

"Us Talumonians got to stick together," replied Ard. "Had to get Sunbeam to safety."

"Kind of blazing name is Sunbeam?"

"She tried to go by Snapjaw for a while," Ard said, "but she didn't feel honest with herself. That just isn't who she is."

The barn door suddenly cracked open and Raek slipped through on foot.

"We've got company," he whispered, sliding the door shut again and leaning his broad back against it.

"The Reggies?" Ard asked.

Raek shook his head, wig flapping. "By the looks of it, I think they've come from the Realm."

That was the most risky line they had planned for this evening, and Ard's hand hovered over his Roller in case it didn't come off right.

"Sparks," muttered Staug. "Oh, sparks." The cursing was certainly a good sign. "Can't be. No way."

"Have a look for yourself." Raek cracked open the barn door just an inch as Staug stepped over. A mere glance, and he ducked out of sight, slamming the door shut with another curse.

"How many of them are out there?" Ard asked.

"I counted ten, but there could be more," said Raek.

"Ten?" shrieked Staug. "I only saw two."

"They were closing on the barn from all angles," Raek followed up.

The two figures Staug had seen were actually nothing more than mirages. Just last night, Ard and Raek had ridden out to the barn wearing different disguises. Under a cloud of Illusion Grit, they had made furtive advances through the surrounding shrubs. Tonight's pot of Illusion Grit, detonated by Raek as he lingered outside, replayed their movements with perfect lifelike realism.

"I don't understand," Ard said to Raek. "We did everything they asked. We got him out safe and sound." He gestured at Staug.

"Me?" the thug cried.

"We've been shadowing you for weeks," Ard continued with

their lie. "The bosses were worried you would talk if the Reggies got you. They didn't want you spilling secrets about how to get to the Realm."

"Flames, I don't know that kind of information," he said. "I'm not even really part of the Realm."

*Part of the Realm . . .*

The way he'd said that made the Realm sound more like a group, or a movement, than a physical place. This was shaping up to be quite an interesting conversation.

"The whole thing was a setup," Raek muttered. "The Realm must have sent the Reggies to break up the ring so we'd isolate Staug. Now they're going to kill all three of us."

"Why?" Staug was panicking perfectly. "I ain't done nothing but what they tell me!"

"You must know too much," Ard said, nodding slowly. "Too much about the Realm."

"I don't know nothing!" he struggled to keep his voice low. "I'm just a common street Hand!"

"What kind of information do you have that you shouldn't?" Ard asked insistently.

"The passphrase?" he wondered. "But all the Hands know it . . . That's how we know the job is coming down from the Realm."

"Maybe you learned the wrong one," Ard said. "How does it go?"

"They say, 'I fear I'm going gray.' And I say, 'Some would call it a mark of wisdom.'"

Well, that was certainly helpful information. "Hmm," Ard said, pretending he understood. "That's the same one we know. What else? What's the name of the boss who's giving you these jobs?"

"Different people for every job," answered Staug. "And they've all got bosses of their own."

"Then who's at the top of all this?" Raek asked.

"Sparks if I know," he muttered. "Gotta go to the meetings to figure that out. Boss says I'm too big to ever get recruited into the Faceless."

Too big? That seemed like a strange qualifier.

"Faceless?" Ard asked.

"Yeah, you know..." said Staug.

"That must be it," whispered Ard. "The information you're not supposed to know."

"But... I've spoke with lots of common Hands that know about the Faceless."

Ard was shaking his head. "No," he said. "My partner and I have been working jobs for the Realm for over a year now." It was a safe statement, since Beska's involvement with the Realm had happened around that time. "We've never heard a peep about any *Faceless*."

"What is it?" Raek asked, his back still against the barn door like he might hold it shut against the imaginary enemies.

"It's where all the jobs come from," Staug said. "They meet in secret. Nobody even knows who anybody else is."

*That would be the definition of secret.*

Everyone flinched as a loud gunshot sounded through the quiet barn. A second one followed, and this time, one of the wooden slats beside the door exploded inward. Raek fell with a grunt as Ard raced to his side.

The shots had both been blanks from a Roller outside, the trigger attached to a cord that ran through a small hole in the wall. A tiny amount of Void Grit tucked into a cracked panel had made the slat explode.

Ard knelt in silence over his partner's still form for a reverent moment. When he looked up, his face was tight with a pretended rage.

"He's dead."

Staug raised both hands to his cover his mouth as if to stop himself from screaming. The panic had fully ripened now.

"I can get us out of this." Ard rose, wiping one hand on his pant leg as though it had been bloodstained. "We just need to survive tonight."

"How?"

"I need to get into one of those Faceless meetings." He was going off script here, but what Staug had already shared gave him a good basis for it. "If they're really as anonymous as you claim, then I can clear our names from the inside. Explain to the Realm that you don't know anything, and you haven't talked."

"You'll never find the meeting." Staug scratched his head. "Not unless you get recruited."

"How does that happen?" asked Ard.

"Do enough jobs," he muttered. "Do them good... Or I guess you could try to mark one for the Realm. But that's suicide if it doesn't work."

"What do you mean?" Ard asked.

"You gotta commit a crime," answered Staug. "All on your own. Something big and loud."

Hadn't he and Raek done that dozens of times? Did it get any bigger than stealing the Royal Regalia right from the throne room?

"That's all?" Ard asked.

"Then you mark the crime in the name of the Realm," he said. "If they like it, they'll come to you."

"Like putting Reek Sauce on the dragon bait," Ard muttered.

"Except you become the bait. And you better pray to the Homeland that the Realm likes what you done," Staug said. "You're in, or you're dead."

Ard raised his eyebrows. That was certainly a motivating ultimatum. "How do you mark the crime?"

"Paint your face. Stark white like a cycle-old corpse," Staug explained. "After that, you just gotta turn yourself in."

"To the Reggies?" Ard cried. "I've done time in a Regulation Stockade. They're not easy to break out of."

"If the Realm likes your little stunt, they'll get you out," said

Staug. "That's why it's gotta be big. Else you spend the rest of your days in a cell."

Another shot fired from outside. Ard hadn't even seen Raek's hand twitch as he tugged the cord.

"We've got to get out of here." Staug moved toward the horses.

"Agreed," Ard said, crossing to the barn door. "I'll lay down cover fire while you ride out. Don't stop until you reach Panes. I'll head back toward Beripent, and it might split their focus enough for both of us to escape."

Staug Raifen climbed into the saddle. "You'll really get us out of this mess?"

"We've got to watch each other's backs," Ard said. "If the Realm is going to turn us against one another like lizards in the ring, then we've got to do something about it." He gripped the door. "Ready?"

The big thug on horseback drew his gun.

"Ride!" Ard yanked open the door and quickly fired two cover shots toward the invisible enemies. The Illusion cloud had likely burned out by now, but fear was the real motivator here. Staug's horse lurched forward, the thug's Roller spitting balls into the darkness. Ard watched him go until he was out of sight down the road.

"Well." Ard waved his hand through the lingering smoke from the gunshots. "That was certainly worth our while."

Raek sat up, stretching as though he were awakening from a nap. "So, the Realm is an organized-crime ring."

"Apparently more secretive than the usual groups."

"And by the sound of it, more organized." Raek pulled off his awful wig and scratched his bare scalp.

"How big do you think this group is?" Ard asked. "Sounds like they've got plenty of common criminals in place to carry out their jobs."

"And if the Faceless are the bosses of the street Hands," Raek said, "then who are the bosses of the Faceless?"

"That's what I intend to find out."

"Now we just need to think of a crime big enough to catch the Realm's eye," said Raek.

"Oh, I've got just the thing." Ard glanced at his partner in the dim barn.

"What do you have in mind?"

"We need a high-profile target. I'm thinking a certain Dronadanian royal who happens to be the former queen of the Greater Chain."

"And our employer," reminded Raek with a groan. "What are you going to do to Lady Abeth Agaul?"

Ard holstered his gun. "I'm going to kill her."

~

*When our threat to their existence grew too strong, they fled.*

# CHAPTER

# 8

Some people called this an evening of proper entertainment. Quarrah Khai called it torture.

Too many memories in the Royal Concert Hall for Quarrah's liking. Constricting gowns, that blazing red wig, the bitter taste of detonated Silence Grit that had hidden her voice while Cinza Ortemion sang from between her knees.

The music swelled, with the first violinist leaning so hard she nearly tumbled off her chair. That was smug Cantibel Tren, whose life appeared shamelessly unaffected by the war and general collapse of society happening around her.

That seemed to be the trend among the patrons here tonight. Mostly noble folk, though Quarrah noticed a few more empty seats than when she'd been Azania Fyse, the imposter soprano that had won the hearts of high society.

Quarrah's gaze shifted back to the woman in seat D18. Her head kept drooping, and Quarrah felt somewhat vindicated that she wasn't the only one who thought this piece had gone on too long.

Outside, a clap of thunder punctuated the music, drawing Quarrah's attention up to the darkened, rain-spattered skylight in the vaulted ceiling. At least she had one good memory of this place, Drift Jumping from the stage with a frightened Ardor Benn in tow.

The music took an unexpected turn, and two of the nobles in front of her glanced at each other with raised eyebrows. Likely, that harmony was the most thrilling thing to cross their paths in cycles. Well, they'd have something else to talk about when they got home and realized that the brooch from the nobleman's ponytail was missing.

Quarrah tucked the jewel into one of the pockets she'd sewn into her dress. It was quite ridiculous that dresses didn't come with pockets straight from the tailor. Even if the wearer wasn't a thief, surely she still needed somewhere to stash a ... well, whatever kinds of trinkets a noble lady typically carried.

Quarrah hadn't come for the brooch. That was just a little bonus to ensure that the evening wasn't a complete waste. Besides, how could she *not* have taken it? What kind of fool dangled a precious jewel in plain sight on the back of his head? The patrons of the Royal Concert Hall were ripe for the picking, and if the environment hadn't borne such toxic memories, Quarrah might have considered making this a regular stop.

But, no. Then she'd have to steal a collection of gowns, since wearing the same one twice was apparently bad form.

The loose-fitting navy gown Quarrah currently wore had earned her disdainful looks from half a dozen patrons before the concert had started. Disdainful was fine. It was *recognition* that Quarrah feared. A pair of thick-rimmed spectacles, a bit of poise, and cycles of training had once made her the most sought-after woman in this hall. But Azania Fyse was more than a year dead, blown to bits in the king's carriage in a tragic assassination attempt. And nobody was looking for her ghost.

Nobody except Quarrah Khai.

The conductor's baton whipped into a dramatic cutoff, and the final note gave way to silence that hung like a heavy blanket over the entire hall. Then the applause rolled forward, enhanced by a second peal of thunder. Still, Quarrah remembered the clapping to be a lot louder when she was on the receiving end.

The conductor stepped off his podium, bowing, bowing. At least it wasn't Lorstan Grale. Quarrah was one of a select few who knew the truth about Elbrig Taut's long-term elaborate disguise as the conductor of the Royal Orchestra. Gratefully, she hadn't seen either of the disguise masters since her last job with Ard.

Where Elbrig was now, Quarrah couldn't begin to guess. Maybe he was on vacation. Maybe he'd been found out. Maybe the new king simply wanted fresh talent on the podium. Although Quarrah had heard that Termain Agaul wasn't much for the music scene.

"We will return shortly with Lagne's *The Wanderer Suite*," the conductor said as the applause faded. "Please make sure you are seated before the intermission Light Grit extinguishes."

Abruptly, the large hall filled with even light. The sparking switch was likely backstage, igniting a surplus of Light Grit that overflowed the pipes in the walls, erupting through the chandeliers and sconces as glowing orb-shaped clouds.

Quarrah waited for the patrons to begin mingling, spilling into the aisles and creating a nice wash of conversation. But the socializing nobles completely obscured her view of the woman in seat D18!

*Great,* Quarrah thought. *Now I have to stand up and make sure no one talks to me. Maybe this was a mistake. Sparks, this probably was a mistake.*

She stepped into the aisle, repositioning herself to get a clear view of the woman. She was still seated, flirting with the man next to her and earning glares from his wife.

The woman wasn't important. Quarrah didn't even know her name. It was her seat that mattered.

Two weeks ago, Quarrah had popped into Ponti's Tavern for a drink and some late supper, only to find that the man behind the bar had a letter for her. Flames! An actual letter addressed to Quarrah Khai! She'd already been feeling the urge to move to a new neighborhood, and that had been the final straw.

The barkeep didn't know it was her, of course. But he'd been asking all his female customers. Quarrah denied ever hearing the name, swiped the letter while his back was turned, and vanished into the night.

Inside the folded parchment had been a ticket to tonight's performance at the Royal Concert Hall. A ticket for seat D18.

Normally, Quarrah would have simply thrown it to the curb or sold it to another criminal. She had no desire to revisit high society's orchestral scene, even with the intriguing message included with the ticket.

*I have a job for you.*

But it was the name signed on the note that really grabbed her by the ears and sat her up straight.

*Sincerely, Azania Fyse*

It was a short list of people who had known about her elaborate disguise as the ginger soprano. And the most dangerous ones were dead—King Pethredote and Prime Isle Chauster. Everyone else who knew of her role had a vested interest in maintaining that secrecy.

So, Azania Fyse had lured her to the Royal Concert Hall once more. Of course, Quarrah didn't take the seat she'd been given.

That was just asking for a marksman to put a Fielder ball through her head.

Quarrah had played it safe by swapping tickets with an unsuspecting patron. A well-timed bump when the ticket was visible, a little sleight of hand... Even if the woman realized that her seat had changed, she wasn't likely to dispute it. She had arrived at the hall unaccompanied, and advancing from row R to row D was a fine upgrade.

Quarrah maneuvered herself down the aisle, attempting to look casual while keeping her original assigned seat in view. In all likelihood, her ticket swap had already spoiled the meeting.

The woman in D18 was alone now. She looked awkward, head swiveling around like a Regulation searchlight, desperate to find a familiar face to latch on to. That was the problem with these royal folks. They couldn't just sit alone and feel content. They were always trying to connect so they could smother each other in dishonest flattery. Especially now, when "who you know" was often the only thing preventing one's family from going to the front lines of the war.

A young man came up the aisle, wearing the black vest of a stagehand. In his grasp was a single flower, the orange bloom large and delicate. He reached out and touched the woman on the shoulder. She promptly stood, anxious for any social attention. Her eyes grew wide when she saw the flower, and she glanced across the hall to see who might be noticing.

Quarrah slipped forward, sliding into row F—the closest she dared come to her assigned seat. With the practiced ear of a master thief, she tuned in to the exchange, trying to block the babble of unimportant conversations around her.

"For me?" The woman was full of mock astonishment.

The young man checked the armrest. "You *are* seated in D18, are you not?"

She cast an anxious glance across the hall and then nodded,

carefully taking the flower from him. Well, it would seem that the game was not spoiled after all.

"To whom shall I direct my thanks for such a favor?" she asked.

Oh, please... Talking all proper, like she hadn't been sneakily picking her nose during the second movement of the symphony tonight.

"He said you'd know who it was from," answered the young man.

She lifted the orange bloom to her chin and took a long sniff. What a fool! Quarrah could think of half a dozen toxins that could be applied unnoticed to the petals of a flower. But the woman didn't immediately swoon, faint, or die, so Quarrah took that as a good sign.

"Yes," continued the servant. "He wanted to make sure you noticed that the flower was out of season, grown in the greenhouse at extra expense. It's an amacea."

Quarrah Khai suddenly felt like *she* might swoon, faint, or die from the instant chill that passed over her.

*Amacea.*

King Pethredote had once threatened Azania Fyse with a rather drawn-out story about the amacea festival at the University in Helizon, promising to cut her down the moment she'd passed her prime. That conversation had happened in Dale Hizror's Avedon apartment, in total secrecy.

"He would like you to sit with him for the second half," the young man said to the woman in seat D18. "He said you'd know where he always sits for these concerts."

A note signed by Azania Fyse. An amacea flower. And this had to be an invitation to the king's box on the grand tier.

By the Homeland! Was Pethredote still alive? No. A hundred eyewitnesses had seen him get devoured by that sow dragon on the palace steps. But someone else clearly knew of Quarrah's history with the crusader monarch. Someone with access to the king's box.

Quarrah knew she should have left right then. This was not

something to get tangled up in. But then, someone had come close to finding her once at Ponti's Tavern. What if next time the message was more deadly than a concert ticket?

Her feet had already carried her to the back of the hall. But instead of exiting into the lobby, she made her way up to the mezzanine, probably two or three minutes remaining before the Light Grit winked out. She took the stairs two at a time, the fabric of her dark dress designedly unrestrictive.

She maneuvered along the front of the mezzanine, pushing her way toward the grand tier that extended on the right side. She could see the king's box, solid wood with ornate draperies adorning the visible side.

Ugh. There were too many people in this building. Too many pretty people spritzed with too many perfumes.

At last, she reached the entrance to the grand tier only to find it roped off and guarded by two red-uniformed Regulators.

Stepping right over the rope wouldn't have been difficult. It barely came to Quarrah's thigh. But the Regulators bristled the moment she drew near. Well, if her theories were correct, then she'd been *invited* to the king's box, so these guards wouldn't stop her. She just needed to explain herself quickly since most of the patrons on the mezzanine were already seated for the second half.

"I've been asked to come to the king's box," Quarrah said, gaze downcast from the unshakable fear that one of them might recognize her.

"I don't think so," said the guard on her right.

Wouldn't the Reggies have been told to watch for the woman from seat D18? Quarrah didn't have to worry about the real occupant of that seat coming up here. The message that had accompanied the flower was cryptic enough that only Quarrah would understand its true meaning. The flower was a coded connection to the king.

It suddenly dawned on her why the Regulators barred her passage.

"I don't have the flower," she said. "The orange amacea that was sent to my seat." At least that got the two men to glance at each other, their exchange a silent conference. "I'm allergic," Quarrah lied. "The bloom was nice, but amaceas cause me to break out in a rash."

Her ability to lie had certainly improved since her ruse with Ardor Benn. At least something useful had worn off on her.

The Light Grit burned out abruptly, without so much as a flicker. Behind her, the few patrons who had dawdled were hurrying to their seats as an anticipatory quiet spread across the hall.

Quarrah wondered just how hard she should press. Maybe she should consider this an omen. Turn and walk away. On the stage below, the orchestra began tuning. Wordlessly, the Reggie on her left detached the thick rope and drew it back.

The other Regulator gave a quiet knock on the box's door before pushing it open, gesturing for Quarrah to enter.

Was she really about to step into the king's box with no knowledge of who would be waiting for her? This was truly uncharacteristic carelessness from Quarrah Khai. She slipped her hand through a slit in her dress. The cut was of her own making and allowed her to grip the handle of the loaded Singler she had holstered to her thigh. Still, what good would one shot be on the grand tier of the Royal Concert Hall? Oh, she'd really dived deep this time.

The front of the box was open, allowing a perfect view over a low railing to the stage below. There were a variety of comfortable seating options, a side table with a few hors d'ouevres, and a small glow of Light Grit burning in a lantern by the entrance.

Two people sat in the king's box and neither of them was King Pethredote. Of course not. It was pure foolishness to even think he could still be alive. Yet, whoever these strangers were, they clearly knew about her past with the crusader monarch.

An artist was sitting off to the side, facing into the box with her back to the railing. Before her was an easel, the framed canvas turned so Quarrah couldn't see the portrait. But the subject sat right before her.

She was an old woman, with a plump, yet wrinkly face, overdone makeup, and an obvious wig of dark hair. She was gazing down at the stage, her profile to the painter, with a long thin pipe clenched in her teeth.

Quarrah didn't let herself relax as the old woman smiled, gesturing for the Regulator to close the door. The old woman and the painter seemed harmless enough, and Quarrah didn't recognize either individual. King Termain was known to have frequent female companions, but Quarrah couldn't imagine he'd go for someone so old. So, what was this woman doing in the box?

Below, the audience broke into a short applause that Quarrah knew heralded the entrance of the conductor. The music began, the first movement of *The Wanderer Suite*, soft and atmospheric.

Quarrah kept her grip on the Singler's hilt, her hand tucked awkwardly through the folds of her dark dress. It was a clumsy arrangement, but at the very least she could draw and fire the ball through the fabric.

From the painter's corner, Quarrah heard the distinct shattering of a clay Grit pot. She tensed but didn't panic as the box filled with the discolored haze of a detonation. At the same time, the orchestra went suddenly silent. Through the box's open front, Quarrah could see that the musicians' bows still skimmed across strings, so they hadn't stopped playing.

Silence Grit.

"Come, have a seat," the old woman said, her lips parting around the stem of her pipe. She didn't whisper or beckon, but spoke in an unapologetic voice, pitched low and awfully raspy. No matter the volume of her grating voice, enclosed in their cloud of Silence Grit, no one outside would be able to hear them speak.

Quarrah didn't move, preferring to stay near the door.

"Oh..." The old woman pulled the pipe out of her mouth.

"Perhaps you don't recognize me without my red wig and spectacles." She grinned, showing yellowed teeth. "It's me. The acclaimed soprano, Azania Fyse!"

"Somehow, I doubt that." Quarrah's stiff reply earned a cackle from the old woman.

"Quarrah Khai. Every bit as practical as I've heard," she said. "Perhaps if I introduce myself, you'll relax a bit."

"I'm plenty relaxed."

"Then I assume that's just a Singler under your dress?"

Sparks, Quarrah had drawn the gun without really realizing it. So much for subtlety.

"My name is Fabra Ment."

*Fabra Ment?* Well, that explained what she was doing in the king's box.

"Yes, yes," the woman said, as though answering a question Quarrah hadn't asked. "You're looking at the beloved queen dowager."

The mother of Termain Agaul, wife of the late Gond Agaul. If Quarrah remembered correctly, Fabra Ment was of the royal bloodline of Strind.

Quarrah took a deep breath and decided that bowing would be the correct thing to do. It was more of a curtsy, as she still hadn't decided whether or not to let go of her gun. "Your Majesty." Was that how the queen dowager wanted to be addressed?

"Such respect from a thief," the old woman answered. "You should call me Fabra." She coughed, dry and wheezy. "Won't you sit? It's breaking my neck to turn like this."

Quarrah finally moved away from the door. If the old woman's reputation was to be believed, she was only a threat to the rabbits on the palace hunting grounds. Fabra pointed to the soft seat beside her, and Quarrah quickly inspected it before sitting down. Now that the widow queen was turned toward the front of the box once more, the painter began sketching with rapid strokes.

"Where's the flower I sent you?" Fabra tugged down the lacy front of her gown with such sharpness that Quarrah was afraid her wrinkled bosoms might pop right out. "I don't suppose you're hiding it under your dress as well."

"No." Should she tell the old woman how she had swapped tickets? Better just to cut to the chase. "Why am I here?"

"Because I have a job for you." Fabra was gazing down at the silently moving orchestra.

"Oh?" Quarrah had heard as much from the note that came with the concert ticket.

"I need you to find Ardor Benn."

Quarrah felt her skin prickle at the mention of his name. Find Ardor Benn? There weren't enough Ashings in the royal treasury to convince her to do that.

"I don't know who that is," Quarrah answered.

Fabra Ment let out something that sounded like a cross between a laugh and a croak. "Don't play the fool with me, Quarrah Khai. Haven't I already delivered sufficient proof that I know you?"

"You've delivered me nothing but a falsely signed note and a single flower." Quarrah tried to weasel out of it, but she was starting to sweat. Sparks, how did the queen dowager know so much?

"Are you worried about Errel?" Fabra gestured to the painter in the corner. She looked a few years older than Quarrah, but thinner. Almost gaunt.

"She doesn't hear," said Fabra. "It's like the poor thing was born with Silence Grit in her ears. Errel's my handmaiden, among a variety of other skills she possesses. Blazing good painter. And fast at it."

It wasn't the handmaiden's presence that kept Quarrah tight-lipped. That job with Ard wasn't something she talked about. Especially not with royal folks.

"I, for one, think it's pure genius the way you got under Pethredote's nose and stole the regalia," continued the old woman. "And how did you survive the carriage explosion after the Grotenisk Festival? I've pieced so much of it together, but still, there are holes I can't seem to fill."

Quarrah stared at her for a long moment, but the queen dowager kept her gaze toward the stage. Finally, Quarrah stood to leave. "I didn't come here to answer questions. And I *certainly* didn't come here to help you find Ardor Benn."

"Oh, good. While you're up, why don't you get me one of those rum-soaked prunes." Fabra pointed to the loaded side table. "Actually, just stick a few of them on a skewer."

Flustered, Quarrah suddenly found herself at the hors d'ouevres instead of the back door. She picked up a wooden skewer and stabbed three of the prunes. Once dried for preservation, these were now plump from the dark rum they'd been soaking in.

"I need the ruse artist," Fabra continued.

"For what?" Quarrah jabbed another prune with so much force that the tip of the skewer broke off in the bowl.

"A job."

"Ard doesn't just take a job," said Quarrah. "He takes obsessions."

"Exactly why I need him." Fabra coughed. "Try as I might, I can't find the blazing rat anywhere."

"But you found me?" That wasn't very comforting.

"Ardor Benn has either left Espar or he's in hiding," replied Fabra. "You're still active in Beripent. Unless there's another person responsible for lifting three hundred Ashings from Lord Zan last cycle."

Fabra was wrong—not about the stolen Ashings, Quarrah had swept in on that safe box easily enough, but Ard wasn't dead or hiding. He was actually being smart for once, protecting his name.

Ardor Benn and the Short Fuse had gained too much attention after everything had gone down with King Pethredote. Now, instead of flaunting his name to get jobs, Ard had simply changed it again. He was going by Androt Penn, mostly. And as of two cycles ago, she knew where to find him—that dingy little apartment he was sharing with Raek in the lower Western Quarter. Sparks, Quarrah even knew that Ard had grown a beard.

It wasn't that she'd wanted to find him. But she knew Ard had been looking for her. And the best way to stay ahead of him was to know where he was and what he was doing—rusing. Like he always did. The man had saved the kingdom and preserved life and time itself, but most nights he was hitting up a pub looking for a new Focus to swindle.

It was different for her. Yes, she'd gone back to thieving, but she wasn't the same. More focused, more centered, more purposeful. More alone.

"Why Ardor Benn?" Quarrah crossed back to the old woman with the skewer of prunes on a small plate. She hadn't taken anything to eat for herself. She'd wait for an invitation...and to make sure that the queen dowager hadn't poisoned her own hors d'oeuvres. "There are other ruse artists."

"But none I know of who have proven their ability to infiltrate an organization as close-knit as royal high society." Fabra took the plate and slurped one of the prunes off the end of the broken skewer.

"How do you know so much about that job?" Quarrah seated herself beside the widow. In the corner, Errel took up painting again after a moment of pause to mix colors on her palette.

"I'm the queen dowager," Fabra said while chewing. "I'm rich and I'm bored."

"The conversation about the amacea festival..." said Quarrah. "Pethredote and I were alone for that."

Fabra chuckled. "What is *alone* for a king? It simply means his guards are listening at the door. And those same guards respond quite well to bribes from an old washed-up queen."

"Hence the Silence Grit." Quarrah waved a hand through the air in the small room.

"And Errel," added Fabra, eating another prune.

"Why all the interest in the stolen regalia?" Quarrah asked. It was more than passive curiosity if Fabra was willing to bribe and pay for information.

"I've always been fascinated by things clandestine," answered the old woman. "Which is why I need Ardor Benn."

"Ard is anything but clandestine," Quarrah scoffed. "He lives for attention."

"And I understand that you live for the shadows." Fabra took the last two prunes in one bite, sliding them off the skewer like a beaver stripping leaves off a branch. "I believe my son is being manipulated by a dangerous organization known as the Realm. Have you heard of it?"

Quarrah shook her head. "Should I have?"

"You've heard of the organized-crime rings?"

"Of course." Almost every significant city in the Greater Chain had one. Beripent alone had four.

"The Realm came first," Fabra said. "The first references show up more than four hundred years ago in texts from the Strondath Era. They're an ancient organization that specializes in manipulating entire kingdoms. Talumon's civil war in 914... The reuniting of Strind and Espar in the early Belmein Era... Sparks, some even say that the Realm manipulated King Kerith into bringing Grotenisk to Beripent."

"And yet, I've never heard of them." Quarrah found that hard to believe, with her years of experience in the criminal world.

"Not surprising," Fabra said. "After all, it is a *secret* organization."

"And what makes you think the king is being manipulated by this... *Realm*?" Quarrah asked.

"A few cycles ago, I was having one of my midday sleeps on the chaise in the north-wing study," the queen dowager began. "I awoke to conversation between one of my son's primary advisors and an associate, who remained hidden behind the balcony curtain. I've always considered Waelis Mordo to be a slippery eel of an advisor. They greeted one another with a strange phrase that got my ears tingling." She sat up tall. "'I fear I'm going gray,' says the one behind the curtain. 'Some would call it a mark of wisdom,' replies Mordo."

Quarrah stared, trying to decide if the queen dowager had lost her mind. "And that makes you think they are part of a secret organization manipulating your son?"

"Waelis Mordo then drew something on a piece of paper and held it around the curtain for the other to see. After that, they spoke of a meeting. A Faceless meeting, they called it."

"What was written on the paper?"

Fabra coughed. "Could you get me one of those smoked eggs? They whip the yolks, and it makes for the lightest filling."

Quarrah stared at her blankly. "That's what he wrote?"

Fabra chuckled. "Oh, no, dearie. I'm asking a favor of you." She pointed back to the table of hors d'oeuvres. Quarrah stood, her mind finding its way back to what the queen dowager had been saying, while absently picking a halved egg and sliding it onto another little plate.

"Waelis Mordo burned the scrap before leaving the study," she continued. "But my curiosity was piqued. I began sending my handmaiden to follow him in secret."

"I thought she can't hear." Quarrah glanced at the silent woman painting in the corner of the box.

"But she can see," replied Fabra. "Thrice she caught the advisor rendezvousing with an unseen associate at the study's balcony. And with a stealthy cloud of Illusion Grit, I was able to witness a silent replay of Mordo's interaction. The Illusion cloud was contained against the curtain, of course, so I couldn't make out who was on the other side. But I am adept enough at reading lips to realize that Waelis Mordo started each meeting with the same strange phrase about going gray."

"You think it's a code of some kind," Quarrah assumed, delivering the smoked egg to the old woman and taking a seat.

Fabra nodded. "And after it was given, he would draw something and show it around the curtain to the other person. With the Illusion Grit, I was able to see that it was some sort of secret symbol, the strokes drawn in precisely the same order each time."

"Anything you recognized?"

"Not at first," answered the elderly woman. "But after hours of study, interspersed with an appropriate amount of catnaps and alcohol, I was able to connect both of these things back to an ancient organization called the Realm. The specific codes and symbols were not recorded, of course, and the books all say that the Realm is a hundred years gone."

"But you think it's back," said Quarrah doubtfully. "Why now?"

"This is the perfect time for its resurgence. Pethredote ruled as a placeholder monarch for forty years, but everyone knew there would be a period of uncertainty when his reign ended. The Realm might have been positioning themselves all those years to make the most impact when the time came."

"And you thought it would be a good idea to hire Ardor Benn to sniff around and see what he can learn about this organization?" It was a crazy enough job for him, assuming that such a Realm really existed.

"Yes, yes. I need him to infiltrate the Realm, learn its secrets, and find out what sway they have over Termain. From what I understand, the ruse artist is skilled enough to pull this off alone."

Quarrah scoffed loudly. She couldn't help it. Alone? What could Ard ever accomplish alone? *She* had been the one to get him through locked doors, Elbrig had costumed him, Raek had Mixed his Grit and carried out his plans.

"I just need you to find him first," said Fabra. "I'll make it worth your time."

"Not going to happen," Quarrah said. "If you want Ardor Benn, you can find him yourself."

"I know you're a criminal, but I'd heard you still had a soul," said Fabra. "Possibly even consider yourself Wayfarist. What I'm asking is for the good of the kingdom. Sparks, we free my son from the grip of a group like the Realm and it'll give him a chance to rule properly. Might even end the war."

Quarrah didn't fool herself into thinking it would be that simple. From what she'd heard, Termain Agaul was not a good person. Removing manipulative advisors wouldn't suddenly make him compassionate.

And then there was the means. Fabra Ment really didn't know what she was suggesting.

"Involving Ardor Benn in any of your affairs will not be for the 'good of the kingdom,'" Quarrah said frankly.

"You don't think he can do it?"

"Oh, he'd get the job done," answered Quarrah. "Problem is, when Ardor Benn is involved, the end of the job just marks the beginning of a bigger one. He won't solve your problems, he'll just create new ones." She took a deep breath. It had been so long since she'd ranted about him like this. "My answer is definitely no."

"Oh, but sweetie, you can't turn me down," said the old woman.

"Is that a threat?" Quarrah genuinely couldn't tell from Fabra's tone.

"I know a lot about you," she said, nibbling the corner of the egg. "Information about your role in Pethredote's demise. There are people who would be very curious..."

Yep. Threat. Quarrah shouldn't have come. Powerful folks made better extortionists than employers.

"Fine. You can ruin my name," Quarrah said. "I'll change it and you'll never find me again."

It was working for Ard. She could do it far better. Before tonight,

Fabra obviously hadn't known Quarrah's face or she wouldn't have had the flower delivered. If there was one skill that outshined all her others, it was Quarrah's ability to blend into the darkness. Ard knew her name *and* her face, and even he hadn't been able to find her this past year and a half.

Quarrah was standing again, not realizing exactly when that had happened. Surprisingly, Fabra Ment didn't seem flustered at all. She slowly chewed her bite of smoked egg and gave Errel a distinct gesture.

Quarrah's attention shifted to the artist in the corner as she turned the canvas around. Ah, flames. The painting wasn't of the queen dowager.

It was a portrait of Quarrah Khai.

And a good one, too. Not like that charcoal sketch of Ard that had once circulated among the Reggies. This was in full color, and the likeness was startling.

Fabra let out an overly jovial laugh. "Look at that! Not bad for a handmaiden! And did I mention she was fast? She could have two dozen of these whipped up and distributed at every checkpoint out of the city before the paint dries." The queen dowager wiped at a bit of yolk at the corner of her mouth. "I need you to bring me Ardor Benn."

Quarrah took a deep breath, fighting to remain calm. She could get out of this. It seemed like the old woman was genuinely trying to do what was best for her son and the kingdom. Perhaps they could strike an accord.

"You're wasting your time," Quarrah said. "And you're insulting me."

"I can see that your feelings for Ardor Benn are—"

"This isn't about my feelings toward Ard," she cut in. "It's about my skill set. You need someone to infiltrate the Realm and find out if they are manipulating the king. You're looking at her."

Fabra Ment raised one eyebrow. "But you're not a ruse artist."

"A thief is just a ruse artist who is never seen," she said.

Fabra gave a crooked smile. "I like you. There's a passion behind you that I hadn't expected. From what I'd heard, Ardor—"

Quarrah held up her hands. "I'll do your blazing job. Let's just agree not to talk about Ard anymore."

This was answered by a low chuckle that turned into a wheezing cough. "Fair enough," Fabra managed. "Consider yourself hired."

This was going to be a very different job than her usual hires. But what choice did she have? The alternative was turning this over to Ardor Benn. Quarrah knew she would do it better. Smarter. And with a lot less drama.

"What's the payout?"

"I'll offer you the same deal I would have offered the ruse artist," said the queen dowager. "Ongoing payment as you bring me information. Whatever you think it's worth—within reason. I'll keep my ear to the palace floor, and the two of us can coordinate what we learn."

Fabra had said it herself—the queen dowager was rich, and she was bored. Quarrah could think of worse qualities to have in an employer.

"Poking around Waelis Mordo's belongings seems like a good place to start," Quarrah said. "Is he still staying in the palace?"

Fabra nodded. "In the south wing. If it helps, I could arrange a time to have him occupied. Maybe leave his door or window unlocked so you can slip in quickly."

"Is tomorrow night too soon?"

"I'll arrange it," she said. "Say, nine o'clock?"

In the corner, Errel turned the canvas around once more and seemed to be adding some final touches to the portrait. Quarrah didn't like that kind of leverage over her hard-earned anonymity. The painting would have to be "misplaced" at the soonest opportunity.

Quarrah sat down beside the old woman once more. "In the meantime, you should probably teach me how to draw that symbol."

~

*There can be no secrets among us, for our eyes can see them.*

# PART II

A day cometh when all must speedily go unto the Homeland. Stumblers have gone before thee, and these silent
ones have heralded thy voyage.

—Wayfarist Voyage, *vol. 1*

Retrace my steps. Make me wise like those great ones
who rose up. Keep me no more blinded, but give me that
promised sight.

—*Ancient Agrodite song*

# CHAPTER

# 9

Professor Wal." San's voice caused Portsend to look up from the scroll. He had fallen into the habit of staring at the rolled page, as though new text might suddenly appear. "It's probably right in front of me, but I can't find the Compounding rate of Barrier Grit on this chart."

Portsend knit his eyebrows, squinting across the laboratory. "Barrier can't Compound, San. It's Jonzan's Seventh Truth." That was basic, even for a first-year student. If they were in the classroom, he'd have made the lad recite it.

*If the natural effect of a Grit type is absolute, it cannot be Compounded.*

An impenetrable Barrier shell couldn't be made *more* impenetrable, just as a Drift cloud couldn't be made *more* weightless. The effect was absolute.

San scolded himself with a light slap to the forehead. A beginner's mistake to be sure, but it was late and San wasn't feeling his best. Besides, he'd been crunching numbers for several hours, working twice as hard without Lomaya.

Her unexpected absence wasn't too concerning, with the winter cycles always bringing a wave of aches and sniffles around campus. San's lingering cough was enough to drive any coworker mad. Mad enough that Portsend had mixed up a hot concoction that was supposed to ease the throat. It was repulsive and bitter, with elm bark, bear root, hodgegrass, and garlic, topped off with a shot of strong coffee. Gloristar had introduced him to the treatment years ago, when he'd refused to miss a guidance session in the Mooring over a sore throat.

San was obviously not too keen on the drink, following his first sip over an hour ago. Well, if he didn't finish, maybe he could drop it off at Lomaya's dormitory once they concluded here tonight. San could give her a full report of what she'd missed. Not that it would be much.

Portsend sighed and slipped the scroll into its leather tube. The three of them had been at this for a full cycle now, meeting every evening without fail. But in more than thirty sessions, they had done little more than deplete the stock of special materials that Gloristar had delivered.

He hadn't seen the Prime Isless since she'd stopped by with the scroll last cycle. He'd sent a written request for more processed materials, though he probably wouldn't get them for another few weeks.

"Did you finish that contamination sheet?" Portsend asked, trying not to make it sound like an overdue assignment. He was anxious to get into the testing.

"I got distracted," San admitted, following up with a bout of coughs.

"Looking for the Compounding rate of Barrier Grit?" questioned Portsend.

"I wasn't thinking straight," answered San. "I just remembered how we Compounded the birchwood to see if it intensified at the same rate as regular Light Grit. I thought we could try the same with the gold dust."

While Portsend appreciated the initiative, the lad's efforts were misplaced. Sporadic, like the first two weeks of research. Portsend took full responsibility for those first fifteen sessions, spent haplessly detonating Grit in the lab's secure chamber, hoping for some unusual outcome.

When the frustration of failure had reached its peak, Portsend had realized that their methods needed to change. Instead of a hopeful widespread approach, he'd instituted a more targeted method—choose one of the materials and put it through every conceivable test with every conceivable variable.

This was exhausting, and in many ways *more* frustrating. Portsend had alphabetized the scroll's seven materials and started at the top. Weeks of dedicated research to birchwood had yielded nothing. Now they had moved on to gold—an interesting material, to be sure.

"It's a fine idea to Compound the gold powder," Portsend validated. They needed to try *everything*, even the impossible. "But that's not what we're doing right now."

San nodded, moving quickly back to the table with a spread of papers before him. "I only have a few more calculations to make." He slid aside the full mug of tea for the dozenth time and started writing.

Tested alone, the gold reacted exactly as it should—like common metal becoming a spherical cloud of Barrier Grit. Hopefully, this calculated mixing with other types would yield something different.

The idea behind San's tedious worksheet was to use the powdered gold as a contaminant, to see if it would produce expected results. To analyze this, they needed to calculate the duration of a cloud with every allowable ratio of contamination.

San coughed, reaching across the table for the abacus. His arm bumped the mug, but he managed to catch it before it tipped. A bit of the dark liquid sloshed over the side and San hurriedly pulled his papers away.

"You don't have to drink that." Portsend tossed him a rag.

"I'd like to," answered San. "I think it could help."

"Not as much, now that it's cooled."

"Grandmum used to make something similar." San wiped the small spill. "Made my tongue go numb. She'd sit across the table and make sure we drank every drop."

"Well, I don't want to compete with your grandmum." Portsend picked up the pail beside the door, bits of broken clay pots rattling in the bottom.

"It's not my favorite, either," Portsend admitted, holding out the pail. Sheepishly, San upended the mug into the metal bin.

"It's definitely no ale," San joked, going to the corner and pouring himself some water now that his mug was free again.

Portsend would need to remember to dump the pail tonight or the whole lab would smell like garlic in the morning.

"Let's go ahead and test a few of the detonations you've already calculated," Portsend said. "You can finish the sheet tomorrow."

He could sense that they both needed a little excitement in order to keep going tonight. And Portsend had readied all the materials while San had prepared the numbers.

"Do you mind if I add the contaminants?" San set down his mug and moved around to Portsend's side of the table.

"That'll be fine. Any reason?"

San made a face as though the answer should be obvious. "It's gold, Professor."

This elicited something of a chuckle from Portsend Wal. That kind of youthful enthusiasm was the reason he had chosen two inexperienced students as research partners. While Portsend saw the materials before him as little more than scientific elements, San still saw them for what they were. And this lad wanted to get his hands into a canister of powdered gold.

Portsend had prepared ten stations across the long table against the lab's east wall. Balance scales, Grit trays, wooden measuring spoons, and a Sifter. They'd be adding the gold as a contaminant to Light Grit, since the effect could be safely observed without going into the detonation chamber.

San pinned the large paper to the corkboard, where both of them would have easy access to it. Portsend slipped on his glasses and studied the first set, muttering the amount he was supposed to weigh.

With years of practice under his belt, Portsend was much faster than his pupil. He moved along, meting out Light Grit to San's specific calculations. Once the measured wood dust was in the tray, San approached each station, carefully adding the right amount of gold dust to serve as contaminant.

Portsend had completed eight stations by the time San was wrapping up his second. Doubling back, the professor used the handheld Sifter to mix San's measured gold dust evenly with the larger quantity of Light Grit.

He loved this, working in silence. And for a moment, Portsend could almost forget about the highly unusual circumstances that had brought him here. Almost forget that the Prime Isless had all but begged him to experiment with a forbidden list of items from the Anchored Tome. For a moment, Portsend was simply mixing— the earthy, musty smell of Grit falling through the Sifter.

There was a knock at the door, causing both men to halt their work and glance at one another. With less than two hours to midnight, it had to be Luthe, the guard on duty tonight.

Portsend churned the remaining bit of Grit into the tray and set down the Sifter. He still found the bodyguards unnecessary, even bothersome with their continuous presence. It wasn't as though he'd discovered anything worth protecting. And his work with San and Lomaya wasn't against any college regulations, as long as they were working in his personal lab.

Portsend pushed up the bar and opened the heavy door. Lomaya was framed in the opening, book satchel over one shoulder, casting furtive glances at Luthe, who loomed in the distance behind her.

"Sorry I'm late," she said. "I wasn't sure if you'd still be here. Or if I should just come in..." As she spoke, the young woman stepped past Portsend and moved into the lab.

"We didn't think you were coming." Portsend shut the door behind her. "You're three hours late." He was proud of himself for not coming down on her harder than that. Lomaya had been consistent until now, and she didn't sound sick. Well, he was sure she'd have a reason.

"I'm sorry," she said again. "There's an exam in Fentall's class tomorrow. I...I didn't feel ready for it."

"You know I don't want your studies to suffer for this." Portsend glanced at San. "Either of you." Then, turning back to Lomaya, "But a little notice would have been nice."

"I'm sorry." A third time. "I couldn't get away. It was Kend's birthday. I promised him we could have dinner together. It ran long."

Portsend furrowed his brow. "I'm not sure I follow. Were you studying for the exam or having dinner with Kend?"

Lomaya winced. "Both were happening simultaneously."

"How romantic," San chimed.

*Homeland*, Portsend thought. *Maybe I'm putting too much on these kids.*

"Perhaps we should call it a night," Portsend said as one of the Light Grit lanterns winked out.

"But I just got here!" Lomaya protested.

"And we're finally doing something other than arithmetic," San added.

Lomaya slid the satchel off her shoulder and dropped it to the floor, shrugging out of her coat as she crossed to San's side as though proving her intent to work. "What are we doing?"

San quickly explained, directing her to the sheet he had pinned to the board. His explanation led to a fit of coughs and he crossed the lab to pour himself another drink of water. Lomaya took up his station, and Portsend ignited more Light Grit in the lantern that had gone out.

A few moments later, the three of them reconvened at the table, picking up with their respective tasks.

"Did you move the Sifter?" Portsend asked San, glancing down the table for it.

Lomaya held it out. "I used it on the first station. San told me that's what we were doing."

"I already Sifted the first two stations," Portsend replied.

"I thought you were measuring Light Grit..." The young woman's expression fell. "I added gold dust as a contaminant to the first station."

"What?" San cried. "How much?"

"Two granules," she answered. "That's what it said on the sheet."

Portsend sighed, clapping his hands together in a definitive manner. "We're done for the night."

If Lomaya had mixed two more granules on top of San's addition, then the first station was ruined, placing the Grit squarely in the waste ratio.

Portsend picked up the tray and carried it across the lab. Sifted as it was, there was no way to separate the gold dust from the Light Grit. They could add more processed wood to tip the ratio back to an operable level, but he was too tired for that. The teacher in him wanted to prove a point—to make sure an error like this never happened again.

"Wait," San said when he saw that Portsend intended to dump the Grit. "We might as well test it."

Portsend paused. The lad was right. The scroll demanded nothing less than complete experimentation. Perhaps this gold dust would miraculously detonate within the waste ratio.

Wordlessly, he placed the tray on the table and separated a little pinch of the Grit. Portsend produced a Slagstone ignitor from his pocket, directing the tip at the tiny pile on the table. A sharp pull of the trigger caused the spring-loaded hammer to snap down, the impact showering precise sparks on the Grit.

Nothing happened.

Well, technically, the Grit ignited, but the detonation had been null—all the powder burning away in a heartbeat, leaving no residual cloud or effect. The little optimism died in his mind. Gold dust wasted the same as every other Grit. It was ordinary. It was all ordinary, and he would have nothing for Gloristar.

In a huff, Portsend slid the tray off the edge of the table, toppling it into the pail of scraps at his feet. He sensed Lomaya and San standing rigid against the east wall.

Portsend touched the scroll tube in his vest pocket. Maybe his pupils would work more efficiently if he told them it was for the Prime Isless. If he told them the materials were listed in the sacred Anchored Tome.

Two more Light Grit lanterns extinguished. He crossed the room and got his coat. "Gold is valuable enough on its own," Portsend said, voice steady. "Much more so after passing through a dragon and processing it into Grit. We cannot be wasteful. We cannot be careless. Let's meet again tomorrow evening. Fresh."

As he spoke, the students obediently tugged on their coats. In the waning light, Portsend cast a glance across his laboratory. Open canisters of Grit, scales half balanced... It was unlike him to leave it in such a state, but ordering San and Lomaya out so he could stay after and clean up would only increase their feeling of failure. He'd swing by before his first lecture in the morning and tidy things up.

Portsend pulled open the heavy door and felt the cold night air rush into the lab. A moment later, the door was locked and the three of them were heading up the hill toward campus.

Luthe met them halfway, seeming to materialize out of the darkness and startling San.

"Do you get paid extra for scaring the slag out of me?" the lad asked, falling into a fit of coughs.

"I'll suggest it to my employer." Luthe's voice always sounded more youthful than Portsend expected. Sparks, the bodyguard couldn't be much older than San. He had the palest of skin and always seemed to be fidgeting with the silver buttons on his dark jacket.

"I don't think the professor heard you," San glanced over at Portsend.

"I did," Portsend replied. *But I'm not his employer.* He wondered again what Gloristar was paying them for this pointless babysitting job.

Of the two, Luthe was more talkative, although it was rare for either to be near enough to engage in conversation beyond simply checking in.

They walked in silence for a moment, passing the campus's outermost building and entering the central courtyard. This late at night, all was quiet—a stark contrast to the flow of students usually crisscrossing the open lawn during the day.

"What have you told Kend?" San asked Lomaya. His voice was quiet, as though wanting to start a private conversation. But Portsend had no trouble picking it up. "I mean, about us."

Oh, Homeland. What was San Green saying? Had the two students taken their extracurricular studies even further? To a personal level? Lomaya looked at him, letting out a little laugh. San suddenly seemed to realize how his statement had sounded.

"About our studies," he floundered. "About *all* of us." He pointed at Portsend and Luthe. "Flames, Lomaya, you know what I meant."

Portsend found the lad's obvious embarrassment endearing.

"I don't want to argue with him," was Lomaya's answer.

"What is there to argue about?" Portsend asked.

"This just takes so much time. Time he'd rather I spend with him."

"Do you enjoy our research in the lab?" Portsend asked. Lomaya nodded emphatically. "Then I don't see why he wouldn't want you to continue."

"It's complicated," she said. "He's complicated. Kend isn't a student. He has a hard time seeing the value in a lot of this."

"Is he a tradesman?" Portsend asked. He really knew nothing about the boyfriend. Lomaya seldom even mentioned him.

"A soldier," she replied.

"So he's stationed here in Beripent?" Harbor patrol, perhaps?

"He was infantry," Lomaya answered. "Injured in Denvad. He's been home nine cycles—almost a year." Her gaze was fixed straight ahead. "He's always talking about going back once he heals. Kend was a good soldier."

No doubt he was. But nine cycles home didn't mean he was likely to go back. Either the injury was serious enough that it wasn't mending properly or the lad was war shocked and just unable to bring himself to reenlist.

"And you're a good student." Portsend didn't want to press her for details.

"That's yet to be seen," answered Lomaya. "Check in with me after that mathematics exam tomorrow..." She stopped in her tracks, halfway across the central courtyard. "Sparks, I left my book satchel in the laboratory."

Portsend sighed and gestured back in the direction they'd just come while the young woman apologized profusely. It was times like these, when his legs were tired from standing all day, that he wished he could give the key to Luthe and send the bodyguard to retrieve the bag. But Portsend knew that without Brase to keep an eye on him, Luthe wouldn't leave his side.

Portsend, Luthe, and Lomaya turned back, bidding good evening to San, whose cough was an announcement that he was in desperate need of rest.

As they walked back to the laboratory, Lomaya probably took Portsend's silence as a sign that he was upset, but it really wasn't that. Portsend was just tired and frustrated by their lack of progress.

Luthe hung back as Portsend unlocked the lab door. Pushing it open didn't reveal any light, which meant that the final lantern had burned out. Fumbling on the rack beside the door, he found a clay pot and smashed it on the wall. A dome of light partially illuminated the room, as the clay shards clattered to the floor.

For Homeland's sake, he was just adding to the mess of his

cluttered workspace. Why hadn't he replaced the scraps pail to catch the falling shards?

Lomaya moved past him as Portsend stooped to gather the biggest pieces of the broken pot and the little fragment of Slagstone.

"There it is..." Lomaya pulled the satchel over her shoulder as Portsend pitched the clay shards into the scraps pail in the middle of the room.

A rush of energy ripped through the lab. There was a deafening sound, a blinding light. Something struck Portsend Wal in the side, throwing him across the table and headlong into a tall set of cabinets.

He grunted, pushing himself up on one elbow only to collapse again. Bright! Suddenly so bright! The thick smoke in his eyes didn't help either. And his ears were ringing with a sound like an incessant peal from a trumpet. Squinting, Portsend used the cabinets to pull himself upright. The ribs on his right side throbbed with a dull ache.

What the blazes?

Ten orbs of Light Grit were glowing along the east wall above the table where they had been measuring. Overlapping one of them was a Barrier cloud, its impenetrable shell wrapping around their work stations and sealing off that side of the room.

Near where Portsend had been standing was another detonation cloud. Through the acrid smoke that filled the room, he couldn't tell what type. One corner of the lab was completely hidden from view, enveloped in a ball of utter blackness. And the south wall leading into the detonation chamber... Half of it was gone, debris scattered across the lab, with flames licking at the timbers that were still in place.

Luthe appeared in the doorway, his arm raised to shield his face against the smoke and light. "Portsend!" he shouted.

"I'm all right!" he called back. "Find Lomaya!"

Luthe pressed forward only to be tossed backward when he encountered the same cloud that had thrown Portsend. "Void

Grit!" Luthe shouted, crawling under the table on hands and knees to avoid it.

Void Grit, Light Grit, Barrier Grit, Shadow Grit... And the lingering smoke and deafening explosion on the south wall was a telltale sign of Blast Grit. Was this sabotage?

"We need to get out of here before those flames reach more Grit!" Luthe shouted.

"Lomaya!" Portsend insisted. Through the rubble and disarray, he couldn't see where Luthe had gone.

"I'm all right." The young woman's voice cut through Portsend's still-ringing ears. Homeland be praised!

Portsend shoved against the table, but he didn't have the strength to hold it with the Void cloud providing constant resistance from the other side. Leaning back against the cabinets again, Portsend coughed from the smoke. He slid to his knees and crawled toward the exit, pushing aside a wooden stool that had toppled in the detonations. He saw Luthe and Lomaya now, dragging themselves into the clear night.

Portsend bumped into the pail of scraps, knocking it over in front of him. Clay shards from a dozen broken pots tumbled out, several of the little Slagstone fragments sparking on the stone floor.

*This!* This was what had caused the detonations! He had tossed a piece of Slagstone into the pail and the resulting spark must have somehow triggered a multi-Grit explosion.

There *had* been Grit in the pail, Portsend remembered. But the mix had been useless, contaminated well into the waste ratio. Besides, the bucket had at least an inch of liquid in the bottom from San's discarded tea. Damp Grit could still ignite, but not if it soaked in a pint of water.

Wait.

Portsend ran his hand across the floor. Dry, despite the toppled pail. No sign of a spill. Seizing the bucket, Portsend reached inside, swiping along the bottom. Sparks! It was dry! Had he dumped

San's mug into a different pail? No, he could still smell the garlic and hodgegrass from the potent drink.

Portsend was still hunched over the pail, mind racing, when Luthe grabbed his arm. "Flames, Portsend! Come on!"

Dropping the pail, the two men moved quickly for the exit. They spilled through the doorway and onto the grass in a billow of smoke. Up the hill, Light Grit detonations were appearing at the edge of campus. The sound of an explosion in the still of night would bring many running. Good, they'd need help getting the fire under control before it ignited more Grit. The lab might still be salvageable if they acted quickly.

"Professor?" Lomaya was seated in the grass, her face smudged with soot from debris, clutching her book satchel like a shield against her chest. "What was that?"

Portsend gazed at the bright open doorway to his laboratory. "A discovery."

~

*Together, we labored in the soil for our food, and when the sun rose high, we shared our shade and our cup.*

# CHAPTER

# 10

Quarrah coiled the heavy rope for the third time. As long as she appeared busy with this task, no one was likely to bother her as the crew of the *Leeward Pride* continued securing the ship.

Quarrah certainly wasn't a legitimate crew member of Lady
Abeth's extravagant Dronodanian transport vessel. She had only
been aboard for the last fifteen minutes, since the moment the ship
had made berth in Beripent's North Central Harbor.

Now she just needed to blend in with the crew and keep an
eye on the cabin, ready to make her move as soon as Lady Abeth
appeared.

Part of her still couldn't believe that she was here, preparing
to go through with this insane plan. As an employer, Fabra Ment
didn't seem entirely stable of the mind, and were it not for the information Quarrah had discovered about the Realm on her own, she
certainly wouldn't be risking everything today.

The intrusion into Waelis Mordo's room had been very enlight-
ening. It hadn't taken much snooping to discover that the king's
advisor was definitely not acting in the Archkingdom's best interest.

She'd found records of illegal Grit sales to representatives of the
Sovereign States. She'd found a stack of blank documents that had
been signed and sealed by King Termain.

She'd found information on the Realm.

It hadn't been much. Just a single letter addressed to someone
called Overseer. From the letter, Quarrah had been able to deduce
several significant things.

The Realm seemed to be made up of three levels. The street
Hands did a lot of the grunt work while not really knowing why or
who they were doing it for. Members of the Faceless seemed to be in
charge of managing the jobs and organizing the Hands. The Faceless took direction from the top tier, known as the Directorate.

Coordination between the Directorate and the Faceless apparently took place at highly secretive and anonymous meetings. If
she wanted to get any real information about the Realm's influence
over King Termain, Quarrah realized she'd need to get herself into
one of those meetings.

She had reported all of this to Fabra Ment, who received the information about the secret organization like a giddy schoolgirl. A few days later, when they'd met again, Quarrah Drift Jumping to the queen dowager's private balcony in the dead of night, Fabra was the one who'd uncovered more information.

The old widow had told Quarrah that she'd overheard another conversation between Waelis Mordo and his unseen associate, in which they'd discussed recruiting to fill some vacant positions in the Faceless. Apparently, the usual method was to reach out to some of the most dependable Hands and bring them in to the secret meetings. There was, however, another way.

Quarrah needed to commit a crime flashy enough to impress the Realm. That would be the easy part. She still wasn't sure about turning herself in, putting all her trust in the unknown Realm to set her free. Luckily, Fabra Ment had given her some additional assurances.

As the king's mother, the queen dowager still had enough reach and influence to spring Quarrah from her cell by the end of the week, if the Realm didn't claim her. The old widow had already proven to be sneaky and resourceful enough to pull that off. And the alternative was letting Fabra disseminate Quarrah's portrait, which might land her behind bars anyway.

Quarrah had already stolen the painting once, the rolled canvas almost begging to be nicked from a shelf in Fabra's chambers. Much to her dismay, an identical copy was waiting in the same place the next time she'd checked in, making a quiet, but obvious point. The only way out of this was to do the job.

Quarrah glanced across the deck of the *Leeward Pride* as the cabin door finally opened. Lady Abeth Agaul quietly stepped out, flanked on both sides by Dronodanian soldiers wearing uniforms of the Sovereign States. The former queen was sporting a white fur coat and a warm hat to match. Even from here, Quarrah could see the large ring on the middle finger of her right hand, fit securely over her pale blue glove.

Quarrah knew a great deal about the Agaul family ring, having recently done plenty of research to be sure that this theft would impress the Realm.

The piece of braided-gold jewelry was topped with a massive three-granule emerald, created for Leonid Agaul, baron of Espar, some three hundred years ago. It was made famous two generations later when Leonid the Third became the first Agaul to rule the Greater Chain, taking the throne from King Kerith, whose entire line had been killed when Grotenisk razed Beripent.

From King Leonid the Third the ring had been passed from king or queen to prince or princess, always adorning the ruler's hand. After Pethredote had defeated King Barrid Agaul and become the crusader monarch, he'd gifted the ring to Remium's grandfather, the rightful successor. Decades later, Remium had been wearing it the day his throat was slit in the palace.

As king, Termain should have been bequeathed the ring through the will of his assassinated cousin, but Abeth had found some sort of loophole. Although an Agaul only by marriage, she had quickly drafted into *her* will that the ring would return to Termain, or a legitimate heir should he ever marry, upon Abeth's death.

Oh, Quarrah knew a spiteful move when she saw one. Lady Abeth was said to always wear the ring in public as an obvious statement against Termain. And short of killing her, there was nothing he could do to get it for himself. Termain didn't technically need it to rule, but the ring represented generations of Agauls giving their blessing to their progeny on the throne.

Acting quickly, Quarrah began uncoiling the rope as Lady Abeth moved across the deck in the direction of the ramp. This would take a bit of careful timing to reach the queen's hand, but Quarrah was confident that the actual theft wouldn't give her any trouble. *The glove is probably the only thing keeping that ring on her dainty hand,* she thought.

She needed to do this without getting caught. Sure, she was

planning to turn herself in, but the Realm would only be impressed if she successfully stole the ring first.

The moment Lady Abeth and her entourage were in position, Quarrah gave a sharp tug on her rope, untying a knot on the other end and loosing a stack of small barrels that Quarrah had turned on their sides. The barrels came rolling across the deck, causing one of the crew members to shout a warning. The soldiers on that side moved to shield Lady Abeth from the obstacles, creating just the opening Quarrah needed to get close.

She executed a simple "bump-and-sorry," slamming her shoulder against Lady Abeth as she pretended to move hastily toward the barrels. This was followed up with a profuse apology, Quarrah's face downcast in shame. Her left hand gripped Abeth's elbow, fingers digging in painfully, while her right clasped the queen's gloved hand as though begging forgiveness.

Lady Abeth winced as Quarrah applied just the right amount of pressure to the woman's elbow, drawing attention away from the fact that she was sliding the loose ring from her finger.

The piece of jewelry was free before the barrels had come to a standstill, and Quarrah slipped across the deck and made her descent to the dock by way of an aft ladder.

*That went well*, Quarrah thought. *Now for the hard part.*

From the anonymity of the gathered crowd, Quarrah watched Lady Abeth move gracefully down the ramp and across the dock. Surprisingly, she seemed not to have noticed that the ring was missing yet. To think! If Quarrah owned an item worth half the value of this ring, she'd notice if someone so much as sneezed within ten feet of it.

For maximum impact, Quarrah had decided to turn herself in once Lady Abeth started publicly panicking. *She better notice soon*, she thought. *I might get second thoughts and hang on to this. It's probably worth more than anything Fabra will pay me.*

Quarrah slipped the ring onto her own finger. It actually fit quite well, even though she found it annoyingly gaudy. How was she supposed to reach a hand in her pocket with such an obstruction rising from her knuckle?

And how had Lady Abeth not noticed yet? Must have been the gloves. She probably couldn't feel the ring on her finger, and she seemed too distracted with the crowds as she made her way up the ramps that led out of the harbor.

The day was clear but chill, and Quarrah could have used a drink to warm her insides. But the small flask at her side was filled with white paint today, as per Fabra Ment's instructions.

Now above the harbor, Quarrah saw the rest of the entourage waiting to escort Lady Abeth to visit the graves of her husband and son. Mounted Reggies, an armed carriage, and a host of citizens who clearly wished that she had been their queen for more than the space of a few hours.

Quarrah swallowed a sudden lump in her throat. That was a lot of public attention. She hoped she wouldn't get shot outright when she stepped forward, waving the ring around.

*Maybe she'll notice it's missing when she gets in the carriage. Come on! Look at your blazing hand.*

A well-dressed butler stepped forward and pulled open the carriage door. He was tall and thin, with a little smile peeking out from beneath his gray mustache. Lady Abeth greeted him warmly and the two of them climbed into the cab, the butler pulling the door shut. With a flick of the reins, the entire processional moved forward.

*Seriously?* Quarrah sighed in annoyance. Well, she was only going to follow them as far as Orchard Avenue. Then she was painting her face and turning herself in, whether the queen noticed her heirloom ring was missing or not.

It was as good a day as any to assassinate a queen. The sky was clear and the midday sun cast its shadow straight down. Here, on the rooftop of the Wry Fox Inn, there was just enough breeze to bring the scent of salt water off the sea, but not enough to require compensation when aiming to fire.

Not that Ardor Benn would be making any actual shots today. He leaned on a long-barreled Fielder whose butt was planted against the shale shingles of the inn. At five stories, the Wry Fox was the tallest building on the block and provided the best tactical viewpoint for the task ahead. Ard had rented the upper room at a steal, since no one wanted it because of the smell. Probably a dead rat in the wall, but it made no difference to Ard. The rental was just to give him access to the roof.

A careful assassin would have stayed hidden in the room and shot through the window. Ard had opted for something more visible. After all, wasn't the entire point of this escapade to turn himself in?

Ard angled his white face northward, peering down the street. The paint was caked in his beard and it made his eyelids feel brittle. The handheld mirror in the room below proved that his appearance was deathly, especially in contrast to his dark coat. Resisting the urge to scratch at his face, Ard had the sudden, discomforting thought that this whole thing could be a setup. What if Staug Raifen's instructions on getting into the Realm were pure hogwash? The big thug might be settling in to watch Ard get arrested and have a good laugh about the painted face.

Well, no sense in doubting the plan now. At least Ard had on his most comfortable shirt. It might be what he'd end up wearing for the rest of his life, locked up in a Reggie Outpost.

Trumpets blared, and Ard saw the excitement among the citizens in the street below. Queen Abeth's retinue came into view, Hedma Sallis at the reins of the carriage. Mounted escorts were heavily armed, carrying the flags of Dronodan and Espar side by side. Well, that was something of a controversy. The former queen's entire visit stood on shaky footing.

Lady Abeth had left the Archkingdom of her own volition when Termain had taken the throne, which was the only reason she was allowed to return now. Still, it was dangerous for her to be in the Archkingdom at all. She was the daughter of the Dronodanian king, and she had obviously opposed Termain's rule.

Abeth's public reason for visiting today was to pay respects to the graves of her husband and son. This would pull at the heartstrings of the citizens enough that Termain wouldn't dare deny her request for fear of his public reputation falling even further—not that he even seemed to care about that.

Visiting the graves was the same reason she'd secretly come to Beripent the night Ard had met her. Abeth hadn't wanted the fanfare of a return then, but it was exactly what they needed now. The queen's assassination needed to be witnessed and verified.

Convincing Lady Abeth to die had been remarkably easy. Once Ard and Raek had their idea fully hatched, the whole conversation had taken place in a series of four letters. The logistics of how it would be done took much more corresponding, but Codley's smugglers had been surprisingly swift with their deliveries.

Today's plan was simple—boringly so, to Ardor Benn. He had suggested half a dozen more interesting methods of faking someone's assassination. Drown her, hang her, behead her, disembowel her... But Raek had talked him down, reminding Ard that simple was better. The focus needed to be on turning himself in. The last thing Ard needed to do was upstage himself with some overly gory display.

They were going with a method tried and true. A blank gunshot, screams, and a shouted proclamation that the queen was hit.

Ard pulled a cartridge from his Grit belt. These Fielder rounds packed a lot of punch. He twisted the lead ball off, keeping the cartridge upright so the wadding and Blast Grit didn't spill. Then he dropped the paper cartridge into the long barrel and rammed the tamping rod down, packing the bundle tightly into the chamber where the sparks from the Slagstone hammer would ignite it.

Ard lifted the gun and placed the wooden butt against his shoulder, sighting down the length of the long barrel. The Fielder was heavy and holding it like this for very long would be impractical if he were actually aiming. But Abeth's carriage was within range now, and Ard needed to be ready to pull the trigger with only five seconds' notice.

Ard was pleased with the way the employees of the Guesthouse Adagio had responded to his plans. Bringing them in on the ruse was an absolute necessity, since Lady Abeth would have to spend the foreseeable future at the guesthouse pretending to be dead.

Codley Hattingson had been waiting for her with a carriage at the harbor. The groundskeeper and equerry, Hedma Sallis, was driving, ensuring that the carriage went the route it was supposed to. And Bannit Lagaday... Well, Ard wasn't sure if the squirrelly cook was ready for field testing yet. He was still at the guesthouse preparing a welcome feast worthy of their long-absent queen.

Below, Hedma pulled back on the reins, bringing the carriage to an abrupt halt. Leaning back, she rapped once on the covered carriage.

Ard began the count. *One... Two... Three...*

The escorts stopped. One of them might have asked Hedma if something was wrong, but Ard couldn't hear the conversation at such a distance.

*Four... Five.*

Ard squeezed the trigger. The Slagstone hammer sparked, the Blast Grit igniting with a deafening crack, spitting flames from the mouth of the long barrel. The heavy gun recoiled enough to knock an inexperienced shooter off his feet, but Ard was braced against the shingles.

Through the smoke, Ard could see that the carriage's side window had broken. That would have been Codley's handiwork, shattering the glass from the inside, exactly five seconds after Hedma had given the signal.

These little details were important to Ardor Benn. In his mind, it was what set his work apart from lazier ruse artists. Still, Ard had held back on the minutia, since Codley wasn't quite as cooperative as he'd hoped. For example, there would be no blood today. That meant they needed to make sure that no one outside the team would get close to her after the shot.

From the street, Ard heard plenty of screams. Some of them would belong to Codley, who would be raising the word that Abeth had been shot. But another cry directed attention to the top of the Wry Fox Inn.

Ard had been spotted. Now the trick was to turn himself in without getting killed first.

The escorts cracked off a pair of shots, sending Ard scrambling back across the shingles. He dropped the Fielder, watching it slide down the angled rooftop and tumble over the side. Ard hoped tossing one's gun like this would seem like an obvious surrender, providing the heavy weapon didn't knock someone over the head five stories below.

Lying flat against the shingles, his feet about ten feet from the edge of the roof, Ard pulled the prepared pot of Barrier Grit from his belt. Raek had mixed just the right amount for the size of detonation that he'd need, and the added string would be the perfect length, assuming it didn't tangle.

Another gunshot sounded from below, and one of the shingles at the edge of the inn's roof exploded, throwing dust onto Ard's boots. He looped the end of the string around a nail he'd placed in the roof and let go of the Barrier Grit pot, watching it roll down the roof's slope. It picked up speed, bouncing gently across the shingles as the string unwound.

*Don't break*, Ard pleaded. Why didn't they make these rooftops smoother?

The Grit pot plummeted over the edge and out of sight. Ard saw the string go taut as the tied-on pot reached the end. It swung like a pendulum back toward the side of the inn, and Ard heard the satisfying sound of the pot breaking against the building.

Ard coaxed himself down the pitched rooftop until his feet hung over the edge. Nobody shot a hole in his sole, so that seemed like a good sign. He sat up, sliding forward until he was perched precariously at the edge.

Just as Raek had calculated, the pot had broken, detonating a dome of Barrier Grit against the wall of the fourth story. The protective cloud protruded from the side of the building, leaving open the access to his fifth-floor window, but blocking the line of fire from the street below.

Hedma Sallis had directed the carriage up to the intersection with Glemond Street. But where the blazes was Raek? He was supposed to be there with the medical coach by now. Hedma was stalling—and that looked suspicious.

It did Ard little good to worry about the parts of the plan he had no control over. He grabbed the edge of the roof and swung himself down, feet finding purchase on the windowsill of his rented room. Being up so high made his heart race. For some reason, he always found it scarier going down than climbing up. If he fell now, he'd strike the cloud of Barrier Grit, but that would hardly break his fall.

Barrier clouds were impossible to successfully stand on. Raek talked about how the hardened shell was actually a plate of Grit in constant motion, swirling and sliding like oil over water. Ard preferred the term "blazing slippery." If Ard fell onto the cloud below, he would just glance off, probably getting filled full of lead as he plummeted uncontrollably to the road below.

Ard tumbled through the window into the room, wrinkling his nose at the rotten stench. Three Ashings a night was still a ripoff here.

He unbuckled his Grit belt and dropped it onto the bed. No sense in turning that in to the Reggies. Raek would swing by later and pick it up. Ard kept a long knife in his boot sheath, even though they'd definitely confiscate it once he was arrested. The blade wasn't worth a lot, and he just couldn't bring himself to go out there completely weaponless.

He exited the room and made for the stairs. Ard didn't encounter the Regulators until he was almost to the ground level. The two men didn't shoot, praise the Homeland, but they trained their Rollers on Ard and started yelling something fierce. They'd obviously identified him as the shooter. Apparently, painting one's face stark white made for a considerably identifiable trait, even while positioned five stories above the road.

Ard held up his hands and slowly dropped to his knees on the stair landing halfway up the flight. "At least tell me if I hit her," he said. "I mean, it's a small carriage, so, pretty good odds, but I was clear up on that rooftop."

"In the name of King Termain Agaul of the Archkingdom, you are under arrest," declared one of the Reggies, drawing a step nearer.

"My name is Androt Penn," Ard stated loudly. "And I shot the former queen, Abeth Agaul."

~

*We shall send their bodies to the depths that once held us.*

# CHAPTER

# 11

You will rise slowly and come without resistance." The second Regulator already had the shackles ready to clap around Ard's wrists. "You will answer for your crimes."

Ard rose to his feet in as nonthreatening a way as possible. Well, that had all gone smoothly. Turned out it was rather easy to turn oneself in. Not nearly as much fun as getting away with it.

Just as the Regulator with the shackles stepped onto the bottom stair, the inn door burst open. A figure moving fast with the element of surprise plowed into the Reggie and sent him tumbling to the floor. Startled, his companion cranked off a shot from his Roller. The ball missed Ard by mere inches, splintering the wooden step behind him.

Ard stumbled in shock, tumbling nearly to the bottom step before he caught himself. The Reggie shot again and again, and Ard realized that, gratefully, he was no longer the target. By the time Ard had pulled himself to his feet, he heard the sizzling snap of a Slagstone hammer throwing sparks without the resounding shot of a Blast cartridge. The gun was empty.

Ard turned to see who had been the recipient of the Reggie's five rounds. The stranger was lying prone atop the first Regulator who had fallen. It was a man with shoulder-length black hair, unkempt and greasy. He wasn't wearing much, and what rags he had were torn and shredded, exposing large areas of bruised skin.

Both men appeared to be dead, a pool of blood soaking the

floorboards beneath the fallen Regulator's head. The attacker, too, was a mess of wounds, with thick scabs formed over countless cuts and lesions.

Ardor Benn took a step toward the fallen duo. At once, the dirty stranger sprang from his position atop the Reggie, cracked mouth open as though uttering some heinous cry. Except, all was silent. And the man's eyes were red like blood—the color of the crimson moon.

*What the blazes?* The man was Moonsick!

The insane man was onto the second Regulator with alarming speed. Hands came down with surprising force, broken fingers wielded like the claws of a deranged animal. The Reggie took the first blow to the face, falling backward against the wall. The Moonsick Bloodeye closed his bleeding hand around the other man's throat, grip tightening like a vise.

"Sparks!" Ard drew his long knife and leapt forward, plunging the blade into the man's exposed back. But it didn't sink in like it should have. Despite the tender, damaged flesh he could see, it felt like stabbing wood. He stabbed again, and a third time.

The Reggie's feet were kicking frantically as he pushed against the creature pinning him. As a last-ditch effort, the man drew a Grit pot blindly from his belt. Ard scrambled backward out of range, but the Bloodeye swatted the pot out of the Reggie's grasp. It fell only a few inches, clay cracking, spilling its powdery contents, but not striking with enough force to detonate.

The empty Roller had fallen beside the steps, and Ard turned away from the fight to retrieve the gun. There would be extra rounds on the Reggie's belt. If the two of them could work together...

The Moonsick man knocked into Ard, bloodying his lip and sending the Roller spinning across the room. Ard swiped his knife wildly, but the Bloodeye had no fear of the blade. He advanced blindly, Ard's steel cutting zigzag lines across his tattered chest.

The strangled Reggie was lying still against the wall, dead or unconscious. Of little help, either way. Still, the man had Grit and Blast cartridges on his belt.

Ard kicked the Moonsick man and lunged for the motionless Reggie, dropping to his knees and pawing over his belt. He pulled two gun cartridges from their loops. At least that would give him two shots if he got to the Roller. He'd still have to load the weapon...

The Bloodeye was on him again, this time pinning Ard under his weight like he had done to the two Reggies. Ard twisted, thrusting the long knife between the man's ribs, blood running over his hand. It wasn't enough. Nothing was enough. Where in Homeland's name had this creature come from?

The man's rough hand found Ard's throat. That iron grip closed, pinching away his breath. Ard tried not to flail like the Regulator had done. He tried to retain his wits. But the face looking down at him was enough to shake any soul.

The man's red eyes roved in constant motion, searching for things they would never see. They were opaque orbs, crying tears of blood, never blinking. He reeked of rotting flesh—like a spoiled fish left too long in the sun. And that wide mouth dangled open above Ard, caught in a terrifying scream of silence, a yawn that might devour...

From the corner of his eye, Ard saw the clay pot that had failed to detonate. Reaching out, he brushed away the cracked pot, his hand skidding through the powdery Grit. His fingers found the little chip of Slagstone and he took hold of it.

Ard felt the veins on his painted face bulging. He fought against the panic of not being able to draw breath. In total desperation, Ard reached up, shoving both gun cartridges and the fragment of Slagstone into the Moonsick man's open mouth.

With his last drib of energy, Ard delivered an uppercut to the Bloodeye's jaw, knocking it closed with teeth-shattering force. Inside the man's mouth, the Slagstone must have sparked, igniting the cartridges.

Ard flinched as the man's head exploded, two lead balls flying in random directions. He felt a warm spray across his face and he gagged, rolling the lifeless body away.

Ardor Benn rose on shaking legs, staggering for the exit. He threw open the door and stumbled into the street, hands above his head. He didn't have time to digest what had happened. He needed to stick to the plan and turn himself in.

"My name is Androt Penn!" he shouted, "and I shot Queen Abeth Agaul." But no one was paying him any attention. "Sparks," Ard cursed. "You've got to be kidding me."

Another Moonsick man was crouching in the street, half hidden behind the carcass of a horse. The rider, one of the armed escorts, was lying dead just yards away. Ball after ball tore into the Bloodeye, and he looked unable to stand. But Ard had seen the one inside spring up from what should have been certain death.

Ard fell back against the wall of the inn, keeping himself out of the line of fire. He counted three Regulators putting down fire, and none of them seemed interested in arresting him!

Maybe getting caught was harder than he'd suspected.

Ard heard the twang of a crossbow and saw a cloud of Barrier Grit appear around the Moonsick man as the bolt struck. Cautiously, the three Regulators stepped out from their protected positions and moved toward the deranged Bloodeye.

The fear was palpable as they surrounded the unthinkable, the improbable—Moonsickness in central Beripent.

Ard couldn't understand it, either, and he knew more about Moonsickness than most. At a week since the last Passing, it was reasonable to think that people exposed to the Moon rays would be well into the violent third stage by now. But what were they doing here? So far out of their right minds, a man with advanced Moonsickness like this certainly couldn't find his way off Pekal.

Ard knew Moonsickness had to be spreading. It had touched the farthest farming community of Espar even before Isle Halavend had been killed. Another outlying township in southern Dronodan had fallen to Moonsickness three cycles later, prompting evacuations from all of the farthest communities throughout the Greater Chain.

The Moon's influence would spread farther with every sow dragon that died on Pekal until the newly hatched bull dragon reached maturity. Once it did, more eggs would be fertilized, more dragons would hatch, and the range of the Moon's rays would retreat to the borders of Pekal as it had been for centuries.

Still, the presence of Moonsick people in Beripent didn't make sense. If a large city were to be touched by the Moon's rays, *everyone* would get sick. How, then, could two Moonsick people show up, seven days into the new cycle, and word of their condition not spread through the neighborhoods like wildfire?

Ard tried to shake aside the questions. The attack had been the very kind of upstaging Raek had been worried about. They needed to salvage this job so the whole assassination wasn't a waste.

Glancing down the street, Ard saw the medical coach, white flag flying. So, Raek had finally showed up! His big partner was transferring the still form of Abeth from her carriage to the coach. Between Codley and Raek, they'd pronounce her dead to the public. Raek would use the medical coach to move her to the undertaker, where they'd smuggle Abeth away to the Guesthouse Adagio.

Ard stepped forward and dropped to his knees in the street. "My name is Androt Penn," he said with significantly less enthusiasm. "When you're done with that Bloodeye, can someone please arrest me?"

Quarrah ducked into a narrow alleyway, breathing heavily as people streamed away from the street where Lady Abeth's carriage had turned. Some were screaming, sobbing in distress, as Quarrah pieced together what the panicked citizens were saying.

The queen had been *shot*?

This certainly didn't bode well for Quarrah's plans.

She needed to act now. Claim the theft of the Agaul family ring before Lady Abeth died. Every minute that passed would only muddy the order of events, making it seem more likely that she'd slipped the ring from the dead queen's finger in the confusion of the assassination. That would hardly be impressive to the Realm.

She opened her flask, tipping back her head and pouring out the white paint. It felt cold, running from the hairline of her braided, dust-colored hair, to her chin.

It was done in a moment, a swipe of Quarrah's hand spreading it evenly across her face as she opened her eyes through the viscous whiteness. Hastily, she wiped her palm on the leg of her black trousers, the Agaul ring remaining shiny and clean on her other hand.

She turned the corner, moving against the flow of fleeing citizens like a fish swimming upstream.

The area was a disaster! Regulators swarmed in all directions, and the queen's carriage stood empty at the end of the street. A cloud of Barrier Grit burned beside a horse and rider who had somehow fallen. Quarrah drew back as a figure within the cloud threw himself against the invisible shell, thrashing wildly. Through the ring of Reggies surrounding the detonation, Quarrah saw a brief glimpse of his twisted face.

Homeland afar! That man was Moonsick!

At once, Quarrah's mind was flooded with disturbing memories. Fighting a Moonsick Ulusal on Pekal—the woman's wrecked face gazing at her through sightless eyes that dripped crimson. The smell of rotting flesh that peeled away from her, fingers scraped to the bone from her savage outbursts. Quarrah had sunk that stout sword into her collar, a warm spray of blood up her arm. Running, hiding. The Moonsick woman sniffing her out...

Quarrah shook off the unsettling images, focusing on what she was here to do. She held up her hand in the chaotic street and shouted.

"I stole the Agaul family ring!"

The pandemonium continued around her, Reggies shouting as they raced through the front door of the Wry Fox Inn next door. She noticed that a cluster of Reggies had pinned a man on the street, clapping shackles firmly around his wrist. Quarrah couldn't see his face, but his hair was long and unkempt.

They must have found their assassin. But that didn't explain why there was a terrible Bloodeye moaning soundlessly inside a sealed Barrier cloud.

"The Agaul family ring!" Quarrah cried again, waving it. "I stole it from her hand!"

Still no response, the turmoil of the street carrying on in indifference to her claims. Oh, flames. She'd been upstaged. Quarrah felt her opportunity slipping between her fingers like an oversized ring on a cold day. There was no way her theft could compete with the urgency of the Bloodeye and the assassin.

Her mind began to race. There had to be a way to salvage this situation. She stepped farther into the street and almost tripped on a discarded Fielder. The barrel was bent and the wooden stock cracked as though the gun had been dropped from a significant height.

Quarrah picked it up, noting that the long barrel was still warm. The weapon had been shot quite recently...

A wildly fresh idea suddenly occurred to Quarrah. As a master thief she'd stolen plenty of Ashings, jewels, and valuables. One time she'd even stolen a breeding horse.

But Quarrah Khai had never stolen a crime before.

*Flames,* she thought, *this is crazy.* It would work. If she turned herself in, the real assassin would be happy to corroborate her story so he could be exonerated. She sucked in a deep breath.

"I shot the former queen, Lady Abeth Agaul!"

Quarrah's voice cut through the chaos as she dropped to her knees on the compact dirt, lifting the Fielder above her head with both hands.

What was she doing? Running a ruse? No, this was still theft. Theft of a deed. Ardor Benn had influenced her in many ways, but not enough for her to change her methods. Or at least, that was what she kept telling herself.

"I shot the queen!" she called again.

Two of the Reggies converged on her like sharks on a wounded fish. She resisted the urge to bolt as the Fielder was ripped from her hands. One of the Reggies kept a Roller trained on her while the other pulled back her arms, fixing shackles around her wrists.

"Chief!" the Reggie called over to his superior. "We've got another white face!"

*Another?*

"Keep her away from her partner," answered the chief. "Don't want them talking."

Quarrah felt hopelessness begin to spread through her body. It started in her stomach and shot outward in all directions like a detonation of Void Grit. This was bad. Oh, Homeland, this was bad!

The assassination of Lady Abeth was *already* being used as a calling card for the Realm!

Quarrah tried to twist her head sideways to see the real shooter, but he had been taken around the inn and out of sight. There was no chance of pulling this off now. No chance at all. She would have to rely on Fabra Ment to save her before the executioner got to her.

"Take her through the east door of the Radge Outpost," the chief said. "We'll sort the two of them out once we get this mess under control." He gestured at the Bloodeye, who was pounding the road with his bare fists.

"Where'd they come from?" the Reggie asked the chief.

"Pekal," he replied with a belittling tone.

"I meant the assassins."

"Doesn't matter where they came from," he said. "What matters is where they're going. They'll see the hangman's noose by morning."

*Morning!* She didn't know if Fabra Ment could get her out that quickly. Quarrah Khai had stolen a crime that didn't belong to her, and now all hope of getting out alive rested on the Realm. And on Quarrah's ability to convince that mysterious organization that she was the one who had killed Lady Abeth.

Hopefully, the real assassin wouldn't be much of a talker.

～

*But all this while it was they who stole from us. Not possessions or goods, but the love of our gods.*

# CHAPTER

# 12

The first thing Quarrah noticed was the freshness of the air. It wasn't a particularly pleasant smell—not like the old days with Ard, when their hideout had been above the bakery on Humont Street. But it wasn't rank and foul, which was what tipped her off that she wasn't in the Regulation Outpost cell anymore.

Quarrah had no idea how much time had passed. She'd been escorted to the Outpost, stripped of all her possessions, including the stolen Agaul ring, and sent to a jail cell to await the inspectors. They'd given her a cup of water to drink. No, that definitely hadn't been water. She'd barely finished swallowing it before the drug had knocked her out cold on the rank cell floor.

Now she sat somewhere soft and comfortable, with something covering her face. It spanned forehead to chin, blocking her vision entirely and causing her breath to feel hot and muggy.

Her senses seemed to return all at once. The moment she realized her hands were free, Quarrah reached up and yanked off the object covering her face.

It was a simple mask, painted white, made of hardened leather. It showed the vague outline of a face, but there were no holes for the eyes or mouth. A wide ribbon had been tied behind her head, holding the frightful thing in place.

Clutching the mask, Quarrah rose to her feet. She'd been seated in a padded chair with stuffed arms, the kind that usually belonged in the sitting room of a nobleman's manor. Despite being ornate, the room was actually quite small and windowless, a detail that Quarrah noticed immediately, filling her with a sudden sense of claustrophobia.

Three little clouds of Light Grit hung over metal sconces on the wall, and from their glow, Quarrah saw a small clock on the mantel above a Heat Grit hearth. It was a curious clock, operating without any noticeable pendulum. She'd heard about these new contraptions, but she hadn't seen any in person yet.

The clock's hands told her that it was almost nine o'clock. Flames! Had she been unconscious for nearly six hours? No wonder she felt groggy and hungry.

There was a round rug on the floor, topped with a knee-high table with carved legs. A framed painting of an unknown Holy Isle hung on the wall beside a large mirror. Quarrah flinched at her own reflection. The white paint was still caked on her face. Some bits had flaked off, while others had smeared from the sweat of being under the thick leather mask. She looked a rather ghastly sight.

The air in the room seemed slightly hazy. Or perhaps Quarrah hadn't fully recovered from her unconsciousness yet. Either way, finding herself in such a luxurious room was disconcerting.

Oh, and there was a man on the couch with a mask on his face.

Quarrah held perfectly still, watching him patiently. His mask was indistinguishable from the leather one she held, tied behind his long brown hair but concealing every inch of his face.

The man was lying down, his head propped against the arm of the couch, chest rising and falling with the steady rhythm of slumber. He was dressed like a working-class citizen; boots, brown trousers, and a dark buttoned-up coat. Tufts of his unruly beard poked out along the sides of his mask.

His gentle snoring could have been an act. This was likely the man who had really assassinated Abeth Agaul. Maybe this was her chance! If she unmasked him quickly, she might be able to use one of these soft pillows to smother him. She could replace the mask before anyone from the Realm arrived and they would assume that he hadn't recovered from whatever drug had likely been in his drink.

Quarrah picked up a pillow from her chair and stepped toward the stranger. Across the room, the door opened.

A figure stood in the doorway, entire head concealed beneath a decorated headpiece, draped in uncut dragon scales, giving it a rough, primal appearance. There wasn't a face, per se, but the two eyeholes looked like pits of blackness nestled between greenish gray scales. A third hole hung like a gaping maw, but it must have been covered with some sort of fabric because, like the eyes, Quarrah could see nothing but flat shadow.

The door shut and the figure strode forward. Perhaps more unsettling than the headpiece was the rest of the attire. The stranger was not very tall but was draped with a heavy shroud of black cloth that concealed any details of the body.

"Welcome, Jerisa Khailar." The voice was husky, and somewhat androgynous, although Quarrah guessed it belonged to a woman.

Jerisa. She'd had to give the Reggies a name when they were locking her up at the Outpost. Ard had always been full of aliases, quick to give them on the fly, but Quarrah rarely even gave her real name. In the pressure of the moment, she had said Jerisa Khailar—the name of her mother.

"I am Overseer." Her speech seemed affected, as though talking through a mouthful of bread. "Tell me of your crime for the Realm."

Sparks! It was time to talk, and that was usually when things started going downhill for Quarrah Khai.

"I committed a crime," she began. "I...I stole the family ring directly off the finger of Lady Abeth Agaul." Might as well start there. If that didn't impress Overseer, then Quarrah could risk claiming the assassination, too.

"Where were you arrested?"

"Radge Street," she answered. "And the corner of Arch."

"You have the ring with you?" the voice asked through the large headpiece.

"Well, no," stammered Quarrah. "The Reggies took it when I got to the Outpost."

A gloved hand suddenly appeared through the wide sleeve of her robe. Nestled in the palm was the Agaul ring.

"This ring is now property of the Realm," spoke Overseer. "Do you have any objection to that?"

Quarrah shook her head slowly at first, then picked up speed as she realized the full impact of the ring's presence here. Not only had the Realm taken her from a secure cell but they had taken what had to be the most valuable thing in the Outpost. And they'd done it in the space of a few hours. Sparks! What kind of reach did this organization have?

"Good." Overseer's fingers closed around the ring. "Your contribution is paltry, with the death of Abeth Agaul. If we were able to spring you from a Regulation Outpost, how simply we could take the heirloom ring from the hand of a corpse."

Quarrah felt her mouth go dry, the sudden onset of a headache. "I shot Lady Abeth Agaul." Well, she was all in, now.

"Say, which was it, child?" asked Overseer. "Did you steal the ring, or did you murder the queen?"

"Both!" Quarrah exclaimed. "I did both. I shot the queen, and then slipped the ring off her finger before turning myself over to the Reggies."

"Was the shot instantly fatal?"

"I don't know," answered Quarrah. "She was in the carriage." Oh, flames, this was risky.

"Now, that is interesting," mused Overseer. "You see, my witnesses said that Lady Abeth's carriage moved a block eastward after the shot, where it met a medical coach with a healer, who took her lifeless body. The corner of Radge and Arch would put you over a block away from the coach. How was it that you managed to acquire the ring?"

Quarrah needed to sit down before the dizziness of anxiety betrayed any shred of confidence that still lingered. She never did get her way with words. Maybe she could dash past Overseer and slip out the door. The leader of the Realm certainly didn't look too agile with that long cloak.

"Where were you standing when you took the shot?" asked Overseer.

"I told you, the corner of Radge and Arch." She was stalling, but what else could she do? The more she answered, the less truth her claim held.

"Where were you positioned?"

Quarrah felt a bead of sweat collecting on her hairline, probably milky from the paint. "I was...I was behind a barrel. Clear line of sight to the carriage."

Overseer remained frighteningly still. "Oh? But my witnesses placed the shooter on the rooftop of the Wry Fox Inn."

"Which was exactly what we *wanted* you to see," spoke a new voice from the couch behind them. The voice was terribly familiar to Quarrah Khai, his inflection savvy and full of wit.

*By the Homeland afar,* Quarrah thought. *There's no way it's him.*

Ardor Benn sat on the edge of the couch, his hands clasped in front of him and the white leather mask resting on his knee. If any-thing, he looked more ragged and shambled than Quarrah, white paint crusted in his long beard, covered in a spattering of dried blood. His hair was long over his ears, and quite frankly, she didn't think it was the right look for him.

But the eyes were the same. And the crooked half smile as he looked at her. As though they weren't in a life-or-death situation.

"I told you, no side jobs," Ard said to Quarrah, rising to his feet. "This was about getting an audience with the Realm, not making a score. And what's this 'Jerisa Khailar' business I'm hearing? You told me your name was Shadow Cat!"

He was standing right in front of her now, and Quarrah didn't know if she wanted to smack him or run.

Ard turned to Overseer and stuck out his hand as though they might shake. "Hullo there. The name's Androt Penn. Pleasure to meet you."

Overseer's hand did not appear for a cordial greeting and Ard raised his eyebrows as though he'd really misread the situation.

"Sorry about the mix-up," he said to Overseer, dropping his hand. "Looks like Shadow Cat got greedy, but she still got the job done." He turned to Quarrah. "When *did* you steal that ring?"

"In the harbor," she answered truthfully. "Before she disembarked."

"Flying sparks, Cat!" Ard cried. "Are you out of your mind? That could have jeopardized the whole plan!"

"But it didn't," she replied. "We killed the queen and now we're here."

"It was never about turning a profit on the ring, was it?" Ard pressed. He leaned close. "You wanted to confess to another crime—try to make me look bad for the Realm. Is that it?"

She squinted, pressing the palms of her hands against her closed eyes. Why was Ard pressuring her like this? Didn't he remember how poorly she lied under pressure? If he backed off the act a bit, they might be able to come through this together.

"Which one of you killed Lady Abeth Agaul?" asked Overseer with a tone of finality.

"We both did," answered Ard. "It takes two dogs to make a puppy." He pointed at Quarrah. "This woman approached me a cycle back and said she was interested in getting into the Realm, and word on the street was that I had the same goal. We hatched a plan to assassinate the former queen, mark the crime for the Realm, and turn ourselves in."

"The Realm does much in collaboration," said Overseer. "We have those who plan, and those who execute. Your joint effort shows no lack of planning, but today I can only accept the one who was also willing to execute. Which one of you pulled the trigger?"

Her gloved hand appeared through the folds of her cloak again. This time it was holding a Singler, the Slagstone hammer already cocked. Overseer didn't point it at either of them, but left it auspiciously angled at the low table.

Ard jumped in with an answer. "We both shot at the same time, signaling each other with a glint from a handheld mirror. You'll find mine in the top-floor room I rented at the Wry Fox. I signaled first from the rooftop, she signaled back. We counted to five and pulled the triggers in unison."

"I find two inconsistencies in your tale," said Overseer. "First, Abeth died of a single Fielder ball. My sources heard the healer proclaim it at the coach."

Quarrah looked to Ard, expecting him to have an answer. And if he didn't, he stalled better than anyone she knew.

"Are you familiar with King Termain's firing squad?" Ard asked.

"Is that a threat?" asked Overseer.

"Flames, no!" Ard backed up a step apologetically. "I'm trying to draw an analogy here."

"Let us pray it is worthwhile," said Overseer.

He cleared his throat. "There are ten people on the king's firing squad, all trained marksmen. At ten yards, they put the ball right through the victim's forehead. You ever see someone get shot in the forehead? A single ball does a number on the skull. With ten, their head would practically explode, and that would be a bit overkill, no pun intended. That's why the ten shooters on the squad only have one gun loaded with an actual ball. The other nine are shooting blanks. I think it's for the mess, but they claim it's supposed to help with the guilt that the shooters might feel. See, none of them knows which one actually shoots the ball, so they can all believe that they shot the blanks."

"You intend to tell me that one of you shot a blank?" assumed Overseer.

"Well, I figured the opposite principle would be true for murderers like Shadow Cat and me," Ard continued. "If one of us shot a blank, there would be no way to turn on each other and claim the crime for ourself." Ard shot Quarrah a pointed glance. "By shooting a blank, it's impossible for you, or even us, to know which of us committed the actual murder. Call it criminal's insurance against each other."

Ard had either talked Overseer into a state of utter confusion or the masked figure accepted his wild theory.

"Second inconsistency," Overseer continued, "my witnesses heard only *one* Fielder shot. From the rooftop. So, why are you defending Jerisa Khailar?" She pointed the Singler at Ard, who promptly raised his hands.

"Maybe your witnesses heard wrong," Ard boldly declared. "I mean, there was a lot of chaos and gunfire with those blazing Moonsick fellows showing up."

"The Bloodeyes had nothing to do with your crime," said Overseer. "I trust my witnesses more than the word of an aspiring criminal like you. There was only one Fielder shot, and it was from the inn's roof."

"She already double-crossed me, stealing that ring." Ard said. "Maybe she never actually shot."

Overseer turned the gun from Ard to Quarrah in an unspoken demand for further explanation. Quarrah took a deep breath. She might actually have thought a way out of this one.

"Silence Grit," Quarrah cut in. "I detonated a small cloud around my Fielder to cover the sound. I figured the Reggies would focus all their fire wherever they heard the gunshot. I made sure that was the rooftop." Ard glared at her, but she thought she could see a glimmer of a smile in his eyes. Quarrah shrugged. "I wanted to turn myself in, not get gunned down."

Overseer's gun swiveled back toward Ard. "She is more clever than you."

Ard opened his mouth to say something, but seemed to think better of it. Now it was Quarrah's turn to hide a grin.

For the first time, Overseer's large headpiece began to move in a satisfied nod. "The complexity of your ruse agrees with me. Clearly, you both have the mind to plan, and the mettle to execute." The Singler disappeared into her cloak. "Welcome to the Realm."

The fact that Quarrah was standing here after all these cycles was nearly too much for Ardor Benn to contain. Her very presence seemed to inspire him, causing him to talk a little more smoothly, lie a little more convincingly.

He had sought her for a year and a half without a single lead. Now she was here, her face painted white and her expression equally ghostly. The sound of her voice hummed in his brain, reaffirming how much he'd missed her. The mere sight of her seemed to resolve something that had festered, broken, since the night she'd left.

Their time apart clearly hadn't turned Quarrah into an expert liar, although she had convincingly sold that bit about Silence Grit around her gun. The look on her face told Ard that Quarrah was just as terrified to be admitted into the Realm as he was. However, the alternative was getting shot by Overseer, so they should both be celebrating this as a win.

Quarrah's glance kept darting to his face and away again, as though a lingering gaze could somehow burn her. Ard thought he caught a glimmer of relief behind her startled eyes, as though she couldn't believe he had awakened just in the nick of time.

In truth, Ard had come to on the couch long before he'd heard Quarrah stand up. By feigning to sleep on, it had given him the chance to collect his thoughts and make a dozen plans for a dozen possible outcomes. Quarrah's presence wasn't one he had predicted.

Hearing her speak to Overseer, Ard's heart had nearly burst from his chest, but he'd lain still, waiting to hear her story. He had joined the conversation at the last possible moment before every-thing spun out of control. Backing up Quarrah's story and patching some obvious holes was the surest way to make sure she didn't turn on him.

What was Quarrah Khai doing mixed up with the Realm? A secret organization of collaborative crime really didn't seem like her thing. Unless she had made a complete about-face, Quarrah was a lone wolf. She'd made that abundantly clear the night Ard had gone back to the palace to rescue Raek, and she had disap-peared into the darkness.

Even now, Ard could see the lingering resentment on her pale face. As if parting ways had been *his* idea! Sparks, she'd been the one who'd demanded he stop the ruse—leaving Raek to rot in the palace dungeon and Pethredote to get away with his crimes. She'd wanted him to change his very nature, and he would have tried, once all the loose ends of the ruse had been wrapped up.

Instead, her departure had only anchored his zeal deeper. He'd run dozens of successful ruses since that night, and his drive had served him well.

But his persistence hadn't been to spite Quarrah. It had been to find her. He'd decided if he didn't stop—if he kept rusing—eventually he'd cross Quarrah's path again. Because Homeland knew *she* wasn't going to stop thieving.

He just hadn't expected it to be *this* job.

"It is rare for the Realm to allow anyone to join its ranks," continued Overseer. "Most crimes marked with the painted face aren't worth breaking the person out of their cell. And those that do gain audience with me usually wind up dead in a room like this one."

"Well, then, I'm glad our crime was worthwhile," Ard said.

"It was bold," admitted Overseer, "but not particularly worthwhile. We already had plans in motion to kill Abeth Agaul. You simply acted a few minutes sooner."

*Sparks!* Good thing everything went off without a hitch.

"Out of curiosity," Ard said. "How were you guys going to do it?"

"I believe you encountered our assassination weapon," answered Overseer. "Forged in the night of the Moon's last Passing."

A chill crossed over Ard as he realized what was implied. Those Bloodeyes had been brought into Beripent. The Realm had released them to murder Abeth Agaul. And this wasn't the first instance. Had the Realm also been behind the Moonsick attack on Strind last cycle?

"Your crime, although redundant, was in line with the goals of the Realm, and efficiently carried out," said Overseer. "I hope you understand how rare it is that I offer you a place in our organization. Rarer still to admit two at once."

"I assure you," Ard replied, glancing at Quarrah, "we'll work well together."

"From here forward, any collaboration between the two of you will be unknowing," said Overseer. "Our organization functions on absolute secrecy."

That was why Ard had decided to spin them as little more than strangers uniting effectively for a job. It made the most sense, really. He knew the Realm thrived on anonymity. Such a group was likely to favor those who kept their personal relationships at arm's length.

"Outside of this room," continued Overseer, "neither of you will be aware that the other is part of the Realm."

"What about this conversation?" Quarrah asked. She'd been silent for a long time, seeming to absorb everything that was being said.

Overseer lifted her hand and made a sweeping gesture through the air in front of them.

"Memory Grit," Overseer answered. "None of this will remain in your minds. You will never recall this interaction with me, or with each other."

It made sense as a precaution. Conversely, it would benefit Ard. Assuming he and Quarrah made it out of this room alive, Overseer wouldn't be able to investigate their story about the assassination.

"But what if I look for Jerisa again when we get out?" Ard asked. "Once I realize she's not dead, and not in the Stockade, I'll be able to deduce that our plan worked and we both made it into the Realm."

"You are not making me feel very confident in my decision." Overseer's hand withdrew into her cloak, and Ard expected it to reappear with the Singler again.

Yeah. Maybe it was time to shut up. Why did Ard feel the need to point out a loophole in the enemy's logic, when that very loophole was helping him stay alive?

"Even if you found me outside—which you won't," Quarrah replied, "I wouldn't reveal anything to you. I'd say I escaped from the Stockade on my own. If you know anything about me, you'll know I'm capable of it."

Overseer nodded. "Once you join us, you will suspect many. But you will tell whatever lies are needed to keep yourself from suspicion. You will protect the secrecy of the Realm with your very life."

"Got it," Ard said. But there was one more thing nagging him. "If we won't remember any of this, then why are you wearing that mask?" He asked the question before he realized how much it sounded like a challenge.

Overseer turned her masked head slowly to focus on Ard. "Some risks are never worth taking." That same gloved hand reappeared, pinching two folded squares of paper. "Consider this your invitation to the next Faceless meeting."

"Faceless?" Ard pretended like he'd never heard of it, stepping forward to take the note.

"I oversee all operations of the Realm, counseling with others who are part of the Directorate," she explained. "Assignments are made to the Faceless, who then hire street Hands as needed to accomplish the jobs."

Ard unfolded his note.

*Deribesh Wax and Candles—27th of 10—8 o'clock morning.*

The twenty-seventh day of the Tenth Cycle was just over a week away! Beneath the writing was a simple symbol. It looked like a square divided into four equal parts, but the top right quadrant was missing.

"You'll find a carriage marked with that symbol waiting for you at those locations," explained Overseer. "Discreetly get inside and the Realm will deliver you to the meeting."

"How are we supposed to remember these instructions after we leave?" Quarrah asked, pocketing her square of paper.

"We will provide the necessary information," assured Overseer.

"And if we decide not to get in?" Ard always found it helpful to explore his options before he agreed to climb into mysterious carriages.

"If you ever fail to attend a Faceless meeting," said Overseer, "you will die."

Ard scrunched his eyebrows together, puzzled. "How do you find us if you won't remember this conversation? In fact, how do you even know who is in your little club?"

"Androt Penn and Jerisa Khailar," answered Overseer. "I authorized your rescue from the Outpost. And I will remain in this room until the Memory Grit burns out. When I find there are no bodies, I will know that both of you have become Faceless in the Realm."

"And if our carriage shows up empty," said Quarrah, "then you'll know we didn't come to the meeting."

"This time, yes," Overseer replied. "Your next pickup location will be given to you anonymously, and at that point I'll have no way to track who is coming and going in each carriage."

That seemed like a major flaw to Ard. And potentially a good way out. "You just expect everyone to keep coming?"

"The Realm provides incentive that will ensure your continued attendance whether we know your name or not," Overseer said. "We call it the Waters of Loyalty. You'll drink it at the beginning of every Faceless meeting."

"I don't tend to drink things from strangers," Quarrah admitted.

"Oh, but you already have."

Ard realized at once what Overseer was referring to. He chided himself for drinking from that cup in his cell, but then again, it was the reason he was here.

"The water at the Outpost," Quarrah muttered.

"An infusion of bluelock put you to sleep," said Overseer, "but that wasn't the only thing in the water."

"Poison?" Ard asked.

"Attend the Faceless meetings, and you will never have to find out," replied Overseer. "The Waters keep everyone loyal."

*And paranoid,* Ard thought, agonizing over the fact that he had no idea what deadly concoction could be churning around inside him right now.

Overseer turned her large, scaly mask toward the door. "We are finished here. There are two carriages outside that door. They will take you separate ways and release you into the city."

*Release,* Ard thought, *like a caged animal.*

"Tie your masks in place at the door and you will be guided out."

Ard and Quarrah followed the instructions, moving side by side to the exit. He pressed the eyeless, white leather mask against his bearded face and reached back to tie the ribbons behind his shaggy hair.

He felt a rush of cold air as the door opened. Impulsively, Ardor

Benn reached out blindly for Quarrah's hand. His fingers wrapped around hers and he whispered her name. There was so much he wanted to say, but she pulled free, and Ard sensed her moving outside.

Going after her, he stepped forward, sightlessly crossing the threshold and feeling with his feet.

He suddenly didn't know where he was. What was covering his face? The last thing Ard remembered was drinking that cup of water in the Outpost cell—obviously drugged. Was the Realm coming for him?

He reached up to untie the mask, but a cold blade suddenly pressed against the bare flesh of his neck.

"Do not speak," said a deep rumble of a voice. "Come with me." An iron grip on his arm guided him several steps forward. He heard the jingle of a harness and knew there must be horses near. Then he was guided up a rickety step. Was he entering a carriage?

The rough hands pushed him into a seat, and Ard felt the person withdraw.

"A carriage will be waiting for you at the location and time on your note," the voice said. "You have been poisoned, but the antidote will be given to you at the Faceless meeting. Leave the mask on the seat when you exit the cab. Welcome to the Realm."

The carriage door slammed shut.

~

*They despised us when we ascended to be like them.*

# CHAPTER

# 13

E xcellent work today, everyone!" Ard announced, abruptly entering through the back door of the Guesthouse Adagio. With his late-night return, he'd expected only Raek to be waiting up for him in the grand salon. But in addition to his partner, Codley Hattingson whirled, a short-barreled Singler appearing in his hand as the butler stood protectively over Lady Abeth Agaul, who was now dressed in the drab garments of a tradeswoman.

"Ashes and soot, Codley!" Ard flinched at the weapon. "It's just *me!*"

Codley swallowed, the apple in his thin neck bobbing visibly. "Thank the Homeland you're alive, Master Ardour!" He tucked the gun into his black vest. "Oh, I thought we were all for the grave, what with Master Raekon's Healer coach arriving late. There were two Moonsick people tearing into the Regulators on the street! *Moonsickness!* Do you hear me? In Beripent!"

"I hear you all right," Ard said, remembering the Bloodeye's head exploding over him in graphic detail.

"Where did they come from?" Lady Abeth asked. She looked well, for a dead woman. The ordeal of falsifying her own assassination didn't appear to shake her as much as Ard had expected. Instead of looking frightened or weary, her eyes seemed almost energized despite the late hour. After all, this was supposed to be drawing them nearer to her missing son.

Ard crossed the spacious room and dropped heavily onto one

of the soft divans near the large picture windows. "It doesn't make sense. Those Bloodeyes obviously originated on Pekal. I can't figure how they found their way into the heart of Beripent."

"Maybe it's spreading," Codley whispered. "Maybe it's finally reached us."

"That's not how it works." Raek sighed. "I've been trying to explain it to them, Ard. Moonsickness can't strike a select few out of the middle of a large population. If it had reached Beripent, we'd all have it."

"I heard rumors of this last cycle," Codley continued. "And not just in Beripent, but other major cities across the Greater Chain."

Lady Abeth nodded. "There was talk of it in Leigh, as well." The capital city of Dronodan wasn't as large as Beripent, but was geographically situated even farther from Pekal.

"The Holy Torch has failed," Codley muttered.

Raek rolled his eyes. "The Holy Torch is a bunch of dogmatic slag cooked up for the sole purpose of making you feel safe."

"That's blasphemy," Codley snapped. "You watch your Settled tongue in this house!"

"Do you also subscribe to the dragon-shield theory, like your partner?" Abeth asked Ard. Unlike her butler, she didn't seem the least bit riled.

"We've got good reason to believe it," Ard said. "Which is why I can join with Raek in assuring you that Moonsickness is *not* spreading into Beripent, or any of the other major cities."

"I saw those poor fellows with my own eyes," said Codley. "They had lost their minds."

"One of them definitely did," said Ard. "Blew it off, myself."

"How could two Moonsick people find their way off Pekal?" Lady Abeth asked.

"Too far to swim," Raek said. "Even for a Trothian."

Ard sighed. It was a good question. "Maybe they hitched a ride first thing after the Passing? Didn't let on that they'd spent the night on Pekal. In the first stage of the sickness, they would have lost their voices, but they wouldn't have been violent or insane for another few days."

"We've had our ears to the cobblestones all afternoon," Raek said, "but nobody has answers about the Bloodeyes. It's just a general feeling of fear in the streets. I suppose it was helpful in some ways."

"Helpful?" Codley cried. "How so?"

"Took some of the pressure off of us," Raek replied. "The sighting of two Bloodeyes in the middle of Beripent has a way of overshadowing anything else that might be going on."

"Like the assassination of the former queen," said Ard. "Or the arrest of the man who shot her."

"Wherever they came from," Raek said, "the Bloodeyes gave us some decent cover. And for the record, I was only late in picking you up because we had trouble hitching the guesthouse horses to the Healer's coach. Keyling is as stubborn as they come—ask Hedma. We finally had to yoke Acorn in her place."

Ard knew the mare had been suffering trauma since Beska had stolen her the night of her murder. Hedma Sallis had been working to rehabilitate the horse with late-night rides through the city.

"How did you get out of the Regulation Outpost?" Lady Abeth asked Ard.

"To be honest, I'm not really sure," he replied. "The Realm must have sprung me, but I was out cold from something they gave me to drink. Next thing I can remember I was being pushed into a carriage, wearing a mask with no eyeholes."

"That seems like a significant design flaw," Raek cut in.

"Uncomfortable, too," Ard added, slipping out of his coat. "I'd let you try it on, but they told me to leave it in the carriage when I got out."

"Which quarter of the city were you in when you got into the carriage?" asked Lady Abeth.

Ard shrugged. "I had that confounded mask on my face."

"You didn't even peek?" Raek asked.

Ard clucked his tongue in disapproval. "A gentleman never peeks." He sniffed self-consciously. "Okay. The carriage windows were blacked out. I couldn't see a thing. But I was in there for at least an hour before the driver dropped me at the Char."

"That would mean you were picked up somewhere near the outskirts of Beripent," said Codley.

"Unless he was driving in circles for an hour," Lady Abeth rebutted. "So, what's next, Inspector?"

Hmm. It was going to be an adjustment with her hiding at the guesthouse. At the very least, Ard would have to start wearing pants when he wanted to make a midnight visit to the kitchen.

"Please," he said. "Call me Ard." The fact that she hadn't yet commented on the inconsistency of his accent probably meant Raek had already told the story they'd prepared. Inspector Ardour Stringer was born on Dronodan, but had actually lived most of his life in Beripent. He'd affected his speech when meeting with the queen that night just to put her at ease.

Now they just had to explain why they'd been living at the guesthouse all this time.

"Once I took off the mask, I found this note in my pocket." Ard handed the small piece of paper to Lady Abeth, who read it aloud. "Deribesh Wax and Candles—North Central Harbor Market—twenty-seventh of Ten—eight o'clock morning." She looked up. "And you have no idea where it came from?"

Ard kicked off his boots, leaning back to put his feet up on the divan. "There must have been Memory Grit in play. The only thing I know is what the man who loaded me into the carriage told me." Ard lowered his voice in a quick impersonation. "A carriage will be waiting for you at the location and time on your note."

"I'm sure he didn't sound like *that*," replied Raek.

"He sounded *exactly* like that."

"So, the meeting's happening in a carriage..." Raek joked.

"I find that highly improbable, Master Raekon," said Codley. "The cab would have to be enormous."

Raek chuckled. "Or maybe the Faceless are all very tiny."

"I'm more concerned about where that carriage is going," Ard said, rescuing Codley from Raek's further sarcasm. "Raek will have to keep an eye on it from a safe distance. Track it to the actual location of the meeting."

"You know I love chasing you through town while you're riding in luxury. Especially when my foot is caught in a rat trap and I'm carrying fifty panweights of clamshells..."

"You're still worked up about the Killgan Ruse?" Ard said. "I barely remember things that happened last cycle, let alone five years ago."

"Well, it was memorable for me," said Raek. "I got a six-inch scar and an irreparable dint in my pride. We never even used those empty clams."

"I thought they'd be important," Ard said in self-defense. "Turned out a Roller was more effective at getting Killgan to talk."

"That sounds like a rather blunt method for an inspector," Codley interjected.

"We were undercover," Ard said.

"*Deep* undercover," seconded Raek.

"Anyway," Ard resumed, "it'll be different this time. Just trace my carriage to the location of the Faceless meeting and wait outside to see if you recognize anyone else."

Raek sighed melodramatically. "Fine. I'll clear my schedule."

"What are you planning to do once you arrive at the Faceless meeting?" asked Lady Abeth.

"I'll have a look around," answered Ard. "Talk to a few folks and see what I can learn about Shad."

"Without attracting too much attention by asking about him," interjected Codley nervously.

"That's a given," said Ard. "Mostly, I just need to get a feel for what these Realm folks do at their get-togethers. I'm hoping there'll be pastries." He wrinkled his brow. "And an antidote."

"Antidote?" Raek repeated.

"The voice that guided me into the carriage told me that I'd been poisoned," Ard explained. "I'll receive the antidote at the Faceless meeting. I suppose that's their way of making sure I go."

"Has the poison already set in?" Codley asked. "You look a bit peaky. How do you feel?"

Ard scoffed. *Peaky.* He still hadn't had a good wash since the face paint. "I feel fine. It must be a very slow-acting poison if I'm meant to survive until the twenty-seventh."

"Or the whole thing is a trick to keep you loyal," said Raek. "Maybe the poison's all in your head."

"I'd prefer not to risk it," Ard replied.

"If it is real, it's not very threatening," Raek continued. "It's easy enough to purge a poison." He dug into his pocket and produced a paper roll like the one he'd used after Ard had "smoked the chimney" in that room above the alley. "Ten minutes in a cloud of Health Grit will eliminate any toxins in your body." He tossed the roll to Ard. There was just a pinch of powder left at one of the twisted ends.

"Good idea," Ard said. "I'll use it tonight." At the very least it could ease some of his aches and bruises from fighting that Bloodeye.

"Just make sure you're lying down when you detonate it," said Raek. "There's a little Compounding Grit mixed with it. A bit on the strong side for me."

Compounded Health Grit? That stuff could be dangerous—and habit forming.

"Found it in Beska's cottage after she ran," Raek explained when he saw Ard's inquisitive look. "A single use shouldn't hurt you, especially if you really were poisoned."

Ard tucked the roll of Grit into his pocket and turned to Lady Abeth Agaul. "Now, on to the matter of your funeral."

"My funeral?" she repeated.

"You were brutally assassinated in the streets of Beripent," Ard pressed. "Your body has to end up somewhere. Word of your death will probably reach Dronodan by tomorrow morning. Your royal parents will be beyond distressed."

"This is the kind of stuff that could start a war," Raek said, "if we didn't already have a humdinger going."

Lady Abeth's countenance seemed to dim a little. Maybe she hadn't thought through this aspect of the ruse. Faking one's own death required total commitment—Ard would know. At least she had the potential of coming back from the dead once this was all over. She'd likely see her parents again, which was a luxury Ardor Benn could not afford.

His first ruse had set up his folks in a nice country home in leeward Espar. Raek had checked on them several cycles back to make sure the war hadn't disrupted their simple life. The Castenacs were fine, yet Ard couldn't help but feel a longing for them when he saw the look on Abeth's face.

"It won't be a true funeral," Ard continued, pushing past his personal thoughts. "Which is unfortunate, because I think you'd have a great time attending."

"What do you have in mind?" she asked.

"We send an empty coffin back to Dronodan on a small ship, but we hire the captain to dump it in the InterIsland Waters," explained Ard. "This convinces Beripent that your body was sent home. At the same time, our dear Codley sends a letter to your parents stating that you had expressed the desire to be interred in Beripent beside your husband and son. This convinces Dronodan. Everyone thinks they know where your body ended up, but it was actually never there."

"Like those fellows in the Char who put a gem under one of their seashells and shuffle them around to confuse you," added Raek.

"This plan sounds inordinately risky," Codley expressed. "It wouldn't take much investigation to determine that both islands had been scurrilously duped."

"We don't need to be totally convincing," said Ard, "just confusing enough to buy us a few weeks so we can find Shad Agaul and reveal the truth."

Lady Abeth nodded. "Let's go ahead with the plan." She sat forward, suddenly wringing her hands. "I have another concern, although it seems trivial in comparison to finding my son."

"What is it?" Ard asked, softening his voice as he often did to convince others to confide in him.

She held out her bare hand. "The Agaul family ring." Beside her, Codley Hattingson muttered something that might have been a curse. "It seems to have slipped off my finger before the assassination."

"And you're just mentioning this *now*?" Codley cried.

"I thought it might have been part of the plan," she answered. "Something Inspector—Ard had failed to mention in the planning letters."

Ard shook his head, mouth set crooked in a sympathetic frown. "I'm afraid not, m'lady."

"When did you first notice it was missing?" Codley asked, visibly struggling to maintain his composure.

"At the harbor. Before you greeted me at the carriage."

"You should have told me!" Codley cried. "You should have stopped the procession and initiated a search!"

"I didn't want to do anything that might jeopardize the success of the assassination!" she shot back. "My life was on the line, if you'll recall."

Her stern reply seemed to remind the butler of his place. He stiffened, tugging at his vest, squeaking out an official apology.

"I shall send someone to the harbor at once," Codley said. "The *Leeward Pride* is not set to depart until morning. I'll have the vessel scoured on the chance that it—"

"That ring is long gone," Raek cut in. "I don't mean to be insensitive, Your Former Highness, but if you drop a giant emerald ring in a crowded harbor, it's walking off with the first person who has a finger to put it on."

"And chances are, it wasn't dropped," Ard added.

"You're suggesting theft?" cried Codley. "The lady was wearing it on her very hand!" He turned to her. "You had it on, didn't you?"

Abeth nodded glumly.

"That doesn't provide you any real security," Ard said. "There are thieves and pickpockets out there with enough skills to steal the shirt right off your back."

"He would know," Raek said. "He was in a relationship with one." Ard shot him a steely glance. "Undercover again," his partner fumbled. "Big case."

Lady Abeth shrugged despondently. "At the very least, I beg you to keep an eye out for it. Perhaps exercise some of your investigative methods on behalf of the family heirloom? After all, if we succeed in finding my son, I'd like it to adorn his finger as further endorsement of his rule."

"Of course," Ard answered. But inwardly, he was shaking his head. He didn't have time to hunt down a stolen ring!

"Thank you," she said, a yawn creeping up on her. "Oh, it's been quite the day. There are plenty of guest cottages across the grounds. The two of you are welcome to stay the night, if you please."

Ard shot a half-panicked look at Raek, who instantly rose, positioning himself between Abeth and the butler. "Codley, my man! I've been meaning to ask you about this portrait over here." He slung one beefy arm around the butler's thin shoulders, steering him across the room. "That fellow with the eyebrows. Was he an Agaul or the inventor of the parasol...?"

Ard quickly took advantage of the distraction to smooth things over with Lady Abeth. "Did Codley not tell you? Oh, sparks. Now I feel like we've been taking advantage..."

"What?" she asked.

"Your butler invited us to stay as soon as we began the investigation," Ard said. "It was so much easier to coordinate our information about the missing prince. I assumed he had your permission."

She waved a hand. "No matter. You do now. And it'll keep us in close contact, since I'll be shut in here for the foreseeable future." She gestured over her shoulder to the royal suite.

"If it's all the same," continued Ard, "maybe don't mention this to Codley. You know how uptight he can get."

She widened her eyes dramatically. "Especially if he thinks he's done something wrong."

"Not wrong by our account. We're quite enjoying our stay." Ardor Benn threw her a winning smile.

～

*We extended our dwellings beyond the boundaries.*

# CHAPTER
# 14

Waiting in the Mooring's large entry room filled Portsend Wal with familiar feelings. The smell of the waterway, the damp saltiness of the air, and his heart beating faster at the thought of soon being alone with Gloristar. All these feelings were no different from the ones he'd felt during years past, waiting in this foyer for one of the young Isles to pole him to Cove 14.

But Portsend acknowledged the new feelings now, as well. Awe for Gloristar's holy position, a mix of excitement and anxiety for the discoveries he'd made, and a harrowing pit in his stomach at the thought of presenting this new Grit to a tyrant like King Termain.

Portsend shuffled his feet, absently examining the large display in the center of the room. It was a dragon egg, gelatinous and unfertilized, suspended in some sort of fluid in a huge glass container. His eyes fell to the placard, inscribed with a verse from *Wayfarist Voyage*.

*"Life is the keeper of life. It is the love of a guardian. A seed in the soil. An unhatched egg."*

"I had expected you to visit me in Cove One." Gloristar's voice caused him to turn, an irresistible smile encroaching onto his face. She looked well—possibly a little sleep deprived, but if that was all the trouble that had befallen her under Termain's thumb, then Portsend considered it a win.

He hadn't allowed himself to visit her new cove. There would be no point to it, aside from socializing and commiserating. And Portsend couldn't allow the distraction right now. Couldn't allow himself to be alone with Gloristar when they were both so afraid and vulnerable.

"I've been so busy," he settled on saying.

And indeed, he had been. Two weeks had passed since the unexpected explosion in the laboratory. They had managed to extinguish the fire before everything was lost, but the lab was unusable. Now he owed the college a whole term at half pay to restore his space to working order.

In the meantime, his only option was to use a student laboratory. It was frustrating in the wake of his incredible, albeit accidental, discovery. Portsend had to work around the student schedules, reserving the lab for limited chunks of private research time with San and Lomaya. And worse, he had to lug all of the scroll's materials to and from his apartment just off campus. Technically, Brase and Luthe did most of the lugging, but Portsend had to make careful plans about which materials he wanted to test in each session.

All of this meant a full week had passed before Portsend's tests yielded consistent results giving him a decent understanding of what they had discovered. Brase had delivered a vague letter to Gloristar, which was answered promptly. But another week had passed before the appointment with Termain had been confirmed.

"The carriage is ready." Portsend gestured outside through the open doors.

"We shouldn't keep His Highness waiting." Gloristar led the way out of the Mooring. Her appearance on the steps sparked a wave of outrage from the gathered crowd of protesters. Portsend had seen them on his way in, but they had been much quieter then.

An attendant opened the carriage door and the two of them quickly climbed inside for the short ride to the palace.

"Do they gather every day?" Portsend asked, drawing the curtain over the window as they moved through the heckling crowd.

She nodded. "They have their demands. And to be honest, I agree with most of them."

"Such as?"

"Some call for my resignation as Prime, or at least a denunciation of King Termain's rule," she answered. "Others demand that I address the issues of the Holy Torch or remove the dragon egg in the Mooring entryway."

"Why haven't you?" Portsend asked. He understood her position with King Termain, but removing the egg seemed like an easy concession. "Or at the least, take down the verse?"

"Will it strengthen their faith to hide everything that may suddenly seem controversial?" Gloristar responded. "This religion is based upon generations of belief. Truth does not change just because a few radicals sow doubt in the streets."

The verse was controversial, all right. Portsend had heard the new theories—that the dragons, not the Holy Torch, protected the islands from Moonsickness. It was blasphemous, and Portsend didn't see the logic to support it.

Advocates of this "new doctrine" claimed that the decline in dragon population was causing the spread of Moonsickness. It was a doomsday theory, since dragons were on the fast path to extinction. But lately, he'd heard rumors about that, too.

"What do you make of the reports about a young bull dragon on Pekal?" Portsend asked. "Falsehood?"

"I think the reports are too many to discredit," she answered.

"But how would that be possible?"

"Perhaps an egg sat dormant, or incubation was somehow drawn out. Or perhaps it was something holier."

"A Paladin Visitant?" Did the fabled fiery beings have that kind of power?

"I cannot say," Gloristar replied. "But the Homeland is good, Portsend. If the bull dragons have indeed returned, I shall call it a miracle."

It was good to talk like this. Like being in Cove 14 in years past. Simply being near Gloristar rekindled his religious beliefs. Her statements, bold and inspiring, made him never want to doubt.

"I'm sorry it took so long to arrange this," she said. "His Majesty did not want to make himself available."

"That surprises me," replied Portsend. "I thought he would be anxious to hear what we had to say."

"He is more anxious to demonstrate his power over me," said Gloristar. She gave him a pained look. "I told him I had information that could greatly benefit the Archkingdom. He is likely desperate to know what it is, but would rather let me stew in my own request for an audience with him. To make me wonder if I'm still relevant at all."

Relevant! She was the Prime Isless of Wayfarism! And didn't Gloristar's endorsement, given under duress, prove that Termain knew exactly how relevant she was?

"Well, a little extra time may have worked in our favor," Portsend replied. "I've made even more advances since my letter."

"I'm anxious to learn about it all," said Gloristar. "But I should warn you. Termain will likely downplay anything you give him. We need to make a convincing case that what you are presenting is worthwhile."

"New Grit, Gloristar," Portsend whispered. "The first new type in nearly two hundred years. How could that not be worthwhile?"

She held up a hand. "Can it be weaponized?"

*Weaponized?* Portsend hadn't told her any details about the Grit, and this was her first question?

"Termain is only interested in things that will help him gain an upper hand in the war," Gloristar explained. "When you speak to him, do everything you can to make your new Grit seem threatening and powerful."

It wouldn't be a stretch to think of the militaristic uses, but Portsend certainly hadn't been planning to lead with those. It frightened him to know that Gloristar had to think this way.

Although the Greater Chain had divided, Wayfarism still had significant influence in Dronodan and Talumon. Gloristar was the Prime Isless over the whole religion. As such, her first responsibility was supposed to be to the followers of her faith—instructing them, nurturing them. That said, the Prime Isle had always professed some political affiliation. It wasn't mandatory for Wayfarists to agree, but it had that effect on most.

As it was, Portsend realized that Gloristar was in a terrible conundrum. She was fulfilling her first obligation to protect Wayfarism by agreeing to Termain's terms. But by so doing, she was helping develop new Grit that could turn the war, leading to hundreds of deaths—most of them likely to be Wayfarists.

"Brase and Luthe are keeping you well?" She changed the subject, parting the curtain just enough to peer out the carriage window.

"I believe this is the first time I've been out of their sight in cycles," answered Portsend. "Good lads."

"And your young research companions?"

"They work with an incredible energy," he reported, "especially after we made our first discovery. I promised to sing their praises to the king."

Gloristar looked sharply at him. "You told them you were meeting with His Majesty?"

Portsend nodded slowly, but her tone and look had already tipped him off to his mistake. "To report our findings."

"You must not mention either of them to the king. For their safety, you claim to work alone." Gloristar looked out the window again.

Portsend took a deep breath and decided to ask it. "How can we end this, Gloristar? How can we get the Anchored Tome back?" Doing so would finally get her out from under Termain's control.

She inhaled sharply, as though to steady herself. "Trust me, I am exploring every option."

"There has to be *something* we can do," he pressed.

"We fulfill the king's demands and help him win the war, for now," said Gloristar. "And we pray to the Homeland that he doesn't destroy the Anchored Tome."

"The Homeland will see you succeed." Portsend tried his best to speak faithfully. "It is your very destiny, Gloristar. It's always been right there, in our verse—"

"Perhaps we should not mention our verse again," she said, cutting him off.

Portsend choked back the sudden well of emotion. Did she truly feel that way? Perhaps their verse seemed trivial or coquettish now that she had become Prime Isless. But it still mattered to him.

"I hardly feel worthy of my namesake anymore," Gloristar whispered as the carriage came to a halt.

Portsend wanted to reassure her, but what could he say that would matter? Instead, he reached out a hand and placed it softly on her knee.

The carriage door opened, Portsend whipping his comforting hand away as the attendant folded out the steps. Portsend followed Gloristar out, trying not to show too much awe as they ascended the palace steps. According to the reports he'd heard, a dragon had stood on these very stones just over a year and a half ago. The reconstructed palace still showed damage, but Portsend was amazed at how quickly they'd been able to rebuild.

They entered the building, following a pair of red-uniformed Regulators up a flight of stairs. Gloristar seemed calm and confident, and Portsend tried to emulate her. The truth was, he was quaking in his boots, taking in the grand masonry, trimmings, and artwork on the walls. He'd never been in the palace before—and he'd certainly never been summoned to meet a king.

It passed in a blur, and soon Portsend found himself in the legendary throne room, staring at the skull of Grotenisk the Destroyer. The giant head of the bull dragon sprawled as a centerpiece, a throne cut from marble atop the skull. Two chimney pipes rose behind the seat like columns, providing ventilation for the bonfire that always blazed in the dragon's mouth.

Except the fire had gone out—even the embers looked cold.

From what Portsend understood, the fire hadn't died in decades. It was an emblem. A symbol of mankind's survival against the dragon that had once destroyed Beripent.

"We're still, um, looking for His Majesty," one of the Regulators said. "I'm sure he will be here shortly." He gestured to his companion and the two of them awkwardly dismissed themselves.

Portsend glanced over his shoulder. There were still two guards at the door, but otherwise, he and Gloristar were alone in the grand room. He stepped aside, examining the empty alcoves that pocked the walls of the triangular-shaped room.

"Those were used to display relics from previous monarchies." Gloristar's quiet voice still echoed through the room. "And those doors lead to the balcony where the kings and queens used to make addresses."

There were unspoken *but*s to both her statements. First, the relics, *but King Termain didn't want to celebrate successful monarchs of the past*. Second, the balcony, *but King Termain refused to address the public*. Now the doors were boarded up, probably soon to be walled over completely.

"Perhaps you should set up your demonstration while we wait," Gloristar suggested, drawing Portsend away from the empty alcoves. He was happy to oblige, as the preparations would calm his nerves during the awkward wait.

Taking a knee, Portsend produced three empty trays from his satchel and placed them several feet apart. To the first, he added a previously measured amount of Light Grit; to the second, Shadow Grit; and to the third, Barrier Grit. He was still tidying the little piles when a voice caused Portsend and Gloristar to turn.

"Good afternoon, ladies!"

King Termain had just entered the throne room. Portsend was puzzled by his greeting. It was definitely morning, Portsend clearly wasn't a lady, and why the blazes was the king *naked*?

Termain had only a small towel wrapped around his waist and he was soaking wet. His unruly black hair was matted and dripping, with three days of stubble across his chin. His skin was pale, especially his legs and hairy torso. He looked somewhat fit, except for a drooping stomach that spoke of too much ale.

The king held his towel in place with one hand as his bare feet padded across the throne room, leaving little puddles with each step. As he passed Portsend's setup, he gestured at the items on the floor.

"What's all this? Who left this slag lying around my throne room?"

Only then did Portsend gain the presence of mind to bow.

Already on one knee, he lowered his head. "It is my demonstration, Your Majesty." Sparks, it was hard to keep his voice from trembling. He rose, daring to look up at the king, who now stood in front of him.

"Who said you could stop bowing?" Termain snapped. Portsend instantly dropped to one knee again.

"Ha! I'm joking!" called Termain. "Homeland, can't you take a joke?"

Portsend faltered, not knowing what to do until Gloristar reached out and placed a hand on his shoulder. He rose to his feet again, trembling.

"So, I had these bathtubs brought up to every floor—the big ones that use Heat Grit to warm the water." Termain moved alongside the dragon skull. "Between the hot water, the wine, and the twins," he shrugged, "I forgot all about this blazing meeting."

He pulled himself up the side of the skull with surprising agility, somehow managing not to lose his towel until he sat down on the throne, legs sprawled wide. Termain reclined, pulling the towel to cover the ugliest bits, but still showing an unfortunate amount of hairy thigh.

"It's freezing in here." He shivered. "Let's hurry up and get this over with. What've you got?"

Portsend held back his fury as Gloristar studied the floor. This was the ruler of the kingdom, sitting naked atop a burned-out throne in an empty room. Well, that seemed to accurately sum up Termain's kingship.

"We're here with information that could be greatly beneficial to the Archkingdom, Your Majesty," Gloristar said, refusing to look at the throne.

"Hopefully something to blow the Sovereign States to little chunks?" he said.

No matter that the king was much different than expected,

Portsend needed to deliver his presentation the way he had rehearsed it. That way, he'd be sure to properly represent the science and mechanics of what he'd discovered. He could add tailored bits about weaponizing the Grit as he went.

Portsend cleared his throat. "I would like to begin by thanking Your Highness for providing the invaluable materials for my experimentation."

"I did? Old Purple Robes did most of the work." He gestured at Gloristar. "I just had to sign off on the papers. It's amazing that this kingdom used to function at all with how much legwork Pethredote had in place. I've only been on the throne for seventeen cycles, and I've got the process down to a single signature in the presence of only one notary." He clapped his hands. "Efficiency!"

*Homeland help us,* Portsend thought. *I'm about to give up powerful secrets to a total imbecile.* But he wasn't doing this for Termain or the Archkingdom. This was for Gloristar's safety and the perpetuity of Wayfarism.

"Throughout all of known history, there have only ever been fifteen types of Grit," Portsend continued, getting back to his prepared speech. "The latest was Illusion Grit, discovered by Usclad Marg in 1029 and believed to be the final type. Until today."

Portsend reached into his satchel and withdrew a small glass vial stopped with a cork. The murky liquid inside was dyed red, and a little fragment of Slagstone had settled at the bottom.

"I present to Your Majesty," Portsend stretched forth his arm, pinching the vial carefully between two fingers, "Ignition Grit."

Termain Agaul leaned forward, squinting at the item in Portsend's hand. "That's no Grit pot."

"This is something entirely new," replied the professor. "A Grit *solution.*"

"You watered it down," stated the king. "I'm supposed to be impressed?"

Portsend was flustered by the frequent interjections. His students certainly never commentated his lectures like this. And it was much more than simply watering down the Grit. Portsend took a deep breath. He could do more than impress the king. He could confuse him.

"The liquid is an infusion of hodgegrass, steeped long enough to bring the balance level of the water to a negative flat five," Portsend said. He hadn't planned on explaining the science, but he was going way off script anyway. Might as well show the brilliance that had gone into this discovery.

"The Grit used in this experiment was processed, powdered gold," Portsend continued, "which, under normal circumstances, would yield a Barrier cloud. Grit is not supposed to be soluble, and diluted like this in water, traditional Grit would never ignite. Yet, this simple liquid infusion of hodgegrass, carefully steeped to the right balance level, effectively dissolved the Grit."

Portsend took a moment to relish in his superior intellect over the king. Termain had turned his attention to the ceiling halfway through Portsend's explanation and had a far-off look in his eye.

"Fascinating!" the naked king shouted, suddenly looking back to Portsend. "But what does it *do*?"

Portsend sucked in a steadying breath. Hopefully, his brief lecture had proven his value and intellect. Now it was time to cater to the king's warmongering appetite.

"It blows things up."

From atop his throne, Termain Agaul grinned. "More potent than Blast Grit?"

"Something altogether different," Portsend said. "Allow me a short demonstration?" It was always considerate to seek permission from others in the room before igniting any type of Grit. Especially in front of a touchy king.

"Let's see what you've got." Termain folded his arms across his bare chest and shivered.

"I have here three types of familiar Grit." Portsend gestured to the trays he'd set out. "And if you'll spare me a moment, I'll prepare another that may benefit Your Highness."

Quickly, Portsend retrieved another tray from his satchel and a pot of Grit he hadn't necessarily planned on using. Removing the wax plug, he emptied the contents onto the fourth tray, stepping back to explain each type.

"Light, Shadow, Barrier, and"—he gestured to the one he'd just placed—"Heat Grit. None of these trays are equipped with Slag-stone or any other catalyst." He held up the vial once more. "This Ignition Grit will cause each type of Grit to ignite simultaneously. Please observe."

Standing more than three yards from the trays, Portsend tossed the vial against the stone floor at his feet. The thin glass shattered and the Slagstone fragment sparked, a rush of energy emanating from the spot. In front of him, the four Grit types detonated, each throwing a visible cloud that hung domelike over the floor, side by side.

King Termain stood up slowly, walking along the top of the huge skull until he perched right atop the nose. It was not a good angle for a man covered only with a damp towel.

"Well, ashes and soot," he muttered. "You just sparked four detonations at once." He scampered down the dragon's nose, com-pletely losing his towel in the effort. Portsend and Gloristar averted their eyes as he gathered it back into place.

King Termain stepped into the fourth cloud, visibly relaxing as the warmth from the Heat Grit enveloped his dripping body. "Your Ignition Grit is a blazing fine parlor trick," he said. "But how does it kill people?"

Portsend swallowed, the weight of the king's statement pressing itself against him. He shuffled his feet, feeling bits of fragile glass crumble under the soles of his boots.

"From a militaristic standpoint, this Ignition Grit could be highly useful," Portsend began hesitantly. "It could be used in a preemptive strike to ignite and eliminate your enemy's Grit supply."

"Not just their Grit," added Termain. "If an infantryman's belt explodes, the soldier wearing it doesn't have much chance. That's good. What else?"

"I should mention that Ignition Grit will only cause other types of Grit to ignite if they are out and exposed," Portsend said. This was the only reason why his *entire* laboratory hadn't exploded. In the aftermath, he had found that there was no reaction from Grit that was held in closed containers.

"So Grit pots won't ignite?" Termain asked.

"Not if they are properly sealed," answered Portsend.

"I'm less impressed. What about Blast Grit cartridges?"

"I can't say," replied Portsend. There was a chance that the Ignition cloud could penetrate the paper wrapping on the gun cartridges. If that were the case, then Portsend's new discovery would be far more deadly on the battlefield than he'd realized.

"What's the radius?" Termain asked.

"Like other Grit types, that depends completely on the quantity detonated," answered Portsend. "It creates what I call a flash cloud. Unlike the lingering detonation clouds of other Grit types, this one exists for only a brief second. Just long enough to set off any other Grit in its radius."

"I'll admit," Termain said, turning to Gloristar. "Your boy found us something that might actually be worth looking into."

Gloristar didn't reply.

Termain turned back to Portsend. "You'll give a full report of this to my chief Mixer. We'll need to begin mass production and distribution to the troops. But we also have to make sure that the Sovereign States don't figure this out. Ignition Grit is the Archkingdom's secret, and I want to keep it that way for as long as possible. Give us a chance to blow apart as many of those Sovs as we can."

As he spoke, Termain stepped out of his cloud of warmth and strode past Portsend and Gloristar, making for the exit.

"Are we finished here?" Gloristar called out. Her voice was terse and she refused to turn around and face him.

Portsend saw the king pause in the doorway just long enough to glance back at them. "Unless you'd like to join me in the bath, Isless." And then he was gone.

~

*They loved what they could control.*

# CHAPTER

# 15

Ardor Benn decided he was in for quite the experience if it took an entire sheet of instructions just to get him dressed for the Faceless meeting.

He had found the carriage waiting for him in front of Deribesh Wax and Candles, which had turned out to be a little shop in the upper Southern Quarter. The black carriage looked just like any one of the hundreds of hired cabs working the city. It was small and drawn by a single standardbred horse. Upon closer inspection, Ard had seen the small symbol from his paper chalked next to the door handle—a divided square with the top right quadrant missing. At the time Ard had climbed in, there hadn't been a driver. But within five minutes, the carriage had lurched forward and Ard knew he was on his way.

Most carriages had curtains for the windows, but Ard had quickly discovered that these were heavier, the hems tacked down, completely obscuring his view out. He was blazing curious to know where he was being taken, but something told him it wouldn't be a good idea to tear up the curtain's edge to see.

Besides, Raek was following from a safe distance, so they'd know exactly where the meeting would take place.

Ard unclasped his Grit belt and Rollers, reluctantly setting them aside on the bench. The instructions he'd found with the disguise clearly stated that no personal items could be brought into a Faceless meeting—that members would be frisked at the door, resulting in a slit throat if so much as an Ashlit was found in a pocket.

Ard sighed. Couldn't someone have mentioned that *before* he got in the carriage? He withdrew his boot knife and a little sack of Ashings that was supposed to be his pastry money for after the meeting.

The sheet informed him that any items left in the carriage would be considered a "donation" to the Realm. Ard preferred to call it "extortion."

The first thing Ard put on was a strange-looking yoke, like the type that secured an ox's neck when pulling a wagon. This one was smaller, obviously built for a human neck. Still, Ard felt uneasy as he clasped a thick leather strap across his throat to keep it in place on his shoulders. At least it had some padding.

Next, he slipped into a pair of leather gloves before unfolding the large bundle of black fabric on the seat next to him. It was an oversized cloak, looking more like a blanket with sleeves. He put his arms through, cinching the sleeves tightly around his wrists. With some effort, he managed to direct his head through the hole, shaking it out over his wooden shoulders.

Ard felt like a walking tent in this thing, but he instantly realized its value. With the yoke across his shoulders, and the cloak shrouding his body, no one would be able to tell if he was male or female, slender or portly.

Suddenly, the carriage stopped. Ard almost panicked, only half-way into his disguise. Outside, he could hear the hubbub of a large crowd. Were they in the Char? No. There were too many whistles blowing. People shouting street names and fares.

This was a carriage station. By the sound of it, North Central Carriage Station.

His cab rolled forward again, leaving the sounds behind before coming to a halt once more. Outside, Ard could hear the jingle of other harnesses, and the creak of many wheels. If he had to guess, he was now in the carriage yard.

This stop didn't last more than a few minutes before he was on the move once more, the hustle of the station fading to the regular thump of the road.

Strange. Maybe the driver needed to pick up directions? Ard turned his attention back to costuming.

The instruction sheet said the voice modifier was optional, but Ard decided to give it a try. It looked like a small cube of soft wax with a thin wooden rod running through it, the stick's rounded ends jutting out a half inch on either side of the wax.

He pressed the wax onto his top teeth, with the rod sitting horizontally in his mouth, the rounded ends pressing against the inside of his cheeks, bulging them like a crazed squirrel. The wax had a sweet taste, but the thing was blazing uncomfortable.

"A troubled Trothian trading tricks is truly trivial," he said, quoting one of the diction warm-ups Cinza had drilled into Quarrah during their singing rehearsals.

Ard found it relatively easy to speak, but the modifier made his voice sound hollow and strange. The wooden rod expanded the resonance of his mouth, slightly lowering the pitch and altering the timbre.

Next to go on was the mask. It was white and largely feature-less, like the one he had worn before. Gratefully, this mask had eye-holes, although a fine black-mesh fabric had been sewn over the inside. Where his mouth would be, there were a series of small vertical slices in the leather to help with ventilation. Ard couldn't help but think that it looked like oversized sutures stitching the mask's mouth shut.

Ard pressed it onto his face, tying it firmly behind his head. Then, as a finishing touch to his costume, he raised the cloak's hood, finding a series of buttonholes in the hem that secured through little hooks around the edge of the mask.

No sooner had he finished than the carriage came to a halt and the door swung open. He had to turn his absurdly broad shoulders to pass through the doorway, stepping down to a graveled road.

Ard had hoped to get a glimpse of his surroundings, but the morning sun was completely blotted out, only a short, dark tunnel leading him to an open door ahead.

*Shadow Grit,* he realized. They had overlapped clouds of Shadow Grit to make an archway of darkness. Oh, Raek was going to like this, from wherever he was watching.

Ard moved to the building, only able to see a few inches of brick trim around the door. Two large guards were waiting at the threshold, black masks concealing their faces, but otherwise undisguised. They gave him a good frisking and, finding nothing unusual, let him pass without a word.

The room he had just entered was some twenty yards wide and as many long. With only two small detonations of Light Grit, it was dimly lit, and fairly hazy.

The haziness, he realized, must have been Silence Grit, because the moment he stepped past the guards, the subtle sounds of the meeting suddenly reached his ears. The Silence Grit made sense for the Realm to ensure secrecy against eavesdroppers from outside.

Ard squinted through his mesh-covered eyeholes. The room was already full of people, their figures masked and cloaked in the exact same fashion as Ard. They milled about, studying each other from behind their white masks, the only sound the swishing of their cloaks and the padding of their feet on the wooden floor. The group looked inhuman and intimidating, like formless ghouls adrift in the dim room.

Another person entered through the doorway behind Ard, prompting him to move forward and explore the space. He walked carefully, trying not to bump into anyone, which proved to be a difficult task with that confounded yoke jutting out beyond his shoulders.

Ard tried to get a head count, but it was surprisingly difficult when everyone looked the same. There were at least thirty people, possibly as many as fifty. The only interactions he observed between Realm members were acknowledging nods. Although he couldn't see any eyes through the mesh coverings, Ard couldn't shake the feeling that they were all studying one another, searching in vain for any identifying clue.

On the opposite side of the room, Ard discovered a raised stage, accessed by three sets of wooden stairs. The front edge of the platform was lined with tin cups. They looked almost decorative, so carefully set and evenly spaced. On the stage was a lectern, and three small tables, each with a candle burning beside an empty bowl.

As Ard studied the setup, four figures descended from a staircase at the back of the stage. They each wore the same cloak, shoulders unnaturally broadened by the yoke-like structure. But each one wore a unique mask. More of a headpiece really, eliminating any need for a hood.

One had antlers rising from what looked like a bleached skull. Another bore brightly colored feathers. The third had a mask adorned with ocean shells. The last one had a single pointed horn that curved upward from a forehead stubbed with barbs.

They were at once majestic and frightening, each showing a twisted face to conceal the real one underneath.

Ard assumed he was looking at members of the Directorate, because their presence immediately changed the attitude of the

Faceless on the floor. Those wearing simple white masks grew still, each turning to face the stage. Ard found himself uncomfortably at the front of the crowd.

The figure with the feathered headpiece raised a gloved hand through an oversized cloak.

"We are the Realm."

Ard startled as everyone in the room began speaking in unison, their voices distorted from the voice modifiers, sounding otherworldly.

"We are the shape of the shadow. The eyes in the darkness. We do not grin or grimace, but we are the cause of both. Faceless, we unite, serving our silent cause until Ashings, so abundant, spill from our very mouths. We are the Realm."

A chill passed through Ardor Benn as the cryptic recitation ended.

"Come, all," spoke Feather Head. Despite the distortion, Ard could tell that it was a man's voice. "Drink of the Waters of Loyalty."

The Waters of Loyalty... Sounded like an antidote to Ard. He had used the Compounded Health Grit several days ago. Raek had been right to warn him against its potency. That stuff had relaxed him so much he hadn't been able to muster the strength to stand. If there had been poison inside him, that cloud would surely have purged it. Still, it seemed like a good idea to err on the side of redundancy and take whatever was being offered here.

All around him, Faceless were taking turns stepping forward, gloved hands appearing through their shrouding cloaks to remove a tin cup from the edge of the stage. As they stepped away, each figure lifted the cup to his or her masked lips, but Ard couldn't see if they were actually drinking anything. How could they, through their masks? They didn't even tip back the cups.

Those that were finished moved to either side of the stage, casting the cups into large barrels, the clattering sounds filling the otherwise silent area.

Ard waited until about half the cups were gone before moving up to the edge of the stage. He peered into the nearest one to see that it was indeed full of some sort of liquid. Now he could also see a length of reed in the cup, thin and woody, long enough to stand a few inches over the cup's rim.

Ard picked up a cup, stepping away from the stage. Lifting it to his mask's mouth, he sniffed sharply, but he couldn't smell anything other than the leather over his nose. He inserted the thin reed through one of the ventilation slits of his mask and curled his lips around it like a drinking straw, taking a sip.

Definitely not plain water. The liquid had an intensely bitter taste, like a bad, unsweetened tea that was neither hot nor cold.

Ard found he couldn't gulp it down as fast as he would have liked while sucking through that thin reed with the voice modifier in his mouth. Still, the cup was soon empty, though the bitterness lingered. He moved across the room and pitched the tin cup into one of the barrels, turning his attention back to the stage.

The figure with the horned mask was positioned behind the lectern off to the side, while the other three stood behind the tall tables, meeting one at a time with the Faceless who had finished drinking the Waters of Loyalty.

The interaction provided very little to see. With their masks in place, it was hard to tell if they were quietly conversing or simply staring at one another.

Antler Head appeared to write on something before passing it to the Faceless, who took up another scribing charcoal and wrote back.

Then Antler Head picked up the scrap of paper and touched it to the candle flame, dropping the note into the metal bowl once it was burning.

Through the smoke wafting upward, they began what Ard assumed was another indecipherable conversation. Antler Head was now holding a large book, turning pages before marking something down.

The Faceless who'd been meeting with Feather Head stepped away from the table, moving over to the lectern. Horn Mask accepted a piece of paper from the Faceless and handed over what was obviously a sack of Ashings.

Immediately, another Faceless took the stage, beginning a process that looked identical to what he'd seen with Antler Head's client.

Ard watched for about a half an hour, trying to detect patterns, or glean any useful information. The Faceless seemed to approach the stage in no particular order or summoning. Once they left the table, they moved to the lectern and received payment from Horn Mask. After that, they lined up at the door and exited one at a time, presumably as quickly as the carriages could pull into the Shadow Grit archway.

Who were these people, coming and going in utmost secrecy? The anonymity of the Realm was surely intended to provide a measure of security for its members. Strangely, Ardor Benn didn't find much confidence at all in hiding behind a mask. He thrived in the spotlight, but this oversized costume put him on the same playing field as everyone else in the room.

The crowd of Faceless was dwindling now, and Ard didn't think it seemed like a smart idea to be the last one in the room. He needed to move onto the stage and speak with one of the superiors. But what would they talk to him about? What if they sniffed him out as an imposter?

Wait. He *wasn't* an imposter. He'd been invited to this meeting fair and square. In a ruse, Ard referred to this as Riding the Milk Cow. It was that moment when enough groundwork had been laid that his presence was actually legitimate. He'd achieved it as Dale Hizror, not only invited to the royal receptions but welcomed as an honored guest. This was still a ruse, and Ard knew he needed to go forward with that same confidence now, even though no one could see his face.

There was an opening on the stairs leading up to Antler Head's table. The moment the Faceless departed, Ard moved in, careful not to trip on the front of his long cloak.

He stepped up to the tall desk, noting the metal bowl full of ash, a plume of smoke trailing upward. In the flickering candlelight, the antlered headpiece looked wicked and morose. The skull was more detailed than Ard had noticed from the floor, likely made from pieces of real bone.

"I fear I'm going gray," Antler Head said. Although altered, the voice was clearly feminine.

"Some would call it a mark of wisdom," Ard replied, hoping Staug Raifen had given them good information.

Antler Head didn't react negatively, so Ard let out a quiet sigh of relief behind his mask.

The woman picked up a scribing charcoal and drew a circle on a piece of paper. She slid it across the desk to Ard, who stared at it, puzzled.

"Ah," she said when he didn't move. "This is your first meeting."

He tried to shrug, but it was too awkward with the yoke on his shoulders. "Gotta start somewhere."

"Welcome," said Antler Head. "You are now Faceless in the Realm—those who wear the white mask of duty. You report only to the Directorate—those who wear the full headpieces."

"Got it. Street Hands, Faceless, Directorate," Ard repeated the levels. "Who does the Directorate answer to?"

"We counsel together in all matters, under the direction of our leader, Overseer. This is the symbol of the Realm." She pointed to the paper.

"A circle?" Ard lifted an eyebrow under his mask. Not as cryptic as he would have guessed.

"The symbol is drawn in stages," she went on. "The Directorate will scribe the circle, to which you will add as many markings as you have learned," she answered. "Each time you complete a job, you have an opportunity to learn the next line of the symbol." She picked up the charcoal and drew a vertical line, dissecting the circle in half. "This is the first."

"And this is how you track our progress," Ard said.

Antler Head nodded. "It is how we know at a glance how capable and trustworthy you are. And how much you will get paid."

."What happens when I learn the whole symbol?" Ard asked.

"You will continue to serve at that maximum level," she said, "making more Ashings than your associates. Waiting to be considered, should a vacancy arise in the Directorate."

Honestly, that was more than Ard had hoped to learn. Being an entry-level Faceless wasn't likely to give him much information— certainly not the kind he needed to learn about Shad Agaul.

"Serve well," said Antler Head, "and you will rise with time."

How much time? The fake assassination had driven Lady Abeth into hiding, and the Archkingdom was a sinking ship under King Termain's rule.

He would have to find a way to move up through the Realm quickly.

Antler Head opened the large book on the desk, angling it so Ard couldn't see the text. "There is a clockmaker in the Western Quarter by the name of Gregious Mas," she said. "He has recently developed a small clock that is not driven by weights or pendulum."

Ard had seen them popping up on the mantelpieces of a few noble manors within the last year. They were boxy and small, quite unlike the upright pendulum clocks that people were familiar with. Raek had pulled one right off Lord Stend's shelf, calling it witchcraft with a curious grin.

"The Realm needs you to steal twenty-five of these chainspring mantel clocks," said Antler Head. "You will deliver them to a Grit Mixer, who goes by the name Ticktock. You can find her in Stylet, operating out of a blue barn on the north end of town."

"How long do I have?" Ard asked. The job certainly didn't sound difficult. He was used to stealing things from places with much higher security than a clockmaker's shop. But the delivery would take some time. Stylet was a good day's ride south of Beripent.

"Until the next Faceless meeting," answered Antler Head. "Exactly one cycle from today."

"What if I don't get the job done?" Might as well ask now while the stakes seemed lower.

"Then you don't get paid," she said. "Faceless who fail enough jobs will not be invited back."

"I imagine their life expectancy isn't too long, at that point," Ard said.

The Realm didn't seem like an organization that would let people go on good terms. But if all identities were kept secret, how would anyone find them to finish them off?

"About fifty days," answered the woman. "That's how long you can survive without the Waters of Loyalty."

"Wait," Ard cried, "I'm still poisoned?"

"The Waters of Loyalty are both poison and antidote," said Antler Head. "Best to be at every meeting."

*Poison and antidote* . . . How did they manage that? Maybe Raek had been right and the whole thing was just a bluff to keep people coming. If so, it wasn't a bluff Ard was willing to call. At least not yet . . .

"Health Grit will not expunge it," Antler Head said, as if predicting he might ask. "The formula has been carefully crafted to withstand the cleansing effect of a Health cloud."

Well, that was disheartening. This was turning out to be quite the complex beverage.

"Might I suggest a sweetener?" Ard said. "Maybe just a drizzle of honey?"

"I assure you," she said, "the bitterness of the Waters is far superior to the fatal effects of not drinking it—blackening of the abdomen as your insides fill up with your own blood."

"Gives new meaning to the term *stiff drink*," Ard commented. There was no way to know if Antler Head was amused by his comment. Reading people was one of Ardor Benn's greatest strengths, but sparks, these costumes made it difficult.

"How would you like to label the job?" asked Antler Head.

Ard drummed his fingers thoughtfully on the tabletop. "Label?"

"The word that ties you to the job for payment?" she explained. "Reporting the word at the next meeting will allow us to know you were the one who received the assignment."

"Of course," Ard said.

It made a great deal of sense, now that he thought about it. A secret label would be more anonymous than attaching even a pseudonym to the job, since a Faceless could change their label with each job to protect their identity.

"'Time,'" Ard said. It felt appropriate for stealing clocks. And it was a topic he had personal experience with, having traveled through it. Antler Head jotted the word down in her book.

"I'm looking forward to the job." Ard grinned behind the mask, but his charm had no power here.

The bitter aftertaste of the Waters of Loyalty lingered in Quarrah's mouth as she stepped onto the stage, moving toward the Directorate figure wearing the seashell headpiece.

It was time to make good on the information Fabra Ment had shared with her. Quarrah had met with the queen dowager briefly after being freed from the Regulation Outpost.

There hadn't been much to report. Quarrah had a strange gap in her memory, which made her think she'd been the victim of Memory Grit. She'd been wearing an eyeless mask, holding a note with a time and place written on it.

Quarrah had picked up a waiting carriage at Jorish and Sons in the Central Quarter, dressing herself according to the instructions left inside the cab.

Now that she was in the room, Quarrah actually found a great deal of comfort in the disguise. Wearing this oversized outfit was second to hiding in the shadows. No one knew her this way, and she didn't have to worry about crossing paths with someone she might once have stolen from.

The wax mouthpiece was beginning to cause some pain in her cheeks, though. Quarrah wished she hadn't put it in, since she didn't plan to speak a word beyond the necessary ones to the Directorate.

"I fear I'm going gray." The man in the seashell-crusted mask had a deep rumble of a voice.

"Some would call it a mark of wisdom," answered Quarrah, her own voice altered and strange. This was the first test of Fabra Ment's information. According to the queen dowager, these were the two phrases she'd heard Waelis Mordo use with his unseen associate.

Quarrah's response must have appeased the Directorate, because the man picked up a scribing charcoal and drew a circle on a piece of paper.

Her heart was racing as he slid it across to her. Now to test what Fabra had seen in the Illusion cloud as she'd spied on the crooked advisor's drawing.

Quarrah lifted her own scribing charcoal and drew a vertical line, dividing the circle in half. Next, she drew another line, beginning just outside the circle on the upper left side and halving the circle on a diagonal. The third line started outside the circle on the upper right, crossing diagonally to form an $X$ with the second line.

At the top right of the $X$, she drew a small circle, looking as if it were in a very tight orbit of the big one that the man had drawn. Next Quarrah drew a small triangle on the bottom left tip of the $X$, making that line look sort of like an arrow piercing the larger circle.

She set down the scribing charcoal and slid the paper back to the man with the shell mask, realizing that she hadn't taken a single breath during the entire drawing.

The man nodded his large headpiece, candlelight flickering against the shiny shells. He picked up the piece of paper and touched it to the flame, dropping it into the ashes in the metal bowl.

"Do you have anything to report?" he asked.

"Not today," Quarrah answered, hoping she'd get away with it, since she was obviously posing as someone with experience in the Realm. She'd observed others taking receipts to the horned figure at the lectern, collecting payment for jobs completed.

"Then you failed your mission?" he asked. "The Realm is displeased. What was the label?"

Oh, flames! What was he even talking about? This was about to fall apart if she couldn't lie her way through it. Quarrah had a difficult enough time smooth talking when she *didn't* have a wooden stick poking the insides of her cheeks.

"I failed my previous assignment," she began hesitantly. "The person I reported to decided to let me sit out a cycle or two as punishment. Unpaid." Wasn't everyone in this for the money? Well, money and power, but the former usually begat the latter.

"Curious," he said, picking up a ledger and leafing through it. "Your knowledge of the complete symbol qualifies you for eligibility in the Directorate. Are you interested?"

"Yes." Whatever that was. If it had to do with the Directorate, she was interested.

"An opening has recently become available," he said. "One of our Directors did not attend the last meeting. He or she has likely already perished without the Waters of Loyalty. As a result, all Faceless with knowledge of the full symbol are eligible to advance into the Directorate."

Yes! This was fantastic! Getting into the Directorate would likely get her a lot more information about the Realm's involvement with King Termain. The sooner she could figure this out, the sooner she could get out from under Fabra Ment's thumb.

"What do I have to do?"

"There is a contest, of sorts," he answered. "Whichever eligible Faceless brings us the greatest quantity of Void Grit will be admitted into the Directorate."

"Void Grit," Quarrah repeated. Excellent. If the contest came down to stealing things, she had a real chance of winning. "When is it due?"

"At the next meeting," answered the man. "You will be allowed to bring your load past the guards at the door if you speak the word *rearguard*."

Quarrah had noticed some of the Faceless delivering items to the horned figure at the lectern and wondered how they'd gotten past the frisking.

"There will be no payment for this job, other than the potential for advancement," he said. "Do you understand?"

She nodded. "I understand."

He turned to the end of the notebook. "The next meeting will take place at eight o'clock on the morning of the twenty-seventh day of the First Cycle. Your carriage will be waiting at Maraked's Haberdashery. This is the marking."

He flipped to the last page and turned the notebook so she could see it. The drawing was a tall rectangle divided horizontally into thirds.

"There is no payment owed, so I will not write you a receipt," concluded the masked man. "The exit word is *plum*." He nodded his large headpiece in obvious dismissal. "We are the Realm."

Quarrah nodded back, stepping away from the table, tilting her head so she could see the steps through the mask's eyeholes. She wondered how many Faceless had come away from this stage having just received an important, possibly society-altering assignment, only to trip and tumble down the stairs.

Quarrah's mind was swimming. So much to keep track of. Remember the street phrase for the working Hands. Remember how to draw the symbol. Remember the marking for the next meeting and the word she needed to bring her stolen Void Grit inside. Remember the exit word, which she expected would get her past those guards at the door with proof that she'd met with the Directorate.

It wasn't as complex as playing Azania Fyse, but it was still more information than Quarrah liked to keep track of. She was made for action, for slipping into locked chambers in the dead of night. Not for exchanging secrets and keeping everything straight.

And then there was the matter of her new job. Stealing Void Grit was in her wheelhouse. But she'd need a lot of it in order to ensure a victory over her competitors.

She reached the doorway and waited with a group of fellow white-masked figures. Not a word was exchanged. Why weren't people this agreeable when she had to look at their faces? One by one, they stepped up to the guards, whispering the exit word and disappearing.

"Plum," Quarrah spoke quietly when her turn finally came. She moved through the dark tunnel of Shadow Grit and climbed into the carriage. As it rolled forward, Quarrah began pulling off her disguise. The instructions had said to leave it in the carriage after the meeting.

She spit the voice modifier onto the seat next to her and rubbed her cheeks, breathing deeply without the leather mask in place.

So that was the Realm...She wondered how many jobs were given this morning. Were they all connected to one big purpose, or was the Realm just tinkering with society?

Fabra Ment would be pleased to know she'd survived the first meeting, but Quarrah thought she might wait to meet with the queen dowager until after she stole the Void Grit.

The fewer meetings the better.

~

*Let it be known that before the changing we were all alike.*

# CHAPTER

# 16

U nder what circumstances will Grit fail to ignite?" Portsend
posed the question to his entire class.

"If it gets wet," answered one student.

"Wet Grit can still detonate," the professor corrected. "But if it is
diluted in enough liquid, it will fail." With certain exceptions that
he couldn't discuss. He called on another student with her hand
raised.

"If it's dispersed."

"Good," said Portsend. "And that begs the question—Can a single particle of Grit ignite?"

"It's Jonzan's First Truth," answered Lomaya without waiting
to be called on. "*All Grit, if properly ignited, will detonate.* But a single
particle would yield an imperceptibly small cloud. So although it
technically ignites, the detonation is undetectable."

It made Portsend nervous when Lomaya and San answered questions in front of the class. They knew so much, and it would be so
easy for them to slip and mention something that they'd sworn to
keep secret. Sadly, of late, he'd avoided calling on them at all in class.
But sometimes they answered without permission, a sign that they'd
grown awfully comfortable with Portsend over the last seven weeks.

"What, then, is the difference between Grit that fails to ignite
and a null detonation?" Portsend couldn't help spinning his lectures to back up his new research. It was all he could think about—
all he wanted to talk about.

"I believe that's another one of Jonzan's Truths," said a student thumbing through his book of notes. "Something about null detonations..."

"The Sixth," said Portsend. "'A null detonation is still a detonation.' But why?"

"'All Grit is consumed upon detonation.'"

Jonzan's Second. Good. At least his students knew the basics.

"'All Grit is consumed upon detonation,'" Portsend repeated. "That means there will be no trace nor dusting of Grit in the aftermath of ignition. It would be a perfectly clean operation if it weren't for all the broken Grit pots." His joke didn't land quite as well as he'd hoped, but it still earned some smiles.

"Can you give us an example of that?" asked one of the students.

"Prolonging Grit," Portsend explained. "It's useless unless added to another type of Grit. If it's ignited alone, the Prolonging Grit simply burns up with no noticeable effect. That's an example of a null detonation."

*Or, if you use a vial of our new liquid Null Grit.*

They'd discovered it just last night—a solution capable of snuffing out existing Grit clouds. It was still too early to have a comprehensive understanding of it—too early even to alert Gloristar. But they had run several successful tests.

The source material was shale. Before the list from the Anchored Tome, shale was considered common stone, often being incorporated into an aggregate of processed stone that made up Prolonging Grit. But Portsend and his two pupils had discovered just the right acidic-balance level to dissolve the shale, creating a whole new solution.

Based on last night's testing, the detonation created another "flash cloud," as opposed to the typical ten-minute cloud of familiar Grit. Unfortunately, their scheduled time at the student laboratory had expired and they hadn't had a chance to test it against all types of Grit. But it had successfully snuffed clouds of Light, Shadow, Void, and even Barrier Grit.

The implications were huge. With this new Grit solution in play, the duration of any cloud could be reduced to mere seconds!

Termain would like their new discovery, as loathe as Portsend was to share it with him. On the battlefield, a vial of Null Grit could cancel the enemy's protective Barrier cloud, leaving them defenseless. It could knock out clouds of Drift Grit used to transport cannons and other heavy weaponry. It could extinguish Light Grit and plunge the enemy camp into darkness.

"Professor Wal?" asked Yunstan, in the third row of the tiered classroom.

Portsend had been so deep in thought he wondered how long she'd had her hand raised.

"Yes?" he said.

"What about an unworthy detonation of Visitant Grit?" she asked. "Would that be a type of null detonation?"

At the side of the classroom, the door suddenly cracked open. All heads turned, Portsend's included. Students often showed up a few minutes late, but they were already halfway through the lecture.

It was a stranger—a rather heavyset fellow who looked to be a good ten years older than the typical student. He nodded to Portsend, giving a brief apologetic wave. "Sorry I'm late," he muttered, slipping into the nearest vacant seat in the front row.

Late? *Was* the man a student? Portsend prided himself on knowing all of his students by name. He had been awfully caught up in his own research lately, but would he forget a student's face entirely?

Portsend shrugged off the late arrival, turning back to Yunstan. "Could you restate the question?"

The man in the front row slowly donned a floppy-brimmed hat, his gaze never leaving Portsend. Odd that he'd wait to put it on until he was inside. The hat made Portsend think of Brase. The bodyguard often wore one just like it.

"I was wondering if a cloud of Visitant Grit that doesn't yield a Paladin Visitant is considered a null detonation," restated Yunstan.

"That is a common misconception," answered Portsend.

The door opened again. Portsend wasn't finished answering, but he couldn't help glancing over at the second interruption. It was another stranger, this man looking close to Portsend's age. He was wiry and short, with the sides of his head shaved smooth.

And the man was wearing Luthe's jacket.

The floppy-brimmed hat had seemed a coincidence, but this surely proved that it wasn't. It was unmistakably Luthe's high-collared jacket with the shiny silver buttons.

From the corner of his eye, Portsend saw San and Lomaya, seated side by side, stiffen at the same realization. The professor's mouth went suddenly dry, and he felt the need to keep talking. Try not to show his hand or the terror that was suddenly wrapping itself around his heart.

"Just because a Paladin Visitant fails to appear," Portsend stumbled on, "does not change the fact that a detonation occurred."

The stranger in Luthe's jacket seated himself beside the other man. Portsend tried not to look at them, but his eyes kept flicking back in their direction, only to find them staring back.

"If it was null," rambled Portsend, "then the Grit would burn up with no cloud. No visible cloud." He glanced at the hourglass by the door. Sparks, there were still at least twenty minutes until the end of class. "In an unworthy Visitant Grit detonation, there is still a cloud." Had he already said that? "The cloud just stands empty for the entire duration because a Paladin will not appear for the worthy...er, pardon me. The *un*worthy."

The strangers had him tripping over his words now. Portsend took a moment to breathe. His mind raced over any possibilities that would make their arrival seem less sinister. They were college administrators who failed to inform Portsend that they'd be sitting in on his lecture this afternoon. Brase could have left his hat on the step outside. And the other man happened to share a tailor with Luthe.

Homeland, who was he kidding? Portsend's bodyguards had been taken, maybe even killed. That made these strangers dangerous. And allowing them to sit in a classroom full of innocent students was a threat that Portsend needed to mitigate.

"We will pick up here next time," Portsend said. "Class dismissed."

His sudden dismissal sent a ripple of surprise up the tiers. It was certainly out of character for Portsend Wal, and most of the students responded with nods of satisfaction at gaining an extra twenty minutes in their afternoon. They quickly gathered notebooks and supplies before pouring out of the room.

Portsend busied himself, packing his own satchel, not willing to check on the men in the front row. Now that he had dismissed the class, he realized that he had likely put himself in an even more perilous situation. If Portsend didn't exit with the flow of students, the strangers would have him alone.

"Is everything all right, Professor?"

No, no! It was San and Lomaya standing on the other side of the table. The twinge in the lad's voice made it apparent that his pupils had sensed the danger. They were afraid and wanted direction from Portsend. As though he knew what to do!

"Decided to end early so I could read through the papers that were due last week." If the thugs were listening, Portsend didn't want to give away any ties to his young partners. "I had other things I'd hoped to do, but they'll have to wait. Why don't you two check in with me tomorrow?"

He saw that his subtlety had not fallen on deaf ears. Lomaya and San would not come down to the laboratory during their scheduled time this evening.

"You should hurry to your next class." Portsend swung his satchel over his shoulder. "I'll see you out."

The three of them moved for the classroom door, merging into the flow of students still exiting. As they passed the front row, the man with Brase's hat stood abruptly.

"Professor?" he said, voice raspy. "I wondered if I could have a moment of your time."

Portsend didn't stop moving, didn't look him in the face. "I'm afraid I'm in a bit of a rush. If you're thinking about joining the class... well, it's past midterm. You'll need to see the administration. Try the Tower building."

The man in Luthe's jacket stepped into Portsend's path, stopping him. "We just have a couple of questions about mixing Grit." He grinned, two of his front teeth missing. "Theoretical questions. Word is, that's your specialty."

Portsend realized that San and Lomaya had stopped beside him, even though their path was clear. He gestured them forward, trying to step around the stranger. The man repositioned himself, and this time Portsend felt something sharp pressing softly into his back.

*Oh, Homeland.* Portsend swooned, light-headed from the rush of fear. Reluctantly, Lomaya and San moved ahead, exiting the classroom with the final students.

Portsend took a shallow breath and cleared his voice. "How can I help you gentlemen?"

The man in the jacket used his head to gesture at the chair he'd been occupying. "Take a seat."

For a fleeting moment, Portsend considered making a run for it. If he leapt forward, he might be able to avoid the knife at his back. He could use his satchel of books to push past the man in front of him and get away.

Portsend sat down in the chair.

Now that he could see the man in the hat, Portsend was glad he hadn't run. The knife was long, with teeth along one edge. But the man's other hand held a small Singler, thumb hovering over the hammer.

"I don't know what you fellows want," Portsend tried, "but I'm sure we can come to some kind of agreement."

"Negotiation is on her way," said the hat. "Just sit tight until she gets here." He kept the gun pointed at Portsend while his companion moved to the door. Cracking it open, he peered into the hallway as though standing guard.

Portsend watched the sand fall through the large classroom hourglass. Minutes certainly passed at a painstaking rate, and he constantly braced himself against the possibility of the pulled trigger.

With about ten minutes left in the hourglass, the man with Luthe's jacket swung the door wide and stepped aside.

A woman entered—another stranger to Portsend Wal. She wasn't very tall, and stouter than either of the men. Her black hair, in a simple braid down her back, matched the color of her long coat. A broad jaw and a prominent nose only served to enhance her stern expression.

As soon as the woman cleared the threshold, the ruffian swung the door shut and positioned himself to keep it so. She crossed to the center of the room and stopped behind Portsend's lecture table. Slowly, she unbuttoned her coat and shrugged out of it. More black garb beneath, the front cut low.

She folded her coat over one arm and laid it on the table in front of her. "You will no longer report your findings to King Termain Agaul." Her voice carried a thick Dronodanian accent.

*Sovereign spies*, Portsend instantly thought. That happened quickly. To his knowledge, Termain's people hadn't even completed mass production of the Ignition Grit solution, let alone distribution to the troops.

"I don't know what you're talking about," Portsend quietly said. This kind of feigned ignorance wasn't likely to get him far, but it was worth a try.

"Can I cut him?" The thug with the hat brandished his knife.

"And leave blood in the classroom?" The woman shook her head. "We cut him outside. If he refuses to cooperate." She leaned forward, planting both hands flatly on the table. "But I think he will."

Portsend took a deep breath, breaking eye contact as the woman bore down on him with a relentless stare.

"We know you developed a liquid solution you refer to as Ignition Grit," she stated when the silence between them became unbearable. "Innovative. Absurdly so. I do not believe such a discovery could have happened by accident or traditional means."

So, she didn't know about Gloristar's list from the Anchored Tome, but she was probing for it. Little did she realize that Portsend's first breakthrough *had* been largely accidental. Still, it never would have happened without the scroll encouraging him to isolate the processed gold dust.

"I was simply following the Urgings of the Homeland," Portsend replied. In a way, that was true, considering the sacred origins of the scroll.

The woman in black raised her bushy eyebrows. "Then I'm sure the Homeland will Urge again." She obviously didn't believe him, Settled as she surely was. "And next time, you're going to share that information with me."

"And, who..." Portsend stammered, "who exactly are you?"

"Your new boss."

Yes. Portsend had gathered that. He was hoping for a name. At least an affiliation. "I don't think there's any need for this." Portsend gestured to the knife and gun. "Perhaps we can reach an accord."

Maybe this could work in everyone's favor. If these criminals were indeed Sovereign spies, then giving them information could help to end the war quicker. And if they coordinated their efforts, they might be able to move fast enough to dethrone Termain before he could strike against Gloristar.

It was incredibly risky. *Too* risky, since Portsend had no idea who his new "boss" swore allegiance to.

A terrifying thought suddenly overshadowed Portsend. What if this was some kind of test? What if Termain Agaul had sent these bruisers to the college to threaten him as a way of gauging his loyalty? Portsend wouldn't put it past the deranged king.

As all these musings tore through Portsend's mind, he realized that there was only one safe way to play this. "Safe" for Gloristar, but certainly not for him.

"There is more at stake here than my life," Portsend bravely proclaimed. "My research must go to His Majesty."

He braced himself for the blade or the ball, in disbelief that his lips had just sworn such allegiance to a man he despised. In terror that he might now die for a cause he didn't support.

But he *did* support Gloristar. And Homeland would see that she learned the truth of what happened to him here.

"Moonsickness is spreading." The woman's abrupt change in topic did nothing to calm Portsend's nerves. "Not just to the outlying communities. It's spreading among us."

It was inexplicable, but true. Supposedly, it had been happening for five cycles now, but Portsend couldn't keep all the reports straight. He'd dismissed them for a while, but as the accounts persisted, they gained more traction and veracity.

"Some say it's the failing Holy Torch, others say it's the dwindling population of the dragon shield." The woman stepped around the edge of the table. "But I say it's the work of ordinary people."

"What are you saying?" Portsend whispered.

"The people I work for have an interesting side business." The boss interlocked her fingers in front of her. "I suppose you could call it a farm. But instead of crops or livestock," she was pacing in front of him now, "they raise Moonsickness."

Sparks! Was this the truth? "How?"

"In cages, of course," she said. "A number of chosen individuals are exposed to the Moon during the night of a Passing and kept locked away until the sickness advances to the third stage."

A flow of disturbing images took over Portsend's imagination. He shook his head. "Pekal's exportation laws...harbor Regulation..."

How was this happening with so many checks in place? Was the entire system corrupt?

"Don't trouble yourself with the logistics," replied the boss. "We have people for that. You, Professor, have been promoted straight to the top of this little business."

Portsend felt cold. "I don't understand."

"For the last few cycles, we've been releasing eight Moonsick Bloodeyes into high-population areas all across the Greater Chain," explained the boss. "Now I'm giving you some control over that number."

"What do you mean?" Portsend was trembling.

"If you cooperate," she said. "If you give us new Grit, then you can help us decide how many we release."

Portsend held up his hands. "Just because I discovered one new Grit type doesn't mean there are more." He couldn't tell her that Null Grit was already well along, or that there were five other items listed on the scroll.

"We shall see." The boss walked back around the table and picked up her long coat. "But if you share any more discoveries with King Termain, the number of Bloodeyes will double. Am I clear?"

Portsend nodded. Was he really going to be responsible for this? Innocent people were going to die. Just last cycle, a pair of Moonsick Bloodeyes had killed Lady Abeth Agaul and three Beripent Regulators.

"And if word of this conversation leaks to anyone..." The boss flung the coat around her shoulders and began fastening the buttons with her stout fingers. "Well, you might find yourself on the inside of a farm cage."

Portsend felt the panic of her approaching departure. He'd been scared to sit in her presence, but in a way it seemed more terrifying to have her leave. Then her manipulation would be in full swing and Portsend would have no choice but to comply with her demands.

"How do I report my findings?" he blurted, wincing at the fact that he had just given in.

"You'll be working closely with your new bodyguards, Brase and Luthe." She gestured to the men in their stolen apparel. "You'll never be out of their sight, and they will let me know when you have something to share with me and my superiors."

A sinking sensation rooted itself in Portsend's stomach. He had expected the two men to leave with their boss.

"Feed them well and they'll watch your back," she said, heading for the exit. "Try to deceive them and they'll put a knife in it."

Imposter Luthe stepped aside and yanked open the door. The woman nodded and disappeared into the hallway.

Portsend wanted to breathe a massive sigh and collapse. He wanted to weep and crawl into his laboratory and lock the door. How could he do this to Gloristar? He couldn't turn his back on her, no matter the cost.

Which calamity would he rather be responsible for, the terror of Moonsickness raging into the public or the possible collapse of Wayfarism should Termain send the Prime Isless away and destroy the Anchored Tome?

"Whom do you work for?" Portsend whispered, turning a steely gaze on the imposter Brase. The portly man had sheathed his knife and holstered his Singler, but he still packed plenty of intimidation.

"You, I suppose." He spat on the classroom floor. "Until further notice."

～

*They came against us, but we stood firmly.*

# PART III

Who will falter at the Homeland's shores? Who will fear the inhabitants of that holy place? They are not strangers, but mothers and fathers past. The worthy will ascend, and we will become like them, transformed into perfection.

—Wayfarist Voyage, *vol. 2*

With four legs, we would be unshakable. A fin would hold us balanced in the waves. With wings we would soar above dragons, and a thicker hide would keep us warm. Rue our feeble and unsteady form, robbed of the greatness we deserve.

—*Ancient Agrodite poem*

# CHAPTER

# 17

This was either going to be a massive success or it was going to get Quarrah killed. She really didn't see a lot of middle ground here. She'd run dangerous thefts before. But this was the war front. People came here to die.

Quarrah had slipped past the Archkingdom's eastern lookouts easily enough. Now she crouched low among the outermost row of tents, not two hundred yards north of the cliff shoreline, which had long faded into the black of night.

A week into the First Cycle meant it was officially spring, although there was still a notable chill in the air. It was hard to believe that this cycle marked two years from the time she had performed at the Grotenisk Spring Festival. Termain had canceled the celebrations again this year, which meant that the memory of Azania Fyse lived on as the last performance. Well, she'd rather be here, anyway, crouched in the dark at the edge of a war camp on the southern side of Strind, waiting.

Quarrah made a mental map of what she could see of the encampment's layout, dotting it with campfires and charting a path toward the center that would avoid the well-lit areas.

She hadn't meant to come to the war front. She hadn't even intended to leave Espar. The original plan would have been much safer and faster, but the munitions shipment had left Beripent a full day ahead of schedule. By the time Quarrah managed to stow away on the next vessel and make her way to the front, the fifty pan-weights of Void Grit had already been delivered to the Archking-dom army.

The war often seemed a distant thing to her, since the fighting hadn't yet touched Espar. But the repercussions of the war had imprinted themselves on everyday life—constantly rising prices of common goods, shortages, a general air of fear and grief.

But here on Strind, following the swath of destruction that the Sovereign States had carved from Middlesway Harbor to Jopham, Quarrah realized that the war was much worse than anything she'd imagined during her lifetime of peace.

Entire towns had been razed, buildings standing as little more than charred framework, populated only by the memories of those who had been sent running for help. These small villages wouldn't have had any support, and the Sovereign States appeared to be showing no mercy in their march toward Drasken.

Quarrah hardly considered herself a tactician, but their strat-egy made sense. Force Strind to buckle. Push across the island with ruthless aggression until the Strindian nobles withdrew support from Espar.

Quarrah realized that stealing an entire shipment of Void Grit wasn't going to do the defending Archkingdom any favors. But to be honest, Quarrah would rather the Sovereign States win any-way. She lived in Beripent for the convenience and opportunity, not because she owed the city some grand allegiance.

She slipped the thin wire-framed spectacles off her face and tucked them into a pocket sewn to their exact specifications. She liked the way the glass lenses sharpened her eyesight, but she rarely wore them for long periods, especially at night, when they glinted like the eyes of a deer in a beam of Light Grit.

The fifty panweights of Void Grit would be kept at the center of the encampment. King Termain had probably authorized such a huge shipment in an attempt to boost morale.

Both the Archkingdom and the Sovereign States had been using Compounded Void Grit in an utterly brutal application. Void Grit scrap bombs. They were unusually large clay pots, roughly the size of a melon, with a special chamber at the bottom that housed highly Compounded Void Grit. The rest of the hollow pot could be packed with dangerous scraps such as old nails or shards of glass.

The bomb could be lofted over an enemy shield wall, shattering behind their exposed backs. As the Compounded Void Grit detonated, it threw the scraps outward in all directions, their velocity nearing the speed of a Singler ball.

A less expensive variation, using Blast Grit as the propellant, had been used in warfare for centuries. But the Void Grit sprayed the scrap projectiles more evenly, and as a bonus, created a ten-minute cloud that served as a frustrating obstacle behind enemy lines.

Quarrah didn't know the detonation rate, but she suspected fifty panweights of Void Grit could blow a significant crater in the ranks of the Sovereign States, if it were detonated all at once. Instead, they'd measure it into the scrap bombs and divvy them out to soldiers of rank, making the supply last well over a cycle.

In truth, it wouldn't last them the night, once Quarrah made off with the load.

She had no idea how many other Realm members had been issued the same challenge, or how they planned to steal their Void Grit. Quarrah had counted nearly fifty Faceless individuals in white masks at the meeting, but she didn't imagine that many of them knew how to draw the full symbol.

Then again, what did she really know about the Realm? The Faceless could pile up for years, dozens of them knowing the full symbol before there was an opening in the Directorate.

She couldn't distract herself with the odds. All she could control was how much Void Grit she stole. And Quarrah was counting on fifty panweights to be enough.

She began her slow and careful approach, sliding between tents and lingering in the deepest pockets of blackness that the night had to offer.

An unexpected duo of soldiers came around one of the tents, and she snapped her fingers on her left hand. The small fragment of Slagstone sewn into the tip of her glove's middle finger sparked with the action. The mesh pocket on her palm was loaded with Shadow Grit tonight, and the resulting cloud concealed her perfectly, remaining motionless as they passed by.

A ruse artist like Ardor Benn certainly would have stolen an Archkingdom uniform and sauntered nonchalantly right up to the munitions tents. But Quarrah didn't operate that way, and she prided herself on having only one uniform for all her jobs—her custom-made black garb. It suited her well for waiting in the darkness.

Patience had always been one of her best qualities. As a young girl, it might have been mistaken for indecision. Sitting in the shadows, a stone's throw from a loaf of bread. Feeling the hunger, but waiting, afraid of what would happen if she were caught. Eventually, a window had always opened and she'd learned to strike fast and disappear. That youthful indecision had sculpted her patience. Now she didn't usually feel the fear of getting caught, but she knew the value of waiting for that opening.

Quarrah nestled herself into a tight spot between two crates and studied the munitions tent. It was pitched in a clearing, campfires and Light Grit providing far too much illumination. Soldiers stood guard at either end of the large tent, but the wind-rustled flaps showed nothing but darkness within.

She'd need a diversion to get across the clearing. Quarrah reached into her pocket and withdrew a coil of fuse. It was cheap stuff that burned at an erratic rate, putting out more smoke than any campfire she'd seen.

She found a fist-sized rock and tied one end of the fuse securely around it. Then, holding tightly to the other end, she pitched the stone across the dimmest end of the clearing.

Snapping her fingers sparked the Slagstone in her gloved middle finger, igniting the other end of the fuse. The moment it was lit, Quarrah flung it forward and retreated between the two tents behind her.

A shout of alarm went up immediately. Quarrah saw both guards spring from their posts at the munitions tent in response to the unexpected threat.

It was a distraction tactic Quarrah had used many times, finding it most effective in the dark when the bright burning fuse would attract all kinds of attention. And in her experience, people were usually far more concerned about where the fuse was leading than where it came from. At least initially. But she only needed a handful of seconds.

Sprinting out of hiding, Quarrah crossed the illuminated clearing and slipped through the loose flaps of the munitions tent. She felt her way forward in the impossible darkness—a crate here, a barrel there.

From her belt, she withdrew a small tea bag containing a bit of Light Grit. Holding it in the palm of her right hand, she snapped her fingers. The Slagstone in her glove ignited the Grit, throwing an orb of light about a foot in diameter. Quarrah pulled her hand out of the glowing cloud, its shape perfectly undisturbed by her movements.

There was more in this tent than Quarrah had suspected. Racks of firearms lined one wall, with bundles of pole arms and tall shields. There were even two cannons, half-covered with a dusty blanket and tucked away in the corner. These would all be extra weapons. The main line of cannons was set at the west end of the encampment, ready to roll out against the Sovereign army at a moment's notice. And Quarrah was sure that the soldiers would be sleeping within arm's reach of their primary weapons.

The rest of the tent was full of boxes, barrels, and crates. There were towers of them, most branded with the Archkingdom's symbol and marked with a wide swatch of colored paint.

Quarrah knew the standardized color-coding system. Void Grit would be marked with teal, and she found the two large boxes in little time. She removed the items stacked on top, struggling under the weight of an obnoxiously heavy box before prying open the lid of the first teal container.

Quarrah had been hoping that the Void Grit would be stored in one big bag, easy to snatch and go. Instead, she found herself staring at individual Grit kegs. She guessed their volume by the size, but she picked one up and checked the markings to be sure. Five panweights. There would be ten of these, then. Looked like five in this box and the rest underneath.

Quarrah pulled off her specialized gloves and slipped the empty backpack from her shoulder. The kegs themselves would be too bulky to fit into a pack this size, so she'd need to empty the contents directly into the large cloth drawstring bag that would fit inside her backpack.

She popped open the first Grit keg, careful not to let the Slagstone fragment fall out of the lid where the trigger pin connected. She angled the vessel toward the light, making sure the contents looked like pulverized granite before upending the keg into her cloth bag and moving on to the next one.

Through the canvas wall of the tent, Quarrah could hear some mild confusion. By the sound of it, they'd cut her fuse and traced it to the useless rock she'd tied around the end. Hearing the bark of a commander, she realized that they were scouring the far area by the tents, suspecting some hidden stash of Grit that the fuse had been intended to reach.

Quarrah moved on to the second box, quickly getting the fifty panweights of Void Grit she'd come for.

Well, now that the thieving was out of the way, it was time to think about how the blazes she was going to get out of this encampment, with all the soldiers awake and on edge.

Best to start by leaving no trace of her theft. Quarrah pulled the drawstring tight and dropped it into her pack. Then she stacked the Void Grit boxes exactly as they'd been, turning to reset the items that had been on top of them.

One was a strange little box, half the height of the others and unpainted, branded only with the Archkingdom seal and the word *Fragile*.

*Probably gun cartridges,* Quarrah thought, sliding it into place at the top of the stack. But why would it be marked "fragile"? Blast cartridges, with their attached lead balls, contained no fragments of Slagstone, so dropping them wasn't likely to cause an accidental ignition. And was that the clink of glass inside the box?

Quarrah knew she should be going, but her Light Grit detonation still had two or three minutes, and the thief's itch was taking control. Curiosity, and the fear of regret. The fear that she'd get safely away only to be kept up at night wondering what extra valuables she could have nicked.

In a flash, the box was open, Quarrah anxiously peering inside. The soft light in the tent glinted off dozens of glass vials, packed in a nest of coarse sawdust. She picked one out, lifting it to the light and squinting at it.

The vial was stopped with a small piece of cork. The liquid inside was bright green, and it looked like there was a small fragment of rock settled at the bottom. Slagstone? In a liquid solution?

"Check the munitions tent." The commander's voice outside snapped through her curiosity, replacing it with haste.

Instinctively, she snatched two more vials and slid them into her pocket, quietly closing the lid on the box of fragile glass.

Time to go dark. And quick! If that tent flap pulled back with the Light Grit still glowing, there'd be nothing left to do but run with fifty panweights of extra baggage on her back.

The mesh pocket on her left glove was still loaded with Shadow Grit. It would create a cloud just large enough to conceal her, which would be more than sufficient to cover the Light cloud.

Quarrah jammed her hand into the glove and leapt forward, pushing her raised fist directly into the hanging orb of light. She snapped her fingers, but the Grit didn't take. She snapped again, and the sparks found their target, throwing a spherical cloud of blackness around the existing Light Grit detonation.

The munitions tent was plunged into darkness, and Quarrah dropped into a crouch behind a barrel just as the tent flaps were pulled open. Dim, flickering light from the campfires outside spilled past her.

Igniting the Shadow Grit in the air meant that it didn't obscure many of the tent's contents. Still, Quarrah could see that the top of a stacked box seemed to disappear, swallowed up in the impossible blackness of the cloud. Hopefully, the natural darkness of the night would be enough to blend the Grit's concealing effect.

The soldier at the entrance scanned the tent. He took a step closer, still holding the canvas flaps open to allow the faint outside light to spill in.

*He knows something's off,* Quarrah thought, keeping her breathing shallow behind the barrel. One more step and he'd see it for sure. Quarrah would have to spring at him. Maybe, with the element of surprise, she could take him down before he raised an alarm.

How exactly did she intend to "take him down"? Slit his throat like some base assassin? That simply wasn't how she operated.

"Clear!" the soldier suddenly shouted in report to his commander. Then the flaps fell shut and the faint light was gone.

Letting out a slow sigh of relief, Quarrah crossed back to the area where she'd been working and found her backpack. Swinging it onto her shoulders, she tread silently toward the opposite tent flaps, parting them just enough to peer out into the clearing. The guard was standing off to the side, conferring with a superior officer. In addition to them, Quarrah counted eight uniformed soldiers who must have been on the night watch. At least a dozen more were milling around by the tents, yawns on their faces and blankets wrapped around their shoulders, clearly having been startled awake.

Too many to sneak past. It was risky, but Quarrah might be able to pull off a walkthrough. It was a simple tactic that she frequently used in the city. When the streets were bustling and Quarrah needed to get in or out of somewhere unnoticed, she had learned that walking casually among the citizens made her almost as invisible as slinking through the shadows. It was considerably more nerve-racking, but it usually worked. And the few times she *did* get spotted by her pursuers, Quarrah could sprint through the crowd and be gone.

She didn't fool herself into thinking this would be the same. This wasn't a crowd of unsuspecting common citizens, fearfully willing to step aside if she was forced to run.

Quarrah moved to the corner of the munitions tent, feeling in the darkness until her hand touched the cold metal of a cannon. Following it up the tube, she gripped the hem of the dusty blanket she'd seen and flung it around her shoulders. With the stuffed backpack in place, the blanket hung loosely behind her. Hopefully, that wouldn't be too distracting. Quarrah thought it might even help to disguise her true form, like the wide-shouldered cloaks at the Faceless meetings.

Taking a deep breath, Quarrah slipped out of the tent and strode purposefully across the illuminated clearing. Sparks! There were more people out here than she'd guessed. And not all of them looked as tired as the ones she'd first seen.

She didn't run—that would only draw attention. Instead, she intentionally passed near one of the campfires as though to prove that she had nothing to hide. A nod to one of the tired soldiers, and then she had made it to the first row of tents.

Quarrah didn't allow herself to hide again until she reached the fifth row. Then she ditched the large blanket and picked up her pace, moving eastward through the encampment, trusting that most of the suspicion would be turned westward toward the Sovereign camps.

This was how Quarrah Khai loved to move. Melding with midnight, her score on her back, not a hundred yards from a host of people wondering what had just happened.

She burst out of the encampment, staying low as she moved into the flat landscape to the east. Now all she had to do was get past the sentries positioned in the brush, but they weren't likely to pose any trouble.

A horn blared through the still night, and Quarrah's heart leapt into her throat. She dropped into the tall grasses, trying to figure out what it meant. The sound was coming from...oh, flames. One of the sentries was running right for her, horn raised and pealing!

Quarrah reached for her belt. He was close now, but he seemed more interested in signaling the others than firing on her. Barrier Grit would contain him, and she could follow up with a cloud of Silence Grit. That might give her enough time to—

A gunshot rang out and the sentry jolted, stumbling forward. He crashed forward on his face, tumbling through the grass and lying still, not five feet from Quarrah. He was dead. Shot in the back.

All at once, Quarrah saw figures rising from the grasses at startlingly close range. They charged forward, whooping and hollering, now that their approach had been spoiled.

Quarrah glanced back toward the encampment she had just robbed. The soldiers were beginning to assemble, most of them still out of uniform as they formed a line before the outermost row of tents. Their quick response no doubt had to do with the fact that so many of them were already awake from Quarrah's little disturbance. Maybe her thieving tonight would actually end up saving lives. Whether she would be counted among the survivors was yet to be seen.

She'd heard the Sovereign army was prone to night raids, but why did they have to pick *tonight*? The way things were shaping up, Quarrah Khai was about to be stuck right in the line of fire between two armies.

Trothians would probably be leading the charge. Their unique eyes, constantly vibrating, took in the energy emanating out of all things, essentially allowing them to see in the dark. They would spot her lying in the grass. They would take her for a sentry and kill her without hesitation.

Quarrah heard the Archkingdom commander shout something, followed by a chorus of gunfire. Lead balls whizzed overhead, cutting into the charging enemies. A trumpet bugled from the east, and the Sovereign soldiers responded to the call immediately. They halted their charge not thirty yards from where Quarrah lay and scrambled to form ranks.

More troops arrived from behind, planting tall rectangular shields at intervals to provide cover for the others. Quarrah could see the tips of countless pole arms bristling like forest treetops after a fire. She knew what would happen next. The shield carriers would begin a slow advance, lines of Fielders systematically firing and reloading. The pikemen would thrust over the shield carriers, protecting the Fielders until the line was breached. At that point, it would be hand to hand with swords, knives, and whatever Grit the common infantry were allotted.

In the darkness, it was impossible to see how far the line of soldiers extended. It would be hopeless to run in front of them, trying to evade shots from both sides.

*I'll never get past*, Quarrah thought. *If they don't shoot me, I'll get trampled in the advance.*

Glancing back, she saw a similar wall of standing shields assembled on the Archkingdom side. Theirs was far tighter, spanning the width of the encampment and looking quite formidable.

Volleys of shots continued overhead, and the acrid smell of Blast smoke reached Quarrah, who was lying at the heart of the field. She inched southward toward the cliff's edge, staying low, maneuvering through the brush like a snake as she tried to find the courage to get up and sprint.

The Sovereign trumpeter signaled an advance, and the troops came forward with alarming speed. This sent Quarrah scrambling westward, back toward the Archkingdom defensive line.

She crawled now, frantic, heavy backpack yanking her side to side as the brush scraped at her face. The Sovs were advancing too quickly behind her. At roughly forty feet, it was a miracle they hadn't shot her yet.

Quarrah broke and ran, heading southwest. She had tried to identify a pattern to the shots, undertaking her sprint just after the nearest group fired en masse, hoping she could make it a few yards while they reloaded.

A lead ball struck her pack, tearing through the fabric and lodging in the valuable contents. Undetonated Void Grit scattered around her as the impact, along with the pack's weight, threw her off balance. Quarrah went down hard on her side, more lead flying in all directions. She felt something break in her hip pocket, the bite of broken glass embedding itself into her skin.

All at once, a series of detonations surrounded her. She was thrown outward, tumbling through the grass some six or eight feet before slamming into the impenetrable wall of a Barrier cloud. Pinned by some unseen force, Quarrah tried to comprehend what had just happened, her breath stolen away by the same powerful wind that was holding her helpless against the Barrier shell.

*Oh, flames,* Quarrah thought. *The Void Grit.*

She didn't know how much of it had detonated, or *how?* But she could feel that her backpack was empty now, the ripped cloth whipping in the strong, unnatural wind.

And the Void Grit wasn't the only thing that had ignited. There were splashes of Light Grit, their spherical shapes unaffected by the wind of the Void cloud. She saw a pocket of Shadow as well as the Barrier dome that currently enclosed her.

Based on the layout, all these detonations had originated in the very spot where Quarrah had fallen. She suddenly realized that it was *her* Grit that had ignited. Not just the stolen Void Grit, but all of it. Everything she had been carrying.

*What the blazes?*

She ached all over from colliding with the Barrier dome, but the pain in her hip was sharper. Quarrah knew she wasn't bleeding much, but that glass had definitely cut her. It wasn't her spectacles. Those were on her other side. No. It was the vials of green liquid she'd stolen from the munitions tent.

There was little use in resisting the Void wind at her back. Caught against the Barrier, she was fairly protected, although a feeling of helplessness threatened to smother her. Agility and movement were two qualities a thief always counted on. Her current predicament was akin to being locked in a glass box.

Minutes passed, and she calmed herself, head turned away from the wind so she could actually breathe, planning the route by which she would flee. Then, all at once, the Void cloud expired. Quarrah rolled away from the Barrier's shell, watching the other detonation clouds fizzle out within seconds of the first.

The Barrier cloud was the last to go out. Quarrah rose on shaky legs, the grasses still splayed outward in all directions from her. She turned this way and that in the vacant field, searching for the armies that had been closing in on both sides.

Gone.

Sparks! They were gone! She squinted into the night, but it was impossible to see anything more than darkness where the Sovereign soldiers had been. And to the west...

The Archkingdom encampment, or what was left of it, was on fire. Entire rows of tents had been uprooted by the Void cloud and strewn about. Campfires had been scattered, the embers setting the rest of the encampment ablaze.

Quarrah stood in shock for a long moment, confused and disoriented. Then she began to check her equipment. Every tea bag she carried was now empty, the Grit burned away. She felt inside her backpack, but there wasn't even a dusting of Void Grit at the bottom of the cloth drawstring bag. Miraculously, her spectacles were undamaged, although her other pocket was full of glass shards. One of the vials had survived.

Holding it up, Quarrah inspected the small glass vial with renewed curiosity and a sudden suspicion. Had this been the cause of the mass detonation? Could the Archkingdom have synthesized some kind of solution to ignite Grit from a distance?

Quarrah turned northward and suddenly found herself staring down the barrel of a Fielder. The Trothian man was less than twenty feet away, his vibrating eyes trained on her.

Her instinct was to run, but that would surely get her shot. Sparks! How had he managed to creep up so quietly?

"Here!" His voice was so heavily accented that it took Quarrah a moment to realize he was calling his companions. "Here! Here!"

A Lander man came blundering through the brush, Roller drawn but held loosely at his side. "You an Archkingdom scout?" he asked, his *R* softened in the accent of the Dronodanians.

"No," she replied.

"What are you doing out here?"

"I robbed the encampment."

The Lander glanced at his Trothian ally with a look of puzzlement. "Before or after the blazing Void wind hit?"

"Before."

"How'd you survive that Void cloud?" he asked. If the Trothian would lower his Fielder, she might think about running.

"Same as you, I suppose," she replied cautiously. Probably wasn't wise to let on that *she* was the source of the detonation.

He shook his head as though her answer didn't satisfy him. "We were a quarter mile back. Just out of range. Stood there watching bodies fly overhead, soaring off the cliff down to the InterIsland Waters."

Just out of range! At a quarter mile? Sweet Homeland, how large had that detonation been?

"Blazing Archies must have used every granule of Void Grit they had," said the Lander. "Don't have to worry about scrap bombs anymore. Suppose that could give us the upper hand with *our* Void Grit…"

A salvage idea came to her. It certainly wasn't her usual method, but given the situation, it seemed like the best option. By the time she sailed back to Beripent, there wouldn't be time to scour the city for large stores of Void Grit, let alone steal them before the next Faceless meeting.

But maybe there was still hope here, on the battlefront.

"I need to speak to your commander," Quarrah blurted.

"Concerning what?" asked the Lander skeptically.

"I've been through the Archkingdom encampment," she answered. "They have something in their munitions tent that I think your superiors would like to know about."

"What is it?" demanded the Trothian.

"I will not speak again unless it is to your commanding officer." Quarrah clenched her jaw.

"Then you will not speak again." The Trothian pressed the stock of his gun tightly against his shoulder and sighted down the long barrel with one quivering eye.

Quarrah tensed, but the Lander put a hand on his companion's shoulder.

"It's worth hearing her out," he said softly. "If she's a spy for the Archkingdom, then the chieftess can deal with her."

The Trothian didn't lower his weapon but used it to indicate that she should start walking. They moved northward in silence until they came upon the recovering Sovereign soldiers.

The group was clearly in a state of emergency, hastening to pull themselves together so they could retreat to the main body of the Sovereign army. The air was full of shouts and moans, while those who were uninjured hastily tended to their companions. Sparks, it looked like they'd already seen combat, but Quarrah knew this was solely the work of the massive blast of Void Grit.

"Where's the chieftess?" the Lander escort asked another soldier.

"Flames," he muttered. "Are the Archies coming?"

"The chieftess!" he snapped, causing the soldier to point sharply to their left.

Quarrah was guided away, but she hadn't gone a hundred feet when she heard a voice she recognized. She stopped abruptly, the Trothian with the Fielder nearly bumping into her as she scanned the crowd to find the speaker.

There, kneeling at the side of a wounded soldier. Quarrah pushed past her guards, stepping forward and shouting her name.

"Lyndel!"

The Agrodite priestess rose, turning to see who had called her. Their eyes locked, Quarrah's steady, Lyndel's in constant flux.

Then Lyndel smiled. In that moment, Quarrah realized that she couldn't recall seeing that expression on the woman's face before.

Lyndel looked well. Thin and rail-backed as ever, yet she walked toward her with a fluid grace. Her long, graying hair was braided into several thick strands, tied together with thin strips of leather.

The two guards caught up, both of them nodding in respect to Lyndel. The Trothian man said something in his own language. But Quarrah understood the Lander.

"Chieftess."

Chieftess? Oh, the Homeland must have been smiling on Quarrah. Her new plan had a far better chance of succeeding now that negotiations would be held with an old ally.

"We found this woman in the field," said the Lander. "She claims to have something of interest to the Sovereign States."

Lyndel motioned the two away with the back of her hand. "Leave us." Without so much as a questioning glance, the two men disappeared.

Lyndel scratched her arm, and Quarrah saw her blue skin looking rather dry and flaky beneath her wrist bands. Perhaps she wasn't doing as well as Quarrah had first thought. Trothian anatomy held several apparent advantages over the Landers, but their need for a regular saltwater soak seemed like a terrible inconvenience. Quarrah couldn't fathom how the Trothian soldiers were managing it while making their steady march across Strind.

"*Omligath*, Quarrah Khai." Lyndel crossed her red-wrapped arms in front of her chest.

Quarrah let out a sigh. "It's good to see you, Lyndel. Chieftess. I don't know where that fits in the chain of command."

"Somewhere near the top," she replied coyly.

Quarrah hadn't seen the priestess in almost two years. Their final interaction had been in Oriar's Square the night that Ard traveled through time to use Grotenisk's fire to fertilize the bull-dragon egg. It was a night forever burned into Quarrah's memory. Lyndel had sided with Ard, her people providing protection while he detonated the Visitant Grit. She had been a stalwart ally through that entire ruse, but time had passed. People changed. Quarrah would have to approach this carefully.

Nearby, a soldier cried out in pain as a Healer set his broken leg. Quarrah could even hear the splintered bone grating. She glanced at the soldier in time to see him pass out.

"Does it ever get to you?" Quarrah muttered under her breath.

"Does what?"

"The fact that we started this. The division of the islands. This war."

Lyndel shook her head. "Pethredote started this when he banished my people from the Greater Chain, sending us back to our islets like a failed experiment."

"But Pethredote might not have done that if we hadn't provoked him with the ruse," said Quarrah, her voice low. "Stealing the royal regalia, uncovering his secrets about poisoning the dragons, killing the Prime Isle...Maybe we didn't start the war, but it certainly seems like we *caused* it."

"You do not believe it was all necessary?"

Quarrah didn't know how to respond. Restoring the dragons had been of paramount importance, protecting all humankind from Moonsickness. They'd saved civilization, but now it was tearing itself apart in the aftermath.

"What if there had been a better way, but we just couldn't see it at the time?" Quarrah asked. Perhaps they had all been a bit blinded by Ardor Benn's zeal and determination. "Some way that wouldn't have provoked the crusader monarch into expelling the Trothian people."

"This war isn't just about us," Lyndel said. "Termain Agaul upholds Pethredote's stance against my people. That is why *we* fight. Dronodan and Talumon are grateful to call us allies, but they have their own reasons."

So many reasons for this war. Maybe Ardor Benn really wasn't one of them. Maybe she'd given him too much credit, and the Greater Chain would have fallen apart even without his meddling.

"I could end this war," Lyndel said. "I could bring the Archkingdom to its knees if the Sovereign war council would give me freedom to act."

"How?"

"Under the council's direction, we exhaust ourselves at sea and on this... this cycles-old march toward Drasken. But it is Pekal we should be targeting."

"Pekal?"

"Cut off the Archkingdom's supply of Grit at the very source," she explained. "Capture the harbors on Pekal and starve them out."

Quarrah nodded. That was a good idea. "Why hasn't anyone tried it yet?"

"The Sovereign war council says it is against the rules of war to attack Pekal," said Lyndel. "Of course Landers must have rules about how they can kill one another..." She shook her head. "They say the Pekal harbors are too well fortified, anyway. The defenses would sink our entire fleet before we reached cannon range. And even if we did capture one of the harbors, they say we would just be forced out to the Redeye line during the next Moon Passing, and the Archkingdom would reclaim it."

"You don't agree?"

"I have a way to take the harbors," said Lyndel. "With the resources of the Sovereign States, I believe I could do it with my Trothian warriors alone."

"How?"

Lyndel stared at her, as though suddenly realizing that she had said too much. As though realizing that Quarrah could easily be an Archkingdom spy, despite the fact that they'd known each other from a life before the war.

"What are you doing here, Quarrah Khai?"

Well, maybe it was best just to get down to business. How well did they really know each other, after all?

"I came here to steal something from the Archkingdom."

"So, you are with us?" Lyndel raised an eyebrow. "I was not made aware of any secret operations."

"I'm working solo," Quarrah said. Not that it should come as a surprise.

"What did you take?"

"Void Grit."

Lyndel sucked in a sharp breath, connecting Quarrah's answer with the unexpected tragedy that had just struck her warriors. "Is that why the Archkingdom detonated it? To prevent you from stealing it?"

"They didn't set it off." Quarrah leaned in, lowering her voice to a mere whisper. "I did."

Lyndel muttered something in her own language, and Quarrah could see the woman struggling to stay composed.

"Not on purpose," Quarrah quickly added. "This is what I needed to talk to you about."

"I'm listening."

Quarrah reached into her pocket and withdrew the surviving glass vial. "Have you ever seen anything like this?"

Lyndel took it, turning it slowly in her fingers, quavering eyes studying it. "Is that a chip of Slagstone?"

"I think this solution caused my stolen Void Grit to detonate," Quarrah said. "And it ignited everything else I was carrying, too."

"Some kind of catalyst?"

"I don't know exactly. But the Archkingdom has a whole box of these in their munitions tent. If these do what I'm guessing, then the Archies could use them to set off huge stores of your Grit."

"You're giving this to me?" Lyndel asked.

Quarrah nodded. "But I need something in return."

"What?"

Quarrah took a deep breath. "I need all of the Sovereign army's Void Grit."

~

*With the strength of our arms we repelled the enemies on the left and on the right.*

# CHAPTER

# 18

"Talk about being underutilized." Ard flicked the reins, though it didn't really inspire the horses to pull the wagon any faster. "At this point, we're little more than delivery boys for the Realm."

It was fine to speak openly here. They were on a Homeland-forsaken road to the little township of Stylet. In the last four hours they'd only passed six groups of travelers.

"At least they trusted you with a job," Raek pointed out.

"Clocks," Ard said. "From an unsuspecting clockmaker. Not like it was difficult."

"Don't pretend like you're put out," Raek said, shivering more than seemed reasonable for the surprisingly warm spring day. "That was a solid ruse with a decent payout." He paused. "There is a decent payout, right?"

Ard shrugged. "I didn't really demand specifics." But Raek was right. Ard had had more fun with this simple ruse than he was willing to admit.

He and Raek had paid Gregious Mas's clock shop a visit the day after the Faceless meeting. The clockmaker was a short man, as round as he was tall, with watery, beady eyes and very little hair.

Ard had found him to be an excessively talkative fellow, and the success of his invention had clearly gone to his head. His new chainspring mantel clocks were surprisingly popular, despite costing an impressive eighty Ashings apiece! The guy must have been as rich as a nobleman by now.

Gregious had plenty of competitors in Beripent and abroad, selling similar clocks for a fraction of the price. But a Gregious Mas clock was in vogue right now, and the quality of his products supposedly outdid those of his competition.

Completing the clock ruse in just one cycle had posed some immediate challenges. The popularity of Gregious's work meant that a new order wouldn't be fulfilled for three cycles. Furthermore, the man never seemed to have twenty-five clocks in his shop at one time. There were three here, five there, with the orders going out as soon as the clocks were completed.

It had taken some good old-fashioned trickery and deceit, but it wasn't something Ardor Benn and the Short Fuse had any trouble with. Or in this case, Androt Penn and the Lit Fuse.

"Think that's our barn?" Raek asked, handing Ard the spyglass and taking the reins.

Ard peered through the lens in the direction Raek had pointed. "It's certainly blue," he said. And it was in the right place, just north of Stylet. "I think you should give the Realm passphrase when we meet Ticktock."

"Is that a bald joke?" Raek accused.

*I fear I'm going gray.* Ard laughed when he realized the irony. "That's not what I meant. If you give the phrase, it takes some of the attention off of me. Makes us both look like street Hands hired for a simple delivery run by the Realm."

Antler Head had given Ard a handful of techniques to allay suspicions of being one of the Realm's Faceless. The first rule was never to take credit for a job. Always make references to the "boss," and never pretend to be more than a common Hand. In fact, Antler Head had encouraged him to stay completely out of the job whenever possible. Suspicion of being Faceless could be mitigated by taking a purely organizational stance, hiring one Hand to hire others. If Ard wanted to be really cautious, he would hire one to hire another to hire a crew. That way everyone was constantly referring to a different "boss," making it much more difficult to track who was actually in charge.

It was all too cloak-and-dagger for Ardor Benn. He hadn't gotten into the rusing business just to sit back and tell other people what to do. Actually, that was *exactly* why he'd gotten into the business, but what made it worthwhile was being there to see it all unfold. Directing common criminals from the shadows would rob him of that.

Ard had taught Raek the phrase, officially "hiring" him into the Realm's workforce of street Hands. Now he could keep the jobs between the two of them, operating much as they always had.

"Clocks," Raek muttered. "Do you think the Realm realizes that they hired the least punctual person in the Greater Chain to move clocks?"

"They better not know who I am," Ard said. "Isn't that the whole purpose in assembling with such great secrecy?"

"Someone has to know that you're part of the group," Raek insisted. "Or at least, that Androt Penn is. What about their leader? Overseer?"

"Never met him," Ard answered truthfully. "But I assume he knows. The Realm broke Androt Penn out of a cell. If I hadn't made it into the organization, I'd either be locked up, or dead. I suppose anyone who catches word of Androt Penn thriving on the streets would be able to figure out that I'd become Faceless, if they knew I'd been arrested with my face painted white."

"That doesn't make you nervous?"

"I can always change my name again," Ard answered. Maybe it was time to retire Androt Penn. Spread the word that he'd died doing something heroic. "Besides," Ard continued. "I've been itching for a haircut lately."

"Don't go too short or you'll look like Ardor Benn again," Raek warned.

"Maybe I'll just cut it halfway."

"The left half or the right?"

"Or maybe I'll shave my head," Ard said. "Then we'd look like twins."

"You realize you don't get this good-looking and muscular just by shaving your head."

"Oh, I know it takes significant preening."

"Which would make you even later for all your appointments."

"Hey, I'm punctual now," Ard said, gesturing over his shoulder to their load. "The Realm demands it."

He hated to think what might happen if he were late to the next pickup location that Antler Head had given him. Likely, the carriage would drive away empty and he'd be abandoned to perish without the Waters of Loyalty. His only hope would be to find the meeting place on his own, which was unlikely, after what Raek had learned from trying to follow him last time.

Ard's cab had been routed through the vast North Central Carriage Station, just as he'd suspected by the sounds. Raek had lost him at the arrivals platform and was unable to identify his carriage again on the departures side. The carriage yard had served as an effective scrambler, probably switching horse and driver, since those were the biggest identifiers on cabs that otherwise looked identical.

By the sound of it, the Realm had figured out a way to make it nearly impossible to track a carriage on its way to a Faceless meeting, although Raek was planning to try again next time.

"I hate the masks," Ard said, thinking of the gathering. "I just wanted to peel them up and see who's hiding under there. That Faceless meeting has got to be full of people we know."

"Then it's probably best that everyone keeps their ugly faces covered," Raek said. "Need I remind you that we have outstanding debts with many of our 'associates'?"

"I thought we were settled up with everyone," said Ard.

"Parthen?" Raek reminded.

"We paid him the amount we first agreed on," Ard said. "He can't go demanding more just because his carriage ended up in that tree."

"Moroy Peng?"

"He got away from Pekal with his life. I consider that payment enough."

"How about Sigg and Gard?" Raek continued.

"They double-crossed us."

"Skenda Plat?"

"She can accuse us all she wants. I know I didn't put sand in that payment box."

"And the crazies?"

"Cinza and Elbrig?" Ard cried. "Please. We're fine. I paid them everything. Mostly. They said they'd be willing to incite the public for free the night the dragon showed up."

"Okay. What about Sormian Dethers?"

"Who?"

"Captain of the *Shiverswift*," Raek said, trying to jog his memory. "He and his pirates towed our Slagstone off Pekal…"

"Sparks! We never paid him?"

"We sort of ran out of funds, remember? Our wealthy Isle died for the cause and we ended up broke. Hence, our outstanding debts."

"Truly outstanding."

"That's reason enough to be grateful that everyone in the Realm hides behind a mask."

"Cowards," Ard muttered. There was no art in facelessness. No craft. People felt powerful when wearing a mask, but it was just a facade. Masks eliminated responsibility and accountability. They made lying and cheating that much easier. Sparks. Pit Ardor Benn face-to-bareface with any of those frauds and he would show them real handling and control.

"I don't think there's anyone in these criminal circles that you'd want to see on the regular," said Raek. "Besides me, of course."

"And Quarrah," Ard said quietly.

"Come on. Do you really see Quarrah Khai mixed up with a bunch like the Realm?"

Ard sighed. "Good point. Wherever she is, she's probably working alone." He snapped his fingers in thought. "Maybe if I can work my way into the Directorate, I could use the Realm network to find her."

"Or maybe—and I'm just throwing this out there—she doesn't want you to find her."

"Don't be absurd, Raek. She just needed some time. I'm a different man now."

Raek scoffed, but Ard meant it. The events from nearly two

years ago had changed him. He wouldn't consider himself more religious—he'd seen firsthand the corruption and discontinuity in Wayfarism. But despite this, he was closer to the Homeland than ever before. He didn't understand exactly what that meant, knowing that the Homeland was a perfect version of the future. But he felt a new responsibility.

Singlehandedly, Ardor Benn had decided to preserve this timeline. As a Paladin Visitant, he could have obliterated the known world with a single word.

But he hadn't.

Now this timeline progressed naturally, and he was its envoy. It was why he was infiltrating the Realm, why he was looking for Shad Agaul. Ard still believed that the Homeland—the *future*—had pushed him to Abeth Agaul's carriage that night. By taking this job, he might be moving them all toward that perfect future.

"You don't seem too different to me," Raek said. "Just poorer. We can't stay in the Agaul guesthouse forever, you know."

"Won't need to," Ard said. "Lady Abeth said she'd pay us handsomely for finding her son. And supposedly, the Realm pays good for its jobs, too. Soon we'll be rolling in it."

"Yeah, yeah. And once you have enough Ashings, you're going to find Tanalin and sweep her off her feet."

"Tanalin?" Ard snapped.

"Oh, did I say Tanalin?" Raek asked in mock apology. "I meant Quarrah. Guess I just got a little confused there. We've had this conversation for so many years. Seems like only the name has changed."

"Hey!" Ard felt a rush of blood to his face. Sometimes Raek said things that only Raek could say. In moments like these, Ard was reminded that his partner was more like a brother. Frank, and sometimes rather annoying.

"Face it, Ard. Every day, Quarrah is looking more like the new Tanalin."

"That's not..." Ard stammered. "You're wrong. Dead wrong. And I don't want to talk about this. Let's talk about some of *your* baggage."

Raek spread his arms in invitation. As if he had nothing to be ashamed of.

"You've..." Ard struggled to find anything. "You've been late a lot."

"I take that as a compliment, coming from you."

"Sometimes you don't even seem to be listening," Ard continued, finding some steam. "You walk out of the room in the middle of a conversation without saying a word."

Come to think of it, these behaviors were rather unusual. Raek had always been the one to anchor the conversation and keep them on task.

"Do I have to make an announcement every time I go piss?" Raek snapped.

"Sure seems to happen a lot."

"My insides aren't what they used to be," he said. "You should try getting a sword rammed through your middle. Tell me how it feels."

That ended the conversation suddenly, both men turning silently to the road ahead. Ard let out a long breath. Poor Raek. It was easy to forget that his friend was still adapting to his injury. But it was impossible to forget that night in the palace. Ard could still feel his friend's warm blood on his hands, watching the life drain out of him.

It was a true miracle that Raekon Dorrel was alive at all. The procedure to install the "chimney" in his chest had not been intended to restore him to a fully functioning individual. It had merely been meant to keep him breathing until Pethredote could torture more information out of him.

Raek had defied the odds. He'd survived without any serious lingering consequences, thank the Homeland. Because where would Ardor Benn be without him?

Raek directed the wagon off the main road and onto a graveled path leading over to the blue-painted barn. Livestock was corralled on both sides—cows and sheep out to pasture, and chickens pecking at the ground. A couple of horses were grazing nearer to the barn, but Ard didn't see anyone around.

"Ho." Raek pulled back on the reins, easing the wagon to a halt.

A woman suddenly appeared around the corner of the barn, a bundle of hay on her back. She was small but tough-looking, instantly reminding Ard of Tanalin Phor. But this woman was much older, her angular face etched with wrinkles.

"Can I help you fellows?" she asked, dropping the bundle and straightening, dark eyes squinting against the late-afternoon sun.

"We're looking for someone who goes by the name of Ticktock," Raek said, taking the lead as Ard had asked.

"That's an unusual name," she answered. "I'm the only one what works out here. You might keep on down the road to Stylet."

"Thanks. The boss will have our heads if we don't get this delivered in time." Raek gestured to the wagonload behind him. "Stressful, running deliveries from Beripent with poor directions." He sighed. "I fear I'm going gray."

"Some would call it a mark of wisdom," the woman answered. "Why don't you pull into the barn and I'll see if I can help you."

Good. This was the right place.

Raek flicked the reins, directing the horses through the large open door of the barn. Once inside, Ard could see that half of the barn was set up like a Grit mixing station—three long tables littered with balance scales, wadding, and blank Grit pots.

The wagon rolled to a stop as Ticktock pulled one side of the massive barn doors shut, giving them some privacy. Ard leapt down from the bench and pulled the blanket off the back of the wagon. The finely crafted cedar boxes looked like they'd traveled well, nestled tightly against one another. Gregious Mas's meticulous craftsmanship showed, even on the clock's packaging.

"Here's the merchandise," Ard said, his voice affecting a bump-kin accent. "Twenty-five Gregious Mas chainspring mantel clocks. Homeland knows what you want with them, but the boss said to bring them here."

"Let's take a look." She snapped her fingers impatiently.

Straightforward, no-nonsense kind of woman. So far, Ard was yet to meet anyone involved with the Realm who had much of a sense of humor.

He pulled the nearest box off the end of the wagon and followed Ticktock to the tables on the other side of the barn. She wedged the thin blade of her long knife under the lid of the box and pried, the shiny nails pulling out of the soft wood with ease.

Out of the corner of his eye, Ard saw Raek moving toward the barn's exit. "Where are you off to?" he called. He could really use his friend's intimidating presence to prevent Ticktock from getting too bold.

"Gotta take a piss," he shouted over his shoulder.

"I guess that's permissible," Ard replied as Raek disappeared outside.

Ticktock reached into the box and began pulling out the top layer of straw that had padded the fragile devices during a long ride. She withdrew the clock, hidden in a protective cloth bag with a drawstring, the initials and official logo of Gregious Mas Clock-works embroidered on the front.

Ticktock plucked off a few clinging pieces of straw and opened the drawstring, carefully sliding out the mantel clock. It was rect-angular, with a domed top and sides made out of a dark-colored wood. The face of the clock was a little bigger than Ard's palm, and the hands were currently motionless, waiting for the inner workings to be wound.

"I'll need you two fellows to stick around until I can verify the authenticity of the merchandise," she said.

Was that a veiled threat? No matter, the clocks were genuine.

And that made Ticktock a captive audience so that he could explain the genius behind the theft. After all, he wanted to impress the Directorate, which meant he'd need to reveal his process on this particular job, all the while pretending he hadn't been involved.

"The others are all the same?" asked Ticktock.

Ard shrugged. "The boss just said to deliver them. Stealing the contraptions was somebody else's job. You hear how they did it?" He gave only a beat, not really expecting the woman to reply before plowing ahead.

"Boss said they went into the shop, posing like they were going to buy a clock. Really, they were casing the place, only to find out that the clockmaker never has twenty-five finished products in his shop at a time. If they're gonna steal them, they gotta figure out where they are first. So they got to asking Mister Gregious who could afford more than one, since the things cost a pretty Ashing. Clock man said he had plenty of return customers. Said some of the noble folk like to buy one for every mantel in their fancy manors. 'What's the record?' Boss asks. Old Gregious says he's got two noblemen in a competition of sorts. They've reached a stalemate, both of them owning fourteen of these clocks. And the only reason they stopped buying is because they've both run out of mantels to put the blazing things on!"

This was all true, and Gregious's story of the feuding noblemen hadn't surprised Ard one bit. He'd spent enough time with the rich and royal to know how incredibly petty they could be. But the clockmaker's willingness to boast had given Ard and Raek just what they'd needed to get the job done.

"Anyhow," Ard continued, as Ticktock opened up the back of the clock to inspect the insides. "Boss decides to buy a clock after all, and gives it to a hired hand to open her up and see what's inside, just like you're doing there."

Inspecting the clock had been Raek's job. Ard's partner had taken quite a delight in dissecting something as intricate as a Gregious Mas mantel clock.

"The hired hand figures out how to tamper with the clock's inner workings," said Ard. "Turns out there's a little bell inside with some sort of hammer that strikes every hour. Is that it?" He pointed over Ticktock's shoulder to a component he knew *wasn't* the bell.

"That's the spring casing," she corrected.

"Anyhow," Ard said again, "after enough tampering, he fixes it so it'll ding every twenty minutes or so. Now the boss and his helper go to the first nobleman's manor." Lord Stailing, though Ard omitted that detail, since a simple delivery man wasn't likely to know or remember. "They go in, posing as chimney sweeps. The helper goes up on the roof with a bag of tools, and the boss goes inside with an excuse to hang around the mantels. Helper drops down a little bucket on a string, and the boss loads it up with the clock when nobody's looking. See, I would have stole them all right then," Ard said. But there were two good reasons why he and Raek hadn't taken the clocks directly from the manors.

First, it would have been difficult for Raek to get off the roof unnoticed with fourteen fragile clocks in his possession.

Second, when Ard had received the job from Antler Head, she had specifically instructed him to steal the clocks from Gregious Mas, not just to steal twenty-five Gregious Mas clocks. He didn't know if that was semantics, but it didn't seem worth the risk. Especially not on his first job for the Realm.

"So, up on the roof, his helper sets the clocks to chime wrong," Ard continued to his unenthused audience of one, "then sends them back down the chimney. The boss goes through the manor, his helper up above, and together they tweak *every last clock*."

In truth, they had only tampered with eight of them in Lord Stailing's manor. Messing with all fourteen would have taken far too long. They had trusted that eight malfunctioning clocks would drive Lord Stailing mad enough.

"Next they go to the other nobleman's place." That had been Lord Einter, whom Ard had made sure was sailing the InterIsland

Waters at the time of their visit. "But the boss is so clever, he didn't go in as a chimney sweep. This time, he goes in as a chimney *installer*! Tells the servants that the lord has requested the installation of another hearth and mantel. The servants must have known about the competition and figured this was the way for their master to get one more clock than the other nobleman. So the boss goes in, with the helper on the roof. They pull the same stunt, tampering with all the clocks and putting them back in place."

Raek walked into the barn, his eyes lingering on the tables of mixing equipment.

"I'm telling her how the boss did it," Ard said.

"Have you told her the part about the trained pigeon yet?" Raek asked.

Oh, great. Now Ard had to work in a trained pigeon. He had been trying to keep this story *mostly* factual.

Raek reached down and picked an item off the table. It was clearly a fragment of Slagstone, but it was attached to a springlike device that Ard hadn't seen before.

"Is this some sort of ignitor?" Raek asked.

"Put that down," Ticktock snapped, looking up sharply from the clock she was dismantling. "Do not touch anything. The items on this table are part of the most intricate craft."

Raek dropped the item as though it had suddenly grown red hot. It hit the table and sparked, causing the big man to take an apprehensive step back.

Ha! She clearly took Raek for the muscle he looked like, not the brain that he actually was. Raekon Dorrel would know the ins and outs of every single item on these tables. He was simply masking his true intelligence.

"Anyhow," Ard said for the third time. "Not a week goes by before the complaints start rolling in to Mister Gregious. He goes a-panicking, and starts sending out letters. 'Bring me your clocks! I'll tune them up right, free of charge!' Next thing you know, these two noblemen have shipped their whole collections back to their maker."

"That was when the pigeon came in," Raek said, casting a glance at Ard to see how he'd deal with it.

"Right," Ard stalled. "Boss had a homing pigeon caged up right outside the clock shop. Paid a ten-year-old kid to watch Gregious's store and release the pigeon as soon as a wagonload of recalled clocks came in."

Hey! That was actually a pretty good idea. Maybe they could use it sometime.

"Boss gets his people into position, waiting for the clock man to fix the chimes, box them up like new, and send them back to the noblemen. At that point, he said it wasn't hard for his goons to intercept the wagons and hold the drivers at the end of a Roller while they loaded the goods into this wagon here."

For this distasteful part of the job, Ard had used the Realm passphrase to hire simple street Hands, who didn't mind making bodily threats.

"All right." Ticktock set down her tools and looked up at him. "This is indeed a Gregious Mas clock."

"'Course it is," Ard said. "Didn't you just hear my story?"

"Mas has several signature parts inside his clocks, if you know what to look for," she said, ignoring him. "Unload the rest of the boxes into that corner and you're free to go." Ticktock picked up the Slagstone item Raek had dropped and inspected it for damage.

Ard started unloading, but Raek stood rooted, staring at the table.

"I hope you know how to put that thing back together the right way." He gestured at the disassembled clock.

"I know what I'm doing." Ticktock set down the Slagstone device and picked up a piece of the clock, beginning to unwind it slowly.

"How long have you been playing with these things?" Raek pressed.

"As long as Gregious Mas has been making them," she replied curtly.

Ard was moving his fourth box when he called out to Raek, who was still standing there, silently observing Ticktock. "Am I gonna have to do all the heavy lifting alone? I'm telling the boss that you owe me a chunk of your pay."

Raek finally pulled himself away. But he worked slowly on the boxes, always keeping an eye on Ticktock.

"Pleasure doing business," Ard called, hoisting himself onto the unloaded wagon. "Keep us in mind for future jobs. We're just up in Beripent. Rol Tarn," he said, by way of belated introduction. "This is my partner, Moonhead."

Ard waited for a reaction from Raek, but his partner seemed distracted, sliding wordlessly onto the driver's bench. Ticktock didn't respond either, head buried in her work. Ard shrugged and took the reins, guiding the horses out the back of the barn.

They picked up the gravel path and rode in silence until they reached the road to Beripent. Finally, Ard turned and punched Raek playfully on the arm.

"Really?" Ard said. "I introduce you as Moonhead, and you don't even crack a smile?"

Raek kept staring ahead, his forehead wrinkled in thought.

"What's the matter?" Ard asked.

"She was building something," Raek said.

"I'm guessing it was a clock," replied Ard.

Raek shook his bald head. "Something *inside* the clock."

Now it was Ard's turn to wrinkle his forehead. "What do you mean?"

"That thing I picked up was the spring mechanism that sounds the chime on a Gregious Mas clock. It was a piece I tampered with when I wanted the bell to go off every twenty minutes."

"But it had a chunk of Slagstone attached to it," Ard pointed out. Even he knew that seemed wrong.

"Exactly. It looked to me like she wanted the insides of the clock to spark when it chimed the hour."

"To detonate Grit," Ard surmised. It was really the only practical reason for creating sparks. "What kind of detonation would be useful inside a clock?"

"Light Grit?" Raek hypothesized. "Make the clock into a lantern? Maybe she's trying to innovate."

"That seems like a pretty benign motive for the Realm," Ard said. "The lady in the antler mask hired me to bring these specific clocks to this specific person."

"Then it's a setup," said Raek. "They're designing the clocks to malfunction in an effort to discredit Gregious Mas."

"That's basically the same ruse we just pulled," Ard said. "But we didn't go loading the clocks with Grit."

"Maybe it's more sinister than discrediting the clockmaker," continued Raek. "What if the Realm is going to frame him? Once the clock gets wound, they could set it to detonate at the chime. Sparks. If Ticktock put Blast Grit in those clocks, she could blow up half a building without being anywhere near it."

It struck Ard like an Urging from the Homeland. The missing piece to an old puzzle. He snapped his fingers and turned to his partner.

"Raek! That's how the Realm murdered Waed."

"Who?"

"Beska Falay's harp student," he said, reminding him. "The body in Shad Agaul's bed."

Raek was nodding. "When the boy went into the prince's room to play the harp, the clock must have already been ticking inside the new mattress."

But wait. The time didn't quite add up. "The clock would have been in there all day."

"I sped the chime up so it would ring every twenty minutes," Raek said. "It would be fairly simple to adjust it the other way.

Ratchet it back far enough and you might be able to get it to sound just once a day."

"This is big, Raek," Ard said. "It's the first theory we've had that explains how the murder could have been committed in a closed room."

"And Ticktock admitted to having been in this business since Mas invented the mantel clock, well over a year ago."

"So the Realm has been using him from the start, but I'm guessing he doesn't know it." Ard wouldn't have needed to steal the clocks if Gregious was part of the Realm. Maybe they wanted him clean and unconnected in case anyone linked an explosion back to one of his devices.

"Then I've got to ask the question," said Raek. "What is the Realm planning to do with twenty-five more of these clock bombs?"

"I'm never going to learn anything valuable as a lowly Faceless." Ard pounded his fist against the bench. "It's like my granddad used to say: if you're not the lead horse, the view's all the same."

"How do you become the lead horse?"

"A good start would be getting into the Directorate," said Ard. "I've got to learn the rest of that symbol."

"So we find someone who knows it," suggested Raek. "Make them an offer they can't turn down."

"I wouldn't even know where to start," Ard replied. "The meeting was downright unsettling. Not an inch of real person could be seen. Heads and hands covered, shape of the body was disguised. They even altered our voices."

"Then find someone on the inside who knows it," suggested Raek. "You don't need to know their identity. Coax the symbol out of them while you're both masked on the floor."

"If I threaten someone, it could make a scene. They might go straight to the Directorate to rat me out."

"Not if they didn't remember it."

"What?" Ard said. "Memory Grit? How am I supposed to get a

pot into the meeting? Those black-masked guards give a thorough frisking at the doorway. I'll be dead before I even get inside."

"You'll have to clench the Grit pot," Raek said with a half grin.

"Have you seen my hindquarters?" Ard cried. "I would shatter that clay pot in two steps."

"Then maybe we need to take a page out of Quarrah Khai's book?"

"What do you mean?"

Raek held up his gloved hand and snapped his fingers.

~

*We have counseled and debated, and this is our best course of action.*

# CHAPTER

# 19

Portsend added forty granules of dried spidertree bark to the pot of boiling water and began stirring it gently. If his calculations were correct, the infusion would simmer to a balance level of positive sharp nine. Their approach had been to systematically increase the balance level, but they hadn't yet tested any of the scroll's materials in a liquid that sharp.

Portsend imagined that the first developments in Grit must have unfolded in a similar manner, some nine hundred years ago. The idea that dragon Slagstone could be processed into something beneficial must have been a huge hurdle. But once the pulverized

Slagstone's properties had been discovered, it gave scientists a formula for success. According to some texts, the five basic types of Grit had all been discovered within a cycle. Eight of the ten types of Specialty Grit had unfolded over the next few decades.

Similarly, Portsend's experiments were progressing at an alarming rate, now that they understood how the new Grit reacted as a solvent.

Stasis Grit had been quick to follow Ignition and Null. It was a solution of isolated birchwood, dissolved in a negative-flat-three solution. The cloud had manifested itself quickly, but after dozens of tests, Portsend and his pupils had no idea what it could do.

Then one evening, Lomaya had observed a cockroach falling unconscious as it entered the detonation radius. That had led to tests on mice, a cat, a goat, and ultimately Lomaya herself.

The results were astounding. While inside the detonation cloud, life-forms were held in a perfectly static state. There was no consciousness, no breathing…Sparks, even the heartbeat was suspended. It all resumed the moment the subject's head was removed from the Stasis cloud, with no noticeable lasting effects.

"That smells like slag," commented the portly man sitting near the laboratory door.

There were few things Portsend Wal hated more than being observed while experimenting. Onlooking students were one thing, but when other professors or professionals breathed over his shoulder, it made him self-conscious.

His constant observers now were hardly academics, but the bodyguards who had replaced Brase and Luthe carried a different air of intimidation. Namely, a loaded Roller.

The two men hadn't left Portsend's sight for nearly four weeks now, and he still only knew them by the obvious nicknames that they called each other. The one who still wore Brase's floppy-brimmed hat was Stubs—aptly assigned since he was missing part of two fingers on his right hand. The leaner one with missing teeth went by Cheery. He was far from that, but Portsend could see how his incessant habit of off-tune whistling might make him seem carefree to an outsider.

Portsend had explained to Lomaya and San that the two men had been hired to replace Brase and Luthe, who'd been called to the war front. The reasoning was hollow, and Portsend's apparent edge around the thugs surely gave away the truth of the matter. His students were not fooled.

Portsend looked up from his pot as San Green opened the heavy door, Lomaya following him in from the observation deck of the detonation chamber.

"We've run a dozen tests," the young woman reported, her voice chipper despite the late hour. Portsend had reserved the latest block of time in the student laboratory. No one cared if they went over, as long as they cleaned and locked up when they finished.

"The cloud is movable, even when the detonation is perfectly spherical," San said. "I've never seen Barrier Grit behave like this."

Portsend raised an eyebrow. "Barrier Grit?"

"Right," San replied. "*Containment* Grit." This was their newest discovery. "Because it's a liquid solution."

"That's not the only thing that differentiates them," Portsend replied. "We must always speak of Barrier Grit and Containment Grit as distinct entities, no matter how similar their clouds might appear."

Both Grit types created an impenetrable, translucent shell upon detonation. And while Barrier Grit was derived from an aggregate of common metals, Containment Grit was created specifically from processed steel. The uneducated citizen would probably not see an immediate difference, but he expected more from San and Lomaya.

Portsend cleared his throat to initiate an impromptu lecture. "What are the two major differences between the two?"

"A cloud of Containment Grit is movable," answered San.

"And that's a direct violation of Jonzan's Fourth," exclaimed Lomaya.

"Which is ... ?" Portsend urged.

"All Grit clouds are immovable unless fully contained," she recited.

"And in terms of Grit," said Portsend, "'containment' means trapping a cloud in a box, or similar vessel, to prevent any part of its edge from reaching its natural spherical shape. Which leads us to the second major departure from traditional Barrier Grit."

"The liquid Grit can, itself, act as a vessel to contain other detonations," Lomaya said.

"And what does that mean, in application?"

"I can move a cloud of Light Grit without a lantern," San said. "The Containment Grit closes around it and makes both clouds movable."

"This will greatly reduce the amount of Drift Grit needed to move heavy items," offered Lomaya. "Instead of detonating multiple overlapping clouds of Drift, you could just enclose one in Containment Grit and move your heavy item inside the movable sphere."

Portsend nodded. "Like a Drift crate, only without the box." There were probably more life-altering applications for Containment Grit, but they were still in the early stages of testing. "Why don't the two of you mix up a few more of those solutions," he said. "I'd like to measure the actual weight of a Containment cloud, and observe what effect gravity might have on a movable detonation."

The two youngsters quickly busied themselves at the scales, measuring consistent amounts of processed steel shavings and pouring dribs of the required liquid.

Homeland, they were making history here. Rather, it would become history if these discoveries were ever released to the public. Under his new "employment," Portsend had been doing all he could to postpone another meeting with King Termain. Gloristar had been sending letters that pained Portsend, her tone growing more impatient, even bordering on desperation.

He knew what was at stake. It was a dangerous game to keep pushing Gloristar back. But if he reported to the king, his new boss would release Moonsick people to rage throughout the city in death and terror.

Portsend had already delivered his information about Null Grit to Stubs and Cheery. It terrified him to think that a woman wicked enough to farm Moonsickness was now in possession of a new Grit type.

He had regretted the decision immediately and decided he would not yield again. If he couldn't report to the king for Gloristar's sake, then he sure as sparks wasn't going to report to the boss. At least not until he absolutely had to.

Portsend told his new guards the same thing he'd written to Gloristar. The new Grit wasn't ready yet. He was on the verge of a breakthrough, but there were still too many unknowns to share.

He'd given Ignition Grit to the king and Null Grit to the boss. But Portsend was keeping Stasis Grit and this new Containment Grit to himself for now, praying to the Homeland that he'd find a way out of this mess.

Portsend noticed that the hourglass beside the stove was empty. He quickly pulled the pot off the heat, hoping not too much extra time had passed. He'd been distracted by his thoughts. A few additional seconds on the heat wouldn't change the balance level too much. He'd leave the infusion to cool and then strain it, bottle it, and label it, adding it to the wide range of liquids they could experiment with.

"We have three solutions ready, Professor," Lomaya said. "Do you want to join us?"

He trusted them to make accurate observations. And staying out here would keep Stubs's eyes off their progress. Portsend was aware that the refinement of each discovery only forced him closer to making a decision. Reveal his information to the king to protect Prime Isless Gloristar, or give in to his oppressors and prevent an attack of Moonsickness in Beripent?

"I'll begin tidying up out here," he answered regretfully. "Take careful notes."

The two students moved onto the observation deck, shutting the heavy door behind them. Portsend shot a quick glance at Stubs to see if he'd picked up on the exchange. The man was sitting on a wooden chair by the entrance to the lab, his cheek packed with tobacco as he spit into a pail.

The lab's exterior door suddenly cracked open. Cheery leaned in, snapping his fingers for attention.

"Stubs," he hissed. "There's somebody here to see you. Said you've got unfinished business."

Stubs sat forward sharply. "I ain't here."

"I can hear your blazing voice, Stubs!" called an unknown voice, deep and resonant, from beyond the door.

"Sparks, Cheery," Stubs snapped. "Kind of bodyguard are you? You're supposed to be keeping back the riffraff."

"He came down the hill like he owned the place," Cheery said. "What was I supposed to do?"

"Shoot him," Stubs whispered. "Stab him. Don't much care how you do it. You know folks from my side business ain't welcome while I'm on duty."

*Side business?* Portsend wondered. But Stubs made a fair point. If Cheery was intimidated by an approaching thug, he wasn't much of a bodyguard.

The door opened sharply, and Portsend saw Cheery shoved aside. A man ducked into the laboratory, among the tallest Portsend had ever seen. Despite the cool spring night, he wore a shirt with cutoff sleeves, his dark skin rippling over massive muscles. His head was bald, but he didn't seem very old. He had a slightly crooked nose that looked like it had been broken in more than one fight, and his face was slick with sweat.

Stubs swallowed audibly. "Homeland, Raekon. You look like slag."

Portsend stayed where he was, hoping to remain inconspicuous near the stove in the corner. Cheery reappeared in the doorway, the glow of the lab's Light Grit glinting on the barrel of his drawn Roller. It seemed the goon was finally taking a stand, now that the stranger had officially trespassed into the lab.

The man named Raekon glanced over his shoulder. "Stow it, Whistler." He grunted threateningly.

Stubs held up a hand to give his companion a signal to relax. "This'll only take a moment." He stood up, the stranger towering over him.

"I don't think you understand how this works," Raekon said. "We make an appointment, I expect you to honor it." He shivered as though a chill had just passed through the stuffy laboratory.

"I took another job," Stubs said. "It conflicted."

"Then you let your clients know you're out," retorted the bigger man. "You don't leave me fixing while my supply runs thin. Makes a fellow blazing disagreeable."

Raekon suddenly held up a little cloth bag, causing Stubs to jolt in surprise. Even across the room, Portsend could hear the clink of Ashings from within.

"I've got the payment." Raekon's hand trembled slightly. "Or I've got half a dozen of your other clients itching to know which rock you're hiding under. So, what do you say? Is business on, like usual?"

Stubs spit, missing the pail. He shrugged. "We can work something out, but I mean...I don't have it with me."

Suddenly Raekon's other hand shot out, seizing Stubs by the front of his shirt and slamming him against the rack on the wall.

Portsend flinched as the clay pots on the rack shifted and clattered. He heard one of them break, but Homeland be praised it didn't have enough force to spark an ignition.

"That's a load of slag!" Raekon called. "I know you couldn't sit on a lazy job like this without fixing a little Heg for yourself."

*Heg.* So this was about Health Grit. Portsend was a silent observer to a shady deal going down between two addicts.

Slowly, as though to show that he wasn't making any sort of threat, Stubs reached into his pocket and withdrew three paper parcels. They looked almost like Blast cartridges used to load guns, but the lead ball was obviously missing, and the diameter of the wrap was too thin.

"Is it Compounded?" Raekon asked, swiping all three paper rolls from his hand.

"One to six," replied Stubs. "That's strong stuff."

With the drawstring of the little bag dangling around his wrist, the man used both big hands to twist open an end on one of the rolls. He tilted it toward the light and inspected the Grit. He sniffed it and then licked the edge of the paper, tasting a little bit of the product against his tongue.

Portsend shuddered. That was human rib bone he was tasting, *after* it had passed through a dragon's digestive tract. The professor had overcome any moral objections to using human-derived Grit decades ago, but tasting it was another matter.

Seemingly satisfied by the quality of the Health Grit, Raekon pushed past Stubs and sat down on the chair that the bodyguard had previously occupied. Portsend stepped sideways to keep the big man in view. It was part curiosity, and part fear that he might do something destructive.

Raekon grabbed the front of his own shirt and pulled it open, revealing a sculpted chest, shiny with sweat. But, Homeland! Something protruded just below the man's sternum! It looked like a shard of pipe—like a bit of shrapnel from one of those Void Grit scrap bombs used in the war. Thick, pale scar tissue had built up around the pipe's opening, incorporating the metal into a grotesque deformation.

Reaching up, Raekon removed what appeared to be a plug in the end of the pipe. Leaning back, he emptied a bit of the Health Grit from the roll directly into his chest! He replaced the plug, giving it a sharp rap, which, judging by the faint sound of grating Slagstone, caused a contained detonation of Health Grit inside the man's body.

No wonder he was addicted. Compounded at a rate of one to six and contained so close to his heart…Portsend wondered if the fellow would even be able to survive without consistent detonations.

Raekon sighed heavily, finally seeming to relax on the chair. "Here," he said, digging out a few Ashings from the bag and handing them to Stubs, who quickly studied the money.

"You only paid me for two rolls."

"Discount for travel," Raekon replied. "I didn't hoof it all the way down to the Southern Quarter to pay full price." He breathed deeply, his trembles subsiding. "You didn't exactly deliver the amount we'd agreed on, either. These rolls won't even get me through the week."

"I'll get you more," promised Stubs. "And you can tell the others that I'm back in the business. Just…" He glanced around the laboratory. "You can't come here again. Spread the word that I'll be back at my regular contact points in the Char."

"Stubs…" muttered Cheery from his place in the open doorway. It was obvious that the second bodyguard didn't understand how his partner was going to make good on that promise while maintaining his new job as Portsend's constant babysitter.

"I can't promise to be there with the same regularity," Stubs clarified to Raekon, "but I'll deal twice the usual amount of Heg to hold you all over."

Portsend turned suddenly as the door from the observation deck opened. Lomaya appeared, San close behind her.

"It's fascinating, Professor," she said, clutching a thin scribing board with a paper tacked onto it. "On its own, the Containment Grit is incredibly lightweight. Our cloud was nearly immeasurable. It weighed slightly more when enclosing a cloud of Light Grit, but we already knew that detonation had measurable mass."

Portsend went rigid. Stubs must have been standing in just the right place to block Lomaya's view of the intruder seated in the chair. Surely, she wouldn't speak so freely in front of a stranger.

"What's more interesting," she went on, moving toward him, "the spherical cloud *is* affected by gravity, but it drops slowly. Almost like a thin piece of paper. Or a feather."

Portsend was shaking his head, silently imploring the young woman to stop talking. His expression must have done the trick, causing her to trail off and glance toward the bodyguards.

Raekon had risen to his feet. It was impossible to overlook him now. His face had a healthy flush to it, and his skin no longer looked clammy in the glow of the Light Grit lanterns.

"*Containment* Grit?" the big man asked, his shirt still hanging open to reveal his old wound.

San and Lomaya froze, looking from Raekon to Portsend, their wide eyes begging for some introduction and assurance that this stranger wasn't here to harm anyone. While Portsend didn't believe Raekon posed much of a threat to anyone but Stubs, it was an assurance he couldn't give.

"You got what you came for," Stubs said. "Now, get out of here."

Raekon crossed the lab in what seemed like half the steps of a regular man. Portsend shuffled hastily backward, burning his elbow on the hot stove.

"Containment Grit," Raekon said again, looming over Portsend. "What is it?"

"Another step and I blow your brains out," Cheery called from the doorway, the Slagstone hammer of his Roller cocked into place.

"It's merely *theoretical*," Portsend stammered. He didn't want

Cheery to shoot, making a mess of another college laboratory. But this man couldn't be allowed to walk out of here with knowledge about one of the new Grit types. Perhaps he could convince this simpleminded thug that the things he'd just overheard were nothing noteworthy.

"My name is Portsend Wal," he continued. "Professor of practical and theoretical Grit mixing. These are two of my first-year students participating in an extracurricular study program that focuses on the theoretical."

"Hmm…" Raekon stroked his chin. "I didn't think the college allowed first-year students into the Grit labs. And this young woman's observation on gravitational pull sounds a lot more like concrete science than mere theory."

"You must have misheard me," Lomaya said. "This is a highly academic setting. We use a lexicon that would likely confuse the common citizen."

Raekon turned to her, his face splitting into a wry grin. "Well, based on what I heard, I'm going to say that Containment Grit creates a Barrier-type cloud capable of enclosing another type of Grit detonation. Furthermore, you can't weigh something that isn't affected by gravity, which means your Containment cloud is movable—in direct violation of Jonzan's Fourth Truth. Floats gradually downward like a *feather*, you say? I find that comparison quite uninspired. Why not say it drops like a thin flake of pastry?"

Flames! This man was hardly a simpleminded thug. When he'd entered the laboratory, he'd seemed frantic and pushy, barely even aware of his surroundings. But now that he'd had his fix of Health Grit, he seemed composed and meticulous, and, quite frankly, brilliant.

"Don't look so surprised." Raekon turned back to Portsend. "My partner and I frequently use pastries to illustrate complicated concepts—actual, *and* theoretical."

"Sir," Portsend began, trying to gather his courage. "You have entered an academic facility without permission. Our research here is highly classified. I must ask you to leave."

Portsend tried not to let his gaze drift as he saw Cheery moving quietly toward them.

"I have a hard time accepting that a fellow like you—obviously reputable and intelligent," said Raekon, "would spend a late night at the college laboratory playing make-believe with a couple of first-year students. And even if I could accept it, I've got to wonder why you have an entire canister labeled 'dragon-processed steel,' when that is considered common metal and there is no need to isolate it from—"

He trailed away as the barrel of Cheery's gun pressed against the back of his neck. "Let's go, big guy," the bodyguard demanded. "This is your last chance to move out peaceful-like."

"Containment Grit," Raekon said a final time, his eyes still lingering on Portsend. "Huh. Wouldn't that be something?"

Raekon turned, his movements careful as Cheery escorted him to the exit. No one in the lab seemed to breathe until Raekon and the bodyguard were gone, the door pulling shut behind them.

"It's all right," Portsend assured Lomaya and San. "The two of you did nothing wrong."

"Who was that?" San asked.

"Just a stranger," Portsend answered. "We'll never see him again."

"Cheery should have pulled that trigger," Stubs said, striking a rather different stance than he'd made while Raekon had been in the room. "One less problem for me to deal with."

"It was your problems that brought him here in the first place," Portsend said, emboldened by the rush of adrenaline he'd just experienced.

"Hey, it was Cheery that let him down here," protested the bodyguard.

"At the very least, you should have handled your side business outside of the laboratory," continued Portsend. "I find you both to blame. What if he'd been sent to destroy this facility?" *Or kill me and steal the scroll*, Portsend thought. "I hardly feel safe with the two of you watching my back."

"Oh, please," Stubs said dismissively. "I know Raekon. If I'd thought he'd do something to endanger you or the materials, we would have disposed of him. We know how to do our jobs."

Wait. Maybe the encounter with Raekon could turn out to be a blessing from the Homeland. Maybe this was the opportunity Portsend needed to get rid of these two.

"We'll have to see if your boss agrees." Portsend had wanted that threat to come out with more confidence. Instead, it had left his lips as little more than a timid whisper. Still, it seemed to do the trick.

Stubs's eye twitched as he stared at the three of them. "Well, I might have some things to say about you, too. About the way you're holding back. I'm no college genius, but I know you've got enough new information to share with the boss."

Portsend had rightfully viewed the bodyguards as half-wits. But even they weren't dense enough to overlook the last few weeks of successful experimentation.

"Then why haven't you reported it?" Portsend asked. This was more than he wanted Lomaya and San to hear. If it wasn't apparent before, they'd definitely realize that Portsend was being manipulated now.

"This is a soft job," Stubs admitted. "Pays nice. Lots of sitting. Not everybody's got it this good."

"So, you're interested in making it last as long as possible?" Portsend said.

"You could say that."

The professor cleared his throat. "I see no reason to report this incident to the boss," he said, "as long as you remain unaware of our progress with the Grit. Do we have an arrangement?"

His heart was hammering in his chest. This could easily come back to bite him, but right now, all Portsend Wal could do was delay a variety of inevitabilities. He had to keep working, and one day the secrets of the scroll might benefit the right people.

"I think I can get Cheery on board with that," Stubs finally replied. "But we never had this conversation."

"Of course not," Portsend answered. He felt another strand of his web of lies wrapping itself around him. The way things were shaping up, he didn't see how this could end favorably for him. These new discoveries were supposed to protect Gloristar from Termain, but so far, it had only put everyone at greater risk. Portsend needed to make sure he didn't lose focus on what was most important.

Stay alive.

Protect San and Lomaya.

Protect Gloristar.

~

*Always, they favored the weak and the simple.*

# CHAPTER

# 20

"Come, all. Drink of the Waters of Loyalty."

The Directorate member who spoke was wearing a mask Ard hadn't seen last time. It was completely draped with long black human hair, bones and beads dangling like ornaments. From this distance, Ard couldn't even see where the eyeholes were.

The figure with the feathered headpiece was on the left this time.

On the right was another new mask, shaped like a savage boar, with long tusks hooking upward from its jowls.

At the payment lectern off to the side of the stage was Antler Head. The room looked identical to the one where the first meeting had taken place. Ard had found his carriage waiting behind Stavrom's Tavern. By the sounds of it, he'd once again been scrambled through North Central Carriage Station before winding up at the meeting.

Ard stepped up to the edge of the stage, dreading the bitter taste of whatever he was about to drink. He threaded the reed through the slit in his mask and downed it quickly, discarding the tin cup in one of the barrels.

As fast as he'd been, he still had to wait a moment before taking an opening at the table with the Boar Face figure.

"I fear I'm going gray." It was a man's voice.

"Some would call it a mark of wisdom," answered Ard.

Boar Face drew a circle on the piece of paper and passed it over. Ard picked up one of the scribing charcoals on the table and drew the single line of the symbol that Antler Head had taught him, dividing the circle in half vertically. He slid it back to the Boar for inspection, but kept his grip on the wooden charcoal stick.

"Do you have anything to report?" Boar Face asked, voice distorted by the wax-and-rod modifier.

"*Time*," answered Ard, giving the label he had assigned to the clocks job. He waited patiently while Boar Face thumbed through the ledger he was holding.

"Our reports say the job was completed," replied Boar Face.

"Of course," answered Ard. "It was my pleasure to serve the Realm."

"And it is our pleasure to compensate you for your efforts." Boar Face wrote something on a piece of paper. His gloved hand rocked a stamp through a pad of ink and he pressed it to the bottom of the note before passing it to Ard.

It was a receipt, the stamp showing a complex sunburst shape. The amount was written for two hundred Ashings. Ard supposed the payment would have been impressive to most, but he and Raek had put a lot of effort into stealing those mantel clocks. To be honest, Ard had been hoping for twice that payment.

"Thank you," Ard said, feeling glad for once that the white mask covered his disappointed expression. He folded the small paper and tucked it into his glove.

"Are you willing to take another assignment?" asked Boar Face.

"Yes," Ard answered. "I'm ready to learn the next part of the symbol."

"That is not what I asked."

"Was the clocks job done inadequately?"

"The Realm was satisfied," he answered. "But that doesn't ensure any sort of advancement. You will be taught the next line of the symbol when *we* are ready. Not you."

Sparks! At this rate, he could be years away from making his way to the top. He would definitely have to implement the backup plan.

"Have you previously performed any tasks related to the farm?" he asked.

*Farm? What kind of farm?* "No, sir."

"Then I shall assign you something very straightforward. The Realm needs you to collect two individuals and deliver them to the farm by the end of the cycle."

That was less than a week away. Good thing Ard wasn't actually planning on doing this job.

"If completed to our satisfaction, *then* you will be eligible to learn more of the symbol," said Boar Face.

By that time, Ard would know the whole thing, if everything went right today. But he had to act excited by the offer, nodding his head enthusiastically. "Where is this farm?"

"Your delivery point will be a half day's ride east of Kennar."

"I didn't think there was anything out that way," Ard admitted.

The township of Kennar was due east of Beripent, and it took a real hardy bunch to live on the windward shore, pelted with near-constant rains and winds.

"That is by design," answered Boar Face.

"Who do I need to bring to this farm?"

"We leave it up to your discretion," replied Boar Face.

"So, anyone will do?" Ard was puzzled.

"Young or old. The captives you deliver needn't be healthy, but they must be alive."

That was an odd criterion. If the people he was supposed to bring in were intended to work as slaves, the unhealthy didn't seem like a smart choice.

"How will you label the job?" Boar Face asked.

"*Oregano*," Ard said. It was the first word that popped into his head. And it didn't really matter if he remembered it, since he had no plans to follow up.

"The exit word is *rancid*," said the man. His boar mask nodded in dismissal. "We are the Realm."

Ard made his way down the steps and began meandering through the other Faceless wandering the floor. He watched people claim their payment, handing Antler Head their receipts in exchange for small burlap sacks bulging with Ashings. From there, those individuals always made a direct line for the door, muttering the exit phrase to the masked guards and moving out to one of the waiting cabs.

Ard couldn't claim his payment. Not yet, at least. But the receipt would serve a more important purpose. He glanced at the scribing charcoal he had swiped.

Time to learn the rest of the symbol.

"I fear I'm going gray," said the man behind the feathered mask.

"Some would call it a mark of wisdom," answered Quarrah, the voice-modifier rod digging into her cheeks.

As the Directorate member drew his circle on a piece of paper,

Quarrah set down both of her bags, stepping on the leather straps to make sure no one could swipe them while she was drawing the symbol.

She quickly drew the five lines of the symbol exactly as she'd done last time, then slid the paper back to the man in the elaborate mask. She held her breath in anticipation of what would happen next. Another job? In a meeting like this, there had to be dozens assigned, probably outlining some bigger picture that no individual member would have a chance of discerning. The Realm had to have a master plan, and like a complicated lock, there would be many independent pins holding it together. Each Faceless was like a tooth in the key, each carrying out his or her own duties that would eventually spring the mechanism.

Quarrah couldn't fathom the amount of planning behind an organization like this. Just to pull off a single meeting was an impressive feat—positioning the carriages and scrambling them through the station, having enough Ashings to pay for every completed job, coordinating assignments...

"Do you have anything to report?" the man asked, interrupting her thoughts as he lit the edge of the paper in the candle's flame and dropped it into the metal bowl.

"Fifty-six panweights of Void Grit," Quarrah said quietly. She had divided it evenly between the two bags, thus making it easier to carry. By speaking the word *rearguard* at the door, the masked guards had let her enter with her score.

Technically, she hadn't stolen this Grit. But she had definitely stolen to get it. Lyndel had been very intrigued by the green vial, but she had decided that one of them was not worth the Sovereign army's entire complement of Void Grit.

Had Lyndel expressed more interest in Quarrah's reason for taking the Grit, she might have explained about the Realm and the possibility that King Termain was under its control. But their conversation had quickly turned into simple negotiation for the Void Grit. Lyndel had agreed to surrender her stores in exchange for all the vials in the Archkingdom encampment. That had sent Quarrah creeping back in to swipe the entire box from the munitions tent just before dawn.

In the end, it had actually worked out even better for Quarrah, coming away with six panweights more than she'd originally stolen from the Archkingdom.

"I'm hoping this will earn me a position in the Directorate," she said.

"Keep it with you," replied the man. "All competitors will remain in this room. Directorate eligibility will be determined after this meeting."

Quarrah couldn't help but cast a glance at the Faceless shuffling around the floor behind her. She'd glimpsed several people holding bags, but none as large as hers. And she had *two* of them!

It really wasn't likely that anyone else could have acquired more than fifty-six panweights of Void Grit in the last three weeks. Or was she underestimating her competitors?

"Your password at the end of the meeting will be *Cataclysm*," said the man.

Quarrah nodded to show that she understood.

"We are the Realm."

Just like that? No exit word, no location for her next pickup… The man with the seashell mask had told her that there would be no payment for this job. But would there be a punishment if she didn't present the most?

She didn't let herself think of that, picking up her bags and stepping away from the table. She would win the competition and take her place in the Directorate. She was sure to get answers about King Termain there. Fabra Ment would at last be satisfied, and Quarrah could part ways with this organization and finally resume her solo work.

It didn't take long for Ard's target to reveal himself—a Faceless figure carrying two black bags. Not only had the person entered the meeting with the luggage, but he didn't show any signs of leaving even after conversing with the Directorate.

Currently, his target Faceless was loitering against one of the walls, back to the bricks in a hypercautious stance. Time to pay him a little visit. Ard double-checked his left glove before closing in on the figure with a determined gait.

"Greetings," he muttered through the awkwardness of the voice modifier. At once, the figure made to flee, but Ard stopped his retreat with another sentence. "The Directorate sent me. There has been a mistake."

The Faceless froze and Ard held his left hand next to the figure's white mask, snapping his fingers. A Slagstone fragment sparked at his fingertip, igniting a small detonation that escaped through the loosened stitches of his glove.

The white-masked head was immediately enclosed in a cloud of Memory Grit. Ardor Benn, however, stood safely just outside the radius. The glove was a direct inspiration from Quarrah Khai. He'd prepared it in the carriage on the way to the meeting, grateful that it had been subtle enough to sneak past the guard's inspection.

"I was sent by the feathered mask," Ard continued. "He failed to communicate some very important information." He slipped the receipt from his glove and used the scribing charcoal to draw a circle on the back. "Of course, I'll need you to complete the symbol before I say anything." He tried to hand the items over, but the white mask simply stared at him, a canvas without a painting. "You understand this is somewhat urgent..." Ard pressed.

"I'm supposed to trust you?" So, it was a woman under all that getup. And by the slurred sound of her voice, that waxen rod was too big for her mouth.

"Trust me or get shot," he said. "I'm just doing my job." Menacingly, Ard reached his left hand into the folds of his shrouding cloak. It was a daring bluff, but he needed to move this along before she took a single step sideways, exiting his Memory cloud.

"You'd never get into this meeting with a gun," she responded.

"Now, that's assuming I'm actually a Faceless."

She cocked her head inquisitively to the side. For a moment, something seemed familiar about her. It was probably just paranoia. Ard couldn't waste time trying to guess the faces behind every mask.

"You don't think the Realm has security on this floor?" Ard pressed. "Dressed to blend in seamlessly with the Faceless?" That got her. He could tell without even seeing her expression. "Believe it or not, I'm actually trying to help you. The Directorate sent me to give you a vital piece of information. If you would just verify…"

The Faceless set down her bags. For a moment, Ard thought about snatching them and running. But that would only cause a stir. And learning the symbol was more important than satisfying his curiosity about the woman's load. Besides, she was now stepping on the straps of the bags to prevent such a theft.

The woman took the paper and charcoal from Ard's gloved hands. He held his breath as she drew the lines—five in total. Whether or not that was the whole symbol, it was certainly cycles ahead of what Ard knew. He took the items back, studying the drawing.

"What do you need to tell me?" she asked, picking up her bags.

Ard's hand shot out, shoving her abruptly sideways and out of the Memory cloud. "I'm sorry," he said. "I mistook you for someone else." A ridiculous statement, given their current apparel. He turned quickly, disappearing through the anonymous figures as the woman shook her masked head in puzzlement.

A moment later, Ard stood across the table from Feather Head, exchanging the passphrase. The man drew the circle and pushed it across the table.

Now it was time to test that woman's honesty.

Ardor Benn took a deep breath and copied the five lines in the exact order that he'd seen the Faceless woman draw it. He slid the paper back to the Directorate member, heart hammering.

He was painfully aware that she could have tricked him. She could have scribbled absolute nonsense just to test him.

Feather Head was studying the paper through his blacked-out eyeholes. Finally, he lifted the scrap to the candle flame. "Do you have anything to report?"

*Praise the Homeland she was an honest criminal!* Now it was time for Ardor Benn to do what he did best. Improvise. Carry on a full conversation about something he knew nothing about, while somehow making the other person feel as if he were the one whose information was lacking.

"I did what was asked," Ard replied vaguely.

"What was the label for your assignment?" He was already thumbing through the notebook.

"I'm not interested in payment this time," said Ard. "Only advancement." Hopefully, this kind of ambitious behavior wouldn't be rewarded with a Roller ball through the forehead.

"You brought the goods with you?" he asked.

"Yes," Ard replied slowly. So, that was why some of the Faceless were carrying bags.

"Keep them with you until the end of the meeting," he replied. "Your password at that time will be *Cataclysm*."

Sparks! What had just happened? Ard stood dumbfounded across the table. That had been *far* easier than he'd expected.

"Thank you," Ard said, backing up numbly, suddenly anxious to get off the stage before his good fortune crumbled around him.

"Thank the Realm," replied Feather Head. "We are the cause of both grin and grimace. Which shall you do for us?"

～

*A third of us were changed, and the gods could not abide it.*

# CHAPTER

# 21

A rd was one of ten Faceless who remained on the floor, lingering after the meeting according to the directions they'd been given. He spotted the woman with two bags right away, pleased that his instincts had been correct about her being part of this. But it didn't provide Ard with a drib of comfort to see that he was the only one not holding a bag or a box.

Six members of the Directorate now stood side by side at the edge of the stage—Antler Head, Feather Head, Boar Face, Hairy Face, Seashell Head, and Horn Mask. One of them spoke, but Ard couldn't determine who.

"Our leader," announced the voice, "Overseer."

A new figure descended the stairs, stepping between Hairy Face and Feather Head at the front of the stage. Dressed in the same oversized shroud, Overseer had a headpiece composed completely of uncut dragon scales. It looked like part of a shed husk, draped over the person's head, the layout forming something of a twisted face with large, curling horns jutting from the crown.

"A member of the Directorate has perished, cut off from the Waters of Loyalty," spoke Overseer.

Ard realized it was a woman. Her voice was rather husky, but it was hard to know its true sound with an obvious voice modifier in place.

"His name," she continued, "was Waelis Mordo."

Sparks! Ard knew the man! During the regalia ruse, Ard had

spent a lot of time at receptions, disguised as Dale Hizror. Elbrig Taut had once counseled him to stay away from Waelis Mordo, citing him as a backbiting gossiper. For the most part, Ard had been successful, but he'd had a handful of run-ins with the nobleman during his time as the famous composer. Mordo was a man of power and influence, and Ard understood that he'd found his way into Termain's ear in the last year.

That certainly showed the reach of the Realm, if the king's own advisor was one of the organization's top members. Then again, Termain himself could be under one of those masks, and Ard would hardly be surprised. That kind of corruption was precisely what had led him here, searching for the missing boy heir.

"His disloyalty caused his insides to rupture, spoiled like rotten meat," continued Overseer. "And now a place at my table has opened. One of you will claim it today." The leader strode down the steps to stand in front of the remaining Faceless. "Form a row, shoulder to shoulder."

Ard positioned himself at the end of the line in case he needed to make a hasty getaway.

"One by one, you will approach me and speak the password. You will deliver your Void Grit to the stage, where it will be verified. The one who delivers the most will join the Directorate."

Void Grit. So, that was what everyone had in their boxes and bags. Ard had only his wits. Great.

On the stage, two of the councillors produced a large set of balance scales as the first Faceless stepped up, whispering to Overseer's satisfaction. The figure handed a box to Boar Face, who opened the container and withdrew a Grit keg. The councillor placed a pinch of the Grit in his palm and struck it with a Slagstone ignitor.

Instantly, Boar Face's hand was thrown downward as an obvious detonation of Void Grit formed in a perfect sphere in the air. It wasn't large. Just enough to prove that the Grit was genuine.

On the table behind, Horn Mask and Feather Head added weights to the scales until they balanced properly. Ard squinted, but he couldn't possibly see what it equaled from this distance. Raek would have been able to guess the weight just by glaring at the keg, but that wasn't Ard's area of expertise.

Feather Head moved down the steps and whispered to Overseer. The leader nodded, motioning aside the Faceless who had just made the delivery.

This process continued for the next half hour, with each sample detonation yielding the same result. The real bottleneck had been the woman with the two duffel bags. After testing and weighing, it had become apparent that she would be the winner of today's contest and thus the newest councillor in the Realm's Directorate. Unless Ard could figure out a way to convince Overseer otherwise.

All too soon, it was Ardor Benn's turn. He'd had the benefit of going last, which bought him as much time as possible to think of a way out of this. He had something of a plan in place, so he decided to approach Overseer with confidence, even though he had nothing to present. In Ard's experience, power in social settings was mostly perceived. If he acted like he had it, others might believe it, too.

"*Cataclysm*," Ard whispered, leaning close to Overseer. Was the mask perfumed? He thought it smelled of pine and sandalwood. Better than recycling stale breath in a mask so tightly woven. Up close, Ard could see that the dragon scales had been polished to a deep green and oiled to give the mask a particular shimmer that only existed on the hide of a living dragon. The headpiece had to be incredibly heavy and its unique material would make it durable enough to stop a Fielder ball at point blank.

"How much did you bring?" asked Overseer after a long, uncomfortable pause.

"See," Ard said, "that's the thing. I don't currently have anything with me..."

"You have nothing?" asked Overseer, tension edging into her disguised voice.

"Well, I wouldn't say nothing. I just—"

"Step back," Overseer demanded with such authority that Ard found himself instantly obeying.

*Well, that could have gone better.* But something told Ard that this wasn't the time to press Overseer. He sucked in a breath, calming himself, hoping for another opportunity.

"The results stand as thus," spoke Overseer. "Fifty-six pan-weights of Void Grit from this Faceless." Her arm extended, pointing two gloved fingers at the woman who had presented the two bags. "Take your place with the Directorate."

She stepped forward, hesitantly at first, but gaining confidence with every step. Ard had exploited that uncertainty earlier, under the cloud of Memory Grit. Maybe he could use her again. Maybe this wasn't over yet.

"This is your new Directorate." Overseer gestured to the stage, where the white masked woman stood awkwardly to the side. "Does any man or woman object to this advancement?"

"I object!" Ard called, stepping forward.

"Your objection is noted," Overseer commented.

*Noted?* He needed to do better than that!

"Anyone else?" Overseer asked.

Silence draped across the room, stretching out until Overseer seemed satisfied. She raised one hand.

"Personally, I want you all to know that your contributions are appreciated. Every granule enhances our cause." Her hand dropped suddenly.

There was a chorus of gunfire. Ard flinched as the Faceless next to him fell. The white mask was torn where the ball had entered, killing the person instantly.

It was over as quickly as it had happened, the smoke from the shots hanging at the edge of the stage like a thundercloud. Ard had meant to run, but the suddenness of the assault left him standing like his legs were carved from stone. Eight people, shot dead in a matter of seconds, their blood seeping out from under their masks and oversized cloaks.

"Blazing sparks!" Ard cursed, his voice and breath finally returning, now that it was too late to flee. "What was…" he trailed away. Eight of the highest-ranking Faceless killed for no reason.

"Your objection has granted you the right to contest the newest member of the Directorate," said Overseer. "You will state your case, hear any rebuttals from the accused, and then the Directorate will evaluate." Overseer gestured for Ard to begin.

"Well, you see…" Ard was shaking. A decent plan had been percolating in his brain before the shock of sudden death around him. He needed to regain his confidence in the lie he was about to sell. "I arrived at this meeting with a whole bag of Void Grit."

"And where would that be now?" asked Feather Head.

"That's just it!" cried Ard. "I was robbed!"

Okay. So all he had to do was convince the majority of the Directorate to believe his completely unfounded accusation. He had no facts. No grounds. Just an off-the-cuff declaration that his Grit had been stolen.

How could this possibly go wrong?

"Robbing Grit was the entire object of the assignment," replied Overseer. "I hardly expected the Void Grit to be obtained legally."

"Now you're changing the rules." Ard held up a finger, decrying injustice. "I was told that whoever brought the most Void Grit into the meeting would join the Directorate. I brought it in, I just wasn't able to present it because it was stolen while I waited for the meeting to conclude. Then I see *her*." Ard turned his finger accusatorially toward the surviving Faceless on the stage. "And I can't help but think that one of her bags looks mighty familiar."

"You think she stole it from you?" asked Hairy Face.

"I know she did," Ard answered.

The woman fidgeted in response. "That's a lie!"

But Overseer silenced her with a raised hand. "How exactly was the bag stolen?" she asked Ard.

He grinned under his white mask. This was the cleverest part of his plan. "I have no recollection of it." Ard held up his hand as if to stave the dismissive comments that were sure to follow. "Which leads me to suspect that I was taken advantage of under a cloud of Memory Grit."

"Are you suggesting that this individual illegally brought Memory Grit into the meeting?" asked Seashell Head, pointing at the Faceless on the stage.

"I'm certainly suggesting that," said Ard. "It would have been easy to smuggle something extra inside the bag she was allowed to bring in."

"Where did you acquire your Void Grit?" asked Horn Mask.

"I hit a Grit-processing factory on Strind," answered Ard. "A private institution. Mordell and Sons." Hopefully that factory was still up and running. Ard hadn't been there since they'd processed the stolen dragon shell almost two years ago. And war had been ravaging Strind.

"Does the bag have any unique features by which you could prove your ownership?" asked Feather Head.

"Oh, yes," Ard said, unable to hold back the sarcasm. "I scribed my name and address on a label inside. That way, if someone stole it, they'd know right where to return it."

"How much Void Grit did you have?" asked Antler Head.

Ard clenched his jaw. "Thirty panweights." Overseer had made the mistake of declaring the winning total. Claiming thirty panweights would leave his competitor with only twenty-six. It was a dangerous bluff, since he had no way of knowing if the Faceless woman had divided the Grit evenly between her bags.

"I might have lost a little in my escape from the factory." Ard added some sheepishness to his voice. "There were watchdogs involved."

There. That gave his lie a little wiggle room.

"Why do you desire to become part of the Directorate?" Overseer's question completely changed the direction of the conversation.

*So I can find out what you really did with Shad Agaul,* Ard instantly thought. But that seemed like a sure way to get shot.

"As a lad growing up in northeastern Talumon, I worked in a factory that manufactured firearms," Ard began instead. "The baron who owned the factory was cruel as sparks. He owned our town and he played with us like a cat with string. We all knew he was dealing illegal Rollers to one of the mob families, but nobody felt like they could do anything about it.

"One day, a couple of fellows start work at the factory— criminals themselves, I would later discover. At the end of every day, they'd leave the factory grounds with a wagonload of dirt. The baron's goons were rightly suspicious, and they sifted through that soil every evening, checking over the entire wagon, certain that these fellows were smuggling guns."

Ard was going somewhere with this story. He just hoped Overseer and the Directorate would be patient enough to appreciate it.

"Then one day we get word that a big deal is going down. The baron comes in wetting himself with worry because the exchange is happening in less than half an hour at the edge of town. Apparently, the mobster was pretty riled up, making all kinds of threats.

"We go to load up the Rollers, and that's when we realize it. There are no wagons. See, those fellows hadn't been smuggling guns. They'd been stealing the transport wagons. We hadn't moved a shipment in about two weeks, so nobody noticed them vanishing.

"All of us who didn't have skin in the game took off. Good thing, too. Wasn't thirty minutes before the mob stormed in. They shot the baron and his cronies, and burned the factory to rubble. You can bet the town changed after that. And all for the better, too."

Those two fellows had profited nicely, as well. Ard and Raek had taken the job from Lord Cubbar, who needed Baron Wolv ousted so he could take over the town and revive the diamond mine on the northern outskirts.

Ard couldn't see the faces of the Directorate, but it was probably best to wrap this story up and make his point.

"Never have been able to find out if those two fellows were part of the Realm, but they taught me something. A well-staged crime can change the fate of an entire town. That's why I want in to the Directorate," he said. "I want to be a part of the big decisions that shape the world."

As if restoring the bull dragons, dethroning King Pethredote, and becoming a hidden Paladin Visitant hadn't been enough.

"I know the Realm has the power to do that," he concluded.

Overseer turned toward the accused Faceless on the stage. "What do you have to say for yourself?"

"He's lying about the Void Grit," she remarked flatly. "I stole all fifty-six panweights myself. I divided them into two bags so they wouldn't be so difficult to carry."

"Where did you come by such a significant load?" asked Horn Mask.

"The war front," she replied. "Both armies keep ample stores. Prime for the taking."

Flames, this woman had actually traveled clear to Strind for that Grit? Not to mention getting herself into the heart of an army encampment. If Ard hadn't been desperate to discredit her, he might have been impressed.

"And you deny the use of Memory Grit in any previous interactions with this man?" asked Hairy Face.

Ha. She couldn't deny it honestly. She was obviously too clever not to realize that she had a short memory lapse while waiting for the meeting to end. Ard hoped her hesitation was as apparent to the Directorate as it was to him.

Finally, the woman answered. "I don't believe I've had any previous interactions with this charlatan."

"Why do you seek a position in the Directorate?" asked Overseer.

"Money," she replied without hesitation. "I've heard the Directorate treats its own very well."

"Move to the floor," Overseer instructed her.

The woman in the white mask carefully made her way down the steps, standing where Overseer indicated, at the opposite end of the line of bodies.

"See, your competitors have fallen between you," said Overseer. Ard didn't want to look at their still figures. In some ways, they looked no different than when they'd been alive, faces and bodies concealed beneath their heavy disguises. But there was death beneath those cloaks now, and it brought a chill that Ard couldn't shake.

"Any of them could have had a place in the Directorate," continued Overseer. "The Realm values individuals with an enterprising spirit. To us, naked ambition weighs the same as fifty-six panweights of Void Grit. Had any of these opposed the decision, they would still be alive to make a case for their admittance."

Overseer turned to the stage. "Let the Directorate vote. Does this man's contestation stand? Or shall he be eliminated straightway?"

"Stand," said Horn Mask.

"Stand," said Boar Face.

"Eliminate," seconded Feather Head.

"Stand," said Hairy Face.

"Eliminate," said Antler Head.

*Come on, Seashell Head*, Ard inwardly pleaded.

"Stand," came the final answer. Praise the Homeland!

"I shall abstain," Overseer said, "as the vote has already moved in your favor."

Ard's heart was racing, but he wasn't exactly clear on what had just happened. "Did I just get voted in to the Directorate?"

"The vote merely allows your contestation to stand," replied

Overseer. "But the laws of the Realm require a Directorate of no more than seven." He glanced between Ard and the woman. "In such an instance, contestation is to be settled by duel. To the death."

What? Ard's face twisted in shock behind his mask. Duel! Oh, flames. This was spiraling out of his control. He'd smooth-talked his way through all of this only to have it come down to a show of physical prowess?

"Both of you will be armed with a Singler, a sword, and one pot of common Grit of your choice," explained Overseer.

As she spoke, two of the councillors descended from the stage. Perhaps this was why so many of them had voted to let his contestation stand. It wasn't because they believed in his case and were moved by his motives. They probably just wanted a show.

Hairy Face approached Ard with the weapons. The Singler was already loaded, he could tell by the weight of it. Ardor Benn was known for being something of a sharpshooter. He was fairly confident that he could hit the woman in a room this size. Whether the single ball would *kill* her, Ard didn't know, since he'd be firing under pressure and speed. He'd really rather not have to finish her off with the sword.

It was a thin-bladed rapier with a basket hilt. Ard had never taken much interest in dueling with swords. In all honesty, Raek was probably a better fencer than he was. Ard preferred to duel with his wits.

Hairy Face unrolled a sash with four clay pots tucked into sewn pockets. "You may select one," he said. "Each has a blast radius of about eight feet."

Ard studied the pots, identifying each by its color code. His options were Blast, Barrier, Drift, and Light.

Ard figured he was too likely to blow himself up with Blast Grit. And Light Grit wouldn't do much beyond casting a nice glow over his opponent in the windowless room.

The choice was really between Barrier and Drift. If Quarrah

were here, she'd definitely have chosen the latter. It could be helpful to Drift Jump, but Ard wasn't nearly as practiced as she was at that particular stunt.

He snatched the pot of Barrier Grit. At the very least, he could trap himself inside and postpone death for about ten minutes. Maybe he could tell a tale so interesting that his opponent wouldn't be able to kill him for fear of never knowing how it ended.

"Among the Faceless, secrecy is life," said Overseer. "But in the Directorate, anonymity yields a little to accountability. As senior-most member of this organization, I have seen the faces of all my councillors. And each has seen the face of the councillors who have joined after. Only the newest member operates without knowing the identity of his or her companions. All of us will see the face of the victor today. And since the other will soon be dead, I see no reason for masks in this duel."

That was actually good news! How was Ard supposed to fight when his eyeholes were so offset he could barely see straight?

Handing the weapons back to Hairy Face, Ard reached up and pulled off his hood. Untying the ribbon behind his head, he lowered the white mask.

Glancing across the mess of dead bodies, Ard saw his opponent's face as she turned toward him. His heart stopped and his blood ran cold at the sight of her.

Oh, flames. This was going to complicate things.

~

*Never at any time have we forbidden the others from becoming like us.*

# CHAPTER

# 22

What was Ardor Benn doing here? Sparks, the man had a way of meddling in business that wasn't his. Now that Quarrah saw his bearded face, she cursed herself for not realizing it was him sooner—the mention of Mordell and Sons Grit Factory, the long-winded side story about some complicated ruse that changed his life...Ard and Raek had probably been the very wagon thieves he'd bragged about.

Quarrah's racing heart had caused a sudden flush to rise to her cheeks, but she had managed to remain otherwise expressionless. She'd let a cluster of conflicting emotions wash over her after the initial surprise—disgust, relief, insecurity, determination—until all that remained was a stunned numbness.

Now she stood mere paces away from dying, thumb on the Slag-stone hammer of her Singler. A thin sword was at her belt, and her other hand clutched the selected pot of Drift Grit. Quarrah's flaxen hair was matted against her neck, sweaty from the hood of the cumbersome costume that she'd just shed.

A duel to the death would be difficult enough if her opponent were an enemy. Sparks, she'd settle for a mere acquaintance. But she had genuinely loved Ardor Benn once, and seeing him here threatened to stir up old feelings. She didn't doubt for a moment that Ard *could* hit her. Their time together had proven that he was a very capable shot. The question was, *would* he?

Had Ard known she was the one under that mask all along? If

so, then she had far more reason to worry about this duel. His mention of Memory Grit corresponded with her short lapse in memories. Had he failed to steal her Void Grit then, forcing him to carry out this riskier backup plan?

"Contestants will stand back to back," announced Overseer.

The councillor with the horned mask who'd helped Quarrah prepare for the duel retreated to the stage, carrying her white mask and cloak.

Quarrah stepped around the dead figures lined on the floor, avoiding the puddles of blood that seeped from their lifeless forms. Ard met her at the place where Overseer was pointing, and for a moment, the two of them stood face-to-face.

Ardor Benn winked at her. It was subtle and fast, the rest of his face remaining expressionless. Then they were back to back, their bodies lightly touching. Her heart rate spiked. Not from the return of physical contact after more than a year apart. Her heart was racing at the thought of killing him. Or worse, being killed by him.

And what was with that wink? Was Ard trying to say "good to see you again," or "I knew it was you all along"? Was it intended to make her relax, letting her know that he had some master plan? Or did he wink to remind her what a good shot he was?

"Ten paces," called Overseer. Quarrah scanned the room. Nowhere to hide. Nowhere to run.

Overseer started counting, Quarrah and Ard taking steps away from each other at a steady rate. At five, she clicked back the Slagstone hammer on her Singler.

Was she really going to shoot him? If she intentionally missed, the Directorate wouldn't know. Sparks, she was likely to miss him even if she didn't mean to.

"Seven. Eight..."

Maybe a ball through the leg. Ard could survive that. She could drop him where he stood and then make a case to the Directorate that his life should be spared. Or maybe Ard would be smart enough to play along and act like the shot had killed him. Homeland knew he had a knack for that sort of thing.

"Nine...Ten!"

Quarrah whirled, her Singler coming up. She spent only a heartbeat sighting down the barrel, aiming at his leg. Then she squeezed the trigger and felt the gun recoil, flame spitting from the muzzle. Through the smoke, she saw she'd missed him completely.

Had he missed her, too? Had he even shot? There was no smoke on his side of the room. Maybe Ard knew she was going to miss and he was using that to take careful aim.

She heard his gun hammer click. The Blast cartridge didn't ignite. That was a bit of sweet luck, but it wasn't going to last. She drew her sword, moving sideways to make herself a more difficult target.

Ard's gun clicked again with no effect. "Sparks," she heard him cursing under his breath. A third time, the hammer came down and the gun failed to fire.

"Rematch!" Ard shouted to the masked figures of the Directorate. "You gave me a blazing dud Singler!"

"The duel goes on!" replied Overseer, who had taken a stand with the others at the edge of the stage.

"Well, I see you're playing favorites!" Ard shouted angrily.

Quarrah charged while he was distracted. She had only a little experience in fencing, but knew that Ard was no expert, either. This duel was suddenly much more evenly matched than it had been with guns. Maybe she could injure him, disarm him, and persuade him to yield. She'd still need to convince the Directorate that he should be granted his life, but by that point, she'd be one of them, and her voice might hold more sway.

At the last moment, Ard threw the useless Singler to the wooden floor and drew his sword. Blades clashed with so much reckless force that it jarred Quarrah to the shoulder.

"My name is Androt Penn," Ard said quietly as their swords slid apart. Between the alias and the unruly facial hair, it was no won-der nobody had been able to find Ardor Benn since the night of Pethredote's death.

"I've been looking for you," he said, parrying one of her thrusts.

She didn't say anything, keeping her focus on the duel. If they were somewhat evenly matched, Quarrah might be able to gain the upper hand just by letting Ard talk. She knew he wasn't great at doing two things at once.

"Have you also, you know..." Ard pressed, "been looking for me?"

Sparks, no! If she'd wanted to find him, she could have done so easily. Besides, he shouldn't be talking about this right now, even with the Realm Directorate likely out of earshot.

Ard made a series of poorly executed lunges that Quarrah eas-ily avoided. But his movement had caused them to circle, and she now found herself with her back to the wall. Ard took a wide stance, ready to stop her from escaping to either side.

His offensive swings increased in velocity until he looked like he was barely in control. Why was he wasting so much energy swing-ing a thin sword? Dueling was all about the thrust. Still, with such force behind his swipes, a single blow was likely to maim her. She was only blocking half of them, and although his blade came close, it never seemed to pose any real threat.

*He's wearing me down,* Quarrah realized. The wide, reckless swings were meant to keep her pinned against the wall, straining her grip on her sword until she could be disarmed.

*Well, might as well give him what he wants.* She knew how to get away from him, but it would be too dangerous to execute the maneuver with a long blade.

Quarrah brought her sword up, meeting Ard's slice as it came at neck level. The moment their blades clashed, she let go of the hilt. Her sword clattered aside, skidding across the floor.

At the same time, she hurled her single pot of Drift Grit at her feet. The detonation cloud formed against the wall, enveloping both of them. But Quarrah was ready for it.

Ard's feet came an inch or two off the floor, the momentum of his latest swing turning him in an ungraceful pirouette from which he could not recover. Floating, Quarrah tucked her feet back, planting them firmly against the wall behind her.

She kicked, her planned trajectory carrying her over Ard's head as he continued to spin. Quarrah exited the cloud headfirst, dropping six feet into a somersault. She sprang up, scanning the area for her discarded sword. It was near the door that led outside, thin blade glinting in the Light Grit glow.

There was no one guarding the door. It was barred, but she might be able to pull it open before the Directorate reached her from the distant stage. But that would mean the end of this job, and Fabra Ment might be upset enough to take it out on her. Better to go for the sword and try to overpower her competitor.

Ard finally spun out of the Drift cloud. Dizzy and tripping, he stumbled, his own sword tumbling from his grasp. He righted himself, sprinting straight for Quarrah.

She made a hasty dash toward her fallen blade. And she would have reached it, if it weren't for the sudden shattering of a clay pot behind her.

Quarrah struck the Barrier wall that had materialized right in front of her. She fell backward, stunned. There was blood on her forehead, and her vision was threatening to go black.

Grunting against the attack, Quarrah sat up. The shimmering shield surrounded her on all sides, confirming that she was trapped inside the dome. With no door or lock to pick, this was a thief's worst enemy.

"So, what are you doing after this?" Ard's voice sounded behind her. "I was thinking maybe we could go for a cup of coffee and a pastry."

She whirled to find him lying on the floor, slightly turned to one side. His legs, from the thighs down, were trapped inside the

Barrier dome with her, but the rest of him was outside. It looked like he'd been attempting some kind of swashbuckling slide to reach the sword before her. Knowing Ard, he had probably misjudged the distance and caught himself in his very own detonation.

"The Bakery on Humont Street sort of exploded," Ard continued casually, sitting up and leaning close to the transparent Barrier, "but I've found this great place just south of the Char..."

"Enough of this!" shouted one of the councillors from the stage. That silenced Ard in a hurry. "This duel is like watching children quarrel. I find them both sorely incapable. Neither worthy of joining the Directorate."

Overseer held up her hand. Her voice wasn't loud, so Quarrah had to strain to hear the reply. "Mastery of the sword is not the determining quality of any councillor. How many of you had to duel for your position?"

In the awkward silence that followed, Quarrah could deduce that she was the first among them.

"We will let the duel play out," continued Overseer.

"Okay," Ard whispered to her. "This is our chance—"

"Quiet," she snapped at him.

"I *am* being quiet," he replied. "They're all the way across the room with their heads wrapped in leather and fabric. This is our chance to team up."

He had a point. They were helplessly trapped for the next ten minutes or so. But the Directorate seemed to be discussing something privately on their own. She could see the figure with the hairy mask leaning close to Overseer's ear.

"What are you even doing here?" she finally whispered.

"Locked in a duel to the death with the woman of my dreams," he answered. "You?"

She groaned, wiping carefully at her forehead. Quarrah hadn't forgotten how utterly irritating he was. But given the circumstances, she'd expected at least a granule of seriousness from him.

"Don't mess with me, *Androt Penn,*" spat Quarrah. "What kind of an alias is that anyway? You liked your real name so much that you made up another one that sounded just like it?"

"That's not…it wasn't…" he stammered. "Ugh. Confusion through similarity. Why doesn't anyone see how clever that is?"

"Did you do this on purpose?" she pressed.

"Do what?"

"All of this." She turned away from him.

Still seated, Quarrah leaned forward, cradling her head between her knees. If they were going to spend the next ten minutes trapped in an insufferable conversation, she needed to make it look like they weren't speaking. The cut on her forehead was the perfect excuse. Besides, short of removing Ard's boots, there wasn't anything she could do to him.

"Honest to Homeland, I didn't know you were here," Ard whispered. "I thought you worked alone."

"The Realm doesn't exactly seem like *your* typical social scene, either," Quarrah hissed.

Ard sighed. She spied out the corner of one eye to see that the hairy-masked councillor was collecting something from the figure with the antlers.

"I'm working a job," Ard whispered. "It's important, Quarrah. Blazing important."

"The last one was, too, right?" she replied. "And the one before that."

"I'm not like that anymore," said Ard, his face an inch from the hazy shield. "I want to tell you everything, Quarrah. I could really use your help on this one."

Ha! He had the audacity to try to recruit her? He probably expected her to say yes. To say how much she'd missed him and how great it would be to team up again. Those words were never going to leave her mouth.

The truth was, she hadn't missed him. She'd missed *aspects* of him, but the man as a whole felt like a Singler ball she'd been lucky to miss.

"I don't think either of our jobs matter much right now," she said. "After all, one of us is about to die."

"I'm not going to kill you!" Ard said, his voice rising louder than Quarrah would have liked.

"I have the feeling a surrender will be just as fatal," she said.

"I've got a plan."

"Of course you do."

"If I get us both out of here, will you let me explain everything?" he asked.

"I'm not making any promises to you," she replied. The man with the hairy mask was moving toward the stairs at the edge of the stage.

"Are you familiar with the Guesthouse Adagio?" Ard whispered.

She glanced over at him. "The estate that belonged to Remium Agaul?" She'd robbed the place several years back.

"Raek and I are living there now," he said. "You should come visit us. We have an intrepid cook. There's plenty of space. You could have your own cottage."

She shook her head. Was he seriously bragging about his living accommodations?

"I'm sure Lady Abeth would love to meet you," he said. "She's staying with us while she's dead."

"Lady…" Quarrah trailed off as everything came together in her head. "You! The assassination…Sparks! It's been you all along, hasn't it!"

"You didn't recognize my style?" Ard said quietly. "You win some, you ruse some. Am I right?"

Homeland, maybe she *had* forgotten how insufferable he was. The hairy-masked councillor was on the floor now, striding purposefully toward them, gloved fist clenched in front of him.

"Here's the plan," Ard began. His back was to the councillor and he surely didn't realize how close he was drawing. "We have to keep fighting once the Barrier cloud drops. Don't hold back. I'm going to—"

Quarrah held up her hand to silence him. Gravely, he turned, spotting the hairy figure coming to a halt just fifteen paces from them. He pitched something from his closed fist, causing Ard to flinch, covering his head. But Quarrah looked on intently, knowing that nothing could touch her inside the Barrier cloud.

Whatever he had thrown broke against the domed shield with the sound of shattering glass. Immediately, she felt the rush of a detonation and somehow the shards of glass rained down on her head, the Barrier detonation inexplicably snuffed out.

A glass vial…an unusual reaction to Grit…This had to be something similar to what she'd encountered at the war front. Only, this vial seemed to have done the opposite of the one she'd broken.

Quarrah realized that the Barrier shell was down before Ard did. She pounced, gripping her sword hilt at last. Turning, she saw that Ard was scrambling toward the stage, the hairy-masked figure quickly making his way back to the steps.

Ard had said to keep fighting. Not to hold back. Quarrah sprinted after him, brandishing the sword for a fatal thrust.

Ard went down. She thought he had tripped, until he turned to defend himself. His discarded Singler was in his hand once again, so hastily retrieved that Ard was gripping it backward. He lifted it above his head, the wooden butt brandished like a club and the barrel pointing toward the stage behind him.

Quarrah had meant to follow through with her thrust, but just as Ard was about to bring the gun down to block, it fired.

Everyone froze, except for Ardor Benn, who dropped the gun under a puff of Blast smoke, cursing. Looking past him, Quarrah watched the councillor with the hairy mask lurch, a strangled cry escaping his lips as he tumbled down the stairs, landing at the bottom in a motionless heap.

At once, the remaining five councillors drew their Rollers, leveling them at the two duelers on the floor. An unmistakable air of fear and panic rippled through the room. Only Overseer seemed to maintain any level of composure, that commanding hand the only thing holding the others back.

"What have you done?" Overseer's words were drawn out and threatening.

As much as it had looked like an accident, Quarrah hoped this was part of Ardor Benn's plan.

This was definitely all part of Ardor Benn's plan.

Well, sort of. He'd actually been hoping to shoot Overseer, but it wasn't too easy to aim behind his back and fire without looking.

It had been a pretty sure bet that he'd hit *someone* in the Directorate. The councillors were all lined up on that stage, practically begging for a firing squad. Old Hairy Face wasn't moving. He must have taken it in the back of the head while moving back up the steps.

The burn on Ard's hand smarted something fierce. Apparently, those gun barrels got mighty hot with all that fire and lead pushing through them. His thumb wasn't in great shape, either. The hammer had split his thumbnail wide open, blood dripping steadily.

"What have you done?" This time, Overseer didn't sound quite as composed.

"It would seem there's been an accident," said Ard.

Finally, Boar Face moved down the steps and crouched beside the fallen councillor.

"He's dead," came the official report.

Ard resisted the urge to sigh with relief. His plan was already sketchy enough without having the councillor hold on to life.

"You murdered him!" Boar Face shouted, rising.

"I murdered him?" Ard cried incredulously. "With a Singler that wouldn't even fire?" He picked up the gun. "I couldn't even shoot the person I was *supposed* to kill with this thing!"

No one could dispute the faultiness of his Singler. Ard had been careful to make a big fuss about it at the start of the duel.

There was actually nothing wrong with the gun. Ard had used his ten paces to remove the Slagstone chip from the hammer, resulting in a dud shot, no matter how many times he pulled the trigger. He had kept the little piece of Slagstone clutched in his sweaty palm, sliding it into place and holding it with his thumb when he finally wanted the Singler to fire. All he had to do was push the trigger with his index finger and the whole thing looked like a misfire.

"You have forfeited the right to contest," spoke Overseer. "The woman will take her place with the Directorate and you will be executed."

"For a mistake?" Ard challenged. "For the accidental discharge of a Singler that *you* provided?" He shook his head. "That's a load of slag! Let me finish the duel. Better yet, let's restart it."

"Sparks, no!" Quarrah cried from behind him; she was still gripping that sword like she might start carving into people. He had to admit, she might have taken him in that duel, all things being equal.

"Your breach of the rules disqualifies you from the duel," said Overseer.

"So, you're just going to shoot me?" Ard said. "Like you did the others?" He gestured to the line of bodies, which had become a macabre centerpiece in the room. "I should warn you. I don't die easily. And that won't solve your problem."

"What problem would that be?" asked Overseer.

With five Rollers pointed in his direction, Ardor Benn had to make this seem natural, as though the idea were just coming to him.

"You'll only have six councillors in the Directorate," he pointed out.

"We will select another through our established methods."

"Another competition?" Ard said. "Who's going to go for that?

Your top contenders are all in this room. But only two of them still have a pulse."

"There are others who know the full symbol," said Overseer.

"Others who were obviously too timid to agree to the competition of Void Grit theft," Ard said, finding his angle. "The best of them will still be little more than a watered-down version of us." He gestured between himself and Quarrah.

"What are you suggesting?" asked Overseer.

No, Ard couldn't say it outright. He needed Overseer to think that the idea was hers. Ard needed to keep presenting the logic until the masked leader saw this as the best option.

"You should let me go," Ard said. "I'll get back out there and spread the word that another Directorate position has opened. In a few weeks, at the next Faceless meeting you can present a new challenge. I can incite some of these second-tier members to give it a try. A few more weeks after that, they can report, and you'll have your new councillor."

Ard suspected that being a person short had put a strain on the Directorate, with their array of responsibilities. They'd already endured this for at least a cycle since Waelis Mordo's death. Ard felt like it might strengthen his case to point out that they were in for at least another cycle of extra work.

"What would be in it for you?" asked Overseer.

"A chance to compete again, obviously," answered Ard. Maybe he'd tipped the conversation too far. This plan was certainly better than getting shot, but he was so close to getting into the council *now*. With Quarrah.

"And you know I'll win," Ard continued, "because I'm guessing the next round of competitors won't be nearly as strong as her." He glanced at Quarrah to see if she'd appreciated the compliment. Her expression was flat.

"Of course, it might raise some questions," Ard said. "Maybe a little confusion as to why two Directorate positions have opened up back to back. People might assume their own leaders have perished without the Waters of Loyalty. Disloyal leaders...That doesn't show the best face. But then, we're an organization of masks, so I'm sure you can cover it up."

It was silent for a long time. And then Overseer spoke slowly. "You have displayed much fortitude and great persuasion. But I have another offer for you."

Ard held his breath.

"Join us today," Overseer said. "The two of you can take the vacant places at our side, completing the Directorate quickly and quietly as we move closer to the Final Era of Utmost Perfection."

"I mean..." Ard began, trying to suppress a grin. "If you insist." He had no idea what that bit meant about "utmost perfection," but everything else had unfolded as *perfectly* as he'd hoped.

Overseer turned to face the five remaining councillors. "Does any member of the Directorate object to the admission of these two individuals?"

Ard's confidence grew in the silence that followed, only to be dashed as the man with the feathered headpiece stepped forward.

"I object. Not to her admission." He pointed at Quarrah. "She played by our rules. But he shot Nexus in the back of the head! He cannot be trusted."

"That was an accident!" Ard said in self-defense. "You saw the—"

Overseer whirled, silencing him with an aggressive wave of her hand. Then turning back to Feather Head. "Do you wish to contest him, Grapple?"

*Oh, great. Not this again.* At least Quarrah wouldn't be involved this time. Ard wasn't the type to be proud of the notches in the butt of his gun, but he wouldn't hesitate to kill this councillor in a fair duel. Although with a name like Grapple, he might make a formidable opponent.

"Not a good idea," Ard said. "Give me a Singler that actually shoots when I pull the trigger and you'll find yourself with an extra eyehole in that mask." At least he'd have the advantage of mobility, since this Grapple fellow surely wouldn't shed his disguise in front of the Directorate.

"I contest," he said.

Overseer's dragon-husk headpiece nodded slowly, resolutely. "The Directorate will now vote to see if Grapple's contestation stands, or whether this man may be admitted into our council straightaway."

"Admit," said Horn Mask.

"Stand," said Boar Face.

"Stand," said Antler Head.

"Admit," said Seashell Head.

It was a tie! *Sparks, what does a tie mean?* Overseer had abstained last time because the vote had already tipped one way. Ard seemed to have won her over a moment ago, but could Feather Head's call for contest have swayed her?

"Admit!" Quarrah's vote called loudly from behind him.

*Quarrah Khai!* What was she doing standing up for him like this? Oh, this was the best thing that had happened yet.

"What?" cried an incensed Feather Head. "You are not... The determining vote goes to Overseer!"

"Not so," said the tall woman with the single horn on her mask. "Your contestation was against the man alone, which means the woman is officially one of us."

"She doesn't even have a name!" spat Feather Head.

"Sleight," Overseer said abruptly. "She will be known among the Directorate as Sleight—a testament to the theft that won her place."

*Sleight.* Ard approved of the name. It was fitting, the way Quarrah's hand seemed to disappear and reappear holding something that didn't belong to her.

Feather Head stood with both hands stiff to his sides, like a toy soldier. "Tell us, *Sleight*, why would you vote in favor of a man who just attempted to kill you?"

"For the benefit of the Realm," Quarrah answered, voice surprisingly calm. "Isn't this the type of relentless personality we need in the Directorate? He is crafty. Innovative." She sucked in a deep breath as if steadying herself against what she was going to say next. "And because he would have made it into the Directorate without contest if I hadn't stolen his portion of the Void Grit."

*Well, look at that,* Ard thought, fighting to stop his excitement and gratitude from showing on his face. Instead, he merely barked, "You see?" and pointed an aggressive finger in her direction.

"When did you take it?" Overseer asked.

"Just after he arrived at the meeting."

"I'm curious to know how it was done," continued the leader. "If there is a flaw in our system, I do not want it to be exploited by our enemies."

"I'm afraid I can't tell you how I stole it," said Quarrah.

Overseer tilted her head disapprovingly, dragon scales clinking on her mask. "We keep no secrets in the Directorate."

"I mean, I don't know how I did it," Quarrah continued. "It happened under a cloud of Memory Grit in the the corner of the room."

Clever. By playing that card, she not only backed up Ard's prior claims, but she also wouldn't have a story to keep straight. Ard glanced at her, but she was staring straight ahead, sword still held at the ready after all this time.

"It is final, then," said Overseer. "Our two newest members, Sleight and Rival."

Ard nodded at his new name. After he'd put up such a fuss, and talked everyone's ear off, Overseer could have called Ard any number of less favorable names. Windbag or Jabberer came to mind.

Overseer gestured for the two of them to take their places on the stage. Feather Head greeted them with a disapproving grunt. Ard would have found it pretty rewarding to see the expression on his face.

"Welcome to the Directorate of the Realm," Overseer continued. "We will meet at noon in ten days. The Old Post Lighthouse. Approach cautiously, wearing your masks."

Ard nodded. He knew the Old Post. It was an abandoned lighthouse in a rare underdeveloped region on the northern shore of Beripent.

"So, do we pick up the outfit somewhere on the way to the lighthouse?" Ard asked.

"We do not bother with the cloaks and voice modifiers when we sit in private council," answered Overseer. "Wear only your masks."

"Okay," said Ard. "So, which one of us has to wear the hairy mask?" He pointed at the dead councillor at the bottom of the stairs.

"You must create your own headpieces," said Overseer. "Might I suggest adequate ventilation when considering a design."

Ard cracked a smile. Was that a bit of humor? Maybe Ard had misread her. Maybe Overseer was just waiting to let her hair down until they were all part of the Directorate.

Ard glanced at Quarrah, but she wouldn't meet his eye. Was it always going to be so complex between them? One minute fighting to the death, and the next vouching for each other?

Well, Ardor Benn would take whatever he could get until he managed to earn her trust again.

~

*We were mighty, but we could still taste death.*

# CHAPTER

# 23

A t least King Termain was clothed this time.

Portsend Wal and Prime Isless Gloristar watched the king pick at a spread of food that would have easily fed an entire family.

The dining hall was an oblong room, the walls pocked with doors that likely led straight into the kitchens. A single long table ran down the center of the hall, lined with at least two dozen chairs. Portsend and Gloristar had not been invited to sit in any of them. They stood at one end while Termain feasted at the other. So far, he had complained about the temperature of the fish soup and sent back the leg of lamb because it smelled of onion, even though he couldn't find any on the platter.

Through all of this, Termain acted as though he were alone, despite the fact that he had summoned them into the hall at the precise time they had appointed to meet.

"Well?" the king finally said over the clinking of his silverware. "Are you going to talk, or do I have to beg?"

Portsend glanced questioningly at Gloristar, who decided to answer. "My apologies, Your Highness. We are not accustomed to speaking to someone of your position without invitation."

"I invited you here, didn't I?" He gestured around the room. "Did you think I just wanted to see your unpleasant faces? I have my mother for that."

He skewered a sizable piece of boiled turroc root with his fork and slid it through a cream-colored sauce before shoving the whole thing into his mouth.

Gloristar nodded for Portsend to speak. He was the reason they were here. After so many weeks of endless petitioning, he couldn't stand to put Gloristar off any longer. He knew the king was circling closer to her, desperate for another advantage in the war.

Reports stated that the Ignition Grit had been highly successful in depleting the Sovereign States' Grit reserves. But Ignition Grit was nearly three cycles old now, and the Sovereign States were taking precautions against it.

"My research continues to move forward at an exciting pace," Portsend said, bringing his voice to the level he did when lecturing, making sure it would reach the distant king. "Although Ignition Grit cannot be Compounded, I've discovered that it does indeed react to Prolonging Grit," said Portsend.

It was something new and truthful, but wasn't likely to be significant enough to tip off the boss that he was giving information to Termain.

"What I previously described as a flash cloud can in fact be sustained with Prolonging Grit," he continued. "A Prolonged cloud of Ignition Grit could effectively create a space where any other type of Grit that entered would ignite. The practical benefits of this could be huge."

"The practical benefits of this could be huge," repeated the king in a mocking voice. "Ignition Grit is old news, Professor. Word is spreading about it. The Sovs are already modifying their transports and stores to make them more secure." He took a long drink from a stemmed glass. "I hope to the Homeland that you didn't come here to tell me more about Ignition Grit. For the sake of the Prime Isless."

Flames. Portsend shouldn't have agreed to this meeting. He should have postponed yet again. That extra bit about Prolonged

Ignition Grit was all he had planned to share. He'd have to stall, but make it satisfying enough to appease Termain.

"Of course not," Portsend said stiffly. "I have a number of other pursuits that are showing promise."

"Such as?" interrupted the king, his mouth full.

"Well," tried Portsend, "after experimenting with a variety of liquid solutions, I managed to achieve a new detonation cloud with another uncommon material." Four new types, actually, but Portsend thought it best to withhold that.

"What does it do?"

Gratefully, Termain hadn't asked what material had yielded the cloud. That kind of information could lead the palace Mixers to uncover the new Grit types as quickly as Portsend had. But Termain didn't seem interested in the development. He wanted a final product that could be implemented now.

"I'm still working toward uncovering the effects of the detonation," Portsend lied. "My style of experimentation is methodical and very systematic. It takes time."

There was some truth to that. Most of the new Grit types they'd discovered had begun as detonation clouds with unknown effects. If it weren't for Lomaya's astute observation of the cockroach, he might have abandoned Stasis Grit altogether.

One of the doors opened and a servant appeared with a replacement platter of lamb leg. She seemed nervous to approach, but the king motioned her over with his knife.

Portsend took the distraction to look at Gloristar. She seemed pale, slightly short of breath, and even thinner than the last time he'd seen her. She caught his gaze and raised her eyebrows, silently imploring him to say more.

"That was all," Portsend whispered as the king said something inappropriate to the servant girl.

Crestfallen, Gloristar looked away, and Portsend felt his heart break inside his chest. She had trusted him and he was lying to her face.

Oh, Homeland, how had he found himself in this impossible situation?

"I don't like waiting," King Termain called to Portsend and Gloristar. "But I do appreciate people who can fix their mistakes." He stooped over the platter of lamb and sniffed deeply.

"I want to share the success of the Archkingdom with you," he said. "I really do. But you don't seem to understand how sharing works. You give me something. I give you something. It's been working since day one. I allowed Gloristar to remain Prime Isless instead of selecting my own—I give. Gloristar gave me the official endorsement of Wayfarism—she gives."

Hardly willingly.

"When the war took a turn for the worse, Gloristar promised information that could help the Archkingdom's military gain the upper hand—she gives. I promise to fund the experiments—I give. Now, it seems, you're running out of things to offer. And last I checked, we haven't won the war yet. See, there's the conundrum."

For once Termain actually seemed engaged in the conversation. Enough so that he'd put down his fork and knife and was staring intently across the long table.

"This is all about winning the war—bringing Dronodan and Talumon back under my rule and sending the Trothians scurrying back to their little islets. Homeland knows they spent generations there without bothering anyone. Why is this such a big deal?"

He sighed heavily and stuck a sugared piece of fruit into his mouth.

"Maybe the Sovereign States surrender tomorrow," he said, a dribble of juice drawing a line down his chin. "Not likely, but if it happens, then our mutual need for one another becomes obsolete and the three of us can merrily go our separate ways. But if not, then you two have to start sharing again. If you don't, I'll be left with no other choice but to send sweet Gloristar off to sea and select a new Prime Isle who *will* do his part."

At Portsend's side, Gloristar drew a sharp breath. It was more than a threat to send her away. It was a threat against all Wayfarism. There was no guarantee that Termain would give the Anchored Tome to the new Prime Isle, either. Without it, no one would have the full knowledge needed to lead the religion.

"You know, it isn't very common for the Wayfarists to send a ship of voyagers in search of the Homeland during wartime," continued Termain. "I think that a crew of devout believers would better serve as infantrymen. But I've already got my people assembling the paperwork for Gloristar's departure."

The king looked down at his array of food. "Sparks! How rude of me not to share."

King Termain picked up his knife and stabbed it sharply through the leg of lamb, hefting it from the platter. He rose to his feet, but didn't stop there. He stepped first onto his chair and then onto the table itself. He strode across the tabletop, his boots toppling a small pitcher of gravy and clanking against fine plates. Once he'd waded through the feast, he stalked across the long table until he towered above Gloristar and Portsend.

He held out the lamb leg, blood and meat juices dripping to the floor between the two of them.

"Go ahead," Termain said. "Take a bite."

Neither moved, and eventually Portsend muttered, "No thank you, Your Majesty."

"I insist."

"I really haven't much of an appetite," Portsend said.

"You will both feast from my knife," Termain demanded, "or I'll have you arrested for defying the king."

Reluctantly, stiffly, Gloristar leaned forward and bit into the large leg of meat. It tore away, greasing her chin as she chewed, eyes downcast. Portsend did the same, his teeth biting through a string of gristle.

"Let's strike a deal," Termain spoke softly. "If you don't have something new for me by tomorrow evening, then that ship sets sail for the Homeland." Patronizingly, he waved goodbye to Gloristar, an expression of mock sadness on his face.

*Tomorrow evening?* The king must have guessed he was withholding, but this wasn't a bluff Portsend was willing to call. He swallowed the meat, but the lump in his throat remained. "I may be able to remember something."

Gloristar turned sharply toward him. Out of the corner of his eye, Portsend could see her puzzled, hurt expression. But he couldn't bring himself to make eye contact.

"How very interesting!" Termain swung the heavy lamb leg behind him, the meat sliding off the knife and landing with a greasy splat on the long table. "I thought you didn't have anything worthwhile."

"I want assurances that Gloristar's ship won't sail," Portsend said.

"It'll buy you another cycle or so," Termain said. "And if you want to stop the ship again, you'll bring me more news."

Portsend's mind raced. He didn't know what kind of counteraction the boss would take when she discovered he had given information to the king. Especially since he had been withholding it from her, too. But he was committed now, and the only thing left to decide was which new Grit type to surrender.

Ignition Grit was already in Termain's pocket. Null Grit seemed much too powerful. The ability to snuff out an existing cloud could change the face of warfare altogether.

Stasis Grit could be equally devastating. A large enough detonation over the enemy could knock them all out, allowing Termain's infantry to fire on the unconscious troops from outside the cloud.

That left Containment Grit, and their newest discovery...

"I call it Weight Grit," he decided. "I didn't consider this ready to share with you, as it was only just discovered three days ago. It's still in development and hasn't been properly tested yet."

That part was true. And by giving Termain an underdeveloped project, Portsend hoped that the palace Mixers would have to do more experimentation on their own, slowing down mass production for the war.

"The source material is pulverized horse vertebrae, which hitherto has been considered a common bone in aggregate with other varieties to form Prolonging Grit," Portsend explained. "Similar to Ignition Grit, the horse vertebrae can be dissolved in a liquid with a balance level of positive sharp one."

"This isn't a lecture, Professor," interrupted the king. "And I'm not your student."

Portsend swallowed, remembering that the king cared much less about *how* something worked than what it did.

"Weight Grit causes any item within its detonation radius to double in weight," Portsend said.

King Termain burst into laughter. "Does it have a use beyond offending my mother?"

Portsend was flustered. He was talking about *new* Grit. Regardless of its effect, this was a groundbreaking discovery. It deserved better than a snide jest, especially considering he was risking so much to explain it.

"I assure you, it is a powerful Grit type," Portsend said in defense. "It can be Compounded to make objects within the cloud exponentially heavier."

"How heavy are you talking about?"

"The upper limit has not yet been reached," answered Portsend, "But my results have already been significant. I have gone so far as to increase the weight of a loaf of bread to nearly five hundred panweights."

"The palace cooks make that all the time." Termain laughed again. "Like chewing on a rock."

"Actually, no," Portsend said, unwilling to yield to the king's mirth. "That is perhaps the most remarkable thing about Weight

Grit. Normally, if you make something heavy enough, the object will eventually collapse on itself. But items within the Weight cloud do not lose structural integrity, even though they feel heavier. That impossibly heavy loaf of bread remained as fresh and airy as though it had just come out of the oven."

"How does it work on people?"

"That depends on how much of the person is inside the detonation," answered Portsend. "If I reach my hand inside, it becomes disproportionately heavy."

"Is it painful?"

"No," Portsend said. "But it becomes difficult, if not impossible, to lift. However, if I position my entire body into the cloud, I become heavier as a whole. I am able to move quite normally, though I weigh a great deal."

"Enhanced strength, then," said Termain.

Not really. But Portsend couldn't keep shutting the king down.

"It does allow you to pick up other items within the same Weight cloud as you," he explained. "If my weight has been increased at the same rate as that five-hundred-panweight loaf, then I will be able to lift it."

"Or you could just lift a normal loaf of bread and do away with this ridiculous Weight Grit altogether," said Termain. "Honestly, your new discovery seems like little more than a gimmick to entertain folks at the next reception." He brandished his greasy knife. "How does it help me win the war?"

*You're asking how it could be weaponized,* Portsend thought. *All right. I've got a few ideas.*

"Clouds of Compounded Weight Grit could be detonated over artillery and other weaponry, making them inaccessible. Too heavy to lift."

Termain picked a little scrap of lamb off the hilt of his knife and popped it into his mouth. "We already have Barrier Grit. It's plenty effective at making things inaccessible."

"But it's not the same," Portsend responded. "Sure it accomplishes the same task, but the methods are different. Like sailing and swimming."

"I don't like doing either," the king moped.

"A cloud of Weight Grit detonated in front of your troops could prevent enemy fire from reaching them," Portsend pressed.

"It could stop Fielder balls?" That got the king's attention.

"It could cause them to drop," Portsend said. *Theoretically.* "If it were sufficiently Compounded."

King Termain tapped the flat of his greasy blade against his chin thoughtfully. "I suppose that could be useful. But the same cloud would cause Archkingdom fire to fall short. You can't fix that?"

"I'm afraid, Your Highness, that gravity is beyond my control." Portsend swallowed. Was that too cheeky? It had come out naturally, like something he would say in a lecture.

Fortunately, King Termain grinned. "What else have you got in that devious mind of yours?"

*Devious* was the mind who manipulated the Prime Isless. Who forced Portsend into revealing dangerous secrets.

Portsend took a deep breath. "It could sink ships." Termain nodded encouragingly. "The Weight Grit could cause them to exceed their buoyancy, pulling them down. Scuttle them in the InterIsland Waters without any cannon fire."

"Well, I'm convinced." Termain stabbed his knife into the wooden tabletop. "Get the information to my palace Mixers and they'll take it from here. Gloristar can give you the next of her little secrets and you'll be back to work for the Archkingdom."

As long as Termain thought Gloristar was leading Portsend, it would keep her relevant. And they'd have to rely on the king's superstition about the Anchored Tome being protected by all the Paladin Visitants.

"One more thing before you go," Termain said. "I've been thinking about visiting the Mooring for some Guidance."

Portsend had a hard time believing that. Anyone who knew Termain Agaul knew he was Wayfarist by word only. And barely even that!

"Some troubling news has reached my royal ear," he went on. "Moonsickness. In Beripent. What did I hear—something like eight Bloodeyes terrorizing the streets after the last Passing?"

Portsend felt a tingling fear begin in his fingertips. He'd heard about it, also. Just two days ago. His silence to the boss had triggered their release, causing the deaths of twelve innocent civilians.

Homeland help him. Was he making the right choice? The Urgings seemed to dissuade him from sharing any information with the stern woman who had taken control of his research, but her threats were not empty. People were dying because of his decision. People were terrified.

Portsend tried to convince himself that it was better for twelve innocents to be slain than the entirety of Wayfarism to collapse with the loss of an irreplaceable Prime Isless. But sometimes it was hard to see the line between that altruistic reasoning and his personal feelings for Gloristar.

"Reports say there were some on Strind, too," continued Termain. "And my spies say it's happening in the major cities on Dronodan and Talumon."

Portsend didn't know anything about those attacks. The way he'd understood it, his arrangement with the boss was for Beripent alone. Still, the same woman, or whatever crime family she might belong to, had to be responsible for all the incidents. She'd told him about the Moonsickness farm. Sparks. Was there one on every island?

King Termain looked down at Gloristar from his standing position atop the table. "Wayfarism is weakening. First with the claims that the dragons were the real protection from Moonsickness, and now with Bloodeyes showing up in the streets. The Greater Chain is already divided. We cannot afford a crisis of faith right now."

Portsend felt a wash of shame take him. Was he doing this? Was he corroding people's faith by resisting the boss's demands? If that was the case, then he was also undermining Gloristar's religious authority. That same authority was the only chip in Gloristar's favor against Termain.

"You're still preaching the slag out of that Holy Torch," the king continued, "but how far are your people willing to turn away from what's happening right in front of them? I need you to fix this, Madame Isless. If we lose Wayfarism, we lose the Archkingdom."

Because Gloristar's endorsement, and the Wayfarist support, was likely the only reason Termain hadn't been forcibly removed from the throne.

"I will continue to preach the Homeland," Gloristar said. "I cannot explain how Moonsickness has stricken people away from Pekal, and I fear that any justification I give would fall short of those who already find themselves doubting the faith. I will preach the Homeland, for that is the source of all faith, and one day the true believers will find its shores and achieve perfection—be that in life or in death."

Never shaken, but unafraid to show her own shortcomings. That was what had drawn Portsend back to Gloristar, week after week. She exuded the moral strength he wished he had.

Portsend thought of their verse. In it, he found hope.

~

*We greatly desired to share the change with all.*

# CHAPTER

# 24

For once in his life, Ardor Benn was early, jogging down the overgrown dirt road toward the Old Post Lighthouse. Good thing, too. Those heavy gray clouds over the ocean looked like they might make landfall in moments. The rain could make a mess of his new leather mask, maybe even rusting the metal components. He'd have to give it a good waxing when he got back to the guesthouse.

Ten days hadn't given him much time to put this mask together. Ard needed it to be grand and terrifying, making a bold statement upon his arrival.

It was a tricky thing, commissioning a mask for a secret organization. Ard assumed that most of the Directorate had eliminated their artists instead of paying them, but that wasn't his style. To keep the secrecy intact, Lady Abeth had insisted that Codley have a go at crafting it.

Ard had been skeptical at first, but the butler had turned out to have quite the hidden talent as a craftsman.

The mask was the sleek face of a fox. It was composed of hardened leather that had been formed into jagged points, like matted fur, overlaid in strips. Thin sheets of metal reinforced the structure and accentuated the design, looking shiny against the leather which had been dyed a burned orange. The fox's mouth was closed, but Codley had inset large dog teeth to give it a menacing snarl.

The mask covered his entire head, with tooled leather fox ears rising at the top. A strap secured it under his chin, and padding along the interior made it rather comfortable. Taking a page from the simple white masks of the Faceless, Ard had instructed Codley to cover the eyeholes with black mesh to prevent anyone seeing in.

Ard had been a little disappointed that Codley hadn't been able to work in the movable Slagstone eyebrows he had suggested. All the Directorate masks were so expressionless, he thought it might've been nice to emote a little, a quizzical raising of a Slagstone eyebrow sending a shower of sparks across his fox muzzle. That would have been highly dramatic.

For the tenth time, Ard shifted the pastry bag from one hand to the other. He'd decided to bring a dozen cinnamon doughnuts to the meeting because, well, he was the new guy. Wasn't that what working citizens did? Although, at this rate, the doughnuts would probably be little more than crumbs by the time he got there.

He'd picked up a carriage on Oxite Avenue, prepaying the driver and asking to be dropped at the Swarthen Apple Orchard, one of the last remaining agricultural lands in Beripent proper. He'd emerged from the carriage wearing his new headpiece, making his way through acres of springtime-budding apple trees before the lighthouse came into view.

The Old Post Lighthouse was, as the name implied, old. Ard supposed it would have once been known simply as the Post Lighthouse, but that would have been a hundred years ago when it was still in operation, positioned on the northern shore to guide ships safely between Espar and Talumon. Sunrise Lighthouse had replaced it, built in a much more accessible and less perilous location.

Ard reached the end of the orchard and paused at the rope bridge. See, this was why the Old Post had shut down. The shoreline cliff was very high here—two hundred feet at least. At some point in ancient history, probably before the Landers had even arrived, a significant piece of the shoreline had cracked, separating a veritable tower of rock from the mainland. For some reason, their

Lander predecessors had decided it was a good idea to build a light-house on that sliver of rock jutting away from Espar.

The building itself was made of limestone, standing about sixty feet tall, with a large square room at the base. From there, the slender lighthouse tapered as it rose. It was weathering well, though Ard doubted that the lighting area at the pinnacle was still operational.

Lighthouses worked almost exactly like the searchlights that Ard had evaded at the Regulation Stockade. A highly Compounded cloud of Light Grit was detonated and directed outward by a parabolic mirror mounted to a manually operated swivel.

Ard stepped onto the hanging bridge. Surely, these ropes weren't as old as the lighthouse they led to. It was nerve-racking enough to cross the rope bridge with just a dozen doughnuts. Ard couldn't imagine bringing panweights of Grit across for the lighthouse's operation.

The Old Post Lighthouse was in the perfect place for a secret meeting, with only one way in and one way out, the acres of apple orchard acting as a natural screen from the public eye.

Still fifteen minutes early, Ard wondered if Quarrah was ahead or behind him. She would probably bound across this fifty-foot bridge in a dozen confident steps, reveling in the fact that there was nothing but a plank of wood between her and a certain-death plunge.

Ard couldn't help but feel immensely disappointed that Quarrah hadn't shown up at the Guesthouse Adagio as he'd asked. The last ten days had been a whiplash of emotions, and Raek must have been tired of hearing him talk about Quarrah Khai. They needed to join forces. Ard could help her with whatever job had brought her to the Realm, and Homeland knew he could use her expertise. They were both in the Directorate now, and they'd be more powerful if they united.

At least he'd see her today. Whether Quarrah agreed to work with him or not, the two of them wouldn't be able to avoid these meetings.

The first drops of rain pattered against his fox mask as he finally stepped off the hanging bridge. Ard moved quickly to the door at the base of the lighthouse, finding it ajar.

Inside, the room was empty. Despite the dampness of the air, dust stirred in the overcast light from a crooked window. During operation, this would have been a storage room for the lighthouse. It had likely held kegs of Grit, and even a cot for the workers to take shifts throughout the night.

Taking up most of the room was the actual round base of the lighthouse. It had clearly been constructed first, with the room being tacked on at a later date. An archway in the stone led to a rather tight spiral staircase winding its way upward.

Ard did a quick sweep of the area to make sure he hadn't missed anything. Maybe he was the first one here. Better head up the stairs and have a look around.

He ducked through the archway and moved up the spiral staircase, the planks that formed the stairs wobbly and moldy. Every so often there was a window through the stone wall. These ports were no bigger than his head, but they provided sufficient light to guide him upward.

He rose higher, the wind whistling through the windows. There was nothing but ocean as far as the eye could see, and Ard began to feel a little vertigo. It didn't seem like it would take much for this whole lighthouse to slip off its precarious perch.

He emerged through an open hatch, rising into the lighting area. It was built like a round pavilion, with a roof overhead and a railing all around the outside. He might have been more amazed by the view if he hadn't discovered Overseer and the entire Directorate already there.

Ard startled at their presence, dropping his bag from the bakery. The group was seated around a circular table where the parabolic mirror would once have stood.

They were all there: Overseer, Feathers, Boar, Horn, Antlers, and Seashell Head. Only, they looked quite different without the bulkiness of their cloaks and shape-masking shoulder yokes. All the councillors wore nondescript clothing with long sleeves and gloves, while Ard had on his usual billowy shirt and a dark blue vest.

Hmm. Maybe that was something to keep in mind for next time.

Ard quickly spotted Quarrah among the group. Unsurprisingly, her mask was completely black. It looked to be made mostly of cloth, with a formed leather piece over the face. There was no ornate decoration or embellishments of any kind. It was slim and held tightly to her head, with no protrusions or formations that could snag her up.

Ever the practical one, Quarrah Khai.

The air was hazy up here, and Ard noticed it was raining now. The droplets were driven on an angle by the wind, but instead of splattering on the table, they were held back by a glimmering shield of detonated Barrier Grit. It was like they were in one of the glassed-in gazebos of the wealthy folks. Except this one was some two hundred and sixty feet above the water.

The breeze rustled the plumes on Feather Head's mask. It was curious how air, smoke, and other Grit clouds could pass through the wall of a Barrier detonation, but elements like water and fire could not. As with most things Grit related, Raek had a theory on that, but Ard couldn't remember what it was.

"I brought doughnuts." Ard picked up his bag from the floor and dropped it on the table. "Thought they might help chase down the Waters of Loyalty."

Ard suddenly realized how foolish his offering was. In order for anyone to eat, they'd have to remove their masks.

"We do not drink the Waters of Loyalty at these meetings," replied Overseer, her voice altered by a modifier, even though she'd specifically said not to bring them to the Directorate meetings. She wore a dark baggy cloak that swallowed her seated figure almost as effectively as that awkward shoulder yoke.

"Nice view up here," Ard said. "Defensible."

"More defensible than you realize," said Overseer, "if I were to learn that my Directorate was in any measure untrustworthy."

*Was that a threat?* Perhaps Ard should have been afraid of more than the heights. It would have been beyond simple to sight a Fielder through one of those small stairway windows and pick off any suspicious councillor crossing the rope bridge.

"Come and sit." She gestured to the only empty chair, situated squarely between Seashell and Antler Head. The former was a surprisingly portly man, and the latter was a squarish, stocky woman.

Ard dropped into the chair, adjusting his fox mask once he was situated. He could tell Quarrah was watching him from across the table. He could almost *feel* her eyes boring into him, demanding that he maintain their estrangement.

"The Directorate of the Realm assembles on this, the seventh day of the Second Cycle," began Overseer. "Each does solemnly swear that all actions and words exchanged here shall be for the benefit of the Realm and its purposes. I, Overseer, do swear it."

"I, Glint, do swear it," said the woman with the antlers.

"I, Grapple, do swear it," said Feather Head.

"I, Trance, do swear it," said the woman with the single horn.

Then it was Quarrah's turn. "I, Sleight, do swear it." She said the name flatly. Ard knew how Quarrah disliked fake names and disguises. Once again, he wondered what had really brought her here.

"I, Radius, do swear it," said Boar Face.

"I, Snare, do swear it," Seashell Head spoke.

Ard was the last to speak. "I, Rival, do swear it." He spoke the name with confidence, as though it were who he'd always been.

"Let us begin with a reading of our oaths and purpose," said Overseer, "for the benefit of Sleight and Rival."

Overseer gestured to Grapple, with the feathered mask, who stood reverently.

"We uphold the truth as it was laid out by the martyr Holy Isle Dreysef in the year 813," he began. "That the Wayfarist Islehood has forsaken their sacred responsibility of preparing for the Great Egress and the Final Era of Utmost Perfection."

Oh, great. The Realm was a religious organization? Now, *that* was a surprise. Most of the street Hands hired to carry out jobs were as Settled as folks came. And executing a line of eight unsuspecting people who thought they were allies definitely didn't seem too righteous.

"The Great Egress, and the what?" Ard asked.

"The Great Egress is the mandatory evacuation from the Greater Chain," said Overseer. "The final exodus when all mankind will leave these islands and set sail for the Homeland. The Final Era of Utmost Perfection is the blessed period that will follow."

"I must have missed that part in my guidance sessions as a youth," Ard followed up. He'd never heard of any mass exodus preached in Wayfarism.

"The Islehood does not preach the Great Egress as an exodus from the islands," Overseer continued. "Over the centuries, they have corrupted the interpretation of certain verses in *Wayfarist Voyage* to pacify their followers with easier doctrines. They now claim that the Egress is a spiritual departure from a Settled lifestyle unto holiness."

"But not us?" Ard clarified. "The Realm believes in a physical exodus?"

"That is the reason Holy Isle Dreysef was barred from the Islehood four centuries ago," explained Overseer. "He took up the first mask, organizing a group of followers with the promise that they could remain anonymous so as to not lose their social standing as good Wayfarists. He called his group the Lowly Realm, taken from one of the misinterpreted verses of scripture. In some form or another the Realm has existed since that date, operating from the shadows, making the hard calls. Shaping society with the end goal of preparing the Greater Chain for the Great Egress."

Ard could see why the Islehood had stopped preaching an exodus. As much as people liked to speak dreamily of an idyllic Homeland, these islands were all anyone knew. The devout had been taking voyages for centuries, but no one had ever returned. Asking everyone who belonged to the religion to set sail at once would have resulted in an abrupt loss of followers.

"The secret codes and symbols of the Realm have passed from generation to generation, sometimes dormant for decades until an Overseer undertakes the cause and rises again. But four hundred years is a long road. Times have changed. Today, people seem more motivated by Ashings than by a holy cause like the Egress."

So, this *wasn't* truly a religious organization. As altruistic as the Realm's initial goals had been when Holy Isle Dreysef had started it, the organization had eroded into the complex ring of crime it now was. Corruption had begat corruption over the course of generations, the masks continually hiding more secrets.

"But you still talk about the Great Egress as though it is the primary motive of the Realm?" Ard asked.

"It is," answered Overseer. "An exodus to the Homeland, followed by an era of perfection."

"It's going to take a lot of convincing to get everyone to leave."

"Not everyone," answered Overseer. "Only those with sufficient faith in Wayfarism. We estimate between thirty and forty percent of the Greater Chain's population will depart."

"I'm afraid I'm missing the point," Ard bluntly declared.

"What is the single greatest influence in maintaining rule over these islands?" Overseer asked.

"Bloodline?" Ard ventured. Weren't they currently fighting a war over that very topic?

"King Pethredote was not of the ruling bloodline," said Overseer, "and yet he was made crusader monarch."

"That's only because his Paladin Visitant happened to show up," said Ard.

"A Paladin Visitant that was entrusted to him by the Islehood." She let the phrase linger until Ard put the pieces together.

"You're suggesting that the Islehood has the greatest influence in maintaining rule?"

"Not just the Islehood but all of Wayfarism," answered Overseer. "One needs only to read the histories to see that the religion has alway gone hand in hand with the rule of the islands. Over the centuries, the Realm has been able to manipulate nearly every aspect of society—politics, economy, education. But religion is a tricky one. Of course, we have people in the Islehood doing their best to alter texts and manipulate doctrines. But the faith of the true believers has proven to be incorruptible, and we ultimately lose any ground we thought we were gaining."

Overseer leaned back, lacing her gloved fingers together. "The Great Egress will solve this problem. With the departure of every believing Wayfarist, including the Prime and all the Holy Isles, the religion will be cut off at the roots. The Realm will be free to rule, and those of us who remain will have an overabundance of wealth, land, goods, power. It will be, as the book says, the Final Era of Utmost Perfection."

Sparks, this wasn't an exodus. It was a purge!

The Realm had twisted Isle Dreysef's centuries-old cause, using a well-established heritage of secrecy and anonymity to purge the Greater Chain of Wayfarism. It was difficult to imagine a world without the religion, but Ard could see the benefit for an organization like the Realm. Wayfarism couldn't be controlled as easily as politics and commerce, since the bulk of its power and influence came from the heartfelt beliefs of its followers. Eliminating it altogether was drastic, but probably more effective than trying to convince people to change their beliefs.

"And when is this mass exodus going to happen?" Ard asked. "Just wondering if I should pack my bags."

"This plan has been under way for well over a year," said

Overseer. "With the aging crusader monarch, the Realm had been stirring for nearly a decade, the Directorate already reestablished. But our plans spurred ahead with great fortune when Pethredote died unexpectedly. The chaos surrounding his death was the perfect opportunity for the Realm to take control."

Ard felt his stomach wrench with guilt. Some of this fell back on him, then. Just as he'd feared. By the sound of it, he'd all but paved the way for the Realm to seize control. They had their fingers in the war, in the politics, in religion. Ard certainly didn't regret saving Raek and sending Pethredote to face the justice of a dragon, but maybe it could have been done in a way that wouldn't have allowed the lurking Realm to flourish. Maybe he should have listened to Quarrah and slowed down.

"We have been moving the pieces ever since that night," continued Overseer, "waiting to bring to pass the signs."

"What signs are you talking about?" Ard asked.

"Grapple will read the passage," said Overseer. Ard turned to see that the man with the feathered mask had opened a small book to a page marked with a long ribbon.

"'A day cometh when all must speedily go unto the Homeland,'" he began. "'Stumblers have gone before thee, and these silent ones have heralded thy voyage. Ye shall know that the great day of egress is upon you when the miserable shall forsake their habitat and walk among you, wild and uncontrolled.'"

"I'm hoping you'll interpret this," Ard cut in. "I've always found the text of *Wayfarist Voyage* to be a little over my head."

Grapple looked to Overseer, as though unsure what to do. Apparently, new members of the Directorate didn't usually ask so many questions.

"The Islehood interprets 'stumblers' and 'silent ones' as the ships of the devout who have sailed in search of the Homeland never to be heard from again," Overseer explained. "And they preach that the 'miserable' who have left their habitat are those who have forsaken

Wayfarism and given in to a Settled lifestyle. The Realm sees both statements as descriptions of Moonsick people leaving Pekal and wandering upon our islands. This is the first sign to precede the Great Egress."

"Brend," Ard said quietly.

"Yes," Overseer responded. "That small village in the southern-most reaches of Espar was struck with Moonsickness a little more than two years ago."

Ard had heard the horrifying reports about how the villagers had torn one another apart. It had been the beginning of an inevitable spreading that Isle Halavend had predicted. As the dragon population shrank, the shield they provided also dwindled, causing the poisoning Moon rays to creep in closer around the edges of the islands.

And Ard had heard that other townships had grown Moonsick since, prompting the evacuation of some of the most distant areas.

"The sickening of Brend was a sign unto us," continued Overseer. "A fulfillment of prophesy, as blatant as could be. But such a distant village was far from the minds and concerns of the general public. Word about it spread, but was quickly extinguished. The fear of Moonsickness on Espar did not take hold as it should have. The sign was too subtle, so we decided to bring it to the forefront, where all of civilization would take proper note. So the Realm founded the farm."

*The farm?* Ard had heard it mentioned at the last Faceless meeting.

"The people cultivated there are greatly appreciated," Overseer said. "They become the very fulfillment of prophesy, helping to prepare the believers for the Great Egress."

Suddenly it all made sense. Sickening, disturbing sense. The Realm was intentionally exposing people to Moonsickness to release them in the cities... He remembered the words Feather Head had used when assigning him the farm job.

*"Young or old. The captives you deliver needn't be healthy, but they must be alive."*

Ard shifted uncomfortably in his seat. Every new detail he learned about this group furthered his desire to take them down.

"Surely, you have heard of the Moonsickness reports in all the major cities across the Greater Chain?" asked Overseer.

Ard couldn't very well admit to killing one of the Bloodeyes at the Wry Fox Inn. Overseer had to know that Androt Penn had been admitted into the Faceless, but she would have no reason to believe that he had already climbed ranks fast enough to infiltrate the Directorate. In fact, maybe Ard could use this little detail to push suspicion even further away.

"I heard about the Bloodeyes in Beripent," he said. "One of them murdered Lady Abeth Agaul."

"That was the plan," Overseer answered. Interesting. So, it was no coincidence that the two Moonsick men had shown up at the precise time Ard was trying to kill Abeth.

"Moonsickness walking among us is the first sign preceding the Great Egress," continued Overseer. "It is well under way. But there is one more sign remaining." She gestured for Grapple to continue reading.

"'In that same day, the waters shall heave up their secret depths to such a height that even the towers upon which mankind hides will not be able to escape. Verily, this cataclysm shall be unto you as a final Urging, bidding all to depart this lowly realm and ascend unto the Homeland. For soon after cometh the Final Era of Utmost Perfection.'"

"The verse prophecies of a massive flood we call the Cataclysm," Overseer explained. "The depths of the sea will spill over our cliff shores and ravage our cities."

What she was describing was unheard of. The sea had never reached them, the high cliff shorelines providing a natural protective barrier.

Freshwater flooding had always been a problem on the islands, between dams breaching and rivers swelling. But the sea was steady and distant, the tide regularly rising and falling only a few feet, with an exception of the Moon Passing, when the range was more than double that.

"What could cause the water to rise so high?" Quarrah asked this question, assuring Ard that she *was* actively listening behind that black mask.

"*We* could," answered Overseer. "The Realm can bring about this cataclysm by submerging a large amount of Compounded Void Grit in the InterIsland Waters."

Ard felt his heart rate quicken. Such a detonation would push the water outward, displacing it with enough force to create a massive wave.

Was this how prophecies were fulfilled? By the cunning trickery of a criminal organization? Ard hadn't decided if he believed in Isle Dreysef's "true" interpretation, but if the Great Egress was real, shouldn't the signs that precede it happen naturally?

But the Realm clearly wasn't interested in the Egress as a way to save civilization. Although that might have been its original purpose, the group had succumbed to corruption. This was about profit now, and that meant forcing these supposed prophecies to occur on the Realm's timetable.

"In the wake of such a disaster," said Overseer, "we shall be positioned to announce the Great Egress and claim the riches of all the islands once the Wayfarist population has departed."

He had to admit, what Overseer described was clever and complex, the types of schemes usually quick to garner approval from Ardor Benn. But their success could mean the deaths of thousands in the Cataclysm. And millions more would die in the Great Egress, following the first Moon Passing beyond the dragons' protective shield. He needed to stop that ship from sailing, both literally and figuratively.

"How is that going to work?" Ard asked. "Once we create the Cataclysm, what makes you think the people will believe it was a sign foretelling an exodus they've never heard about before?"

"There is a final piece to this plan," said Overseer. "Something that assures it will all come together." She leaned forward, placing both hands flat on the table. "We have Shad Agaul."

Ard held his breath, letting the silence hang, allowing for the perfect duration of stunned speechlessness before reacting.

Quarrah went and spoiled all that.

"Shad Agaul?" she cried, nearly coming out of her seat. "Son of King Remium? But he was killed the same night as his father..."

Based on her exuberant reaction, it was clear that this was the first Quarrah Khai had heard of it, which meant her reasons for infiltrating the Realm were not the same as his.

"The boy's death was fabricated," Overseer said.

"How?" asked Ard. It was time to see how much of this story they had figured out correctly. "If I remember right, the boy's death was very conclusive. His body was greatly burned, but whole enough to inter."

"The body was a decoy, belonging to a young harp student that the Realm convinced to spend a night alone in the prince's chambers."

So Ard had been right about Beska Falay's unfortunate student. Using a lad like that... Ard wanted to reach over and strip off Overseer's mask to see what kind of face could be so heartless.

"The boy detonated the Blast Grit, then?" Ard probed, trying to keep his voice aloof.

"We did not trust him to end his own life," she replied. "Fortunately, the Realm has developed a way to detonate Grit without anyone being present."

"Fuses?" Ard asked, keeping the topic rolling.

"Clocks," answered Overseer. "They can be altered to set off an explosion at a specific time."

Raek would be thrilled to know that he had deduced such an intricate detail.

"How ingenious," Ard commented. "I can think of a hundred useful instances for such a contraption."

"Indeed," said Overseer. "We keep a significant stock available for the Realm's purposes. The prince's falsified death was one such. It needed to be done tactfully in order to manipulate the political scene into what it is today."

"To bring about the war," Ard said, cutting right to it.

"The Realm understands that sometimes things must get worse before they can get better," she replied. "The war causes division and grief. It reminds people what life was like before, and they yearn for that to return. Shad Agaul will provide that. The Cataclysm will be a necessary reminder that nature is a common enemy more powerful than either army. In the stunned aftermath of the flood, Shad Agaul will appear, taking the throne from Termain. The Greater Chain will gladly reunite under his rule. He will then exercise his right to select a new Prime Isle, who will preach the doctrine of the Great Egress and lead every faithful Wayfarist man, woman, and child speedily unto the Homeland."

"What?" cried Ard. "How can you be sure that Shad Agaul does what you need him to do?"

"Measures have been taken to assure the lad's compliance," Overseer responded. "When the time comes for the prince to appear, his mind will be properly molded to our needs."

What was that supposed to mean? Were they torturing the kid? Sparks, these people kept getting more awful!

"Then there's the issue of where the prince has been for the last year and a half," Ard said. Hopefully, the answer would give him a clue as to the boy's current whereabouts.

"He will simply explain that he was being held captive by Termain's retinue," answered Overseer. "He was able to escape in the destruction of the flood."

"Does the boy actually believe that?" pressed Ard.

"Shad Agaul is in no state to believe or disbelieve anything until we allow him to. The boy will not give us any trouble."

That was quite the definitive statement. But Ard would keep digging until he found a weak root.

"And the new Prime Isle?" Ard asked.

"One of our own," she said. "He will change the interpretation of the verses and preach the Great Egress."

Ah. Now they'd hit on a topic in which Ardor Benn had some practical experience.

"Not going to work," Ard said flatly.

Overseer cleared her throat. "Elements of this plan have been in the works for nearly a decade," she said. "I assure you, we have considered every angle."

"Not going to work," Ard repeated. Something was brewing in his mind. Not a plan yet, but the arousal of one. Like the gentle touch of young lovers just before they found the hayloft.

"You can't control what people believe." He glanced around the table. "Isn't that basically what Overseer just explained? That's always been the Wayfarist thorn in the Realm's side. Take the Holy Torch, for example. Certain information came forward that the Torch is a meaningless tradition and that true protection comes from the dragons, who absorb the Moon's toxic rays on Pekal. People still don't believe it, even with your Moonsick Bloodeyes terrorizing the streets after each Passing. Belief dies hard, I'm telling you."

"The information against the Holy Torch was spread with no discernible source." It was Trance who spoke. Ard was pleased to be getting input from someone other than Overseer. It meant this was now a conversation instead of a lecture.

"Our new interpretation of doctrines will come from the next Prime Isle," Glint added. "It will gain traction and people will follow."

"Or," dared Ard, "it will simply splinter Wayfarism into more sects, keeping the faith alive even after the Great Egress."

Radius turned his boar-tusk mask toward Overseer. "This newcomer sits among us only to sow doubt into plans that have passed years of scrutiny. You were right to call him Rival. I worry that he guns for your mask, Overseer. I do not like the way he speaks."

Sparks. Ard was pushing too hard. "I'm not saying the plan is bad. I'm just saying that it doesn't hurt to have a fresh mind think through some of the details."

"What about Sleight?" asked Trance. "She's a fresh mind, and yet she says nothing against our plans."

"Let's hear from her," seconded Glint. "What does Sleight have to say about our efforts to bring about the Great Egress?"

All hidden eyes went to Quarrah. Ard found himself holding his breath again.

"I think," she began, "that Rival is wrong. The Directorate's plan strikes me as one that will work well."

Ard let out his breath in a disappointed sigh. Was she playing an angle? Or was she merely disagreeing to spite him now that their lives weren't on the line?

"I must admit," said Snare, "I *can* see some merit in Rival's concerns. In my life outside, I am surrounded by devout Wayfarists. It is difficult to imagine them changing core beliefs simply because their new leader proclaims it."

*Thank you,* Ard thought. *I knew I liked you.*

"True believers will come around in time," Grapple said. "There is no higher authority among Wayfarists than the Prime Isle."

"Actually..." Ard said. His plan was finally coming together, carried on his thoughts like a cloud on the breeze, suddenly shifting from an amorphous wisp into a shape so well defined that even a child could point into the sky and know what it was.

"There is a higher authority," he continued. "One whose word would be received unquestioningly. Someone who is greater and even more powerful than a Prime Isle or a king."

"Are you referring to a Paladin Visitant?" Trance asked incredulously.

*Not quite,* Ard thought. But it was a good place to start. "What do people believe about Paladin Visitants?"

"Visitors from the Homeland," answered Glint, "too holy for the eye to behold or the ear to hear."

That was the response Ard had hoped for, proving that the Realm didn't know the truth. In actuality, the fiery beings were travelers displaced across time through the use of two geographically linked detonations of Visitant Grit.

As far as Ard was aware, there had only been seven people privy to the truth about the Paladin Visitants: Ard, Raek, Quarrah, Lyndel, Halavend, Pethredote, and Prime Isle Chauster. Three of them were dead now, and Ard had to believe that Quarrah and Lyndel fully realized the danger and kept the secret.

"What if we introduced a Paladin Visitant that *could* speak to the people?" Ard continued. "A Homelander in his true form, without the fire and destructive glory."

"You're talking about a ruse?" Overseer asked.

"Yes!" Ard slapped his hand on the table. "A ruse! Great idea!"

"What would be the purpose of this?" asked Grapple, a skeptical tilt of his feathered mask.

"Just imagine…" Ard stood up. He could no longer contain himself. "As the waters of the Cataclysm recede, an unknown ship sails into Beripent's harbor, flying a flag never before seen. Onboard is an entire crew of Homelanders. They're exotic, mystical. Maybe they look different. Talk different." He was circling the table, using his most captivating tone. "Why have they come? To supersede the Prime Isless and correct the erroneous interpretation of the scriptures. To tell all people to prepare for the Great Egress. There would be no one better suited for this announcement.

They've come from the Homeland, so they'll know the way back. I don't know about you, but I'd be far more likely to sail away from here knowing that I had a guide, rather than blindly following the hundreds of ships that have never been heard from again."

Ard let the idea hang in a moment of silence, the wind whistling through the open top of the lighthouse and the rain splattering against the Barrier shell.

"He makes an interesting proposal," Snare finally said.

"It is too much of a deviation from our current plan," argued Grapple. "Putting the young Agaul back on the throne is everything we've worked for. These imposter Homelanders would overshadow his ascension."

"I agree," added Glint. "We need to keep the focus on the prince and his newly appointed Prime Isle. They are already under our control. Why would we trade that for an unpredictable plan like the one Rival proposes?"

"I'm not suggesting we give up Shad Agaul," said Ard. It was time to deliver his final piece—the reason he had suggested this complex ruse in the first place. Everything had been gearing up to this, and if they agreed to it, Ard would finally get what he needed.

"We'll need a captain for the Homeland vessel," Ard said. "Who better than the late Prince Shad Agaul?"

This earned him a wide range of reactions, from guffaws to outright laughter. With the masks on, it was difficult to know what emotion accompanied these responses.

"Wayfarists believe that when a worthy person dies, his soul goes to dwell in the Homeland, right?" Ard continued. "We can maintain that Shad Agaul died in that assassination explosion more than a year ago. No one questions his worthiness to have entered the Homeland. Now he returns from the dead, livened by the Homeland's power. Shad takes the throne from his father's cousin and at the same time he prepares people for the Great Egress."

This time, he didn't need facial expressions to know that his words had made a profound impression. He could taste it in the salty sea air.

"That would certainly keep the focus where we want it," Radius said. "And possibly even maximize the impact of the prince's return."

"It is also a tighter explanation of where the prince has been," said Snare. "And it doesn't leave any lingering questions about his disappearance that could point fingers back to us."

Grapple leaned back, shaking his head. "It just doesn't seem feasible to pull off such a massive trick."

"It's obviously a job bigger than the eight of us can handle," Ard said, "but we've got the entire Realm at our disposal. We can hire the experts we need to make it work."

"We'd need a blazing-sharp mind to spearhead a project of this size," said Trance.

"I couldn't agree more," replied Ard.

"And you think you could do it?" Grapple challenged.

"Me?" Ard cried. "Sparks, no! But I know of someone who could."

Ard paused and waited for the inevitable question to come. It was Glint who asked it. "Who?"

"The best ruse artist in the Greater Chain," he replied. "His name is Ardor Benn."

The name danced across the table. Ard thought their silence was the result of awe, until Trance said, "Who, now?"

"Ardor Benn," Ard repeated. "Surely you've heard of him. He's kind of a big deal. Pulled off some seriously high-profile crimes."

"Oh, yes," replied Radius as though it had just dawned on him. "He was that fellow who assassinated Lady Abeth Agaul. Wasn't he arrested?"

"No, no," corrected Glint. "That was *Androt Penn*."

Ard swallowed, his mask suddenly growing hot. Well, at least the confusion through similarity was working here.

"Didn't that Androt Penn bloke get shivved in the Reggie Stockade?" Ard asked. So much for a heroic death... "From what I understand, Ardor Benn would never be careless enough to get arrested."

"Yes," Overseer followed up, causing everyone to become quiet. "I believe he was the ruse artist involved with that famous soprano who performed at the Grotenisk Festival two years back."

Oh, good. At least the most important person in the room had heard of him. And Ard could only imagine what was happening behind Quarrah's black mask at the mention of Azania Fyse.

"I was under the impression that Ardor Benn had left Espar," continued Overseer.

"I might have a lead on how to contact him," Ard replied.

Overseer's dragon-scale mask nodded slowly. "I am intrigued, but I do not fully trust you. This is your first meeting and you seem to disagree with everything."

"Not everything—"

"My point exactly," she said, cutting him off. "Still, you have raised some interesting thoughts and your proposal is worth investigating. You may extend the offer to Ardor Benn, withholding the Realm's involvement and ultimate motive."

"Of course." Ard's heart was racing. "Thank you."

"Understand that I reserve the right to terminate this operation at any moment, should your motives or methods become any more suspicious than they already are."

"Yes." Ard nodded agreeably.

"Sleight will be running checks and security on this job," Overseer casually assigned.

"What?" Quarrah sat bolt upright in her chair. "Why me?"

"You are both new in the Directorate," Overseer said. "Consider this a way to prove your loyalty."

"What exactly do I have to do?" asked Quarrah.

"You, or someone you hire, will find Ardor Benn and join his operation," said Overseer. "You will monitor and report, making sure he does the job correctly, without knowing of the Realm's involvement."

Quarrah sat back, her face turning slightly toward Ard. "Very well."

Under his mask, Ardor Benn couldn't hold back a grin.

It was time for a shave and a haircut.

~

*Our decision to leave is unanimous.*

# PART IV

It is the nature of all flesh to yearn for a Homeland. The Wayfarist admits his estrangement, while the Settled feign ignorance to its draw. Even the Trothian, with his tireless eyes and azure skin, must feel a pull to whatever distant land once birthed him.

—*Wayfarist Voyage, vol. 3*

Let the Moon turn red from the blushing of our praise. Take us back into your womb. It is our only desire.

—*Ancient Agrodite song*

# CHAPTER

# 25

In Quarrah's experience, overgrown bushes were typically a safe place to hide. But usually, there wasn't a madwoman with a Fielder taking random shots into any vegetation that so much as quivered. Quarrah had been hiding in the garden, waiting for an opportunity to approach the palace so she could meet with Fabra Ment. Instead, the old widow had come outside for a bit of sport shooting.

The queen dowager took another crack at a hedge not thirty yards from Quarrah's hiding spot. Fabra Ment was wearing a large sun hat with the floppiest of brims. Her bright red riding boots came clear up to her knees, and she sported a jerkin made of the same dyed leather. She was shaped somewhat like a wedge, Quarrah realized, observing her from a distance. Rather wide up top and narrow at the bottom.

A handkerchief was tied loosely around her neck and she pulled it up over her mouth and nose every time she took a shot. Presumably, this was to protect her from the gun smoke. The irony was not lost on Quarrah, however, as Fabra had to remove her smoking pipe every time she pulled up the handkerchief. Each shot was then taken with her pipe clutched awkwardly in the two littlest fingers of her trigger hand.

Errel, the mute handmaiden, was at her side, loading Fielders as quickly as Fabra could shoot them. The only thing stopping

Quarrah from jumping up and waving her hands was that blazing Regulator lounging under a tree nearby.

Well, that and the fact that Fabra was likely to shoot before realizing that Quarrah wasn't a rodent.

She repositioned herself, trying to see if she recognized the Reggie who was clearly supposed to be keeping an eye on the queen dowager. Hard to say. They all looked alike to her in those red palace uniforms. She'd never been one for remembering faces, but she was too paranoid that people would remember hers.

There had been a whole group of Reggies just before Fabra arrived. They'd swept the grounds west of the palace in what appeared to be a frantic attempt to clear anyone or anything valuable before the old widow started shooting. That had presented a significant challenge for Quarrah, who had barely managed to stay hidden in some ferns, doubling back behind the Reggie sweep to climb a tree.

Now she just needed to get rid of this last one before she could risk an approach to give her employer a report.

Quarrah flinched as the Fielder spit flame. That shot had been aimed frightfully high, ripping through the upper branches of a large tree. A large black bird came crashing down, and Fabra gave a mighty whoop of victory, tugging down her handkerchief and slipping the end of the pipe between her lips.

She whirled on the Reggie under the tree behind her. "Well?" she rasped loudly enough that Quarrah could easily hear. "Fetch!"

With a weary sigh, the Regulator hauled himself to his feet and sauntered down the hill to the dead bird. His gait told Quarrah that babysitting the queen dowager was not a coveted shift among the Reggies. This guy might have even lost a bet.

Quarrah took advantage of the distraction to move a bit closer, concealing herself behind a large rock. By the time the Reggie stooped to retrieve the kill, she was within earshot of the entire conversation.

THE SHATTERED REALM OF ARDOR BENN   367

"That's the biggest one yet!" Fabra cried merrily. "Take it to Strompsen right away. Tell him to pluck and roast it and serve it to my son."

"It's..." started the Reggie. "It's a *crow*, my lady."

Fabra started to laugh. "That's why it's funny!"

He dropped the bird, but Fabra suddenly leveled the empty Fielder at him, the butt tucked under her armpit. "I gave you an order, Soldier."

"You're serious?" he cried.

"And bring me another pint on your way back," said the widow. "My first one's run out already."

The Regulator picked up the dead crow again and set off toward the palace. He didn't look happy about the message he was supposed to relay, but the spring in his step told Quarrah he didn't mind getting some distance from the old woman.

Fabra turned to Errel, handing her the spent Fielder in exchange for the one the handmaiden had just reloaded. With surprising speed, Fabra whirled, bringing the long gun to her shoulder and pulling the trigger without taking any significant aim. The shot ripped the bush where Quarrah had previously been.

"Sparks!" Fabra cursed to herself. She'd fired with such haste that the pipe was still clenched between her teeth and the handkerchief around her wrinkly neck. "Could've sworn I'd seen that bush a-wagging."

This was Quarrah's moment to emerge—while the Reggie was far enough up the hill not to notice, and the old queen's Fielder was empty. She rose from behind the rock, hands in the air as she stepped into plain view.

"Well, piss in my pipe," said the queen dowager. "I was beginning to think I'd never see you again."

Quarrah moved toward her so she didn't have to speak loudly. It was bad enough to be out in the open like this. "You're not an easy person to reach."

"On the contrary," said Fabra. "I've got nothing but time on my hands. All you have to do is make an appointment and I'll work you in between morning naps."

"I can't make appointments in the palace," Quarrah said, "for reasons that should be obvious to you." Too many familiar workers since Pethredote's reign. Any one of them might remember her and call for an arrest on the spot.

"I've been watching the palace for days," Quarrah continued, "trying to determine your routine so I could get you aside."

"Routine?" Fabra cackled. "Not even my bowels are regular, honey. I do what I want to do, when I want to do it."

"Is there somewhere more private we can talk?"

"Not as many people know you as you'd like to think." Fabra took a puff on her pipe. "I hung that painting of you in the palace."

"You did what?" Quarrah cried. Hadn't she agreed to this job so that Fabra *wouldn't* display her likeness? This seemed like a huge breach of trust.

"It's been a cycle and a half without a peep from you," Fabra said. "I thought you'd abandoned me. You should be glad I didn't have Errel whip up a couple more paintings to circulate."

"I was busy," Quarrah said. Since then, she'd been to two Faceless meetings, sailed to the war front and back, earned her way into the Directorate, and gone to a secret meeting in the Old Post Lighthouse. Quarrah would have given a quick report sooner, but it took some dedicated loitering to reach the queen dowager.

"I want that painting taken down," Quarrah insisted.

"Relax," Fabra dismissed. "Nobody's even made a comment about it. Hung it up in the north wing, right outside the door to my personal chambers."

"Still..." Quarrah said. "And I'd feel more comfortable talking somewhere private."

"Walk with me," said the old queen. She handed the empty Fielder to Errel and moved toward a more forested area of the grounds. The thin handmaiden hoisted both guns over her shoulders and trailed after the two women.

"I assume you have news?" Fabra asked.

So much news, Quarrah wasn't sure where to begin. And to be honest, she wasn't sure how much to share.

"Waelis Mordo," Quarrah began, "the advisor whom you feared was influencing your son..."

"He's dead," Fabra said, tipping back her sun hat as they entered the shade of the trees, where a springtime chill still lingered. "Blazing fool must have eaten something that didn't agree with him. They found him in his bed, black and blue. Bloated like a dead dog on the roadside."

"You were right about him," Quarrah confirmed. "All the information you gave me was accurate. Waelis Mordo wasn't just involved in the Realm, he was one of seven people that forms the Directorate. They counsel with their leader, a woman called Overseer, and together they make all the assignments for the Faceless."

"What do they say about my son?" Fabra asked.

"As far as I can tell, the Realm is using him to make sure the war continues," said Quarrah. "They're setting up Termain to fail."

Fabra snorted. "Not sure they need to try very hard."

"Termain can't be part of the Realm," said Quarrah. "If he were, he'd know that they were undermining his rule."

*Unless it's all an act,* Quarrah suddenly thought. *Unless the aims and goals of the Realm are more important to Termain Agaul than the Archkingdom, and his incompetence is merely a prolonged act.*

It was a chilling thought, and Quarrah couldn't get herself to discount it completely. The Directorate of the Realm seemed to be made up of some frightfully dedicated people.

"Either way," said Fabra, "we can't have this kind of power calling the shots from the shadows. The Realm needs to be shut down."

Quarrah held up her hands. "You hired me to find out how they were manipulating your son. I've done just that."

*And I'm happy to be finished with you,* she thought. Unfortunately, her association with the Realm couldn't end quite yet. Not until she figured out what was in that blazing Waters of Loyalty. The last thing she wanted was to end up black and blue, bloated like a dead dog on the roadside.

"I said you could name your price," Fabra said. "I'll get you paid by tomorrow morning. Just tell me what getting that information was worth to you."

Well, the anxiety and tension of the Realm meetings aside, Quarrah had sailed all the way to Strind, blown up an army, negotiated with the Sovereign States, and dueled Ard to the death. And now she'd apparently drunk something that would kill her painfully unless she kept going back for more.

"Ten thousand Ashings."

Even that seemed low, once she said it out loud. At one moment she'd held the Agaul family ring, and later, fifty-six panweights of Void Grit. Both represented fortunes she'd willingly surrendered.

"Ehh," Fabra made a waffling sound, as though she were debating whether or not to let Quarrah's asking price stand. "You know how many rugs you could buy with ten thousand Ashings? Even your rugs could have rugs."

"I'm not going to buy rugs," Quarrah said.

She always found it downright impolite when someone asked what she was planning to do with a payout.

She'd use it up little by little, or maybe she'd spend it all in a week. She was renting hideout apartments in every quarter of Beripent. They helped make her comings and goings difficult for others to trace. A payout that large would certainly allow her to buy several of them outright and still have enough to replenish her stores of Grit.

"I'll get you the ten thousand," Fabra said. "But I hate to see our relationship end. If the Realm is meddling with my son and the Archkingdom affairs, I'd like to see it dismantled."

"Easier said than done."

"Name your price."

"Me?" Quarrah cried. "You want me to dismantle the Realm?"

"As I said at the concert hall, you were not my first pick." Fabra coughed. "But I must admit, you're proving to be just as effective as Ardor Benn."

"More so," Quarrah countered.

"Then you accept?" asked the queen.

"What do you have in mind?"

Fabra shrugged. "You're the one who's been to their meetings. We need to find a weakness. Some way we can expose their secrets." They moved silently down the path for a moment. "Where do they meet?"

"I don't know about the Faceless meetings," answered Quarrah. "I was only given the location for a carriage pickup. I think they scramble the cabs through the North Central Carriage Station to make them impossible to trace."

"That doesn't give us much."

Quarrah almost said something about the Old Post Lighthouse, but stopped herself. She couldn't risk telling Fabra Ment that she'd earned a spot in the Directorate. The woman seemed prone to gossip, and drawn to drama. If Fabra spilled any of the Realm's plans, it would no doubt get back to Overseer, making Ard and Quarrah the prime suspects. Best only to tell her information that any of the Faceless could uncover. That way, if she blabbed, everyone in a white mask would become a suspect.

Fabra's resources might be useful, however. If an opportunity presented itself to take down the Realm, the queen dowager might have the manpower and Ashings to make it happen. The smart move for Quarrah was to keep digging deeper into the Directorate until a fatal flaw exposed itself. Then she could tell Fabra Ment everything.

"So, what's next?" asked the old widow.

"The purpose of the Faceless meetings is to assign a string of jobs," Quarrah explained. "I assume they all serve some purpose in the Realm's grand plans, but each seems disconnected enough that the people carrying them out could never hope to piece it all together."

"And you have a job?" she asked.

"I'm supposed to be overseeing one of the assignments," Quarrah answered. "I'm guessing it will be pointlessly complex."

"What makes you say that?"

"The Realm is hiring it out to..." Quarrah trailed off. Did she want to mention him?

"To whom?" Fabra pressed, licking her lips.

Quarrah swallowed. "Ardor Benn."

Fabra suddenly stopped her mosey down the path, pipe wobbling as her face cracked into a giddy grin. "He's part of the Realm?"

Quarrah waved a hand. "Sparks, no." She might as well use this opportunity to convince Fabra that she'd made the right choice hiring her over Ard. No need to mention that he'd also finagled his way into the organization.

"But you know where to find him?" pressed Fabra.

What was her obsession with Ard? Was his name really such a legend around the palace? Maybe she felt a strange sense of obligation to him, since his actions had brought down Pethredote and ultimately put her son on the throne.

"I will soon enough," Quarrah answered. "One of the councillors in the Directorate should be making contact with him. He'll let me know once he does."

It was important to keep Rival and Ardor Benn separate in her mind. It wasn't unlike the way she'd compartmentalized Ard and Dale Hizror, his composer persona.

"What's the job?" she asked.

"I believe he'll be putting together a crew," replied Quarrah.

"They're going to Pekal?"

She shook her head. "It's really not clear. I'm hoping to get more details once I speak with him."

"Any chance you could bring him in for a second job?" asked the queen dowager. "Two heads are always better than one. Imagine what the two of you could accomplish. The Realm wouldn't stand a chance if you united."

Maybe there was some truth to that, but Ard and Quarrah would certainly not be uniting under Fabra's flag. Quarrah was out to prove a point to the old queen, and that meant keeping Ard away from her.

"I don't think that would be wise," she said. "Involving Ardor any more than he already is could jeopardize my place in the Realm. Overseer doesn't know we have any connection, and I need to keep it that way."

Fabra rubbed her hands together. "Oh, but it's all rather exciting, wouldn't you say? Secret schemes, daring thieves, and ruse artists. You agree to continue for me, then?"

What choice did Quarrah have? She'd gotten into this mess because the queen dowager had twisted her arm with that painting. The portrait didn't seem to be going away, and now that she was in, the real threat was the Waters of Loyalty. She might as well get paid extra for keeping Fabra in the loop.

"My lady!" The shout came from the direction of the palace beyond the wooded grove they now walked.

"Ah. My pint is wondering where I've wandered off to," said Fabra. "He's quite a strapping lad. I could introduce you if you want to stick around. He looks like he'd be good for a night or two, at the least."

Quarrah was hardly interested in the old woman's impertinent offer. She was already slipping off the trail into the heavy underbrush that would provide her cover until she reached the wall.

"My regards to Ardor Benn," called Fabra Ment.

Ha! As if Quarrah would be sharing any pleasantries with Ard. This time, it would be strictly business.

~

*They will wonder how we survived.*

# CHAPTER

# 26

"Meet Ardor Benn, ruse artist extraordinaire." Ard stepped into the guesthouse salon, taking a slight bow. "Well? What do you think?"

"I think we're going to be late," Raek replied, leaning in the hallway and clearly itching to move outside.

"Hey. A shave this smooth takes finesse," replied Ard, rubbing a hand over his chin.

"It's a monumental improvement, Master Ardor," said Codley Hattingson, softly clapping his hands.

"You look very dapper," agreed Lady Abeth, seated on a padded chair in the corner.

"The haircut's not half bad, either," said Ard. It had taken a little extra pomade to style it the way he liked, but Codley had done a fair job.

It was good to have his old look back. Time for the legendary ruse artist to return. Ard simply hoped that two years was long enough for his enemies to forget his face.

"Yes, well. I've been cutting Mister Lagaday's hair for years," Codley said.

Ard winced. "If you'd told me that before, I wouldn't have let you within arm's reach of my silken locks. I thought I could trust a guy with a mustache like yours. Seriously, Cod. It's a masterpiece in wax."

The butler reached up and twirled the ends of his mustache self-consciously. "I should..." he stammered under the praise. "I ought to tidy up the washroom." He disappeared from the grand salon.

One of the kitchen doors swung open and Ard turned, expecting to find Bannit Lagaday with a fresh cup for Lady Abeth. But the figure in the doorway was not the small cook.

Quarrah Khai.

Ardor Benn's heart was suddenly hammering in his chest, and not just from her surprise appearance. She had finally come! Right when he was late for an appointment...

"I know it's not your style," he said to her, trying to remain calm, "but you could have simply knocked."

"I was checking your security," Quarrah answered. "There wasn't any."

"Well, to be fair, we don't have much to secure."

"What about her?" Quarrah pointed to Lady Abeth, who had just shrunk down in her seat, bringing her napkin up to hide her face.

"You knew she was alive," Ard said. "I told you during the duel."

"Sure," Quarrah replied. "But other people don't know that."

"Other people aren't sneaking in through the kitchen unannounced."

"But they *could*," snapped Quarrah. "And I just proved that they'd take you off guard."

"Enough!" Raek bellowed, stepping between them. "Great to see you, too, Quarrah."

"Hi, Raek."

"Glad you're here," Raek continued. "But we need to get in the carriage. We're already running late."

"Surprise, surprise," she muttered.

The door to the washroom suddenly opened and Codley stepped out, a short-barreled Singler in his grasp. His thumb clicked the Slagstone hammer into place as he pointed the gun at Quarrah.

"Who is this intruder?" demanded the butler.

"Who, indeed?" seconded Abeth, still concealed behind her napkin.

"Everyone, this is my old partner, Quarrah Khai," Ard said.

"You may have heard Ard mention her, oh, a few thousand times," Raek threw in. "Most recently, when they dueled to the death."

"Codley," Ard snapped, trying to draw attention away from Raek's addition, "put that thing away."

The butler slowly released the hammer and tucked the small gun into his vest.

"So, is she with us?" Lady Abeth peered at Quarrah from behind her napkin.

"Yes," Ard said at the precise moment that Quarrah said, "No." They looked at each other across the room. Ard preferred to think that was a playful glare.

"I'll tell you what," Ard said to Abeth. "We will sort all this out on the way and fill you in the moment we get back."

"Where are we going?" Quarrah asked.

"To the Mooring," called Ard as he followed Raek out of the guesthouse. He resisted the urge to look over his shoulder to see if Quarrah was following. He hated rushing their reunion like this, but maybe it was better. It certainly clamped a lid on all the emotions that were threatening to burst out of him.

Quarrah had caught up to Ard and Raek by the time they reached the carriage. The groundskeeper, Hedma Sallis, was already seated on the driving bench. The horses, Goldrun and

Acorn, stamped their hooves impatiently. Ard noticed that Keyling still wasn't feeling up to pulling, despite Hedma's attempts to rehabilitate her.

"Where did she come from?" Hedma asked, eyeing Quarrah.

"She got past our perimeter defenses," scolded Ard.

"We don't have perimeter defenses," the woman replied.

Out of the corner of his eye, Ard couldn't miss the smirk on Quarrah's face. Perhaps they had been too lackadaisical about security at the Guesthouse Adagio. Now that Quarrah was here, she'd surely have some ideas on how to make the area more secure.

"Look at the three of us." Ard sighed as they climbed into the carriage and got situated. "Just like old times."

Hedma flicked the reins, and the cab lurched forward.

"Quite the accommodations you've got here," Quarrah said, watching out the window as the front of the guesthouse passed by, its huge stone dragon statue still damp from last night's rain.

"A little bigger than the Bakery on Humont Street," Ard agreed. "Where are you staying these days?"

"Wouldn't you like to know?" she retorted.

"I was just trying to say that there's plenty of room at the guesthouse," said Ard. "You can come and go as you like, of course."

"I can do that anyway," Quarrah said, "without your permission."

Ard swallowed a retort. She was mad at him. Almost as mad as she'd been the night the bull-dragon egg was fertilized. Wasn't time supposed to mend hard feelings? And whatever happened to distance making the heart grow fonder? Sparks, he was really going to have to be on his best behavior.

"Clever, hiring yourself at the Directorate meeting," Quarrah said.

"Oh, you knew that was me? I thought my foxy mask was supposed to protect my identity."

"You're after the prince, aren't you," she said. "Somehow, Lady Abeth knew her son was still alive and she hired you to find him.

You swayed the Directorate to accept your Homelander ruse so you'd get access to the boy."

There it was, in a nutshell. And while Quarrah had so astutely deduced his motives, he honestly had no guess as to hers.

"Shad Agaul is the key to everything," Ard began. "Overseer said so herself. Removing him will cause the Realm's entire plan to collapse."

"But what are you going to do with him once he's free?" asked Quarrah.

"He can take the throne from Termain and reunite the islands the correct way," said Ard. "Not under the manipulation of the Realm. The Homelander ruse is our best chance of getting him. But I'll need your help to pull it off."

"Why?" she asked. "Because I'm supposed to report on you to Overseer?"

"That's one good reason," said Ard. "And your expertise. I'm sure there will be plenty of things to steal between now and the time that fake Homeland ship sails in. We may even need you to steal a missing prince." He took a deep breath. "And I could use your company, Quarrah."

"Umm," Raek cut in. "You know I'm still here, right?"

Quarrah wouldn't look at him, her eyes glued to the carriage window. "This isn't going to be like last time, Ard. I've learned too much to fall for that again."

"Fall for what?" he exclaimed.

She clenched her fist. "That every ruse you undertake is a matter of life and death. That the fate of the world hangs by a string and you've got it tied around your finger."

"I'm not..." Ard sighed. It would do him no good to defend himself to her. "You'll see that I'm different, so long as you're willing to give it a chance."

"Give what a chance?"

"Working together," Ard said. "Nothing more." Of course he was desperate for more, but he couldn't lead with that.

"I don't know why you're begging me—" Quarrah began.

"Well, I wouldn't say *begging*," Ard interrupted.

"It seems we have little choice but to work together. We do what the Realm orders, or we die without the Waters of Loyalty."

"I'm hoping you know more about that," Ard said. "What it *really* is?"

"Some kind of slow-acting poison," she said. "Or is it the antidote?"

"At my first meeting as a Faceless, they told me it was both poison and antidote," replied Ard.

"That doesn't make any sense," said Raek.

"Maybe it's a suppressant but not a true antidote," suggested Quarrah, "since we have to take it with regularity."

"I told Ard to purge the poison with Health Grit," Raek said.

"Did it work?" she asked.

Ard shook his head. "Antler Head—Glint—told me the poison is somehow immune to the effects of a Health cloud."

"That's all good information to have," Quarrah added. "I came into the meeting posing as a high-level Faceless, so they didn't tell me any of the basics."

Ard nodded. "See, this is why we need to work together! We have a much better chance of uncovering the Realm's secrets if we share everything we learn with each other. You know my motives. So, who are you working for? The Realm certainly doesn't seem like the type of organization Quarrah Khai would seek out on her own."

"The queen dowager hired me," Quarrah said.

"Termain's coot of a mother?" Raek cried.

"She was afraid the king was being manipulated by the Realm."

"I'd say he is," Ard admitted. "They're just setting him up to make a mess of the islands so they can take him down on their terms."

"That's what I told Fabra."

"*Fabra?*" repeated Raek. "You and the queen dowager are on a first-name basis?"

"She's . . . informal," said Quarrah. "I met with her yesterday to report my findings. She seems just as interested in taking down the Realm as you are, since its primary goals go against her son's rule."

"Did you tell her that Shad Agaul was alive?" Ard asked.

Quarrah shook her head. "I didn't tell her much. I don't see the use in involving Fabra Ment until her resources can benefit us in dismantling the Realm."

Ard smiled. Smart and cautious. Every bit the Quarrah Khai he remembered.

The rest of the carriage ride turned into a series of questions and answers. Ard was completely honest with her, and as far as he could tell, Quarrah told him everything she knew.

Their individual paths into the Directorate had been so indicative of who they were: Quarrah thieving, slipping through the shadows, and legitimately earning her place, while Ard came forward with all kinds of fanfare and attention, cheating his way into a spot at Overseer's table.

Everything they shared only served to further convince Ard that this was right. He and Quarrah were like the contents of a Grit pot: Slagstone and powder—so different from each other, but more powerful together.

The carriage came to a halt. Raek popped open the door, and the three of them climbed out.

"I'll be waiting in the shade over there," said Hedma, guiding the horses toward a copse of trees on the roadside.

Ard, Quarrah, and Raek descended the grassy hill until they reached the double doors to the Mooring, open wide as if encouraging visitors. What it really seemed to encourage was protestors.

They loitered on the steps and around the front lawn, speaking all kinds of horrible things about Prime Isless Gloristar.

Why was it that a wholly corrupt Prime Isle like Frid Chauster had been nothing but lauded while his replacement received all the hate? Sure, Prime Isless Gloristar had made a terrible choice in endorsing King Termain, but otherwise, Ard thought she was doing a respectable job of holding Wayfarism together across war-torn borders.

The three of them entered the spacious foyer, sunlight filtering through stained glass overhead. Ard paused before the glass case displaying the gelatinous, unfertilized dragon egg.

"Brings back memories, eh?" Ard said quietly to Quarrah. "Can't help but be amazed when I think of how you stole one of these right from Pekal," he praised. "Single-handedly."

Quarrah shrugged casually at his side. "Mine was bigger." Then she moved around the display to where Raek was already conversing with the Holy Isle on duty.

"I know we're a few minutes late," Raek was saying as Ard joined them, "but we had an appointment with Isless Glemher in Cove Seventeen."

According to Raek's inquiries, Glemher was one of the Islehood's leading experts in the study of the Homeland. They expected her to have some nice resources compiled.

"I believe she's still waiting," said the Isle, gesturing down the stairs that led to the Mooring waterway. "Isle Tonn will guide you."

Isle Tonn was a broad-shouldered fellow who looked more like he belonged at the war front more than in the Mooring. Ard imagined an Isle of his stature was frequently asked to pole visitors to their coves.

In silence, Isle Tonn poled the raft past the huge, empty brazier of the Holy Torch at the heart of the waterway. The Islehood was still lighting it for the Moon Passings, even after all the truth had come out about the dragons being the actual shield.

Ard shouldn't have been surprised. He'd meant what he'd said in the Directorate meeting. *Belief dies hard.*

"Do you expect your appointment to be long?" asked Isle Tonn, the raft bumping into the dock of Cove 17.

"Possibly," Ard said as the three of them disembarked.

"Then I won't wait for you here," the Isle replied, drifting away from the dock. "Ring the bell when your session has concluded and I'll come straightaway."

Ard went to knock, but the cove door was ajar. He pushed it inward to find Isless Glemher seated at the only desk in the small rectangular room. She waved them in, a pleasant smile on her wrinkled face.

"I apologize for our tardiness," Raek said. "Getting these two anywhere is like herding cats."

"No matter," said the aged Isless. Her white hair was a stark contrast to her dark skin. She looked plump and undeniably grandmotherly. Half-circle reading spectacles rested on the end of her nose, and her head trembled just enough that Ard wondered if they'd slip off. "Please have a seat. I am in no rush this morning."

Ard liked her already. The three of them seated themselves on the cove's long bench, Ard in the middle.

"Your request stated that you have a special interest in learning more about the Homeland?" Her voice warbled, reminding Ard of the coo of an evening bird.

"That is correct."

"Has something spurred your interest of late?"

*You could say that,* Ard thought. *Better learn all I can about the place before I claim to have come from there.*

"We've been troubled with questions of a deeply spiritual nature," Ard said instead. "A virulent strain of sickness passed through our village during the winter cycles." Did he dare go here? Why not? "We lost our precious daughter."

Ard reached out and put a hand on Quarrah's back. Without a

drib of subtlety, she swatted it away and slid all the way to the end of the long bench. Well, such a tragedy would test any couple, so perhaps her reaction wasn't totally inconceivable.

Isless Glemher frowned deeply and the compassionate look in her eyes actually made Ard feel sad. "How old was she?"

"Barely a year," Ard replied.

"Surely, she has found her way to the Homeland," said the Isless.

"I have little doubt of that," said Ard. "But we want to know more about what it's like there. To give us some measure of comfort here."

"Yes," said Isless Glemher. "I have prepared passages and quotes from the many descriptions of the Homeland that have been written over the last seven centuries. Personally, I've found none to be truer or more concise than this one put down by Isle Sheroy in 854." Her kind eyes peered down through spectacles as her shaky finger scrolled under the text while she read. "'The Homeland is perfection.'" She looked up, smiling. "Isn't that nice?"

*True and concise, all right,* Ard thought, *but not very educational.*

"Very nice," he responded.

"The Homeland is the core of our beliefs," said the Isless. "It is the place from which all Landers originally came. And it is the place to which all the faithful will return, whether on a devoted Wayfarist Voyage or in death."

According to Pethredote's claims, the Homeland was a perfected version of the future, not a distant physical place. But it was too mind-bending to think that the Lander ancestors had actually come from the future.

Ard shouldn't compare everything Isless Glemher said to what Pethredote had told him. After all, the purpose of this ruse wasn't to impersonate *actual* Homelanders, it was to create a convincing representation of what the majority of Landers *thought* to be Homelanders.

"Do we know where the Homeland lies?" Ard asked. "At least

the general direction?" He seemed to remember the Voyager ships departing any which way.

"No one is certain of its exact location," answered Isless Glemher. "Several verses indicate that it lies to starboard. Many interpret this to mean eastward."

She traced along a line of text as she read it: "'The keel of every soul turns them hard to starboard, from whence we came, and unto where we long to return.' That is from the second volume of *Wayfarist Voyage*. And from the third: 'Why dost thou turn thy heart away from the Homeland, as a ship listing to port?' Perhaps the most apparent is this verse: 'The journey to the Homeland is long, and many shall perish ere they reach that holy shore. From port, send thine aid. But glory, starboard, for it shall mark thy way to everlasting perfection.'"

The bit about starboard might be useful when sailing in on the fake ship. They'd need to come from the eastern sea.

At his side, Ard noticed that Raek was diligently taking notes on a pad of paper, the scribing charcoal looking small in his big hand.

"Only the dead can be sure of its exact location." Isless Glemher began reading again. "'Death becomes the wind in the soul's sails, bearing it back to those blessed shores. Verily, those who have not Settled in life will take up habitation among their worthy ancestors and live in perfection forevermore.'"

"So, who lives there now?" Quarrah asked. She seemed to have recovered from Ard's unwanted backstory. "Just the dead and the most devout Wayfarist Voyagers?"

"And let's be honest, the latter probably became the former after a cycle or so at sea," Raek spoke out the side of his mouth.

"Countless faithful souls from generations past now reside in the Homeland," answered the Isless. "It is a place of peace and respite. War and discord cannot exist there because all who dwell have a perfected mind, unified in thought and deed."

By the sound of it, there would be no place for a ruse artist in a culture like that...

Isless Glemher had given them a bit of general information, but Ard still needed something more concrete to build this ruse on. "What else do you know?"

Isless Glemher looked down and began reading again: "'A day cometh when all must speedily go unto the Homeland.'"

"*All*?" Ard cut her off, instantly recognizing the verse as the one Grapple had read at the Old Post Lighthouse. Now he was curious to hear the Islehood's interpretation of it. "I thought you just explained that only the faithful will make it."

"All people will have the opportunity to go *unto* the Homeland's crystal shores," she explained, "but only the faithful will be allowed *into* that holy place."

"What about Trothians?" Raek asked. "Do they get to go back to the Homeland?"

Isless Glemher nearly gasped, hand coming to her heart. "I should think not. The Trothian race did not originate in the Homeland. Records state that they arrived in ships that the eye could not behold, slaughtering thousands of Landers before we managed to overpower them and drive them to their isolated islets."

"Invisible ships?" Quarrah's voice didn't hide her skepticism. "And I'm pretty sure the slaughtering was on both sides if the Landers *forced* them off the islands."

Isless Glemher clucked her tongue disapprovingly. "Regardless, there is no place for Trothians in the Homeland. They believe in physical gods. They participate in heathen rituals. Such behavior is hardly worthy of such a sacred place."

"To be fair, the saltwater soak is also a health necessity for the Trothians as well as an Agrodite ritual," Raek said, twirling his scribing charcoal between his fingers. "Requiring them to give it up would be like asking you to stop sleeping."

Ard decided to steer the conversation back on track before the old Isless croaked of repugnance. "Can you keep reading that verse?" He pointed to her notes, and Glemher looked down, happy to bury her wrinkly nose in the familiar text.

" 'Stumblers have gone before thee,' " she read, " 'and these silent ones have heralded thy voyage. Ye shall know that the great day of egress is upon you when the miserable shall forsake their habitat and walk among you, wild and uncontrolled.' "

" 'Great day of egress'?" Ard asked.

"The time when every soul must decide whether to stay in Settled disbelief or let their heart make the exodus of faith to the Homeland."

"Interesting," Ard said. "Go on."

" 'In that same day, the waters shall heave up their secret depths to such a height that even the towers upon which mankind resides will not be able to escape. Verily, this cataclysm shall be unto you as a final Urging, bidding all to depart this lowly realm and ascend unto the Homeland.' "

" 'Cataclysm'?" Ard interrupted again.

"A trial of faith," answered the old Isless, "as deep as the ocean. But instead of drowning in the disbelief that surrounds us, the Homeland Urges us to rise above it."

So, the Islehood's interpretation of these verses was wholly symbolic, while the Realm took it all to be quite literal. Ard didn't know which one he believed.

"What is it like in the Homeland?" he asked. "Is our daughter happy? Will we recognize her when we go there after death?"

Glemher smiled slowly. "Prime Isless Erevis saw the Homeland and its perfected residents in a dream in 713. Her vision is considered doctrinal, since it helped to interpret so many scriptural verses."

Seriously? The Islehood was taking some lady's dream as doctrine? Good thing Ard wasn't the Prime Isle. He'd recently had a strange one about a raccoon auditioning for the Royal Orchestra. That rodent had played a mean string bass.

The old Isless found the passage and began reading in her shaky voice.

"'I was whisked away to starboard, speeding over crashing waves as though I were the wind itself. Days and nights passed in the blink of an eye, and how many cycles I traveled, I do not know. Then at once, the Homeland was displayed before my eyes in all its grandeur. There was no foreboding cliff, but the gentlest shore, the sand of which was like pure crystal. I continued inland, passing trees and vegetation whose likeness I had never before seen. There were no thorns or briars, and every plant bore its own ever-ripe fruit.'"

Isless Glemher looked up over the top of her spectacles. "Well, I can stop there. The rest of her dream was focused more on the Homelanders."

"Go on," Ard nearly shouted. Finally! Here was some information around which they could base a convincing ruse. It was always necessary to back up the lie with bits of truth. Or in this case, what Wayfarists *perceived* as truth. If there were descriptions of the Homelanders, Ard certainly needed to hear them.

Isless Glemher looked at the page again, taking a moment to find where she'd left off.

"'And then I beheld the inhabitants of this majestic place. I scarce can call them humans, although I know that is what they had once been. They had ascended into something greater, as a caterpillar emerging from its chrysalis with the wings of a butterfly. No blade or needle could mar their resplendent skin that shimmered as golden and lustrous as a freshly stamped coin. They neither thirsted nor hungered, and their eyes blazed like hot coals. They were as one great family, and all things among them were equal. One could not whisper without all hearing, and none could act without the knowledge of all.'"

Sparks! That sounded like a terrible place! Ard hoped the

dreaming Isless was way off, or he'd have to do a few more highly Settled deeds before he died to make sure he didn't end up there.

"'I opened my mouth to speak and awakened at once, every detail of my vision engrained in my mind.'" Isless Glemher looked up, the passage apparently concluded.

Okay. That was all useful stuff. Raek finished scribing something and gestured to the Isless's notes.

"You said this dream made references to other scriptures?" Raek asked. "Could I get a list of those for further study?"

Isless Glemher nodded her trembly head, sifting through several of the papers before offering one to Raek, who began copying it.

"Is there anything else I can do for the three of you?" she asked.

"One more question," Ard said. "Do you think it would be possible for a Homelander to leave those crystal shores and visit us here?"

"It has happened many times," she said.

*Oh, flames.* "It has?"

"That is the definition of a Paladin Visitant," said the Isless. "A Homelander who has condescended to the Greater Chain."

*Not quite, you sweet old Isless,* Ard thought.

"That's not exactly what I mean," said Ard. "Paladin Visitants appear because a worthy person summons them with a Grit detonation. But would it be possible for a Homelander to visit the Greater Chain on his own? Maybe sail here on a ship?"

"I have never heard such an idea..." Isless Glemher looked short of breath. "It has certainly never happened."

"But *could* it?" Ard asked. "Have you come across anything in your studies that says it wouldn't be possible?"

"Nothing is impossible for one who has stepped foot on the Homeland and ascended to perfection."

Ard nodded. Good. That would be one less hoop to jump through.

Raek stood up and handed the list of references back to Isless Glemher. "Thank you for your time."

The Isless bowed respectfully to them. She turned as Quarrah rose from the end of the bench. "My sincerest condolences to you, madam."

"For what?" Quarrah snapped.

Ard shot her an incredulous glance, and then addressed the Isless. "Thank you. We all deal with grief differently. At times, I wonder if she even remembers that we had a child."

Quarrah stalked across the small cove and yanked open the door. By the time Ard and Raek stepped onto the dock, she had already rung the bell three times.

"Sorry about that," Ard tried. "We needed a story to frame our interest. It seemed natural."

"Well, next time, why don't you have Raek be the father of your child?" She stood with her arms folded across her chest.

Raek shrugged. "I already feel like Ard's father half the time."

"Will you come back to the guesthouse with us?" Ard asked her. "There's a lot to plan and I could use your perspective."

"I've got somewhere else I need to be," she replied. "And personally, I think you've overextended yourself, Ardor Benn."

"You don't think we can pull this off?" Not having her vote of confidence actually stung him more than he'd expected. "We already saved the world and time itself. I was feeling like this was kind of a step down."

"You're going to dress up a whole crew of Paladin Visitants?" Quarrah said.

"Nah. Raek already perfected that costume," Ard said. "This time we're going to do something that won't catch anyone on fire. And hopefully no one explodes."

"Or gets stabbed," added Raek.

"That goes without saying," said Ard.

"But exploding doesn't?" Quarrah muttered.

"The point is," said Ard, "this isn't about dressing people up like Paladin Visitants. The Homelanders are something different. Fiery eyes, golden skin... This is going to be much more complex."

Quarrah shook her head. "Exactly. It's too big."

"We're not doing this alone." He lowered his voice. "We have the Realm's resources at our disposal. And I've been waiting for the right job to reconnect with some old friends."

"You don't mean..." Raek started.

"I do," said Ard. "We're going to need convincing disguises, unusual speech patterns, and knowledge of a land that no one has ever been to. That's going to take careful coaching and rehearsal."

"Oh, flames," muttered Quarrah as she seemed to realize whom Ard was talking about.

"Who better for the job than Cinza Ortemion and Elbrig Taut?"

~

*Will they remember our home?*

# CHAPTER

# 27

Portsend paused on the hillside, setting down the box of supplies and wiping a bead of sweat from his forehead. The Passing two nights ago had marked the beginning of the Third Cycle, and with it, the official onset of summer.

"I cannot wait to be able to leave this stuff in the lab again," San said, widening his stance but choosing not to set down his load. Cheery stood a few feet behind him, whistling absentmindedly through his missing teeth.

"I don't know," replied Lomaya, "I think some of my motivation for working hard was to use it all up." She dropped her box to the grass a little less gently than Portsend would have liked. "Now that we're back in Professor Wal's lab, I might spend more time sipping some of those teas he brews."

"Now, now. Those infusions are strictly for scientific purposes," Portsend said, his tone every bit the professor. "Most of them are toxic, anyway."

He agreed wholeheartedly with his pupils. It would indeed be a blessing from the Homeland to have his private laboratory back. Repairs had been completed ahead of schedule, allowing Portsend to deliver the bulk of the load in a wagon last night. He'd tinkered for hours, setting it up exactly how it had been before the accident. Just the way he liked it. No more hunting around drawers for items that students misplaced. No more stopping in the middle of a critical experiment to yield the lab to the next person on the schedule.

Two weeks had passed since he had delivered his findings on Weight Grit to King Termain. Portsend had raced back to the college and told Stubs and Cheery that he wanted to meet with the boss. He found it strange that she hadn't answered his request yet. The Moon Passing had come and gone, and the city seemed to be holding its breath. The poor victims at the farm would need time to reach the third stage of Moonsickness, so the Bloodeyes probably wouldn't appear for another day or two. Maybe the boss would still show up in time for him to surrender some information and prevent this next round of terror.

As much as it pained him, Portsend had decided that this was the best course of action. He needed to stop the Moonsickness to maintain Gloristar's religious authority.

The hurt look on her face still haunted him. Gloristar had stormed out of the dining hall the moment their meeting was over, taking her own carriage back to the Mooring and leaving Portsend with a dreadful knot in his stomach.

He picked up his box once more, shooting a scathing glance at Cheery, who stood empty-handed. Brase and Luthe, Homeland rest their souls, had always been so willing to carry a heavy load, or open a door.

"Where do you want to start today, Professor?" Lomaya asked, grunting against her box as well.

"We'll continue with the Gather Grit," he answered, leading them down the hill.

They'd discovered yet another new type of detonation just under a week ago. A liquid solution of processed marble with a balance level of positive sharp six. This one worked much like the opposite of Void Grit. Instead of pushing things outward, it sucked everything inward to one central point at the heart of the detonation.

"I thought we could test the Gather Grit's Compounding rate," Portsend said. "Have you seen the slide stakes we use for measuring the push of Void clouds?"

"I've read about them," Lomaya answered, which was just another way of saying no.

"We stake them into the floor in the detonation chamber," Portsend explained. "The top of the instrument is a rod with a series of graduating weights that slide along it. The strength of the Void cloud can be measured by how many of the weights it manages to push along the rod."

"And you think we could measure the Gather Grit by setting up the slide scales backward?" said San. "To measure the pull instead of the push."

"I assume that will work," Portsend replied. "I'll show the two of you how to set up the slides and then leave you to it."

"What will you be doing?" Lomaya asked.

*Praying to the Homeland,* Portsend thought. "I'm going to begin testing another material to see if I can strike the correct balance level to make it dissolve."

"What material?" Lomaya asked.

"Oh, I haven't decided yet," Portsend lied. He knew the answer. There was only one more material on the list from the Anchored Tome.

Pulverized Grit derived from the teeth of a dragon.

Portsend could only imagine what lengths were taken to produce it. He knew dragons lost their teeth much like human children. Only, the beasts did it up to four times throughout their life span.

Portsend had been judicious with his use of the powdered dragon teeth. Even still, he had already used about half of his supply. Gloristar had told him he could request more, but Portsend couldn't stand the thought of asking such a favor of King Termain.

They reached the door to the laboratory and Portsend found it slightly ajar. He turned sharply on Cheery, who was still several paces behind his pupils.

"Have you been down here today?" he asked the oaf. Cheery and Stubs both had keys, obtained when the lock was replaced with the new door.

"Stubs said he was coming down to check things out." The lean man took a break from his whistling to answer.

Portsend used the corner of his box to swing the heavy door open. He peered into the dim space, where two Light Grit lanterns were already glowing. Stubs had his back to the door, absently flicking at one side of a balance scale, watching it level out. That was a Resger Two Hundred—worth more than the ruffian probably made in a year.

"Don't touch what isn't yours," Portsend remarked, striding into the lab and depositing his box on the nearest table. He'd grown bolder in speaking to Stubs and Cheery since that big Hegger, Raekon, had barged into the lab. Knowing something about Stubs's private life had given Portsend a little confidence.

Stubs whirled around, seeming startled by the intrusion. San and Lomaya slid their boxes onto the table beside Portsend's as Cheery shut the door.

"What the blazes, Cheer?" Stubs remarked. "He was supposed to come alone."

"Come alone?" Portsend's heart began to beat faster with the first indication that something was wrong.

"I didn't know his ducklings were going to help him haul his slag down here," answered Cheery. "I thought it would have been more suspicious if I'd tried to separate them."

Portsend moved for the closed door, motioning for his pupils to follow him. Whatever this was, he wanted no part in it. A voice from behind stopped him halfway there.

"It's nothing to worry about. Perhaps it will be even more meaningful this way."

The boss was standing in the doorway to the observation deck, her black hair pulled back in an impossibly tight braid. A Roller in her hand.

"San. Lomaya," whispered Portsend. "I think the two of you ought to wait outside."

"And go for help?" said the boss. "I think not. Anyone who moves for the door will answer to Cheery's knife."

In response, the man produced a long-bladed dagger with a hilt that glinted in the lantern light.

"Do you know why I am here, Portsend Wal?" she asked, stepping forward.

"Because I requested we meet," he answered. "I've been waiting for you."

"I do not come at your every beck and call," she said.

"Perhaps you'll wish you had," dared Portsend. "I have something rather significant to share with you."

"Oh?"

"Progress," he said, "on a new type of Grit."

She had said that information would satisfy her. That didn't mean Portsend needed to tell her *everything*. He would give her

Weight Grit today and hope that would be enough to stave off this round of Bloodeyes.

Portsend turned to the box he'd carried in, rummaging through his papers until he found the folder he was looking for. All his research was duplicated in notebooks at his apartment, so parting with these research papers would be no loss to him.

"I call it Weight Grit." He stepped forward and handed the folder to the boss.

"Intriguing." She flipped briefly through the loose pages, obviously not pausing long enough to interpret any of his notes or figures. "My superiors will be pleased with your progress." She shut the folder. "What more?"

"More?" Portsend did his best to feign surprise. "I'm afraid that's all we've been able to discover thus far. An incredible feat, really, considering the Ignition Grit and the Null Grit, which you already have. Three new Grit types is more than we've seen in the last three centuries. You'll have to be patient. Assuming there is anything more to discover."

"I want something new."

"This *is* new!" Portsend's mouth was dry.

"Something you *didn't* give to King Termain."

Portsend felt suddenly dizzy. She knew, spark it all. She already knew about the meeting!

"I didn't—" he began.

"What about Containment Grit?" the boss spat. "And Stasis Grit, and most recently, Gather Grit. Have you forgotten about those?"

Portsend felt the floor slipping out from under him. He grasped the edge of the table for support.

"Stubs told me everything," said the boss. "Now I'd like to hear your side of it."

That blazing moron! Well, if the man was going to turn his back on their agreement, then Portsend saw no need to defend him.

"You shouldn't trust everything your men tell you," he said. "Perhaps they have not been fully honest."

"People in their line of work seldom are."

"Dealing Heg behind his employer's back," Portsend said. "Jeopardizing the secrecy of my research with his untrustworthy clients..."

"Yes," she said. "Stubs and I have addressed his side business, and he knows how I feel about it."

Portsend whirled on the bodyguard, only to find that Stubs had slunk to the far side of the lab, his back to the wall and his face in the shadows.

"But he did the right thing, coming forward with the truth," the boss continued. "And his punishment was lessened to one-tenth of what it could have been. Well, I suppose in his case, there were only eight-tenths to begin with."

In the corner, Stubs cradled his hand, and Portsend now noticed that it was wrapped in a thick bandage.

A shiver passed through him. This woman, and presumably her superiors, seemed to thrive on punishment. Stubs must have known that he couldn't keep his stalemate with Portsend forever and he wanted the truth to come out on his terms.

"Containment Grit," Portsend finally said. "And Stasis Grit. And, yes, Gather Grit." He turned to his box once more, producing the three corresponding folders. "This is all we have on them." With a sickening wrench in his stomach, he handed the documents to the boss.

"Professor," hissed San. The lad was clenching both fists at his sides. Portsend reached out and put a steadying hand on his shoulder. *Now is not the time to do anything rash.*

"Seems it was a more productive cycle than you first let on," said the boss, not even opening the folders.

Portsend nodded. "That's everything I have," he whispered.

"There is still time for you to hold off the release of the Moonsick people."

"I will honor our agreement," she said. "Tomorrow we will only release eight Bloodeyes."

Portsend's hand slipped from San's shoulder into a fist of his own. "That was not our agreement! I cooperated!"

"Professor?" Lomaya's voice was soft and confused at his side.

"Which is why we aren't releasing sixteen," the boss continued. "You doubled the usual number when you gave that information to King Termain."

"I'm sorry." He felt numb, petrified by regret and fear. "It won't happen again. With luck, there is still one more new type of Grit to uncover. I will share all developments with you as soon as we learn them."

"I appreciate your sincerity," she said. "And I suppose only time will tell if you are speaking the truth."

"Then you'll call off the Bloodeyes?" Portsend tried again.

"People in my organization believe that punishment must be compartmentalized," replied the boss. "The release of the savages is punishment for a specific past transgression—meeting with King Termain. I want to be very clear about that. Your actions today cannot fix what went wrong yesterday."

The boss strode forward, pausing beside the expensive balance scales. "Now let us talk about your other mistake. Withholding information from me when it was ready. There must be a punishment for *all* your errors."

"What are you going to do to him?" Lomaya finally cut in.

"Him?" cried the boss. "He's much too important in these developments."

The hollowness in Portsend's chest expanded as he realized what the boss might be implying. He stepped in front of San and Lomaya, arms extended as if to corral the students behind him.

"Perhaps you do not understand how significant these two are in the research process," he said. "If you hope for any new developments this cycle, they must remain untouched."

The boss dismissed his comment with a wave of her hand. "Stubs and Cheery have already told me as much. I would be a fool to slow the three of you down. You seem to be an effective team."

Not them? Portsend's protective arms slowly lowered. Then who?

The boss opened one of the folders and turned slowly through its pages, finally seeming to read some of the information presented there. Portsend and his pupils stood uncomfortably in the silence until the boss finally looked up, flicking the edge of the scale's pan, just as Stubs had been doing when they came in.

"Measure a detonation of Gather Grit for me," she said.

"What?" Portsend was taken aback by the unexpected request.

"Gather Grit," she repeated. "That *is* what you're calling your newest discovery, is it not?"

"I . . . yes," said Portsend.

She stepped aside, slapping the folder down on the table next to the scales.

"I require a demonstration of the product."

"What size?" Portsend asked.

"A radius of four feet ought to be sufficient."

Portsend stood rigid for a moment, his mind suddenly as blank as though he'd never heard of Gather Grit. Then the information began to flow back into his brain. Not in an exciting remembrance, but rather a flood of panic.

"San," he said. "Would you mind fetching the powdered marble? I've set things up the way we used to have it. We'll need just two and a half granules." The lad nodded curtly, moving toward some canisters on the far side.

"Lomaya." Portsend turned to find her. "We'll need the purple solution with the balance level of positive sharp four. We should still have several cupweights in the jug. Measure out about twenty-five dribs." The young woman moved to fulfill her assignment.

Portsend crossed to a shallow drawer, keenly aware of the boss's Roller lifted in his direction. "No tricks," she said.

He had none intended. The drawer, as she soon saw, was full of glass vials.

"Your notes say it can be Compounded?" interrupted the boss. She was pointing at the chart they'd created.

"That's right." Portsend plucked out a small vial. "Creates a stronger inward pull."

"I want you to add half a panweight of Compounding Grit to this solution."

"Half a panweight?" Portsend cried. That was so far off the charts it seemed ludicrous. "We have no way of knowing what it would do."

"Isn't experimentation the way to find out?" asked the boss.

"But that would be a ratio of nearly a hundred to one," Portsend protested.

"Oh, doesn't a part of you ever want to throw out the arithmetic and just see what happens?"

No part of Portsend Wal wanted that. But the woman with the gun held a special kind of persuasion in the room.

"Lomaya," he called. "We'll need a full cupweight of the solution." A half a panweight of Compounding Grit would barely turn twenty-five dribs into a paste. "And two hundred and twenty-five granules of Compounding Grit, San."

Portsend replaced the little vial and closed the drawer, selecting a glass bottle from a nearby shelf instead. There wasn't a vial large enough to accommodate the highly imbalanced mix they'd just been ordered to create.

Portsend retrieved a canister and tipped it, shaking the contents into his palm. It was mostly full of powdered clay made from broken pots. Nestled into that packing were dozens of Slagstone fragments, chipped to size and ready for use in a detonation pot, ignitor, or gun hammer. The clay anti-ignition material prevented the pieces from accidentally sparking, which could have catastrophic results in a lab full of loose Grit.

He plucked out one of the fragments and dusted the rest of the packing powder back into the canister. San and Lomaya were waiting for him at the central table, and the three of them carefully mixed all the ingredients into the bottle under close supervision of the boss's gun.

Did the stern woman even care that she was witnessing ground-breaking discoveries—the Grit miraculously dissolving in the purplish liquid when it should have merely settled to the bottom of the bottle?

Ever so carefully, Portsend plunked the fragment of Slagstone into the solution, watching it drift slowly to the bottom before sealing the bottle shut with a cork.

"Handle it carefully," Portsend urged as the boss picked it up from the table. "Glass doesn't share the same anti-ignition properties as a standard Grit pot. And that detonation could be incredibly dangerous, Compounded at such a level."

"Why don't the three of you come with me?" the boss demanded, turning toward the secure detonation chamber. "We can test this in a safe place." She gestured at Stubs before ducking through the open doorway.

"You heard the lady." Stubs finally stepped out of the shadows with a gun of his own clutched in his nonbandaged hand. "Get in there."

San went first, his classmate a step behind him. No sooner had she stepped onto the observation deck, than Lomaya let out a blood-curdling scream. Portsend staggered forward, his heart leaping ahead of him. If that woman laid a hand on either of his pupils...

There was a young man seated in the detonation chamber.

Portsend didn't recognize him, shoulders broad and arms thick. Despite his obvious strength, he was strapped to a sturdy wooden chair, ropes tied tightly around his ankles and arms. His head looked like it had been shaved recently, with just a fuzz of dark stubble growing in. The lad's eyes were wide with a look of panic and frenzy, but a red handkerchief was tied in place to gag him.

"Kend!" Lomaya screamed. The observation window was already sealed off with a blast of Barrier Grit, so the frantic young woman went for the hatch into the chamber.

Stubs appeared on the deck, striking her face with the butt of his Roller. Lomaya collapsed, gasping in pain. San leapt forward, arm outstretched for the Gather Grit bottle in the boss's hand. She pulled it out of reach, leveling the gun against the lad's head and pinning him against the wall.

Through it all, Portsend stood immobile, now filling with remorse. He should have moved with San to overpower the woman. He should have ducked back into the lab to collect any sort of prepared Grit pot to use as a weapon. Cheery blocked the way now, having responded to the sounds of commotion.

Lomaya was crawling forward, her face bleeding. She pulled herself up, sobbing, hand pressing against the spherical window of Barrier Grit. In the chamber, Kend thrashed in a futile attempt to loose himself from the chair.

"Punishment!" cried the boss, her face flushed from the moment of action. She stepped away from San, her Roller still leveled at his forehead and the bottle clutched in her other hand.

"You have no family," she said, passing Portsend on the deck. "You have no colleagues that you consider friends. You care only for the Prime Isless and these two students, all of whom are too valuable to take out of play."

The boss pushed open the hatch. How long had Lomaya's boyfriend been tied up here? His muffled screams were hoarse.

"If we cannot hurt someone you care about," she continued,

"then we'll have to hurt someone who loves someone you care about."

"No," Portsend begged. "Don't do this. Please." He saw Lomaya gasping, weeping. "If you need a subject for that detonation, use it on me. On *me*!" His voice had risen to a strangled cry and he took a pleading step forward.

The boss hurled the bottle into the detonation chamber.

It struck at Kend's feet, the glass breaking with a gut-wrenching shatter. The Slagstone sparked and the cloud of highly Compounded Gather Grit ignited. It completely enveloped Kend, instantly pulling him toward the center, just in front of him.

The force of the pull snapped the wooden chair, the legs splintering, driving downward and in. The lad was sucked to the floor with such violence that his body seemed to break as he struck the stone.

Lomaya let out a shriek that split the air. It was the sound of pure grief, akin to the howl Portsend's heart had made when his son had died.

Kend curled inward, compressing more and more at the heart of the detonation until his skin began to tear. In seconds, he was indistinguishable from the chair he'd been sitting on, and Portsend shut his eyes. But the image hung there, horribly etched onto the backs of his eyelids.

"You should be more prepared for our next meeting, Professor Wal." The boss's voice cut through the sudden silence on the observation deck. He heard a shuffle of footsteps and knew she'd gone.

Still, it was some time before Portsend could open his eyes. When he finally managed, he saw San crying in the corner. Lomaya was unconscious, her hand still pressed against the Barrier that had separated her from her murdered boyfriend.

*Homeland,* he thought. *What have I done?* He never should have involved these two. He'd been reckless and selfish—worried only about Gloristar and the research. Now a man was dead in his detonation chamber, and none of them would ever be the same.

It was time to tell San and Lomaya everything. The list from the Anchored Tome, the Prime Isless's plea for help, King Termain's manipulation and threats, the boss's demands, the Moonsickness... *Everything.*

At least the truth might help them understand *why* Kend had died. But Portsend knew that even the truth couldn't heal this wound.

Nothing could.

~

*Our streets have been washed away, but they are not forgotten.*

# CHAPTER

# 28

Renting an entire tavern seemed like overkill to Quarrah Khai. But that was the way Ardor Benn did things. She knew it better than anyone.

The Whispering Pines was a seedy place to start with, located in Beripent's lower Eastern Quarter. Ard had rented the place for the entire week out of his own pocket. Or, more likely, Lady Abeth's pocket, with the hope that he could get a reimbursement as Rival at the next Realm meeting.

The same was true for the exorbitant fees already racked up by Cinza and Elbrig. The disguise managers shouldn't have charged so much. After all, this time they weren't selling off one of their long-term curated personas. They were inventing from scratch, which meant they weren't out anything to get started.

Still, they had driven a hard bargain. But ultimately the payment, the unique high-risk nature of the job, and Ard's charms won them over. Not necessarily in that order.

"Break is over, people!" Elbrig shouted, clapping his hands. "Look lively! This Homelander ship isn't going to sail itself!"

The disguise manager didn't look anything like Quarrah had remembered. His pitch-black hair was pulled into a ponytail and he wore two large hoop earrings. The man's teeth, which Quarrah knew to be as false as the rest of him, were small and yellowed. Even his nose seemed different, with wide nostrils that seemed to be permanently flared.

Quarrah took one last swig from her water cup and rose from the chair where she'd been resting in the corner. The others seemed as weary as she did to resume their places on the tavern floor. Well, except for Ard. He hadn't even taken the break.

This was the third day of rehearsals, and it was proving to be the most tedious. The first had mostly been spent "auditioning" candidates for the job. She and Ard were shoo-ins, both of them having had past experience with Cinza and Elbrig. Although, mentioning that job seemed to be taboo.

The disguise managers themselves had flat out refused to be part of the crew. They'd said a job like this would require too keen an eye in rehearsal and participating might cause them to miss important details. That left Ard with the unique challenge of finding six other willing criminals.

They didn't just need criminals who knew the Realm street code, they needed criminals who could act. Essentially, although Ard wouldn't admit it, they'd needed to find six more ruse artists.

So Ardor Benn had hatched a plan. To Quarrah's surprise, he had actually credited the idea to the guesthouse butler, Codley Hattingson.

A one-act play.

Ard, Raek, and Quarrah had spread the word that auditions were happening for a play that would be performed at an upcoming royal function. Word on the street was that the Realm was directing, and the play would actually be used to get trusted criminals close to the rich and noble for whatever number of reasons Ard had invented.

Eighteen of the Realm's street Hands had shown up to audition. Quarrah, Ard, Raek, Elbrig, and Cinza had really put them through the ringer.

*"Move this way. Move that way. Pick up the chair. Now pick it up slower. Now pick it up whimsically."*

These physical demonstrations had been followed by tests of dialect and speech in an endless string of eye-rolling one-liners like, "You wanna get to the Homeland? You've gotta get through me."

*"Now say it angrier. Now say it sweetly! Now say it sensually!"*

Through it all, the judges had scribed notes and deliberated about strengths and weaknesses after each actor left the tavern.

Well, really just Ard and the crazies had done the deliberating. Raek had mostly guarded the door, and Quarrah had had no constructive thoughts to share. If it were up to her, she wouldn't have hired any of them. Criminals with a flare for the dramatic led to nothing but trouble.

They'd found their six criminals, however. And yesterday they had assembled for the first time. Ardor Benn had introduced himself and told them that unfortunately the play had been canceled. At least, that was the word they were supposed to spread, once Ard had let them in on the barest of details about their real job to impersonate Homelanders.

Quarrah certainly didn't trust them. Three women and three men, all in the prime of their lives. Quarrah admired the bodies of all of the women, and the men were like walking sculptures. From all the discussion she'd overheard during "casting," looks and physique had been highly important. After all, the Homeland was supposed to be populated with perfect people. Hard company to keep. Quarrah wondered how many push-ups Ard would be doing between now and when they set sail...

"Glide-stepping," called Elbrig, now that all eight of them were assembled again on the tavern floor. "The graceful movement of the Homelanders. Form a line." He pointed at Garew Sleet, the man standing next to Ard, to start them off. "Demonstrate!"

Garew strode forward, executing what Quarrah considered to be a decent glide step. "Keep it in the knees!" criticized Elbrig while motioning for the next person to go.

Ruge Harban set off after Garew, her movement considerably stiffer than that of her predecessor. "Relax your neck," said Elbrig. "Look about the room as you go."

Keel Belu went next, the tight curls of her short hair making the unevenness of her step that much more apparent. Elbrig threw his hands up. "Too *much* in the knees! You look like you're climbing invisible stairs. Ardy, show them how it's done."

Ard moved next, and Elbrig smiled contentedly. "That's it. That's it. Is everybody taking note here?"

Quarrah didn't think Ard's step looked much better than Garew's. Why did he always get the praise? Blazing man had his life handed to him on a silver platter.

According to Elbrig Taut, a perfect glide-step allowed a person to walk without her or his upper body moving at all. The shoulders and head should appear to float smoothly without bobbing. Somehow this was supposed to be done while still managing to look around and speak.

The two remaining men, Yalan Steir and Paver Boret, went next, with plenty of criticism from the coach. Then it was Quarrah's turn. She stepped forward, trying to roll her feet from heel to toe the way Elbrig had first demonstrated it. Glide-stepping made Quarrah feel like quite a putz. She could leap from rooftop to rooftop through clouds of Drift Grit, but walking like this was just unnatural.

"Not as bad as I'd expected," Elbrig said. "We'll just have to put a bustle on your outfit if you keep sticking out your rump like that."

Quarrah quickly remembered how much she hated being under the tutelage of Elbrig and Cinza. She hadn't wanted to volunteer for one of the spots on the Homeland crew, but Overseer's assignment overruled her personal feelings.

Ard certainly would have let her hang around the tavern and observe the preparations, but that would be difficult to explain to the Directorate without revealing that she and Ard had a history. Meting herself into the middle of this ruse was the best way to convincingly make her report at the next Directorate meeting.

The last crew member, Palia Neberel, demonstrated her glide-step, but Quarrah was too busy recovering from the embarrassment of unwanted attention to hear what Elbrig said about her.

"Overall, that was dismal." Elbrig crossed to the tavern bar. "You all need to be able to walk like this in your sleep." He picked up an hourglass and made a dramatic display of turning it over. "Ten minutes," he said, pointing a finger for them to begin.

The Whispering Pines really wasn't large enough for all of them to practice the glide-step at once. They'd done it twice already, and it inevitably led to awkwardness, bumping into one another as they circled the open floor. Quarrah had already lifted half a dozen Ashings off her crewmates that morning.

The door cracked open and Raek's head appeared, followed by a hand beckoning for his partner. Ard glide-stepped a few more paces and then broke away from the group, heading to check in with Raek.

Well, if Ardor Benn wasn't going to put in his ten minutes of independent stepping, then Quarrah didn't need to, either. Ard himself had said that she was an equal partner in this ruse. Whatever they were meeting about at the door certainly concerned her.

"The fruit guy's here," Raek said as Quarrah and Ard reached him simultaneously.

Ard nodded. "Send him in." Raek ducked out to the dark street once more.

"Fruit guy?" Quarrah asked.

"We have to be thorough," he replied. "Every plant in the Homeland bore its own ever-ripe fruit. Weren't you listening to that old Isless in the Mooring?"

"I was," she defended. "But somehow, exotic fruit wasn't what I took away from that meeting." Of course, Ard had focused on what the Homelanders could *eat*.

"Ever-ripe," said Ard. "When we sail into that harbor claiming to have been at sea for over a year, the fact that we have fresh ripe fruit is going to astonish and amaze. Persuasion is in the details, Quarrah."

The door opened again and a small round man followed Raek through, clutching a large cloth-covered basket in both hands. Ard guided him to the nearest table, where he set down his wares and stretched his arms as though he'd been hauling the load a long time.

"I'll be honest," said the man, "I found your request highly unusual."

"We don't always understand the jobs we carry out," replied Ard.

"But jobs that follow that phrase typically have a worthwhile payout," he said.

At least Ard and Raek had hired another Realm street Hand for their superfluous fruits.

"Now, let's not get ahead of ourselves." Ard pointed to the basket. "Let's take a look at what you've brought."

He peeled back the covering just enough to reach inside. "What do you think of this?"

"It looks like a peeled orange," said Ard, taking it from his grasp. "With a twig stuck in the top."

The fruiter nodded. "I wasn't sure how unusual you meant."

Ard ripped the orange in half, the twig falling to the floor. He popped a slice into his mouth and handed one-half to Raek and the rest to Quarrah, juice dribbling out. She set it on the table, wiping her fingers on her pants.

"I'm not sure he's our guy," Ard said to her and Raek.

The fruiter held up a hand. "Not so fast. That was just an appetizer. I've got some really weird stuff, if that's what you're after."

In a flash, he produced another fruit. It was clearly a pear—at least by size and shape. But the color of its skin was the most unnatural blue Quarrah had ever seen.

"Paint?" Ard examined the fruit. He wiped it against the sleeve of his shirt, but the color didn't smudge.

"Soaked in a blue dye," explained the fruiter. "The color penetrates halfway to the core."

"Is it safe to eat?" Quarrah asked.

"I don't think a bite or two would do any harm."

Ard handed the pear back. "Blue is too Trothian for our purposes. But I like this direction." He thought for a moment, tapping his smooth chin. "Any way you could make it glow?"

The fruiter raised his eyebrows and then began to chuckle as though it were a joke. Clearly he'd never spoken with Ardor Benn before.

"What else have you got?" Raek asked.

The fruiter produced a bunch of grapes, but the skin was stark white and looked completely artificial. Quarrah plucked one off the vine as the man passed the bunch to Ard.

It was too firm and it felt strange between her fingers. Ard popped one in his mouth, bit down, and promptly spit it out.

"That's like chewing on a candle," he said.

"The idea was that you'd peel off the wax before eating it," said the fruiter.

Quarrah scraped at the white wax with her fingernail until she exposed the pale green grape underneath.

"You dipped each grape?" she asked, noticing that the vine looked untouched. That would have been quite the tedious task.

He nodded. "If they're kept cool in a cloud of Cold Grit, the wax breaks off quite easily."

"Haven't you ever just wanted to sit back and crack into a vine of grapes?" Raek asked.

"By the time we got through eating them, we could tell our grandchildren about the good ole days when it didn't take two hands to eat grapes." Ard discarded the dipped bunch on the table. "Besides, the wax looks too much like a preservative. We need everything to appear fresh."

"I have one more thing," said the fruiter, producing a summer melon. It looked perfectly normal, a bit bigger than Raek's fist, with smooth yellowish skin. The only thing that seemed out of place was the large stem, which looked to be made of hardwood.

The man handed the melon to Ard, who didn't look overly impressed. "Go ahead and cut into it," said the fruiter.

Ard reached down and drew his long knife. Setting the small melon on the table, he cut the fruit in half. Gelatinous goo spilled all over the tabletop, but otherwise, the melon was empty. Most of the meat was gone and all of the seeds had somehow been removed while keeping the rind intact.

The fruiter stretched out a finger and swiped through the unknown substance, licking it clean with a satisfied smile. "Sweetened gelatin."

"Not the most appetizing fruit," Raek commented.

"But delightfully foreign," said Ard, tasting some of the goo for himself. He gestured for Quarrah to give it a try, but she simply raised one eyebrow.

"I bored a small hole into the top of the melon and reamed out the insides," explained the fruiter. "Then I added the sweetened gelatin and plugged the hole with an artificial stem. Again, the melon is meant to stay cool. The gelatin is much firmer that way."

Ard reached out and shook the fruiter's hand enthusiastically. "We'll take two dozen of those jelly melons and fifteen glowing pears."

"Glowing pears..." the man stammered.

"Is there a problem?" Ard asked. "My employer has very high expectations for these fruits."

"No problem at all, sir." The fruiter gathered his basket, and Raek followed him out the tavern door. When Quarrah turned back, Elbrig was standing there, sampling the gelatinous insides of the melon that were now dripping off the table's edge.

"Isn't your shipwright supposed to be here?" the disguise manager asked Ard.

"Raek's waiting for her," he said. "Don't worry about all that. You just make sure the Homelanders are ready for public scrutiny. I'll see to the rest."

"I don't want the shipwright here when Cinza does her presentation," he said.

"Is she ready?" Ard asked.

"Moments away," said Elbrig.

"Raek will hold the shipwright at the door until Cinza's finished."

Quarrah noticed that the hourglass timer must have finally run out since the eight crew members were no longer glide-stepping in circles.

Elbrig clapped his hands to get everyone's attention. "Is anyone hungry?"

Everyone looked interested, Paver and Keel starting forward as though Elbrig might be offering something.

"Wrong!" shouted the disguise manager. "Homelanders feel no hunger or thirst. You may eat and drink, but only as a novelty. And be sure to express criticism for everything that enters your mouths. You're used to food and beverage that has been perfected."

"Like Damarin whiskey," said Yalan, to a chuckle from Garew.

"Homeland whiskey makes the Damarin stuff taste like dragon

bile," snapped Elbrig. "What do you say if people ask you if you've seen their dead loved ones?"

" 'The Homeland's a big place. I haven't had the chance to meet your grandfather yet,' " answered Ruge.

"That's right," said Elbrig. "You can know anybody from Prime Isle Klikson to Queen Melsioba, but if there's a chance anyone still alive might have known them, you haven't met them."

"I don't see why not," said Keel. "Wouldn't it help sell the bit to tell them we've seen their loved ones?"

"Too many inconsistencies," said Elbrig. "What if the person they're asking about had lived a Settled life? Or what if he'd masqueraded as a good Wayfarist, but someone knew he'd meddled in Settled acts that would have barred him from the Homeland?"

To Quarrah that sounded like an apt description of everyone in the Realm. They claimed their cause was religious, but they had become the heart of crime and corruption in Beripent. Possibly in the entire Greater Chain.

"Now," said Elbrig, "let us practice our dialect. We always place the empha*sis* on the fi*nal* sylla*ble* of the word. Home*land*. Home*land*."

Soon, the tavern was filled with a chorus of repeating voices. Quarrah drilled a few of the words that Elbrig put forth, but she didn't even sound convincing to herself. Well, there had to be a few Homelanders who weren't very talkative, right? If Quarrah had to go along with this ridiculous ruse, she'd just keep her mouth shut and let the excess of actors in the crew do the rest.

They were all repeating the word "sau*sage*" when the door to the kitchen opened and Cinza appeared. Really, the only reason Quarrah knew it was her was because she'd heard Elbrig say she'd be arriving any moment.

Cinza Ortemion looked like she'd been smelted out of pure gold. Every inch of her exposed flesh glimmered in the tavern's lantern light. The paint was applied so heavily that her skin looked thick and tight. Her unnaturally golden wig was obviously made up of something other than human hair. Each strand was nearly as thick as a scribing charcoal, and the locks fell almost a foot past her shoulders.

Quarrah felt like the noble folk made some pretty outlandish wardrobe choices, but Cinza's attire really took it to the next level.

It was a purple dress, or maybe some kind of robe. The sleeves were tight and went all the way to her wrists. But the elbows were cut out as though a rip had been hemmed open instead of sewn shut.

One side of the robe hung nearly to the floor, but the other didn't even reach the knee. The exposed leg was completely covered with a ridiculously tall white stocking. More of a leg sleeve, really, since her gold-painted feet were bare, adorned with simple sandals.

But the most bizarre bit of the entire costume was Cinza's face. Aside from being completely golden, the structure of her face was different. This must have been something similar to the false forehead Ard had worn as Dale Hizror, but at least he had still looked human!

This prosthetic started as a ridge at the center of the forehead and spread in both directions, covering her eyebrows and wrapping around the sockets of her eyes until it tapered down into the cheekbones. It gave her an almost skeletal look, making her eyes, which Quarrah noticed were somehow a bright yellow, seem farther back in her skull.

Cinza strode around the end of the bar, expertly glide-stepping. Quarrah had to admit, the entire appearance was striking. Although, she couldn't decide if it was convincing, or just plain distracting.

"Behold, the glorious appearance of the Homelanders," she said, perfectly demonstrating that strange lilting dialect.

Ard whistled softly at Quarrah's side. "Well, isn't that something?"

"What are the men supposed to wear?" asked Paver Boret.

"The same," answered Cinza. "In the Homeland, all things are equal."

Ard turned quietly to Elbrig. "What about the, ah…?" He reached up and tapped the corner of his eye. "Did it work out like we planned?"

Elbrig raised his voice for all to hear. "They look upon the past with eyes transfigured," he began, quoting one of the verses that Quarrah recognized from Raek's copied list of references. "With unbridled effulgence they will judge our deeds to see if we are fit for the Homeland."

Cinza tapped the side of her artificial eye sockets in a similar manner to what Ard had just done. Suddenly, her eyes illuminated. Sparks, they were actually *glowing*! Well, not her eyeballs, but the enlarged surrounding sockets were shining brightly, giving the impression that her eyes were ablaze.

A coo of wonderment passed through the onlooking crew, while Ard smiled broadly. He clapped his hands in applause, stepping toward Cinza and taking command of the room.

"They say a ruse artist never reveals his secrets," Ard said. "But all of you are going to be wearing this costume, so let's hear how it works." He gestured for Cinza to explain.

The disguise manager dropped her proper Homelander posture and started speaking with the abrasive voice that Quarrah remembered all too well.

"The fabric of the wardrobe is light and breathable. Just make sure no one seduces you because we're only painting what can be seen." To prove her point, Cinza bent down and pulled up the sleeve on her exposed leg. The gold paint tapered off about mid shin.

"The paint is sprayed onto your skin to ensure a thick, even application," Cinza continued. "We add flakes of pyrite to a yellow base to give it the appropriate shimmer."

"How do you spray it?" asked Palia. So, Quarrah wasn't the only one concerned about letting the disguise managers spray mineral-flecked paint in her face.

"Using our highly original, one-of-a-kind Void Grit sprayer," answered Elbrig. "Paint goes into a bladder at the top. It's then incrementally pumped into a small tube, where it meets a detonation of Void Grit. The cloud sprays the paint down the tube and through a coarse filter at the end, assuring even dispersement."

That explanation didn't do much to ease Quarrah's concerns. Especially if the spraying device was in the hands of Cinza Ortemion.

"How did you do the eyes?" asked Ruge, pointing at Cinza's still-glowing sockets.

"Oh, we'll use drops of dye to color your eyes a bright yellow," Cinza answered, clearly not answering the question Ruge had intended. "It doesn't affect your vision in any way, but you'll need to plan your outings accordingly since the dye lasts around twelve hours."

"I meant the glowing," Ruge clarified, unamused.

"The bulk of the face modifications are made from hardened clay," Cinza said. "You'll use an adhesive to secure them, and some putty to smooth out the edges. The paint goes on thick enough to convincingly conceal any blemishes. The formations around the eyes are hollow. Before putting them in place, they can be loaded with Light Grit. Tiny pieces of Slagstone are embedded in the sides. All you have to do is give them a tap and the sparks will ignite the Grit, keeping it fully contained within the facial structure. When sufficiently Compounded, the light shines through the artificial eye sockets and you're left with this effect."

"Slagstone eyebrows," Ard said proudly. "I've been sitting on that idea for some time now."

"So it'll only last about ten minutes?" asked Yalan. "And we'll only be able to do it once?"

"Once each time you put on the disguise. And Prolonging Grit can stretch it a few more minutes," answered Elbrig, "but the effect is definitely not permanent."

"It all stems from that verse that Elbrig just quoted," explained

Ard. "Supposedly, the Homelanders use their glowing eyes to judge others. We can use that to our advantage when we're in costume. If somebody does something you consider to be Settled, then light up your eyes and make them reconsider their actions."

The tavern door cracked open and Raek's head reappeared. "Ard! Your next appointment is here."

"Boo, Raekon!" Cinza called. "Spoiling all the fun. I shall make myself scarce so you can get on to less important things." She glide-stepped around the bar and disappeared into the kitchen.

"This isn't a break for the rest of you," Elbrig barked. "I want you paired off in twos to practice the dialect. I'll be coming around to listen and correct you."

Quarrah backed away before anyone could ask her to partner up. She'd keep the numbers even by joining Ard in his conversation with the shipwright.

Raek led the woman into the tavern. She was tall, built like a willow, holding a bundle of large papers rolled into tight scrolls. Quarrah met them at an empty table in the opposite corner from where the fruiter had shown his wares.

"Rumor has it you're the best shipwright with knowledge of a certain phrase," Ard said as she placed her scrolls on the table.

"You could have stopped after 'best shipwright,'" she said. "And the rumors are true." She cleared her throat. "I have a number of designs for vessels that are ideal for an eight-person crew."

She opened one of the scrolls and spread it out, displaying carefully inked to-scale plans. "What do you think of this sloop? They're very common in the war right now as maneuverable trans-port vessels."

"Common is exactly what we're trying to avoid." Ard waved for her to roll up the plans.

She pushed it aside and unrolled another. "Perhaps a schooner? The gaff sails do very well against the adverse winds in the Inter-Island Waters."

Ard sighed, glancing at Raek. "Didn't you tell her we'd be taking it out?" He turned back to the shipwright. "I need something small, but capable of getting my crew all the way to the Homeland if we find the need."

She nodded. "A clipper, then." She shuffled through her remaining scrolls until she found the one she wanted. The plans for this one had a single mast and a long stem.

"I like it," Ard admitted, "but I don't want it to look like a common clipper. Sparks, I don't want it to look like a kind of ship anyone's ever seen before."

"These models are already built," said the shipwright. "With the time frame you gave me I wouldn't have time to craft something from scratch."

"Then alter it. Put the mast on an angle…" Ard mused, "add an aft stem, or some out-riggings. This needs to be the finest ship that has ever been constructed."

She scratched her head. "I cannot guarantee my work if I make such significant alterations."

"She just needs to be seaworthy and mighty fine to look at," said Ard. "In fact, I don't want your guarantee, or your mark on any of it. No one can know you built this."

She scoffed. "Shipbuilding is an art form, sir. We each have our own methods and preferences that become like a signature. The ship will certainly look like mine if anyone knows what to look for."

Ard shook his head. "Then we'll have to cover it up."

"What do you mean?"

"If ships are that easily identifiable, then we'll have to disguise it," he replied. "I want the entire vessel covered in clay from bow to stern." He paused as if doubting himself. "Will that make it sink?"

"Well, no, but—"

"Then do it," said Ard. "Make the clay white. Maybe add some flecks of pyrite for some glitter."

Quarrah rolled her eyes. *Wonder where he got that idea.*

"I'll see what I can do." The shipwright gathered her scrolls and headed for the tavern exit.

"I'm sure I don't need to remind you that the ship must be kept in total secrecy," Ard called, "with a team of workers who share our respect for the Realm."

She looked back. "I understand." Then she disappeared outside.

"I don't like using so many contractors," Ard said, glancing around the tavern.

"We're all working for the same organization," assured Raek.

"An organization that thrives on corruption and manipulation," said Ard. He glanced at Quarrah. "What do you think?"

"I think you're pushing it," she replied. "Even if everyone does what you require of them, there's still a lot of risk."

"I keep reminding myself that none of this actually has to work," Ard said quietly.

"Doesn't have to work?" Quarrah repeated, struggling to keep her voice low. What was he talking about?

"Overseer expects us to put out the Homeland ship and sail into Beripent's harbor immediately following the Cataclysm," Ard explained. "That means they'll have to give us the prince before the flood so we can be in position. Once we have him, we forget about this ruse and hustle the boy straight to the throne room so he can start issuing warnings. With any luck, the harbor Regulation will apprehend the Void Grit device before it is submerged."

"'With any luck' is not a phrase I like to use when thousands of lives are on the line," Quarrah said.

"Fair," Ard replied. "But with Shad on the throne at least the people will have a little warning if the flood can't be stopped. They could evacuate the Northern Quarter. Detonate Barrier Grit..."

"Why are we putting so much work into this ruse if it's never even going to happen?" Quarrah asked.

"It has to be convincing enough that the Realm will give us the prince," he said.

"Is that why you've left holes in the plan?" Raek asked.

Ard turned on him. "I haven't left holes in the plan!"

"What about getting the Homeland ship into the water without anyone noticing?" Raek pressed. "Our shipwright builds her vessels in the Western Quarter, and we're supposed to be sailing in from the east on a one-way trip from the Homeland."

"Okay," Ard conceded. "Maybe that's a tiny little hole. But it doesn't actually matter. We're not going to have to take the ship out. The Realm is going to give us Shad Agaul before the Cataclysm hits, and we'll use him to stop it."

Quarrah folded her arms, annoyed that it had taken Ard this long to be honest with her. "If we're not *actually* going to be Homelanders," she said, "then I'm not practicing that blazing dialect for another minute."

Ard tilted his head disapprovingly. "The Realm has eyes and ears everywhere. This has to be convincing. We press forward like it's happening—"

"Ignoring the little holes," Raek cut in.

"—And soon we'll all be sitting in the throne room with His Majesty Shad Agaul, sharing a gelatin-filled summer melon and having a good laugh about how we were so close to being Homelanders."

~

*In the still of night, the gods made preparations.*

# CHAPTER

# 29

The excitement Portsend had once seen in his pupils was utterly extinguished now, making this one of the most uncomfortable floats he had ever taken through the Mooring's waterway.

The three of them sat in perfect silence, each staring in a different direction into the water as the young Isle poled their craft along.

Despite his many visits over the years, he'd never been this far into the Mooring. The water looked deeper here. Darker, as they approached Cove 1.

Portsend was glad Lomaya had agreed to join them. He hadn't seen the young woman since the afternoon of Kend's gruesome death two weeks ago. Portsend had told them everything that night, and his two pupils had departed the lab in speechless shock.

For three days following, Portsend Wal had worked alone. Then, after news had reached him about eight Moonsick Bloodeyes staggering through the Char and killing twelve innocent civilians, San Green showed up at the lab at their usual time.

The lad was a shell of his former self. Homeland, they all were, after what they had witnessed! But San had returned to the lab with an undercurrent of determination that bordered on vengeance. Perhaps he would have made a good soldier after all.

Portsend vividly remembered the conversation that had brought them to the Mooring today.

"We have to tell the Prime Isless," San had said. "Tell her that you're being manipulated."

"That is the very sort of thing that got Kend killed," Portsend had answered. "I swore to that woman that I would not speak with Gloristar or the king again."

"But *I* made no such promise," the lad had replied. "If you won't tell the Prime Isless, then I will."

So, here they were, Portsend determined to come along but maintain his silence so he could truthfully report to the boss that he had not gone against their agreement.

He had told Cheery and Stubs that they were going to make a request for more materials. Stubs had nursed his bandaged hand, throwing out all kinds of threats if the conversation went anywhere other than the petition.

As a complete surprise, Lomaya had arrived at the laboratory just before they'd set out to the Mooring this morning.

"San told me you were going to see the Prime Isless," she had said. "I'd like to meet her."

The meeting could be good for the young woman. Portsend understood better than anyone how healing Gloristar's words could be in a time of loss. If she had once been able to put together some of Portsend's shattered heart, then surely she could also help Lomaya find peace.

The raft bumped softly against the floating dock, the Isle using his long pole to anchor it against the bed of the waterway. Portsend stepped off, a chill passing over him.

Cove 1.

He knocked on the grand door, the emblem of a white anchor painted on the hardwood. San and Lomaya were at his elbows when it opened.

"Prime Isless Gloristar." Portsend nodded in respect. She looked sorry to see him, her expression possibly bordering on disgust. Well, soon enough, she'd realize why he had pretended not to have any new developments in front of King Termain. She'd realize that it had all been to protect her.

"These are my trusted associates, Lomaya Vans and San Green."

"You may come in." She stepped aside to let them enter.

The room was almost twice the size of any cove Portsend had ever seen, but it wasn't extravagant. There was a large desk against one wall, and the middle of the room was occupied by a round table and a dozen chairs. Comfortable-looking, upholstered seating filled each corner, with a chaise long enough for someone to lie down on.

Books were strewn about, lying open on nearly every surface. Still, the floor-to-ceiling bookshelf that made up the cove's back wall hardly looked depleted.

At the center of the bookcase was a small door, framed by shelves of colorful books. Portsend's eyes must have lingered there, studying the shiny padlock and chain that sealed off the door.

"The Sanctum," Gloristar explained. "Wherein is kept the Anchored Tome."

"They know the Tome is gone, Gloristar," Portsend said. "I've told them everything."

The Prime Isless sighed heavily, motioning for them all to be seated at the table in the middle of the room.

Portsend watched his pupils move slowly, their eyes darting back and forth to take it all in.

"What have you been studying?" Portsend glanced at the title of one of the books as he took a seat at the table. *The Weight of Holiness* by Prime Isle Palk. The dark circles under Gloristar's eyes certainly reflected that weight.

"Sacred topics," replied Gloristar. "Anything in an attempt to jog my memory so I can better re-create the passages I've read in the Anchored Tome."

"Is it going well?"

"It is a futile attempt," she replied coldly. "I was never able to read the full Tome before it was taken."

"The Homeland will Urge and inspire you," Portsend tried. He began to quote their verse. " 'But glory, starboard, for—' "

"Why are you here, Portsend?" she asked, cutting him off.

So terse. So unlike her. She needed the truth quickly before her displeasure in him could solidify any more.

"San," Portsend encouraged his young pupil to begin.

"Most holy Prime Isless." The lad's voice was tense, rightfully nervous. "I speak for Professor Wal, since he has given his word not to share any of this with you."

"Given his word to whom?" she asked, gaze piercing into Portsend's soul.

"You are both being manipulated by powers out of your control," San continued. "A group has taken control of Professor Wal's research."

"How?" she cried. "When?"

Portsend was desperate to answer, but he held his tongue, letting San continue.

"They came just weeks after your first meeting with King Termain," said San. "They replaced Brase and Luthe with bodyguards of their own, demanding that the professor give them information about every development he made. He has been doing his best to withhold our findings from them, but as punishment, they've been releasing people with Moonsickness into Beripent. After the king threatened you at your last meeting, Professor Wal knew he couldn't allow the presence of the Bloodeyes to keep undermining Wayfarist belief."

"The Moonsickness is staged?" Gloristar muttered.

"Professor Wal has surrendered all of our research with hopes that his manipulators will uphold their end of the arrangement and stop releasing the Bloodeyes," San continued. "In total, we have developed six new types of liquid Grit, with one more undiscovered from your secret list of materials."

"Six new Grit types," Gloristar whispered, obviously crestfallen. "You should have come to me, Portsend. You should have—"

"I did!" Portsend finally snapped, unable to remain a silent observer. "I gave Termain information on Weight Grit, and now a man is dead because of it!"

He was gripping the edge of the table, half expecting Lomaya to fall into tears. She sat motionless at his side.

"His name was Kend Apashian." Portsend's voice was quiet now. Defeated. "He was someone very dear to Lomaya."

"He was involved?" Gloristar asked.

"Only by association with her," said Portsend. "I'd never met the lad, and Lomaya was always careful to keep the truth of our studies from him."

"Tell me about him," Gloristar said.

Lomaya stared straight ahead, unwilling to open up.

"I'd met him once or twice," San offered. "Big fellow. Strong. A veteran. He'd been an infantryman for the Archkingdom. Fifth Legion?"

"Third," corrected Lomaya. Her voice sounded raw and under-used. "He was shot in the leg, and that sent him home. He was going to go out again. As soon as he healed up all right."

"Had you been together long?"

"I knew Kend from before he went to war," the young woman answered. "He always made me laugh. Treated me like I was the only person who mattered." Lomaya paused, her breathing slightly changed. "He was different after the war. He'd seen things. Done things...Made him feel like he couldn't be a Wayfarist anymore. His tenderness was gone, but I was fighting for it. I was seeing more of it every day."

Gloristar rose, purple robes swishing about her as she glided around the table toward Lomaya. "'Progress is the rising sun,'" she quoted a scripture that Portsend quickly recognized, "'preceded by the requisite darkness of night. First, it is a subtle lightening, and then a glowing beam of color that doth steadily increase until the perfection of full day spills across the land.'"

The Prime Isless reached out and placed a comforting hand on the younger woman's shoulder. "You were helping him rise from the darkness of war, Lomaya. It is thanks to you that your friend now rests in the Homeland," Gloristar spoke softly. "I know that doesn't make it any easier right now. But you will see him again, perfected as only a Homelander can be, if you do not let yourself Settle in his absence."

Still, Lomaya did not cry. It seemed she was past tears. Instead, she nodded resolutely and touched Gloristar's hand.

"What do you know about this group that is manipulating you?" the Prime Isless asked, turning to Portsend.

"Very little," he answered. "I get the impression that the bodyguards who keep watch over us are little more than grunt labor. The 'boss,' as we've been told to call her, seems to be higher on the list of importance, but even she has mentioned superiors."

"Does she have any qualities that might distinguish her?"

Portsend thought about it. "She's stocky. Black hair..." He shrugged. "I don't know."

"I'm sending a regiment of Regulators back with you," she said. "They can arrest the two criminals and stand guard while you finish working on the final material from the Anchored Tome."

Portsend shook his head. "You can't do that. These people are beyond Settled, Gloristar. They are intentionally exposing people to Moonsickness. Farming them and releasing them into cities all over the Greater Chain."

"Homeland," the Prime Isless whispered. "How do we stop them?"

"I don't think we can," Portsend replied. "Not yet, anyway. Whatever this group is, it has eyes and ears in the palace. You can bet they're among the Regulation as well. Until we get a chance to understand them better, I don't think we can make a move against them that won't end with the three of us dead."

"We have to level the playing field," said San. The lad reached into his satchel and produced four folders, identical to the ones Portsend had surrendered to the boss.

"Professor Wal told us that he has already given Ignition Grit and Weight Grit to the Archkingdom Mixers," San said. "This is all the information regarding the remaining four that we've discovered. Null Grit, Stasis Grit, Weight Grit, and Gather Grit." He slid the folders across the table to where Gloristar was still standing beside Lomaya.

"We've actually achieved a detonation cloud with the final material, but we don't know what it does yet, so I didn't record it in my notes," said San.

He was talking about the processed dragon teeth. Portsend and San had been working on it since Kend's death, albeit with limited progress and enthusiasm.

"What am I to do with these?" Gloristar leafed through the pages in the folders.

"We assume that the boss does not want the Archkingdom to have these new developments," San said. "So it follows that giving them to His Highness would go against them."

"You want me to give all these to the king?" Gloristar asked.

"From what Professor Wal has told us, that information will provide you some protection against His Majesty's threats."

"But it will also put four new types of Grit into the hands of an entitled man-child," Gloristar spoke freely. "Is this really our best course of action?"

"The Grit solutions are already in the hands of a lunatic," Portsend said. "Giving them to Termain could provide complications to the boss and her superiors. If it causes them to unravel enough, we might be able to slip out from under their thumb."

"With these kinds of advantages, the Archkingdom could win the war," said Gloristar.

"Isn't that the only way things end favorably for you?" Portsend said.

"The Sovereign States coming under Termain's control will not be favorable for anyone." Gloristar set down the folders. "Besides, surrendering these developments to King Termain is too dangerous for the three of you. Once this 'boss' woman finds out what you've done..."

"We need to fool her," Lomaya suddenly spoke. "Maybe we can frame this whole thing to look like an accident."

"What do you have in mind?" asked Portsend. He couldn't tell if the young woman was cooking up an idea on the spot or if she'd already crafted it during what must have been endless hours of channeling hatred toward the boss.

"We can stage a break-in at the laboratory tomorrow night," she said. "When Stubs and Cheery find out about it, we tell them that the folders were stolen. The Prime Isless delivers them to the king, claiming that a Regulator discovered them in a stolen satchel, discarded on the roadside."

"You're suggesting a lie?" Gloristar said. "Some sort of elaborate ruse?"

"It could work," Portsend said. "I don't know why a Regulator would deliver them to Gloristar..."

"Perhaps it goes the other way around," said San. "The Prime Isless gives them to the Reggie, with orders to take them to the king."

"Then where did I find the folders?" asked Gloristar.

"Perhaps we should cut the Prime Isless out of this altogether," suggested Lomaya. "Leave the folders somewhere we're certain they'll be picked up."

Portsend shook his head. "Too much risk that it could fall into the wrong hands. Besides, it needs to come from Gloristar, or the king won't have any reason to be pleased with her for it."

"Maybe it was I who orchestrated the break-in," Gloristar said. "I could tell the king that I was growing suspicious of you, suspecting you had more developments that you weren't sharing."

"That could work," Portsend said. "We just need a scapegoat. Someone who could believably break into my laboratory and make the theft on Gloristar's behalf."

"One of the Isles?" San suggested.

"Homeland, no," Portsend said. "Whoever we blame will likely have the boss and her superiors coming after them. We can't pin it on an Isle. Nor is that believable. Gloristar should contract with a criminal for this kind of illegality."

"What about that big fellow?" Lomaya asked. "The one who barged in looking for Heg?"

Portsend nodded. "His name was Raekon, if I remember correctly. We could pin it on him."

"Raekon," repeated the Prime Isless. "When do we do this?"

"I can leave the door to the lab open tomorrow night," Portsend said. "You should wait a day or two after that before presenting the folders to King Termain."

"This could still come back to hurt you, Portsend," she said. "Termain will not be happy that you withheld information from him."

"That's a risk I'm willing to take," he replied. "I'll be counting on him to be pleased enough with his new Grit types that he won't come after me. We have only one more material on the scroll. This will all be over soon."

Gloristar sighed, reaching out to rest a hand on a stack of books. "Once I'm in the king's good graces, perhaps I won't need these studies."

Somehow, Portsend doubted that even winning the war would satisfy Termain Agaul's strange desire for power over Gloristar. The reason might change, but he had a feeling the manipulation would persist.

The Prime Isless stepped away from the table, prompting the other three to stand.

"It was an honor to meet you." San nodded respectfully. "I can't imagine the strength it must take to lead Wayfarism. Especially in these trying times."

Gloristar smiled sadly. "Many marvel at the station of the Prime Isless, but I am simply doing what is expected of me. I see true strength and bravery in the three of you."

She reached out and touched Lomaya's arm again. "No one expects you to take these risks, but I can assure you that the Homeland is grateful. And it Urges you to be careful."

They all shuffled quietly to the exit, San leaving the folders on the table for Gloristar. Portsend was filled with concern about their plan to deceive the boss, but he was proud of Lomaya for having conceived it. The young woman seemed different already, walking with slightly more purpose, head held a little higher. The visit to Gloristar had redirected her, filling her with the faith not to Settle.

Or perhaps it was just a fuel for vengeance. Either way, Portsend Wal was glad she had come.

The Prime Isless pulled open the door and the two pupils stepped onto the floating dock. But Gloristar caught Portsend's arm as he passed, eyes boring into him.

"A moment?" she implored.

Portsend nodded to his students and swung the door shut. In a heartbeat, Gloristar was in his arms. It was as though she had collapsed, her strength utterly sapped as her head pressed against his chest.

She was crying. Sparks, *he* was crying, too, arms surrounding her, holding her tightly. That forbidden night from three years ago had started this very way—with tears and a comforting embrace. It had ended with a long kiss, resulting in an awkwardness that neither of them had spoken of again.

Portsend would not let it escalate today. As much as he wanted to feel her lips on his again, she was the Prime Isless of all Wayfarism. This would only be fuel for their enemies.

"I'm sorry..." she whispered, but she didn't pull away. "I never should have brought you into this. There are other Mixers I could have turned to."

He smiled, tears clearing. "I'm trying not to take that as an insult."

Gloristar managed to sneak a laugh between two sobs. "Other Mixers, who don't mean as much to me."

"For years I have turned to you for help," he said. "As you said before...Isn't it time to set the scripture straight?" She had asked him not to speak of their verse again. But here, with a tender vulnerability stewing between them, Portsend found himself speaking the words in soft recitation. "'The journey to the Homeland is long, and many shall perish, ere they reach that holy shore...'"

"'From port, send thine aid,'" Gloristar continued.

"'But glory, starboard, for it shall mark thy way to everlasting perfection.'"

From the sixth chapter in the first volume of *Wayfarist Voyage*. Portsend had known the verse since he was a child, his devout Wayfarist parents having given him a name derived from that very text.

He was a portsend. An aide. His mother had always told him to help others and serve them freely. It was in his very name.

The fact that Gloristar had been named after the same verse had united them in Cove 14 all those years ago. Her parents, both Holy Isles themselves, would have been so proud to see her fill the robes of Prime, leading the way to the Homeland and its everlasting perfection.

"I'm here for you, Glori," he whispered. "Always."

They held each other in silence for a long moment before drawing slowly apart. "They're so young." She was staring as though she could see through the door.

"San and Lomaya are remarkable," he said. "The brightest I've seen."

"That poor girl," she said. "I feel responsible for that tragedy."

"No," he said. "If anyone is to blame, it's me. But this is nearly finished. We must keep moving forward. I believe our plan will work."

"And what if it doesn't?" She turned her large eyes, still shiny with lingering tears, on Portsend. "I cannot afford to lose you. Any of you."

"Are you saying we shouldn't go through with it?"

"Perhaps it would be better if the three of you simply vanish," she said.

He turned sharply to her. "They will find us."

"I could arrange passage for you all to leave Espar. Leave the Archkingdom for good."

"What about the final material from the Anchored Tome?" *What about seeing you again?*

"Forget the final material."

Portsend shook his head. "With the foundation already paved for liquid Grit solutions, it will only be a matter of time before someone else discovers it. Better to have it come to light on our terms, under our control."

"We've already lost control! Don't you see?" Her voice was full of pleading. "This isn't safe, Portsend. It has to end. I will tell Termain about the list and I'll convince him that we milked it dry."

"He'll find it in the Tome," Portsend said.

"He won't dare open it."

"And if he does?" Portsend said. Was the sacred book *actually* protected by the Paladin Visitants outside the Sanctum? He had a hard time believing that was anything more than carefully crafted superstition. "He'll know you lied to him." Portsend folded his arms stubbornly across his chest. "I'm staying to see this through."

The look on Gloristar's face melted his insides. His knees felt weak, but his resolution stronger.

*I love you,* he wanted to say. Portsend was sure she already knew it, but he longed for her to hear it from his mouth, not just his heart.

"You're a good man, Portsend Wal." She pulled open the door. "Homeland bless and keep you."

He felt suddenly exposed, his two students and the Isle on the raft looking in on his lingering emotions. Portsend nodded to Gloristar and stepped onto the dock, feeling it shift under his feet. The cove door closed behind him, but Portsend didn't look back, choosing to focus on the raft instead.

"What did she say?" San finally asked as the Isle pushed them away from Cove 1.

The professor looked at the young faces of his pupils and his heart ached. Where would they be if he hadn't recruited them to his secret endeavors? San Green would be at the war. Portsend had thought to save him from that sort of fear and ugliness. Instead he had brought it to the lad's doorstep.

And Lomaya . . . If it weren't for Portsend's demands on her time, she might still be with Kend. The two of them could have been living happily while she thrived in her studies.

"The Prime Isless thanks you both for your assistance," Portsend said. "But she has ordered you to leave."

"Leave?" cried San. "And go where?"

"She will arrange passage off Espar," Portsend continued. "The two of us agreed that this has become too dangerous. I will remain to finish working on the final material alone."

"When?" San followed up.

"Tomorrow," answered Portsend. Hopefully, Gloristar could make good on her offer in such a short time. He would send her a sealed letter the moment he got back to the college. After their discussion, he could keep it vague and she would know what he meant.

"What about our plan?" Lomaya asked.

"We'll go through with it," Portsend replied. "It hardly takes three of us to leave the laboratory unlocked and claim a burglary."

"This isn't fair," San muttered through clenched teeth.

"No, it isn't," he said. "It wasn't fair of me to put this kind of pressure on you in the first place."

"I'm not going," San said. "What we're doing is important."

*Blazing stubbornness of youth.* "You wanted to be a soldier, but you obviously can't take orders," Portsend snapped, his voice assuming a disciplinary edge. "This is how it's going to work. My laboratory is locked, and I will no longer be allowing first-year students to access it. You can take the Prime Isless's offer and I will put a hold on your enrollment, allowing you back into the college without question as soon as things blow over." He took a deep breath. "Or I can report a long list of broken rules to the administration and they can forcibly remove you."

Homeland, he hated doing this to them. Threatening and extorting his prize pupils. Was he any better than King Termain, or the "boss"? This was for their safety. And Portsend felt the Homeland Urging him to be stern.

"I'll go," Lomaya said softly.

*Oh, thank you, dear girl.* She'd already been through enough.

"And San will come with me," she continued.

The lad was staring into the water as it swirled along the edge of the raft. "It seems I have no choice." His voice was barely audible.

Portsend turned away so they couldn't see his face, his expression tightening with sorrow. "This is for the best." And he believed it. But that didn't stop his tears from falling into the sacred waters of the Mooring.

~

*Then at last, we will breathe true air and feel the warmth
of the sun on our necks once again.*

# CHAPTER

# 30

Beautiful though the view was from the top of Old Post Light-house, Quarrah found she couldn't enjoy it. Perhaps it had something to do with being in a place that had only one exit, surrounded by masked figures who distrusted her.

The afternoon was clear and bright, but a wall of Barrier Grit still surrounded the pavilion-like room at the top of the tower. *Probably to prevent anyone from being able to shoot into the meeting*, Quarrah thought. *Or maybe to prevent any of us from jumping out.*

There wasn't much sense in trying to run away from the Realm. Not while the Waters of Loyalty swam inside her as an unidentifiable threat.

Quarrah had swallowed another dose of the bitter liquid at the Faceless meeting last week. Aside from drinking the Waters of Loyalty, the meeting itself hadn't turned out to mean much for her and Ard.

She had climbed into a carriage at Finder's Meat Shop, just as she'd done when she was a lowly Faceless. Only this time, she'd donned her own handmade black mask inside the cab and entered the building through a back door and a flight of stairs.

Overseer and the rest of the Directorate had taken the Waters of Loyalty and made sure no pressing matters needed to be resolved before meeting the Faceless downstairs.

Radius, Snare, Glint, and Trance had gone down to carry out the meeting, leaving Quarrah and Ard in the cabin with Grapple and Overseer. Ard had tried to give a report on the Homeland ruse, but Overseer had told him to save it for the lighthouse. Then she'd left the building and hadn't come back. Grapple had spent nearly an hour instructing Quarrah and Ard on the operations of these large Faceless meetings. The ledgers and the lists were long and complex, and Quarrah hoped she would never have a turn at one of the assignment tables.

"By now, I am sure you have all heard the news." Overseer looked around the table, late-afternoon sunlight shining on the rough scales of her headpiece. "As of this morning, Trothian forces have taken both of the Archkingdom's harbors on Pekal."

Murmurs passed around the table. Whispers and gasps interjected with outcries of disbelief. This was news to Quarrah, but she immediately knew who was behind it.

*Lyndel. She's taken the harbors just like she said she could.*

"How?" asked Grapple. "Those harbors were easily defensible, and there were terms of agreement in place with the Sovereign States. This was against the rules!"

Rules in war. Quarrah knew that Lyndel had little regard for Lander rules of any kind. She was only interested in ending the war as quickly as possible.

"They weaponized a Trans-Island Carriage," answered Overseer.

Quarrah's mouth dropped open behind her black mask. Oh, flames. Flying warships? This was going to change the entire face of warfare.

"The carriages flew overhead and dropped panweights of Blast Grit on the harbor defenses. Once they were crippled, it only took a very small fleet of ships on the water to gain control."

"How does this affect us?" Glint asked.

"Very gravely. The Realm keeps significant resources on Pekal," Overseer answered, "including an element that is necessary for the Cataclysm."

"We have all the Void Grit needed for—" Snare tried.

"The kegs!" Overseer suddenly shrieked in an uncharacteristic outburst. "Or have you all forgotten about the Cataclysm kegs?"

The table fell to tense silence. Ardor Benn slowly raised his hand. "I don't think I ever heard about the Cataclysm kegs," he dared.

"The upcoming Faceless meeting is scheduled for noon on the second, just twelve hours before the Cataclysm," Overseer said. "We have promised to distribute a keg to every Faceless, marked with the symbol of a wave. A keg for protection against the flooding and collateral damage."

"Barrier Grit?" Ard ventured.

"Nothing so simple, I'm afraid," answered Overseer. "Suffice it to say that the kegs are irreplaceable, and the Cataclysm mustn't happen without them."

Quarrah puzzled over that behind her mask. What kind of Grit was irreplaceable? Visitant Grit? The thought caused the skin on her arms and neck to prickle. She glanced at the other members of the Directorate. Did they know what was so important about these kegs?

"This can't last," said Glint. "The Trothians will surely lose the harbor by the beginning of next cycle. They will have to leave for the Moon Passing, and the Archkingdom will be sure to beat them back into the harbors. It will be tight, but I believe we can get the kegs in time for the Faceless meeting."

"No." Overseer's voice was tight, her speech deliberate. "We need to move the resources off Pekal *before* the Moon Passing. To ensure that they are here in time."

"Don't we have people on the Sovereign side?" asked Grapple. "People who could get the kegs to us?"

"We do," answered Overseer. "But we have significantly fewer associates among the Trothians. Early reports are stating that this was not a sanctioned attack by the Sovereign States. Rumor is that the Trothians acted independently, under the direction of a warrior priestess with her own plans to speed the war's end."

"Then we forget about the two Trothian harbors," suggested

Snare. "Let us use our contacts in the western harbor that the Sovereign States have always controlled."

"That will not work," said Overseer. "The kegs we need are on the eastern side of Pekal, which will require our team to cross the island on foot. With only twelve days until the Passing, there is no way we can get a team in and out before the Moonsickness strikes."

"Then what are you suggesting?" asked Trance.

"Our crew will have to scale the cliff," Overseer said.

"Shoreline security is going to be tighter than ever with all the attention on Pekal," said Radius. "Are you sure it's worth the risk?"

Overseer slammed her hand against the table. "When I say that the kegs are irreplaceable, do you think I jest?"

Behind the boar's mask, Radius cleared his throat. "I'm only seconding Glint's proposal to wait and extract the kegs first thing in the new cycle, when the Archkingdom has reclaimed the harbors."

"*If* the Archkingdom has reclaimed the harbors," Overseer said. "We are the Realm. We should not be frightened of Regulation shoreline patrol. Grapple will take charge of this venture, with Trance and Radius assisting as needed."

"An operation like this will require highly skilled professionals," said Grapple. "It will take a few days to coordinate, but I swear we will have the resources removed from Pekal before the Moon Passing."

Overseer took a visibly large breath, her indistinguishable form settling a little under her heavy cloak.

"Let us move on to more positive news," said Overseer. "Glint has taken a very effective approach with our Mixer, Portsend Wal." She gestured across the table for the stocky woman to explain.

Glint stood, the antlers on her mask nearly brushing Snare's seashells beside her. She retrieved a large box from behind her chair and set it on the table. Pulling off the lid, Quarrah saw that the box was filled with little glass vials of various colors.

*Oh, great,* she thought. *Not more of this stuff…*

*       *       *

Ard leaned forward, peering curiously at the little glass vials as Glint displayed one of each color on the table.

"Professor Portsend Wal has successfully developed six types of liquid Grit."

*Six types of...*

"Hold on," Ard interjected, holding out his hand. "*Liquid* Grit?" What the blazes was this woman talking about?

"There is new Grit research in development," explained Glint. "A professor at the Southern Quarter College of Beripent has created liquid Grit solutions that yield effects unlike anything we've ever seen."

*Well, feed me a Karvan lizard egg!* Ard thought. New Grit types...

Ard remembered the duel, when Hairy Face had shattered a glass vial that seemed to have extinguished the Barrier cloud. Ard had talked to Raek about it, but his partner had simply shaken his head, saying it wasn't possible. There were fifteen types of Grit— Ard knew them all.

Until now, apparently.

"The Realm is funding this research?" asked Quarrah from across the table.

"King Termain is funding it," answered Glint, "in partnership with Prime Isless Gloristar."

"These new Grit types pose a tremendous threat to society," Overseer said. "If given to Termain, it could turn the war in favor of the Archkingdom. So it became necessary for the Realm to step in."

"We acquired Ignition Grit," Glint pointed to the green vial, "from a source in the palace mixing laboratory." Then she pointed to the yellow vial. "The professor yielded Null Grit to the Realm directly."

From their names, Ard could extrapolate the new Grit's purpose. Ignition, and Null. The latter was likely what Hairy Face had used to extinguish the Barrier.

"The blue vial is Weight Grit," continued Glint. "It functions as something of an opposite to Drift Grit, causing items within the cloud to increase in weight. The orange is Stasis Grit, causing any living thing inside its radius to go into a fully suspended, dormant state. Red is Containment Grit. It creates a Barrier-like shell that can effectively enclose another detonation cloud and make them both mobile. Lastly, this purple vial is Gather Grit. It pulls everything inward to the point of ignition. I had a chance to experiment with this one myself. If sufficiently Compounded, it has the power to crush a human being at its center."

Ard stared speechlessly at the vials. Six new types of Grit! Oh, Raek would be dying to hear about this.

"I'll spare you any sort of demonstration today," continued Glint. "But I've prepared a box like this for each of you to take home for your own experimentation."

"And you may request more at any time," said Overseer. "We've got Realm Mixers working to reproduce them from the professor's notes."

"What does the Archkingdom know of these?" Snare asked, plucking up the red vial and examining it through the eyeholes of his seashell mask.

"Early on, the professor gave Termain the formula for Ignition Grit," explained Glint. "He later gave him Weight Grit. Most recently, the Prime Isless attempted to turn over the rest."

"She was not successful?" asked Trance.

"It seems that the Prime Isless grew suspicious of the professor," said Glint. "She had someone break into his laboratory and take the folders containing his research on the four remaining Grit solutions. Once she had the formulas, she presented them to King Termain. Fortunately, our contacts in the palace picked up on it immediately. One of them was able to destroy the papers before they reached the mixing laboratories."

"A close call," said Overseer.

"I'm curious to know who the holy Prime Isless used for such a job," said Radius. "It had to be someone familiar with the professor's research. One of his young assistants?"

"No," answered Glint. "My last visit to the lab has apparently driven off the professor's students. They have withdrawn from the college, and my sources say they have fled Espar altogether. Word is that the Prime Isless actually hired a criminal." She folded her arms. "A large fellow by the name of Raekon Dorrel."

Ard suddenly felt his breath coming hot and fast under his leather fox mask. Raek? There must have been some mix-up. Surely Glint was referring to someone else. His Raek absolutely would have told him if the Prime Isless had hired him for a job. He would have come skipping back to the Guesthouse Adagio with a self-important smirk on his face. This was a mistake. Sparks, maybe even a setup. Ard needed to diffuse this claim right now.

"How did you learn his name?" he asked with feigned indifference.

"It was mentioned by Gloristar in the palace, and I confirmed it with one of the Hands I have positioned to guard the professor," Glint replied. "He admitted that Raekon Dorrel was a client of his. A big fellow with a shaved head. Only weeks before the break-in, my man admitted that Raekon had forced entry into the lab and pressed the professor about his research."

No! This didn't make sense! "What kind of client?" Ard's voice was at half its usual volume.

"My Hand is an illegal Health Grit dealer," answered Glint. "For this breach of trust, I gave him extra reason to use his own product."

Health Grit...

Flames, a *lot* of things suddenly made sense. Raek's occasional tardiness and his unexplained disappearances. His cold sweats and shaky hands...Raek was addicted to Health Grit. It was why he always seemed to have some on hand when they needed it. That blazing pipe in his chest had saved his life, but now Ard's best friend was a Hegger. And he hadn't said a word about it to Ard.

In that moment, heart pounding as he sat forward on his chair, stunned by the news, Ard found that he wasn't angry or even disappointed in Raek. He was simply filled with sorrow. Sorrow and guilt that he'd been too blind to notice. It had been Ard's plans that'd gone awry, causing Raek to get stabbed. Now his friend still suffered, more than two years later. Apparently, there was a price for cheating death.

Ard had known plenty of addicts in his life. The desire for Heg drove them to do nearly anything. But Raek certainly hadn't done a secret job for the Prime Isless. She and Portsend Wal must have been using him as a scapegoat. If the professor had seen Raek sniffing around for Health Grit, it would make sense that they'd frame him for the break-in.

"We'll circulate his name among the Faceless and Hands," said Overseer. "Teach this *Raekon* not to take a job that doesn't align with the Realm's purposes."

"It's a lie," Ard blurted. He looked across the table at Quarrah. She'd probably put it together by now, too. Ard didn't expect her to come to his aid on this, but as long as she kept her mouth shut, he might be able to fix this. He sure as sparks couldn't leave this meeting knowing there was a target on Raek's back.

"The break-in was clearly staged," he continued. "You punished Portsend for revealing information to the king, so the professor decided to trick you this time."

"It is possible," Glint said.

"Not just possible," answered Ard. "It's absolutely true."

"What makes you so sure of this?"

Ard took a deep breath. "Because *I* am Raekon Dorrel."

It was silent around the Directorate table. Ard's heartbeat hammered in his ears, echoing inside his snarling fox mask. It was a risky statement, especially since they had all seen his face during the duel against Quarrah.

"I know we aren't supposed to reveal our identities," Ard said. "But I can't have you sending goons out after me on the street."

Glint tilted her head curiously. "They said the man was massive."

"Yeah. Well, of course your Hands weren't going to admit to being overpowered by someone their size," Ard pointed out. "And since I know you're all wondering about it, I'd like to announce that I've shaved my head since the duel."

"What were you doing at the professor's laboratory?" asked Overseer.

"Looking for Heg." He repeated what Glint had just said. "My dealer was there."

"And you pressured the professor for information?"

"To be honest, it'd been a while since my last fix and I was pretty desperate," said Ard. "I don't remember much of what went down. But I didn't do any sort of burglary for the Prime Isless. That much I remember."

Overseer turned to Glint. "It seems the professor intended to dupe you. I expect you'll make this right?"

Glint's hands clenched into tight fists. "Of course."

Ard leaned back in his chair, trying not to sigh with relief. Claiming to be Raek had been a risky play, but Overseer had seemed to buy it with surprising ease. Poor Raek. It made Ard positively sick to imagine him storming into a college laboratory, throwing his weight around and threatening an innocent professor.

Ard would fix this. He would talk to Raek and make a plan to help him stop abusing the Health Grit—

"Let us discuss the final phase of our plans," said Overseer, interrupting Ard's thoughts with an abrupt change of subject. "Timing is everything now."

"Which plans?" chimed Grapple. "The ones we spent years developing? Or Rival's elaborate Homeland ruse?"

Overseer held up her hand. "I hear your concerns. What is the status of the Cataclysm device?"

"It's loaded and ready," reported Snare.

"You have tested it empty?" Overseer checked.

He nodded his seashell-crusted mask. "We've run twelve simulations at the depth and location we have planned for the Cataclysm to originate. The device worked flawlessly every time, the chamber completely empty, which indicates that the plain Prolonging Grit ignited underwater exactly as planned." Smart, since Prolonging Grit by itself would not yield any sort of cloud.

"How are you detonating the Grit so far under the surface?" Ard asked. This seemed like a good thing to know if he ever planned on stopping the detonation.

"Fuses," answered Overseer. "A slow-burning fuse designed to burn for an hour. Snare will submerge the device at eleven o'clock, and precisely an hour later, the waters of the deep will heave upon the land, just as it is prophesied in *Wayfarist Voyage.*"

*Good,* Ard thought. *We just need to make sure Shad Agaul is on the throne by eight or nine o'clock.* That would give them plenty of time to shut down the harbors and make sure the Cataclysm device didn't go out.

"Where exactly will the device go down?" asked Trance.

Snare pointed northward over the lighthouse's railing. "There. Equidistant between Talumon and Espar."

"What is the anticipated reach of the floodwaters?" Radius asked.

"On the Beripent side, we estimate it will decimate everything north of the Char," answered Snare. "Significant damage should extend south as well."

Everything north of the Char! That was more than half the city! If they went through with the Cataclysm, it would mean the death of thousands.

"Talumon will experience similar impact in Grisn and other

coastal cities," Snare said. "The most favorable projections also have the waves breeching the southwest cliff of Strind."

"Excellent," Overseer said. "Let us have a report on Rival's progress with his Homelander ruse."

Ard stood up, full of confidence. "Well, things are coming along—"

"From Sleight," Overseer cut him off. That mask of dragon scales swiveled to look at Quarrah. "I would prefer to hear the report from Sleight."

Ard opened his mouth to protest but decided to sit down instead. Of course Overseer wanted to hear from her. She'd basically made Quarrah the babysitter over Rival's project.

"We made contact with the ruse artist Ardor Benn." Quarrah stayed seated during the report. Not a speck of showmanship with her. "I hired a very capable spy to infiltrate his crew."

Ard smiled to hear Quarrah ingratiate herself a bit. Homeland knew he did it all the time.

"Surprisingly, her reports indicate that the ruse *is* likely to be successful," continued Quarrah. "There will be eight convincing Homelanders accompanying the prince, ready to sail into North Central Harbor as the waters of the Cataclysm recede."

"In what ways will these Homelanders be convincing?" asked Radius.

"They're being disguised and rehearsed to look, move, and speak like people from another world altogether," said Quarrah. "Everything from the fruit they carry to the ship they stand on will support the lie."

"Pah!" cried Grapple. "Costumes and props will only go so far."

"There is no greater skeptic than me," Quarrah said. "Especially when it comes to ruse artists." She shot a glance at Ard. "But everything my source tells me makes me think this could actually work."

And it could. Except for the fact that there was no plan to actually get the Homeland ship into the water unnoticed. But none of this was going to happen anyway, once the Realm handed them Shad Agaul.

Overseer turned her large masked head to Ard. "Is there anything Rival would like to add to the report?"

Ard stood up again. "I just want to thank the Realm for supporting this plan. I have full confidence in it. I also need to get a few little reimbursements. Just wondering how I submit those."

Okay. Maybe not so little. But weren't the Realm's funds nigh unlimited?

"You can give them to Trance or Snare," said Overseer. "They are currently handling our finances. I leave it up to them to decide what amount will be reimbursed."

Ard nodded agreeably. It would be no skin off his teeth if the full amount didn't go through. Lady Abeth was paying Ardour Stringer anything he needed for information on her missing son.

"You believe the Homelanders will be convincing?" Overseer checked.

"Absolutely," Ard confirmed.

"Convincing enough to fool even the Prime Isless?"

"I am sure of it."

"Good," Overseer said. "Because there has been a change of plans."

"Excuse me?" Ard felt his heart leap into his throat. *Change of plans* could be a deadly trio of words for a ruse artist. Across the table, Quarrah drummed her fingers in a steady pattern that exposed her nervousness.

"Your ruse artist and his ship of faux Homelanders is needed *before* the Cataclysm," Overseer explained.

Ard gritted his teeth. But maybe this could be to their benefit. If Shad was scheduled to arrive before the flood, it would only give them more time to try to stop it.

"The prince cannot come before the Cataclysm," barked Radius.

"Or before his birthday," added Grapple. "Arriving before his legal age to rule will only cause confusion and complications."

"I am not suggesting that," said Overseer. "I understand better than any that there is a specific order to this. We distribute the kegs to the Faceless at noon. The flood happens at midnight, and on the morning of the second, the boy arrives to claim the throne from Termain."

"And where do Rival's Homelanders fit in?" Quarrah asked. Good of her to be concerned, since she was one of the golden beauties.

"Their ship will arrive before the next Moon Passing," she answered. "Four days before the Cataclysm."

"But that…" Ard stammered. "That doesn't work. The prince…"

"The prince will no longer be sailing with the Homelanders."

Well, there went everything, flopping over the railing of this lighthouse and plummeting two hundred feet to the sea below. If they didn't get Shad Agaul, then they'd actually have to carry out this extensive ruse. And ahead of schedule!

"What?" Ard cried.

"Before each symphony concert, the rich and royal gather for a reception in the palace," said Overseer. "Prime Isless Gloristar will be in attendance to support the king to whom she pledges her endorsement. I want the Homelanders to make their debut at that event."

"I don't understand," said Ard. "The entire purpose of this ruse was to establish Shad Agaul as a Homelander. If he doesn't arrive on that ship—"

"The reception will serve as a trial run," Overseer said. "If your false Homelanders pass scrutiny of even the Prime Isless, then you'll be trusted with the prince."

"But it'll be too late," Ard protested. "Do you plan to design a second Homeland ship patterned after the first? Another crew trained to behave like exotic Homelanders?"

"Nothing so complex," said Overseer. "On the morning of his fourteenth birthday, as the floodwaters subside, the young Agaul will step out of a detonation of Visitant Grit in the throne room, descending from the fiery form of a Paladin Visitant to the familiar beloved boy who had been assassinated. I trust your ruse artist can make that look convincing."

Ard swallowed. "He can." This sudden change provided a load of complications, but it only spurred Ardor Benn forward. If the ruse was convincing—and they'd certainly planned it to be—he'd likely still get access to Shad Agaul on the night before the flood.

"Your Homelanders will say nothing of the Cataclysm, since it will not yet have happened," said Overseer. "Nor shall they speak of the Moonsickness, or the Great Egress."

Those were all the major talking points that the crew was rehearsing! "What's left to discuss?" Ard spat. "The weather?"

"If it pleases you," said Overseer. "I hope you can understand our caution, Rival. Your plan has great merit, but the Realm has not come this far to take such a massive risk with Shad Agaul."

Ard nodded slowly. All was not lost. It just meant they had a lot more work ahead of them. Starting with the pesky detail of getting their Homeland ship into the water undetected.

"I understand," he said. "And I believe Ardor Benn and his Homelanders will impress you."

"I will meet you and Sleight after the reception for a full report," said Overseer.

"Here?" Quarrah asked.

Overseer shook her head. "Somewhere more convenient for you to oversee your ruse artist. Let us rendezvous on the palace grounds, by the east fishing pond. Say, ten o'clock evening?"

"That works for me," Ard said. "I won't have anything else going on that night."

~

*None can oppose our mighty works.*

# CHAPTER

# 31

Ardor Benn sat in the perfect darkness of the cottage, the rattling doorknob causing his mind and body to go as tight as a ship's main halyard. He didn't make a sound as Raek's broad form filled the doorway, silhouetted against the soft glow of the starlit night.

Ard watched his partner fumble in the darkness for a moment before a small orb of Light Grit appeared, instantly flooding the comfortable room with visibility.

"Where have you been?" Ard asked before either of their eyes had time to adjust.

Raek let out a long stream of curses, blundering for a moment like a dragon in a potter's shop. Then he let out a good-natured laugh. "Flames, Ard! You're not my mother."

"You're right," he said. "Fact is, we don't have mothers anymore. All we really have is each other."

"Aw," Raek cooed. "That's awful sweet..."

"I'm not trying to be sweet," Ard snapped. Couldn't his friend hear the seriousness in his voice? Couldn't he see the creases of sincerity on his face? Enough jokes. This needed to be an honest conversation, their facetious exteriors torn open and their true intentions laid bare.

"Where have you been?" he asked again. It had been sundown by the time Ard had returned from the Directorate meeting at the Old Post Lighthouse. He'd been waiting hours for this conversation, playing it out more than a dozen ways in his head.

"I had some business." Raek's tone was finally somber, and Ard could already see him beginning to put up his defensive walls. "Checking up on some of your Homelander actors. Making sure they're keeping their secrets."

*Or keeping your own.* Had he been out to get a fix? Buying more Heg? Sparks, Ard hated the thought of his best friend expired in a dingy alleyway, a contained detonation of Compounded Health Grit seeping into his wounded chest.

"Your name came up at the Directorate meeting this afternoon," Ard said.

"What?" His forehead wrinkled in confusion.

"The rumor is that you did a simple break-in for the Prime Isless."

Raek let out an incredulous laugh. "That's absurd! I've never even spoken to her!"

"I know," said Ard. "Someone was trying to set you up. I covered for you, and the Directorate seemed to accept it."

"I don't understand," Raek muttered. "Who would try to set me up?"

"Portsend Wal."

"Who?" he asked.

"Professor at Beripent's Southern Quarter College?" Ard probed.

"I don't know who that is."

"Well, he apparently knows you," said Ard. "Word has it that a big fellow named Raekon paid a visit to his Grit laboratory. He was looking for Health Grit."

Raek opened his mouth to say something, but closed it again. Ard could tell he was searching for the right words. But what would he do with them—come clean, or keep denying it?

"This is ridiculous," he muttered, turning for the exit. So, he'd just try to avoid this conversation altogether. Ard knew him well enough to anticipate that possibility. He stood up abruptly, hurling the small pot of Grit he had taken from one of Raek's shelves. It smashed against the door, erupting into a Barrier dome that sealed off the exit.

Raek whirled, his face an angry sneer. "What the blazes, Ard!"

"You know, it all makes sense," he began. "The sweats, the shakes... The way you've been slipping off without a word. You always seem to have it on hand."

He stalked toward the bigger man, who stood like a great immovable tree. "You knew Beska Falay because of the Heg. Maybe not her name, but when you saw her face, you got downright skittish. She raided your room the night she fled the guesthouse. Looking for Health Grit. The pinch you gave me to purge the poison wasn't from Beska. It came from *your* stash and it was Compounded to dangerous levels. It all makes perfect sense. There's only one thing I don't understand." They stood so close that Ard could feel Raek's breath coming fast and agitated. "Why didn't you tell me?"

Raek let out a bellow, his fist rising. Now it was Ard's turn to stand fast. He didn't think Raek would strike him—not out of rage like this. Still, he flinched as the chair beside him went careening across the room from Raek's blow.

"What could you have done, Ard?" he yelled. "Why would I tell you?"

"This isn't your fault!" Ard shouted back. "Listen to me. What they did to you in the palace..." He took a deep breath and lowered his voice. "I can help you. I can fix this."

*Homeland knows it's my fault that you're in this situation in the first place.*

Raek closed his eyes and let out a sardonic chuckle. They stood in silence for a moment, and when Raek's eyes opened, Ard saw them shimmering.

"I've got to stop." His voice was soft. "It's not like I *want* to use it. Feels like someone else sometimes. Like someone else is moving me to buy the Heg, take the hits. Once I've got it in me, I feel right again, and it seems like the fixing happened so long ago. I'm in control and it's not a problem. Then it wears off and it takes me again and my feet are walking the same blazing routes..."

It'd been years since Ard had seen his friend cry—since the cycles following the death of his parents. Raek had always been the steady one, while Ard often wore his emotions on his billowy sleeve.

"I can help you," Ard said again. "This isn't something to be ashamed of. We can make sure you get the Health Grit you need to always feel your best."

"No!" he snapped. "If you want to help, then don't enable me! I need to *stop* using it. Didn't you hear what I just said? I have to stop, but at this point I honestly don't know if I can survive without it."

Ard sighed. "This is my fault."

"It's not always about you, Ard."

"You wouldn't have been stabbed if I hadn't dressed you up as a Paladin Visitant and paraded you in front of King Pethredote."

"I knew the risks," Raek said. "I've always known that hanging around with you was likely to get one of us killed."

"And it would have. But you cheated death."

"There are times when I wish I hadn't." Raek sniffed. "Times when I'm in the throes of the Heg and I can't think right and my whole body aches like I can almost feel his sword still inside me." His chin quivered slightly. "This isn't who I am."

"You're my brother." Ard reached up and gripped his muscled shoulder. "I'll take you any way you are."

Raek shook his head. "It isn't fair to you. It puts everything at risk."

"It's fine," Ard said. "I convinced the Directorate that you weren't working for the Prime Isless."

"But if I hadn't been going after the Heg, my name wouldn't have come up at all." He shrugged Ard's hand away. "And it's not just that. I don't have the focus I used to have. I either feel great, or I feel like a pile of slag. The stuff makes me careless, and I've fallen in with the types of people we've spent our whole careers avoiding."

"Like who?" Ard asked.

"Dealers, users..." he said. "People like Beska Falay. She stole every granule of Health Grit she could find in here."

"Did you have a lot of it?" Ard asked. "*Do* you have a lot of it?"

Raek reached into his pocket and pulled out two paper rolls with the ends twisted tightly. With a single quick motion, Ard swiped the items.

"How fast are you going through this stuff?"

"Depends on how Compounded it is. If it's Prolonged..." Raek drew a steadying breath. "Usually around eighty minutes a day."

"Eighty minutes a day!" Ard cried. *How have I been so blind to this?* "That's a cloud every, what, three hours? When have you been doing this? I've been with you for longer stretches than that and I haven't—"

"You wouldn't notice." Raek reached up and tapped his chest. Of course. Ard had seen him carry a contained detonation inside that wretched pipe.

"Honestly, I probably seem most like myself when a cloud's burning," Raek explained. "That's the problem with Heg. The villain comes out *after* the effects wear off—when I'm trying to go clean."

"So, one of these rolls will last you...?"

"About two days," he answered quietly. The shame in his voice twisted Ard's insides. The only thing Raek should have been ashamed of was sticking around with Ard after he'd brought this upon his friend.

"Okay." Ard pressed one of the rolls back into Raek's palm. "This one's going to last you *three* days."

Raek looked skeptical. "And then...what?"

"Then you get this one." Ard held up the second roll. "But it has to last you four days."

"You're *weaning* me?"

Ard nodded. "Like a little piglet."

Raek exhaled slowly. "You've always got a plan, don't you."

"Usually two or three." Ard tucked the paper wad of Health Grit into his pocket. "Now, it's time to clean out your stashes."

"Stashes?"

Ard punched him in the arm. "Are you serious about quitting, or not?"

Raek's eyes glazed for a moment and he seemed to teeter on the brink of decision. As if to tempt him to flee, the Barrier cloud that had been covering the door winked out.

Then he moved with abrupt, determined steps to the bookcase against the wall. Ard recognized many of the texts on the shelf— Grit mixing books that Raek had brought with him from their old apartment. His broad hand spanned the spines of all three volumes of *Necessary Combinations* and he pulled them aside. Reaching behind the books with his other hand, Raek produced a bundle of cloth the size of his fist.

Before he could have second thoughts, Ard seized the parcel. The bookcase was quickly accessible, but not the clever hiding spot he would expect from Raekon Dorrel.

"And the rest of it?" Ard said expectantly.

Raek nodded, looking almost pleased that Ard hadn't let him off so easily. He crossed to a padded armchair and lifted one of the decorative pillows. His knife flashed from its sheath and he sliced through the fine fabric, sending downy feathers floating across the room like whispers of morning fog.

"Been hiding it better since Beska cleaned me out," Raek explained, digging into the flayed pillow and coming up with a little leather drawstring bag. He tossed it to Ard, who was surprised to feel how bulging it was. How many rolls did Raek have? This must have cost him a fortune!

"That's all I've got here," he said with a definitive tone.

*Here?* They knew each other too well, and Raek was too careful to expect Ard to miss that. "All right. Now, where's your secret stash?"

"Outside." Raek headed for the door. "You know that statue over the front door of the guesthouse?"

"That big mossy dragon?"

"Yeah." He grinned. "I hid some up its nose."

Quarrah thought she'd be the first one to the Whispering Pines for this afternoon's rehearsal. She'd been out on the streets all morning, following up on a few leads regarding the Agaul family ring.

The Regulation claimed not to have the emerald jewelry, despite the fact that she remembered turning it over to them when she was arrested. It didn't take much to deduce that the Realm had confiscated it at the same time they'd sprung her from the Outpost. That meant finding the ring could give her a clue as to the identity behind someone in a Realm mask.

It wasn't an avenue of investigation she was sharing with Ard. He had no idea that she'd stolen it in the first place, and he was too close to Lady Abeth. Besides, finding the ring on her own would give her a chance to sell it to the highest bidder.

She opened the tavern door and stopped in surprise to see Ard, Elbrig, and Cinza already settled in to the musty room. As usual, the yellowed curtains were drawn over the windows, filtering sunlight into more of a soft evening glow.

"Ah, Quarrah!" Ard clapped his hands in delight at the sight of her. "Were your ears burning?"

"No," she answered, closing the door behind her. "I was going to put my feet up for an hour or two before the rehearsal started."

"Well, I'm glad you're here," he continued enthusiastically. "I wanted to call a meeting, but I don't have any way of contacting you..."

"By design," she said, glancing around the room. "Where's Raek?"

"He's coming," Ard said. "Meeting with the shipwright probably went a little long."

*Or he's out buying Heg.* "Did you talk to him?"

"Of course." Ard tried to look casual, but she could see that he was still shaken from the revelation at the Directorate meeting.

"And?"

"I'm handling it," he responded. "Raek's been through worse. He will be fine."

Quarrah tried not to scoff. How very Ardor Benn of him, to think he was "handling" Raek's problem.

"I just told Cinza and Elbrig that Overseer moved up our time-line," he continued.

"I'm not sure the crew will be ready," said Elbrig. "Although Yalan and Ruge have shown significant improvement lately."

"Now, if only we could get Quarrah Khai to speak," Cinza chimed in; she was seated at one of the pushed-aside tavern tables, putting stitches into a large bolt of fabric rolled out in front of her.

"I speak when I want to," she answered sharply.

"You're doing great, Quarrah," said Ard.

Sometimes it felt as if no time had passed between them at all. Back at it again, side by side under the tutelage of the disguise managers. Maybe it was the way he said her name, a look of total sincerity in his eyes. Her feelings for him, so distant and cold, sometimes threatened to come to a boil, like a kettle whistling on the stovetop. But she remembered getting burned by the steam, and Quarrah had built her whole life around learning from her mistakes.

"I was showing these two some of the Realm's new developments." Ard moved around the bar and retrieved the small wooden box that they had all been issued at the end of the Directorate meeting. "I'm not sure I'm remembering the colors right." He pointed at each one as he rattled off the list. "Stasis, Gather, Ignition—"

"Ignition is green," Quarrah corrected him.

Ard shrugged. "How do they expect us to keep all of them straight?"

"The code is written on the underside of the lid." Quarrah

stepped closer and flipped it over. But she didn't need the code to remember what that green vial could do.

"Anyway," Ard resumed. "Here's Null, Weight, and Containment Grit. I showed them to Raek this morning and he started tinkering right away. These vials do stuff I've never seen Grit do."

"Hmm." Cinza paused in her stitching long enough to spread the bolt across the table so the others could see how it was shaping up. "Do you think this circle's big enough?"

Quarrah didn't let herself react to Cinza's feigned disinterest in something as earth-shattering as new types of Grit. The strange woman thrived on shock and awe, so Quarrah simply stepped closer to inspect her project.

It was clearly a large flag, the top half blue and the bottom green, with a plain gold circle in the center. The stitching was precise. "It looks rather plain," Quarrah said.

Cinza hissed at her like a cat and pulled the fabric away as if Quarrah might spit on it. "It's not about complexity. It's about symbolism." Her voice was pouty. "Isn't that right, Ardy?"

"Right." Ard pointed. "The blue represents the sky, and the green... well, that's the color of the Islehood robes. It represents the sea, and people here already associate it with holiness. The circle is actually the symbol of the Homeland."

"I thought it was the anchor," said Quarrah.

"That's for Wayfarism," Ard corrected. "Raek found a nice little verse on that list of scriptures. Apparently, the Islehood considered the Homeland circle too sacred to display, so they went with the anchor instead. But we're going to fly that circle high. That flag's going to be the icing on the top of our ship, Cinza," Ard said in praise. "And I'm beginning to think there's nothing you're not good at."

"Obeying the law," she replied, diving back in with her long needle.

The tavern door suddenly opened and Raek appeared, a smile

on his wide face. Nothing had visibly changed about the man, but Quarrah thought he seemed a little different now that she and Ard knew about his addiction. Perhaps it was an air of relief, like a permanent sigh at not having to maintain the secret anymore.

"Ladies and gentlemen," Raek said, holding something delicately in his huge hands. "I give you the *Holy Breath*."

He set the item down on top of Cinza's flag, and Quarrah saw that it was a model ship. The whole vessel was no longer than Raek's forearm, but the detail was rich, with rectangles of white sailcloth billowing along the single mast.

The similarities between the model and a standard clipper ended there, however. For starters, the vessel was nearly round, like a raft. Still, it had the high bulwarks of a traditional sailing ship, and an extra-large keel along the bottom. Instead of individual planks, the entire thing looked to be sculpted out of white clay and sealed with something that made it look durable and glossy. The whole design seemed highly impractical at sea, but it would fit the extravagance of Ard's ruse.

Quarrah squinted at the back of the model, where the words the *Holy Breath* were painted in scrolling gold letters. "Are we sure about the name?"

"Picked it myself," Ard said. "You don't like it?"

She shrugged. "Just sounds sort of..." She breathed out in an exasperated sigh.

"It's supposed to evoke images of a holy wind filling her sails and bearing her from the Homeland," Ard explained.

"The real thing's looking good," reported Raek. "Might even have her ready by Overseer's new deadline."

"Great," said Ard. "Now we've just got to figure out how to get this thing clear out into the eastern sea without anyone noticing." He picked up the model ship. "Where is she now?"

"Under a massive tent in the Western Quarter. Not a mile from the harbor there."

"We can't launch from a harbor," said Quarrah. All of Beripent's were on the InterIsland Waters side. "That would be far too conspicuous."

"Then what are we supposed to do?" asked Ard. "Throw the ship off the edge of a cliff?"

"Maybe," said Raek. "We could lower it down to the water through a chain of overlapping Drift clouds. That's actually fairly common practice for moving large vessels to the water after construction."

"But we'd need to put her down on the easternmost side of Espar," said Ard. "That means we'd have to transport an eight-person clipper all the way across Beripent and another day's journey out of town without anyone seeing it." He shook his head. "I can't even think of enough streets that would be wide enough to accommodate it, let alone the attention we would draw moving it."

"Maybe we could dismantle the ship," suggested Quarrah. "Take it across town in pieces and rebuild her on the east side."

"Not with the clay finish they're sealing her with," Raek said. "Besides, sailing would be easier and faster than taking her over land."

"The way around Beripent is one of the busiest sailing routes," Quarrah noted. "And if we take her too far out, everyone in Talumon will see her. We're talking about sailing this bizarre ship between the two largest cities in the Greater Chain without anyone noticing."

"Remind me why we didn't have the shipwright build her on the east side of Espar in the first place?" asked Raek.

"That's on Ard," Quarrah shot. "He claimed we'd never have to actually set sail once the Realm gave us what we wanted." She didn't dare specifically mention the prince in front of Elbrig and Cinza.

"That was the plan!" Ard defended. "How was I supposed to know that Overseer would unexpectedly change it?"

"I thought you were priding yourself on the fact that this ruse *could* actually be successful if we had to pull it off," continued Quarrah.

"That was before I knew we'd have to pull it off!"

"Wait." Elbrig cut in. "You never actually planned to execute this ruse?"

Cinza threw down her needle and thread. "Then what the blazes am I sewing this for?"

Ard held up his hands as if trying to retake control of the situation. "This doesn't change anything. You two are still getting paid. And now we *will* be going through with it. So it's a good thing we had our ducks in a row."

"I'd say our ducks are staggering, at best," said Raek.

"Let's hope they stagger all the way to the eastern sea," Cinza remarked, resuming her needlework.

"What if we hide the ship in a detonation of Shadow Grit?" suggested Ard. "Nobody will notice a cloud of darkness on the water in the middle of the night."

"That might have worked a few years ago," Raek said. "But wartime is different. We'll have a hard enough time avoiding the searchlights of the shoreline patrol while getting the ship down to the water. That route will be swarming with lights from the Archkingdom and the Sovs."

"What if we had another ship—an ordinary ship—tow it out to the eastern sea?" said Quarrah. "We could cover the *Holy Breath* until we get into position. Then the towing vessel heads back to Espar while we wait a few hours and follow them in."

"That's a good idea," said Ard.

"Towing vessels are the first to get searched in the route between Talumon and Espar," Raek countered. "Especially if we've bundled up our load nice and suspiciously."

"What if they couldn't see it?" Ard suggested.

"You're back to the Shadow Grit?" said Raek. "They're going to spot the cloud—"

"Not Shadow Grit," Ard said. "What if the ship was *underwater*?"

Sparks. Did the man have to say things so dramatically?

"You want to scuttle it?" Raek cried. "We'd never be able to raise it once we reach open water. And there'd be no telling what shape it'd be in at that point."

"Maybe we could protect it somehow," said Ard. "Like a ship in a bottle." He touched the rounded prow of the model vessel thoughtfully.

"With Barrier Grit?" Cinza asked.

"It doesn't work that way," Elbrig countered.

"What about the *new* Barrier Grit?" Ard asked. "What did Glint call it... *Containment* Grit?"

Quarrah nodded. "She said it's as impenetrable as Barrier Grit, but it's movable. Even when it's spherical."

"Even if you could move a Barrier cloud—" said Elbrig.

"Containment cloud," Raek corrected.

"It would still float," the disguise manager continued as if he hadn't been interrupted. "A ship in a bottle is going to float."

"Unless the ship is ridiculously heavy," Ard proposed with a knowing smirk.

Raek snapped his fingers. "Weight Grit!" He crossed to Ard's little wooden box on the bar and took out a blue vial. "It'll increase the weight of the ship without compromising its structural integrity. And the Containment Grit can enclose the Weight cloud to make them movable—like a Drift crate without the box."

Ard smiled. "And the *Holy Breath* is safe within a watertight bubble below the surface."

"Won't that be like an anchor for the towing ship?" Quarrah asked.

"An anchor only works if it hits bottom," Raek said, "which is pretty much limited to the harbors. The InterIsland Waters are too deep to drop anchor."

"Really, Raekon," Cinza scolded. "The whole ship is just supposed to drag along underwater?"

Raek nodded. "The real trick will be making it heavy enough to pull the Barrier bubble down, but not so heavy that it sinks the tow ship. Ideally, the *Holy Breath* will sit about fifteen feet under the surface. There'll be a lot of drag resistance, but a good tow ship is built for that."

Raek pursed his lips in thought. "I'll need to do some experimenting with the model." He quickly counted the vials in the box. "Any chance you can get more of these?"

"I can donate my supply," offered Quarrah. After the Ignition Grit fiasco at the war front, she'd been hesitant to experiment with her allotment of liquid Grit from the Realm. Besides, now they needed to pour all their resources into making sure this ruse would work.

"And Overseer said we could leave requests for more at the Old Post Lighthouse," added Ard. "So, we've got nine days to figure this out. That ship has to make berth in the North Central Harbor on the evening of the twenty-eighth."

"Why did Overseer assign that date?" Elbrig asked.

"There's a royal reception going on at the palace," explained Ard. "We're supposed to drop in and impress everyone—including Prime Isless Gloristar."

"And eat your fill of those little cheese-and-herb balls you were always carrying on about," said Raek. "This time I expect you to smuggle me a plate of your favorites."

"Slices of glazed bacon..." Ard said wistfully. "Those apple fritters..."

"All right, you two," Quarrah cut in. "The Homelanders don't feel hunger or thirst, remember?"

"But we can still eat for the novelty of it," Ard replied. "Elbrig said so."

"Just don't get drunk," Elbrig reminded him.

"Let's reiterate that to the crew when they get here," said Ard. "Although the more I think about it, the more I'm counting on alcohol to lubricate this ruse. We'll need to arrive at the reception late, giving the patrons plenty of time to have one drink too many."

"I hear Termain makes a habit of that at social functions," Cinza said.

"Good," replied Ard. "The king will be setting the tone for the other nobles. He'll be that much easier to convince if he has a hard time walking straight."

"It's Gloristar I'm worried about," said Quarrah. "The Prime Isless doesn't need to impress the king, and she's not likely to get drunk."

"And like it or not, her opinion on the Homelanders might hold more weight than the king's," Raek added.

"If only you had people planted at the reception," Elbrig said with overt wistfulness. "Influential people who could quickly buy in to the Homelanders and help sway the other patrons."

Ard's jaw actually dropped. "Are you . . . I thought Lorstan Grale retired!"

Oh, that *was* worth dropping a jaw! Lorstan Grale had been the conductor of the Royal Orchestra throughout the latter years of Pethredote's rule. By the sound of it, Elbrig was offering to dust off that disguise.

"Well, he didn't *die!*" Elbrig stated. "But old Lorstan is living quite luxuriously in a country villa in central Espar. He won't be making the trip up to Beripent for free."

Ard smiled, clapping his hands in excitement. "Name his price."

"Six hundred."

"Come on, Elbrig," Ard cried. "That's a gouge, and you know it. I think I could talk my employer into two."

"Five hundred."

"Maybe three."

"Four hundred Ashings," Elbrig said. "And we'll throw Cinza in as a server."

"I'm not going as a server," she croaked, going cross-eyed on a stitch. "And you don't 'throw me in' anywhere, Elby." Cinza cleared her throat. "I'll be going as the entertainment. I've got a burlesque dancer—"

"It's not that kind of party," Ard interrupted, but not before Quarrah shuddered at the mental image.

"Fine," Cinza spat. "I'll squeeze into a gown and go as someone boring. But it'll cost you two hundred. And that's a bargain, because I like you, Ardy."

"All right," Ard gave in. "I'll talk to my employer."

Quarrah caught a wink between the disguise managers. Surely, Ard realized he'd just been played, ultimately agreeing to pay the first amount Elbrig had proposed.

"We'll do everything in our power to turn the reception in your favor," Elbrig promised. "But every element of your ruse needs to come together flawlessly. The crew has to be convincing."

"We can't make peach pie out of potatoes," seconded Cinza.

"Paver Boret is definitely a potato right now," Elbrig muttered.

Ard grunted in frustration. "Oh, what if this doesn't work?"

"Whoa! What happened to Mister Confidence?" Raek heckled, calling him on his uncharacteristic pessimism. "A moment ago, you were bragging that the ruse had always been designed to be successful."

"Still, what if it's not enough?"

"What more can we do?" Quarrah asked. The ruse couldn't possibly get more complex. They'd touched on everything— appearance, dialect, food, transportation...

"We need one more element," Ard mused. "Something to make our arrival undeniably momentous."

"We've already got that outlandish ship, which we're supposed to sink and tow underwater." Quarrah pointed to the model. "How could you make it any more impressive?"

Ard smiled, a roguish idea twinkling in his eye. "We make it fly."

~

*When the unchanged settle to such terrible depths, they will be greeted by our words.*

# CHAPTER

# 32

The *Holy Breath* looked even more bizarre at full size. Quarrah stared at the strange ship under the construction tent, orbs of Light Grit illuminating the crew as they nailed large canvas coverings over the hull to conceal its unique finish.

Quarrah knew there were a lot of ways this could go wrong. For starters, the mast would have to be erected once at sea, since it was currently strapped onto the deck for ease of transport.

The shipwright ran past, shouting at one of the crew members, who must have been doing something wrong. What did she expect? These were ruse artists—actors—not true sailors. Most people in the Greater Chain had *some* sailing experience, and the return journey in the *Holy Breath* would be short, with favorable winds. Quarrah had her reservations about taking the ship skyward, but Ard was convinced it would work.

"You ready to see our ship in a bottle?" Ard asked, coming

alongside her. There was a bit of sweat on his forehead, but she couldn't figure out why. Ardor Benn rarely did the pulling and lifting. Like the shipwright, he'd mostly been racing around directing everyone else.

"How's Raek?" she asked.

"He's excited to put his calculations to the test," said Ard. "Worked perfectly on the model every time we tried it."

"I mean, how is he *today*?" asked Quarrah.

Ard studied his friend as Raek tinkered with a keg of Grit. "He's been six days on the last roll I gave him. Clearheaded as ever. We'll be fine."

In the nine days since Ard had confronted him, Quarrah hadn't noticed much of a difference in Raek. If he'd been tapering off the Heg like Ard claimed, shouldn't he be showing more signs of withdrawal? She had a sneaking suspicion of what that meant, but Ard obviously wanted to feign naivety for now.

"Stand ready!" Raek called from the covered deck of the *Holy Breath*. He bent down and tugged the ignition pin on the keg. The powder detonated, enveloping the entire ship in a huge cloud of Drift Grit.

Raek, whose feet had come off the deck, grabbed onto the bulwark and angled himself toward Quarrah and Ard, floating lazily until he tumbled through the perimeter and scrambled to his feet.

"Pull the supports!" he shouted to the crew.

Quarrah watched the shipwright and all six members of the Homeland crew pull at a series of ropes from outside the perimeter of the Drift cloud. The construction frame beneath the *Holy Breath*'s hull ripped free, support bucks spinning through the cloud until they exited, falling heavily to the packed earth.

"You ready for this?" Raek asked quietly. A small glass jar full of red liquid appeared in his big hand. With careful precision, he lobbed it onto the deck of the floating ship. Quarrah heard the glass shatter, and a new cloud sprung up to surround the vessel.

"Containment Grit—not your mother's Barrier Grit." Raek stepped forward and patted the transparent shell. "Behold the Drift crate of the future. The container is weightless, transparent, and indestructible."

They had requested more liquid Grit by leaving a coded note at the Old Post Lighthouse. When Ard had checked back two days later, a large box had been waiting in the holding room at the light-house's base.

Ard moved next to his partner, rubbing a hand across the smooth surface. "If only it had handles."

As if in response to Ard's statement, Raek barked another command to the crew. "Poles ready!"

Keel and Garew moved into position at the ship's stern, Palia and Yalan on the left, with Ruge and Paver on the right. They each carried a long pole, the tips dressed with bundled rags to improve traction as they pressed them against the transparent shell of the Containment cloud.

"Forward!" Raek bellowed.

Garew and Keel leaned into their poles with apparently little effort and Quarrah took a deep breath as the ship moved forward. The *Holy Breath* stayed upright in its Drift cloud, swaying this way and that, knocking gently against the hard Containment shell as it passed through the tent's enormous opening and into the darkness.

"Now, that's not something you see every day," Ard muttered.

But it probably would be in time. Raek had been right. This was the future of Grit. Drift crates would soon be obsolete. Light Grit lanterns, too. Those items had been developed to contain Grit clouds so they could be moved. Now they had a Barrier cloud that was itself mobile. What kind of genius was this Portsend Wal?

Quarrah, Ard, and Raek followed a few yards behind the ship, the crew members using their poles to nudge the Containment cloud from all directions to keep it moving forward. They didn't expect many onlookers in the dark of the early morning. Even if someone did see, floating ships across land wasn't entirely uncommon. Only, it was usually done through a series of overlapping traditional Drift clouds.

"Do you think they'll display this ship in front of the Mooring when we're finished with her?" Raek asked. "Folks'll come from miles around to see the magnificent Homelander vessel."

"Unless we smash her to kindling," Quarrah remarked, distracted by the way the tall grasses flattened in the wake of the Containment cloud. She couldn't tell if the sphere was actually rolling or just sliding forward.

"Our ship-in-a-bottle trick is going to work perfectly," Raek assured her.

"That's not the part I'm worried about."

"Quarrah doesn't want to fly her," Ard cut in.

"It's excessive," she retorted. "Excessively dangerous. Won't we be convincing enough in our awful Homelander getup?"

"There's no such thing as *convincing enough*," replied Ard. "Besides, you've ridden the Trans-Island Carriage System."

"Don't try to tell me it's the same thing," Quarrah snapped. "Those carriages were built for flight. This is a boat." She pointed at the strange vessel rolling forward. "I'm not even sure it's built for water."

"We made some modifications for flying," Raek said, trying to reassure her. "Attached additional sails designed specifically to catch an updraft once you're in the air."

*Special little sails. Ha!* That hardly made her feel better. And why hadn't she been informed of the addition? She sighed. There was probably a lot of valuable information she could learn if she were only willing to spend extra time with Ardor Benn. But for the most part, she had limited herself to seeing him only at rehearsals with the rest of the crew.

"And Raek triple-checked the calculations and measurements we need to lift off once Beripent comes into view," said Ard.

His comment wasn't any more reassuring, although Quarrah actually had great confidence in Raek's work.

Raek's attention suddenly shifted and he sprinted ahead, shouting, "Ease off! Don't let her go over the edge!"

Quarrah followed Ard over to the clifftop as Keel and Garew stopped pushing the Containment cloud. The spherical detonation, along with its housed clipper, came to a halt almost like a ball rolling to a stop.

"The *Iron Arm* is almost in place." Ard pointed to the InterIsland Waters far below.

Quarrah could see the lights on the tow ship as it moved toward their position. Cinza and Elbrig would be onboard with a crew of street Hands who knew the Realm codes. They'd tow them across the busy route between Espar and Talumon and eastward to the sea, bringing up the *Holy Breath* once they were beyond sight of the islands. The disguise managers would then paint and costume the crew before sailing back to Beripent hours ahead of the Homeland vessel.

"Do you have a spare bit of Light Grit?" Ard asked, patting his pockets. "I need to signal the tow ship."

She produced a little tea bag from a pocket on her thigh. "Why didn't you bring one?"

He took the Grit. "Must have forgotten. There was a lot to pack." Ard clapped his hands, catching the tea bag in the impact between his palms. The Slagstone sparked and the resulting Light cloud was no bigger than his fist. Ard passed the flat of his hand back and forth in front of the glowing orb to signal the ship below.

"Besides," he remarked, "I knew you'd be prepared."

Raek ambled over to them, cursing. "Blazing nitwits nearly pushed her over the edge!"

Quarrah looked back at the *Holy Breath*. It was now resting in the dirt at the cliff's edge, the clouds of Drift and Containment Grit extinguished.

"Isn't that the plan?" Quarrah asked.

"Well, yes. But not until we're ready." He glanced down at the *Iron Arm* as one of the ship's lights blinked in response to Ard's signal. Then he turned back to the *Holy Breath*. "Throw the ropes!"

Paver, Keel, Ruge, and Yalan scrambled onto the ship, carefully walking out to the prow, which was hanging precariously several feet over the edge of the cliff. In a moment, they had heaved two great lengths of thick rope over the bulwark, letting them uncoil as they stretched down to the water below.

"Quarrah?" Raek said. "I wondered if you could do the honors." He held out a Slagstone ignitor. "It's all in place midship. You'll just need to ride the floating ship out over the edge, light the fuse, and jump back over to us before the liquid Grit ignites."

"Me?" Wouldn't Raek want to detonate his own carefully crafted chain of liquid Grit jars?

"There's no debating who's the best Drift jumper in the group," Ard said, the sincerity in his voice causing her cheeks to flush. "And we need an expert. If you don't get out before the Grit ignites, you'll be trapped inside the bubble and sink with the ship."

Good thing she was an expert, then. Quarrah pocketed the Slagstone ignitor and followed Raek around the *Holy Breath*. The others had just climbed down from the vessel as Garew detonated a fresh cloud of Drift Grit. This one encompassed the ship, and Quarrah saw that it overlapped a second Drift cloud already hanging in place beyond the edge of the cliff.

"All aboard." Raek gestured for her to take her place on the ship. Quarrah inched up to the perimeter of the Drift cloud, crouching with her toes just inside. Then she sprang like a pouncing cat, angling her body and using her momentum to soar through the weightless cloud.

Her hands reached out, gripping the rail and using it to steady herself before pushing off and drifting toward the middle of the ship.

She saw the jars immediately, each made of opaque clay like the material of a regular Grit pot. A length of fuse ran between each one, intended to set them off at regular intervals to keep the Grit effects safely overlapping.

Although she couldn't see the careful mix of liquids, she knew what the jars contained. Weight Grit would make the ship heavy enough to sink, and Containment Grit would enclose the detonation and protect the vessel from the surrounding water. Raek had also mentioned Prolonging Grit, stretching the effects of the Weight and Containment for as long as possible before the Barrier-like shell would start taking water.

"The *Iron Arm* signaled again," Ard called in report. "They have the ropes."

"You ready, Quarrah?" asked Raek from below.

"Ready!" she answered.

The *Holy Breath* suddenly lurched as the crew members used their poles to push the vessel over the edge of the cliff. This time, the two overlapping Drift clouds were stationary, and the ship slid out of one and into the other.

Crouched midship, clinging to the canvas covering the deck, Quarrah couldn't see over the edge, but she knew the *Holy Breath* was now hovering in midair, some sixty feet above the InterIsland Waters.

The ship jolted to a halt, and Quarrah cast a glance back to see Ruge and Palia holding another rope that had stopped the *Holy Breath* from floating through the other side of the cloud.

"Okay, Quarrah!" Raek shouted. "Let's get that ship into the bottle!"

Quarrah turned her attention back to the jars. She found the loose end of the fuse and pulled the Slagstone ignitor from her pocket. She sent sparks dancing across the deck, but it took three strikes to finally ignite the fuse, which burned brightly in the night, smoking and hissing.

*Time to get out of here.* She remembered Ard's warning about getting trapped in the bubble. Quarrah got her feet down and looked back to the clifftop. This was a bigger jump than she'd done in a long time. If she didn't get the angle right, she could risk hitting the rocks and plummeting to the InterIsland Waters. And she doubted Elbrig and Cinza would care enough to fish her out.

Drawing a deep breath, she aligned her trajectory and kicked off the deck, speeding horizontally toward the people waiting on the clifftop.

Her hands came forward, bracing for impact against the hard earth. But it was never a good idea to completely stop her momentum with her hands—that could break wrists. Instead, she merely used her hands to flip herself forward when she touched the dirt, bearing the brunt of the impact on her shoulders. Her back slammed against the ground and she bounced once before exiting the cloud and rolling through her momentum.

Ard was immediately there to help her up, but she leapt agilely to her feet. She'd just jumped forty feet. Why would she need help standing up?

"That was incredible," Ard said, in an effort to compliment her. "I would have hit the cliff nine times out of ten."

She didn't respond to the praise, but she absorbed it nonetheless. Wordlessly, Quarrah turned back to the ship in time to see the first jar of liquid Grit detonate. At once, the *Holy Breath* was surrounded by a transparent bubble of Containment Grit. Raek waved his hand through the signaling Light Grit and the ship began a slow descent toward the water.

"Didn't the Weight Grit take?" Quarrah asked. "Why is it falling so slowly?"

"That first jar had only Containment Grit," Raek explained. "It captured the Drift Grit and made the whole thing lightweight enough for the *Iron Arm* to draw it down with the tow ropes."

"We're trying to avoid kindling, remember?" said Ard.

Quarrah nodded in understanding. A ship weighing hundreds of thousands of panweights wouldn't likely survive a sixty-foot drop, even inside an impenetrable bubble.

"They'll pull it down to the surface," Raek continued. "After it's been afloat for a few minutes, the next jar will detonate. That one will have the Weight Grit it needs to sink our ship in a bottle."

Flames. Ard and Raek really had thought of everything. Maybe this ruse *did* have a chance at succeeding, after all.

The shipwright approached, her wiry figure stepping between Ard and Quarrah. "Can't say I'm not curious about what you fellows are up to with my ship," she said. "But I've done enough work for this employer to realize that I'll live longer if I don't know the details. You got the rest of my payment?"

Ard produced a bag of Ashings and handed it to her. "Our employer thanks you for your good work."

The shipwright cast one more glance at the *Holy Breath*, which was now bobbing on the water next to the *Iron Arm*. Then she vanished into the early-morning darkness, heading back in the direction of the construction tent.

"It astounds me how many people are working for the Realm," Ard said. "Do you feel like we were the only two criminals in Beripent that didn't know about this organization?"

The thought *had* crossed Quarrah's mind. "They don't necessarily know it's the Realm," she said. "I've done plenty of jobs for employers who put codes and passphrases in place."

"Well, so have I," Ard was quick to add.

"Did it ever cross your mind that one of those jobs might have been for the Realm?" she followed up. It wasn't very often that Quarrah said something to elicit pure surprise from Ardor Benn. But she could tell by the look on his face that he hadn't considered this before. He probably took it as a blow that one of his highly creative ruses could have been little more than an assignment for a lowly street Hand.

"There she goes," Raek said, looking over the edge.

Quarrah glanced down to the water just in time to see the *Holy Breath* plunge out of sight, fiercely rocking the *Iron Arm* in the waves of displaced water.

*Hopefully, that's not our entire ruse sinking,* Quarrah thought. There was a lot depending on that fuse chain of liquid Grit jars. She knew the final jar wouldn't contain any Weight Grit, causing the Containment bubble to instantly float to the surface. Once the ship's hull was above water, they'd hit it with a detonation of Null Grit to extinguish the bubble and set it floating like a natural ship.

"You ready?" Ard stepped up to the edge of the cliff.

"We're not jumping," Quarrah snapped. This whole experience was starting to become reminiscent of the time they encased a Slagstone in ice and threw it over the cliff to steal it from Pekal.

"Not unless you want to die," said Ard. "The *Double Take* is in the Western Harbor. We'll all pile aboard and shuttle out to the *Iron Arm.*" He smiled at her. "It's time to set sail for the Homeland."

<hr/>

*All this time, we have been concealed before their very eyes. And when they behold us at last, we will be upon them.*

# CHAPTER

# 33

The last colors of sunset had faded from the sky as the *Holy Breath* flew high above North Central Harbor.

Ard adjusted his golden sandaled feet in the stirrups that kept him anchored to the circular deck, the weightlessness of the Drift cloud otherwise threatening to float him over the edge. Quarrah stood rooted not arm's length away, the thick strands of her hair flouncing like lazy snakes beside her painted face.

Cinza and Elbrig had done an impeccable job costuming the eight crew members, obsessing over the thickness of the paint and the position of the artificial facial features. Then they'd clamored onto the *Iron Arm* and sailed back toward Beripent several hours ahead of the *Holy Breath*.

"They're not going to shoot," Keel Belu's statement was almost a question. "Not the cannons, at least."

"Just like I told you," Ard said. If he'd learned anything from the Trothian attack against the Pekal harbors, it was that mounted cannons were not equipped for overhead threats. And Fielder balls would ping off their impenetrable Containment shell with little impact.

The *Holy Breath* had sailed normally until the harbor was in sight. Then the crew had executed the precise launching maneuver that Raek had calculated on the miniature model ship.

It was the same technique that lifted a Trans-Island Carriage— a highly Compounded cloud of Heat Grit lifting a vessel whose weight was minimized by Drift Grit. The only real difference was that Containment Grit had been used to trap the clouds instead of a wooden box and a sailcloth balloon. Once they'd reached the desired altitude, Null Grit had been used to extinguish the Heat cloud. They'd unfurled the *Holy Breath*'s sails, catching the wind and pushing them forward as if they were still on the water.

"We'll need to drop altitude or we'll sail right over the palace," called Garew from his position on the mast.

"I'd rather be too high than too low," Ard shouted back. Adjustments in every other direction were working well, but the updraft sails hadn't been quite as effective as they'd hoped.

"How long do we have to stay at the reception?" Quarrah asked at his side. Her tone made it sound as if she wasn't having any fun sailing above Beripent's Western Quarter.

"The crew is welcome to linger as late as they'd like," answered Ard, "with the understanding that they don't get drunk or go home with anyone. But I believe you and I have an appointment beside the palace fishing pond at ten o'clock."

"So we're just supposed to slip away?" Quarrah said. "We're going to be the most watched people at this lousy reception."

"I thought slipping away was your specialty," Ard retorted. He let it hang, but she didn't reply. "They're going to offer a place for the Homelanders to stay," he continued. "Likely in the palace. We can ask to retire early. We sneak into the garden at ten, throw on our masks, and give our report to Overseer."

"Assuming our masks are in place," Quarrah said.

"They'll be there," Ard replied. For an additional twenty Ashings, Elbrig and Cinza had promised to place their masks and two cloaks near the statue of a stag just a hundred yards south of the fishing pond.

"We're drifting too far to starboard," called Yalan Steir from the prow, a spyglass to his eye and a compass in his shiny hand.

"Run out some Void Grit along the starboard yardarm pipe," ordered Ard.

Inspired in part by Raek's "chimney," they had attached long pipes protruding out all sides of the ship. When the Containment cloud had closed them in, the tip of the mast and these pipes extended just inches beyond the protective shell.

Ard watched as Keel Belu fed a pot of Void Grit into the yardarm pipe, using a rod to ram it down the length. The pot exited on the right side of the ship, just outside the Containment wall. It sparked on the pipe's end, igniting a forceful detonation that pushed against the shell, nudging them back on course.

The *Holy Breath* lurched and Ard caught Quarrah's arm for

stability. He didn't let go, and surprisingly she didn't pull away, even after the vessel had stabilized.

"I haven't decided if I'm coming back to the palace after we report to Overseer," Quarrah said quietly.

Ard glanced at her to see if she was serious. Her face barely looked familiar with those prosthetic enhancements ringing her yellowed eyes. He let go of her arm.

"That's not an option, Quarrah. If one of the Homelanders goes missing, it could erode the entire ruse."

"I agreed to be a Homelander because I originally thought we'd be coming in *after* the Cataclysm," she argued. "This was supposed to be a temporary gig. Drop off the prince, show our golden faces, and get the sparks out of there."

"It's still temporary," Ard said. "I'm not asking you to be a Homelander permanently."

Quarrah shut her eyes. "For how long, exactly?"

Ard could tell she was already feeling trapped. This was shaping up to be Azania Fyse and Dale Hizror all over again, only this time with golden skin and a flying ship.

"Four days until the Cataclysm," Ard responded. "Once the Realm hands us the prince, we'll be free to wash off this paint for good. Until then, we get to enjoy the hospitality of the palace. You probably won't even have to leave your room if you don't want to."

"Palace is directly ahead," announced Yalan, lowering the spyglass with a rakish grin. "We've got a lot of fancy folks waiting for us on that balcony."

"They've spotted us?" checked Paver Boret.

"Oh, yes," answered Yalan. "Lots of pointing and waving."

Ard and Quarrah shared a quick glance. Sounded like Elbrig and Cinza had already started their job.

"Well, they'd better get their oversized bustles out of the way," replied Ruge Harban. "Don't they know they're standing on our dock?"

"Everyone in character from here on," Ard instructed. He noticed an almost immediate change in all of them—posture stiffened, demeanors refined. Except for Quarrah, who muttered some disparaging remark about the absurd complexity of the ruse.

By the time they were close enough for Ard to see the large balcony, the wealthy reception-goers had been replaced by a row of red-uniformed Regulators, thin swords glinting between loaded Rollers.

Paver and Palia had been making subtle adjustments to the sails, and now the ship was barely inching forward. Still, Ard knew that the stone wall of the palace was going to have to serve as a backstop. Hopefully, that didn't cause too much damage...to the building.

They were right over the balcony now, the ship's bottom maybe fifteen feet above the heads of the Regulators below.

"Fall back!" came the shout, the command accompanied by the noisy interjections of the rich and royal.

The Containment shell surrounding the *Holy Breath* slammed into the palace wall, and Ard saw two of the detonation pipes snap off at the prow. Quarrah grabbed Ard's arm this time, and the two of them fought to stay upright, all while trying to maintain an air of perfection.

Before the protected ship could bounce away from the wall, Garew launched a pot of Void Grit up the mast, the overhead blast pushing them straight downward. There was another rough jolt as the ship touched down, signaling Ruge to smash a vial of Null Grit against the deck.

At once, the Containment and Drift clouds extinguished. The full weight of the *Holy Breath* rest upon the large balcony, and Ard heard the stone crack.

Well, that would certainly put the ruse to a quick end, with all of the supposed Homelanders crashing to the grounds below in a heap of timbers and stone.

*Better get off quickly.* Ard slipped his feet out of the stirrups, pulling away from Quarrah as he swiftly glide-stepped across the deck.

"Greetings!" he called, emphasizing the last syllable in Elbrig's invented Homelander dialect. He counted a dozen armed Regulators standing in the open doorway that led from the balcony into the reception hall. The patrons were crowded behind the false security of the Reggies, breaking their necks to get a glimpse of what was happening.

"State your business!" shouted the chief. "Whose colors are those?"

*Really?* Ard thought. *A shipful of people who look like golden statues flies in, docks on your balcony, and you're worried about whose flag we're waving?*

"We bring peace and perfection," answered Ard, projecting the best he could. He didn't want to shout, but his voice needed to carry. "Many cycles upon the great sea have led us to you, lost dwellers in a land far-flung." That sounded appropriately Homelandish. "We are those who have gone before. We are the inhabitants of that holy place, the very aspiration of the believers. We are Homelanders."

Ardor Benn leapt from the bulwark, landing on an open portion of the balcony in a dramatic crouch. Head still bowed, his thick shoulder-length wig spilling around his face, Ard heard gun hammers clicking into place. Reaching up, he rapped sharply on the prosthetic pieces that rimmed his eye sockets. The Light Grit ignited on the first try, and Ard slowly rose.

With the darkness of the night at his back, the effect was greatly enhanced. It was downright uncomfortable to have light shining into his yellow-dyed eyes, and Ard tried very hard not to squint. Despite the glare, he could see that the trick had taken a powerful hold over everyone within sight. Curses and prayers bounced between them, and Ard let the awe linger, turning his glowing gaze slowly from one person to the next.

"What are you?" one of the nobles cried from inside the reception hall.

"We are the inhabitants of the Homeland." Was he just going to be repeating that sentence all night long?

"Do you come in peace?" asked a woman's voice from inside.

Perhaps it was Cinza's. Regardless, the wonder of the patrons was beginning to overpower the Regulators' precaution.

"We know nothing but peace," Ard answered. "Do you have a ruler?"

He peered into the reception hall. The room appeared not to have sustained much damage from the dragon attack two years ago. It looked the same as he remembered—wide and spacious, with massive Light Grit chandeliers fueled through a system of pipes in the walls. The hall was draped in greenery, with a large tree making the centerpiece.

"That would be me!" shouted a figure, advancing toward Ard through the parting crowd. "Termain Agaul," he said, introducing himself and taking a rather stumbling bow. "King of the Archkingdom."

*Good. The man was plenty drunk already.* By morning he might not even remember the Homelanders at all.

Termain looked no older than Ard. He was well built, but his face was not as handsome as Ard had expected, given his reputation with the ladies. Then again, such encounters probably had little to do with physical attraction. He looked several days' unshaven, which Ard sensed was more about laziness than style. With no royal regalia of dragon shell, Termain had resorted back to a golden crown bedecked with jewels. His white shoulder cape was extra long, reaching almost to the floor.

Palia Neberel had set out a ramp, and the crew was quickly glide-stepping to Ard's side. He was the only one to have ignited his Light Grit eyes so far. The plan was to stagger the effect, lighting their eyes one at a time throughout the evening to maximize the impact. These were actors. They'd wait for their moment in the limelight before letting sparks fly.

"I am called Abricus," Ard said, by way of introduction. "This is my clan. Tomileu, Bosliut, Gamaran, Kalatris, Merien, Elesey, and Navara."

*Except, Quarrah still seems to be hiding on the ship.* He glanced back in time to see her finally moving down the ramp, holding one of the fruit baskets to disguise her unpracticed step.

"Whoa. I'm not much for remembering names," said Termain, "but I like the way the lot of you look." He reached out and stroked Ruge's exposed elbow.

"We have sailed far to reach you," interjected Ard, sensing Ruge's discomfort and hoping she wouldn't lose her temper. "We have many holy words to speak with your people. May we enter your humble establishment?"

"So I can show off my new golden friends to a room full of important people?" Termain said. "Absolutely."

"Your Majesty," said the Regulator chief. "I must object. We do not know who these people are, or where they're from."

"Homelanders!" Termain cried. "Hot sparks! Don't you believe in the Homeland, Chief?" Termain smiled at Ard and the others as though embarrassed by the Regulator's strictness. "Oh, this is going to thrill the Prime Isless, I'll tell you that much. Blazing good thing, too." He lowered his voice to a whisper. "Just between us, I feel that Wayfarism has been on the decline of late."

"There is great power in Wayfarism," said Ard. "But when compared to the purity of the Homeland, it is as a cloud of Light Grit next to the sun."

"That sounds dangerously like poetry to me." The king straightened his crown. "Come in. Let's get you all something to drink."

The Reggie chief took a bold step in front of the king. "Your Majesty! We cannot allow these strangers inside." He lowered his voice. "They could be Sovereign spies, for all we know."

Ard reached out a hand and touched the man's shoulder. "We bear no threat to any soul. But let our peaceful intentions be proven unto you. With my right hand, I can strike you dead. And with my left, restore you unto life."

Ard clenched his right fist, breaking the glass on a ring filled with Grit solution. At once, a cloud of Stasis Grit ignited around the chief's head, too small and wispy to easily be seen in the dim light of the balcony.

The chief instantly went limp. The crowd gasped. Reggies raised their weapons. Before the chief could fall, Ard caught him by the front of his uniform and held him upright.

"He does not breathe. Nor does his heart beat," Ard said. "Inspect him with your own eyes."

One of the other Regulators came forward aggressively, but the king routed her with a wave of his hand. Then Termain pressed his fingers against the chief's neck to feel for a pulse.

"You killed him?" the king cried, sounding almost amused.

"Death is but a temporary respite in the Homeland," Ard replied, extending his left hand and crushing an identical ring. This one contained Null Grit, instantly snuffing the Stasis cloud and reviving the chief. He gasped, staggering a step backward, eyes wide in confusion and awe.

The miracle earned a wave of gasps and murmurs throughout the reception hall. King Termain applauded.

"The night is young," cried a voice. Ard searched through the crowd and saw that the speaker was Lorstan Grale. "Bring them inside!"

The Regulator chief, clearly shaken from his near-death experience, took a resigned bow. The way was finally open, with the crowd humming in a low frenzy.

"Your religious leader, the Prime Isless..." Ard spoke to the king. "Is she in attendance tonight?"

"Glori!" Termain whistled, patting his thigh like someone calling a dog. "Oh, Glori! Where'd you run off to? Shiny Homelander wants to meet you!"

The crowd parted and Gloristar stepped forward, purple robes swishing, black hair down. At least ten years older than Ard, she had a particular beauty that came with age, and an unmistakable weariness that came with too much responsibility. Her presence actually quieted the patrons, and the night seemed to tense as all ears tuned in to what the Prime Isless of all Wayfarism might say to these Home-landers. Ard had a lot riding on her reaction, too. Impress Gloristar and the Realm might sign off on giving him Shad Agaul.

"This is Prime Isless Gloristar," Termain said. "She is the great-est of our faith."

"Not so, Your Highness," answered Gloristar, keeping her dis-tance. Her voice was cold and notably sober. "The faith of any believing Wayfarist can easily equal my own. I have simply been trusted with a greater portion of responsibility."

"How do you handle such a weight?" Ard asked.

"One day at a time," Gloristar answered tersely. He could see the distrust in her expression. Glowing eyes and a complex costume weren't going to be enough to win her over.

"I perceive that you guide the believers through a difficult time." Ard stretched forth his golden hand as Gloristar's eyes darted over to Termain suspiciously. "But who guides the guide?"

The Prime Isless drew a deep breath. Instead of speaking, she turned suddenly, moving through the astonished crowd toward the back of the reception hall.

Well, they had all night to work on her. Ard would give her some time to think before circling around to speak with her again. For now, it was best to focus on keeping the wealthy patrons wholly con-vinced of their claims.

"Have you come to help the Archkingdom win the war?" asked one of the ladies in a green gown. It could have been Cinza, for all Ard knew.

"Kingdoms and borders mean nothing to us," answered Ard. "We have no titles or stations in the Homeland. All are equal."

"Sparks! Not sure how I feel about that," admitted Termain. To be honest, Ard wasn't sure, either. If all were equal, what was left to work for?

"Then why have you come?" asked Lorstan Grale. Elbrig was seeding this question very nicely for them.

Yalan Steir picked up the cue immediately. "We bring wisdom. And knowledge of the way Home."

"I can see your doubts," said Keel Belu, tapping the sides of her eyes and igniting the Light Grit to shocked cries from the crowd. She glided forward, scanning over the faces. "The light of the Homeland lingers in me, and your apprehensions are plainly displayed before my eyes."

"Long have we searched for our lost ones," said Palia Neberel, also moving into the hall. She reached out, touching the hands of several at the nearest table. This gesture seemed to bolster some of the more fearful onlookers. "Now we have found you at last."

As the golden crew dispersed into the room, the patrons began to ask more questions. Ard heard all the ones they'd predicted and rehearsed for, and soon the actors were hard at work, conversations blossoming all around the hall. Quarrah was nowhere in sight, and Ard wondered when she had wandered off.

Termain cursed, shaking his empty glass. "Why even have servants if they can't keep a blazing glass full?" He staggered away from Ard, which emboldened a few nobles to draw nearer.

"What is it like?" came the predictable question from a woman with wide eyes and a lavender gown.

"It is unlike anything you have ever beheld," said Ard. "You would find it both familiar and shockingly different. Standing on its crystal shores will fill a gap in your soul that you may not have even known you had."

"Have you seen my son there?" asked a man with a drooping mustache. "Casbar Ellow. He would be just a lad."

"The Homeland's inhabitants are as innumerable as the stars in the sky, good fellow," answered Ard. "I have been there for nine hundred of your years and still my associations seem sorely limited.

If your son is there, I can assure you he is surrounded by loving ancestors from many generations."

"Is it far from here?" asked a woman, fidgeting with her gaudy necklace.

"It cannot be reached by the faint of heart," Ard answered. "But the journey is possible, and many of your devout ships have reached us safely. And many more of your loved ones have found their way to us in death."

"There has surely been much of that lately," muttered another man.

"Yes," said Ard. "We sense wars and hatred among the inhabitants of these long-forsaken islands. Such contentions are hardly worthy of the Homeland's perfection."

"What are you saying?" asked a woman.

"The Homeland is displeased with this war," Ard said. "Worthiness is found in peace."

"We had many decades of peace before your arrival," replied the mustached man. "Prime Isle Chauster and the crusader monarch wiped the land clean of violence and hatred."

Ard felt his face flush slightly beneath his heavy makeup. Despite all efforts to spread the truth, Chauster and Pethredote were still considered heroes. How astonishingly simple it was for the rich and noble to look past the crimes and wrongdoings of the powerful people who surrounded them.

"Why do your eyes dim?" asked the woman.

Ard hadn't realized that his lights were stretched thin with Prolonging Grit, ready to wink out at any moment. "Talk of war and evil takes a toll upon my perfected mind."

A servant approached the group with a large tray balanced on his open hand. "A selection of fruits from the Homeland?"

One side of the tray contained wedges of that gelatin-filled summer melon. It had been kept cold enough on the *Holy Breath* that the substance still held nicely to the rind.

The fruiter had not been able to make the pears glow, as per Ard's request, but the slices on the tray were dyed such a vibrant red that they looked like paintings of a sunset.

A wax-covered plum had been the concession for the fruiter's inability to deliver. Ard was pleased with the way they looked, their pits full of Slagstone bits, which sparked when the plums were cut open.

While the folks around him gawked at the fruit, Ard took advantage of the distraction to glance across the room. His crew seemed to be doing an excellent job. Keel's glowing eyes had faded, but it looked like Yalan had just ignited his. The nobles currently flocked to him the most, drawn like moths to the Light Grit.

It took him a moment to locate Quarrah. She was in the far corner by the entrance to the kitchens. But she wasn't alone. A small servant woman stood before her, making rather large gestures with her hands. Quarrah's posture had drooped, making her look noticeably less Homelandish.

"If you'll excuse me," Ard said to his followers, who were now moaning about the deliciousness of that otherworldly fruit.

By the time he had glide-stepped halfway to Quarrah, the conversation had ended and the servant had vanished through the door. Ard avoided getting detained by a curious group of nobles and reached Quarrah in the corner.

"I thought you weren't going to start any conversations," Ard said quietly, maintaining his dialect even though it was unlikely anyone could hear him.

"She recognized me," Quarrah hissed, her expression much too contentious for someone claiming to be from the peaceful Homeland.

Ard held up a finger to indicate that she should pause a moment. Digging in the pocket of his strange robe, he withdrew a small bag of Silence Grit. Raek had mixed it for him in the mesh tea bags he'd seen Quarrah use. He had prepared for just an occasion such as this, knowing that Quarrah had a bad habit of blurting things out that could get them into trouble. Especially when she was under pressure.

Ard held the bag on the flat of his palm and clapped his hands sharply together, sparking the Slagstone and igniting the small cloud of Silence Grit around both of their heads. The reception hall instantly went eerily quiet, despite seeing continued chatter and the clink of glasses.

"Who was she?" Ard dropped the accent now that they couldn't be overheard. All they needed to do was maintain the posture of the Homelanders. People were certainly watching, but no one dared approach them while they conversed in the corner.

"That was the handmaiden to the queen dowager," Quarrah said. "I think she was trying to warn us."

"What did she say?" Ard asked.

Quarrah shook her head. "She doesn't speak."

"Then I'm sure the two of you get along swimmingly." If the handmaiden was mute, then that explained the large gesturing. "She knew you were going to be here?"

"Errel's deaf, too," answered Quarrah. "She wouldn't know about this ruse unless Fabra wrote it out for her after I left. She was nervous, Ard. I think she was trying to tell us to leave."

"Leave?" Ard cried. "We barely just arrived." He glanced at the clock on the wall. "We still have nearly an hour until we're scheduled to meet Overseer in the garden. I only need half that time to win over Gloristar. Everything's going according to plan."

"I haven't seen Fabra in the crowd," Quarrah said.

"That's good." From what Ard had heard about the old widow, she was something of a loose cannon. She knew about the ruse from Quarrah's reports, and having her here was a risk Ard hadn't accounted for.

Quarrah shook her head, face creased with worry. "Something's not right. Why would Errel be here without Fabra? I've only ever seen the two of them together."

"This is a big night." Ard gestured around. "I'm sure the palace staff needs all the help they can get. Besides, if you were in danger, wouldn't Fabra Ment have come herself to protect her investement? Or at the very least, sent you a clearer message?"

Quarrah gasped. "What if the queen dowager's been discovered by the Realm? We know they have eyes and ears in the palace. Fabra could be in trouble. Maybe that's what Errel was trying to say! If the Realm has her, they might already know we're working against them. This whole reception could be a setup. We need to go now. Fabra's chambers are in the north wing. We need to see if she's—"

"I'm not going anywhere," Ard cut her off. "Your paranoia is hampering this ruse, Quarrah. You need to get ahold of yourself."

Quarrah held very still for a moment, and Ard could tell she was debating whether or not to reply. Then she looked right into his yellow eyes.

"It's funny how you think you've changed, Ardor Benn."

Quarrah turned and strode out of their private Silence cloud, remembering to glide-step only after she was three or four paces away.

Ard bristled. Well, maybe he hadn't handled that as tactfully as he could have, but it didn't change his position. Gloristar needed more convincing. If she left the reception still doubting, the Realm would never give Shad Agaul over to Rival.

Looking over the room, he saw the Prime Isless standing alone beside a table of cheese and fried bread. He glide-stepped toward her, pointedly ignoring two groups of nobles who attempted to engage him in conversation.

"You are the leader of many," Ard said, coming up behind her. "And yet, you stand alone."

She whirled, startled. But as soon as she saw it was him, her eyes dropped to the floor. "Well, I'm not exactly the most popular Prime Isless who has ever led Wayfarism."

"It has been centuries since the very notion of 'popularity' has crossed my mind. Is it troubling to you?"

Gloristar shrugged. "I find popularity to be like a sword without a hilt. The tighter you cling to it, the more painful it becomes."

"And how tightly are you clinging?"

"Oh, I had to let go a long time ago," she answered, still staring at the floor. "The people may not know it, but I am doing what is best to preserve Wayfarism."

*Preserve it?* That was a strange choice of words. Ard knew people were leaving the faith, but Wayfarism certainly wasn't on the brink of dying out completely, unless the Realm succeeded in bringing about the Great Egress.

"Why will you not look at me?" Ard asked. "I sense great doubt in your heart regarding my presence."

"I have spent decades trying to attune my heart to the Homeland's Urgings," she said. "And yet, I feel nothing when I look at you."

"Look again," Ard said. What was he suggesting? He couldn't falsify a feeling inside her! But if the perfect future wanted Shad Agaul alive, maybe Gloristar would feel an actual Urging.

The Prime Isless raised her eyes slowly until they locked with his. The emotions hiding there were complex and many. Ard considered each one, trying to decide which to manipulate.

"I sense great distress," he stated. It was perhaps the most apparent in her eyes.

"How can I trust you?"

"The Homeland grants us perfect wisdom," he said, "and knowledge of all things secret." It was a vague answer, borrowed almost verbatim from one of the scriptures Elbrig had drilled them on. Then an idea occurred to him. Something concrete, with the potential to be utterly convincing. "I can speak a secret known only to the Prime."

Her brows folded together in apprehension. "What?"

"The true nature," he whispered, "of the Paladin Visitants."

Gloristar gasped, a hand lifting to her mouth. "I'm afraid that knowledge is lost on me."

*Lost?* "Is it not one of the sacred responsibilities passed from Prime to Prime?"

"Through the Anchored Tome," she replied. As a youth, Ard had heard his parents speak of the fabled book stored in the Mooring's Sanctum at the back of Cove 1. More recently, he'd deduced that Prime Isle Chauster had learned the true nature of the Paladin Visitants from that sacred book, before insensibly passing the information to King Pethredote.

"Was there not a chapter on Paladin Visitants?" Ard asked.

"There was," she replied. "But the pages were missing."

*Missing?* Ard tried not to shriek in disbelief. *Prime Isle Chauster, you self-righteous Bloodeye.* He must have torn out the pages that revealed the true nature of a Paladin Visitant as a traveler through time. Chauster and Pethredote had been so afraid that anyone would reset the timeline and erase the good they'd done that the former Prime Isle had made sure the secret would die with him.

"I have come to fill in the lost pages," Ard said. He wasn't going to tell her the truth. At least not today. If that chapter was missing, Ard could make up anything he wanted.

Gloristar's eyes shimmered in the chandelier Light Grit. She wasn't truly crying, but they welled with a new emotion that Ard recognized as hope.

"You know the contents of the Anchored Tome?" She breathed out the words like a prayer.

Well, this could get rocky in a hurry. "If the Homeland grants it," he said hesitantly. "You have other questions regarding the Tome?"

"The book is currently...inaccessible to me," Gloristar whispered. What the blazes did she mean by that? Had she lost the key to the Sanctum and was too stubborn to have a locksmith enter Cove 1?

"It is not something I can freely speak of here." Gloristar's dark eyes flicked over to where King Termain was drinking from a bottle.

Suddenly, it all came together in Ardor Benn's mind. Gloristar wasn't endorsing the king because she believed in his regime. He was leveraging her. Whether Termain had stolen the Anchored Tome or somehow sealed off the Sanctum, the result would be the same, putting the entire future of Wayfarism on the cusp of being forever leaderless.

"I have done everything I could think of to get it back on my own," she continued. "I recently risked a great deal pursuing an avenue that should have given me some security." Her shoulders fell a little more. "It has left me in even greater danger."

She had to be talking about the staged burglary at Portsend Wal's laboratory. It wasn't her fault that the papers had been destroyed. Was Termain taking that out on her as well?

"I have come to the conclusion that the only solution is to create a new copy of the Anchored Tome," she said. "Would it be within the Homeland's power for you to help me do that?"

"All things are within the Homeland's power," he said, stalling.

"Then, you could do it?"

Flames, what was he getting himself into? But agreeing to this preposterous request would certainly gain the Prime Isless's approval and trust. And Ard only needed to hold her trust until Overseer gave him the prince.

"I can," he said. "It will demand several days of meditation and prayer. Perhaps we can meet again on the second week of the coming cycle?"

Gloristar nodded, filled with a hope that actually made Ard feel like a terrible person. But he was Ardor Benn, ruse artist extraordinaire. He'd lied to hundreds of faces and never felt a pang of guilt. Was it so different because Gloristar was the Prime Isless? Or because her request was so sincere, and, if Ard was right about the Anchored Tome, could determine the fate of Wayfarism?

"This is a truly sacred matter," Gloristar said. "I trust that you will speak of it with no one."

"Not even my clan," Ard answered.

"Praise the Homeland you have come," said Gloristar. "You are indeed an answer to many prayers."

The Prime Isless was obviously ecstatic, but did she feel an actual Urging when she looked at him now? Surely not, and yet she followed her feelings. Ard wondered how many times he had done the same, chasing after something he wanted so badly that he'd even managed to fool his own heart.

~

*Yet, we were not esteemed but spurned. Not lauded but reproached.*

# CHAPTER
# 34

Portsend Wal watched the liquid solution ignite under the sparks from his Slagstone ignitor, the resulting spherical cloud hovering just above the laboratory tabletop.

It was only three dribs of the negative-flat-one solution, with a meager half granule of powdered dragon teeth dissolved in it. He didn't need a large detonation to run his tests, and conserving the material was more important than ever before, with the loss of the Pekal harbors.

Many dismissed the news as a temporary setback, saying that the Trothians had attacked without permission from the Sovereign States. Along with that rumor came a certain reassurance that the harbors would be retaken in just a few more days, once everyone evacuated for the Moon Passing.

Using his straight ruler, Portsend measured the cloud's diameter— just over eight inches. He opened his notebook and copied down the information with a scribing charcoal that had grown so short it was difficult to grip.

Near the door, Stubs kept reaching behind his back, tossing a Grit pot over his shoulder and catching it in front of him. Lately, the ruffian was always doing something obnoxious or distracting. Or maybe Portsend was just noticing it more since he didn't have San and Lomaya to engage with in educated, worthwhile conversation.

"You're going to drop that," Portsend said without looking away from his notebook.

"What's the fuss?" the man replied. "This isn't Blast Grit."

"You're being careless with my resources," said Portsend. It didn't really matter what type of Grit was in the pot. If the Archkingdom didn't take back their Pekal harbors, all prices would soar. "Resources are expensive. And you're distracting me from my work. Is that the report you'd like me to give to the boss next time she pays a visit?"

Stubs made a discontented sound in the back of his throat and deposited the pot on the rack against the wall. He slumped down on a chair and began massaging the blunt ends of his severed fingers.

Portsend reached into the cloud of dragon-teeth Grit, turning his hand this way and that. Unlike Gather and Weight Grit, the detonation had no noticeable effect on his hand. No noticeable *immediate* effect, he corrected himself. Perhaps an extended period of exposure would manifest something, although Portsend was reluctant to try it on his own appendage.

He'd get one of the rats next time. Lomaya was better at handling them, and the critters certainly favored the girl, but Portsend could probably coax one into his grasp with a crumble of cheese.

"And I thought it was boring when there were three of you to watch," Stubs said. "At least the girl was something to look at." Apparently, *all* kinds of rats took a liking to Lomaya. "Any idea when they'll be coming back?"

Portsend ignored him. Partly because the conversation was distracting, but mostly because thoughts of his two pupils always threatened to send him into a depression. He had brought terrors before their eyes when all he'd meant to do was give them opportunities.

Praise the Homeland, they were safe now! By design, Portsend didn't know where they'd gone. He'd felt it was better that way, allowing Gloristar to make all of the arrangements for their departure without his knowledge.

It was enough to know that they weren't in Beripent anymore. Likely, they had left Espar altogether. He would find them when all of this was over. Gloristar would tell him their whereabouts, and Portsend would spare no expense to bring them back to the college to complete their studies.

The door to the lab cracked open, finally convincing Portsend to turn away from his experiment.

It was the boss, her stocky form silhouetted in the last glow of rosy light from the sunset.

Portsend sucked in a deep breath and turned back to his detonation, feigning disinterest in her arrival. In truth, he'd been expecting her for weeks, ever since they'd falsified the break-in at the lab. He'd rehearsed the conversation more than a dozen times in his mind. All he had to do was stick to the story.

"I trust you've been well?" she said, walking into the lab. Behind her, Cheery appeared holding a large box. He waddled in and deposited his load on the floor beside Stubs, kicking the door shut behind him.

That was an unusually friendly greeting. Maybe she didn't know about the break-in yet. By now, Gloristar surely would have given all the information to King Termain, although Portsend still hadn't heard anything about how it had been received.

"Well enough." Portsend turned his full attention to her as the unknown cloud of dragon-teeth Grit went out with a puff.

"I need you to mix a few things for me," said the boss.

Portsend swallowed. The last time she had come in here, placing an order like this, a young man had died. He'd be more wary this time.

"I need a vial of Ignition Grit that will yield a cloud with a radius of two feet," she expounded, "and a measure of Compounded Void Grit the same size. I need a small amount of Compounded Heat Grit that will result in a cloud hot enough to fry an egg. I also need a spoon, some rope, and a vial of Weight Grit, Compounded to make the items in the cloud feel like they weigh a hundred panweights."

"That will depend entirely on the original weight of the objects you want to affect," he said.

"I'm guessing these items weigh between ten and fifteen panweights," she answered. "I'd like the detonation radius to be about a foot and a half."

Portsend reviewed the order in his mind. He was very good at remembering lists. Sometimes his entire career felt like little more than a fulfillment of them.

He moved across the laboratory and opened a cabinet, selecting a large glass jug full of green liquid. This was premixed Ignition Grit, although he'd only need a few dribs for the size of detonation the boss had requested. On the inside of the cabinet door, Portsend checked the charts he had created with San and Lomaya to verify just how much he'd need.

In moments, he had it measured and transferred to one of his smallest glass vials. Still it only filled a quarter of the vessel, and the chip of Slagstone he slid into it was barely submerged.

He corked the Ignition Grit, setting it aside as he turned to a canister of processed, powdered granite. He'd been working so much with liquid Grit lately that it almost felt strange to measure out the Void Grit without adding it to a solution.

"How Compounded would you like it?" he asked, opening the canister of processed quartzite.

"Twice its natural force will do," she answered.

Portsend consulted the chart of Compounding rates hanging on the wall. Then he carefully measured out the granules and let the scales balance.

"How would you like it stored?" he asked.

"On a tray or a dish will suffice."

"Not in a pot?"

The boss shook her head. "I want it loose. And no need to add any Slagstone. I'd hate for it to detonate accidentally."

Portsend removed the little tray from the scales and set it next to the Ignition vial. He set aside a prepared pot that contained Heat Grit, Compounded enough to quickly boil water for his herbal infusions.

Next, Portsend returned to the cabinet and retrieved the blue jug of Weight Grit. They certainly didn't have complete charts for Compounding it, but with an amount so small, Portsend was able to make the calculations rather easily.

"What else did you need?" he asked, once he finished preparing the Weight Grit vial.

"A spoon," said the boss flatly.

Portsend picked up one of the wooden spoons used for scooping Grit out of the canisters. "Something like this?"

She stepped over and took it from his hands. "We'll spare you from searching for rope, as Stubs seems to have acquired a coil while you were measuring."

"Nothing else, then?" Homeland, it would be good if she left without asking any questions.

"Just a few more matters of business." She stepped forward and picked up the blue vial he had just measured. When she turned to face him again, there was a Roller in her hand.

Portsend felt the all-too-familiar rush of fear as the shiny barrel leveled in his direction. Hadn't he seen this coming? The boss's thumb clicked back the hammer, and she gestured with the gun for him to move.

"Step away from the Grit," she threatened.

Portsend obliged, trying to keep his breathing steady and his head on straight. She wouldn't shoot him. Especially now that San and Lomaya were gone and he was working alone. Like Termain, she clearly wanted to twist his arm until there was nothing more to gain. But she'd have no way of knowing how many more types of liquid Grit were yet to be discovered.

"Stop," she ordered.

Portsend obeyed, coming to a halt in the very middle of the laboratory. Here there was absolutely nothing within reach. The boss suddenly dashed the glass vial at Portsend's feet. Instantly, the Compounded Weight cloud sprang up in a domed shape against the floor, encompassing both of his legs from the knees down. He tried to step back, but...his feet! The effect of the cloud had made them both feel like a hundred panweights. Portsend almost toppled backward, but he managed to right himself, arms pinwheeling madly.

"Bind his upper arms," she snapped at Stubs. He came forward, unwinding the length of rope. "At his sides," the boss instructed, "tightly down to the elbows."

Under the watchful gun, Portsend had no choice but to allow the man to begin wrapping him. He felt like little more than a trembling autumn leaf, with the dread sensation that a terrible storm was about to hit. One that might strip him clean of his branch and leave him in tatters.

"Now tie his wrists together."

Stubs's knife flashed as he sliced through the heavy rope. With the second piece, he cinched Portsend's wrists together in front of him.

"Now that you're not going anywhere..." said the boss, setting her gun on the empty table, the barrel still pointed his way.

She walked back to the counter and picked up the loose tray of Compounded Void Grit that he had just Mixed. Returning to him, she set the tray on the floor just outside the perimeter of the Weight cloud. She gave it a good flick, sliding it into the cloud at Portsend's heavy feet. It didn't skid far once the Weight Grit took effect on the little tray, but it came to rest just inches from his toe.

Pulling the wooden spoon from her jacket pocket, the boss shoved it into his hands. Then she circled back to the counter once more to pick up the vial of Ignition Grit and the Heat Grit pot.

"You must be a creative man to have discovered what you did." She stepped closer to him. "So, I hope you can appreciate the creativity in what I'm setting up, here."

Slowly, she reached out and balanced the vial of Ignition Grit in the bowl of the wooden spoon.

"I want you to hold this for me. Of course, you know what would happen if it were to drop."

Portsend swallowed, his hands suddenly sweaty against the shaft of the spoon. Shattering the Ignition vial would detonate the Void Grit at his feet. At the rate it was Compounded, the outward force would throw his legs in opposite directions. And his feet currently happened to weigh a hundred panweights apiece. At best, it would break both of his knees. At worst, every bone from the knee down.

"We need you alive," she said, "but we don't necessarily need you walking." She dropped the pot of Compounded Heat Grit on the floor next to her. The cloud appeared, instantly hot enough to sear flesh. Drawing a long knife from a sheath on her thigh, the boss reached down and pushed the tip of the blade into the Heat cloud.

"Now, I'm going to ask you a few questions," she said. "If I don't like your answers, you'll get a special brand." She withdrew the knife from the cloud, and Portsend could see that the tip was glowing red. "Are you ready to begin?"

Portsend didn't answer, his jaw clenched so tightly he feared his teeth might break.

"Since our last meeting, have you given King Termain any new information?"

"No," he whispered, eyes fixed on the vial of Ignition Grit balanced on the end of his spoon.

"Have you spoken with Prime Isless Gloristar?"

"Yes," he answered, "but I give you my word that I did not give her any new information regarding the liquid Grit. My associates were…distressed after your last visit. I took them to the Prime Isless for healing of a spiritual nature."

"Are you aware that your laboratory was broken into the night after your visit to the Mooring?"

"Of course I am aware," said Portsend. "Several leafs of important data were stolen. Along with hundreds of Ashings' worth of Grit." He had moved the Grit out himself, so as to provide better motive for a burglar.

"Did you ever find out who the intruder was?"

"Unfortunately, no."

"Supposedly, the thief was a man named Raekon, hired by the Prime Isless after she grew suspicious of you withholding information."

"I've never heard of the man."

"That was your first lie."

The boss reached out and touched the searing-hot tip of the knife against the bare flesh of Portsend's neck. He couldn't tell if it had cut him in addition to the burn, but he let out a wheezing breath to steady himself. His eyes stayed on the Ignition Grit in his spoon, fighting not to let his hands shake against the hot pain. A burn on his neck might leave a scar, but it wouldn't cause lasting damage like two broken legs.

"It has come to my attention that the man, Raekon, is in the employ of my superiors," said the boss, finally withdrawing her blade and plunging its tip into the Heat cloud again. "He denied any knowledge of meeting with Prime Isless Gloristar, or breaking into this laboratory."

"Of course he lied," Portsend spit the words out. "He's a criminal. If he's one of yours, then he must have double-crossed you."

"Or the entire story was fabricated so you could fake innocence when King Termain received information about the new Grit," she said. "You'll be pleased to know he didn't."

"Didn't what?" Portsend whispered.

"Termain didn't receive the information that Gloristar gave him," answered the boss. "The papers were intercepted and destroyed."

Portsend felt a sinking in the pit of his stomach. If that was true, Gloristar could be in hotter water than ever. He needed to reach out to her. Why hadn't he heard from her if their plan had failed?

"Next question," said the boss, pulling the knife from the Heat cloud. "What happened to your young companions?"

"They stopped helping me after your last visit," said Portsend.

"Where are they now?"

"I don't know..." said Portsend. "Likely in their dormitories for the night."

"That is your second lie."

The glowing tip of the boss's knife touched the other side of his neck. Portsend let out a cry so raw that it grated his throat. His face was dripping sweat now, and drool ran from his bottom lip as he quavered in agony. All his focus was on keeping the spoon steady in his hands. Such a small thing. Such a simple task.

This interrogation couldn't go on forever. The Compounded Weight Grit around his feet would give out in less than ten minutes, and he'd be mobile again. But his arms would still be bound. And with the boss and her two brutes standing between him and the doorway, Portsend was cornered like a frightened boar in the hunt.

"We know your two pupils left Espar," the boss continued, returning the knife to the Heat cloud. "You'll be pleased to know that they've come back." She waved for Cheery, who picked up the box and moved to her side.

"Back?" Portsend shuddered, the vial clattering in his spoon.

"Yes," said the boss. "They're back in southern Beripent." She snapped her fingers. "Well, at least *some* of them."

Cheery removed the lid, angling the box so Portsend could see inside.

Homeland. Their heads.

The heads of his two dear pupils were boxed in straw like common goods to be shipped. Portsend's insides were suddenly ripped with a new wave of pain. This one made him sick and he shut his eyes against it, wailing in a way that he had not done in years.

Monsters. These people were absolute monsters. *Kill me now,* Portsend thought. If they were smart, they would finish him off immediately. Because, Homeland help him, if he got out of this, these wretches were going to pay with their lives.

"Our people found them in northern Talumon, near Octowyn," said the boss. She waved at Cheery, who replaced the lid and set the box on the table.

"Why?" Portsend moaned, his wailing subsided to a defeated weeping. "Why?"

"We talked about this," continued the boss. "There must be a punishment for your violations, or what good is having an agreement at all? I wanted to believe that you had changed. But until you do, we have no choice but to prod you along."

The boss held up the hot knife. "Shall we continue? My next round of questions will help me determine how long you need to stay alive, so answer carefully. How many more Grit types are you currently developing?"

Portsend quaked, tears streaming down his tingling face. It was truly a miracle that he hadn't dropped the Ignition Grit yet. He could barely hear the boss's voice anymore, his ears ringing with the deafening buzz of pain and grief.

"How many more Grit types do you expect to find?" she rephrased.

Portsend Wal lifted his chin slowly to look her in the face. Then he let out the loudest scream of defiance that his grief-wracked body could muster.

The woman reached out with the knife, but this time her threat was cut short.

The laboratory door banged open, but Portsend couldn't see who stood in the darkened threshold. A gunshot rang out, and Stubs staggered backward.

The boss moved for her Roller on the table, the barrel still pointing toward Portsend, the Slagstone hammer cocked and ready to fire.

Wait.

If the hammer was back, then there would be a tiny opening clear down to the cartridge of Blast Grit. And the boss had just stepped into the line of fire.

Portsend flicked his wrists, launching the vial of Ignition Grit from his spoon. It sailed over the boss's shoulder and shattered on the table in front of her. The Ignition cloud extended over the gun, finding its way through the small opening and detonating the Blast Grit. The Roller fired, the lead ball tearing into the woman a fraction of a second before she reached it.

She fell, grunting, slipping to the floor as blood streamed from her abdomen. She twisted, landing face first in the small detonation of Compounded Heat Grit, the cloud instantly searing the flesh on the left side of her head.

Another shot sounded in the lab, and Portsend saw Cheery crash into a rack of Grit pots. More than a dozen shattered, sparks igniting orbs of Light Grit, which illuminated the lab in a sudden flash.

Portsend squinted against the brightness, straining to see who had rescued him. The man stepped forward, a smoking Roller in each hand.

It was Raekon!

Portsend didn't know how to react. This wasn't the rescue he'd been hoping for. The big fellow had probably come looking for more Heg. What was going to stop him from killing Portsend to leave no witnesses?

"Professor?" he asked, his voice a low rumble.

Stubs suddenly came careening in from the side, knife glinting in his hand. Raekon fired one of his guns, but the shot went wide, chipping into the ceiling. The two men grappled, Stubs knocking one of Raekon's Rollers away and holding back the other with one hand as he tried to stab at his torso.

Raekon's free hand came around, seizing Stubs's throat. With a mighty heave, the big man picked up the guard and slammed him against the countertop, toppling the canisters and causing something to spark.

Drift Grit detonated in a cloud that filled a third of the laboratory. Stubs sprang from his perch, sailing directly over Raekon's head as the other man raised his gun and pulled the trigger.

Blood droplets floated in all directions and the impact of the shot sent Stubs upward, bumping along the ceiling, but otherwise motionless. Raekon kicked off, drifting up and catching himself on the ceiling next to Stubs. Hanging in the air, he turned the dead man over, patting him down and reaching into his pockets.

At last, the cloud of Weight Grit around Portsend's feet burned out. He stumbled backward, his legs giving out. He fell to his knees, staring at the boss, who was barely alive, torso bleeding and head terribly burned.

Raekon came floating over a table, catching himself as he left the perimeter of the Drift cloud. He landed beside the boss, startling as she twitched on the floor.

"Whoa," he said. "This one's still kicking."

Portsend rose on shaking legs. "She can...Let her suffer..." His voice warbled, his mind too cloudy to form a more coherent sentence.

"Fine by me." Raekon opened his shirt, and Portsend saw a paper roll of Heg in his hand. Just like their last encounter, he watched the man shake a pinch of the Health Grit into that scarred mess of a hole in his chest, seal it off, and detonate it.

"Steadies the nerves a little," he explained, drawing a long knife from his belt and stepping toward Portsend. Now that his feet were free, he considered running, but the expression on Raekon's face seemed totally nonthreatening. Still, Portsend couldn't help but flinch as he slid the blade between his wrists and severed the ropes. A moment later, Raekon had cut the wraps around Portsend's chest, and his arms were free.

"You all right?" the big man asked.

Portsend couldn't answer. Now that the adrenaline of the fight was subsiding, he found that he couldn't speak at all, his eyes looking anywhere but at that dreadful box on the table.

The laboratory was a mess, but it wasn't destroyed this time. Canisters and jars hung lazily in the Drift cloud. He knew it would be a good idea to gather them before they came crashing down, but he suddenly didn't care enough. He no longer felt present in the room. His body was there, motionless, staring at his dying enemy and the wreckage around her. But his mind was submerged in so much grief and shock that nothing seemed to reach it.

"Well, you don't see that every day," Raekon's voice sounded shallow and distant, echoing down the vacant corridors of Portsend's mind. The big man was peering into the box on the table—*the* box—and it jarred Portsend from his reverie with a gut-wrenching wave of nausea.

"Please," he rasped, throat already raw from his sobs. "They—"

"Professor," Raekon cut him off. "I'm guessing you don't see a lot of severed heads in your line of work. Because these"—he reached into the box—"are wax."

Raekon withdrew Lomaya's head, Portsend flinching, his heart in his throat.

"Wax," the man said again. "Put a wick in them and they might as well be candles." He scraped a line down the girl's cheek with his fingernail. "I know half a dozen forgers good enough to pull off something like this. Isn't hard to imagine that the Realm has a few of them on retainer." He held out the fake head for Portsend's inspection.

Swallowing the lump in his throat, he tried to see past the realism of the object dangling in front of him. The longer he stared at it, the less convincing it seemed. How had he been fooled so deeply? "So, that means…"

"The Realm was playing with you."

Portsend felt the walls of horror and grief begin to crumble. He had to reconstruct his mind, shaping it back into a world where San and Lomaya were still safe. "They're alive," he whispered, as if to set it in stone.

"Probably," Raek said. "I mean, there's always a chance that they got struck by lightning or something. But the fact that the Realm went to such lengths to falsify these heads tells me that they actually have no idea where your young friends are."

Portsend broke down again, this time grinning through his tears. Raekon reached out a large hand and squeezed his shoulder. "Raekon Dorrel," the man said. "I think it's time the two of us officially met."

"Portsend," he gasped, through a relieved sob. "Portsend Wal."

"Oh, I know," Raekon said. "That's why I'm here. Now, let's pack this place up and get out of here."

"Where are we going?"

"Somewhere the Realm won't find you." He set the wax head back in the box.

"The Realm?"

"I'll explain on the way. Stubs and his partner are both dead. We just need to make sure this one is, too, before we go." Raekon nudged the boss with his toe. She was lying still now, breaths coming in ragged, short gasps.

A moment ago, nothing had mattered in the shadow of his slaughtered students. Now he was filled with a renewed hope. Portsend crossed to the filing cabinet and began pulling out every scrap of paper with information regarding the liquid Grit solutions.

"How did you know I was in danger?" Portsend asked, depositing the documents in an empty box as he began to take down the Grit charts tacked to the walls.

"The tortured screaming was a pretty good indicator." Raekon moved into the Drift cloud to retrieve the floating jars and canisters, lining them up at the edge of the table.

"You were waiting outside?" Portsend secured the lid on the container of processed dragon teeth and set it aside. Out of everything in the lab, this and the documents were probably the most important to him. "How long had you been out there?"

"Just arrived, actually. Had to run a ship out to the eastern sea and didn't get back until recently. Figured this was my chance to get down here while my partner's tied up at that reception."

"You came just to check on me?" Portsend grabbed the boss's discharged Roller off the table. He gently lowered the hammer and tucked the gun into his belt.

"That's the story we're going with," Raekon answered. "And I'd be much obliged if you don't mention the other bit."

"Killing these three?" Portsend clarified.

"Oh, Ard will be pleased that we eliminated some of the Realm's Hands. That one might have been a Faceless." He gestured toward the boss lady, who was finally still. Likely dead by now. "Maybe even in the Directorate."

*Realm. Faceless. Directorate.* Portsend only understood half of what the man was saying. Raekon seemed to know a lot about the people who had been controlling him. Maybe Portsend would finally get some answers.

"It's the Health Grit that needs to be our little secret, okay?" Raekon continued. "Ard took my entire stash. Even took my secret stash. And I'd just about burned through everything in my *secret* secret stash just to be able to think straight while we were planning the ruse."

"I won't mention it," said Portsend. Homeland, he owed the man his unbroken legs, if not his life itself. Keeping quiet about the Heg was the least he could do.

"That's everything?" Raekon said, looking over the supplies they'd gathered.

"I need to get a message to Prime Isless Gloristar," he said. Find out if Termain had punished her when the new Grit papers were lost. At the very least, let her know he was alive.

"That's not a good idea," Raekon said. "The Realm knows about your connection with her. That's the first avenue they'll be watching. I'm afraid it's got to be total silence from here out. For your safety. And hers."

Portsend picked up his box of papers. "How far are we going?"

"Upper Eastern Quarter," Raekon answered. "The Guesthouse Adagio is already harboring a couple of ruse artists and an allegedly dead queen. The Realm hasn't found us yet, so I think we'll be okay. Plus, the accommodations are first-rate."

Raekon pulled back the hammer on his Roller and shot the boss once more to make sure she was dead.

"We even have a stuffy butler."

~

*We rose up against our encroaching madness.*

# CHAPTER

# 35

Quarrah ducked into the shadows of the hallway as a red-uniformed Regulator on patrol strolled lazily past. She cursed the shimmery golden coating on her skin as the antithesis of subtlety. Still, her expertise, coupled with the Reggie's carelessness, kept her effectively hidden.

She was fuming about Ard's nonchalant response to the warning she'd received from Errel. The handmaiden had clearly been in some degree of distress, which had resonated with Quarrah despite the fact that the two of them couldn't communicate accurately. It wasn't dismissible paranoia.

During their ruse for the royal regalia, Quarrah never would have given up on Ard so easily. Now she simply didn't care. He'd been warned, which was all she could do. If that stubborn man wanted to stay in the reception hall and face whatever danger Errel was trying to warn them about, then that was his choice. As for Quarrah, she was going to check on her employer.

She had left the reception hall mere moments after her argument with Ard. Taking a lap around the hall had given her a chance to shake lingering stares from the noble folk and verify that Fabra Ment was indeed not in attendance.

Then it had been a simple matter of waiting until Ruge Harban had ignited her glowing eyes. In the sudden draw of attention, it had been easy to slip into the hallway through one of the unguarded doors on the far wall.

Quarrah ducked her head and moved swiftly down the hallway, bare feet absolutely silent against the cold stone floor. The loose fit of her sandals had caused an audible slap when she needed to move quickly, so Quarrah was now holding them.

She'd made it to the north wing of the palace. This area was completely new since the sow-dragon attack, and Quarrah was essentially wandering blindly through its dim passages.

She was looking for the portrait of herself, painted by Errel in the king's box at the Royal Concert Hall. Fabra had said it was hanging just outside her chambers in the north wing. And while Quarrah had demanded that she take it down at their last meeting, Fabra didn't really strike her as the type to follow through promptly.

She found it with little trouble, mounted to the wall beside a locked door. It really would be a fine piece of art if the subject matter were different. Squinting briefly, Quarrah saw that Errel had even captured the subtle bags under her eyes. Sparks, the handmaiden could have done without those.

Glancing down the vacant hallway, Quarrah twisted awkwardly, reaching up the short side of her robe to the band of tools she'd tied around her thigh. Her picks were out in a moment, and the mortise lock posed no difficulty, even in the dim lighting.

Quarrah cracked open the door and peered inside. It was definitely Fabra Ment's room, still illuminated by a waning detonation of Prolonged Light Grit in a bracket on the wall. She could see the queen dowager's large sun hat that she'd worn while shooting around the palace grounds. And her pipe was on the desk beside a tin of tobacco.

Relieved to find all quiet, Quarrah pushed open the door the rest of the way, stepping inside. The chamber was unnecessarily large and highly decorated, with two bay windows latched from within. There was a poster bed, its drapes drawn tidily, and a footed tub behind a curtained partition. A mirror taller than Quarrah was mounted to one wall, and the reflected image startled her with its full-sized movement. There was no shortage of comfortable places to lounge, which bespoke the same idleness the queen dowager was always bragging about.

Several animal heads were mounted to the walls, their glass eyes glinting in the meager light. Apparently, Fabra hunted more than just the rabbits and crows on the palace grounds. There was a buffalo head that must have come from southern Dronodan, a wild boar, and a buck deer likely from Pekal.

Quarrah shut the door and locked it behind her. "Fabra?" she whispered into the room, moving toward the high-back padded chairs facing the hearth. The seats were vacant, but Quarrah noticed the soft ticking of one of those Gregious Mas mantel clocks. Only a half hour until their meeting at ten.

"Fabra?" she called again, this time a little louder. She saw two doors in the south wall. Presumably, those would lead to ancillary rooms with more amenities. As if anyone needed more than this luxurious room...

Quarrah crossed the chamber and tested the first door. Locked. But it was no more complex than the one to the hallway. She took a knee on the animal-skin rug, shuddering under the steady gaze of the deer staring down at her.

The lock sprang, and Quarrah eased the door open to complete darkness. In the little light that spilled in, she saw an extravagant closet.

Clothing lined both sides and the back wall, hanging from rods like vacant soldiers standing at attention. There were hat boxes on shelves above, and more shoes than Quarrah could fathom. Didn't most people have only two feet?

As she pulled the door shut, her jagpin tool snagged on some lacy material and got tugged out of her grasp.

"Sparks," Quarrah muttered, dropping to her knees on the floor, feeling blindly for the fallen tool. In resigned frustration, Quarrah reached up and tapped sharply on the piece of Slagstone embedded

beside her right eye. The Light Grit detonated, nearly blinding her
with the sudden contrast. In a moment, her vision had adjusted and
she saw the metal tool glinting. She crawled forward on hands and
knees...

Why did the rug extend all the way to the back wall of the closet?
And the fibers looked worn, as though a footpath continued directly
under the row of hanging clothes.

Grabbing her jagpin, Quarrah pushed aside the hanging clothing and shone her glowing eye at the closet's back wall. There was
a hinged panel, at least four feet tall, secured with a latch and a
single-pin hanging lock.

She was through the lock in a matter of seconds, pushing the
panel inward on its hinges. Another secret closet came into view,
easily as large as the one she was kneeling in.

Quarrah crawled forward, rising to her feet as she came through
the small doorway. She couldn't take it all in at once, but one
thing drew her attention most, the light from her eye casting it in a
dreaded glow.

Overseer's mask.

By the Homeland, that was Overseer's dragon-scale mask on the
shelf! Realizing what it all meant, Quarrah began to tremble. She
wanted to shed her uncomfortable disguise and flee at once.

She had stumbled into the lair of the Realm's leader, Fabra Ment.
Why?

The question kept cascading through Quarrah's mind. Why
would the queen dowager hire her to infiltrate her own secret organization? Quarrah thought back to the reason she'd been hired.
Fabra had been afraid Termain was being manipulated by the
Realm. She clearly knew he was.

Quarrah must not have accomplished what Fabra had truly
wanted, because the queen dowager had begged to keep her on. To
probe the Realm for signs of weakness and report back to her.

*She's checking her own security,* Quarrah realized. This whole time,

Fabra would have known, as Overseer, that Quarrah was not loyal to the Realm. *So why hasn't she eliminated me yet? Why keep me going?*

Maybe the Realm's security had been compromised and Fabra still didn't know where the problem was. Quarrah was supposed to ferret it out, but she...

Oh, flames. It was Ardor Benn.

Fabra Ment had been obsessed with him from the start. The only reason she had hired Quarrah was because she hadn't been able to get to Ard. Somehow, she must have known Ardor Benn was infiltrating the Realm, an organization she believed to be watertight. Fabra had likely hired Quarrah only because of her past association with the ruse artist. Because if anyone could draw out Ardor Benn, it was Quarrah Khai.

This whole job was a setup! The decision to move the Homeland ruse up a few days to avoid letting them reach Shad Agaul. The meeting with Overseer in the garden tonight...Sparks, she needed to stop Ard from going!

Quarrah turned to leave, but paused, her thief's instinct kicking in. She had just uncovered a secret that no one in the Directorate even knew. This was Overseer's base of operations. It had to be full of valuable information. She'd have a look around and get out fast enough to reach Ard before he went to the garden.

In addition to the uncut-dragon-husk headpiece, Quarrah saw a few other familiar items. Resting on the shelf were a pair of leather gloves and a voice-modifying wax mouthpiece. Hanging beside the mask were a few heavy black robes—the kind Quarrah had seen Overseer wear at the Directorate meetings.

On another shelf, Quarrah spotted a pair of Rollers with metal-capped butts. A Grit belt and holsters hung beside them, with plenty of Blast cartridges for reloading.

But what the blazes was *this*? Quarrah's light shone on a series of glass jars on another shelf. She picked one up and peered closely at it. Instead of a lid, mesh fabric was tied over the top. Inside, there was a large black worm clinging to a mossy stick. The worm had spines running from one bulbous end to the other. Some viscous, amber-colored liquid filled the bottom inch of the jar, and bits of rotting meat were swimming in it.

Repulsed, she set it down and examined the other jars to find that they all housed at least one of the same disgusting black worms. The final jar in the row held only the amber liquid. As her light shone through it, she could see little round flecks not much larger than grains of salt.

*Eggs,* Quarrah realized. *Disgusting, squishy little worm eggs.* Why would Overseer be keeping...

The Waters of Loyalty!

Of course! It wasn't poison, it was a parasite. Since the worms were living creatures, exposing them to Health Grit would only make them stronger. These eggs were easily small enough to pass through the drinking reed and be swallowed without detection.

Quarrah shuddered, thinking of a colony of unhatched worms swimming inside her. With each swallow of Loyalty, the Faceless would be introducing more eggs into their body, while simultaneously consuming some kind of suppressant that postponed their hatching. Clever.

Quarrah set down the jar and moved to examine the little writing desk against the opposing wall. She pulled out the shallow drawer and found a ledger, flipping it open to the first page.

*Faceless Meeting—Fourteenth of Nine—Noon*

*Nexus—Widehart's Millinery*

*Grapple—Fardal and Sons*

*Snare—Baubles and Knickknacks*

*Radius—Thatch Fishmonger*

*Glint—Dem Haberdashery*

*Hedge—Chansel Library and Paperworks*

*Trance—Floura Fishmonger*

Quarrah flipped to the next page.

*Faceless Meeting—Thirtieth of Nine—8 o'clock morning*

A similar list of names and locations followed. Quarrah skipped through the ledger until the name *Sleight* appeared. The date at the top of the page corresponded with her first meeting as one of the Directorate, and she was marked down for pickup at Jorish and Sons in the Central Quarter, where her marked carriage had awaited her.

Quarrah thumbed to the last page with text and read the details.

*Faceless Meeting—Second of Four—Noon*

This was the upcoming Faceless meeting, scheduled for the day Shad Agaul was set to arrive, with the Cataclysm happening that night.

Shuffling through the drawer, Quarrah found a blank scrap of paper and a scribing charcoal. Her Light Grit eye had just started to dim, but she'd still have several more minutes of sufficient illumination. Quarrah scrawled the date and time of the meeting, followed by the code name of each Directorate member and their pickup location.

What else was in this desk drawer? There were a lot of blank pages and loose leafs with seemingly meaningless notes scribbled on them. Peering to the back of the drawer, Quarrah noticed a tightly scrolled page that had rolled out of sight. She retrieved it, freezing when she saw what held it bound.

The Agaul family ring.

Well, well. Quarrah hadn't expected to see this again. And what kind of paper was important enough to be stored in the heirloom ring? She pocketed the jewelry and unrolled the page.

It was a map of Pekal, or at least the eastern slopes, extending from the Archkingdom's southern harbor up to North Pointe.

Distinct symbols were scrawled across the map—mostly *X*s and circles, with a handful of symbols that denoted Ashings.

These had to be the locations of the resources that Overseer had mentioned in the last meeting, although Quarrah had no way of knowing what each marking represented.

A distinct sound sent a sudden jolt of panic through her. It was a key rattling in the lock from the hallway.

Quarrah dumped the ledger into the drawer and pushed it closed. But she held on to the map and the notes she had written. With the Agaul family ring in her pocket, she lunged through the opening into the clothes closet, pulling the panel door shut and clicking the padlock into place.

The large bedchamber was dark now, but sparks, her eye was still glowing! As if her shiny golden skin wasn't bad enough. In a pinch decision, Quarrah closed herself in the closet just as the chamber door swung open from the hallway.

With probably only fifteen minutes until their predetermined rendezvous, this would definitely be Fabra Ment. And she'd be coming right for this closet to retrieve Overseer's mask.

Quarrah parted the rack of clothes hanging on the left side of the closet and wriggled behind them. Her back touched the wall and she tucked in her painted feet. In her normal attire, she would have felt quite confident in this hiding spot, even with the queen dowager passing within arm's reach. As it was, her dimming eye light was shining through the clothes like a lighthouse beacon.

Quarrah heard the key in the closet door. She hadn't locked it behind her, but Fabra's key would turn in the hole just the same, hopefully making the queen dowager think she'd opened it.

Quarrah grabbed the closest item hanging in front of her face, a nice thick wool fabric. Against all her instincts, she buried her face to hide the light. She breathed slowly, hearing Fabra clear her throat as she stepped into the closet. The keys jingled again and the padlock scraped through the latch.

This was her chance. Quarrah let go of the wool coat and peered through the clothes. Nobody else was in the closet, but the queen dowager would be costuming just on the other side of that rack.

Ever so quietly, but with a practiced speed, Quarrah eased herself out from behind the clothes, taking the wool coat with her as she slipped out of the closet on bare feet. The door to the hallway remained unlocked and Quarrah passed through it without so much as a squeak of a hinge.

Then she was racing down the hallway, desperate to find Ardor Benn before he left the reception hall.

"A toast!" cried King Termain, pushing out the nearest chair and stepping onto it. In Ard's opinion, the man had already had too many, and the reception didn't show any signs of winding down.

Ard glanced at the large pendulum clock in the corner of the room. He could only stay a few more minutes anyway. It would be unwise to keep Overseer waiting in the garden.

"Eight glasses of the finest we have," Termain shouted at the servants. "Only the best for our Homelanders!"

"Seven glasses." Ard decided to address it now on his terms rather than waiting for one of the nobility to notice that Quarrah had vanished. "I'm afraid Navara grew uncomfortable in the confines of such a small room and had to step outside for some fresh air." It was ludicrous, since the reception hall was one of the vastest chambers in the palace. But it furthered the lie that buildings in the Homeland were unimaginably grand.

"No matter!" the king continued. "I'll drink with seven or seven hundred Homelanders. This is a night to be remembered!"

Although the king would probably be remembering very little in the morning.

"The intention is kind, good sir," Garew responded to the king. "But our bodies have no need for nourishment since our feet have touched the Homeland. We have been elevated beyond such frailty."

"Nourishment, ha!" Termain's speech was a bit slurred. "This is purely recreational. If the Homeland doesn't value that, methinks I want no part of it!"

"On the contrary," said Ruge. "We can still find great pleasure in partaking of such things. Offer your toast, King. We shall gratify you with a drink."

A servant returned with seven stemmed glasses on a tray. He handed one to Ard and then distributed the rest to the other Homelanders.

"To the Homeland!" shouted Termain, raising the latest glass he'd been nursing. "May we all reach her crystal shores!"

"To the Homeland!" went up a chorus from the rest of the wealthy people in the room.

Ard lifted the glass to his lips and took a sip. Sparks, this *was* the finest he'd had. And soon he'd get to brag to Raek that he'd been served fancy drinks by *two* kings in as many years.

"I suppose I had forgotten how simple and flavorless drinks were before the Homeland," remarked Yalan, smacking his lips softly.

"Simple and flavorless?" King Termain laughed. "I love this guy! What a riot!"

"I meant no mirth," answered Yalan. "I was merely remarking that wines in the Homeland have an elevated complexity not found anywhere..." He coughed. "Excuse me."

He coughed again. And beside him, Palia made a sound as though she might vomit. The king's laughter increased until Yalan fell to his knees, the glass slipping from his hand and shattering on the floor.

"Sparks!" Termain cried, leaping down from his chair, face twisted up in sudden genuine concern. "What the blazes?"

Garew suddenly went down at Ard's side, yellow foam appearing on his lips, streaming out his nose. The crowd gasped and screamed.

Ardor Benn staggered a step backward, glancing at the drink

in his hand. Oh, flames. What was happening? Ruge and Keel lurched forward, hacking and vomiting that same foamy substance.

"It was the wine!" someone cried, a voice above the rest. "Poison!"

Yalan and Palia were now dead on the floor. Ard could see the glazed lifelessness in their yellow eyes. He kept backing up as the crowd closed tighter, gawking at the spectacle of six golden figures writhing on the floor of the reception hall.

"Who would do such a thing?" shouted another.

"It was the Prime Isless! She's been skeptical since the moment they arrived!"

Ard saw Gloristar standing against the wall, shaking her head in dumbfounded shock. "Homelanders cannot be poisoned," she said. "Their perfected bodies should be immune to such threats."

Ard looked again at his glass, waiting in dread for whatever poison was tearing through the rest of his crew. Reaching out, he set it on one of the tall tables.

"Imposters!" someone shouted. "Sovereign spies!"

Ard's steady backward retreat had led him to the doorway. All eyes were on the center of the room, and he turned and fled into the hallway.

He ran down whichever corridor appeared the dimmest, anxious to put distance between himself and the reception hall. Why wasn't he dying? Why hadn't the poison struck him yet?

Quarrah had been right. Sparks, he should have listened to her! Fabra Ment's handmaiden must have known that the queen dowager had been found out. This whole reception had been nothing more than a setup—a way to effectively eliminate anyone who had been involved in Ard's Homelander ruse.

Overseer obviously didn't trust Rival. Had she ever? Flames, how long had she been playing him?

Ard had no idea where he was when Quarrah Khai emerged from the shadows and grabbed him by the shoulders. The shock toppled him to his knees and he stayed down, gasping for breath.

"Are you all right?" she asked. A long wool coat concealed her foreign Homeland attire. She'd removed her wig and face ridges, doing her best to wipe off the thick paint.

"I've been poisoned, Quarrah," he gasped. "It killed the others. All of them! Someone poisoned the wine." He sucked in a deep breath, but still felt no pain or discomfort inside. "The whole reception was a trap to expose the ruse and kill everyone involved. Everything's ruined..."

Quarrah crossed the dim hallway and tested the door. It swung open and she pulled Ard inside. The room was unoccupied, gratefully, and appeared to be some kind of instrumental rehearsal space. Music stands stood like skeletal trees, and a covered harpsichord sat in the corner.

Quarrah grabbed Ard's wig and pulled it off with a sharp tug. He winced, letting out a grunt of pain as the clips came free. She whipped the cloth cover off the harpsichord and tossed it at his feet.

"Put this on," she said. "We've got to get out of here."

"You don't understand," he cried, painfully stripping away the artificial ridges on his face and scratching at the leftover adhesive. "We can't go to the meeting in the garden."

"I know," she snapped. "Fabra Ment is Overseer."

Ard froze, the final prosthetic hanging halfway attached around his eye. "The queen dowager? But that doesn't make sense. She's..."

"My employer," Quarrah finished. "She must have hired me as a security check. She never trusted me, but she needed me to work my way up so that I could tell her how to catch you."

"Me?" Ard cried. "I've never even met the old lady!" He shook his head, peeling off the last bit of his disguise. "How did you learn all of this?"

"I got into Fabra's staging room," she replied. "The closet she uses as Overseer."

He grunted. "I should have come with you."

"If you had, you'd probably have gotten us killed," she answered.

"I'm dying anyway..."

"Oh, please. You weren't poisoned, Ard. If the others died within seconds of drinking, then why are you still alive?"

He exhaled in relief. She made an excellent point. "I thought my superior physique was delaying the poison's effect."

Quarrah rolled her eyes. "Those other three Homelander men made you look like an overfed slug." She cracked open the door and peered into the corridor.

Ard touched her arm. "We can't go out there without a plan. If we flee tonight, Overseer will know we got away, and the Realm will put everything they've got into finding us."

"What are you suggesting?"

"We know who Overseer is," said Ard. "And we know where she's going to be. Let's use this opportunity to take her down."

"What are we supposed to do, storm into the garden and shoot her? She's the king's mother!"

"We can arrest her," said Ard. "Make her crimes public." He thought she'd appreciate this plan. It was more in line with what Quarrah had wanted to do to Pethredote before Ard had called the dragon to destroy him.

"We're not Regulators," Quarrah reminded him.

"Then we send the Reggies into the garden," he said.

"And how do you plan to convince them?"

"I have my ways," he defended.

Quarrah looked into his eyes for the first time since they'd entered the rehearsal room. "That could work. It would be dangerous for the Reggies."

"They'll have her outnumbered," Ard persuaded, "with the element of surprise." He picked up the harpsichord cover and slung it around his shoulders. A piece of paper fluttered to the floor and he stooped to retrieve it. Just a sheet of music—a sonatina.

Footsteps suddenly sounded down the corridor. Ard peered out as Quarrah closed the door to a mere sliver.

"Now, if that's not a sign from the Homeland..." Ard said, folding the page of music in his hands. The footsteps belonged to a Regulator, who was walking so fast she looked like she might break into a jog at any moment.

"I don't like this," Quarrah whispered.

Ard lifted his hand to the door and shoved it open just as the Reggie was level with them in the hallway.

The sharp movement caused the Regulator to whirl, drawing her Roller. Ard stood in the doorway with his hands raised peacefully, the cover of the harpsichord concealing his strange garb. Most of his face and hands were still golden, not to mention his dyed yellow eyes.

"My name is Inspector Stringer," he spoke quickly, flashing the folded sheet of music as though it were proper paperwork. "I'm licensed to work privately in all quarters of the city. My partner and I need your help to make an arrest on a case we've been working for several cycles."

"Why do you look like that?" The woman gestured at Ard's appearance with the barrel of her gun.

"Surely you've heard about the Homelanders," Ard answered. Their ship had only arrived a few hours ago, but news of this magnitude was bound to spread fast. Especially around the palace.

The Regulator nodded suspiciously.

"Golden skin, yellow eyes..." Ard gestured to himself.

"You're not one of—"

"Of course not!" Ard cut her off. "The Homelanders are all fake." Behind him, Quarrah drew in a sharp breath. But there was no sense in trying to keep the ruse intact now.

The Regulator's suspicious nod turned more genuine. Ard could see in her eyes that she believed him. She'd probably been dubious of the Homelander reports all along.

"The entire thing was a ruse set up by the criminal we've been following," Ard continued. "He was planning to use his counterfeit

Homelanders to assassinate His Majesty, but we managed to get hired onto his team so we could expose the plot and protect the king."

"Then why haven't you arrested him?"

"The man is skittish," said Ard. "He's been coordinating all this from the shadows, so we haven't had a chance to reach him."

"Until tonight," Quarrah said. Ard glanced back at her with a smirk. It was good to have her backing him up.

"We have a meeting with him in the east garden," Ard explained. "Near the fishing pond. You need to assemble the troops and get down there. Our rendezvous was set for ten o'clock sharp. We can't expect him to wait much longer."

The Reggie tilted her head. "I'm not a commanding officer. I can't simply assemble the palace Regulation—"

"Then go get someone who can!" Ard shouted. "This is the kind of arrest that's going to turn a lot of heads."

"Who's the crook?"

"His name is Ardor Benn," he answered. "You may remember him as the ruse artist who put a gun to King Pethredote's head and then escaped from the Regulation Stockade?"

The size of the Reggie's eyes indicated that she did indeed recognize the name. "Why is he meeting you in the garden?"

"To get paid," Ard said. "Ardor Benn is part of a massive crime ring. We were going to pose as his superiors and tell him where he could pick up his payment."

"Dressed like that?" she cried. "He's bound to recognize you as part of the Homelander crew."

"We were going to wear masks," Quarrah added.

"You have them with you?"

Ard shook his head. "Our disguises are hidden behind the lilac bush near the statue of the stag." There was no telling if the Reggie would check that detail, but the more truth he could sprinkle into this story, the better it might hold up.

"It was a risky plan," Ard admitted. "And we only hoped to get close enough to apprehend him. But you..." He gestured at her uniform in open admiration. "An entire brigade of Regulators closing in on his position is a much better way to get the job done."

Finally, the Regulator nodded. "I'll take this to Assistant Chief Dime. This could get him the promotion he's been after." She gestured down the corridor. "Come this way."

Ard pulled a hesitant face, pointing back at Quarrah in the dim room. "I'm afraid she turned her ankle when we were fleeing the reception hall." On cue, Quarrah twisted her face into something of a grimace and leaned against the doorjamb. *Nice touch.* "We'll only slow you down, and Ardor Benn demands punctuality." Good thing Raek wasn't here to scoff at that line. "We'll meet you at the infirmary after you make the arrest. Homeland speed you."

The Reggie seemed to hesitate for only a moment before continuing down the hallway, breaking into the jog she'd been bordering on earlier.

"Can you get us to a balcony on the east side of the palace?" Ard asked Quarrah the moment the Reggie was out of sight.

"Balcony?"

"I thought you'd like to watch the arrest," he said. "See your employer get her comeuppance."

Ard dropped the folded sheet of music as Quarrah slipped past him, leading the way in the opposite direction.

Following Quarrah through the palace while some harebrained idea threatened to fold at any moment made Ard feel alive in a way that he hadn't since they'd separated. His words, smooth and cunning, striking in tandem with Quarrah's impeccable memory and sense of direction. There was passion when they worked together like this. Why didn't she see it? Why didn't she *feel* it?

Soon, they were cutting through a vacant guest room, finding their way onto an east-facing balcony. As dark as the night was, Ard could barely make out the reflection of the stars in the fishing pond partway across the garden.

He and Quarrah crouched in silence, peering through the metal balusters of the balcony's railing. "They're taking too long," Ard whispered, eyes straining for any sign of the Reggie brigade that should have been closing in. "Overseer will be gone by now."

"There." Quarrah pointed. Ard could just make out two figures on the graveled path leading out to the pond, making no attempt at stealth. Squinting, Ard realized why.

They were wearing the Directorate masks of Rival and Sleight.

"What are they doing?" Quarrah whispered.

"Are those our Reggies?"

Suddenly, a small gush of flames flared beside the pond and the figure wearing Quarrah's black mask fell with a strangled cry. A second muzzle flash showed in the night, dropping the person wearing Ard's fox mask. From above, Ard thought he could hear the Roller ball fatally cracking into the figure's chest.

Ard gasped, and Quarrah covered her mouth. The shots had been perfectly noiseless, no doubt concealed in a cloud of Silence Grit. Neither of the figures stirred from where they'd been shot, but Ard suddenly saw Overseer moving toward their downed figures, her large headpiece of uncut dragon scales shimmering in a beam of light that spilled from a palace window.

"She's going to unmask them," Quarrah whispered at his side. And the moment she did, she'd know it had been a trick.

"Help!" Ard shouted as loudly as he could. Below, Overseer froze on the path, her dragon-scale mask tilting upward to the sound of the cry.

"Help!" Ard yelled again. "They've been shot! Murder! Murder!"

Still ten feet from the dead pair, Overseer suddenly turned and vanished into the darkness of the garden.

Within moments, a trio of Regulators responded, detonating

Light Grit above the deceased and pulling back their masks and cloaks to reveal their identities. Both were wearing red uniforms. Ard was sure that the one in Quarrah's mask had been the same Reggie they'd convinced to make the arrest.

"Why?" he whispered. "Why didn't she close in on Overseer like we'd suggested?"

"Maybe she was part of the Realm," said Quarrah. "We know they have influence inside the palace."

"Or maybe she and the assistant chief were hoping for an even bigger arrest than Ardor Benn."

"What do you mean?"

"We told her that Ardor Benn was part of a crime ring," Ard said. "Maybe she thought they could go through with the meeting and hope to make a connection that could take down the entire ring."

"Overseer killed them," Quarrah muttered.

True. It didn't really matter *why* the two Regulators below had disguised themselves to go through with the meeting. What mattered was that Overseer fired the moment she saw their masks.

"That would have been us," Quarrah whispered. "But why not just poison us along with the others?"

"That was probably the primary plan. And it would have taken care of Ardor Benn and Quarrah Khai," said Ard. "But Overseer needed to make sure she killed Rival and Sleight as well."

If the ruse artist and Rival had been different people, as Ard had been playing it, then Fabra needed to finish him off with a Roller in the garden.

"The Realm thinks we're dead," Quarrah suddenly whispered. "This could be our chance to get out."

Ard grimaced. "Except we still need the Waters of Loyalty."

"I may have a lead on that."

"You..." Ard grinned his widest yet.

"From Overseer's closet," she pressed on. "Some kind of insect eggs, I think. She was harvesting them from black worms kept in glass jars."

"Of course," he said. "Did you happen to swipe a specimen?"

She shook her head. "I was interrupted. But I took this." She produced a paper from the pocket of her wool coat. Based on its shape, it had obviously been scrolled, although nothing was tied around it.

Quarrah unrolled the page and held it out for Ard's inspection. "The Realm's resources on Pekal."

A map. Brilliant! One of the markings caught Ard's eye as he squinted down at it. "That symbol…" His heart beat faster.

"I didn't notice it before," Quarrah whispered. "Overseer said that the Faceless expected to receive special kegs for the Cataclysm." She pointed. "Marked with a wave."

Ard shook his head. Quarrah was probably right about the Cataclysm kegs, but that wasn't what had seized him. "*That* symbol." He pointed to a mark at the top of Parnan's Canyon.

"The star?" she asked.

"That's no star." Ard's voice was tight. It was the only one on the map. A capital letter 'A,' the bottom crossed to look like a star with the top point standing tall. "That's the Agaul *A*. It's hanging all over the Guesthouse Adagio."

"So, the Realm is hiding something they stole from King Termain—"

"Not Termain," Ard corrected. "That's *Remium's* family symbol."

Quarrah's voice was barely a whisper at his side. "Shad."

Ard nodded. "It's the perfect hiding place."

"No," she responded. "It's not. Not for a child. Not for anyone." She sounded distressed. "How are they keeping him from getting Moonsick?"

"They must be moving him off the island every thirty days." Ard snapped his fingers. "That's why Overseer was so bent out of shape about moving the resources off Pekal *before* the Moon Passing!"

"The Cataclysm kegs were a front," said Quarrah. "A justification for her panic attack."

"I mean, I'm sure the Realm wants to get them, too," Ard said, "but if they're just full of Grit, they're not going to spoil under the Moon Passing like Shad Agaul."

"So the extraction team Grapple is organizing might not even be going for the kegs," said Quarrah. "But they're definitely going for the prince."

Ard shrugged. "Unless we beat them there." He tapped the symbol at the top of Parnan's Canyon. "You ready to go back to Pekal?"

~

*We slaughtered them without resistance, ourselves grieved to turn blades on our former brothers and sisters.*

# PART V

---

How can we achieve such glory as those who walk upon the Homeland? Verily, their eyes stream with a blessed glow, and their will is made known to one another in wordless unity.

—Wayfarist Voyage, *vol. 2*

Our eyes are further livened by the shards. Through plates of red, the shimmering Glass, its sacred aura shining, will always show the way to truth.

—*Ancient Agrodite poem*

# CHAPTER

# 36

Quarrah looked up at the looming mountains of Pekal. Hadn't she sworn never to come back to this island of death and nightmares? She'd finally reached a point where her closed eyes weren't haunted by visions of dragons tearing through her companions. Where a malodorous smell didn't remind her of hacking a sword into the shoulder of that Moonsick Trothian. *And don't even get me started on eggs…*

Well, this time it would be different. She was more prepared. And she wasn't simply going to follow Ardor Benn's half-baked plans.

"It had to be Glint, don't you think?" Ard said, leaning on the rudder of the *Double Take*. Quarrah thought they were much too close to Pekal's harbor to be rehashing this casual conversation. She could actually see individuals in the wreckage of the docks and half-sunken ships.

It would appear that the Trothians were planning to hold out until the very last second before the Moon Passing. The Archkingdom and the Sovereign States both had small fleets waiting beyond the red-line zone. But instead of firing on one another, they both seemed to be waiting for the Trothians' inevitable departure.

It had been risky to sail around the two fleets and head straight for the harbor, but the *Double Take* was a fast ship, and small enough that the fleets had apparently deemed it unthreatening. Either that, or by the time they realized the *Double Take* was heading for the harbor, engaging them would have put them within range of the Trothian cannons. Maybe that wasn't a risk they were willing to take.

"Everything the professor said about her corresponds with what we've seen of Glint," Ard carried on. "Shorter woman with a stocky build charged with overseeing Portsend's progress…"

Quarrah agreed that the woman Portsend had killed probably had been Glint. That would mean three openings in the Directorate, with Sleight and Rival presumed dead.

She and Ard had not stuck around long after witnessing the shooting from the balcony. Before they had even escaped the palace, Quarrah had heard people confirming that the fraudulent Homelanders were Sovereign spies. The queen dowager had managed to spin the whole debacle in the Realm's favor, exposing the ruse to further tensions between both sides.

Fabra Ment would order the Realm to return to the original plan with Shad Agaul, having him appear after the Cataclysm, claiming to have been a captive of King Termain.

Unless, of course, Quarrah and Ard got to him first. That was why they'd left before dawn, sailing with favorable winds not twelve hours after the disaster at the reception.

"Whoever she was," Raek said, "she put the poor professor through a lot."

"It was good thinking to check on him," Ard said.

"Thought I could clear things up with the professor so he wouldn't try to frame me for anything else," Raek said. "Things escalated quickly once I got inside the lab."

"You did the right thing," Ard assured. "He'll be safe with Codley and the others."

Quarrah was the only one who thought it was a bad idea to invite Portsend Wal to stay at the Guesthouse Adagio. He was too close to the Prime Isless and too much of a target for the Realm. And while

Quarrah was off to Pekal, she wanted as few people sniffing around the guesthouse grounds as possible. After all, she'd had little choice but to stash the Agaul family ring behind a loose brick on the back of the carriage house.

She hadn't decided what to do with the enormous jewel yet. Quarrah had rightfully stolen it, and now the ring had come back to her. She'd wait to see how things panned out with the prince before deciding whether to give it back to the Agauls or sell it for a hefty sum.

"Steady as she goes," Ard said, eking a little more out of the sails as Raek dropped onto the rowing bench and readied the oars.

On the clifflike sides of the harbor, Quarrah saw the shine of metal in the defensible gun ports. The *Double Take* was flying a white flag, but that was their only assurance that the Trothians wouldn't open fire.

The harbor was actually in worse shape than she'd originally thought. The Trans-Island Carriages that had made the initial flyby attack were nowhere to be seen. Quarrah knew firsthand that Pekal was not equipped to receive the air vessels, and landing one successfully on the mountain slopes was virtually impossible. Likely, the ones used to drop the Grit had flown on, circling back to land on Talumon or Dronodan.

From what she'd heard, that attack had only been intended to cripple the harbor defenses and make it possible for a fleet of warships to get in and finish the job. The Trothians had used Sovereign ships for this, and those were what Quarrah saw now, large brigantines at rest among the flotsam cluttering the harbor.

The *Double Take* maneuvered its way through the big ships, Raek's powerful arms pulling at the oars. There were thousands of Trothians, mingled with a few Landers, who must have been excited about taking a more aggressive approach than the Sovereign officials would authorize.

In all honesty, Quarrah couldn't ever remember seeing so many

Trothians in one place at a time. The largest group she'd previously seen had been on the night in Oriar's Square when Ard had taken the dragon egg back in time for Grotenisk to fertilize. She'd felt their power then, but it had been intense and rather frenzied. Here in the harbor, the Trothians exuded a quiet authority. They had taken this harbor from the Archkingdom and she sensed no regret or fear that they'd lose it.

The prow of the *Double Take* bumped into a dock that looked slightly charred. Ard tossed a rope to a Trothian woman, who began lashing the boat in place. Behind her, a row of armed Trothians held pikes, with guns holstered at their sides. A few carried Trothian swords, which were significantly wider and heavier than the dueling blades common among the Landers. Despite their treasonous act, most wore the colors and helmets of the Sovereign States.

"Quite the welcoming committee," Ard muttered.

"What is your business here?" called one of the men. He wasn't wearing a helmet, and his dark eyes were blurry as he studied them.

"We seek an audience with your chieftess, Lyndel," Ard said.

Quarrah held her breath. There had been no way to be sure she'd really be here, but this was the bigger and busier of the two captured harbors, and Quarrah knew the attack had been Lyndel's plan all along.

"We're old friends," Ard said after a moment of awkward silence. "You can give her our names…"

"This way." The man gestured for them to follow. Quarrah grabbed her pack and climbed onto the dock, following until they came to one of the checkpoint huts. One that was still intact, at least.

The man rapped on the door and cracked it open. He spoke briefly in the Trothian tongue, and Quarrah breathed a sigh of relief to hear Lyndel's voice responding. A moment later, he pushed open the door and stepped back to allow the three Landers to enter.

Lyndel was not alone in the room. Three other Trothians and

one Lander woman with deep brown skin were gathered around her. The Lander was bent over a table spread with maps and other documents, reading the text that the Trothians' unique eyes could not perceive.

The chieftess looked healthier than the last time Quarrah had seen her. Come to think of it, all the Trothians did. Their dark blue skin looked smooth and lush. This close to the water, Lyndel was probably making sure all her warriors received an adequate saltwater soak. That alone might have been sufficient incentive to pull the Trothian forces from the inland march to execute an unsanctioned attack at the harbors.

"*Omligath*, Lyndel!" Ard cried merrily, as if he spoke their language. "Hard to believe it's been two years! You don't look a day older."

Quarrah found the greeting to be a bit more familiar than was indicative of their relationship. Sure, Ard and Lyndel had worked together to coordinate the gathering in Oriar's Square, but they had never been chummy.

Lyndel must have felt the same as Quarrah, since her response was simple. "Ardor Benn."

"How have you been?" he asked cordially. "When Quarrah told me you were in command of the Trothian armed forces, I thought to myself, 'Of course she is. No one better suited in my mind.'"

Sparks, Ard was really buttering her up. Lyndel didn't strike Quarrah as someone who would succumb to flowery flattery. In her experience, the priestess had been rather blunt and very direct. She did what she felt needed to be done, regardless of how others would perceive it.

"I assume you are not simply here to lend your support to my actions," Lyndel said. "What have you come to ask of me?"

"Well, first of all, congratulations on taking the Archkingdom's harbors," Ard belabored. "I found your tactics revolutionary and—"

"We need your people to let us onto the island," Quarrah interjected. Ard was handling this all wrong. At the rate he was speaking, the Moon Passing would be on them before they even left this hut.

"A Harvesting operation?" Lyndel asked.

"Not this time," answered Quarrah. "We need to find something that was hidden in the mountains and bring it out before the Passing."

Lyndel seemed to ponder it for a moment, glancing around the room at her companions. Quarrah wondered if the other Trothians understood Landerian well enough to follow the conversation. By the looks on their faces, they could. And they didn't seem to approve.

"We cannot," Lyndel answered. "This harbor must remain closed to citizens of the Archkingdom."

"I wouldn't exactly call us citizens..." Ard protested.

"Do you not live in Beripent?" she asked.

"Well, yes, but..."

"Then you are citizens of the Archkingdom."

"Nobody has to know that," he said.

"How can I trust you?" Lyndel asked. "I know your reputation and your occupation. You are likely here because someone in Beripent hired you. Perhaps you are abusing your connection with me in order to gain access to Pekal and do something that will benefit the Archkingdom."

"What we're doing isn't for your enemies," Ard continued. "This might even be the key to ending the war. Your people can just look the other way and we'll disappear into the trees. It's going to be a quick job. Has to be, with that Passing coming."

"You'd be too late for a major expedition anyway," Lyndel said. "All the Harvesters who were here this cycle have already departed."

"You let them go?" Raek asked.

"We are not merciless murderers," Lyndel replied. "We captured the harbors to cut off the Archkingdom's supply of new Grit. We confiscated the Slagstone mounds and all the equipment we could, but we let the crews sail out of here peacefully. Most of their ships had been damaged beyond repair during the attack, but we provided vessels sufficient for their departure. We hope word of their fair treatment will spread. We are doing what we can to ensure that this tactic does not become mistaken for a Trothian-Lander war."

"By the looks of it, I wouldn't say the Sovs have your back," Raek said. "There's a whole fleet of them waiting at the Redeye line."

"Yes," Lyndel said. "We are aware of both fleets."

"And the fact that they're not fighting each other?" Ard said. "This doesn't look good for you, Lyndel."

"There is a Trothian saying," replied Lyndel. "Take away the *jakna* before the young ones get sick."

"What's a *jakna*?" asked Raek.

"It is a Trothian sweet drink," Lyndel answered. "Too much can sour a child's stomach."

"Not sure what that has to do with the fleets waiting for you," Ard mentioned.

"A child is often angry with a parent for taking away the *jakna*. But the parent knows best," said Lyndel. "I did what was needed for the Sovereign States to keep the upper hand, yet they are angry with me."

"The Landers have another phrase for that," said Ard. "Better to ask forgiveness than to ask permission."

"I asked permission," said Lyndel, "at the Sovereign war council last cycle. And the cycle before that. They are blinded by tradition and they refuse to see a more effective way to win the war."

"So, what will happen when you sail out of here?" Quarrah asked.

"There is word out for my arrest from the Sovereign States," she answered.

"And probably your head from the Archkingdom," muttered Raek.

"I will be taken to tribunal. They are calling it treason."

"They have a funny way of labeling things," Ard said. "I'd call it a stratagem."

"What about the other harbor?" Quarrah asked.

"I have left Darbu in command there."

"Darbu!" Ard cried. "Did I ever tell you about the time he held on to King Pethredote's coat during a visit to the apartment on Avedon Street? What a guy!"

"His harbor is under the same situation," Lyndel continued as though Ard had not interjected. "Between the two locations, we have pulled almost every Trothian warrior from the Sovereign forces."

"Are you worried what they'll do to your people?" Quarrah asked.

"More worried about whether or not the Archkingdom will fire on us when we sail out," she said. "I believe the Sovereign States will only hold me, Darbu, and a few of my other chiefs responsible. They will try to reincorporate the Trothian warriors into their army once again. We are too great a boon to be rejected completely."

"So, worst-case scenario, the Archkingdom fleet sprays you with lead the moment you set sail," said Ard. "Best-case scenario, you get arrested, go to tribunal, and most likely face the firing squad or the noose."

"That is the way things stand," said Lyndel. "Obviously, I had hoped that the Sovereign States would see the benefit of what I'd done and back my position in maintaining the harbors."

"What if you could do something to win back favor with the Sovs?" Ard mused.

"I believe we are past that point," she said.

He held up a thoughtful finger. "What if your cause and our cause happened to align once again?"

Quarrah saw where Ard was going with this. As much as she wanted to cut him off and save Lyndel from his manipulation, she realized that this might actually be their best play for getting onto the island.

Ard glanced around the hut. "I don't suppose there is any way we could speak more privately?"

Quarrah could see the struggle in Lyndel's vibrating eyes. It was the desire not to give in to Ardor Benn, but the fear of not hearing what he had to say. Because, like it or not, the man usually said something interesting.

Lyndel turned to her companions and spoke a few words in Trothian. Whether the Lander woman understood, or simply followed the others, the hut was soon vacated as per Ard's request.

"Isle Halavend never fully trusted you," Lyndel said, once the door shut.

"Ouch," Ard said. "And here I thought the old Isle and I were pals."

"But he trusted that you could make things happen," she continued. "And I saw firsthand what you accomplished. I extend that same limited trust to you now. What is your proposal?"

"We plan to bring down King Termain Agaul," said Ard.

"How?" Her reply was flat and rather emotionless, considering it followed a statement like that. It was as though she'd heard that sentence a dozen times in her Sovereign war councils.

"The rightful heir to the throne is Termain's cousin's son, Shad Agaul," said Ard.

Lyndel nodded. "The boy was killed."

"That assassination was fake," said Ard. "Falsified by a secret organization called the Realm. Prince Shad Agaul is very much alive and he's being held against his will. He's here, Lyndel. On Pekal."

Lyndel turned to Quarrah. "Is this true?"

She felt a burst of pride that Lyndel considered her more honest than Ard. But this time, the ruse artist wasn't spinning any yarn. "We believe he's being held somewhere up Parnan's Canyon."

"That isn't too far from here," Ard said. "If your people let us through, we'll gather the boy and sail out with you. I'm guessing the Archkingdom isn't going to fire on your ships if the prince is with us. And who knows, maybe the Sovs will go easy on you at tribunal. Single-handedly ending the war has to carry some weight, don't you think?"

Lyndel folded her arms, wrapped in the religious red cloth of her Agrodite station. Quarrah could see she was considering it. Ard's proposal had been made with a bit more melodrama than Quarrah liked, but he hadn't exaggerated. If Lyndel let them get the prince, it could be her ticket out of here.

"There is one thing I do not understand," said Lyndel. "If the boy has been held on Pekal for all these cycles, won't he be deep into the third stage of Moonsickness?"

Ard shook his head. "He's healthy. For nearly two years, the Realm has been planning to put him on the throne under their control. I don't think a Moonsick king is going to convincingly unite the islands."

"How has he survived the Moon Passings, then?" asked Lyndel.

"We think his captors have moved him out to the Redeye line with every Passing," Quarrah explained. "The Realm leader basically panicked when she shared the news that you had captured the Archkingdom's harbors. She's attempting to send a team up the face of the cliff to extract the Realm's 'resource.'"

"The 'resource' being the boy?" clarified Lyndel.

"Yes," said Ard. "But the Realm has also stashed some rather significant Grit kegs here."

"What type of Grit?" asked Lyndel.

"We don't know."

"And it doesn't matter," Quarrah said.

"I wouldn't go that far," Ard retorted. "Overseer promised them to every member of the Faceless. I can't imagine the Cataclysm kegs are *useless.*"

"They will be if we stop the Cataclysm," Quarrah pointed out.

"Cataclysm?" ventured Lyndel.

"Big flood," Raek answered. "The Realm's engineering it to happen four nights from now."

"Besides," Quarrah said, "there isn't time to go for the kegs *and* Shad Agaul before the Moon Passing."

"How well do you know the island?" Lyndel asked.

"Ard and I used to be Harvesters," Raek said. "Which means Ard has no idea where he's going."

"But you do?"

"It's been years," said Raek. "On my own, I'd probably be sunk. But with Quarrah's map and her sense of direction, I think we can get to Parnan's Canyon and find the boy."

"It's getting back in time that has me worried," Quarrah admitted. "We're cutting this close."

"With no assurance that the prince will still be there," added Lyndel.

She was right. If the Realm's team had succeeded in getting onto Pekal, they could have already reached Shad. And if they weren't using the harbors, they could extract him at any point along the shoreline.

"Guess that means we'd better hurry," Ard said. "Beat the Realm's team to the prince."

"Very well," said Lyndel after a moment's pause. "Your chances of making it back in time will increase if I come with you."

"You know Pekal?" Ard asked, his voice surprised.

"Nuki does," said Lyndel. "But she doesn't speak a word of Landerian."

"So you'd be coming as a translator?" Ard said.

"You can tell me what's on the map, and I can tell Nuki." Lyndel crossed to the door and cracked it open, speaking in her native tongue to the man waiting outside.

"The Trothians need your leadership right now, and last time we went into the wilds of Pekal, not very many of us came back," Raek said as Lyndel shut the door again. "Are you sure it's right for you to leave?"

"We have a chain of command," said Lyndel. "I will leave Rabar as acting chief with instructions to sail from the harbor at the last possible moment if we have not returned."

Ard sighed obnoxiously. "This isn't really about translating, is it? You're demanding to come because you don't *fully* trust us."

"If the Agaul prince is actually alive, I am sure you can respect my decision not to leave him in the hands of ruse artists and thieves."

"I thought you knew us better than that, Lyndel," said Ard. "We may be ruse artists and thieves, but we hold ourselves to a higher law."

Quarrah scoffed, and even Raek rolled his eyes at that comment.

"Haven't we proven that we aren't interested in death and destruction?" Ard continued. "Sparks, if we'd wanted civilization to fall apart, we would have given up on the Visitant Grit after Isle Halavend was killed and any chance of getting paid went out the window."

"The stakes were higher then."

"Right. This time, we're just trying to end a war and stop a cataclysmic flood from killing thousands." Ard stared at her. "This is important. And time is of the essence."

"And yet, here you stand," said Lyndel, "talking."

Quarrah didn't resist the smile that spread across her face. Even Ard smirked.

There was a knock at the door, and Lyndel gestured for Raek to open it. A Trothian woman entered. She looked younger than Quarrah, her black hair cut short on both sides. She greeted Lyndel, and the two of them spoke briefly in their language.

"Nuki says it's about a six-hour hike to the top of Parnan's Canyon from here."

"That probably means they won't move the prince until morning," Raek said. "Even if the extraction team gets to him."

"What time do the ships need to sail out tomorrow?" Quarrah asked.

"We plan at least three hours of sailing to reach the Redeye line," said Lyndel, "assuming the weather is favorable. This time of year, six o'clock would be the absolute latest to ensure that we are safely away by the time the Moon rises."

"Then that gives us plenty of time," said Ard. "We can be to the prince by nightfall. Even if we catch a few hours of sleep and leave at dawn, we'll be back to the harbor by noon."

"That's only if everything goes smoothly," Quarrah said. In her experience, it didn't.

"I'll assemble five of my Trothian warriors to accompany us," said Lyndel. "In case there is trouble with the prince." She spoke some orders to Nuki, who immediately exited the hut.

"We leave in thirty minutes," Lyndel said. "And for all our sakes, the Agaul prince had better be where you say he is."

*No one knows the way, save it be upward.*

# CHAPTER

# 37

Ard yawned, glancing eastward where the first light of dawn glimmered through the trees, not yet rich with the colors of sunrise.

Why had he even bothered to string up his hammock? He

couldn't have slept for more than three hours, and he was still dizzy with fatigue. They should have found the prince by now. They should have been breaking camp to head back to the harbor.

But Pekal had a way of shaking up even the best-laid plans.

They had reached the top of Parnan's Canyon just after sunset, but a search of the surroundings had revealed no prince. Well into the night, they had traversed the area, hoping to see something they had missed on the way up, but it had eventually become obvious that they would find nothing until morning.

"How do you say 'tree' in Trothian?" Ard asked, untying his hammock and stuffing it into his pack.

"*Dalish*," answered Lyndel.

"What about 'crooked tree'?"

"*Dalish emokney.*"

"Sparks, Ard," Raek said. "You're back to the Trothian vocabulary already? Since when have you ever been interested in saying anything more than 'We'll pay you later'?"

"Hey," Ard defended. "I figured this was a good time to learn a few basic directions and some landmarks. You know, in case our translator falls off a cliff and we can't find our way back to the harbor."

It was true that he'd asked about a lot of words while they'd hiked yesterday. And his justifications were flimsy, since two of the other Trothians Lyndel had brought along also spoke passable Landerian. Ard had his own reasons for brushing up on their language, but he wasn't ready to reveal his plans yet. He needed to see how much time they'd have after finding Shad Agaul.

"We must split up to increase our chances of finding the boy," said Lyndel. She'd suggested it last night, but Ard hadn't been too keen on the idea. Trothian night vision was far superior to that of the Landers, since their eyes took in the energy emanating from everything around.

Lyndel switched to her native tongue, speaking for a moment with Nuki and the five other Trothian warriors. They were good company on Pekal, each of them built for strenuous expeditions. Everyone was traveling light, but Oronat and Gorus were quite heavily armed. And Ard knew that Sopar, Pula, and Staj carried a significant supply of Grit in their backpacks.

Lyndel finished what she was saying, and the six of them went out in different directions.

"We'll meet at this spot before noon," Lyndel said to Ard, Raek, and Quarrah. "If you find the boy, fire two shots and wait for everyone to join you before engaging him." She cinched her Grit belt and moved out of sight.

"I think it makes the most sense for the three of us to stick together," Ard said to his companions. "I've got snacks."

Wordlessly, Quarrah turned and disappeared into the trees. Ard faced his big friend, who was standing like a sentinel with his arms folded, watching the skies for any signs of a dragon.

"If I leave you on your own," Raek said, "what do you think would be the likelihood of you ever finding your way back to this spot?"

"I could do it," Ard defended. "It might take me a week, but I could do it."

"Let's go." Raek headed uphill.

In some places, Parnan's Canyon was nearly a quarter mile wide, while other spots narrowed so much that the stream rambling along its bottom could hardly be avoided. The walls of the canyon were quite steep, formed mostly of mossy rock. Clusters of dense trees pocked the entire area.

Ard didn't like being nestled down in the deep canyon with only two ways to go—up or down. And if this made *him* feel trapped, he wondered how Quarrah was dealing with the canyon's confines. She was probably watching the rocky sides, always evaluating the best route to climb out.

The sun rose slowly behind them, the bottom of the canyon remaining in pleasant cool shadow.

"What's the plan once we get the kid?" Raek asked. "You really intend to let Lyndel use him to get herself out of trouble?"

"We don't have much choice but to sail out with the Trothian ships," said Ard. "We just have to figure out how to use the waiting fleets to our advantage."

"Turn him over to the Sovs," Raek suggested. "They could provide the military power needed to make sure he takes the throne."

"Doesn't that just continue the war?" Ard said.

"Well, turning him over to the Archkingdom fleet doesn't seem like the best idea. With the king's mother being Overseer, we might as well just give him to the Realm."

"So, maybe we don't give him to either side," said Ard. "Maybe we keep him for ourselves."

"To be our own personal king," Raek said in mock reverence.

Ard snorted. "I'm saying we sneak him into the palace and dethrone Termain quietly from within. That way Shad doesn't become a pawn for either side to manipulate. By the time anyone knows he's still alive, he's already wearing the crown."

"But that can't happen until his birthday," reminded Raek. "So we'll have to shelter him at the guesthouse along with all our other strays."

They were hiking right up against the north wall of the canyon, and Ard stopped beside a trickle of fresh water tumbling down the green rocks.

"What do you think about our professor? You've spent more time with him than any of us." He let some of the water pool in his hand. It was clear and cold, and he used it to rinse the sweat that was already collecting on his forehead.

"The man is a genius." Raek uncorked his water skin and took a swallow. "Two hundred years since the discovery of Illusion Grit, and Portsend Wal goes and creates seven new Grit types in less than four cycles."

"Seven?" Ard said. "The Realm only knows about six."

"He's developed a sustainable cloud for a seventh type, but he doesn't know what it does yet."

"Seems fishy," said Ard. "I don't think he's telling us everything. Did he talk to you about his relationship with the Prime Isless?"

"He used to go to her for guidance," said Raek, "and they hatched a plot to get the information about the new Grit to the king. Not sure why."

"Termain is controlling her," Ard said. "I think he's stolen the Anchored Tome out of the Sanctum. When I was a Homelander, Gloristar asked me to help her create a new copy."

"Interesting," Raek said. "That actually makes sense . . ."

He trailed off as a gunshot pealed through the canyon. A second shot followed, and then a third.

"Which way did that come from?" Ard whispered. The echo had made it hard to determine. Raek squinted up the canyon, pointing to a flock of birds that had just been spooked from a tree.

It wasn't far. The big man broke into a run, Ard following, wondering how Raek seemed to have so much energy when Ard was supposed to be the healthy one. Weaning him off the Health Grit had been a complete success.

They moved away from the rock wall, eventually splashing through the ankle-deep stream that dissected the bottom of the wide canyon. Ard nearly drew his Roller when Nuki and Sopar emerged from the trees to join them at a sprint.

Another gunshot sounded. This time the ball tore through the branches above Ard's head. The surprise caused him to tumble as a second shot chipped into a large tree trunk.

"This way!" Raek cried, adjusting their course based on the direction of fire. Ard pulled himself up, Roller clearing his holster as he now found himself at the back of the group.

They were almost to the south wall of the canyon when Ard saw their enemies hunkered behind a cluster of boulders. He counted five men—two of them with beards that looked as overgrown as

Pekal's vegetation. Their position was considerably defensible, placed at the top of a steep slope, cleared of everything but grass, the high wall to their backs.

Ard couldn't decide if the placement of the boulders was natural or constructed, but they ringed the top of the little hill like battlements on a turret. The only way in and out was through a gap between the two largest boulders.

Lying in the opening was the still figure of one of Lyndel's warriors. He must have been inspecting the unusual arrangement of rocks when he happened upon the goons at close range.

Ard dropped his pack in the underbrush, pressing his back against a large tree at the bottom of the open hill. Nuki was positioned to his left and Sopar to his right. A short distance away, Raek was hastily trying to assemble his crossbow. Why was he wasting his time with nonlethal weapons, when he had a Roller? These were clearly Realm Hands intent on killing them. Sparks. It was probably the extraction team.

One of the bearded men leaned through the gap, snapping off a shot that went high of Nuki. The shooter ducked out of sight again, presumably to reload while his partners covered the opening.

From seemingly out of nowhere, Lyndel appeared, flanked closely by Oronat and Pula. That still left Quarrah and one of the Trothians unaccounted for.

Sopar said something to Lyndel and she responded sharply, sending her two companions circling around to both sides of the knoll. Lyndel sheltered behind the tree directly next to Ard.

She was holding an object in both hands, cradling it in a manner that made it seem fairly heavy. It looked like a wad of broad leaves, about the size of a summer melon, crisscrossed with twine to hold it loosely together.

"What is that thing?" Ard hissed.

"Void Grit scrap bomb," she answered.

"The kind they're using on the war front?" Ard had heard about the brutal bombs, but he hadn't imagined them to look so...rustic.

"Not like this," said Lyndel. "I had to improvise."

"With leaves?"

"There is a pot of Compounded Void Grit at its center," she replied. "The leaves are holding stones instead of scrap metal."

Now, that was engineering on the fly. A creation so clever could even give Raekon Dorrel a run for his money.

"I need you to lay down fire from all angles," she spoke loudly enough for Ard and Raek to hear. He got the impression she was merely repeating the instructions she'd just given to her warriors. "Allow me to get far enough up the hill to throw this behind their boulders."

"Wait a minute!" Ard's admiration quickly gave way to hesitation. "What if the prince is up there?"

"He is not," she answered.

"How can you be so sure?"

"You said the boy is almost fourteen years old?" she verified.

"What does that have to do with anything?"

"There are only adults behind those rocks," she explained. "A teenage male Lander gives off a very *distinctive* energy."

Ard didn't know exactly what that meant, but he trusted Lyndel's enhanced Trothian vision.

"On my call, Oronat and Pula will advance from the sides," she continued. "I'll charge up the middle with the four of you firing to keep them pinned."

It was a bold plan, and the risks were readily obvious. If Lyndel tripped, or was shot, the bomb could detonate and spray her with high-velocity pebbles. Ard and the others might be safe behind the trees, but her two advancing warriors would likely be struck as well.

Out of the corner of his eye, Ard saw Raek drop his freshly assembled crossbow and draw his Roller. He spun through the chambers, making sure they were loaded properly before giving Lyndel a nod.

The priestess shouted something—Ard didn't know if it was a Trothian word or simply a phonic cry—and whirled around her tree, clutching the makeshift Void Grit scrap bomb under one arm.

The call was answered on both sides of the knoll, and Ard saw a flash of blue skin as the two Trothian warriors emerged onto opposing sides of the slope, staying close to the steep canyon wall.

Ard leaned around his protective tree trunk and fired blindly up the hill, aiming only well enough to make sure he didn't hit anyone in the advancing trio. The trees were quickly filled with the haze of gun smoke, and the barrage of balls ensured that none of the Hands would dare peer out to take a shot of their own.

Lyndel was halfway up the hill, and Ard had just pulled his trigger for the third time, when Quarrah's voice cut through the gaps between shots.

"Marksman!" Her shout was desperate and breathless. "There's a marksman in the cliff!"

A Fielder sounded. Ard didn't see the muzzle flash, but Lyndel suddenly went down, turning at the last moment to prevent the scrap bomb from striking the hillside.

Ard popped off one more shot while Raek, Nuki, and Sopar continued firing. Quarrah might have charged right into the open if Ard hadn't grabbed her by the arm and pulled her against the tree with him.

On the slope, Oronat had crossed to the fallen priestess and was struggling to pull her to her feet. Lyndel was still alive, praise the Homeland, but she was clearly injured. And the two of them were sitting ducks.

"We've got to take him out before he reloads," Quarrah insisted, trying to pull away from Ard.

"You can't go out there," he said. "We can't even see him!"

"I know where he is. There's a ledge in the cliff about twenty feet above those boulders. To the right."

"And you're just going to climb up there?"

"I could Drift jump," she said. "I just need some extra Grit to get me higher."

"It's too dangerous!"

"Quarrah!" Raek's deep voice cut over to them. "I've got you! Just give me a sign for the jump. Go!"

Without another word, she ripped free of Ard's grasp and sprinted into the open, moving up the hillside faster than any of the Trothians had.

Ard whirled on his partner, a look of betrayal on his face. Raek had exchanged his Roller for the crossbow again. Now he was quickly loading a Drift bolt into the powerful weapon.

Lyndel and Oronat were struggling. The warrior seemed insistent on getting her back to the safety of the trees, while Lyndel kept shouting at him and holding out the leaf-wrapped pot of Void Grit.

Quarrah sprinted wide of them, traversing the hillside on an upward angle. She raised her hand for half a dozen steps and then waved it down in a signal for Raek. He stepped out, sighting down the crossbow and squeezing the trigger. The bolt flew, striking the canyon wall and detonating the Grit on impact.

Without missing a step, Quarrah entered the cloud and leapt. Her body flew upward through the weightless environment, exiting out the top of the cloud and landing adroitly on a lip of rock that jutted out of the cliff face.

Ard finally saw the marksman, lying prone on the shelf with a freshly loaded Fielder tucked into his shoulder. Quarrah grabbed the long barrel and yanked it from his grasp. Before she could turn the weapon on him, the marksman swiped her legs, knocking her against the cliff.

The Fielder discharged sideways into the treetops, but the flames rushing through the metal barrel must have burned Quarrah's hands. She let go, the big gun spiraling through the Drift cloud, striking the grassy earth, and floating up again.

The marksman was on his feet now, but he clearly underestimated Quarrah's balance on the ledge. She leapt for him, kicking his knee sideways. The man tumbled from his perch, drifting down through the detonation cloud and crashing into the ground. He gripped fistfuls of tall grass, preventing himself from floating out of control. But he only hovered there for a moment before Pula finished him with two rounds from her Roller.

Ard turned his attention back to Lyndel. She was alone on the hillside now, lying on her back, face twisted in pain. Oronat had clearly lost the argument and now bore the makeshift Void Grit bomb. As Nuki and Sopar emptied their Rollers at the boulders above, Oronat hurled the explosive, diving back down the hill and covering his head as quickly as he could.

Ard didn't see the leaf-wrapped parcel land, falling out of sight behind the nearest boulder. He heard the screams, though, as a spray of small stones blasted out the top of the enemies' protective shelter.

Then all was quiet.

Ard broke cover and raced for Lyndel.

"I am fine," she said before he'd even reached her. "The ball only grazed my leg. I have Health Grit in my pack to keep me going."

That looked like a lot more blood than Ard would expect from a graze. And judging by the way she was holding her thigh, the ball had passed clear through.

"Sparks," Ard muttered. This was going to slow them down tremendously. A cloud or two of Health Grit might stop the bleeding and temporarily relieve the pain, but a wound like that wasn't going to heal without more significant attention from a Healer.

Nuki and Sopar were suddenly crowding around their leader, the conversation turning to a language Ard could not understand.

He glanced up at the cliff face, but Quarrah was already on the ground again, having used the Drift cloud to float safely down. She was headed toward the ring of boulders that the goons had been guarding.

Ard moved up the hill to intercept her, joining Raek, Oronat, and Pula as they cautiously approached the gap entrance between the big rocks. He saw now that the dead Trothian at the opening was Staj, his skull cracked from a ball fired at close range.

The five of them halted beside their downed comrade. From this angle, all Ard could see was a thin sliver of the Void Grit cloud that still raged behind the natural walls of the hideout.

Raek signaled them to ready their weapons. Ard holstered his half-empty Roller and drew his second gun, only then noticing that Quarrah stood beside him with nothing but a knife. Didn't she have a gun? Sparks, who came to Pekal without a firearm? Wordlessly, he passed the Roller to her, pleased that she accepted it without hesitation.

Ard popped open the cylinder on his other Roller and quickly reloaded, noticing Pula doing the same. Raek waited until the group was fully armed. Then he held out a small glass vial of yellow liquid. Null Grit, right? That would certainly make sense, as they couldn't enter the ring of boulders until that Void cloud extinguished.

Raek stepped into the opening and pitched the vial into the Void cloud. It penetrated only an inch or two before being hurtled outward on a new trajectory, shattering against the inside of one of the boulders. The liquid Grit detonated, and Ard glimpsed the flash of a cloud that immediately snuffed out the active Void Grit.

The five of them poured through the opening, guns panning over every inch of the area. The five Hands were dead, fistfuls of pebbles from the scrap bomb embedded into their heads and torsos. Ard grimaced. Lyndel's weapon had been brutally effective, almost to the point of seeming cheap. Those men hadn't stood a chance against it. The priestess definitely got results, with a level of straightforward no-nonsense about her methods.

Inside the ring of boulders, Ard saw a cave entrance in the canyon wall, easily tall enough for Raek to enter without stooping. The uniformity of the dark tunnel told Ard that it was man-made.

"Looks like an evil hideout to me," Raek said, squinting at a glimmer of dim light deep inside.

"I'll hang on to these." Quarrah held up a ring of keys that she'd taken from one of the dead Hands. She was something of a walking key herself, but having the actual ones would certainly be faster than picking locks.

"Who wants to go first?" Ard asked, glancing at the group. Gorus, the final Trothian warrior, had at last shown up, but Nuki was still tending to Lyndel on the hillside.

When no one replied to his question, Ard lifted his Roller and strode into the tunnel entrance, the other six falling into step behind him. He moved slowly and cautiously, listening for any sounds as he drew nearer to the soft glow ahead.

In moments, the seven of them emerged from the tunnel into the cavern proper. Like the entrance, Ard suspected that this had been a natural chamber carefully enlarged by human hands. He could even see chisel marks in the glow of the two Prolonged Light Grit lanterns.

The space was surprisingly large and heavily stocked with supplies. Boxes and barrels lined the left wall, some unopened while others had their contents carelessly strewn about. At a glance, Ard could see everything, from foodstuffs to ammunition and Grit. Against the back wall were three sagging cots and a small table. In front of those was a Drift crate, which explained why the tunnel entrance needed to be so wide.

The other half of the cave was a jail cell. Metal bars had been set into the stone, rising from floor to ceiling. Inside was another dirty cot and a couple of bedpans on the uneven floor. The door to the single cell hung ajar, and Ard could see that the space was vacant.

"Flames," Raek muttered. "They must have moved the boy before we got here."

Gorus rattled the lock on the Drift-crate hatch, waving for Quarrah to bring the keys. She hurried over, matching key to lock on her first try. Gorus pulled open the hatch, instantly releasing a detonation cloud that had been fully contained inside. Losing containment, the hazy air assumed a rounded shape, the cloud becoming immovable as it spilled just a foot or two through the box's opening.

Ard peered into the open crate as Raek held one of the Light Grit lanterns to illuminate its contents—bags and packs, boxes and buckets.

And huddled at the center of the supplies was a frightened-looking boy.

Shad Agaul did not look much like the portrait hanging in the grand salon of the Guesthouse Adagio, although Ard could see the resemblance if he looked past the long, filthy hair and dirty face. His skin was deathly pale, as though he hadn't seen the sun in cycles. He was several years older than the boy in the painting, just days away from his fourteenth birthday and his legal right to rule. Strange to think of a child on the throne. Especially one who looked so terrified and confused.

"Hullo there, Your Majesty," Ard said, putting on a friendly smile. "You ready to go home?"

"Home?" whispered the boy, as though the word were foreign to him. "Where is home?"

"Currently, your family's guesthouse in northeastern Beripent," said Ard. "Your mother is waiting for you there."

The boy's eyes widened and he lifted his chin from where it had been tucked against his bent knees. "I have a mother?"

Ard cast a puzzled glance at Quarrah and Raek, who were watching the exchange carefully. "Of course," Ard said to the boy. "Technically, everyone does. Just so happens yours is a queen."

"Queen of what?" he asked.

"Boy," Quarrah said, peering into the crate beside Ard. "What's your name?"

"No name," he replied. "I'm just lucky to be alive."

"Sparks," Ard whispered. "Is that what they tell you? The brutes who take care of you?"

"I'm just lucky to be alive," he said again in what appeared to be a rote statement.

Ard felt the worry creeping in. This *was* Shad Agaul, wasn't it? The boy had been gone for two years, but that wasn't long enough to make someone forget his own name...

"Hold on a minute." Raek passed the lantern to Gorus and nudged Ard aside. "Ask me a question."

"What question?" replied Ard.

"Anything," Raek answered. "Something easy." Then he leaned forward, sticking his bald head into the Grit cloud that had overflowed the Crate.

"Who is king of the Archkingdom?" Ard asked.

"His Rottenness, King Termain Agaul." Raek pulled his head out of the cloud. "Did you ask it yet?"

"Yes," said Ard. "And you answered me."

"Flames," Raek muttered. "It's Memory Grit." He waved his hand through the cloud.

"But Memory Grit only affects your mind while you're within the cloud," Quarrah said. "It doesn't remove memories from *before*."

"There's a theory about this," Raek said. "Stomad Farn wrote a whole book on it. Long-term exposure to Memory Grit can decay regular memories that occurred before the detonation cloud. It's exacerbated by Prolonging Grit and, theoretically, even Compounding Grit. With enough exposure, the subjects can become completely brainwashed to the point where they cannot retain information whether they're inside a cloud of Memory Grit or not. Their mind becomes like a blank slate. Motor skills aren't affected, and it seems like he's able to maintain at least some degree of language."

"This makes sense," said Quarrah. "When you asked Overseer how she could be sure that the prince would do what the Realm needed him to do, she responded that it wouldn't be an issue."

Ard nodded. "Because Overseer was confident that they could make him think anything the Realm needed. He wasn't just going to preach the Great Egress. He was going to believe it."

"Is it reversible?" Quarrah asked.

Raek shrugged. "Up until right now I thought this theory had only ever been tested on animals. Some of them got royally messed up after regular exposure ended. Farn introduced them to a variety of elements, and the subjects supposedly assimilated whatever traits were first imposed on them. One of the dogs thought it was a fish and drowned itself in an irrigation canal."

"What about getting old memories back?" Ard asked. "*Real* memories."

"It's hypothesized that a strong stimulus can jog lost memories. Something like that seemed to work on one of the test animals when exposed to its familiar pen after cycles of Memory Grit exposure. But other animals showed no recovery, so it was deemed inconclusive."

"We've got to get him out of there," Quarrah whispered.

"No," Ard said. "He stays in the Memory cloud until we get back to Beripent. Another day or so isn't likely to make his condition worse, and we need to make sure he comes out of this under the right circumstances."

"You mean, when you have time to indoctrinate him with your altruistic perspectives?" Quarrah snapped.

"Not me," Ard replied. "We need to get that boy to someone who can stimulate the memories of who he really is."

"His mother..."

Ard nodded. "We'll keep him surrounded with Memory Grit until we get back to Lady Abeth. When that cloud finally comes down, I want the first thing this boy sees to be his mother's face."

A gunshot resonated through the cave, causing everyone to

jump. Gorus went down, gripping his neck. Ard whirled as another ball flew past him, close enough that he could feel the rush of wind against his sleeve. It sailed through the open hatch and into the Drift crate, followed by another, and another.

A final Hand had been concealed beneath the cots, but he was on his feet now, staggering forward like a madman, shooting so rapidly into the crate that his Roller was empty before Ard could draw his gun.

The Hand succumbed to a flurry of lead balls, which all seemed to strike him in unison as the surprised crew surrounding the Drift crate finally managed to respond. Sopar and Pula instantly went to Gorus's aid, but Ard could tell that the warrior was already dead. Oronat moved over to the downed enemy, but Ard turned all of his attention back to the Drift crate.

A horrid, pungent odor wafted from the crate's opening, causing Ard to gag. Fighting the stench, he saw that Shad Agaul was still huddled at the center of the crate. He looked uninjured, praise the Homeland, but the goon's haphazard shots had damaged the supplies around him. Something wet had sprayed all over the prince and was running across the bottom of the Drift crate. Shad was pinching his nose, obviously trying not to gag.

Ard almost wretched again, covering his nose and mouth with his hand. "What the blazes?" he muttered through the muffle.

"*Aptonus Siliamitrus*," came Raek's choked reply.

"This isn't the time for Trothian curse words." Ard had no idea what his partner had said.

"Reek Sauce in concentrate," Raek clarified. "Officially, *Aptonus Siliamitrus*."

No wonder the Harvesters had given the stuff a nickname. Who had room in their brain to remember big words like that?

Sparks! Now the prince was covered in dragon attractant? Once Raek had pointed it out, Ard recognized the odor. He'd avoided it during his Harvester days, never sticking around long enough to watch the Feeder apply the awful-smelling liquid to the bait. Still, he'd had a good whiff of it that night when he'd tricked King Pethredote into dumping a flask of the Reek Sauce on his own head.

"They've got a lot of Feeder equipment in there," Raek said, peering in.

"Maybe that's how they planned to get off the island," Ard said. "Posing as members of a Harvesting crew who had been separated and lost. They could take advantage of the Trothians' mercy at the harbor and they wouldn't have to risk the shoreline cliffs."

"Sparks," Quarrah muttered. "Now the prince smells like dragon bait?"

"And there's a reason they tell you not to get this stuff on your skin," said Ard.

Raek grimaced. "Doesn't wash out for a week."

Inside the Drift crate, young Shad Agaul finally vomited.

~

*But no tears were shed for our losses.*

# CHAPTER

# 38

Quarrah watched Nuki talking with Ard. Talking *at* Ard would be more appropriate, since he couldn't understand her language. Still, she seemed to get her point across with a few gestures and a nod of her head as Ard repeated a few of the Trothian words he had been practicing.

"Halt!" shouted Ard, holding up his hand to the company. "It's time to replace the Pichar boughs. Fan out and shout if you find anything." They had stopped in a beautiful glen with a spring-fed pond blossoming with lily pads.

Sopar did his best to translate Ard's commands to Pula and Nuki, then the three of them spread out into the surrounding trees. At the back of the group, Raek and Oronat slowly lowered the Drift crate to the ground. The way it smelled, there was a reason for keeping it downwind of the others.

Quarrah wondered how Lyndel and the prince were faring inside. By now, they'd either be numb to the stench or passed out.

Carrying the Agrodite priestess in the crate was really their only option, with a wound through her leg. Health Grit had stabilized her, and they were adding more clouds to the Drift crate from time to time, hoping that she'd recover enough to hike the final stretch down to the harbor.

At least Lyndel wouldn't remember the odiferous journey, since the prince needed to be contained in a cloud of Memory Grit. The cave had been stocked with a fortune's worth of the stuff—clearly, the Realm had spared no expense keeping Shad Agaul hidden and secure.

Getting the Drift crate out of the cavern hideout had taken a little longer than planned. First they'd emptied it of everything but the boy. Then they'd taken turns wiping it out until they couldn't get up any more of the spilled Reek Sauce. After that, they'd restocked the crate with loaded Grit pots, which were the most useful and valuable items in the cave.

Raek had been pleased to discover several boxes of the new liquid Grit vials, likely brought in by the extraction team to safeguard Shad Agaul's exit with the most up-to-date materials.

Once the Drift crate was restocked, they'd maneuvered it outside, detonating a stack of overlapping Drift clouds that allowed them to float the Crate up and over, landing it safely on the grassy slope.

Raek lumbered up to Ard, who was picking at a blister on his palm. "We don't have time for this, Ard," Quarrah heard the big man say. "We don't even know if the Pichar boughs are doing anything besides making us *feel* safer."

"I agree," she decided to chime in. "Our best choice is to press on as fast as we can to the harbor. We've only got, what... two hours before the ships set sail? And we're probably still an hour from the harbor."

"An hour and a half," Ard corrected. "According to Nuki."

"You can't even speak her language," said Raek.

"I understood enough," he replied. "Besides, panic is fairly universal, and I have a feeling she'd be doing that if we weren't on track to make it in time. Sure, we'll be cutting it close, but we're going to make it."

Quarrah stalked over to the Drift crate, gesturing for Oronat to stand aside as she unlatched the hatch.

"What are you doing?" Ard asked.

"If we're stopping, I'm going to give our poor passengers a breath of fresh air," she said, pulling it open. The contained cloud rushed out, a mix of Drift and Memory. The young prince was floating, stretched out in a resigned position as though being carted around in a horrid-smelling box was routine for him. Lyndel, on the other hand, looked absolutely miserable.

Quarrah backed up until she stood just outside the perimeter of the detonation cloud.

"Have we arrived?" Lyndel pushed off the thin wooden wall and floated toward the exit.

"Not yet," Quarrah said. "We've stopped for more Pichar boughs."

It had been hours since they'd found the first tree. They'd rubbed the crate, trying to get the needles to release their scent-masking oils. Quarrah hadn't noticed a real difference, but at least it was emotionally reassuring. A few more fresh branches had been lashed to the top, but several of them had fallen off during the hike.

"How much farther?" Lyndel asked. She was still within the overspilled cloud, steadying herself against the Drift crate's opening and trying to get her feet down on the ground. The priestess winced, grabbing the bandaged wound on her thigh.

"Depends on whom you ask," answered Quarrah.

"That boy is not well."

"How so?"

Lyndel reached up and tapped the side of her head. "He will not speak unless I ask him direct questions. Even then, it is as though he only comprehends half of what I am saying. I would think him dim-witted if I didn't know the situation."

Oronat reached into the detonation cloud, lending a supportive arm and helping Lyndel outside the perimeter. The priestess would have instantly forgotten what she'd said about Shad Agaul, but her words lingered in Quarrah's mind. How far gone was the young prince?

"How much farther?" Lyndel asked again.

Before Quarrah could answer, she tensed at the sound of someone shouting through the trees. The cry was in Trothian, and Quarrah didn't know if it was a report on Pichar boughs or a warning of a dragon.

"That is Pula," said Lyndel. "She has found something."

"A Pichar tree?"

Lyndel squinted. "Something else."

Quarrah saw Ard and Raek move off in the direction of the call.

Lyndel patted her holster. "Oronat and I will stay to guard the boy," she said, giving Quarrah permission to go investigate. The big Trothian warrior helped her slowly to the ground, back resting stiffly against the Drift crate.

Quarrah cut through the trees, leaving behind the glen with the small pond. As the late-afternoon light filtered through the branches, she saw the group standing in a half circle. Ard and Raek had beat her there, and as she approached, the ruse artist gave her a winning smile.

"Would you look at this?" he cried, pointing at a wall of vegetation. It took her a moment to realize what was beneath the vines and moss. "Another Drift crate!"

Pula had peeled away the greenery around the hatch and was picking at the lock.

"Quarrah," Ard said. "Would you mind saving us some time?" He gestured for her to replace Pula. As much as she didn't want to oblige him, she felt the call of a sealed box. Before she realized it, she had drawn the lock-picking tools from her pocket and taken Pula's place.

The lock was rusty, which always complicated things a bit. A rusty lock was like a stubborn old horse—it knew the route it was supposed to run, it had done it a hundred times, but it liked to stop and poke its head down every other side road, sniffing for apples.

At last, the lock was sprung and Quarrah yanked the Drift crate open through vines that stretched and snapped. Ard was suddenly at her shoulder, breathing heavily with anticipation as they peered into the portable box.

It was stocked with Grit kegs. Ard reached in and pulled one out, Quarrah studying it as he turned it over in his hand. It was large, almost too big around for Ard to grip with one hand, and it was marked with a symbol.

The symbol of a wave.

"The Cataclysm kegs," Quarrah whispered.

Ard chuckled. "What a blazing coincidence!"

If that was truly what they were, then there would be a keg for every Faceless—well over fifty. Overseer had wanted these for the next Faceless meeting, but she'd been willing to abandon them to rescue Shad Agaul instead.

"Let's get this uncovered," Ard said, replacing the keg. "We can transfer Lyndel and the boy into this clean crate and continue on."

The Cataclysm kegs...Quarrah reached into her pocket and pulled out the map she'd taken from Overseer's drawer. She quickly located Parnan's Canyon and scanned the drawing until she saw the label for the Cataclysm kegs.

Her gaze snapped up to find Ard. "You knew!"

"What?" he turned innocently.

"This wasn't a coincidence. You learned enough Trothian to convince Nuki to guide us here."

That explained his sudden interest in their language, and the number of times he'd tried to communicate with their guide since leaving Shad's cave. Sparks, he was probably grateful Lyndel had been injured, keeping her out of the way so she didn't catch on to what he was doing.

"You've been planning this since we got to Pekal," she continued. And the fact that Ard didn't instantly refute her only seemed to confirm it. Raek was paying attention now, too. And the three Trothians. They'd understand her tone, even if they didn't comprehend all her words.

"Did you know about this, too?" she turned on Raek.

"About the kegs?" he clarified. "How would I know about—"

"It's on the map." She held it up for all of them to see. "This little symbol. The wave. Labeled right here, by this pond in the glen at the top of Crooked Ravine. *South* of the harbor." She spit out the word one more time, for emphasis. "*South!*"

They had taken a different route back, and Quarrah had been fooled into thinking it was for the ease of carrying the Drift crate. They'd stayed inland, moving south, but they should have cut eastward to the harbor some time ago. According to their placement on the map, they'd gone too far and would now have to double back to the northeast to reach it.

"Look," Ard began, "Nuki said we'd still have time."

"Oh, sparks," Raek said, whirling on his companion. "Are you blazing kidding me?"

"It's a short detour," he continued, playing it off casually. "Well worth it for this score."

"We don't even know what's in these kegs!" Raek shouted.

"Overseer said they were irreplaceable," said Ard. "I've got plans for them. It's important, or we wouldn't be here."

Quarrah let out a bitter laugh. "We're literally pulling around dragon bait and you took us on a detour." She turned away, lifting a hand to her forehead. "Did we even need to stay inland? Flames, we should have cut straight down to the shoreline the moment we left Parnan's."

Dragons had free range over the entire island, but even Quarrah knew that the beasts typically preferred to stay hidden farther up the slopes.

"Let's just cut this crate free of the vines and get moving," Ard said.

"You're an absolute egomaniac," she muttered, grabbing fistfuls of vines and ripping them away from the overgrown crate.

With Sopar's short underbrush sword, the crate was quickly cleared. Pula, Nuki, Raek, and Ard carried it back to the glen without a Drift detonation while Quarrah stormed through the foliage ahead of them.

"Did you find more Pichar boughs?" Lyndel called when she saw Quarrah.

"We found something better!" shouted Ard as they lumbered into view. The four of them deposited the crate beside the one they'd taken from the cave.

They quickly transferred all the cargo from the foul-smelling crate into the fresh one. By the time they finished, Quarrah wondered if there would still be room in there for Lyndel and Shad. The boy was still inside the old crate, docile and confused under a cloud of Prolonged Memory Grit.

"I believe I can hike now," Lyndel said.

"Excellent," Ard replied. "Let's get that mix of Drift and Memory Grit ready. We need to transfer the prince quickly…"

He trailed off as a massive shadow suddenly blotted the afternoon sunlight. Quarrah looked up in time to see the dragon drop out of the sky like a bolt of lightning.

She landed in the glen, one huge claw crushing the life out of Pula. The dragon's mouth closed around the reeking Drift crate, the prince still inside. She pulled it off the ground, jaws snapping together in a spray of broken wood. Shad was ejected from the rubble, somehow whole and unbitten, landing in a motionless heap at the edge of the pond.

The crew finally erupted, their actions painfully postponed by the absolute shock of the dragon's sudden arrival. Already a person down, half a dozen guns spit hot lead at the towering beast, but Quarrah knew that Roller balls couldn't penetrate those steely scales.

The dragon reared, sniffing sharply, emerald eyes finding the still boy by the pond. Ard and Raek were racing toward him, but they wouldn't get there in time if she decided to strike. Even if they did, what could they do against her mighty jaws?

Quarrah saw Ard pull a Grit pot from his belt and pitch it at the fallen prince. It struck just in time, a dome of Barrier Grit enclosing him as the dragon's head came down. Her steaming muzzle slammed into the protective shell and she drew back, irritated.

That was effective, but it would only buy them ten minutes or so.

Quarrah had a feeling that Lyndel would be next on the menu, having spent the last several hours enclosed in the Reek Sauce–saturated Drift crate.

Quarrah pulled a Barrier Grit pot from her own belt and tossed it to the priestess. "Don't wait too long to use it."

Then Quarrah was sprinting toward the pond where Ard and Raek were slowly backing away from the prince. The dragon was still struggling to reach the boy, drawing back each time her nose hit the invisible shield.

"We have to distract her!" Ard cried. He fired another shot at the dragon's head, causing her to twitch and grunt, twin tendrils of heat vapor rising from her nostrils.

The dragon changed tactics, springing back up the glen for Lyndel. The priestess managed to get one useless shot off before dashing the Barrier pot at her own feet.

If the dragon was irritated before, the fact that she couldn't reach either of the baited specimens put her over the edge. She bellowed, a sound that ripped at Quarrah like sleet in a strong wind.

Her tail came around, the tip catching a tree at the edge of the clearing and snapping it off at the trunk.

"We need to get to the heavier Grit if we have any hope of taking her down," Raek called.

"We can't afford to kill her," Ard countered. "Until our little bull dragon reaches maturity, she's one of the last things protecting us from Moonsickness."

"That bull had better grow some balls in the next ten minutes, then," replied Raek. "Because I don't see how we're getting out of here with the prince while this gal's alive."

There was a sudden *thwack* of a crossbow string, resulting in an explosion of fiery Blast Grit against the dragon's left shoulder.

"Yeah!" Raek hollered. "That's what I'm talking about!"

Beside the new Drift crate, Nuki had assembled Raek's crossbow and shot the explosive bolt. She was ratcheting another into place when the dragon swiped one muscled foreleg, catching Nuki and throwing her into the trees, bones breaking like twigs.

"Sparks," Quarrah cursed. A feeling of helplessness seemed to hang over everyone in the glen. She was going to side with Raek on this one. They needed to kill that dragon.

"We've got to get her to hit the new Drift crate," Quarrah said. "It'll detonate everything we've got." And if that didn't stop her, nothing would.

"What? No!" Ard cried. "We need that Grit! And those Cataclysm kegs!"

"Not if you're dead," said Quarrah, racing toward the crate. Oronat was crouched nearby, the last of Lyndel's warriors. Maybe the two of them could...

The dragon snapped Oronat off the ground with her teeth and shook him back and forth like a dog with a scrap of leather. Quarrah came to a grinding halt and watched the beast slowly swallow the man whole.

Once more, the dragon turned her attention back to Shad Agaul, nostrils flaring at the tempting scent of the Reek Sauce.

Quarrah took advantage of the moment to scramble the rest of the way to the Drift crate and leap inside. There had to be something she could use in here. Something powerful enough to drop a mature dragon in her tracks.

What about one of the professor's new Grit types?

Quarrah tried to review them in her mind. Ignition, Null, Gather, Weight... Sparks, she knew she was forgetting some. She moved one of the boxes, and a label caught her eye. She hadn't used this kind before. Would it be powerful enough to take down a creature that size? How fast would it work?

She pried open the lid and snatched three little vials of the orange liquid in each hand. Then she ducked out of the Drift crate and raced across the glen toward the sow dragon.

Ard and Raek had abandoned Shad, helplessly retreating toward the trees at the border of the clearing. Ard shouted her name. He was trying to tell her to stop, probably claiming that he had some brilliant plan. But Quarrah Khai was tired of waiting on Ard. This time she had the plan, and it was going to work.

Oh, Homeland, she hoped it would work.

Quarrah's legs desperately wanted to carry her in the other direction, or to give out entirely, but she continued running until the dragon finally sprang for her.

The sow's head came down, jaws wide. Quarrah hurled the three vials in her right hand, hearing the thin glass smash on the creature's armored nose. The spherical detonation cloud sprang up at once, enveloping the monster's entire horned head.

The dragon collapsed, unconscious.

Her eyes rolled back and that giant hulking body went completely limp, slumping forward and crashing into the clear pond. Her head passed through the cloud of Stasis Grit and struck the grassy meadow just inches from Quarrah.

As soon as she was down, the dragon came to, eyes snapping open before they had even fully shut. She raised her massive head, coming in contact once again with the Stasis cloud hovering above.

Unconsciousness took her and she fell anew, startling awake again with a twitch of her entire deep green body. Before she could rise up, Quarrah pitched her second handful of vials, breaking them between the beast's eyes and detonating another cloud as big as the one overhead.

The dragon went limp again, but this time, Quarrah's second cloud surrounded her head where it rested in the tall grass.

Shaking, wholly stunned at her success, Quarrah's legs finally gave out and she crumpled to the soft ground just outside the perimeter of the Stasis cloud.

She sat there, feeling the heat from the dragon's face only a stone's throw away. After a moment, she realized she was waiting for Ard to rush over and fill her ear with his praise and adulation. When he didn't come, she turned to find him rooting around in the Drift crate.

"Blazing brilliant, Quarrah Khai!" This was from Raek, as he came running toward her. The compliment was genuine, but somehow didn't reach her in the same way that Ard's usually did. Well, maybe she'd spurned his accolades enough times that he'd finally gotten the picture.

Strangely, that bothered her, though she would never admit it aloud. She was annoyed with herself for even coming to expect his applause. Quarrah had taken down a dragon singlehandedly.

Having Ard sing her praises didn't change anything about that spectacular feat.

Raek tossed a Grit vial against the Barrier shell surrounding Shad Agaul. It detonated in a flash cloud, instantly extinguishing the shield.

Quarrah glanced across the glen to see that Ard was doing the same for Lyndel. When she looked back, Raek was standing beside her, the malnourished prince flung over one shoulder like a sack of flour. The big man offered her a hand, and Quarrah took it, feeling the steadiness return to her legs as she rose.

"We've got less than ten minutes to get out of here before the beast wakes up," Raek said as they trekked back toward the crate.

"She covers ground a lot faster than we do," Quarrah pointed out. "She'll just smell the prince again."

"I'm with you," Raek replied. "We should kill her while she's down."

That wasn't what she'd meant. Now that the dragon was defenseless, killing her seemed unnecessary. Besides, Ard had made a fair point about her being part of the shield against Moonsickness. If she was one of the eleven dragons still alive, then her death could advance the spread of Moonsickness into the Greater Chain by miles.

They met up with Ard and Lyndel at the crate. The priestess's blue face was sweaty, her expression tight from the lingering pain of her injury.

"How's the prince?" Ard asked.

"Better than he has any right to be," answered Raek. "He could have a concussion, but a cloud of Health Grit ought to bring him around."

"Let's get him into the Drift crate." Ard turned to Lyndel. "Are you riding or walking?"

"Better to die out here where the air is fresh," she said.

"I don't know," said Raek. "Ard is out here."

"You're not exactly a fresh patch of flowers, either," retorted Ard.

In truth, they probably all carried the lingering stench of the Reek Sauce. The Trothian warriors had worked especially hard to scrub out the first crate, and they'd paid for it with their lives.

Quarrah felt sick just thinking about it. She'd now survived two dragon strikes on Pekal. They happened so quickly, lives snuffed out like a swift detonation of Null Grit. In those moments, Quarrah felt her mettle tested. This time she was proud of the way she'd reacted.

It took Raek longer than expected to load the mixed Grit into the hopper of the Drift crate. By now, they likely had no more than three or four minutes before the dragon awakened. That wasn't much of a head start against a creature that could cover so much ground with a single beat of her wings.

Ard and Raek hefted the Drift crate and set off across the glen, Lyndel close behind. Quarrah didn't find it a good idea to let Ardor Benn lead, so she dashed a short way ahead and turned their course northeast. With only an hour and a half until the Trothian fleet's departure from the harbor, they were going to be hard pressed to make it in time.

They weren't even to the trees when the dragon sprang up in a hot rush of wind and a spray of cold spring water.

"Sparks," Quarrah muttered.

"We can't outrun her!" cried Raek, the dragon turning in mid-air to locate them. She dove like a falcon. Raek and Ard ground to a halt in the meadow.

"Quarrah!" Lyndel shouted, causing her to jump back as the priestess slammed a pot of Barrier Grit against the side of the wooden crate.

It sheltered all of them, the dome forming just inches over Quarrah's head. Raek and Ard lowered the Drift crate to the grass at the center of the detonation.

"Now what?" Quarrah cried. Trapping themselves inside an impenetrable cloud didn't seem like the best long-term solution. And if the dragon breathed fire, they'd be cooked like loaves in an oven. But Quarrah had heard that dragons seldom used their fire. Reckless breathing would make quick desolation of their singular island habitat.

"Now we wait," said Ard. The dragon struck the transparent shield, causing all four of them to flinch.

"Wait?" she shouted. "And hope the dragon gets bored and flies away in less than ten minutes?"

In response, Raek gestured to his belt, freshly stocked with blue-dyed Barrier Grit pots. "We can stay here all night."

"No!" Quarrah cried. "We can't! We can't even stay here an hour!"

"She won't bother us for long," Ard said, gesturing to the dragon. The normal levity in his voice had been replaced with a surliness that he didn't even try to hide. Quarrah could tell he was feeling guilty for the detour. Guilty for Nuki, and Pula, and Oronat. And he should. They should have already made it to the harbor by now. They should have all been alive.

The dragon struck again, long teeth clacking against the Barrier as she tried to gnaw, fetid hot breath wafting down on them.

"She doesn't seem interested in leaving," Quarrah remarked. Bloody saliva streamed down the side of the dome.

"Tonight's the Moon Passing," Ard said. "The dragons swarm. She has to leave us eventually so she can get to the peak of the island and absorb the direct Moon rays."

"The same Moon rays that will spill down the mountainside and eventually kill us," Quarrah said deliberately.

"She'll leave," Ard said in hopeful insistence. "We'll still have time to get to the harbor. We'll make it off Pekal."

The dragon struck again.

～

*The dragons slept at our borders, full of judgment and swift wrath.*

# CHAPTER

# 39

Portsend Wal found his guesthouse cottage delightful and surprisingly spacious. A large soft bed, plush pillows, and a washing area that drained through the wall with the pull of a plug. There was plenty of table space for his research, with shelves to accommodate most of his materials.

The butler gave continual disclaimers, reminding him how understaffed and underfunded they were for such a facility, but Portsend hardly minded. He was accustomed to changing his own wash water and fixing his own meals, so any services rendered made his stay feel purely luxurious.

Overall, the Guesthouse Adagio was by far the nicest place he had ever spent a night. Nicer even than that villa in Octowyn where he had taken his wife after their wedding. He'd been a young man then. It seemed a lifetime ago.

Portsend measured just two dribs into the smallest beaker he had. Still, the liquid barely covered the bottom. In its natural state, it looked slightly murky, almost milky, as he hadn't yet decided on a color to dye it.

He had less than two cupweights of the solution left. There would be no more when this ran out. Who could he turn to with a request for dragon teeth to be fed to one of the beasts, extracted from the Slagstone, and processed into powder?

King Termain or Gloristar might have been willing to try to get it for him, but at this point, neither of them knew if he was even alive. As much as he wanted to reach out to the Prime Isless, he couldn't jeopardize the security of the guesthouse after he'd been so generously sheltered here.

Portsend knew he was close to determining this cloud's purpose. Almost like an Urging from the Homeland, he could sense that he was only a few detonations away from discovering the truth. He was confident that he'd get there before the solution ran out, but that wouldn't leave him with much to use after its secrets were uncovered.

What was he to do with those findings, anyway? Would they really help Gloristar if he gave them to the king? Or would his research just be destroyed again, making Termain even more upset?

Regardless, he felt a desperate compulsion to see this through, even after so many awful things had happened. Maybe it was *because* of those awful things. He certainly felt like he owed it to San and Lomaya to uncover this final detonation.

Portsend placed the small beaker on an empty table and drew a Slagstone ignitor from his vest pocket. Instead of throwing the sparks, he sat and stared blankly at the dribs of discolored liquid. His notes were all around him, but what would he write that he hadn't already recorded a dozen times? Why did he expect this detonation to be any different?

All the optimism he'd felt while measuring the liquid Grit dissolved into hopelessness. It settled on his shoulders and he hunched forward slightly, no longer staring at the beaker but seeming to stare *through* it.

He didn't know how much time had passed when a sharp rap on the cottage door jolted him out of his reverie. Heart suddenly pounding, he moved quickly and quietly to the bed's side table. Easing open the drawer, he withdrew his loaded Roller, thumb hovering on the Slagstone hammer.

"Come in," he called, body tensed.

The door swung open and the thin figure of Codley Hattingson was silhouetted against the late-afternoon light. Portsend relaxed, slipping the gun back into the drawer and pushing it shut with his thigh. Would the Realm have knocked politely if they'd discovered where he was hiding?

"Good afternoon, Professor," said the butler. "Is there anything I can do for you?"

"I'm all right, Mister Hattingson. Just a bit startled."

"Yes, well, many say they feel anxious on the night of a Moon Passing," he said. "Understandable, with the increase of Moonsickness as of late."

Portsend only wished that his anxiety was limited to one evening each cycle. And feeling responsible for the spreading Moonsickness did nothing to ease his nerves.

"Is there anything else?" Portsend asked when the man didn't move.

"Actually, yes," said Hattingson. "I wondered if I could get your opinion on a certain matter. As a man of science."

"Certainly," Portsend replied, grateful that he hadn't used up one of his precious detonations with this sudden distraction. "Come in."

The butler stooped and picked up a large wicker basket that Portsend hadn't noticed just outside the doorway. He stepped into the cottage, holding the basket on one narrow hip as he closed the door behind him.

"Before her rushed departure, Quarrah Khai asked me to look into a certain matter. I'm sure you noticed I was gone all day."

Portsend hadn't noticed. But then, he'd hardly left his own cottage, as wrapped up in his own experiments as he'd been.

The butler set the basket on the table, and Portsend found it full of small glass containers. There was greenery in each jar, and a square of mesh fabric tied across the opening like a lid.

"While inside Overseer's hidden closet," said Hattingson, removing the jars and lining them up as though on display, "Quarrah discovered a set of jars containing a sort of black, spiny worm. She believes the eggs produced by the worm are being ingested by Realm members to ensure their loyalty."

"How does that work?"

"At every meeting, each member of the organization drinks a beverage they call the Waters of Loyalty. They are informed that this is both poison and antidote. Based on Quarrah's findings, it would seem that the Waters of Loyalty are in fact a way to continually introduce new worm eggs into the members. The drink must also contain some sort of herb or chemical that prevents the eggs from hatching inside the host."

"Ah," Portsend said. "Seems like an effective way to keep everyone loyal."

"And to ensure that they attend each meeting." The basket was empty now, and Hattingson set it on the floor. "Quarrah asked me to collect a variety of specimens matching the description of the worm she saw."

Portsend reached across the table and picked up one of the jars. "Did you collect these around the guesthouse grounds?"

"One or two," he replied. "I acquired the majority of the specimens from an entomologist at the North Harbor Market."

It had always seemed a strange field of study to Portsend. Professor Harwood at the Southern Quarter College of Beripent was an entomologist, and she was always carrying on about the benefits of this bug or that worm. She'd even made a pretty Ashing selling certain insects to Healers for medicinal purposes.

"According to Quarrah," said the butler, "going without the Waters of Loyalty is quite devastating. Severe bruising that turns to open wounds, ending with a fatal fit of vomiting blood."

"Homeland," muttered Portsend. Why did everything the Realm have its fingers in result in such graphic consequences? "And that's the result of the eggs hatching inside the host?"

"Precisely," Hattingson said. "I know so little of these creeping varieties, I wondered if you could give them a glance. Would you have any suggestions on how we might test them to see if one of these could be capable of producing such... undesirable results?"

"Not sure I'm the right person to ask," admitted Portsend, examining another specimen. "But how likely do you think it would be that a public entomologist at the North Harbor Market would sell you worms that could do such a thing?"

The tall man sighed. "Probably not likely. However, my connections are quite lacking when it comes to the darker side of business. I have never found much occasion to associate with poisoners or exterminators."

"How did Quarrah describe the bugs?" Portsend asked.

"Inadequately," answered the butler. "Black, roughly an inch long, with bulbous ends. She said they had hairlike spines along their entire length."

"Well, these two aren't worms at all. At least, not technically." Portsend slid two of the jars to the side. "These are spanworms— the larval stage of a moth. And this one is a caterpillar." He moved aside another jar. "I think we can rule them out."

Codley Hattingson stiffened. "I am aware of the difference between a worm and a caterpillar. I thought, however, that Quarrah might not be. Her description could just as easily have been one of these."

"Except, they don't lay eggs," said Portsend. "Spanworms and caterpillars are immature until they undergo metamorphosis. Their adult versions—moths and butterflies—are the ones that lay the eggs."

"Still, the ones Quarrah saw could have hatched from the eggs. She said there were many tiny eggs in the bottom of each jar."

"Of course," said Portsend. "Because Overseer was likely harvesting eggs from the worms, not vice versa."

"Very well." Hattingson stiffly moved the three jars off the table and into his basket. "What about these others?"

"We should be looking for something parasitic. I would start by introducing raw meat to each of these specimens and record their reaction to it."

"Yes." He held up a finger. "Quarrah did mention that there appeared to be bits of rotten meat in the jars she found."

"In order to get such a severe reaction out of a host, I would venture that the worm will be quite hardy, and aggressive," Portsend said. "Again, not likely something you'll find from an entomologist at the North Harbor Market."

"Would you happen to know any distributors of black worms with undesirable parasitic attributes?"

Portsend thought about giving him Professor Harwood's name, but he couldn't bring himself to say it. Any connection back to the Southern Quarter College seemed unnecessarily risky. If Codley Hattingson went snooping around for worms that matched the description of something the Realm used, Harwood and Hattingson could both end up dead. And Portsend couldn't have another soul on his conscience.

"I don't," he replied. "Although, I'd suspect that the origins of such a severe worm would be linked to Pekal. That island has a way of breeding the most extreme forms of life."

Hattingson nodded resignedly, lifting his basket and gathering up the remaining jars. "Well, I suppose I shall head back to the guesthouse and give these a bite of Mister Lagaday's leftover meatloaf. If that doesn't bring out the barbarism in them, I don't know what will." He smiled cordially, and Portsend chuckled at the joke.

"I very much appreciate you taking the time to discuss this with me," said the butler. "Time is something of the essence, as both Quarrah and Ardor have ingested these eggs and are not welcome to return to any of the Realm's meetings. They likely have only a few weeks to learn what other component is in the Waters of Loyalty to eradicate them."

"I'd be happy to give it all of my attention," Portsend said, "as soon as I am finished with my current project."

Was that selfish of him? He was so close to understanding this final Grit cloud. Another couple of days and then he could divert all his attention to the black worm eggs.

"That would be wonderful," said the butler. "I'm sure you are very busy. I would like to officially express my amazement at your accomplishments. Your discoveries have been truly unprecedented."

Portsend bowed his head slightly at the compliments. He'd heard similar language from the others, Raekon and his partner, Ardor Benn. Even the former Queen Abeth Agaul, whose presence here was almost more than Portsend could comprehend, had lauded his creation of the liquid Grit solutions. He didn't revel in the praise of his rescuers, but it was better to let them say it than to reveal his connection to something as sacred as a list from the Anchored Tome.

"I was humbled to have your input on my project," Hattingson said as he picked up his basket.

Portsend hardly felt like he'd contributed anything significant. Still, he certainly knew the value of talking through a theory with someone. Perhaps that was what he'd been missing with this final type of Grit.

"Mister Hattingson," Portsend said as the butler turned to go.

"Hmm?"

Now that he'd stopped him, Portsend hesitated. Would speaking of his project with the butler doom the man to inevitable death at the hands of the Realm? Maybe he was doomed already. Codley Hattingson certainly wasn't working innocently, as Portsend's pupils had done for so many weeks. If anything, the butler knew more about the Realm's organization than he did.

"Perhaps you could return the favor of lending your thoughts on a particular experiment that has been giving me some difficulty."

"I would be delighted," Hattingson said, setting down the basket, "and highly unqualified."

Portsend was committed now. He would just show the man the small detonation cloud and see if he had any new thoughts toward determining its usefulness.

"I have managed to create yet another new Grit type, using processed dragon teeth as the source material," Portsend began, holding aloft his little beaker and tilting it so that the liquid pooled more visibly to the side. "Like the others, the Grit dissolves in an infusion with a unique balance level, creating a liquid solution that detonates much like powdered Grit."

He picked up the Slagstone ignitor in his other hand and angled it into the tilted beaker, sending sparks dancing down the glass. The moment they touched the solution, it detonated, leaving the beaker suddenly empty and dry.

The vaporous cloud formed in a perfect sphere around his hands, no more than a foot in diameter. He withdrew the beaker and ignitor, his movement doing nothing to disturb the orb that hung at shoulder height above the table.

"What does it do?" Hattingson asked, moving around to view it from another angle.

"That's the question. It seems to have no effect whatsoever."

"Likely whoever first discovered Illusion Grit thought the same thing."

Usclad Marg. Yes. Portsend had read his research and it was fraught with long periods of frustration before he discovered that two clouds detonated in the same space could connect an image through time. But this was different.

"I've tried repeat detonations in the exact same location," said Portsend. "And I've tried mixing this with every other Grit type, save Visitant Grit, for obvious reasons."

The butler reached his hand into the detonation. "No discernible temperature or pressure change?"

"None that my instruments can detect," replied Portsend. "I'd appreciate any new ideas. Homeland knows I've exhausted all of mine. I've tested this detonation on everything from a slice of bread to an experimentation rat."

"How do you test them?"

"By simply passing the subject through the cloud and observing any reaction."

To demonstrate, Portsend snatched one of the jars from the butler's basket and passed it quickly through the hanging detonation. "No noticeable effect on glass, vegetation, or animal life." He set it on the table again.

"Could it be an issue with the person detonating?"

"Me?"

"I'm only thinking of familiar Grit. Your mention of Visitant made me think of the worthiness that is required to successfully make a Paladin Visitant appear."

"You don't think I'm worthy to detonate this?" Portsend asked.

"I realize how that sounds," said Hattingson. "And it is not what I meant. I'm only suggesting that perhaps there is another attribute of the person detonating that determines the success of this particular cloud."

It was something Portsend had never considered. As the butler had mentioned, he was a man of science. Portsend liked things that could be measured and quantified. Things like worthiness were better left to be determined by the Islehood. And yet, that *was* his understanding of the way Visitant Grit worked. Perhaps Hattingson was on to something.

"Say, for example, that this particular type of Grit only yields its effect when detonated by a woman," continued the butler. "Or a child. Or perhaps a Trothian."

"This does open a new set of variables for me to test," Portsend said. Although, at the onset, the list seemed daunting and full of endless possibilities.

"Oh, what do I know?" the butler suddenly pulled his hand out of the cloud, seeming somewhat sheepish for having been caught up in a theory.

"No shame in swapping ideas," Portsend validated. "You're welcome to stick around and watch it burn out. But the duration is nothing unusual, so you probably have better things to do with your time."

Portsend picked up the jar he had taken from the basket and offered it to the butler. It wasn't until Hattingson's eyes went wide that Portsend realized what he was holding.

A butterfly.

Not daring to breathe, he lifted the jar for a closer inspection. The butterfly was perched on the leafy twig, its fragile wings a glorious display of vibrant purple-and-yellow spots.

"Fascinating," whispered Codley Hattingson.

Portsend had a dozen other words to match. He set down the butterfly and pulled one of the spanworm jars from the butler's basket.

Slowly, ceremoniously, he moved the container into the hanging sphere. The cloud passed easily through the mesh over the jar's top, and Portsend watched as the most miraculous thing occurred.

In the course of just a few seconds, the spanworm underwent the complete process of metamorphosis. Or perhaps it had skipped the process altogether. There was no cocoon or gradual emergence from a pupal state. One moment, the thin, black spanworm was inching along a broad leaf, and the next, it had fully formed dusty wings lying flat along its back, feathered antennae flicking curiously.

"Another," Portsend muttered, setting the large brown moth beside the butterfly. Hattingson handed him the other moth jar, and Portsend held it into the cloud, repeating the instant transformation in the exact same manner.

"One of the worms," Portsend said, beckoning as he set down the second moth.

The butler handed him a jar with a long black worm coiled on a bed of soil at the bottom. His heart pounding, Portsend thrust it into the detonation cloud, his eyes trained on the insect.

"Nothing," whispered Hattingson.

"Which is what I expected," replied Portsend. "The worm is already in its mature form. It isn't meant to transform into something new."

"It happened so quickly," Hattingson said, picking up the butterfly.

"We need to test this again," Portsend said.

"I can easily acquire another caterpillar."

Portsend nodded. "Yes. And I'd like to test it on a pupa as well. Either a moth already in a cocoon, or a butterfly in its chrysalis."

The butler set down the butterfly jar. "It is indeed astounding. But I fail to see its usefulness. Metamorphosis Grit seems to have an incredibly narrow field of application."

"And we don't even know if it will work on all life-forms that undergo a change," said Portsend. "We need to continue testing everything we can. Butterflies, moths..." He snapped his fingers in thought. "What else does it?"

"A variety of amphibians," answered Hattingson. "Frogs, newts..."

Portsend nodded. "Where can we find tadpoles?"

"Frogs are abundant in the guesthouse fishing pond. This time of year, there are likely still tadpoles swimming about."

"Good," said Portsend. "Bring me as many as you can reasonably scoop up."

"Now?" he asked.

"I'm sorry," Portsend said. "I'm overstepping." He'd mistakenly thought that his level of enthusiasm was shared by the butler. And while Hattingson certainly seemed impressed, he had duties and other guests to attend to.

"I'll see to it myself," Portsend said, "if you could help me find the supplies I need."

"Homeland, no!" cried the butler. "You are Professor Portsend Wal, a name I expect to be sung throughout history. I shan't have you fishing about for tadpoles under the Red Moon. I'll bring you the specimens shortly."

He bowed slightly and hastily exited the cottage, leaving behind his basket of curated worms.

Portsend waved his hand through the floating orb in amazement, then stooped to study the three transformed larvae.

Metamorphosis Grit.

After all his tinkering and experimenting, Portsend Wal was now on the final stretch.

~

*They were like insects beneath our feet.*

# CHAPTER

# 40

Ardor Benn stared down at the empty harbor. Even from his elevated viewpoint, the fleet of Trothian ships was completely out of sight as evening was coming on.

"They even took the *Double Take*," Raek muttered in disbelief. "If I ever find the rat who stole my ship, I'm gonna use him as an anchor."

"That's what you're raving about?" Quarrah said. She was pacing anxiously, an erratic pattern, as though she kept striking out to go somewhere only to forget her destination three steps in. "We've got to get down there."

"And do what? Swim?" Lyndel retorted, leaning against the Drift crate to take weight off her injured leg.

"We could salvage one of those scuttled ships," Quarrah said. "Maybe there's a personnel rowboat still intact."

"A rowboat!" Raek laughed. "Even if we had the *Double Take*, in all her speed and glory, we couldn't get to the Redeye line before the Moon comes up."

"So...what?" she barked. "We just stand here and enjoy the view? Or do we plan who gets a ball through the brain first? Because, Homeland help me, I'm not letting Moonsickness take me."

Ard kicked a small rock, watching it plummet over the steep edge and clatter along the ramps that led to the docks below. He didn't feel too different from that rock. Dull, worthless. A broken piece from a larger stone that had once been significant and notable.

So, this was how it was going to end. He really wouldn't have expected it. He'd spent nearly the last decade thinking it would be a shot in the head or a knife in the ribs. He thought it would happen quickly, although not entirely unexpectedly.

Somehow, this was worse. Marooned on Pekal during a Moon Passing. Now he had to decide how he'd spend his last day instead of just living it like any other. That kind of pressure could really spoil his evening.

"I'm not hearing anyone else sharing ideas," Quarrah continued.

"None to share," said Raek. "The ship has sailed...literally. Nothing to do but wait now. Personally, I think I'm going to look the best with red eyes."

"No!" Quarrah yelled, coming to a halt. "No jokes. This isn't just another one of your ruses gone slightly awry. Sparks! We're going to die here. And for what? *Barrier Grit?*"

Her words twisted the knife in Ard's emotions. Oh, he'd done it this time. The detour to pick up the Cataclysm kegs in Crooked Ravine had ended up costing them everything. And after all that sacrifice, the only thing they contained was simple Barrier Grit.

Overseer's overtures about the kegs had truly been nothing more than a cover. The Grit inside was not *irreplaceable*, as she'd touted. Raek had identified it as regular Barrier Grit and they'd tested one of the kegs not ten minutes ago when they realized the fleet had abandoned them.

"Don't you want to kill him?" Quarrah pointed an accusatory finger at Ard.

"That's not really a new sensation," Raek replied. "And I don't see how that's going to get us off this island. Besides, by the looks of it, Ard's killing himself right now."

Ard kicked another rock over the edge without looking up. He wasn't ready to speak yet. Words had always been his greatest weapon, and he refused to use them until they were appropriately sharpened for the occasion. But in this case, he felt like the man who had brought a knife to a gunfight.

He remained still in the maelstrom of nervous bickering that surrounded him, searching for the right break in the storm and realizing that it would probably never come.

They should have made it in time. Had things gone smoothly—had that blazing dragon not pinned them under the Barrier cloud for nearly two hours before flying off for the summit—they would have been safely on the *Double Take* sailing with the Trothian fleet.

Now what? They'd fall to Moonsickness, and Overseer would probably carry out the Cataclysm as planned. Thousands of people would lose their lives.

Well, at least now the crooked queen dowager wouldn't be able to use Shad Agaul.

Was that just selfish justification? The notion that it was better for the fourteen-year-old boy to die of Moonsickness on Pekal than to live out his days as a king under the Realm's control? Ard was chilled by his own thoughts.

He shut his eyes. Maybe he *was* a terrible person. Maybe he was all the things Quarrah said she hated about him, and none of the good that he saw in himself.

"There has to be another way," Quarrah said. "Barrier Grit. We scored enough from Shad's hideout to keep us covered all night. Not to mention the Cataclysm kegs."

"Barrier Grit will not stop the rays," Lyndel said. "It has been tried before."

"Then what about a cave or a hole in the ground that we can hide in..."

"Grumont's Theory," said Raek, shaking his bald head. "The entire island becomes a conduit for the Moonsickness and—"

"That's a *theory*, Raek!" she cried. "The four of us know the real cause of Moonsickness."

"Doesn't disprove Grumont's concepts," he rebutted. "That the island itself gets saturated with the poisoning rays from the Moon. He taught that the sickness seeps through rocks and soil—"

"Well, I still say we look for some kind of shelter," Quarrah said. "This Grumont idiot probably would have done the same thing if he'd been marooned here during a Passing!"

"Actually, that's how he died," said Raek. "Testing his *theory*. The Islehood considered some of his teachings heretical and he was marooned here during the Ninth Cycle Passing in the early eleven hundreds. A Harvesting crew found him two years later in a crevasse so narrow that he hadn't been able to get out. But he was almost a quarter mile underground and as stark-raving sick as any Bloodeye."

"He was still alive when they found him?" Lyndel asked.

"Sparks, yeah. He'd worn off his hands clear to the wrists trying to claw his way out. Grumont's Crevasse. It's a marked site on the windward side of Pekal. Ard and I visited, what, nine years ago?

You can still see Grumont's finger marks in the sandstone. You remember that, Ard?"

Ard opened his eyes again, but only to kick another little stone down to the harbor. There was something cathartic about watching them tumble, seeing which ones would make it to the water below.

"Stop it!" Quarrah suddenly snapped. "Stop telling stories and kicking rocks! You got us into this mess, Ardor Benn, and before your voice gets ripped out of your throat forever, I want to know if you even care."

Ard kicked another rock, which was apparently not the right thing to do. Quarrah sprang at him, shoving him sideways and not even seeming to care that he stumbled near the drop-off.

Finally, he looked at the faces of his companions. Quarrah was terrified—he'd heard that in her voice. Lyndel just looked angry, with deep blue lines creasing her face in a scowl. Shad Agaul was asleep in the open Drift crate, and Raek...

Raek was sitting in the dirt, a keg of Grit between his knees as he unbuttoned his shirt. He looked resigned, if anything, and Ard watched in confusion as he took a pinch of Grit and loaded it into the opening in his chest.

"What are you doing?" Ard's first words tumbled out sharp and accusatory.

Raek looked up casually, replacing the cork in the pipe and sparking the detonation. He let out a slow breath. "Figured there was all this Health Grit in the crate. Pity to let it go to waste."

Ard felt his cheeks flush. *No!* Not this again! Raek hadn't needed Health Grit for days. Ard had gotten him through it ...

He stalked the short distance to his friend and yanked the keg out from between his knees. "What the blazes, Raek? Why would you do this?"

"Umm ... Because I'd like to be as healthy as possible when I get Moonsickness tonight?" The big man did not look amused, despite the attempt at humor lingering in his deep voice.

"We talked about this!" Ard slammed the lid of the keg shut. The anger in his voice was compounding, and he realized that Raek's Heg abuse was little more than a metaphor for their current situation. Ardor Benn had landed Raek on death's doorstep once again. Only this time, there wouldn't be a team of palace Healers ready to save him. And it wasn't just Raekon Dorrel.

"*You* talked about it," Raek returned. "*You* came up with a plan—"

"And it was working!" Ard clutched the Grit keg in both hands. "You were getting better!"

"Oh, really? How would you know?" Raek slowly rose to his feet, towering over Ard as the afternoon sun highlighted the scars and crooked angles of his face. "You just hand me a roll every few days and tell me how long it's supposed to last. You've never actually *asked* me how it's going!"

"Did I need to?" Ard cried. "It was a solid plan!"

"For *you*!" spat Raek. "It was a solid plan to make you feel better. Make you feel like you were in control of the situation. But, surprise... I never stopped. The rolls you gave me would last a day—maybe two. Then I was back on the streets, drumming up my contacts, refilling my stashes."

If Raek had punched him in the stomach, it would have come as no less of a blow. But deep inside, Ard wasn't surprised by the confession. He'd intentionally blinded himself to Raek's problem because it numbed his own guilt. He'd concocted a solution that was straightforward and simple, two qualities that completely misrepresented everything in his life.

Ard sighed, grimacing. His voice was soft and defeated. "I think I really missed the mark on this one."

"Well, it was never your mark to hit." Raek reached out and peeled the keg of Health Grit from Ard's grasp. "This is something I've got to do. It's something I've got to *want* to do."

Ard stared at his partner, and for a moment he saw the teenage face that he'd befriended all those years ago. Despite all they'd been through, in many ways, they were no different from the mischievous boys they'd been back then. Ard suddenly felt entirely overwhelmed and filled with regret.

*I'm not ready to die,* he realized. *Not like this*—a disappointment to his friends. An overinflated failure.

Ard turned away from Raek in frustration and despair, too embarrassed to look at Quarrah and Lyndel. He kicked his largest rock yet, hurting his foot as it barely tumbled over the cliff's edge.

So, he was back to envying the lifeless stones, watching them sink away from the hopeless situation on Pekal, plunging out of reach of the Moon's sickening rays...

Ard froze. Like a whetstone sharpening a blade, he felt his mind honing a wild and hopeful idea. The falling stone had sparked it, and Ard's brain was responding with a detonation of thought.

"Ship in a bottle." His eyes snapped up, finding the strained faces of his companions.

"What are you talking about?" Quarrah asked. He couldn't miss the hopeful notes in her voice. "The *Holy Breath*?"

"Yes," he said. "And no. How much time do we have until the Moon rises?"

"Just over an hour," answered Lyndel. "But even if we had a vessel, there is no way we could sail out of range fast enough."

"Not *out* of range," Ard said. "*Down.*"

Raek began to chuckle, and Ard knew his partner was following. "That's crazy, Ard. You're crazy."

"Right now, I'd say this kind of crazy is better than Moonsickness," Ard replied. "Could we do it? We have enough Grit, right?"

"I'll need to double-check and run a few numbers," Raek said. "And we have no guarantee that the Moon rays won't reach us."

"What are you talking about?" Lyndel finally cut in. Based on the look on Quarrah's face, she wasn't fully following either. Ard couldn't blame them, he and Raek had been finishing each other's sentences for so many years. Other people required more than twice the explanation.

"We close ourselves into one of those newfangled Containment clouds," Ard explained. "We throw ourselves over the cliff and go straight down into the InterIsland Waters, as fast and deep as we can."

"We will float," said Lyndel.

"We've already worked out the wrinkles on that," Ard said. "We can use Compounded Weight Grit to make ourselves heavy. Not just heavy enough to bob under the surface like the *Holy Breath*, but to really sink fast."

"How deep will we need to go?" Lyndel asked. "It's fifteen miles to the Redeye line, but I cannot imagine the InterIsland Waters being that deep."

"Then we go to the bottom. How deep would you wager that is?" Ard asked.

"No one really knows," she answered. "Anchors go down in the harbors up to fifty yards. Out there," she pointed into the Inter-Island Waters, "the depth is unknown. The bottom has never been reached."

"Well, that sounds plenty deep to me." His voice was full of optimism, meant to ease the doubts of the others. Not that he'd need to do much convincing for this plan. It was really their only option, whether it seemed like it would work or not.

"Besides," Ard continued, "we'll be counting on the water overhead to stop the Moon rays."

"What about that theory?" Quarrah said. "The guy who scratched his hands off?"

"Grumont's Theory has to do with the geomorphic features of Pekal," Raek explained. "The island works like a conduit for the rays, but nothing suggests the water will."

"Nothing suggests it won't," Quarrah pointed out.

"If water were an effective conduit for the Moon rays," Raek rebutted, "what would stop it from spreading through the entire InterIsland Waters instead of tapering off at the Redeye line? We have to assume the rays are just falling on the surface."

"Assume," repeated Quarrah.

"A moment ago, you were begging for ideas," Raek said. "I think an assumption is the best we're going to get. This kind of thing has definitely never been tested before."

"How do we come back up?" Lyndel asked.

"Simple," answered Ard. "We let the Weight Grit wear off and rise with the natural buoyancy of the Containment bubble."

"We have enough liquid Containment Grit to do this?" Lyndel asked.

Raek tilted his head. "Doubtful."

"But we've got plenty of Barrier Grit," Ard said. "Even without using the Cataclysm kegs."

"How does that help us?" Quarrah asked. "Barrier Grit is immovable."

"So we only use the Containment Grit on our way down and our way back up," Ard said. "Once we get to a safe depth, we can detonate regular Barrier Grit that'll hold us in place under the water. We won't even need Weight Grit at that point."

"That should work," said Raek. "And once we're ready to come up, we'll switch back to the liquid stuff and the movable Containment cloud will just float to the surface like an empty jug."

"How will we breathe?" Lyndel asked. "We are talking about spending an entire night in an enclosed space under water. How big will this bubble be?"

"Just big enough to hold the five of us," Raek said. "That's not going to give us much air."

"How long could we last?" Quarrah asked.

Raek shrugged. "Hard to know. Say the diameter of our detonation cloud is twelve feet. With five of us breathing..."

"Could we somehow slow down our air consumption?" Ard asked.

"Holding our breath?" Raek raised an eyebrow.

"I can hold my breath for at least thirty minutes at a time," contributed Lyndel.

"Oh," Raek said. "Well, those of us that aren't Trothian can only manage a minute or so."

"And then we'll all be gasping and using it up twice as fast," said Quarrah.

"Stasis Grit!" Ard cried.

"Won't that just knock us unconscious?" Quarrah said. "We'd still be breathing, right?"

"Not according to the professor," Raek said. "Stasis Grit suspends a person's body in a state of perfect inactivity. It's not sleep or unconsciousness. It's *stasis*. That means no movement, no heartbeat, no breathing."

"Is it safe?" Quarrah asked.

"Portsend kept a rat in stasis overnight and it revived just fine," said Raek.

"I will remain awake throughout the night," Lyndel volunteered. "Someone will need to detonate fresh Containment and Weight Grit every ten minutes or so. I can limit my breath and stay alert to do what is needed."

"That's what I call a plan!" Ard clapped his hands.

"Now, I assume you're counting on me to make sure this actually works?" Raek said.

"That is the way we generally do things."

"We don't have a lot of time," Lyndel said. "There is no telling how deep the rays will penetrate into the water."

"Let's move north along the shoreline," Raek said. "We need to make sure we don't drop into the harbor since it might not be deep enough. Once we find a good section of overhang on the cliff, we'll get ourselves into position."

"What do we do with the Drift crate?" Ard asked.

"We leave it here," answered Quarrah.

"What about the Cataclysm kegs?" Ard said. Just because they were full of simple Barrier Grit didn't change the plan Ard had for them. If they came out of this alive, he'd need those kegs.

"Are you serious?" Quarrah shouted. "What is your obsession with those blazing useless kegs?"

He'd tell her the plan later, when she wasn't so worked up. They had plenty of other things to focus on now.

"Actually," Raek said, "we might want to take the Drift crate."

"Why?" Lyndel asked.

"Well, you're going to need some way to stay out of the Stasis cloud that's keeping the rest of us down."

"You're suggesting that the three of us pile in with Shad Agaul?" Ard asked.

Raek nodded. "We'll have to lose some of the cargo to make room—not the Cataclysm kegs," he said, as if anticipating Ard's objection. "It'll be easy for Lyndel to feed Stasis Grit into the hopper and keep the four of us out cold."

"How is the Drift crate going to fit inside the Containment cloud?" Quarrah asked.

"We can saw off the handles," answered Raek. "When we detonate the Containment Grit, it'll settle into the bottom of the sphere like a box resting inside a bowl."

"Or a coffin," Quarrah muttered.

"We don't have much time," Lyndel said.

Ard was feeling genuinely hopeful. This had worked with the *Holy Breath*, and there was no reason it wouldn't work with them inside the bubble. The only elements that couldn't be calculated were the depth of the InterIsland Waters, and the penetration of the rays through the surface. Admittedly, those were some major variables. But what other option did they have?

It was moments like these that Ardor Benn lived for. When the brilliance of keen minds came together to hatch a plan so wild and daring that it seemed to defy logic and even fate itself.

Ard took a deep breath. "Let's go for a dive."

~

*Fishes and sharks they piled upon our heads and left us for dead.*

# CHAPTER

# 41

Quarrah awoke with a start. It was perfectly dark and cold enough that she wondered how she'd been sleeping through it. Her mind felt fuzzy, her heart racing unusually fast, and her breaths coming in ragged gasps.

She suddenly remembered where she was —in a Drift crate inside a bubble of Containment Grit sinking to the bottom of the InterIsland Waters.

Quarrah's first cohesive thought was that something had gone wrong. Lyndel wasn't supposed to bring them out of the Stasis cloud until morning, but it couldn't be time already.

Pressed uncomfortably beside her, Quarrah heard Ard grunt as though trying to shake away the confusion of suddenly coming to. In the darkness, young Shad Agaul was muttering, "Dark. Dark. Why is it dark?"

Quarrah heard the sound of the Drift crate's hatch opening, but no light filtered in. Sparks. Why *was* it still dark? If Lyndel was letting them out of the crate, shouldn't it be morning? Shouldn't they be back to the surface?

"Lyndel?" Quarrah spoke anxiously.

"It's all right," came her Trothian-accented voice.

"What's going on?" Ard asked.

"We have reached the bottom of the InterIsland Waters," Lyndel answered.

"What?" Raek's voice sounded harsh. "We don't have the air for this!"

"I believe we now have all the air we need."

"What are you talking about?" Raek cried.

"You should come out and see this," said the priestess.

"It's pitch-dark, Lyndel," Ard pointed out. "We don't all have Trothian eyes."

Quarrah heard some rustling and then the shattering of a clay pot. At once, their bubble was flooded with the bright glow of Light Grit. Quarrah squinted against it, Ard and Raek cursing at the sudden illumination. Shad Agaul cried out as though he'd been struck.

The Drift crate's loading hatch had fallen open, the door now leaning against the shell of the Barrier bubble like a platform. Quarrah was the first to scramble out onto it, peering up at where Lyndel sat atop the wooden box. All the supplies she needed for their descent were stocked in backpacks surrounding her.

"Do you see it now?" Lyndel asked.

"What are we looking at?" Ard crawled out of their confines, stretching. Quarrah, too, felt the lingering stiffness of having been in stasis.

"Our bubble sank for over an hour," Lyndel said.

"Then the Moon's up by now." Raek's added weight on the door caused the wooden platform to bow and creak.

Quarrah looked up, and there was no red glow above. That was a good sign, right?

"So we either missed the rays or we're already Moonsick," Ard surmised.

"I believe we are safe," said Lyndel. "We have descended deeper than any living soul."

Quarrah felt a chill from something other than the pervasive cold. Had they really reached the bottom of the InterIsland Waters?

Ard leaned forward, cupping his hands around his face and pressing them to the side of the Barrier bubble, peering outward through the darkness.

"Holy sparks," he whispered, his tone so somber and sincere that Quarrah felt another chill. She mimicked Ard's stance like someone in a bright room peering out at the night through a window. In the glow of Lyndel's lantern, she saw the object of Ard's exclamation.

It was a massive red spire of shimmering glass, smooth and broad at the base, but tapering as it rose to unseen heights.

"Agrodite Moon Glass," Lyndel said reverently.

Quarrah thought back to two years ago, when the four of them had sat in Lyndel's apartment, the floor littered with Halavend's books that the priestess's eyes could not read. Lyndel had shown them a shard of the red glass—sacred to her people. As Quarrah remembered it, looking through the Moon Glass caused Landers to see the way Trothian eyes did. And supposedly, it did even more to enhance Trothian vision.

Lyndel had once given her piece of Moon Glass to Halavend's young pupil, Isless Malla. She had carried it to the summit of Pekal on a journey that had ended in her death by Moonsickness. Through the Glass, Isless Malla had been able to confirm the theory that the dragons were absorbing the toxic Moon rays, drawing them away from the habitable islands and shielding all of humankind.

"There are but three known pieces of Moon Glass throughout all our islets," Lyndel said. "It is the sacred duty of the Agrodite priestesses to safeguard them."

"Looks like somebody dropped a piece," Raek said. The spire outside was gigantic—at least thirty feet in diameter at its base.

"There is something more." The priestess's vibrating eyes gazed outward through their transparent vessel. "We are not under water anymore."

Not under water? What was she talking about? This was the bottom of the sea!

"That spire of Moon Glass is completely dry," Lyndel expounded, "surrounded by air."

"Air?" Ard said dubiously.

"A pocket of air," Lyndel verified. "I cannot explain it. The pocket appears to be quite vast. My eyes cannot behold the end of it."

"That isn't possible," Raek muttered.

"I saw the air pocket as we sank toward it," explained Lyndel, "so I had a pot of Drift Grit ready when we fell into it. I was able to detonate it and reduce our weight, preventing us from falling to our deaths."

Ard waved a hand through the air. "The Drift Grit already extinguished?"

Lyndel nodded. "I have been debating whether or not to awaken you for some time now. But I believe we have been brought here for a reason. In Agrodite belief, Moon Glass is a symbol of knowledge and wisdom. It brings clarity and purpose." Her dark eyes were staring at the spire. "We must go out to it."

"Whoa!" Ard shouted. "I appreciate the religious enthusiasm, but you need to get ahold of yourself. We're on the bottom of the sea here."

"Miles deep, if I had to guess," agreed Lyndel. "But the Moon Glass would not lead us into danger." There was a frightening calmness about the priestess. Whatever they had just stumbled upon connected with her in a deeply spiritual way. "It always shows the path to truth."

"Truth is," said Raek, "that oceans are full of water."

Lyndel nodded. "There is an ocean's worth of water above us. But that spire has guided us here, to this pocket of air. We must go out and examine the Glass."

"We're not going anywhere," insisted Ard. "Maybe it looks dry to your eyes, but we have no idea what's really out there."

"This is a test of faith, Ardor Benn. If you will not take it, then I must go to the spire alone."

"That's not really how this works," Ard said. "We can't exactly open a door and let you out. We all have to stay together."

"Or we all have to go," said Lyndel. She held up her hand and Quarrah saw a vial of yellow liquid Null Grit glinting in the Light cloud!

"Flames, Lyndel!" Quarrah called out. "What are you thinking?"

"You are welcome to hold your breath if you think I am wrong," Lyndel said. "But the Moon Glass will show us the truth of all things."

She dashed the glass vial against the side of the Barrier shield. The Slagstone chip in the liquid sparked and the Grit ignited in a flash cloud, instantly extinguishing their only protection.

Quarrah flinched, drawing her hands around her head. The handleless Drift crate fell two or three feet, Lyndel holding on to the top as Quarrah, Ard, and Raek tumbled off the open door that had served as a platform.

Quarrah sucked in a breath. Air. No crushing water poured in around her or whisked her off her feet. She stood, breathing, shivering from the cold, at the bottom of the InterIsland Waters.

"Well, this raises more eyebrows than I currently have," Raek said.

The Null flash cloud hadn't snuffed the sealed Light Grit lantern, but its illumination seemed pitifully small in such a vast darkness.

What was this place?

Quarrah turned as Ard shut the door on the Drift crate, sealing the dazed young prince inside once more.

"We need to get him back in a Stasis cloud," Ard said. "I really don't think this is the first message we want to imprint on his tender brain."

"Let's use Memory Grit," Quarrah suggested. "Save the Stasis for the way back up."

She grabbed one of the loaded backpacks from the top of the Drift crate as Lyndel climbed down. Rummaging through, Quarrah found a pot of Memory Grit marked with identifying gray paint. She dropped it into the hopper and pulled the trigger, hearing the clay crunch as the detonation filled the crate.

By that point, Raek had produced a couple of Compounded Light Grit pots from another pack, fitting them with a very short fuse. Once they were lit, he threw them straight into the air, the Grit detonating at the apex of his toss.

In the increased glow, Quarrah could better see her surroundings. It was, just as Lyndel had said, some kind of underwater air pocket. The stone floor was smooth and dry beneath her feet, more like a paved courtyard than a seabed.

And around them was a wall of pure seawater, as far as Quarrah could see. It rose unnaturally, extending on both sides into the darkness. It curled overhead, forming a liquid roof that glimmered in Raek's Light detonations. Looking up, it was like staring at the InterIsland Waters on a dark night—only upside down.

Lyndel's voice caused Quarrah to turn. The priestess was at the base of the glass spire, muttering something in her native tongue, arms crossed over her chest in a respectful gesture.

The red Moon Glass was indeed extraordinary. It rose out of a square base of stone that appeared to be chiseled directly from the ocean's bedrock. The glass column reached nearly to the water ceiling, some forty feet above their heads.

"Where are we?" Ard whispered, turning slowly.

"And how the blazes are we going to get back up there?" Raek asked.

"We'll have to launch from here," Ard said.

"We have no buoyancy," Raek pointed out. "We're not under water."

"Then we'll have to detonate a Containment cloud around ourselves and force it into that wall of water so we can float up," said Ard.

Raek reached out and touched the water, his fingers passing into it as easily as if it were a regular pond. The disrupted surface caused a few droplets of cold, salty water to spray in their faces.

"I don't think I like it here." Raek quickly withdrew his hand, drying it on the leg of his pants.

"Nice to visit, though," Ard said.

"If we detonate our movable Containment cloud here," Raek swept his arm in a wide motion, "then we just need some sort of push to get us into the water."

"Void Grit," Quarrah suggested. "If it's Compounded enough, it should be able to shove us in some general direction."

Raek nodded. "That'll work. We might as well pass the rest of the night down here where we know we have air. Then Lyndel can put us back into a Stasis cloud and we can float up to where things are . . . *normal*."

"If she even decides to come back with us." Ard pointed over at her.

Lyndel had her back to them, one hand stretched out to touch the smooth glass spire.

"Maybe she sees something we don't," Quarrah remarked, leading them over to where Lyndel stood in a worshipful reverie.

"Any idea how a spire of sacred Agrodite glass ended up clear down here?" Quarrah asked as they drew near. Lyndel turned to face them, and Quarrah leapt back, letting out a cry of alarm.

The priestess's eyes were glowing. Bright red, like the color of a setting sun.

Her blue hand dropped from the column and her eyes faded so quickly that Quarrah wondered if it had been a trick of the light.

But the fact that Ard had his Roller out was an indication that he'd seen it, too.

"Sparks, Lyndel." Quarrah shuddered. "What was that? Are you all right?"

"It is a testament," she said, her eyes dark and vibrating once again at their usual rate.

"Testament?" Raek repeated incredulously. "How can you be sure?"

"I... read it," she said.

"Hold on a minute." Ard stepped forward. "*Read* it? I don't even see any words."

Not to mention the fact that Lyndel's eyes weren't supposed to be able to perceive the written word.

"I cannot fully explain it," Lyndel replied. "It was not 'reading' in any conventional sense that you are familiar with. Rather, I heard the words with my eyes. And I saw them with my touch."

"Then this isn't Agrodite Moon Glass?" Quarrah asked.

"It is the same."

"Does your shard of Glass back home do this?" Ard asked.

"Never before," she answered.

Ard reached out and pressed his hand against the glass column. "Did you break it?" he asked after a moment of nothing.

"I do not think it will react to your plain Lander constitution," Lyndel said. "And yet, the words in my mind were as straightforward as if someone were speaking them into my ear."

"What did they say?"

"Very little. But I sense there is more. I was startled and I pulled away."

Turning her attention back to the large glass, Lyndel stretched out her hand and placed it once more on the smooth spire, the dark blue of her skin contrasting starkly with the shimmering rosiness of the glass. At once, her eyes began to vibrate faster and faster until suddenly they lit from within. A red glow.

*"This is our final testament,"* she began to speak. *"We have forged this glass in our might and power, and should we die up there, our glory shall not be forgotten, for this shall remain forever incorruptible. None can oppose our mighty works. We were wronged, but from that mistreatment came our strength.*

*"Let it be known, that before the changing we were all alike. Together, we labored in the soil for our food, and when the sun rose high, we shared our shade and our cup. We were no strangers to conflicts, but we resolved them in our own way, without the meddling of gods.*

*"The dragons slept at our borders, full of judgment and swift wrath. But at length, we defied them. We extended our dwellings beyond the boundaries.*

*"The gods grew angry at our progress and they smote us with a plague of mind and body. But we were many in number, and we rose up against our encroaching madness, taking salvation out of the open mouths of the dragons. From their teeth we rose to higher heights, granted new sight and power beyond our imaginings.*

*"A third of us were changed, and the gods could not abide it. In truth, we greatly desired to share the change with all. Never at any time have we forbidden others from becoming like us. For our minds are keener and our bodies pure, even unto a state of utter perfection. Yet, we were not esteemed, but spurned. Not lauded, but reproached. But all this while it was they who stole from us. Not possessions or goods, but the love of our gods.*

*"They came against us, but we stood firmly. We were mighty, but we could still taste death. With the strength of our arms we repelled the enemies on the left and on the right.*

*"The unchanged stood with the gods, but they were like insects beneath our feet. We slaughtered them without resistance, ourselves grieved to turn blades on our former brothers and sisters. Nevertheless, they would not relent.*

*"The gods wept when they saw how many of the unchanged had fallen by our blades. But no tears were shed for our losses. Always, they favored the weak and the simple. And when our threat to their existence grew too strong, they fled.*

*"In the still of night, the gods made preparations, building towers of stone and soil reaching almost to the Red Moon itself. Then, taking the last remaining unchanged, they whisked them high up out of our reach.*

*"The gods were spent from such expenditure of their power. Already, we saw them begin to decay. They had sacrificed themselves for the unchanged, and given us nothing but scorn. They loved what they could control, and they despised us when we ascended to be like them.*

*"With their final measure of power, the gods filled our kingdom with the depths of the sea. Fishes and sharks they piled upon our heads and left us for dead.*

*"But we did not perish.*

*"Our streets have been washed away, but they are not forgotten. We swam in the depths as the centuries passed above our heads, dwelling in the dry pockets that the gods' waning power was insufficient to fill. We thrived on the sole of the sea, isolated and forsaken.*

*"We have hidden in the depths, but no longer. On the morrow, we shall go up at last. After all this time, our bodies are strong enough within the water to make the journey. No one knows the way, save it be upward.*

*"Will they remember our home? All this time, we have been concealed before their very eyes. And when they behold us at last, we will be upon them, rising from the sea like mist to finish the war they fled from.*

*"They will wonder how we survived, but our only answer will be a blade between their ribs. Their kings and queens will bow down before us and they will be filled with regret. We shall send their bodies to the depths that once held us. Then at last, we will breathe true air and feel the warmth of the sun on our necks once again.*

*"Our decision to leave is unanimous. There can be no secrets among us, for our eyes can see them. We have counseled and debated, and this is our best course of action.*

*"We take no glass with us, but leave spires like this scattered by the thousands across the ocean floor. When the unchanged settle to such terrible depths, they will be greeted by our words.*

*"You have abandoned us, favored of the gods.*

*"Now we are coming for you."*

Lyndel's hand dropped from the spire and she stepped back, her glowing eyes darkening. She was breathing heavily, as though translating the words had exacted great effort of body and mind.

"This is the Homeland." Ard was the first to speak in the silence that followed.

Lyndel nodded. "We were once the same, you and I. Landers and Trothians."

Quarrah lifted a hand to her head. The text that Lyndel had spoken was confusing at best. Once there had been dragons down here? And *gods*? What did that even mean? As far as she knew, there was never any mention of gods in Wayfarism.

"Let me make sure I got all that straight," Raek said. "Landers and Trothians were once the same race living in some sort of civilization down here? A third of them went out of bounds and the gods struck them with a plague?"

"That's what it sounded like to me," said Ard.

"Moonsickness?" Quarrah asked. "Isn't that what happens if we go 'out of bounds'?"

"Interesting," Ard mused. "But they didn't die."

"It sounds like they fought some dragons and somehow stayed alive."

"They didn't just stay alive," Quarrah said. "They changed."

"Into what?"

"Something more powerful than they'd been," said Raek. "And it displeased the 'gods.'"

"That has to be talking about Trothian gods?" Ard clarified.

Lyndel shook her head. "I do not believe so. My religion teaches that the gods were the first family of Trothians, born out of the Crimson Moon. But instead of suckle, the Moon gave them sickness. So our ancestor gods hid from the Moon that birthed them. They used their great strength to heap up all the earth into one point, and they formed Pekal so that its high peak would push the Moon away."

"I thought Agrodites worshiped the Moon," Quarrah said. While Landers tended to hide inside during the Passings, Quarrah knew that many Trothians gathered outside under its red glow.

"We do," she answered. "We pray to our gods, asking them to

flatter the Moon into loving us once more. Agrodites believe that one day, instead of sickness, the Red Moon will fill us with power. And instead of blindness, we will be given new sight."

"So the Agrodite gods are basically your Trothian ancestors, who were the first to 'change,'" said Ard.

"Which means that the gods they were writing about were something altogether different, since they existed *before* the Trothian transformation," said Raek.

"The gods of our gods," muttered Lyndel.

"Well, whoever these gods were, it sounded like they feared the ancient Trothians enough to take the Landers and flee," said Quarrah.

"And that fear never really died," Ard said. "Accounts from our Lander ancestors say that the first Trothians arrived suddenly in 'ships that the eye could not behold.'"

"Because they swam up from the deep," said Raek. "They were clearly a superior race, so they managed to slaughter thousands of Landers without any difficulty."

"So, what happened?" Ard said. "Why are Trothians… Trothians, instead of those godlike beings Lyndel just read about?"

"We must have decayed," said Lyndel. "Over time, far above our place of origin, we must have digressed back into what we'd been before."

"But not exactly," said Raek. "You must have evolved into a new race altogether."

"Was there anything more in the spire?" Quarrah asked.

Lyndel shook her head. "That was all."

"Blazing lucky our bubble came down where it did," Ard pointed out. "All the vastness of the InterIsland Waters, and we showed up *here*?"

"They said there were thousands of these testament spires across the seabed," Quarrah reminded him.

"Still…" said Ard.

"I believe we were drawn here," said Lyndel. "In Agrodite belief, Moon Glass holds great power. Perhaps even power to pull us to it."

"But your shards of Moon Glass don't hold any testament or secret message, do they?" Ard asked, double-checking.

"I am beginning to think that they might have, long ago," said Lyndel. "It seems likely that the power of our Moon Glass, or perhaps just our ability to access it, could have waned and decayed just as our race did. What was once recorded history then became wholly oral, changing slightly with each generation."

"All this time…" Ard muttered. "The Homeland has been *beneath* us." He held out his hands as though feeling the air.

"I'll admit it," said Raek. "You've finally made me a believer."

"I don't think this is what Wayfarism is preaching about," said Ard.

"Yeah," added Quarrah. "What about those crystal shores and lush jungles?"

"This place could very well have been that, once," Lyndel pointed out.

"That's not exactly what I mean," said Ard. "Think about what Wayfarism preaches. Always striving to progress. Never Settle. Push for perfection."

"So?" Raek said.

"Pethredote told me that the true Homeland was not a place at all but a perfected version of the future," he explained. "The testament stated that after undergoing the change, they considered themselves perfect."

"You're saying that it wasn't necessarily this *place*," said Lyndel, "but rather the people—my *ancestors*—who were the Homeland?"

Ard nodded. "In both the sense of place and being. If they were really as strong and powerful as the testament makes them sound, there had to be a degree of jealousy from the unchanged. That could have easily carried into Lander belief and formed the very basis of Wayfarism."

"I'll let you explain that one to the Prime Isless when we get back," Raek said.

Ard waved his hand. "It doesn't matter anyway. There's obviously no way for anyone to become one of these 'changed Homelanders' now. It's not even clear how they did it back then, what with gods and curses and all…"

"It wasn't a curse," Quarrah said. "It was a plague."

"I thought it said the gods cursed them with a plague."

"Maybe we should hear it again," suggested Raek. "After all, we've got all night."

Lyndel pressed her hand to the glass spire, and her eyes flared red.

~

*We thrived on the sole of the sea, isolated and forsaken.*

# CHAPTER

# 42

A rd clambered out of the Drift crate, the whole thing suddenly pitching sideways, causing him to slam against the transparent shell of the Containment cloud.

He slid helplessly down the slippery surface, coming to rest in the bowled section beneath the handleless Crate.

There was water all around him, but the midmorning sky was clear and bright overhead.

They'd made it to the surface!

He had expected it to be just past dawn, but they must have mis-judged the passage of time so deep under water. Well, better that they'd erred on the side of caution, since the Red Moon was now long gone.

They'd listened to the testament more than a dozen times and actually caught a little sleep before using a detonation of Compounded Void Grit to push their movable Containment cloud into the wall of water. Buoyancy had done the rest, Lyndel remaining outside the Stasis-filled crate to detonate the vials they needed to see them all the way up.

There was a loud boom, and the whole Containment sphere skipped across the water's surface, the Drift crate jolting sideways and pitching Raek out of its open side. The big man slid down the slick Containment shell, colliding with Ard at the bottom of the bubble, a couple of loose Cataclysm kegs nestling in beside them.

"Sparks!" Ard yelled. "What was that?"

"Cannon fire!" replied Lyndel. Ard pushed against Raek, but it was impossible to find purchase on the utterly smooth surface beneath him.

"Cannon fire?" Raek repeated.

Lyndel's blue hand suddenly appeared over the side of the crate. Ard took it, and with a little boost from Raek, he managed to slide out from under the crate, scrambling up the side to join Lyndel and Quarrah, who were clinging to the top of the box.

Finally above the surface, Ard could see that the undercurrents of the sea had caused their bubble to come up several miles from Pekal's harbor...

Right in the middle of a war zone.

At a glance, Ard spotted Archkingdom ships and Sovereign vessels, half of which were crewed by Trothians.

"Your people survived the night," Raek said as Lyndel helped him scramble onto the top of the Drift crate with the others.

"Yes," replied the priestess. "My warriors are attempting to reclaim the harbor."

"How do the Sovs feel about that?" Ard asked. Half of the Sovereign fleet appeared to be firing on the Archkingdom's vessels, while the other half took cracks at the Trothians.

"They seem divided," Lyndel answered. "Willing to sink a few of their own ships as a warning to call back my warriors."

"They've been fighting all night?" Ard asked, as if Lyndel would know the answer.

"Perhaps there was a period of negotiation and questioning," she replied, "as they tried to learn our motives."

"Looks like that must have gone well," muttered Raek.

Quarrah suddenly gasped, gripping the top of the Drift crate. "Incoming!"

Ard turned in time to see the cannonball strike the water not five feet in front of their Containment cloud. It sent their spherical vessel reeling, the open Drift crate spilling out a few more of the Cataclysm kegs.

"I think we've been spotted," Raek said.

"That's one of *our* ships!" cried Lyndel, staring in the direction where the shot had come from. Ard saw the large brigantine, Sovereign colors flying from both masts.

"Maybe you should tell them not to shoot at their chieftess," Ard said.

"I thought that was common knowledge," added Raek.

Lyndel rose to her feet on top of the Drift crate, unable to stand tall with the Containment shield curving overhead. She began shouting in the Trothian tongue, waving her red-wrapped arms frantically.

"They're turning toward us," Ard said. "That's a good sign, right?"

"That ship doesn't have a cannon at the bow," Lyndel said. "If she's coming toward us, that means I've been recognized."

"How much time do we have left on this detonation?" Raek asked. "We don't want it winking out before they reach us. We can swim, but I wouldn't count on Shad Agaul to know how. And these crates aren't made to float."

In response to Raek's question, Lyndel held up the ten-minute hourglass that she'd been using to time the detonations. The top chamber had cracked, and sand was spilling out.

"Flames, Lyndel!" Raek hissed, digging through one of the packs for a measured vial of liquid Containment Grit. "Have you just been guessing?"

"It wasn't like this the whole way up!" Lyndel defended. "We were struck by a cannonball the moment we surfaced. It must have broken in the impact."

To the accompaniment of surrounding Archkingdom cannon fire, Ard decided to recover the kegs that had spilled to the bottom of their Containment bubble. With Quarrah's help, he gathered them into the crate and latched the door, closing Shad inside.

"I don't think we want to shape the prince's fragile mind with the screams of war," Ard said, dropping a pot of Memory Grit into the Crate's hopper and detonating it.

"For being the most important person in the Greater Chain, he certainly has spent a lot of time closed up in a box," Quarrah said.

"It's for the best."

Keeping Shad Agaul inside the Drift crate might only have been postponing the inevitable truth that his mind was too far gone. But Ard had to believe that the right stimulus at the right time could bring the boy around.

The Trothian brigantine was nearly on top of them now, and Raek had detonated a fresh vial of Containment Grit to make sure they would stay protected. For a moment, they were extrasafe, housed inside two spheres of the same exact size. The first one would extinguish at any moment, but it wouldn't be noticeable with the fresh one already in place.

"Are they going to ram us?" Quarrah asked. "Sparks! They're going to ram us!"

The prow of the large ship bumped into their impenetrable sphere, throwing Lyndel and Raek off the crate and sending the bubble skittering across the water like a skipping rock.

Lyndel braced herself against the side of the crate, feet against the Containment wall, yelling furiously. Ard didn't need to speak Trothian to get the gist of it.

Suddenly, a large cargo net was flung overboard and a handful of shirtless Trothians dove from the bulwarks. Ard watched them work, securing the net around their Containment bubble, amazed at how long they could remain beneath the surface of the sea, how fluid their bodies were within the water.

*On the morrow, we shall go up at last,* Ard remembered the words from the testament spire. *After all this time, our bodies are strong enough within the water to make the journey.*

It was no wonder the Trothians were so adept in the sea, or why they needed the *fajumar* saltwater soak. They had descended from beings who swam from the very depths of the ocean.

Soon, the Trothians had drawn their sphere right up to the ship's hull. A pot of Drift Grit was thrown from the deck of the brigantine, and Ard saw the water around him form into weightless airborne orbs. A second pot of Drift Grit formed against the side of the ship, and the netted cargo was drawn upward quickly through the overlapping clouds.

The moment they were onboard, Raek smashed a vial of Null Grit, extinguishing all their detonations and dropping the crate to the deck.

One of the Trothian sailors shouted a shrill command, causing the rest of the crew to duck and brace. Ard was still trying to interpret what it meant, when the starboard rail exploded in a spray of shattered timbers.

The brigantine pitched hard, throwing Ard, Raek, Quarrah, and Lyndel from the top of the Drift crate as it slid across the deck. In a heartbeat, the priestess was on her feet, engaged in half a dozen conversations at once.

Ard wiped a bit of blood from his scuffed elbow and peered off the starboard side of the ship. An Archkingdom vessel had come broadside, three open gun ports facing the Trothian ship.

Lyndel moved to open the Drift crate, but Ard scrambled over to her.

"What are you doing?" he cried.

"We have to alert the Archkingdom ship that we have Shad Agaul onboard," Lyndel said.

"No!" he yelled. "That's an *Archkingdom* ship! Loyal to King Termain. Showing them the prince will only be further incentive to blow us to bits."

"They could spread the word," Lyndel argued. "The Sovereign fleet could rally to us."

"The prince stays hidden, Lyndel!" Ard snapped. This was the very confrontation they would have had if they'd sailed out with the Trothian fleet last evening. Ard had been hoping that a night under water would have helped them avoid this.

The shrill cry came again, and this time Ard knew to brace for impact. He flopped to the deck of the ship, covering his head as Lyndel did the same.

This time, the cannonball went high, clipping a yardarm on the port side.

*"Hadjavas! Hadjavas!"* Lyndel screamed, rising to her knees.

Two of the starboard cannons on the Trothian brigantine responded to her order with a thundering boom, spitting a pair of eighteen-panweight cast-iron balls at the enemy ship.

"Call a retreat," Ard said. "If not for your whole fleet, then at least for this ship."

"My warriors have not died all morning to surrender," Lyndel answered. "If we can make it to the harbor, its defenses will help us hold it for another cycle."

"We can't go back to Pekal!" Ard shouted. He continued with his voice much lower. "We have Shad Agaul. The Realm will be coming for him, and they don't play by the rules. We have to get the boy back to Beripent and put him on the throne in time to help us stop the Cataclysm."

Lyndel took a deep breath, standing just inches away from him, her blurred eyes locked with his.

"Call the retreat," Ard insisted. "The Archies will leave us alone if they see us sailing east."

"Ardor Benn," she breathed. "You have made an enemy of me this day." Lyndel turned away from him sharply, her braided hair flying out behind her as she began barking commands to the crew. Almost immediately, the brigantine began turning hard to port in what Ard assumed was an about-face.

"That was the right call," Raek reassured him, coming up behind Ard. "Going back to Pekal would do us no good. Assuming we even survived long enough to reach the harbor."

"How are we supposed to make berth in Beripent?" Quarrah followed up. "We're in a Trothian ship with Sovereign flags."

"We'll have to commandeer another vessel once we get away from the fighting," Ard said.

Quarrah raised her eyebrows. "We're pirates now?"

"Nothing so sinister," he replied. "We'll just sidle up to the first fishing vessel flying Archkingdom colors that we see. A little smooth talking—"

"And the promise of Ashings," Raek added.

"—and we'll have safe passage into any one of Beripent's harbors."

"What about Lyndel?" Quarrah asked.

"Something tells me she won't be joining us," answered Ard.

"She's dead set on reclaiming Pekal's harbor. I have a feeling she'll be taking this ship back to the fight the moment we step off."

"And the prince?"

"He comes with us, obviously. We keep him hidden in a cloud of Memory Grit until we reach the Guesthouse Adagio."

The cry sounded across the deck once more, causing Ard, Quarrah, and Raek to drop and take shelter. The cannonball struck high on the stern, timbers cracking and Trothians shouting.

Raek pushed himself up. "Sounds like they could use some help rolling out the stern chasers. Send those blazing Archies to the Homeland."

Ard realized that that statement might never have been truer.

*We shall send their bodies to the depths that once held us.* He thought of the testament spire again. *When the unchanged settle to such terrible depths, they will be greeted by our words.*

Quarrah Khai was beyond grateful to find her feet on the familiar streets of Beripent once again. It was approaching midnight, and the lights of the Guesthouse Adagio were finally coming into view. They had walked most of the way from the harbor, awkwardly toting their handleless Drift crate covered with a large canvas Quarrah had nicked along the way. She had felt as though everyone they'd passed was looking right through their portable box to the young prince hidden inside.

More than twenty-four hours had passed since the Red Moon had risen, and Ardor Benn was still jabbering away, so Quarrah finally felt confident that they weren't going to catch Moonsickness.

Submerging themselves under water had done more than shield them from the toxic rays. It had taken them to the bottom of the InterIsland Waters, shown them the remnants of an ancient kingdom, and taught them the truth of the Trothian origins and the place from whence all Landers had come.

In essence, Quarrah Khai had been to the Homeland.

She led the way up the graveled road toward the guesthouse, Ard and Raek lugging the Drift crate a few steps behind. Just as Ard had predicted, Lyndel had sailed back to Pekal on the Trothian brigantine the moment the three of them had moved the hidden prince's Drift crate onto the Archkingdom fishing vessel they'd commandeered.

Lyndel had been livid with Ardor Benn. Quarrah completely understood, as she'd been there many times herself. Shad Agaul could have been the bargaining chip needed to save the rogue Trothian fleet. But Ard always thought his own ideas were the most important, even if it meant leaving thousands of sailors in a futile struggle.

Ard and Raek lowered the crate to the lawn and unlatched it, the Drift and Memory clouds losing containment as they spilled out of the wooden box. Ard reached inside, extracting a timid, confused Shad Agaul. The ruse artist put an arm around the smelly boy and used his other hand to cover his eyes as though leading him to a birthday surprise.

In a way, Quarrah supposed it was, since this was happening just the day before he turned fourteen.

Raek pounded on the guesthouse door as the four of them huddled on the porch under the stone dragon head. Quarrah kept glancing back over the dark grounds, sure someone would spot them and recognize the boy. But that was highly unlikely. With his hair so unkempt and his face so dirty, she wondered if even his mother would recognize him.

At last, the door swung open to reveal Codley Hattingson. The butler's expression quickly turned from annoyed to surprised to overjoyed. He beckoned them in out of the darkness.

"Is it true? Is it him?" In the dim foyer, Codley reached past Ard and touched the prince's face. "Why are you holding him that way?"

"He's not quite himself yet," Ard said, keeping his hand over

Shad's eyes. "This setting could be familiar to him, and we don't want to dilute the effect that seeing his mother could have."

"What on earth are you talking about?" asked Codley.

"Just get us to Lady Abeth," demanded Ard.

"Her Majesty is dozing in the grand salon," Codley reported. "I was waiting for the stroke of midnight to see her to her cottage. Right this way."

They followed him into the large room, where Bannit Lagaday was clearing away some used dishes. The cook also looked startled to see them, but his expression gave way to a grin when he realized who they were.

"I knew they'd be back," he whispered. "Didn't I say it?"

"I certainly hope you weren't casting bets *against* us," said Raek as the butler moved around to where Abeth was sleeping on the couch.

"I'll fetch the professor," Bannit said. "He wanted us to tell him if...*when* you made it back. I think he will..." His sentence trailed off as he deposited the dishes back on the table and scurried toward the exit.

The clink of the dishes caused Lady Abeth to stir, and Ard quickly moved her son into position before her eyes opened. Ard pulled his hand away from the boy's face, and Shad stared at his mother flatly, it seemed without a drib of recognition.

Lady Abeth Agaul sat up sharply, blinking against the sleep that had taken her. Tears seemed to come before she was even completely awake. Her mouth opened, but only a rasp of shock and disbelief escaped. Then she sprang forward, her arms wrapping around the thin boy as she pulled him into a weeping embrace.

Quarrah turned away, feeling awkward about witnessing such raw emotion. For a fraction of a second, she thought of her own mother, possibly still alive if the drink and Heg hadn't taken her by now. Quarrah was envious of the reunion, knowing that no one would likely ever show such a pure reaction to her presence. It was powerful, and if she hadn't spent a lifetime distracting herself from such thoughts, her own emotions might have risen to the surface like their bubble of Containment Grit on the waves.

"We believe your son has been held in a series of Prolonged Memory Grit clouds over the last two years," Ard's voice softly narrated beside Abeth's unyielding embrace. "He has forgotten much of who he is and the world around him. We believe if anyone can get through to him, it will be his mother."

"Thank you," Abeth sobbed, lifting her head from her son's rancid neck. "Homeland keep you, Ardour Stringer."

That kind of tainted the moment for Quarrah. All this time, and the former queen still didn't know who she was thanking. It didn't seem to bother Ard, however, and he stepped away from the couch.

"We'll leave the two of you alone for a moment," he said, leading Quarrah and the others across the grand salon to the dining table at the far end.

Quarrah thought of the Agaul family ring, tucked behind a brick on the back of the carriage house. She glanced back at the ailing boy, her options nagging at her. She could put the jewel on Shad's finger, where it belonged. Or she could sell it for thousands of Ashings.

The back door opened, pulling Quarrah's attention to Bannit Lagaday, who entered with Portsend Wal. Granted, it was the middle of the night, but the professor looked exhausted. He was holding a large basket filled with an assortment of mesh-covered jars.

Portsend nodded to Raek. "You were successful in your expedition to Pekal, I presume?"

In response, Raek merely pointed to the couch across the room. The prince was now seated beside his mother, one of her hands holding his and the other resting gently on his back. She was speaking into his ear, but her words were so soft that Quarrah couldn't make them out.

"Is that...?" Portsend stammered.

"Shad Agaul," answered Ard. "Rightful heir to the throne and legal to rule in almost exactly twenty-four hours."

"The Realm had plans to use him," said Raek, "but we got to him first."

The professor stared unabashedly for a moment before seeming to remember his sense of propriety. Then, shaking away the surprising sight, he turned to Quarrah. "You can thank Mister Hattingson for the collection." He set down the basket.

"I did my best to compile an assortment of worms for your examination," said the butler. "Today's efforts were perhaps more appropriate than my first attempt." He began taking the jars from the basket and setting them on the table.

"Where did you find these?" Quarrah peered at the black worms wriggling among their little vegetative habitats.

"After some encouragement"—he glanced at Portsend—"I reached out to a rather unsavory dealer of illegal artifacts from Pekal. He connected me with someone even seedier, from whom I purchased these eight options. All of them parasitic, matching the description you gave me."

"It was this one." Quarrah picked up the jar to examine it from all angles. The sight of it made her shudder, thinking that its eggs could be swimming inside her.

"You're sure?" Ard nosed in. "They all look basically the same to me."

"I'm sure." She took a small step away from him. Locks probably all looked the same to him as well, but Quarrah had spent her entire life trying to identify minute differences in things that other people glossed over.

"What number is it?" Codley asked, producing a small notepad from the basket.

Quarrah spun the jar, finding the number painted near the rim. "Four."

Codley studied his notebook. "That is the Black Ripeworm.

Native to Pekal. Its eggs can live inside a host for up to two cycles before hatching."

"Well, that's not what we want," Ard said. "How do we kill them?"

"I'm far from an expert on the matter," said Codley, "but I believe this particular variety cannot be exterminated early within a host."

"What?" Ard shouted.

Codley held up a gloved hand. "Supposedly, chemicals released from steeping wideblade wetgrass in boiling water create an effective suppressant."

"Supposedly?" muttered Ard, but Quarrah was beyond grateful for any kind of antidote.

"If you drink the tea regularly over the next three cycles, it will keep the eggs from hatching and they will die naturally."

"The man works quickly," Portsend vouched. "A day ago, I'm not sure he knew the difference between a parasite and a caterpillar."

"He took a class from the professor?" Raek asked.

"I'm no entomologist, either," replied Portsend. "But I was keeping the worms in my cottage after we discovered that some of the ones Hattingson collected were valuable to my experiments."

"How so?" asked Raek.

"I finally achieved results with that new Grit type I'd been struggling with."

"More Grit?" Ard said. "This new one doesn't happen to restore lost memories, does it?" He glanced at the prince.

"I'm afraid not," replied Portsend. "I'm calling it Metamorphosis Grit."

"Ooh," Ard cooed sarcastically. "Let me guess... It makes butterflies?"

"Well, yes, actually," said Portsend. "It immediately transforms any life-form that undergoes metamorphosis into its mature state."

"That's it?" Ard asked. Quarrah, too, was a little disappointed, but she knew how to hide it better. An aggressive new type of Grit could have given them the element of surprise, since the Realm already had the first six of the professor's developments.

"Caterpillars to butterflies, spanworms to moths, tadpoles to frogs," listed Portsend proudly. "It has also metamorphosed a handful of newts, and I'm currently gathering other specimens."

"I'll definitely be taking some of that to my next gunfight," Ard remarked.

"What is the formula?" Raek asked.

"It was the one I mentioned after you rescued me," answered Portsend. "A liquid with a balance level of negative flat five. I discovered it weeks ago."

"What's the source material for the Grit?"

"Unique, to be sure," answered Portsend. "It is derived from the teeth of a dragon."

"Dragon teeth?" Raek repeated, a distant look in his eye.

Portsend nodded. "It's treated much the same as any other source material. The teeth are incorporated into the bait and passed through the dragon, later to be extracted from the Slagstone and isolated as it gets processed into powder. Technically, it fits into the category of bone-derived Grit, but—"

Portsend was cut off as the door flew open and the groundskeeper, Hedma Sallis, came stumbling in. Her breath came in gasps, and her short hair was sweaty against her face.

"Sparks, Hedma!" Ard cried, holstering the Roller he'd just instinctively drawn. "You can't barge in on us like that!"

"We need to move!" the woman spoke, her voice tense.

"What's going on?" Lady Abeth looked up from where she'd been holding her son on the couch.

"There's an army of goons at the Creekstone Watermill," she said. "At least a hundred-strong. Heavily armed."

"Calm down," Ard said, trying to sooth her. "Creekstone Watermill is nearly a mile from here, and we're off the beaten path. There's no reason for them to pass by."

"They're coming *here!*" Hedma shouted.

"How do you know?" Raek asked.

"I was working with Keyling on one of our nighttime rides," she answered. "She froze up at the sound of a crowd crossing the bridge by the watermill. I got closer on foot. They mentioned the guesthouse!"

"Flames," Ard cursed.

"The Realm?" Quarrah ventured.

"Has to be," muttered Ard. "How did they find us? After all this time..." He whirled on Portsend. "Have you told anyone you were staying here?"

"Homeland, no!" he answered. "I've had no communication with anyone but you lot since I arrived."

"How much time do we have?" asked Raek.

"At the rate they were moving, I'd say thirty minutes at most."

"We have to leave," Quarrah said.

Ard nodded. "Hedma. Ready the carriages and every horse we've got."

"I'll pack my things." Portsend promptly exited through the back door toward the cottages.

Suddenly Shad Agaul let out a laugh. It wasn't boisterous or obnoxious, but rather innocent and sincere. "Is it ready yet, Mum?" he asked.

Quarrah followed Ard around the end of the couch so they could see his face. In what seemed like the first genuine display of emotion, the prince was grinning.

Lady Abeth touched his knee. "Is *what* ready, Shaddy?"

"The midwinter cake," he said. "I know you said it wouldn't be done until Father got here, but Loora said it was out of the oven an hour ago."

Lady Abeth glanced up at the faces of her observers, looking unsure about how to respond. Ard nodded encouragingly, his eyebrows raised as though telling her to play along.

Abeth turned back to her son's eager face. "Loora lets you snitch too often. Just think about how much better it will taste if you wait." She didn't sound very genuine speaking those words.

"It's just not as fun to wait without Scratcher." The boy leaned forward, elbows on his knees with his face cradled in his hands.

Lady Abeth stood abruptly, stepping away from the boy and lowering her voice to the others.

"He seems to think it is midwinter, the cycle after his dog died."

"How long ago was that?" Quarrah asked.

"Three and a half years back. We left the city and came to stay at the guesthouse for a week. It was a wonderful time."

"Your Majesty," Hedma said to Abeth. "We have to go."

"Wait," Ard said. "Ask him something else. Something he should obviously know the answer to."

"Shaddy," she said. "Can you tell me Father's name?"

"Name?" he asked. "Why do we name it? Does it rain here?"

"He's still unstable," Raek said. "But you're making progress."

"I insist that we leave at once!" Hedma cried.

"I have to agree," added Codley. "We can resume this conversation in a safer locale."

"Codley!" Shad cried, turning to the butler. "How long have you been in here?" He chuckled nervously. "You didn't see that, did you?"

Ard put a hand on the butler's back. His mustache twitched in irritation as he replied to the prince. "See what, Your Majesty?"

"Now you're just trying to trick me into telling you," Shad replied. "If you didn't see it, then it didn't happen."

Codley cleared his throat. "Would you be referring to a certain punctured portrait?" He pointed to the wall of paintings.

"Sparks," the boy cursed. "I didn't mean to get that close. I was only waving the sword in his direction. You won't tell Father?"

"I shall tell him that the portrait was removed for maintenance," Codley answered. "Which is only the truth."

"I don't have to. I don't have to!" shouted the boy manically. "Not right now!"

"Aaaand he's lost again," Ard said.

"What was he talking about?" asked Quarrah.

"An incident from four summers ago," Codley said. "Lord Remium and Lady Abeth were abroad to Dronodan and I brought the prince to stay out here at the guesthouse. He put a slice in Grandfather Fidor Agaul's painting while fiddling with a dueling blade that was much too heavy for him."

Lady Abeth rose, taking her foggy-minded son by both hands and helping him up.

"We can't leave," Ard suddenly said.

"You're welcome to stay," replied Hedma Sallis, "but the royal family and I are leaving."

"No," Ard pressed. "I thought the boy's mother would restore his memories, but—no offense Your Majesty—it isn't you. It's this *place*. The Guesthouse Adagio is providing the stimulus he needs to find his way home."

"You can't be certain of that," said Hedma. "And we can't risk staying here. There are a hundred armed thugs on their way right now!"

"And there are..."—Ard quickly counted on his fingers—"nine of us. Well, eight, since the prince might not shoot."

"You're suggesting we stay and *fight*?" cried the groundskeeper. Of course he was. Odds meant nothing to Ardor Benn.

"He's had crazier ideas in the last few days," contributed Quarrah.

"I'm saying, if we move the prince now, we could lose him," argued Ard. "None of us really knows how this memory restoration is supposed to work, but we're seeing progress, and it seems to be linked to this very room."

"Father's taking me hunting soon," Shad contributed. "He says there are more grouse than usual in the fields to the west. He said I can even fire the gun, as long as I'm not shooting back toward the guesthouse."

"See? Nine of us," declared Ard. "Turns out the boy knows how to shoot after all!"

~

*Nevertheless, they would not relent.*

## CHAPTER

# 43

From the flat roof of the guesthouse, Ardor Benn watched the lights of the mob drawing closer to the outer gate. Thirty minutes hadn't been much time to form a strategy and get everything in place. Everyone had done their part, but Raek and Portsend had proved themselves indispensable, measuring and mixing Grit as fast as their scales could balance.

Ard sighted down the long barrel of his Fielder. Nothing to do but wait now.

As in most things Ard considered worth doing, their odds weren't great. It was seven against a hundred. They'd decided not to arm Lady Abeth or her son. The two of them remained on the couch in the room below, sharing memories and trying to get the boy to discover the present. It was actually coming along nicely, which made Ard feel justified in their decision to stay and fight. A chorus of gunfire and explosives probably wasn't going to make the right mark on the prince's impressionable mind, so he and his mother were wrapped in a cloud of Silence Grit. If all went well, they'd never even hear the attack, and the prince would be back to himself by sunrise.

Beside him, Quarrah fidgeted, checking her gun's Slagstone hammer for the umpteenth time.

The fact that she'd decided to stay at the guesthouse meant everything to Ard. He never would have found the prince without her, and he believed that the Homeland had Urged them back together.

But which Homeland was it? The underwater pre-Trothian kingdom? Or some esoteric perfected version of the future? Ard didn't know what to think anymore.

"I'm sorry about what happened on Pekal," he said quietly. "You were right. I shouldn't have risked the detour to Crooked Ravine."

He'd told her of his plan for the Cataclysm kegs, and it had gone over better than he'd expected. In fact, to Ard's great surprise, she had agreed to help him carry it out if they survived the night.

"I should have seen it coming," she replied. "I know who you are, and yet I keep letting myself be surprised by the stupid things you do."

"To be fair, I sometimes surprise myself."

He wasn't giving up on her, but Ard had finally conceded that things would never return to what they'd been during the regalia ruse—the thrill and wonder of romantic pursuit. They knew each other too well now. But that didn't have to mean it was hopeless between them. Maybe they could forge something new—more honest and substantial. After all, the main course always came after the appetizer.

Codley strode over, setting two more Fielders between them. "I found these in one of the sheds," said the butler.

"They look...dusty," Ard pointed out. "How likely are they to blow up in our faces?"

"They are fine weapons, loaded and ready to fire," Codley

assured him. "Both of them are Yanok models, with the trademark padded stock. His Majesty only considered two or three gunsmiths to be reputable. Those Fielders will shoot true even after years in the shed."

That upped their guns to seventeen—five Fielders, eight Rollers, and four Singlers. They had two crossbows, six swords, and not nearly as much Grit or ammunition as Ard had hoped for.

"Is everyone ready down below?" Ard asked.

"Master Raekon and Hedma are double-checking the traps," Codley replied. "They should be up shortly."

"We should leave someone else with the Agauls," Quarrah said.

"Bannit and the professor have them covered," answered Ard.

"That's why I'm concerned."

"It should be noted that I don't believe Bannit Lagaday has ever fired a gun," mentioned Codley.

"Well, maybe he'll shoot like he cooks."

"How's that?" Quarrah asked.

"Unyieldingly."

They'd made the decision to hole everyone into the guesthouse instead of spreading across the entire estate. Ard realized that it was probably the least defensible of the many structures, what with three entrances and the entire east side formed of large viewing windows.

A cottage, or certainly one of the sheds, might have been small enough to enclose in a dome of Barrier Grit for the night, but the mob wasn't likely to give up and move away by sunrise. Outlasting the enemy was not an option here. They had to eliminate them.

Besides, Shad Agaul was responding to the grand salon, and Ard didn't want to risk their progress by moving him out to one of the cottages where he likely hadn't spent much time.

Codley took a knee beside Ard. "Whatever happens here tonight, I want you to know that I am eternally grateful to you for what you have accomplished. I truly never thought I would see that boy again, but I now have hope that the family I have dedicated my life to serving can continue on long after I'm gone. I'll admit, I had my reservations about you when we first met, but you have never ceased to amaze me, Inspector."

Ard took a deep breath. "You're a good man, Codley Hattingson." Quarrah scoffed at his side, and Ard knew what he had to do. Not just to impress her but because the butler deserved the truth. "There's something I want to tell you."

"Let me guess," replied Codley. "You are not actually Inspector Ardour Stringer, nor were you *ever* Inspector Ardour Stringer."

"Flames," Ard muttered. "How long have you known?"

"Since the day after you showed up at the guesthouse," he said. "I paid a visit to the *actual* inspector's office. The man bore little resemblance to you."

"I mean...I'd say *no* resemblance, really," Ard said. "Did you tell him about me?"

"I did not," answered Codley. "You seemed so genuine in your efforts to find the prince that I decided to wait and see how things played out. Homeland forgive me for saying this, but I believe you may have been the better choice for getting the job done."

"That means a lot coming from you," Ard said. "But don't be fooled into thinking all ruse artists are like me."

"I stole the Agaul family ring," Quarrah suddenly blurted.

"Pardon?" Codley leaned around Ard to look at her.

"Stole it right off Lady Abeth's finger at the docks," she continued.

"And you're telling me this, why?" asked the butler.

"I just thought... While we're in the spirit of full disclosure." She reached into her pocket and produced the large emerald ring. "I'm not a common thief, you know."

Now it was Ard's turn to scoff. Of course Quarrah had the ring. Too big and shiny for her not to.

"Well..." Codley's mustache twitched in displeasure. "You two make quite the pair."

"That's what I've been trying to say!" Ard cried.

Quarrah held out the gaudy ring to the butler. "Take it."

"In this life, there are few feelings greater than making recompense for one's mistakes," Codley said. "I would be cruel to deprive you of the chance to do so."

"You're trusting me to give it to the prince myself?" Quarrah asked. "I'm not sure my offer will stand..."

"I wouldn't expect it to," Codley said, "if you were a common thief."

A rustling behind them caught their attention as Hedma Sallis and Raek climbed through the hole in the rooftop. The opening had been cut just fifteen minutes ago, with Codley wincing at every stroke of the saw. Lady Abeth had given them permission to do whatever they needed to do, which was good since Ard was going to do it anyway. With any luck, the salon below would remain intact. Ard could not promise the same for any of the other structures on the property.

"You ready for this?" Ard asked his partner.

"Do you remember that shortcut we used to take on our delivery route after school?"

"That alley full of stray dogs?"

"The other one." Raek rolled out a sash of ammunition for his crossbow, the bolts tipped with clay Grit pots and little glass vials lashed in place with waxy twine. "Where we had to cut through that old lady's house."

"Oh, right. Grandma Three-Teeth. Her house always smelled like pickles."

"And *traps*," Raek said.

"I told you not to go that day," Ard reminisced. "I knew she was catching on to us."

"Well, that's about how I'm feeling right now." Raek sighted down his crossbow. "Except I'm the grandma."

There was a soundless explosion at the estate gate as the first goons blew apart the heavy lock under a cloud of Silence Grit. The enemies began pouring through the opening in the stone wall, polished steel from their guns and blades winking in the glow of the few Light Grit lanterns among them. As they moved stealthily up the road, Ard could see that they were a ragtag group of hardened men and women.

Hands of the Realm. Maybe even Faceless among them.

This was it. The anticipation was palpable on the rooftop, carried on the salty breeze rolling off the nearby sea. The only sound was Ard's own heavy breathing, and the steady crash of the waves against the base of the cliff far below.

"Now?" Codley whispered.

"Not yet." Ard glanced at Raek and Hedma to make sure they were ready. Both were sighting down their crossbows, steady and waiting.

More than half of the mob was through the gate now, the leaders almost to the fork in the gravel road. The left would lead them to the carriage house, and the right to the guesthouse.

"Let 'em have it," Ard gave the command.

The crossbows sounded in unison, their bolts tipped with vials of Ignition Grit. Raek's hit the stone wall next to the entrance, where he had previously poured piles of Blast Grit. The wall exploded in a crushing maelstrom of rock and debris.

At the same time, Hedma's bolt struck a pile of Compounded Void Grit poured onto the road. Scraps of rusty metal and old nails from the sheds had been heaped over the pile and the Grit sent them flying in a deadly spray of shrapnel, instantly dropping the leading Hands. Their screams reached Ard on the rooftop and he shuddered against what they had just started.

The bulk of the group suddenly found themselves caught between the explosion at the wall and the scrap-studded Void Grit mine.

In their moment of panic and confusion, Quarrah gave a sharp tug on the end of a string that drooped clear across the property like a clothesline, connecting to the top of the carriage house doors. Pulling it sparked a Slagstone ignitor, detonating their final pot of Void Grit. The forceful cloud threw open the carriage house doors, which ripped the stops out from under the two cabs inside. Pitched at a steep angle across a crude ramp of scrap wood, the carriages rolled forward, picking up speed as they came down the sloped road toward the mob waiting at the fork.

Driverless and horseless, the carriages careened. One went off course, bumping over the edge of the road and toppling to its side. The other stayed true, its wheels locked straight. Instinctively, the gang opened fire on the approaching cab, scattering to avoid being run down.

When the carriage was in the midst of the group, Raek shot another bolt of Ignition Grit. The cab exploded in a fiery burst of Blast Grit, flaming pieces of wreckage falling like deadly hail.

"Fire away!" Ard called to his companions on the rooftop. He sighted down his Fielder and squeezed the trigger, catching one of the men in the back. Hedma shot at the same time, the two of them reloading while Quarrah and Codley fired the next volley.

Ard was trying hard to keep himself disconnected from the violence below, and he hoped the others could, too. None of the rooftop defenders were trained soldiers or ruthless killers, but the Realm had sent a private war to their very doorstep. This wasn't just a ruse anymore. It was a matter of base survival. To kill, or be killed.

"They're looking for us," Raek called. "Cease fire. It's time to draw them up to the cottages."

He released another crossbow bolt, this time aiming at the tall picket fence that spanned between the guesthouse and the sta-bles. The bolt detonated, throwing up a cloud of Illusion Grit that encompassed the fence's main gate.

This was the second detonation of Illusion Grit to occupy that spot, and it immediately began displaying an image of what had happened in the first cloud, detonated just fifteen minutes ago.

Below, Ard saw Raek's image rise from a shrub, a Light Grit lantern in one hand and a Roller in the other. He dashed through the open gate and dove behind a hedge on the other side of the fence. A moment later, the image of Quarrah sprang up from behind a rock, sprinting through the gate and ducking behind the same hedge.

The enemies flooded upward, the sight of the figures drawing the majority of them toward the fence instead of taking the fork in the road over to the guesthouse entrance.

Below, Ard's image made a break for it, and a chorus of gunshots spit lead in his direction. He'd added a bit of personal flare, making a crude gesture before taking shelter behind the hedge. Codley's image was the last one they had recorded, and it drew even more fire and attention as he made the sprint.

In a moment, there were a fair number of goons at the fence, pausing just outside the gate to take blind shots into the hedge. Merciless, without any idea that they were standing in a cloud of Illusion Grit, chasing ghosts.

On the rooftop, Raek sighted down his crossbow and squeezed the trigger. The vial on the bolt was Gather Grit, and it shattered on the rock that Quarrah's image had been hiding behind.

Immediately, the nearest woman was pulled down, slamming her head on the rock and dropping her gun. Six other figures were caught in the detonation, sucking them inward until they were a wriggling mass.

Five bales' worth of straw had been spread at the gateway, and in a heartbeat, it was also gathered inward until the squirming figures looked like a prickly ball.

Flickering fire on the rooftop caught the corner of Ard's eye. He turned to see Hedma aiming her crossbow at the struggling group in the Gather cloud. The tip of the bolt was alight, wrapped in a tar-soaked rag that fed the flames as she took the shot.

The straw, which had been drenched in oil, caught fire at once, the seven doomed Hands going up in a bright blaze of screams.

Ard had no experience with Gather Grit, and its application here quite horrified him. It was working exactly as the professor had said it would, but seeing those people writhe and scream, unable to extricate themselves as smoke rose from their burning flesh...Well, there was a reason Ardor Benn had never wanted to be a soldier.

Goons were jumping the fence now, their rough voices shouting that the hedge was empty. Ard and the others crouched low on the flat roof, watching a group of them sprint to the nearest cottage. They moved up the steps, kicking open the door and tripping a line that instantly detonated a chain of Blast Grit kegs.

The entire cottage exploded with a thunder that shook the whole property. In the ensuing rain of brick and splintered lumber, Ard saw Codley grimace.

"The royal Cannilsons once slept in that cottage." The butler's voice was a requiem.

"So did I," Ard answered.

"I thought you were in Cottage Seven," Raek said.

"I tried out all the beds during the first week."

Every one of the cottages was rigged to explode. As sad as it was to lose such fine accommodations, Ard hoped the thugs set off a few more before they decided to focus everything on the main guesthouse.

The grounds were a mess now, with multiple fires raging. Hedma had wet the walls of the guesthouse, and doused the immediate surroundings with an anti-ignition solution that would hopefully keep the fires from reaching the Agauls inside.

It was difficult to get an accurate head count as the figures ran in all directions below. Ard guessed that at least half of them were dead or burning from the various explosions. But they still had a long way to go before the night was won.

"They're at the front door!" Hedma called, moving across the rooftop.

Ard wiped a bead of sweat from his forehead, leaning out to see a cluster of goons gathered on the steps. Three men and one woman, each wearing an enraged expression that seemed to bespeak a lust for blood in vengeance for their slain comrades. Finding the guest-house's front door barred and nailed shut, the group was placing kegs of Blast Grit and spooling off a length of fuse.

"Drop the dragon!" Ard called.

The groundskeeper picked up a vial of blue liquid and tossed it down to the large statue of the dragon head that protruded from the front of the guesthouse. The glass vial smashed between the dragon's horns, the Slagstone sparking and igniting the solution. A Compounded cloud of Weight Grit formed, increasing the statue's weight by more than four times. It cracked free of its foundation and plummeted, smashing the four thugs below and breaking into a pile of rubble that further blocked the door.

"We've got company at the kitchen entrance, as well," Codley called, peering over the back edge.

"Time to put Bannit's cooking to the test." Ard crossed to a bar-rel of frying oil perched near the roof's edge. The cloud of Com-pounded Heat Grit had extinguished several minutes ago, but even the wood of the barrel was still almost too hot to touch.

He and Codley put their shoulders to the top of the barrel and tipped it over, the scalding oil pouring out onto the enemy batter-ing the kitchen door below. The barrel slipped, spinning sideways and rolling off the edge. It splintered into kindling as it struck the ground in the midst of the screaming enemies.

"They have a cannon!" Quarrah suddenly cried.

"What?" Ard raced back to the corner, peering down to where a wheeled cannon was being staked into the grass. "Where'd they come from?"

"Just got through the gate," she answered. "Must have kept the heavy artillery behind the main group. They floated that cannon right over the rubble in a cloud of Drift Grit."

"They're going to blow a hole right through the south wall," Raek said, commenting on the cannon's positioning.

The cannoneers were loading it now, packing a parcel of Blast Grit and rolling the heavy ball into place. The five of them did not operate with the same reckless frenzy as the rest of the invading brutes. They communicated through the loading process with hand signals and obvious discipline. The only thing missing were the uniforms.

"Those are Archkingdom cannoneers," Ard hissed, turning to Raek. "Remember the Spesmain ruse?" It was one of the first jobs they'd run as Androt Penn and the Lit Fuse after the war had started. They'd run afoul with some Archkingdom cannoneers, and it had cost their entire payout just to repair the *Double Take*.

"What does that mean?" Quarrah cried.

"It means they can reload and fire a round in under four minutes," Ard replied. If they were lucky, these particular cannoneers might be deserters. It wouldn't make them any less skillful, but maybe they wouldn't be as well equipped.

"It means we've got to take these suckers out." Raek wound his crossbow and dropped a Grit bolt into place.

A Roller ball suddenly whizzed past Ard's head, causing him to stumble backward and sprawl on the roof.

"It would seem the others have spotted us as well," Codley stated. Raek tried to ease upward to take the shot, but another Roller ball cracked into the edge of the roof, forcing him back.

There was a resounding *boom*, and Ard felt the guesthouse quake as though its very foundation had been shaken.

"Direct hit from the cannon!" cried Hedma. "South wall. Just beside the front door."

Raek popped over the edge and took the shot, Ard peering down to see the result. The cannon and all five of its operators were trapped under Raek's dome of Barrier Grit.

"That'll hold them off," Raek reported.

"Or not," Quarrah said.

Ard peered back over the edge to see that the Barrier dome was completely gone, the skilled cannoneers reloading.

"Null Grit," said Quarrah. "They came prepared."

So much for hoping they were underequipped. Ard realized that it didn't matter whether the cannoneers were deserters or not. They worked for the Realm, and Overseer was sparing nothing in tying up any potential loose ends.

On the east side of the guesthouse there was a sound so sharp and distinctive that it caused every muscle in Ard's body to tense. The glass wall had shattered. Cursing, he scampered across the roof and peered down.

Below, there was no more than ten feet of easement before the abrupt edge of the cliff, dropping away to the sea below. Half a dozen ruffians were climbing over the threshold of broken glass, finally discovering the people they'd surely been hired to kill.

"Bannit!" Ard screamed. Why hadn't he pulled the stake yet?

Two gunshots sounded from the room below, followed by a loud twang as Bannit presumably pulled the stake out of the wooden floor. The stretched cord released like the string of a giant crossbow, catching all six men in the middle and flinging them out through the shattered glass panels. They tumbled over the easement and fell screaming to the dark sea below.

At once, Ard saw the glass replaced by the domed surface of a large Barrier cloud. Portsend would have mixed that with Prolonging Grit, which would hopefully buy them twenty minutes before the shell grew soft enough to shoot a ball through. The professor had one more detonation to replace it after that, and two more small pots to cover the royal mother and son. Then they'd have to break into the Realm's Cataclysm kegs if they needed more Barrier Grit. That would be a fine alternative to dying, but Ard hoped they wouldn't disturb that stash he had squirreled away in the adjoining royal boudoir.

The guesthouse shook again, as if thunder itself had pounded the south wall with a mighty fist.

"The wall is breached!" Hedma shouted. "They're clearing the rubble with Drift Grit!"

The cry sent everyone scrambling for the manhole in the roof. Ard was the first to drop into the room below. He glimpsed Abeth and Shad sitting calmly on the couch, speaking words that could not escape the cloud of Silence Grit around them. She looked visibly frightened, but the boy laughed as she brushed back his filthy long hair. They were a strange sight, like a pair of delicate flowers in a hailstorm.

"Ardor!" Portsend croaked. He spotted the professor kneeling on the floor beside the spot where the clothesline stake had been nailed down. Bannit Lagaday was lying prone in front of him, a pool of red surrounding the awkward little cook. His jet-black hair was the starkest contrast to his ashen, expressionless face.

"He's dead," Portsend whispered. "The stake was too…He tried to pull it…"

Ard wanted time to grieve, but he could hear the debris being cleared down the hallway in the foyer. Raek and Hedma moved past him, Quarrah on their heels. Codley Hattingson froze at the bottom of the ladder, his eyes on the dead cook.

Gunfire sounded from the foyer and Codley looked up, his face suddenly twisted in a mix of rage and determination. He drew his dueling sword from its scabbard and ran for the breach, Ard joining him as they rounded the corner.

The hole in the wall was slightly larger than a doorway. Two thugs had already been dispatched in the foyer, their bodies lying still amidst the dust and rubble.

Raek and Hedma were firing steady shots through the breach, forcing the enemy back.

"Cannonball!" Quarrah leapt against the foyer's back wall and covered her head. Ard and the others did the same, Raek barely retreating before the wall exploded again. A piece of rock struck Ard in the back and he grunted in pain, falling to his chest and gasping for breath through the chalky dust.

"We have to take out that cannon!" Hedma shouted, quickly resuming her station beside Raek, firing against the next wave of goons that rushed toward the widening gap in the wall.

Codley suddenly cried out, falling onto his side. One of the men whom they'd presumed dead had reached through the rubble and seized the butler's ankle. Codley whirled, raising his sword to strike, but Ard grabbed his arm.

"Wait!" He crawled over to the injured man, taking him by the lapels of his coat and pulling him into a sitting position against the foyer's back wall.

"Who hired you?" Ard demanded.

The man's breathing was ragged. There was no telling how long he could hold on. He responded with a defiant sneer. This fellow knew he was a dead man. Ard needed to convince him to speak from his death bed.

"I fear I'm going gray," Ard said, earning him a puzzled glare. "Yes, I'm part of the Realm. They sent me ahead to scout out the guesthouse. I got inside."

"Some would call it a mark of wisdom," the man rasped. Ard didn't know if he'd gained his trust, but in his weakened state, the fellow seemed confused enough to speak now.

"What was the job?" Ard asked.

"Kill everyone." He coughed, blood spilling onto his stubbled chin. "Kill the queen. The Dronodanian Agaul."

Sparks, they knew about Lady Abeth? How?

"Who hired you?" Ard asked again. This was the Realm, so he knew he wouldn't get a straight answer. There would always be an unknown boss.

"Galgall," he muttered. The name meant nothing to Ard. "Galgall Staves. Got the funds to hire a team."

Codley Hattingson had gone ash white—pale beyond the layer of dust on his face. "Galgall Staves," he whispered.

"You know him?" Ard asked.

"Flames, Ardor, this is all my fault."

"What are you talking about?"

"The man I met with, the one who sold me that Black Ripeworm…"

"Galgall Staves," Ard finished. "He must be Overseer's supplier, too. He got suspicious of your interest in the worms and followed you back to the guesthouse."

"Saw the queen," Codley continued, "and returned with an army to make sure her assassination was done properly this time."

From the crumbled opening in the south wall, Raek shouted. "We've taken out two of the cannoneers, but they're still reloading! We need Barrier Grit if we want to survive another hit!"

Ard sighed. *Guess it's time to break into my precious Cataclysm kegs.* He grabbed the dying Hand by the front of his jacket and dragged him down the short hallway and around the corner into the grand salon. Portsend Wal was still kneeling over Bannit's body, but he looked up when Ard dropped the man to the floor.

"Get this guy to tell us everything he knows," Ard said. "Use Health Grit to keep him conscious if you have to."

"I'm sorry, Ardor, but you're suggesting torture?" The professor rose slowly to his feet.

"We need to find out if everyone knows that Shad Agaul is still alive," Ard said. "He knew about Lady Abeth. We've got to press him to see what else he's got."

From the foyer, Ard suddenly heard his companions shouting. Leaving the dying Hand on the floor, he raced back down the hallway to see what new development had caused such a cry of alarm.

Quarrah, Raek, and Hedma still fired through the broken wall. But…

"Where's Codley?" Ard asked.

Quarrah pointed outside into the burning night, her grim face smudged with dirt and sweat. Ard felt his stomach drop as he peered through the gap. Codley was out there, sprinting toward the cannon through a storm of flying Roller balls, thin sword glinting in the firelight.

*He's going for the cannon,* Ard realized. He could almost hear the butler's voice. *In this life, there are few feelings greater than making recompense for one's mistakes.*

After so many successful cycles hiding in the Guesthouse Adagio, Codley Hattingson had accidentally led an army of goons right to their doorstep. Sparks, it was probably the first real mistake the man had ever made in his life. And now he was paying for it.

The butler made it almost twenty yards before the first ball struck him. Ard couldn't tell where it hit, but he saw Codley twitch and fall. Then he was up again, sword slashing through two nearby enemies as he lurched another few yards toward the cannon.

Ard leveled his Roller and joined the others, alternating shots in an attempt to provide the butler some cover. Codley's sword parried a blow, and he thrust, skewering an opponent. A Singler appeared in his other hand and he spent the shot on one of the three remaining cannoneers.

With the large weapon almost loaded, the surviving pair of cannoneers turned on him. Before they could reach him, Codley pitched something through the darkness. Drift Grit detonated around the artillery, sending the two cannoneers floating unsteadily.

The injured butler pushed forward, skirting the Drift cloud and reaching the ammunition chest. Ard saw him gather four parcels of Blast Grit before rolling into the Drift cloud. Pulling out the rammer, which had been left halfway in the barrel, Codley shoved all the Grit into the cannon.

Planting his feet against the ground, he heaved the weightless gun upward. It tipped forward easily, and Codley guided it down, mouth of the big barrel pressed into the grass.

Whether he sparked the Blast parcels or used a vial of Ignition Grit, Ard couldn't tell. The cannon fired straight down into the ground. With the added parcels in the weightless cloud, the recoil on the big gun was unlike anything Ard had ever witnessed.

The cannon kicked forcefully into the air, all smoke and hot metal. It struck Codley, throwing him sideways as it exited the top of the Drift cloud at an angle, the artillery careening eastward across the grounds. The cannon landed in the grass, plowing an impressive groove all the way to the edge of the cliff before tumbling out of sight to the sea below.

In the chaos of it all, it took Ard a moment to see that Codley's body had been hurtled all the way to the gravel road. Lying still, his tall figure broken and spent, the encroaching flames enveloped him in death's embrace, and he disappeared in the glow.

With such a dramatic end to the cannon, any real hope the Hands had of getting through the guesthouse wall seemed to fade. They could keep rushing the breach, but by doing so, they made themselves easy targets for Ard and his team sheltered in the foyer.

Ard watched their numbers dwindle as the enemies began to retreat, trickling steadily away from the guesthouse property. The last ones in sight were quickly shot down, and the night finally seemed to rest. A breeze rustled across the grounds like a weary sigh following a long quarrel. Fires raged, and the darkness was punctuated by the moans and cries of those who were still resisting death.

But the guesthouse was intact.

The four of them stood in the foyer without speaking a word, the weight of Codley's sacrifice hanging over them like a cloud of Silence Grit.

"We should wet the walls again," Hedma Sallis finally said. "I'll make a sweep of the grounds to round up any survivors."

Ard took a deep breath and turned to Raek and Quarrah. "And we need to prep those Cataclysm kegs and make our final preparations. Only a few hours to go until our carriages will be in position to pick us up. We've got a Faceless meeting to steal."

The stillness was suddenly broken by the sound of a lone gunshot from around the corner. It sounded reprehensible and out of place, like a single clap falling much too late after an applause had quieted.

Ard sprinted down the hallway into the grand salon. Aside from the shattered glass wall, most of the damage had been sustained on the south wall, out of Shad Agaul's sight. Good thing, too, since they'd fought and died to keep this room in shape to restore the boy's memories. Shad and his mother still looked frightfully peaceful on the couch, their backs to the action.

Portsend Wal was standing across the room, a smoking Singler in his hand. When he heard Ard's footsteps, he turned. The thug was seated in a chair against the wall, a fresh ball wound hollowing his skull.

"They don't say much after you shoot them in the head," Ard cried. Sparks! There was a darkness behind the professor's eyes that he wouldn't have suspected.

"They have her," Portsend whispered.

"Who?" Quarrah asked.

Portsend shut his eyes. "Prime Isless Gloristar." He swallowed visibly. "They took her to the farm."

Ard raised a hand to his mouth in shock.

"The moment I disappeared, they took her," he explained. "They were waiting in the Mooring when she got back from the reception."

"Why would they do that?" Ard asked. The Realm had never been interested in eliminating the Prime Isless.

"To lure me out of hiding," Portsend said.

"Is she...?" Ard started.

"She was there for the Moon Passing," Portsend replied. "She's going to die."

"'Taking salvation out of the open mouths of the dragons.'" Raek spoke quietly, his eyes closed in concentration.

Ard turned to his partner. He recognized the phrase from the glass testament spire. They'd heard Lyndel recite it more than a dozen times.

"What are you thinking?" Ard asked.

"'They were struck with a plague of body and mind. Encroaching madness...'" he muttered. "'But they received new sight, and power...from the teeth of the dragons.'" Raek opened his eyes. "Metamorphosis Grit."

"Homeland afar," Ard muttered. "Are you saying...? You think that...?"

"Moonsickness is an immature state," explained Raek. "A precursor to some kind of human metamorphosis."

Ard thought back to that passage that Isless Glemher had read them in the Mooring. He had reread the section dozens of times while preparing the Homelander ruse and rehearsing with Cinza and Elbrig. He even had it somewhat memorized.

"'I saw the inhabitants of the Homeland,'" he did his best to quote. "'I can barely call them humans, although I know that's what they had once been. Now they had ascended into something greater, as a caterpillar emerging from its chrysalis with the wings of a butterfly.'" Flames! The answer had been right there all along!

"You're saying..." Portsend began tentatively. "You're saying that Gloristar could survive this. That she could...*transform*? Into what?"

Ardor Benn looked him in the eyes. "Into a Homelander."

~

*But we did not perish.*

# CHAPTER

# 44

Portsend's horse came out of a gallop. The poor animals were exhausted. The horses they'd picked up in Kennar weren't as strong as the ones they'd taken from the Guesthouse Adagio. But even those had been ridden weary, and they'd left them in the township in a trade for fresh mounts.

The road out here was little more than a trail, with natural ruts formed on either side for the wheels of a wagon. The last thing they needed to do was turn one of the horses' ankles.

Behind him, Raekon slowed to a trot. The man was starting to look ragged again. Portsend hadn't seen him use any Health Grit since the outskirts of Beripent just before dawn.

"The Faceless meeting should be starting about now," Raekon said, glancing up as the sun neared it zenith. Riding due east, it had been blinding them all morning.

"You don't think they'll recognize Ardor and Quarrah?" Portsend asked.

"That's the downfall of the Realm," replied Raekon. "Everyone wears a mask. Too much secrecy can be a bad thing. There's probably a Trothian saying about that. They've got a saying for just about every occasion. It's why they're wiser than us. Maybe if we'd had so many good sayings, *we* would have been the ones to transform into all-powerful Homelanders."

Raekon had explained it all on the ride out of Beripent. The truth about the Trothian origins and the true nature of the Homeland. It was boggling to Portsend's scientific mind, but he found he couldn't doubt their conviction.

Landers and Trothians had once been the same race. A third of them had contracted Moonsickness and used Grit derived from dragon teeth to transform into elevated, perfected beings. This power made them dangerous, and they turned against their gods and the remaining unperfected humans. Fearing for their annihilation, the gods took the humans and raised them up on towers of stone to keep them safe. The rest of the world was filled with water, in the hope of drowning the evolved Trothians.

Eventually, the powerful beings had found their way up to the islands. Hundreds of years had passed for the Landers above, but those below were still the first generation, left to drown and unfavored by the gods.

And who were these gods anyway? Wayfarism bore no mention of any deity other than the Homeland, and Raekon didn't have any answers about them. Portsend wondered where these forgotten gods were now, or if they had been there when the perfected Trothian ancestors rose from the sea to slaughter thousands out of anger and vengeance. Regardless, something had caused the elevated race to devolve into modern Trothians. The Landers had soon overpowered them, forcing them off the islands of the Greater Chain and onto their own secluded islets of sand.

Raekon's brief explanation in the guesthouse had left Portsend confused at first. But the big man had clarified that Trothians were not Homelanders. Rather, they—and the Landers—could *become* Homelanders through exposure to the toxic Moon rays followed by a detonation of Metamorphosis Grit.

After all of his experiments yesterday, Portsend had only two small vials of the solution remaining. Still, that would be plenty. Each vial would produce a cloud with nearly a seven-foot diameter. He only needed to encompass Gloristar.

"Do you think Ardor's plan will succeed?" Portsend asked.

"They always seem to have a way of working out," answered Raekon. "Maybe not exactly the way he wants, but he's remarkably adaptable."

"I'm sure he could have used your help making alterations to those Cataclysm kegs," Portsend said.

"He'll figure it out," replied Raekon. "Ard is actually more capable than he thinks he is. He just prefers to have other people do the work for him. I left him with all the calculations and measurements he'll need. Besides, we've got to save the Prime Isless."

A fresh wash of despair flowed through Portsend. Gloristar had been taken because of him. By now, she'd be starting into the second phase of Moonsickness. Her voice would be gone, and her vision would be fading, if her eyes hadn't already turned blood red.

Homeland, he hoped he wasn't arriving too late. He hoped that their hypothesis would work at all. He was confident in the new Grit, and Raekon seemed sure about their theory. It would have to be enough. What other hope did he have of saving her?

They rode in silence through orchards and fields, the trail finally necking down and growing even fainter as it entered an untamed wood. The thick shade was refreshing, but the vegetation required them to slow their horses to a careful walk.

After a few minutes, they emerged quite suddenly on the other side of the small forest. The trees had made an effective visual barrier and Portsend was almost to the gate before he even realized it was there. He sprang from the saddle, turning the horse back into the shelter of the trees until they could get a better glimpse of the space ahead.

The Realm had constructed their terrible farm on a natural stone peninsula. It was maybe two hundred feet wide at the point where it joined the mainland, tapering to what looked like a mere fifty feet at the tip. It protruded at least a hundred yards from the otherwise straight cliff edge of the shore.

The terrain was flat, treeless and grassy in places where regular foot traffic hadn't worn it to packed dirt. A few horses were tethered to the fence that spanned the peninsula's width, and a couple of covered wagons probably served as shelter for the guards.

But the cages were what caught Portsend's eye.

He couldn't count them, ringing the outer edge of the peninsula. A few were empty, but most held some unfortunate soul who was dithering away in the third stage of Moonsickness. Some individuals made steady, almost rhythmic strikes against the bars. Others lay still as though dead, only to leap up in a violent rage and slam against the bars like frightened animals.

Was this to be Gloristar's fate? The Prime Isless wouldn't be this far gone already, so Portsend scanned the cages in search of someone who might still be clinging to their sanity.

"I count only four workers," Raekon said, his voice so close that it caused Portsend to jump. He'd been so wrapped up in the decaying Bloodeyes, that he had looked right past the workers seated by a fire pit on the other side of the gate.

"Minimal crew," Raekon continued, voice low. "Anyone involved with the Faceless will be in Beripent for the meeting. How's your aim, Professor?"

He'd hunted with his father as a teenager, but he'd found that academics gave him more of a thrill. "At this range," said Portsend, "I could manage it with a Fielder."

They'd brought two of the long guns from the guesthouse, assuming that they'd need to eliminate whatever security they might encounter at the farm.

"All right," whispered Raekon, hitching the horses to a tree and readying the Fielders. "We each pick a different target and we fire in unison. That'll leave only two for us to deal with when we hop the fence."

Portsend swallowed. He was still rattled from executing that ruffian in the guesthouse. He'd never murdered anyone before, and now he was preparing to do it again? After interrogating that fellow, he'd been seized by a wild anger. The man had taunted him, making light of Gloristar's capture and saying that Portsend was to blame. He'd squeezed the trigger almost before he'd known what he was really doing. This was different. The men on the other side of the fence were relaxed in conversation, one of them poking at the coals of the dying cooking fire.

*For Gloristar,* he thought, as Raekon handed him one of the guns he'd just loaded. Even if he hadn't known her personally—perhaps *too* personally—Portsend told himself that the Prime Isless was worth killing for. These guards were Settled ingrates, supporting the worst debauchery Portsend had ever heard of.

"Isn't that your Prime Isless in the last cage at the tip of the peninsula?" Raekon handed him the spyglass he'd just been peering through. Filled with both hope and dread, Portsend raised it to his eye.

He found it hard to keep his hand steady. But even through his shakiness, he could see that it was her. The magnifying lens of the spyglass wasn't powerful enough to show him details, but from this distance, at least, Gloristar still looked . . . human. Maybe she hadn't contracted Moonsickness after all. Maybe the Hand at the guesthouse had been wrong and Gloristar hadn't arrived until after the Passing.

"Figures they'd stick her in the farthest cage at the edge of the cliff," Raekon muttered.

"Hardest to reach for a rescue," presumed Portsend.

"First to suck up the Moon rays during the Passing," he corrected. The big man sighted down his Fielder. "I'm taking the one with the blue shirt. You should go for the guy poking at the fire."

"Why him?" Portsend asked.

"Looks like he's got the biggest head."

Portsend shuddered, bringing the gunstock against his shoulder and dead resting the long barrel in the low crook of a tree branch.

"Once we fire, ditch the Fielders and move in," Raekon continued. "I'll take care of the last two guys. You just get down to the
Prime Isless as quickly as you can. Ready?"

Portsend's sweaty hand shifted, thumb cocking the hammer. He
shut one eye and sighted down the gun. "Ready."

"On three. One. Two. Three!"

Portsend pulled the trigger, his stomach a mass of knots and
unease. His aim was true, and the man with the stick fell into the
fire. At the same time, his companion in the blue shirt toppled without a cry. The other two scrambled frantically to their feet. One
drew a Roller, taking two aimless shots into the dense trees.

"Go!" Raekon yelled, firing his own Roller as he moved forward.

Portsend sprinted from his hiding place, one hand over his vest
pocket. Once, the leather scroll tube had worn a spot there, but
that list had been milked of all its mysteries. In its place were the
two vials of Metamorphosis Grit, too valuable to carry in his hand
should he fall.

He made it to the fence, breathing hard before he even reached
the hundred-yard dash to Gloristar's cage. He found footing on one
of the horizontal fence slats and hoisted himself up.

Out of the corner of his eye, he saw Raekon's gun spit flame,
dropping the closest guard. The second had made a hasty retreat
toward the nearest bank of cages.

Portsend swung his leg over the top of the fence and dropped to
the other side, landing with less agility than he'd hoped. Righting
himself, he prepared to make the run when the sound of grating
metal caused him to falter.

At the row of cages, the guard was heaving against a crank
wheel, lifting a bar that ran across the front of all five cells on that
block. As it rose, the cage doors lifted with it, opening from the bottom like portcullises.

The engineering made sense on a farm where the product was

insane, absurdly violent people. They'd need to transport the Bloodeyes somehow, and opening a typical hinged door would require the wild people to be herded into the wagons. This way, a wagon could be backed right up to the cages and when the bars slid up, the Bloodeyes would fling themselves into it, probably thrashing in transit the entire way.

Raekon put a ball into the guard, but the man held on to the crank, the Bloodeyes inside the cages growing frantic as an exit began to present itself. The second Roller ball finished the man, who managed only half a turn more before collapsing to the ground.

Portsend had guessed that the wheel would spin back, the weight of the bar closing the cages again. But bloody, mangled hands had already found purchase on the rising bar from inside the cages.

With inhuman strength, they heaved it upward far enough to worm their way out. It was done in a moment, the bar crashing back to the ground behind them.

Five blind Bloodeyes stood free, sniffing at the air, their mouths opening and closing in silent screams.

Portsend's feet had put down roots and he felt like he would never be able to move again. Then Raekon's Roller sounded and the nearest Bloodeye fell to the ground. The shot would probably have been fatal to a regular woman, but the Bloodeye righted herself at once, yellowish foam clotting at the wound to keep her alive.

"This might be a good time to test our theory!" Raekon shouted, taking another shot as the five Moonsick people sprang at the sound.

It took Portsend a moment to realize what he meant. The Metamorphosis Grit! He had been so focused on saving the detonation for Gloristar that he'd almost forgotten he had *two* vials.

His hand shot into his breast pocket and he withdrew one. With a grunt, he pitched it at the two nearest Moonsick people, hearing the confirmation of shattering glass against the packed dirt. The detonation cloud sprang up, catching both Bloodeyes in its radius.

His heart began to sink. The Grit had no immediate effect on them as it'd had on all the creatures in his tests. The Bloodeyes staggered out of the cloud and came toward him, arms swiping blindly.

"Maybe it takes longer on the ripe ones," Raekon called.

*That's it!* Every test he'd preformed on actual chrysalises or cocoons had failed. Portsend had determined that the pupal state of the insects was too far advanced to be affected by the Metamorphosis Grit. Maybe there was still hope for Gloristar, even if these third-stage Bloodeyes were beyond any susceptibility for transformation.

Portsend jumped back, hitting the fence as the first Bloodeye lunged for him. Fumbling, he drew his Singler, firing the ball into the man's head at a distance of just five feet. He flew backward, striking the ground in silence before rising slowly.

Raw terror clutched at his hammering heart. The creatures before him were an embodiment of death—relentless, inevitable.

"Portsend! Go!" Raekon's voice cut through his paralyzing fear. His Roller must have been empty, because he used it like a club now, battering back a Moonsick woman with enough force to send her spinning. The big man ditched the gun and drew two long knives, jumping back from a blind grasp and slicing deeply into both sides of the Bloodeye's arm.

Raekon was doing his best to draw them away, but these monsters were not going down easily. Portsend would simply have to outrun them to Gloristar's cage.

Casting aside the empty Singler, Portsend drew his own dagger.

"'The journey to the Homeland is long...'" He began the quote, his voice soft as he sprinted forward. At the sound of his movement, the two nearest Bloodeyes immediately turned for him.

"'...and many shall perish...'" Without breaking step, he slashed at the man beside him. "'...ere they reach that holy shore.'"

Portsend felt the blade of his knife connect, tearing through what rags of clothing remained. But the flesh of the Bloodeye's chest seemed as rough and impenetrable as tree bark. Portsend's feet pounded the ground, steady and determined. Only halfway there, and his lungs felt like bursting.

"'From port, send thine aid...'"

One of the Bloodeyes tackled him from behind. They rolled forward, crooked fingers raking across the back of Portsend's head, pulling out fistfuls of his graying hair.

Portsend twisted, thrusting behind him with the dagger. He felt the tip strike, but the man's skin was too hard. Pounding the pommel with his other fist, he managed to drive the blade in nearly to the hilt.

"'But glory, starboard...!'" he screamed, rising to his feet, hands soaked in warm blood as he yanked out the dagger. The stabbed Moonsick man showed no signs of dying, but at least he was momentarily slowed.

The second Bloodeye pounced at him like a cat, but Portsend managed to shake her off and continue his scramble toward Gloristar's cage.

"'... for it shall mark thy way...'"

He could see her now, kneeling in the cage, her hands gripping the bars. Her mouth was forming the shape of his name in a silent scream. Her once-dark eyes looked like they had just begun to change—pale, swollen, with a deep redness creeping in at the sides.

With tears streaming down his face, Portsend reached into his pocket and withdrew the final vial of Metamorphosis Grit.

One of the Bloodeyes struck him from behind and he fell, stars dancing across his vision as he fought to stay conscious. His dagger had tumbled away, but his bloody fist still clutched the vial securely. He looked up, locking eyes with Gloristar as he pulled back his arm.

"'... to everlasting perfection.'"

Portsend hurled the vial, watching it turn end for end in the midday sunlight. He heard the glass break, but he could not see it as the Bloodeye descended with a horrid fury on the side of his unprotected head.

He heard his spine break, a cracking sound like a tree branch splintering in a windstorm. At once, his body went still and the pain of the attacks was gone. Helpless panic gripped him. He tried to move, but his arms and legs felt like solid lead.

Portsend Wal screamed. It wasn't from the pain of the two Bloodeyes ravaging his torso, for he was numb. Nor was it a cry for help to Raekon, for he knew that moment had passed.

It was a scream of despair. Of having a sure knowledge that his life was quickly coming to an end and his wounds had already crossed the threshold for any chance of recovery.

It was despair at thinking that he would never see Gloristar again. That his final image would be of her kneeling in that cage, already half blinded, with her mouth open in a silent shout of his name.

His vision was just starting to cloud when his two Moonsick attackers suddenly fell away from his paralyzed body like broken pieces of a clay Grit pot to the waste pail.

Seemingly out of nowhere, Gloristar was in his view, standing above him like a guardian. Portsend knew it was she, despite the fact that the figure bore so little resemblance to the woman he'd loved.

She was towering above her natural height. From his prone position in the grass, Portsend would have guessed her to be even taller than Raekon. Her black hair had disappeared entirely, and her smooth scalp seemed to be made of shimmering red glass that started just above her eyebrows and continued down the back of her skull.

Gloristar's clothing, ripped by her enlargement, hung in shreds over skin of the palest blue. It was several shades lighter than Trothian flesh, and appeared almost translucent in the sunlight. Glistening beneath her skin was a network of veins and arteries that seemed to course with liquid gold. She was muscular and shapely, the perfected specimen of all humankind.

Her face was perhaps the only thing truly familiar to Portsend, but even that was chillingly foreign. Gloristar's eyes blazed a deep red, not akin to fire or the yellow glow of Light Grit. This was something else altogether, like two wells of power cradled in the middle of her face.

Like Moons.

The two Bloodeyes, apparently recovered from whatever initial blow Gloristar had dealt them, came scrambling back, clawing madly with bloodied hands.

Gloristar caught the Moonsick man as he leapt for Portsend. Seizing him by the neck, she lifted him entirely into the air as though he were weightless. The second Bloodeye sprang for them, but Gloristar brought the first one around like a swinging club.

She slammed their heads together with such impossible force that Portsend saw both of their skulls split like overripened melons. Their motionless bodies tumbled aside, their regenerative healing abilities outmatched by sudden death.

"Oh, Portsend...my dear Portsend," Gloristar whispered, her radiant eyes turning on him as she fell to her knees by his side. It was her voice, but it seemed to pierce straight to his heart. It was as if her words were accompanied by the richness of musical instruments that only he could hear.

She was weeping over him, crimson tears that drew lines upon her shimmering golden-blue face. Her sorrow seemed to linger over his broken body, and Portsend finally glanced downward to see what the Bloodeyes had done to him.

His stomach was split wide, entrails visible through his shredded vest. It was the strangest sensation as he looked upon it without a trace of pain. That couldn't be his body, so mangled and spent. Surely he was looking at a lifeless corpse.

Gloristar's powerful arms scooped him up, and she rose, cradling him against her breast. Now lifted from the ground, Portsend could see Raekon racing toward them, two more of the Bloodeyes still scrambling after him.

Gloristar would protect Raekon now. She would make everything right. She was dredged in power unlike anything Portsend had ever perceived. She had become a Homelander, and borne in her golden arms, he, too, had reached the Homeland.

Portsend Wal took one final breath.

*Glory, starboard.*

~

*You have abandoned us, favored of the gods. Now we are coming for you.*

# CHAPTER

# 45

"Turns out it's not so difficult to get a meeting with King Termain when you show up at the palace with the legitimate heir," Ard said to Quarrah as they strode down the corridor toward the throne room. Beside them, Lady Abeth had one arm wrapped tightly around her son. The four of them were surrounded by half a dozen palace Regulator escorts, who had quickly let them in at the sight of the living, breathing Agaul mother and son.

Ard really hadn't expected much trouble. It was only an hour until midnight, and any Faceless who normally worked in the palace would be getting ready to detonate their Cataclysm kegs.

The Faceless meeting had gone remarkably well, and Ard had received confirmation that everything was in place. There was no way the Cataclysm could happen now. The Void Grit device would never leave the harbor, and they didn't even need Shad Agaul to put out a search for it.

Now for the grand finale.

Ard had been to this throne room enough times to know the way himself. The guards at the door stepped aside to let the group enter. Fresh spheres of Light Grit glowed steadily in sconces on the walls, but the alcoves that had once displayed royal relics stood empty.

And there was good old Grotenisk. Surprisingly, there was no bonfire in his skull, but the stone throne still looked highly impressive, mounted to its top, twin chimney columns rising to the ceiling.

Behind the dark throne, the door to the balcony was open, the curtains waving gently in the night breeze. Ard found it odd that the exterior door hadn't been barred off for good. Termain Agaul wasn't one to make public speeches. But then, a man like him probably liked to stand on that balcony and survey his subjects, making him feel highly important as the quality of life for the citizens of Beripent continued to corrode under his misrule.

The king had not arrived yet, which didn't surprise Ard, given the very short notice to appear. The only person in the large room was a servant with a wrinkled cravat and a sleepless look in his eyes.

"His Majesty has been notified of your presence," the servant said. "He will arrive shortly."

"And the queen dowager?" Quarrah asked.

"Slightly more difficult to rouse from slumber, if you can believe it," he replied. "And she has a habit of not granting audiences or following through with appointments."

"Did you tell her who was here?" Ard asked.

Ard and Quarrah hadn't given their own names. Those were best kept hushed in this palace. Besides, in this case, the names of Abeth and Shad Agaul would carry much more weight.

"I have a feeling that'll get even an old maid like her dressed in record time," Ard finished.

"Please," snapped the servant. "Show some respect for the king's aging mother."

"She's used up all my respect," said Quarrah flatly.

Ard agreed. Seeing Overseer at noon for the Faceless meeting had almost been too much. They could have easily overpowered her then, hidden behind masks she trusted as she gave them all the information they needed to carry out the meeting. But Ard had insisted they wait. A takedown in secret would only have caused backlash and confusion. This way, they'd get the queen dowager with reputable witnesses, and the public would receive the drama much better.

"I know we're still an hour early," said Ard, turning to the prince, who was in his mother's arms, "but why don't you get up there and try out your birthday present?"

Shad's eyes turned to the dragon-skull throne, a look of determination instead of the overwhelmed expression Ard had expected to see. The skinny youth stepped forward, his mother reluctantly letting go of him.

"For years, I imagined how Father would look on this throne," Shad said. "He was always a king to me, even though the crusader monarch filled his place."

"I am confident that your father would have done better than old Pethredote," Ard said.

"You were born for this, my boy," said Lady Abeth, her voice choked with emotion.

"Will they accept me?" Shad asked.

"You were trained and schooled for this moment," Abeth said. "Necessity is bringing it to pass sooner than any of us had expected. But that same necessity will win you the hearts of all people."

"Shad," Quarrah suddenly spoke as the boy stepped toward the skull. "Er... Your Highness?"

The prince turned back to look at her, his eyes growing wide when he saw what she held.

"Where did you find this?" he asked, taking the emerald Agaul family ring from her grasp. "Mother told me it was stolen."

"I . . ." Quarrah stammered. "I stole it back for you."

He slipped it onto the middle finger of his right hand, grinning. "It's a little big."

"I'm sure you'll grow into it," she said.

*More than a common thief.* Ard nodded to her, but Quarrah wouldn't look over at him. That ring could have set her up comfortably, maybe for the rest of her life. But giving it to the prince was the right choice. He'd be king in less than an hour. And being on good terms with him might end up being more beneficial than thousands of Ashings in her pocket.

Shad Agaul moved to the side of the skull and climbed up the natural divots in the dragon's bone structure that served as crude steps.

Ard expected the Reggies to try to stop him. He certainly expected the servant to protest. But no one moved and no one said a word. To Ard, it was a testament to how tired those in the palace had grown of Termain's self-centered rule.

Shad reached the top of the skull and turned out to face them. "I, Shad Agaul, only son of Remium Agaul and Abeth Ostel, and rightful heir to the throne, do swear to serve these islands in justice, purity, and truth. To move forward in a manner both steady and effective. I swear to maintain—"

"Hold on," Ard interrupted. "What are you doing?"

"He's had the oaths of kingship memorized since he was eight years old," Abeth answered for her son. "He can recite the entire thing without any notes or prompting."

"At least we know his memory's holding," Quarrah muttered.

"That's good, kid," said Ard. "But you need to save it for an hour. I promise we'll get all the official people in here and you can say your bit. Right now, we're really just trying to prove a point. Why don't you have a seat and relax for a bit . . . Your Highness?"

Shad nodded. Reaching back, he gripped both stone armrests and slid his backside into the throne. He suddenly looked much smaller and even younger than his fourteen years. Maybe it was the fine clothes he was wearing, taken from his room at the guesthouse, but quite ill-fitting due to his added height.

Lady Abeth had given him something of a haircut before they came, and he'd bathed in some of the water Hedma had drawn to put out the fires. His appearance, and odor, were much improved, but Ard thought that seeing him seated in that grand throne made him look more like a little boy than a king.

"What the blazes is going on?" King Termain's voice caused them all to whirl. He had arrived, hair tousled and dressed in a pair of loose cotton pants and a shirt with an open front.

"Arrest him!" Termain shouted, pointing to the boy on the throne. "Sparks! Just shoot him now and save the firing squad the hassle!"

*It's a good thing Termain is unarmed,* Ard thought as the king stormed toward the skull throne. Suddenly Termain pulled a Singler from his billowy shirt. So much for that...

Ard leaped forward, pushing the king's arm aside as he pulled the trigger. The shot went wide, but it caused the young prince to spring to his feet, panic on his face. Ard wrenched the hot gun out of Termain's hand, the king stumbling backward.

"Who are you traitors?" he hissed.

"I assume you remember your cousin's wife?" Ard gestured to her. "Lady Abeth Agaul, former queen of the Greater Chain."

Termain's face twisted as he looked from Abeth to the prince. "You... *how?*"

"Didn't the servants tell you it was us?" Lady Abeth asked, standing with confidence against the despicable man.

"If I'd believed them," said Termain, "I'd be expecting ghosts."

"Ooh, snarky," Ard cut in. "The two of us could have gotten along, if you weren't such a self-centered egomaniac."

Quarrah cleared her throat conspicuously behind him. *What...* Ard thought. *There's only room for one of us.*

"So, you've come to take my kingdom?" Termain said stiffly, as though trying to make an implied threat.

"The kingdom should never have been yours," Lady Abeth replied.

"She's right," Ard explained. "You were manipulated into the throne so that you'd do a bang-up job. You didn't let them down."

"What are you talking about?" Termain asked. "I was manipulated by no man."

"No *man*," agreed Quarrah. "By your own mother."

That had to sting, but Termain didn't show it. In fact he seemed to refuse the idea, shaking his head rapidly back and forth.

"Fabra Ment is the leader of a criminal organization called the Realm," explained Quarrah. "She had your cousin assassinated, and staged the death of Shad Agaul."

"But she didn't stop there," Ard continued. "The queen dowager kept your palace swarming with eyes and ears faithful to the Realm, including your advisor, Waelis Mordo. She manipulated you into maintaining the conflict with the Sovereign States with the ultimate goal of replacing you and using the prince to restore peace to the Greater Chain on her terms."

"No," Termain whispered, still shaking his head.

"Your mother is a ruthless killer," Ard insisted. "While you might think she's sleeping peacefully in her chambers, she's more likely preparing for tonight's activities, which happen to include mass genocide."

"No," Termain said again. "My mother is little more than a hapless widow, whose mind is past its useful years."

The sound of boots in the hallway caused Ard to glance over his shoulder. Perfect timing.

"Don't believe us?" Ard asked Termain. "Ask her yourself."

Fabra Ment staggered into sight, seeming to keep herself upright only with the support of a cane in one hand and her deaf hand-maiden in the other. The old queen was wearing a nightgown without any sort of sash or belt, so it hung formlessly around her plump form. Her slippered feet padded along, those skinny legs visible from her midshin down. She wore a white nightcap, which tied under the chin with a tidy bow. Clenched between her teeth was a long pipe. Ard didn't think it was lit yet, but her mouth seemed to be shaped around it.

Hobbling forward, bleary-eyed and slightly whiskery, Fabra Ment certainly didn't look like a criminal mastermind. But then, that was probably exactly what she was counting on. The queen dowager was a master of misdirection.

"Good of you to join us," Ard said. "I was just describing some of your . . . *hobbies* to the king here."

"Is it true, Mother?" Termain asked with the same whiny tone of a spoiled child. "Tell me it's not true."

"Well, Quarrah Khai," said Fabra, "I thought for certain you had died with those imposter Homelanders. I heard they were poisoned."

"Some of us were shot," Quarrah said. "You can drop the act, Fabra."

"Mother!" Termain cried. "What have you done? How do you know these people?"

"Sweet boy," the queen dowager said to her son. "This woman is a thief. I hired her to infiltrate a wicked organization known as the Realm. I was worried that your old advisor, Waelis Mordo, was—"

"Enough!" Ard shouted, his voice echoing through the spacious room.

"I found your mask," Quarrah picked up in the resulting silence. "I found the hidden room in the back of the closet. The map of Pekal, the ring, the ledgers, the ripeworms—"

"What in the great blazes are you talking about?" Fabra rasped.

"We know who you are," Quarrah said, "Overseer."

Fabra Ment began to chuckle, the laughter growing big enough that she had to take the pipe out of her mouth to keep it from falling. "Me?" she cried. "Overseer? Homeland! Wouldn't *that* be something! Tell me...If that were true, why would I hire you to take me down?"

"The whole job was a security check against Ardor Benn," said Quarrah. "You must have grown suspicious that he was making his way into the Realm, so you hired me, knowing that I was the best candidate to be able to sniff him out."

"Sparks," Fabra muttered. "How very clever of me. Clever indeed."

"It's over, Fabra," Ard said. He was tired of her mock innocence, clearly intended to keep her simpleminded son on her side. It was time to provoke her into a confession. "The Cataclysm is called off, and every Faceless member of the Realm is about to be arrested at the stroke of midnight."

"This is the man?" Fabra asked Quarrah, taking a step closer to Ard. "This is the famous ruse artist who brought down the crusader monarch?"

"I'd been specializing in crooked kings," Ard said, "but I'm willing to branch out to include washed-up old queens."

She grinned around her pipe. "I like the way he talks."

"Thanks to Quarrah's resourcefulness," Ard continued, unabashed by the flattery, "we got everything we needed. The Agaul prince, recently restored to his full and regular mental capacity." He gestured to the boy who was still standing in front of the throne. "While we were on Pekal, we swung by Crooked Ravine and picked up a Drift crate full of Cataclysm kegs that you had promised to pass out to every one of the Faceless. We fulfilled your promise at the meeting earlier today with specific instructions to detonate the kegs at the stroke of midnight. Just as you planned, a cloud of Barrier Grit will safely cover them, but at the same time a cupweight of Harvester tracer's dye will spray the hand that detonates each keg.

Then, nicely contained in an inescapable dome, with their hands dyed crimson, every one of your worker bees will be caught, quite literally, red-handed."

"What are you saying...?" Fabra muttered.

"To make it easy on the Regulators," Ard pressed on, "we told all of the Faceless to detonate the protection kegs in the Char. Then I tipped off a friend of mine, a certain private inspector for the city of Beripent. Inspector Ardour Stringer was able to file the paperwork he needed to have a significant patrol of Reggies standing by in the Char to make the expected arrests. Honestly, it won't be difficult. They're basically imprisoning themselves with your kegs."

A gunshot suddenly robbed him of his moment. Reeling away from the queen dowager, Ard drew his own gun, scanning the throne room. A pained whimper drew his attention to the throne.

Shad Agaul had fallen back into the large throne, his chest bloody and his eyes wet with tears. His lips trembled, and his hands gripped the armrests, unwilling to touch the wound where the ball had entered.

Lady Abeth's scream filled the room, its grief cutting Ard to the bone. She ran forward, clamoring up the side of the dragon skull and falling on her child.

By the time Ard turned back, the smoking Roller was on the floor in front of a Reggie with an empty holster. His face looked shocked as he turned to the figure beside him.

Fabra Ment's handmaiden sprang into action. Leaping up with remarkable agility, she wrapped one leg over the Reggie's shoulder. A knife appeared in her hand, slicing across the Regulator's throat as she threw her weight, toppling the big man.

Ard leveled his gun and fired, missing by a hair as the woman ripped a Grit pot from the Reggie's belt. She hurtled the knife, the blade passing just inches to the side of Ard's shoulder. Then she smashed the clay pot against the floor. An instant shield surrounded her as half a dozen shots were fired from the remaining

Reggies. The lead balls pinged off the Barrier's exterior, ricocheting dangerously across the throne room.

"Errel?" Quarrah whispered, taking a step closer to the assassin. The handmaiden was still crouched over the dead man, her simple tunic stained red.

"Mother!" This strangled cry came from King Termain, causing Ard yet again to divert his focus.

Behind him, the queen dowager had fallen to the floor, her white nightgown blossoming with red as she gripped the hilt of the knife that had struck her just below the collarbone. She gurgled, her teeth clenched tighter than ever around that pipe.

"You actually fell for it," came a voice from inside the Barrier cloud. Errel had risen to her feet, staring impassively at the dying old widow.

"You?" Quarrah shook her head in disbelief.

"Me," the handmaiden answered.

"Fabra Ment was never Overseer," Quarrah whispered, staring through the Barrier cloud at Errel.

The handmaiden didn't answer, but her silence seemed to confirm it. Sparks! How had Quarrah been so blind? Errel had been there all the time, listening, learning. Using the queen dowager as a front.

From the throne, Lady Abeth wailed. Two of the Regulators were attending to the prince, clouds of Health Grit springing up around him in what Quarrah thought was probably a futile attempt to save his life. Blazing ironic to get him all the way to the throne, only to have him die on it.

The queen dowager was also being attended to with Health Grit, the king frittering at her side and letting out long streams of profane language.

"Did Fabra know?" Quarrah asked.

"She knew what I wanted her to know," answered Errel.

"Did she know you could speak?"

"That was our secret," she said. "Oh, Fabra Ment loved secrets. To tell them. To hear them. To hold them for no good reason. I was her eyes and ears around the palace. People spoke freely in front of me, and I told Fabra enough secrets to make sure I was indispensable."

"*You* poisoned the wine at the reception to kill the Homelanders," Quarrah said.

"They were loose ends," answered Errel. "The Homelander ruse could have been successful, but Rival lost my trust."

"When did you suspect it?" Ard asked. "How?"

"It really goes clear back to Beska Falay," said Errel.

"The harp tuner?" Ard asked.

"We had people looking for her," explained Errel. "She had become a problem even before you found her. When my Hands caught her trying to flee Espar, she mentioned the name Ardor Benn. My ears perked up because I'd been around the palace long enough to hear your connection to Pethredote and the theft of the Royal Regalia. Before she died, Beska said that you were inside the Realm and you knew how to take us down."

"She jumped the gun a bit with that statement," said Ard, "but ultimately, she was right."

"That's why you hired me," Quarrah said. "To find Ard inside the Realm and report his activities back to Fabra."

"I convinced the old lady that Termain was being manipulated, which was only the truth. As Overseer, I ordered one of the Directorate, Waelis Mordo, to expose the Realm codes and symbol to Fabra."

"You were the one on the other side of the curtain," Quarrah assumed.

"Yes," answered Errel. "And once you were accepted into the Faceless, I killed Waelis Mordo in order to open a position in my council. When Ardor shot *another* opening into the Directorate, I decided to let him enter. Keep your enemies close, don't they say?"

"You knew it was me?" Ard cried.

"I highly suspected it," she said. "But there was no way to be certain in the moment, since you both did such a remarkable job of pretending not to recognize each other. During the duel, I was actually convinced that Quarrah felt nothing but hatred for you."

Well, maybe that hadn't been far from the truth. Perhaps her bitter feelings had saved Ard's life.

"When Quarrah didn't report to Fabra that she'd found you, I began to doubt," said Errel. "It wasn't until the incident with Raekon Dorrel that I began to be sure again. See, I was familiar enough with the Short Fuse, known associate of Ardor Benn, to know that Rival did not match his physical description. When you claimed to be him in the lighthouse, it finally tipped your hand."

"But you let us go through with the Homelander ruse," Ard said. "Why?"

"I needed to be absolutely sure that Ardor Benn, Androt Penn, Rival, and the captain of the Homelanders were all the same person," said Errel. "Besides, if I had shut down your ruse entirely, it could have raised a red flag. I needed you to think that I trusted you. At the reception, I identified Quarrah as one of the Homelanders because I expected her to be there. Warning her about the poison was supposed to draw you both out, where I could shoot you and confirm that the faces under the masks were indeed the people I suspected."

"And there lies the problem with your secret club," Ard said. "*Anyone* can put on a mask."

"I suppose it doesn't matter now," said Errel. "The prince will die, which could slow down the reunification of the Greater Chain. But the Great Egress will happen sooner or later. And the islands will be ours to spoil, free of Wayfarism."

"Funny you still consider yourself a free woman," Ard said. "Once that Barrier cloud comes down, every Reggie in the palace will fall on you."

She held up another Grit pot. "Then I will stall."

"Stall for what?" Quarrah asked. "You can't hope to outlast us."

"When I heard of your arrival, I sent out a signal to the Director-ate," she said. "Three lights upon Old Post Lighthouse. It means the palace is compromised and they should bring the largest force they can muster to plunder it. An exciting prospect for an organization of criminals."

Ard started to chuckle, scratching at his chin and turning to Quarrah. "Do you want to tell her, or should I?"

"You go ahead," Quarrah answered. It would take longer this way, but she could tell he was dying to explain it.

"Rispit Born, Chal Ovent, Moyer Tane, and Daret Bonds," Ard said. "Well, technically, there was Saff Eri, but our mutual friend, Portsend Wal, took care of her. In case you didn't know, those are the names of everyone in the Directorate. If you'd like to talk to them, you'll find the four who are still alive in the palace dungeon. They've been there since noon."

"That's not possible." Errel swallowed visibly. "I spoke with them at that very time, just before the Faceless meeting."

"Rather, you spoke with four people wearing their masks," Ard corrected. "It's like I said. That's the problem with your secret club."

"I found the list of pickup locations in the drawer of your hidden closet," Quarrah said.

"We made sure a few of *our* marked carriages were there to pick them up instead," explained Ard.

"*Regulator* carriages," Quarrah clarified. "They brought them to the palace dungeon, because the Outposts are clearly under Realm control."

"Stasis Grit knocked them right out," explained Ard, "allowing us to take their masks and lock them each in a separate jail cell."

"You're probably wondering whom you met with at noon," Quarrah said to Errel. "I went as Trance."

"I went as Snare," said Ard. "And I'll tell you, that seashell mask smells like a dead fish on the inside." He exhaled sharply. "Grapple and Radius were played by two of our other acquaintances, who have a penchant for complicated disguises."

Quarrah was still impressed that Cinza had convincingly portrayed the portly man with the boar's-head mask. The meeting had been brief enough that Ard had done all the talking, pulling off a rather convincing impersonation of Snare.

"The Realm is shattered," Ard concluded. "You were the final broken piece to pick up."

"Others will take our place," said Errel. "Others who know the symbols and speak the phrases. Did you think the Realm only thrived in Beripent? This organization is centuries old. It has survived through worse, and someone else will continue the push for Egress."

"Maybe," said Quarrah. "But not tonight."

Errel laughed bitterly. "You think you've stopped the Cataclysm, don't you?"

"Snare was overseeing it," Ard said. "And he's been out of the picture since noon. We spread word to the Faceless that all previous jobs must be halted at once. Getting to the Char and detonating the Cataclysm kegs is their only remaining task."

Errel shook her head, and for the first time Quarrah thought she could see some resemblance to the masked Overseer.

"Snare submerged the device this morning," she said with a wry smile.

"What?" Ard cried. "How? The fuse would have to burn for over twelve hours."

"There was never a fuse on the Cataclysm device," said the handmaiden. "Long fuses are unreliable enough *above* water."

"Then how…" Ard trailed away as Errel held up her finger, swinging it back and forth like a pendulum while clicking her tongue in a steady *tick tock tick tock*.

"Sparks," Quarrah whispered. "The mantel clocks." It was the same innovative method the Realm had used to ignite the Blast Grit in Shad Agaul's bedroom.

"At the stroke of midnight, the Gregious Mas clock inside the Cataclysm device will spark." Errel opened her fists, fingers splayed out as her mouth made the sound of an explosion. "Time stops for no one."

From across the room, King Termain let out a maniacal cry. He sprinted forward, throwing himself uselessly against the Barrier cloud. Sliding off the shell, he crumpled to his side on the floor.

"I will kill you myself," he hissed through the invisible shield. "I will tear your limbs from your body. I'll hang your right arm in front of the palace, your left arm on Strind, and your legs in Talumon and Dronodan. But I'm keeping your head to use your jaw as a boot scraper."

Quarrah looked across the throne room. Fabra Ment was clearly dead, but atop Grotenisk's skull, Healers had arrived, still working on Shad Agaul within a Health cloud.

Ard cursed. His face looked tense from Overseer's final, unanticipated sting. The looming, ticking clock.

"We need to evacuate the city," Quarrah said.

Ard shrugged hopelessly. "It's the middle of the night. We've got less than half an hour."

"We have to do *something*," Quarrah cried. She turned to Termain, who was now kneeling beside the Barrier shell. "You are the king," she said. "Whether Shad Agaul survives or not, you are still the king for the next half hour. You need to call for an immediate evacuation of the city, starting with the Northern Quarter."

Termain slowly turned his sneer on her. "You don't understand... She killed my blazing mother!"

"There's a flood coming," Ard stepped in. "From the ocean. One large enough to wipe out half of Beripent. We need to warn the people."

"You expect me to make a fool of myself in the middle of the night?" he shouted. "The easier to replace me if I seem to be going mad."

"It's the truth," Quarrah insisted. "There's a device loaded with Compounded Void Grit. When it detonates below the sea, it's going to displace a lot of water very quickly."

"There has never been a flood from the InterIsland Waters," said Termain. "You will not make a fool of me!"

"The fearful make fools of themselves," came a new voice from the balcony.

Quarrah turned as the curtains parted, and what she saw nearly sent her reeling backward in astonishment.

The majestic being who stepped into sight towered over everyone in the room, shockingly beautiful and terrifying at the same time. Her skin looked both blue and gold, shimmering in the Light Grit as her eyes blazed an inhuman crimson. Her head was bare, the scalp made of a similar thick red glass to the testament spire they'd seen at the bottom of the sea.

The woman strode into the room, her gait confident and sure even as two dozen guns pointed in her direction. She moved past Grotenisk's skull and stopped not ten feet from King Termain.

"Gloristar?" he finally whispered in fearful recognition.

It was the Prime Isless.

Portsend's experiment must have worked! He had successfully transformed the Moonsick Prime Isless into . . . *this*.

Into a Homelander.

"All these cycles you have loomed over me." Her voice carried an unnatural resonance. "But I see now that I never had any reason to despair. All things form a great Sphere. And I have now come to the top."

Termain was trembling, his face wrenched with a twisted fury. "Don't threaten me, woman. Homeland knows what happened to you, but you'd be wise to remember that I still have the Anchored Tome. Without that book, there can be no—"

Gloristar reached out and put a hand on his bare chest. Without moving a muscle, she somehow sent the king flying backward to the sound of breaking bones. For a moment, Quarrah thought she saw a detonation cloud issuing from the Prime Isless's hand. But it didn't look right, stretched into a point like a spearhead. Then it was gone.

At once, the Reggies in the room opened fire. Gloristar twitched as the first balls struck her, dropping to her knees on the stone floor. Quarrah watched for the blood, but the Roller balls didn't seem to penetrate her majestic flesh. Then her hand was outstretched again, and this time Quarrah definitely saw a cloud.

It was Barrier Grit, or at least it appeared to be, blocking the incoming balls with ease. Instead of its natural spherical shape, the Barrier cloud had formed into a flat disk, hanging vertically in the air before her like a giant transparent shield. The moment the Slagstone gun hammers began to click on empty chambers, Gloristar dropped her hand, and the shield disappeared. Several of the Reggies fled, while others fell back, frantically trying to reload.

Gloristar moved over to the king once more, her steps indescribably graceful. Termain had slid to a halt on his back, still attempting to breathe, while his chest looked completely collapsed.

"There is no more need for the Anchored Tome," she said. "No more need for the Prime Isles. Wayfarism is a spent Grit pot. I am the spark and the detonation."

Termain wheezed in an obvious attempt to grovel.

Gloristar picked him up and threw him straight across the room with tremendous force. Termain sailed unnaturally through some sort of oblong detonation streaming from Gloristar's hand, until the king struck the front of Grotenisk's skull. The bottom teeth impaled Termain as his top half fell limply into the dragon's mouth.

In a wink, the Barrier cloud over Errel extinguished. She seemed to have been the only one ready for it, and there were notably fewer guns in the room now.

The handmaiden sprinted for the balcony, throwing her second pot of Barrier Grit. It smashed against the floor at Quarrah's feet, enclosing her and Ard under the impenetrable dome.

With superhuman speed, Gloristar crossed the throne room, catching the fleeing assassin by the back of the neck like a cat snatching a runaway mouse. Errel swung upward, managing to wrap both legs around the transformed woman's muscular shoulder, pulling down against her arm. Trying to break free.

"What are you?" Errel shrieked, voice choked by the strong hand around her neck. "Sparks! What demon are you?"

"I am the Homeland," she answered calmly. "I am time and space perfected."

A flurry of Roller balls struck Gloristar's back as two of the Regulators made a daring advance. The assault gave Errel the chance she needed to squirm free, landing on her side and scrambling for the balcony.

"I am not your enemy!" Gloristar shouted, whirling on the Regulators. Detonation clouds billowed from her palms, sending both of them skidding across the floor.

By the time Gloristar turned back, Errel had vanished. The Prime Isless waved her hands, somehow using more of her detonations to push aside the curtains from a distance of at least twenty feet.

The balcony was empty.

"You let her get away!" Ard cried.

Quarrah shot him a glare. Hadn't he just seen this woman destroy the king with her bare hands?

Slowly Gloristar turned to face them. Under the gaze of her red eyes, Quarrah felt herself begin to tremble. At least there was a cloud of Barrier Grit shielding them.

Gloristar stretched out one bluish-gold hand, gently touching the smooth surface of the Barrier shield. In a heartbeat, the cloud disappeared as though it had been absorbed through her fingertips.

"Umm. I don't believe we've been properly introduced," Ard said.

Seriously? Like he was at a social event?

"My name is Ardor Benn. Portsend Wal was a good friend of ours."

That was a bit of an exaggeration, as they'd only known the professor for a short time.

"Given your...current state," Ard continued. "I'm guessing the professor found you."

Gloristar's unblinking, glowing eyes seemed to dim with sorrow. "He perished in my arms."

"Flames," Quarrah whispered.

"Our condolences," said Ard. "Our companion was with him. A large fellow..."

"Raekon Dorrel," finished Gloristar. "His return to Beripent was not as swift as mine. Still, your friend should be arriving soon."

At the throne, one of the Healers stood, hands red and a somber look on his face. "Shad Agaul, son of Remium Agaul and Abeth Ostel, has died," he announced to the room. Lady Abeth was slumped at the base of the throne, taken by silent sobs. "May he find the shores of the Homeland swiftly."

Flames. The poor boy. He'd come so far. Survived so long. Quarrah turned to Gloristar. "Is there anything you can do for him?"

The Prime Isless slowly shook her head, Light Grit reflecting on the red glass of her smooth scalp. "Not until the Sphere is complete. For now, there is an order to life and a time for death."

Quarrah didn't understand her cryptic words, but the failure of losing Shad Agaul settled on her with a degree of grief and numbness.

"What about our other problem?" Ard asked. "We don't have much time left. Do you know how to stop a massive flood that is about to drown Beripent?"

Gloristar flexed her fingers. "I will need more Barrier Grit."

"The armory," Quarrah said. "I know the way." It was on the lowest level, so reconstruction probably wouldn't have affected it.

"I will also need to reach a high vantage point," Gloristar said. "Somewhere I can clearly see out over the InterIsland Waters."

"You mean, you don't fly?" Ard asked. "You sure had a few other surprising skill sets."

Sparks, did he have to be so casual with the most powerful being in the known world?

"A high point..." Quarrah mused. "I think I know just the place."

~

*Their kings and queens will bow down before us, and they will be filled with regret.*

# CHAPTER

# 46

Ardor Benn was out of breath by the time they reached the light-room at the top of the Old Post Lighthouse. Quarrah was leading the way, with the transformed Prime Isless close behind.

Ard and Quarrah had taken horses from the palace stables, giving them their head whenever they had a long enough stretch of road. But Gloristar had gone on foot. It was the most unsettling thing to see a woman, standing nearly Ard's height on horseback, running at the speed of a gallop without ever appearing to tire.

*It's a blazing good thing she's on our side,* Ard kept thinking.

The cool night wind whipped Ard's hair as he slipped out of the backpack and set it on the table. The chairs around it were empty now, and in the midst of all the tension, Ard let himself feel a kiss of satisfaction that the masked Directorate would not be meeting here again.

He glanced out over the InterIsland Waters, but it simply looked like a vast expanse of blackness. Talumon's big cities, Grisn, Helizon, and surrounding outskirts were out there somewhere across the water, completely unaware that a cataclysmic flood could decimate them in a matter of minutes.

The lights of Beripent drew his eye, the lay of the city stretching beyond Ard's sight. Large pieces of the Northern Quarter were dark, their inhabitants surely fast asleep. But here and there, little orbs of Light Grit shone like steady stars, and small fires winked and flickered playfully.

Each light represented a person—or *people,* more likely—with thousands filling the darkness in between.

*Homeland,* Ard thought. *Please let this work.*

He caught himself praying and wondered what good it did. If the Homeland was far beneath them, that ancient underwater kingdom certainly wasn't receiving silently expressed hopes and desires.

In the throne room, Gloristar had called herself the Homeland. That, more than anything, made sense with what Pethredote had once told him—a perfect version of the future. But if Gloristar had successfully reached her perfect future through transformation, then what would stop others from creating Metamorphosis Grit and doing the same?

It was a terrifying thought.

Quarrah ignited a little Light Grit and opened the backpack, producing three large Grit kegs. Taken from the armory, each had a couple of panweights of Barrier Grit inside. These kegs were meant for storage, not detonation, so Quarrah had to pop off the lid, a bit of the fine metal dust kicking up in the breeze.

Quarrah quickly produced a Slagstone ignitor, but before she could use it, Gloristar reached her index finger into the keg. Ard saw a sizzle of sparks and the Grit detonated.

Unlike that rainy meeting when the Barrier cloud had barely encompassed the open patio area, this detonation stretched so far into the darkness that Ard couldn't see it.

Quarrah removed the lids on the other two kegs, and Gloristar ignited the Grit with her sparking finger. The air around them was very hazy now, with three overlapping Barrier clouds enveloping them.

Lifting both hands into the air, Gloristar closed her eyes. Ard watched in pure fascination as the three clouds were absorbed into her palms. It was done in a moment, the air around them clear once more.

"How do you do that?" Ard asked in awe.

"I hold the clouds within me," she answered. "Reshape them as I need."

Well, that was quite the trick. *Raek's going to be a jealous fool when he sees it.*

"Any minute now." Quarrah was quietly studying the dark horizon.

He wished she'd turn and look at him. Not just look, but really see him the way she had before. All this time working together... had it brought them any closer? Why did he need her so badly? Was it just because he had a hard time letting go of things that had once fulfilled him? Was she another Tanalin Phor, as Raek had accused? He'd loved the memory of Tanalin, but once he had confronted her, the longing had died.

Ard's feelings for Quarrah were different. His heart still beat for her despite the fact that she might never love him back.

"It is happening," Gloristar said ominously. She stepped out onto the little catwalk surrounding the upper room of the lighthouse, stretching out her hands.

Somewhere in the depths of the sea, contained within its clever device, a Gregious Mas clock would be chiming, the mechanism throwing sparks into fifty-six panweights of Compounded Void Grit.

Ard heard a sound like a raging wind or the crashing of a massive wave. In response, Grit clouds streamed from the palms of Gloristar's hands, rushing out and downward toward the InterIsland Waters.

"Is it working?" Ard asked anxiously, squinting into the darkness.

"'A day cometh when all must speedily go unto the Homeland.'" As Gloristar spoke, ribbons of detonated Light Grit burst from her hands, flowing out to illuminate what she had done.

Her Barrier cloud covered everything below, as far as Ard could see in the illumination. The water roiled and crashed beneath the flattened shell, but the dangerous waves were contained.

"'Stumblers have gone before thee, and these silent ones have heralded thy voyage,'" Gloristar continued her recitation.

*Moonsickness truly heralded the voyage to the Homeland,* Ard realized. Over the centuries, thousands had been sickened by the Moon, never knowing that it was a necessary prerequisite to becoming a perfected Homelander.

Gloristar rippled the light cloud eastward, and Ard could now see that she was funneling the water away from the islands, pushing the massive waves out into the eastern sea.

"'Ye shall know that the great day of egress is upon you,'" she continued, "'when the miserable shall forsake their habitat and walk among you, wild and uncontrolled.'"

The first sign to precede the Great Egress. Despite the Realm's meddling, the prophesy had been fulfilled naturally with the sickening of Brend two years ago.

"'In that same day,'" she muttered, "'the waters shall heave up their secret depths to such a height that even the towers upon which mankind hides will not be able to escape.'"

Well, at least they'd stopped that part of the prophesy. Ard felt a sudden chill. An Urging from the Homeland? Standing behind the transformed Prime Isless Gloristar, watching her manipulate Grit in an unfathomable way, Ard suddenly realized that they hadn't stopped any of the prophecies.

*Secret depths.*

Sparks! The verse had never been about a flood at all!

Secrets. Knowledge. From the depths of the InterIsland Waters.

What Ard and the others had learned at the testament spire had given Portsend what he needed to truly understand what the Metamorphosis Grit could do.

The Homeland had indeed been found to starboard. Not the direction, but rather the namesake.

"'Verily,'" said Gloristar, "'this cataclysm shall be unto you as a final Urging, bidding all to depart this lowly realm and ascend unto the Homeland.'"

The Great Egress. Was it going to happen after all? The rest of the writings had certainly come to pass. Would it be a literal egress, like the Realm foresaw, or a spiritual one, like the Islehood taught? Maybe it would be something else altogether.

Gloristar held steady for a few more moments, then the Grit clouds extinguished and she lowered her powerful hands.

"'For soon after cometh the Final Era of Utmost Perfection.'"

Far below, there was a sudden, resounding *crack*, like a peal of thunder that shook the entire lighthouse. Gloristar whirled, her fiery, glowing eyes wide with a new intensity. "Blast Grit," she whispered.

"Blast—" Ard's repetition was cut short as a second *boom* sounded from below, infinitesimally louder than the first.

The Old Post Lighthouse bucked like a wild stallion, timbers and stone splitting apart and raining down. Ard scrambled backward, tripping over the undulating floor and sprawling on his back just in time to see the roof coming down on them.

Somehow still on her feet, Gloristar stretched out her shimmery blue hand, throwing a domed shield of Barrier Grit over Ard and Quarrah. Debris clattered on the protective cover above them, spilling over all sides like raindrops on a parasol.

Ard gripped Quarrah's hand, a helpless reassurance as he realized that the entire structure was about to crumble. Her breathing was fast and heavy in his ear, exhalations of pure terror.

One of the last remaining trusses overhead snapped free, the heavy beam sliding on a downward angle like an oversized spear. It struck Gloristar squarely in the back of the head, throwing her, face first, onto the cracking floor.

The Barrier over Ard and Quarrah instantly winked out. But with the lighthouse's roof collapsed, the fear of falling rubble had mostly passed. Now the danger was their teetering pedestal of a building. Even as Ard rose onto his knees, never letting go of Quarrah, he saw the north side of the lighthouse slough away, carrying the fallen Gloristar with it.

The mighty woman threw down her hand, Barrier Grit flowing out of her fingers to form a flat plate beneath her. She knelt on the translucent shield, nothing but the harrowing midnight darkness beneath her. As she turned, Ard saw the damage the loose wooden beam had done.

Gloristar's red glass skull was cracked, innumerable fractures spiderwebbing in a crown of jagged lines. Her eyes still shone like hot coals in the night, but her face was twisted in a snarl of pain.

"Go!" she shrieked, free hand snapping forward and throwing an elongated cloud toward the mainland. It shot past Ard and Quarrah, a veritable tunnel of hazy Grit. Ard knelt rooted, watching chunks of stone and splinters of wood floating through the Drift Grit pathway.

Then Quarrah yanked him up, their hands still inseparable in a sweaty grip. She led him in a dead sprint across the collapsing floor, parallel to the Drift tunnel, wind whipping at her hair.

*We're going to Drift Jump,* Ard realized in horror.

"Hang on!" Quarrah shouted, preparing to spring into the elongated Drift cloud. Just then, the Old Post Lighthouse finally collapsed beneath them, stealing away the stones beneath their feet at the precise moment they needed them.

They barely tumbled into the Drift cloud, spinning awkwardly, with no momentum behind their jump. In seconds, they would spiral out the other side and plummet through the night to their certain deaths.

Turning head over heels, Ard could see that the lighthouse was gone, its broken pieces clattering to the sea below. He glimpsed Gloristar still out there, seeming to hover on her transparent disk of Barrier Grit, her other hand sustaining the Drift cloud that was supposed to lead them to safety.

On his next revolution, Ard saw her glowing eyes close. She raised the hand that was maintaining the Barrier cloud, the action tossing her slightly upward as the shield snuffed out. For a brief second, her hand was leveled directly at Ard and Quarrah, sighting down the shaft of Drift Grit.

Ard didn't see the column of Void Grit leave Gloristar's fingers, but he felt it strike him in the back, redirecting his out-of-control flight and pushing him and Quarrah speedily along the tunnel-like Drift cloud. They clung to each other, a pair of helpless airborne mortals delivered by the Homeland herself.

At the last moment, the Drift cloud extinguished around them, but the momentum of Gloristar's Void push was just enough to throw them the final few feet to the mainland. They tumbled, Ard feeling his right arm break as he absorbed the bulk of their fall. He cried out in pain as they rolled to a stop at the edge of the orchard.

Quarrah was the first to recover, her breathing ragged. "Are you all right?"

Ard grunted, vision blurred from the pain. "I'll be fine." He sat up, cradling his arm.

Quarrah stumbled to the edge of the cliff. "The Prime Isless..."

Ard had seen her fall. She'd given up her Barrier cloud footing to redirect them with that Void Grit. "If anyone can survive that fall…" But he trailed off. The entire lighthouse had gone down with her—into the sea with thousands of panweights of devastating debris. The testament spire had said that the changed race could still taste death.

And Gloristar's skull…Had Quarrah seen the fractured glass of her cranium?

"Blast Grit?" Quarrah repeated what Gloristar had said.

"Did it take out the lighthouse from the base?" Ard couldn't bring himself to get up with the dizzying pain in his arm.

"More than that. It blew out half the stone column it was built on," Quarrah answered. "What happened?"

"Overseer," Ard surmised. "She must have had the lighthouse rigged with Blast Grit all along."

"In case she grew suspicious of the Directorate," said Quarrah.

Ard nodded. "She could wait until they were all convened and then sink everyone into the InterIsland Waters." He cursed. "She told us the lighthouse was more defensible than we realized."

"We have to get down there," Quarrah continued. "Search for Gloristar."

"Not sure I'm up for scaling cliffs," he admitted.

"Then I'll go alone."

And leave him here? His heart began an accelerando toward the moment he'd been dreading.

"I can be to the rubble by daybreak if I take a boat from North Central Harbor," Quarrah continued.

"You'll come back?" Ard blurted. He hadn't meant for it to sound so desperate, and his stomach sank when her answer was nothing but silence. Quietly, she moved toward the trees.

"Quarrah." He said her name with such passion that it seemed to freeze her in place. "Don't leave. Not yet." *Not after everything we've been through.*

He closed his eyes. With the Realm broken up, would this be the end of their association? If Quarrah left now, would he ever find her again, or would she simply vanish into the city, a ghost to him once more?

"Goodbye, Ard."

He opened his eyes just in time to see her disappear into the darkness of the orchard. Ard wasn't naïve enough to think he could keep up with her, so only his heart followed, his injured body slumped in the scrubby grasses near the cliff's edge.

The minutes passed, Ard trying to gather the strength and desire to rise, grunting against the constant pain and discouragement. He watched the dust from the rubble dance in the starlight, swirling and shifting in a postlude of destruction.

What had he done this time? Had his meddling left the islands a better place? They'd dismantled the Realm. That had to count for something. The surviving members of the Directorate had been imprisoned, and by now the rest of the Faceless would be arrested. And then there was the Cataclysm...Gloristar had saved thousands of lives tonight.

But Shad Agaul was dead. And with King Termain perishing on the same night, the pure Agaul bloodline had come to an end. What did that mean for the Archkingdom and the Sovereign States?

His thoughts were interrupted by a rustling of the underbrush behind him. Quarrah! Had she decided to give him another chance? But why would she have circled the orchard to approach from the other side...?

Ard whirled, his hope disintegrating into dread at the sight of the assassin handmaiden materializing through the trees.

Overseer.

Of course she was here! Someone would've had to be nearby to detonate the Blast Grit under the lighthouse.

Ard went for his Roller, but it was on his right, the draw made awkward with his broken arm. A clay pot shattered on the ground between them, and the night seemed to grow quieter. Then Errel's Singler sounded, and Ard felt the hot lead tear into his leg. He screamed, losing his left-handed grip on his Roller. Overseer came forward swiftly, like a shadow of death itself. She cast aside her spent gun and drew a thin sword, metal ringing through the still night.

"You were supposed to go down with the Old Post." Her voice cut like glass—familiar as Overseer, and yet so foreign without her mask. "You were supposed to die by the fishing pond, on Pekal, at the guesthouse... I keep giving you chances."

Ard rolled sideways, grasping his Roller once more. But before he could bring it up, the handmaiden's shoe came down on his wrist with her full weight. Maneuvering his thumb, he cocked the hammer and fired anyway, the ball tattering the nearest tuft of a bush. He fired again. Maybe Quarrah would hear the shots. He fired again. Maybe she would come back for him. He pulled the trigger yet again, but this time the Slagstone sparked into an empty chamber.

"Silence Grit," Overseer said, swishing her sword through the hazy air around them. It was as if she could read his thoughts— always predicting his moves. One step ahead. "I'll finish you quietly and catch up to Quarrah Khai before she leaves the orchard."

Errel lowered her sword to his chest, but Ard's attention was on movement in the trees behind her. He knew it wasn't Quarrah. She had abandoned him. But he still had a friend in this world. Someone who always came back. Someone who wouldn't leave him to die on this Homeland-forsaken shoreline.

And thanks to the Silence Grit, Overseer couldn't hear him coming.

Raekon Dorrel barreled into the cloud, his battle cry well under way before it reached Ard's ears. The huge man struck the lithe assassin, lifting her clear off her feet. The dueling sword flew from her hand, doing a complete revolution before staking itself in the ground mere inches from Ard's head.

Ard tried to sit up, screaming in pain. His good hand was pressed tightly against the wound in his thigh, but the blood still seeped through. He felt himself growing faint, the darkness at his periphery blacker than the night alone.

Rolling back his head, Ard spotted Raek and Errel. The handmaiden was clinging to the big man's back like a barnacle. Her legs wrapped around his middle, ankles locked, while her arms tightened around Raek's neck with the force of a Slagstone chipping vise.

Sparks! His friend wasn't winning this fight! Raek's arms thrashed, his face already a deep shade of red. Their struggle had carried them just beyond the perimeter of the Silence cloud, so the fight was absolutely noiseless to Ard. But he doubted his partner was making much sound anyway, mouth agape with a string of drool streaming from his bottom lip.

Raek staggered toward Ard. One step. Two. They entered the Silence cloud, and Ard heard Errel's grunts, but still not a sound from Raek. He managed two more steps before Errel brought him to his knees. Her legs unwound from his middle, but only so that her feet could find better leverage on the ground. With this new vantage, she seemed to double the pressure around his neck, deepening the shade of his cheeks to purple.

They were only feet away, but what help could Ard possibly give when he couldn't even stand up?

Raek's bulging eyes locked with Ard's in the darkness. Panic was setting in, but the Short Fuse was too calculated a man to let it take control. Reaching up, he ripped open his shirt, exposing his scarred bare chest.

Ardor Benn knew exactly what to do. Twisting sideways, he snatched the hilt of Overseer's dueling sword and plucked it from the ground. With an uncontrolled lurch, he made a desperate lunge at his partner. Raek's hand came up, catching the flat of the blade against his palm and guiding the tip directly into the pipe in his chest. Ard let go and Raek fell forward, the hilt of the sword butting against the hard ground and the blade running him all the way through.

Errel made a sound like a gurgling cough, her arms releasing from around Raek's neck. Her body twitched atop his before going limp with the telltale stillness of death.

"Raek," Ard called. "Raek, old pal. You still alive?" Ard knew he was. His partner's desperate wheezing for breath was a dead giveaway.

Raek pushed himself up onto his elbows, the handmaiden's corpse pinned to his back. "No thanks to you. I've got to find a friend who doesn't keep shooting and stabbing me."

"How'd you know I was here?" He might not have been, if Raek's arrival had come a moment later.

"I was riding for the palace when I heard the lighthouse come crashing down. Probably woke up half of Beripent." He managed to get to his knees, grimacing as Errel's limp body slipped off the end of the sword. "The palace, the guesthouse, the lighthouse... See, Ard. This is why we can't have nice things. Where's Quarrah?"

"She..." He didn't want to admit it. "Left."

Raek sighed. "I can think of half a dozen worse ways to end that sentence." He reached up and grabbed the hilt buried in his bare chest. Slowly, and with what appeared to be a significant amount of pain, he withdrew the long, thin blade. With a disgusted look, he dumped the bloody weapon beside Errel's body. "Who was she? With the Realm?"

Ard exhaled, suddenly realizing how much had happened since they'd parted ways at the guesthouse. "Overseer."

"But I thought—"

Ard waved a bloody hand at him. "The *real* Overseer. For someone half your size, she had you in quite the choke hold."

Raek merely grunted. "Wouldn't have happened if I'd had a proper supper. You know I don't like fighting on an empty stomach."

"Why didn't you just shoot her from the trees?"

"Spent all my ammunition on those Bloodeyes back at the farm," answered Raek, producing a paper roll of Health Grit. "Got bad out there."

"Not much better here." There was so much to tell. So much death. And Gloristar...

With trembling hands, Raek poured a bit of Health Grit into his palm and produced a little Slagstone ignitor. "Don't tell me our employer died..."

"Lady Abeth is alive." *At least, she was when I left the palace.* But poor Shad...

Raek lit the Grit. The resulting cloud hanging between them was larger than Ard had expected. "Get over here." He held up a hand as if expecting a rebuttal. "And don't give me slag about using this. You've got to stop that bleeding, and your arm looks like a string noodle."

Resignedly, Ard clawed a few feet through the dirt until the cloud of Health Grit encompassed both his wounds. "I don't think this is over, Raek."

"What do you mean? We're not getting paid?"

Ard remembered Gloristar's voice as she'd recited the verses. She'd been transformed into power and perfection, a literal fulfillment of the text she'd quoted.

"I'm talking about the Great Egress," Ard said.

"You're worried that the Realm will continue their plans? Form a new Directorate?"

Ard shook his head. "I don't think the Realm understood it. Or the Islehood. I don't think anyone really knows what's about to come."

Raek scoffed. "Except for you. *You* know."

"Not this time," said Ardor Benn. And that was what terrified him most.

~

*We rose to higher heights, granted new sight and power beyond our imaginings.*

The story continues in…

*The Last Lies of Ardor Benn*

Kingdom of Grit: Book Three

# ACKNOWLEDGMENTS

Thank you for continuing with my series and reading this book! Writing it was so fun and rewarding. At the same time, it was one of the most difficult books I've written. I'll tell you, Ardor Benn is not an easy fellow to keep up with! I hope this was a worthy sequel, and don't worry, I have some big things in store for the final installment.

A huge thanks to the entire team at Orbit. Bradley Englert and Emily Byron for your guiding editorial assistance. Thanks to Lauren Panepinto for her excellent art direction, and Ben Zweifel for his majestic cover art, and Serena Malyon for the beautiful map of the Greater Chain.

Thank you to my agent Ammi-Joan Paquette. She's always in my corner and works tirelessly on my behalf.

Thanks to my earliest readers, who provided some insightful feedback: Celeste and Brad Baillio, Jamie and Carson Younker, Spencer Munyon, and Rob Davis. Grateful to have you all on my rusing crew!

I dedicated this book to my high school literature teacher, Mr. Barfuss. He took me under his wing when I showed an interest in writing, and believed in me enough to create a one-on-one class period to coach me on the process of "writing to publish."

Thanks to my parents for nurturing my creativity as a kid and always being proud of my work.

Of course, the biggest thanks goes to my wife, Connie. She lives with Ard and the gang on a daily basis, and believe me, they can be quite demanding. The three-year-old told me that his imaginary friends are reading Ardor Benn, so it's nice to know I've found an audience.

# extras

orbit

www.orbitbooks.net

# about the author

**Tyler Whitesides** is the author of bestselling children's series Janitors and The Wishmakers. *The Thousand Deaths of Ardor Benn* is his adult debut. When he's not writing, Tyler enjoys playing percussion, hiking, fly-fishing, cooking, and the theater. He lives in the mountains of northern Utah with his wife and two sons.

Find out more about Tyler Whitesides and other Orbit authors by registering for the free monthly newsletter at www.orbitbooks.net.

**if you enjoyed**

# THE SHATTERED REALM OF ARDOR BENN

**look out for**

# AGE OF ASSASSINS

## The Wounded Kingdom: Book One

**by**

# RJ Barker

*Girton Club-Foot, apprentice to the land's best assassin, still has much to learn about the art of taking lives. But his latest mission tasks Girton and his master with a far more difficult challenge: to save a life. Someone, or many someones, is trying to kill the heir to the throne, and it is up to Girton and his master to uncover the traitor and prevent the prince's murder.*

*In a kingdom on the brink of civil war and a castle thick with lies Girton finds friends he never expected, responsibilities he never wanted, and a conspiracy that could destroy an entire land.*

# Prologue

Darik the smith was last among the desolate. The Landsman made him kneel with a kick to the back of his knees, forcing his head down so he knelt and stared at the line between the good green grass and the putrid yellow desert of the sourlands. Nothing grew in the sourlands. A sorcerer had taken the life of the land for his own magics many years ago, before Darik's parents were born, and only death was found there now. A foul-smelling wind blew his long brown hair into his face and, ten paces away, the first of the desolate was weeping as she waited for the blade – Kina the herdsgirl, no more than a child and the only other from his village. The voice of the Landsman, huge and strong in his grass-green armour, was surprisingly gentle as he spoke to her, a whisper no louder than the knife leaving its scabbard.

"Shh, child. Soonest done, soonest over," he said, and then the knife bit into her neck and her tears were stilled for ever. Darik glanced between the bars of his hair and saw Kina's body jerking as blood fountained from her neck and made dark, twisting, red patterns on the stinking yellow ground – silhouettes of death and life.

He had hoped to marry Kina when she came of age.

Darik was cold but it was not the wind that made him shiver; he had been cold ever since the sorcerer hunters had come for him. It was the first time in fifteen years of life that the sweat on his skin wasn't because of the fierce heat of the forge. The moisture that had clung to him since was a different sweat, a new sweat, a cold frightened animal sweat that hadn't stopped since they locked the shackles on his wrists. It seemed so long ago now.

The weeks of marching across the Tired Lands had been like a dream but, looking back, the most dreamlike moment of all was that moment when they had called his name. He hadn't been surprised – it was as if he'd sold himself to a hedge spirit long ago and had been waiting for someone to come and collect on the debt his whole life.

"Shh, child. Soonest done, soonest over." The knife does its necessary work on another of the desolate, and a second set of bloody sigils spatters out on the filthy yellow ground. Is there meaning there? Is there some message for him? In this place between life and death, close to embracing the watery darkness that swallowed the dead gods, are they talking to him?

Or is it just blood?

And death.

And fear.

"Shh, child. Soonest done, soonest over." The next one begs for life in the moments before the blade bites. Darik doesn't know that one's name, never asked him, never saw the point because once you're one of the desolate you're dead. There is no way out, no point running. The brand on your forehead shows you for what they think you are – magic user, destroyer, abomination, *sorcerer*. You're only good for bleeding out on the dry dead earth, a sacrifice of blood to heal the land. No one will hide you, no one will pity you when magic has made the dirt so weak people can barely feed their children. There is the sound of choking, fighting, begging as the knife does its work and the thirsty ground drinks the life stolen from it.

Does Darik feel something in that moment of death? Is there a vibration? Is there a twinge that runs from Darik's knees, up his legs through his blood to squirm in his belly? Or is that only fear?

"Shh, child. Soonest done, soonest over."

The slice, the cough, blood on the ground, and this time it is unmistakable – a *something* that shoots up through his body. It sets his teeth on edge, it makes the roots of his hair hurt. Everything starts changing around him: the land is a lens and he is its focus, his mind a bright burning spot of light. What is this feeling? What is it? Were they right?

*Are they right?*

A hand on his forehead.

*Dark worms moving through his flesh.*

The hiss of the blade leaving the scabbard.

*He sweats, hot as any day at the forge.*

His head pulled back, his neck stretched.

*Closing his eyes, he sees a world of silvered lines and shadows.*

The cold touch of the blade against his neck.

*A pause, like the hiss of hot metal in water, like the moment before the geyser of scorching steam hisses out around his hand and the blade is set.*

The sting of a sharp edge against his skin.

*And the grass is talking, and the land is talking, and the trees are talking, and all in a language he cannot understand but at the same time he knows exactly what is being said. Is this what a hedging lord sounds like?*

The creak of leather armour.

"I will save you." *Is it the voice of Fitchgrass of the fields?*

"No!"

"Only listen . . ." *This near the souring is it Coil the yellower?*

"Shh, shh, child." The Landsman's voice, soothing, calming. "Soonest done, soonest over."

"I can save you." *Too far from the rivers for Blue Watta.*

"No." But Darik's word is a whisper drowned in fear of the approaching void. Time slows further as the knife slices though his skin, cutting through layer after layer in search of the black vessels of his life.

"*Let me save you.*" *Or is it the worst of all of them? Is it Dark Ungar speaking?*

"No," he says. But the word is weak and the will to fight is gone.

"*Let us?*"

"Yes!"

An explosion of . . . of?

*Something.*

Something he doesn't know or understand but he recognises it – it has always been within him. It is something he's fought, denied, run from. A familiar voice from his childhood, the imaginary friend that frightened his mother and she told him to forget so he pushed it away, far away. But now, when he needs it the most, it is there.

The blade is gone from his neck.

He opens his eyes.

The world is out of focus – a haze of yellows – and a high whine fills his ears the way it would when his father clouted him for "dangerous talk". The green grass beneath Darik's knees is gone, replaced by yellow fronds that flake away at his touch like morning ash in the forge. He stares at his hands. They are the same – the same scars, the same half-healed cuts and nicks, the same old burns and calluses.

Around him is perfect half-circle of dead grass, as if the sourlands have taken a bite out of the lush grasslands at their edge

His wrists are no longer bound in cold metal.

Is he lost, gone? Has he made a deal with something terrible? But it doesn't feel like that; it feels like this was something in him, something that has always been in him, just waiting for the right moment.

He can feel the souring like an ache.

There had been four Landsmen to guard the five desolate. Now the guards are blurry smears of torn, angular metal, red flesh and sharp white bone.

Darik rubbed his eyes and forced himself up, staggering like a man waking from too long a sleep. A movement in the corner of his eye pulled at his attention. One of the Landsmen was still alive, on his back and trying to scuttle away on his elbows as Darik approached. The smith knelt by the Landsman and placed his big hands on either side of his head. It would be easy to finish him, just a single twist of his big arms and the Landsman's neck would snap like a charcoaled stick. He willed his arms to move but instead found himself staring at the Landsman. Not much older than he was and scared, so scared. The Landsman's lips were moving and at first the only sound is the high whine of the world, then the words come like the approaching thunder of a mount's feet as it gallops towards him.

"I'msorryI'msorryI'msorryI'msorry . . ."

"It's wrong," Darik said, "this is all wrong," but the Landsman's eyes were far away, lost in fear and past under-standing. His mouth moving.

". . . I'msorryI'msorryI'msorry . . ."

Darik stared a little longer, the killing muscles in his arms tensing. Now his vision had cleared he saw beyond the broken bodies of the other Landsmen to the shattered corpses of those who had died beside him. They had been picked up and tossed away on the winds of his fury.

Darik leaned in close to the Landsman.

"This has to stop," he said, and let go of the man's head. The words kept coming.

". . . I'msorryI'msorryI'msorry."

He could see Kina's corpse, dead at the hand of the knights then shredded into a red mess by his magic.

"I forgive you," said Darik through tears. The Landsman slumped to the floor, eyes wide in shock as the smith walked away.

Inside the thick muscles of Darik's arms black veins are screaming.

# Chapter 1

We were attempting to enter Castle Maniyadoc through the night soil gate and my master was in the sort of foul mood only an assassin forced to wade through a week's worth of shit can be. I was far more sanguine about our situation. As an assassin's apprentice you become inured to foulness. It is your lot.

"Girton," said Merela Karn. That is my master's true name, though if I were to refer to her as anything other than "Master" I would be swiftly and painfully reprimanded. "Girton," she said, "if one more king, queen or any other member of the blessed classes thinks a night soil gate is the best way to make an unseen entrance to their castle, you are to run them through."

"Really, Master?"

"No, not really," she whispered into the night, her breath a cloud in the cold air. "Of course not really. You are to politely suggest that walking in the main gate dressed as masked priests of the dead gods is less conspicuous. Show me a blessed who doesn't know that the night soil gate is an easy way in for an enemy and I will show you a corpse."

"You have shown me many corpses, Master."

"Be quiet, Girton."

My master is not a lover of humour. Not many assassins are; it is a profession that attracts the miserable and the melancholic. I would never put myself into either of those categories, but I was bought into the profession and did not join by choice.

"Dead gods in their watery graves!" hissed my master into the night. "They have not even opened the grate for us." She swung herself aside whispering, "Move, Girton!" I slipped and slid crabwise on the filthy grass of the slope running from the river below us up to the base of the towering castle walls. Foulness farted out of the grating to join the oozing stream that ran down the motte and joined the river.

A silvery smudge marred the riverbank in the distance; it looked like a giant paint-covered thumb had been placed over it. In the moonlight it was quite beautiful, but we had passed near as we sneaked in, and I knew it was the same livid yellow as the other sourings which scarred the Tired Lands. There was no telling how old this souring was, and I wondered how big it had been originally and how much blood had been spilled to shrink it to its present size. I glanced up at the keep. This side had few windows and I thought the small souring could be new, but that was a silly, childish thought. The blades of the Landsmen kept us safe from sorcerers and the magic which sucked the life from the land. There had been no significant magic used in the Tired Lands since the Black Sorcerer had risen, and he had died before I had been born. No, what I saw was simply one of many sores on the land – a place as dead as the ancient sorcerer who made it. I turned from the souring and did my best to imagine it wasn't there, though I was sure I could smell it, even over the high stink of the night soil drain.

"Someone will pay for arranging this, Girton, I swear," said my master. Her head vanished into the darkness as she bobbed down to examine the grate once more. "This is sealed with a simple five-lever lock." She did not even breathe heavily despite holding her entire weight on one arm and one leg jammed into stonework the black of old wounds. "You can open this, Girton. You need as much practice with locks as you can get."

"Thank you, Master," I said. I did not mean it. It was cold, and a lock is far harder to manipulate when it is cold.

And when it is covered in shit.

Unlike my master, I am no great acrobat. I am hampered by a clubbed foot, so I used my weight to hold me tight against the grating even though it meant getting covered in filth. On the stone columns either side of the grate the forlorn remains of minor gods had been almost chipped away. On my right only a pair of intricately carved antlers remained, and on my left a pair of horns and one solemn eye stared out at me. I turned from the eye and brought out my picks, sliding them into the lock with shaking fingers and feeling within using the slim metal rods.

"What if there are dogs, Master?"

"We kill them, Girton."

There is something rewarding in picking a lock. Something very satisfying about the click of the barrels and the pressure vanishing as the lock gives way to skill. It is not quite as rewarding done while a castle's toilets empty themselves over your body, but a happy life is one where you take your pleasures where you can.

"It is open, Master."

"Good. You took too long."

"Thank you, Master." It was difficult to tell in the darkness, but I was sure she smiled before she nodded me forward. I hesitated at the edge of the pitch-dark drain.

"It looks like the sort of place you'd find Dark Ungar, Master."

"The hedgings are just like the gods, Girton — stories to scare the weak-minded. There's nothing in there but stink and filth. You've been through worse. Go."

I slithered through the gate, managing to make sure no part of my skin or clothing remained clean, and into the tunnel that led through the keep's curtain wall. Somewhere beyond I could hear the lumpy splashes of night soil being shovelled into the stream that ran over my feet. The living classes in the villages keep their piss and night soil and sell it to the tanneries and dye makers, but the blessed classes are far too grand for that, and their castles shovel their filth out into the rivers − as if to gift it to the populace. I have crawled through plenty of filth in my fifteen years, from the thankful, the living and the blessed; it all smells equally bad.

Once we had squeezed through the opening we were able to stand, and my master lit a glow-worm lamp, a small wick that burns with a dim light that can be amplified or shut off by a cleverly interlocking set of mirrors. Then she lifted a gloved hand and pointed at her ear.

I listened.

Above the happy gurgle of the stream running down the channel − water cares nothing for the medium it travels through − I heard the voices of men as they worked. We would have to wait for them to move before we could proceed into the castle proper, and whenever we have to wait I count out the seconds the way my master taught me − one, my master. Two, my master. Three, my master − ticking away in my mind like the balls of a water clock as I stand idle, filth swirling round my ankles and my heart beating out a nervous tattoo.

You get used to the smell. That is what people say.

It is not true.

Eight minutes and nineteen seconds passed before we finally heard the men laugh and move on. Another signal from my master and I started to count again. Five minutes this time. Human nature being the way it is you cannot guarantee someone will not leave something and come back for it.

When the five minutes had passed we made our way up the night soil passage until we could see dim light dancing on walls caked with centuries of filth. My own height plus a half above us was the shovelling room. Above us the door creaked and then we heard footsteps, followed by voices.

". . . so now we're done and Alsa's in the heir's guard. Fancy armour and more pay."

"It's a hedging's deal. I'd sooner poke out my own eyes and find magic in my hand than serve the fat bear, he's a right yellower."

"Service is mother though, aye?"

Laughter followed. My master glanced up through the hole, chewing on her lip. She held up two fingers before speaking in the Whisper-That-Flies-to-the-Ear so only I could hear her.

"Guards. You will have to take care of them," she said. I nodded and started to move. "Don't kill them unless you absolutely have to."

"It will be harder."

"I know," she said and leaned over, putting her hands together to make a stirrup. "But I will be here."

*I breathe out.*

*I breathe in.*

I placed my foot on her hands and, with a heave, she propelled me up and into the room. I came out of the hole landing with my back to the two men. *Seventeenth iteration: the Drunk's Reversal.* Rolling forward, twisting and coming up facing guards dressed in kilted skirts, leather helms and poorly kept-up boiled-leather chest pieces splashed with red paint. They stared at me dumbly, as if I were the hedging lord Blue Watta appearing from the deeps. Both of them held clubs, though they had stabswords at their sides. I wondered if they were here to guard against rats rather than people.

"Assassin?" said the guard on the left. He was smaller than his friend, though both were bigger than me.

"Aye," said the other, a huge man. "Assassin." His grip shifted on his club.

They should have gone for the door and reinforcements.

My hand was hovering over the throwing knives at my belt in case they did. Instead the smaller man grinned, showing missing teeth and black stumps.

"I imagine there's a good price on the head of an assassin, Joam, even if it's a crippled child." He started forward. The bigger man grinned and followed his friend's lead. They split up to avoid the hole in the centre of the room and I made my move. *Second iteration: the Quicksteps*. Darting forward, I chose the smaller of the two as my first target – the other had not drawn his blade. He swung at me with his club and I stepped backwards, feeling the draught of the hard wood through the air. He thrust with his dagger but was too far away to reach my flesh. When his swipe missed he jumped back, expecting me to counter-attack, but I remained unmoving. All I had wanted was to get an idea of his skill before I closed with him. He did not impress me, his friend impressed me even less; rather than joining the attack he was watching, slack-jawed, as if we put on a show for him.

"Joam," shouted my opponent, "don't be just standing there!" The bigger man trundled forward, though he was in no hurry. I didn't want to be fighting two at the same time if I could help it so decided to finish the smaller man quickly. *First iteration: the Precise Steps*. Forward into the range of his weapons. He thrust with his stabsword. *Ninth iteration: the Bow*. Middle of my body bowing backwards to avoid the blade. With his other hand he swung his club at my head. I ducked. As his arm came over my head I grabbed his elbow and pushed, making him lose his balance, and as he struggled to right himself I found purchase on the rim of his chest piece. *Tenth iteration: the Broom*. Sweeping my leg round I knocked his feet from under him. With a push I sent him flailing into the hole so he cracked his head on the edge of it on his way down.

I turned to his friend, Joam.

Had the dead gods given Joam any sense he would have

seen his friend easily beaten and made for the door. Instead, Joam's face had the same look on it I had seen on a bull as it smashed its head against a wall in a useless attempt to get at a heifer beyond – the look of something too stupid and angry to know it was in a fight it couldn't win.

"I'm a kill you, assassin," he said and lumbered slowly forward, smacking his club against his hand. I had no time to wait for him; the longer we fought the more likely it was that someone would hear us and bring more guards. I jumped over the hole and landed behind Joam. He turned, swinging his club. *Fifteenth Iteration: the Oar.* Bending at the hip and bringing my body down and round so it went under his swing. At the lowest point I punched forward, landing a solid blow between Joam's legs. He screeched, dropping his weapon and doubling over. With a jerk I brought my body up so the back of my skull smashed into his face, sending the big man staggering back, blood streaming from a broken nose. It was a blow that would have felled most, but Joam was a strong man. Though his eyes were bleary and unfocused he still stood. *Eighteenth iteration: the Water Clock.* I ran at him, grabbing his thick belt and using it as a fulcrum to swing myself round and up so I could lock my legs around his throat. Joam's hand grasped blindly for the blade at his hip. I drew it and tossed it away before he reached it. His hands spidered down my body searching for and locking around my throat, but Joam's strength, though great, was fleeing as he choked. I wormed my thumb underneath his fingers and grabbed his little finger and third finger, breaking them. I expected a grunt of pain as he let go of me, but the man was already unconscious and fell back, sliding down the wall to the floor. I squirmed free of his weight and checked he was still breathing. Once I was sure he was alive I rolled his body over to the hole.

"Look out, Master," I whispered. Then pushed the limp body into the hole. I took a moment, a second only, to check and see if I had been heard, then I knelt to pull up my master.

She was not heavy.

For the first time I had a moment to look around, and the room we stood in was a strange one. Small in length and breadth but far higher than it needed to be. I barely had time for that thought to form on the surface of my mind before my master shouted,

"This is wrong, Girton! Back!"

I jumped for the grate, as did she, but before either of us fell back into the midden a hidden gate clanked into place across the hole. Four pikers squeezed into the room, dressed in boiled-leather armour, wide-brimmed helms and skirts sewn with chunks of metal. Below the knee they wore leather greaves with strips of metal cut into the material to protect their shins, and as they brandished their weapons they assaulted us with the smell of unwashed bodies and the rancid fat they used to oil their armour. In such a small room their stink was a more effective weapon than the pikes; they would have been far better bringing long shields and short swords. They would realise quickly enough.

"Hostages," said my master as I reached for the blade on my back.

I let go of the hilt.

And was among the guards. Bare-handed and violent. The unmistakable fleshy crack of a nose being broken followed by a man squealing like a gelded mount came from behind me as my master engaged the pikers. I shoved one pike aside to get in close and drove my elbow into the throat of the man in front of me – not a killing blow but enough to put the man out of action. The second piker, a woman, was off balance, and it was easy enough for me to twist her so she was held in front of me like a shield with my razor-tipped thumbnail at her throat. My master had her piker in a similar embrace. Blood ran down his face and another guard lay unconscious on the floor next to the man I had elbowed in the throat.

"Open the grating," she shouted to the walls. "Let us go or we will kill these guards."

The sound of a man laughing came from above, and the reason for the room's height became clear as murder holes opened in the walls. Each was big enough for a crossbow to be pointed down at the room and eight weapons threatened us with taut bows and stubby little bolts which would pass straight through armour.

"Open the grate. We will leave and your troops will live," shouted my master.

More laughter.

"I think not," came a voice. Male, sure of himself, amused.

*One, my master. Two, my master . . .*

The twang of crossbows, echoing through the silence like the sound of rocks falling down a cliff face will echo through a quiet wood. Bolts buried themselves in the unconscious guards on the floor in front of us. Laughter from above.

"Together," hissed my master, and I pulled my guard round so that we hid behind the bodies of our prisoners.

"Let me go, please," said my guard, her voice shivering like her body. "Aydor doesn't care about us guards. He's worse than Dark Ungar and he'll kill us all if he wants yer."

"Quiet!" I said and pushed my razor-edged thumb harder against her neck, making the blood flow. I felt warmth on my thigh as her bladder let go in fear.

"Look at them," came from above. "Cowardly little assassins hiding behind troops brave enough to face death head on like real warriors."

"Coil's piss, no," murmured the guard in my arms.

"Your loyalty will be remembered," came the voice again. "No!"

Crossbows spat out bolts and the woman in my arms stiffened and arched in my embrace. One moment she was alive and then, almost magically, a bolt was vibrating in front of my nose like a conduit for life to flee her body.

"Master?" I said. Her guard was spasming as he died, a bolt sticking out of his neck and blood spattering onto the floor. "They are playing with us, Master."

Laughter from above and the crossbows fired again, thudding bolts into the body in my arms and making me cringe down further behind the corpse. The laughter stopped and a second voice, female, commanding, said something, though I could not make out what it was. Then the woman shouted down to us.

"We only want you, Merela Karn. Lay on the floor and make no move to harm those who come for you or I will have your fellow shot."

Did something cross my master's face at hearing her name spoken by a stranger? Was she surprised? Did her dark skin grey slightly in shock? I had never, in all our years together, seen my master shocked. Though I was sure she was known throughout the Tired Lands — Merela Karn, the best of the assassins — few would know her face or that she was a woman.

"Drop the body, Girton," she said, letting hers fall face down on the tiled and bloody floor. "This is not what it seems."

As always I did as I was told, though I braced every muscle, waiting for the bite of a bolt which never came.

"Lie on the floor, both of you," said the male voice from above.

We did as instructed and the room was suddenly buzzing with guards. I took a few kicks to the ribs, and luckily for the owners of those feet I could not see their faces to mark them for my attention later. We were quickly bound — well enough for amateurs — and hauled to our feet in front of a man as big as any I have seen, though he was as much fat as muscle.

"Shall I take their masks off?" asked a guard to my left.

"No. Take any weapons from them and put them in the cells. Then you can all go and wash their shit off yourselves and forget this ever happened."

"I think it's your shit, actually," I said. My master stared at the floor, shaking her head, and the man backhanded me across the face. It was a poor blow. Children have hurt me more with harsh words.

"You should remember," he said, "we don't need you; we only need her."

Before I could reply bags were put over our heads for a swift, dark and rough trip to the cells. *Five hundred paces against the clock walking across stone. Turn left and twenty paces across thick carpet. Down two sets of spiral stairs into a place that stinks of human misery.*

Dungeons are usually full of the flotsam of humanity, but this one sounded empty of prisoners apart from my master and I. We were placed in filthy cells, still tied though the bonds did not hold me long. Once free I removed the sack from my head and coughed out a wire I had half swallowed and had been holding in my gullet. It was a simple job to get my arm through the barred window of my door and pick the lock. Outside was a surprisingly wide area with a table, chairs and braziers, cold now. I tiptoed to my master's cell door.

"Master, I am out."

"Well done, Girton, but go back to your cell," she said softly. "Be calm. Wait."

I stood before the door of her cell for a moment. An assassin cannot expect much mercy once captured. A blood gibbet or maybe a public dissection. Something drawn out and painful always awaited us if we were caught, unless another assassin got to us first – my master says the loose association that makes up the Open Circle guards its secrets jealously. It would have been easy enough for me to slip into the castle proper and find some servant. I could take his clothes and become anonymous and from there I could escape out into the country. I knew the assassins' scratch language and could find the drop boxes to pick up work. Many would have done that in my situation.

But my master had told me to go back to my cell and wait, so I did. I locked the door behind me and slipped my sack and bonds back on. I imagined a circle filled with air, then let the top quarter of the circle open and breathed the air out. I let go of fear and became nothing but an instrument, a weapon.

I waited.

"One, my master. Two, my master. Three, my master . . ."